HUNT THE
REAPER

THE REAPER SERIES, BOOK 2

TODD HOSEA

 GRANDIZER

ALSO BY TODD HOSEA

Steal the Reaper
Hunt the Reaper

For my brother, Ryan

ACKNOWLEDGMENTS

I am eternally grateful to my wife, Cindy. You have been my greatest supporter and I cannot thank you enough for our countless conversations, bouncing around ideas, and all of the time you've spent helping me edit. The Reaper Series would be nothing without you.

Thank you to Kristin Campbell at C&D Editing for your editing prowess. I also want to thank Jarrod, Susan, Mitch, and Doris for your help on this project. Every baby is ugly at the start, but you helped me craft this book into the best story it could be.

To my family, friends, vendors, and, most importantly, you, the reader, thank you so much for your support. From buying the book and leaving a review to giving me words of encouragement to help keep this dream going, thank you, thank you, thank you!

Lastly, I want to give a shout-out to some of my artistic heroes whose out-of-this-world talents had a profound influence on my life. Your visions sparked a young boy's imagination and directly affected to the stories I tell today. Thank you, Steven Spielberg, George Lucas, John Williams, Irvin Kirshner, and everyone at Industrial Light & Magic.

"He who defends everything, defends nothing."

- Frederick the Great

PROLOGUE

Aiwan Mothership
En route to Earth, somewhere in hyperspace …

Luna shook her head, grinning. As she admired the sleek contours of the Reaper's hull, she had to admit the prototype was impressive.

"I must say, when you disobey the king, you certainly do it with style," she quipped.

Standing on the grated bridge overlooking the mothership's cargo bay, Prince Kypa and Luna leaned against the metal railing and gazed at the Reaper. This was Luna's first glimpse of the prototype since it had been brought aboard. She approved the vessel's unique design; it was a vast departure from other Aiwan ships.

Noticing Kypa's silence, Luna glanced at her childhood friend, who was tapping his foot incessantly. She turned to face him. "Nervous?"

Kypa gave her a sidelong look then realized his tell and flattened his foot. "I am fine," he assured her. "Thank you."

Luna nodded but knew it to be untrue. It pained her that Kypa felt the need to carry this burden alone.

"We are taking an awful risk," she reminded him. "If you want to turn back …"

"No, there is no turning back now," Kypa insisted, saying it more for his own sake than hers. "I must see this through."

Luna was right, Kypa admitted to himself. If the High Court discovered he had diverted precious resources away from Aiwa's war-fighting efforts to build the Reaper, he could be charged with treason—a crime punishable by death.

Luna smiled warmly, respecting her friend's unwavering devotion to their cause. Changing the subject, she remarked, "I am impressed by how well you kept all of this a secret. How did you manage it?"

"I had help," he said with a sly smile. "Your cloaking technology proved quite useful."

"Ah, so you are not alone in this after all?" She playfully punched his arm. "Glad I could contribute to your deviance. Does Commodore Boa know?"

Judging by Kypa's feigned ignorance, Luna realized it was a silly question.

"Never mind," she said dryly. "At least Captain Torga supports what we are doing."

"Indeed," Kypa said. "Torga hand-selected the crew, requiring each member to take the mission without knowing any details. He also logged a false flight plan so we could rendezvous with the Reaper in a discreet location, away from prying eyes."

"It seems you have thought of everything."

Kypa took a long breath. "I hope."

A moment of silence passed. "You seem confident about this site," Luna remarked without preamble.

Kypa nodded. "I am, actually. I have never seen readings so high," he marveled. "The magnetarite deposits on this planet must be enormous. I just hope other harvesters have not discovered this world already."

"Is it inhabited?"

"Unknown, but we will find out soon enough." Kypa leaned against the railing once again, looking out at his creation. "Just think, Luna, if all goes to plan, we will bring back enough crystals for Boa's fleet to defeat Krunig's horde once and for all." Kypa paused, imagining the possibility of peace restored to his people. "Then we will show everyone how the Reaper can rebuild our world."

Luna cocked her eyebrow. "Everyone?"

Kypa gave her a determined look. "Yes, everyone," he insisted. "Even my father will see the Reaper's merits."

Luna held his look with empathy. As a refugee of Cirros, she understood better than most that Kypa had been unfairly blamed for its destruction. But it was not the court of public opinion that troubled her friend.

As the former head of Aiwa's harvesting efforts, Kypa had done everything in his power to avert the quakes, but his warnings had fallen on deaf ears. Most notably, King Loka's, his father. Their relationship had never healed after that, not that they had been particularly close before the tragedy. Except now, in light of Kypa's theft of precious resources to fund his unauthorized science experiment, he would be hard-pressed to find support from anyone back home if this mission failed. With Aiwa's defenses weakening, and pressure to resume crystal harvesting at an all-time high, Kypa was right—the fate of their world depended on the Reaper.

The sound of a door opening interrupted their quiet conversation. Kypa and Luna both turned and spotted two handlers entering the empty cargo bin below. They were escorting a reptilian beast—an obercai—into the storage compartment, prodding it forward with long-handled electrodes tipped with blue energy arcs.

The obercai immediately sensed the presence of Kypa and Luna through its large nostrils and forked tongue. Homing in on their scents, the creature's beady, yellow eyes shot upward and locked on to them. Stopping to hiss, the obercai earned a zap in the back from one of the handlers. The beast protested, only to receive more jolts to quell its behavior.

Obercais were apex predators on Aiwa and, while highly dangerous, they made perfect beasts of burden for harvesting. They could survive underwater for long periods, even at crushing depths. And with their herculean strength, these beasts were able to move heavy objects, such as boulders, when powered equipment was unavailable or impractical.

There were obvious downsides to using obercais. They were cunning and lethal, even at a young age, and immune to Aiwan telepathy. This made domestication a tedious and dangerous affair.

Kypa recognized this particular obercai—a juvenile—from its dark scales and nasty disposition. He knew it to be early in the training process, this being the creature's first trip off-world.

Kypa and Luna watched as the handlers led the beast inside the bin directly beneath them. Once the door closed behind them, they activated a hologram to simulate an underwater excavation site.

"Let us leave them to their work," Kypa suggested after a few minutes of observing the training process through the open ceiling. "We should be getting close—"

Suddenly, the entire ship shuddered violently, knocking Kypa and Luna off balance. Kypa steadied himself against the railing, but Luna stumbled backward. Unable to stop herself, she let out a scream as she fell over the railing.

Kypa snatched her wrist at the last second. Momentum nearly pulled him over the side with her, but he managed to plant his feet on the grated floor and stop them both from plummeting to their deaths.

Hanging upside down with her knees hooked over the railing, Luna found herself looking down at the obercai. They locked eyes and, in that dreadful moment, she saw the creature's predator instincts activate.

"Give me your other hand!" Kypa called down to her. He was bent over the railing, holding her left wrist firmly with both hands.

Luna focused her attention on Kypa. Ready to time her move, she felt something brush against her right hand as it dangled freely. Giving a sideways glance, Luna's bulbous blue eyes flashed at the sight of the obercai landing on its massive hind legs. A loud, metal thud echoed in the bay.

The obercai's first attempt to snag its prey fell short, which seemed to invigorate the beast. Smelling Luna's fear, the obercai readied to spring another attack when the two handlers intervened, jolting the creature with several electric shocks.

With the handlers distracting the beast, Luna rolled herself up so Kypa could grab her free hand and pull her to safety. As soon as she was back on solid footing, Luna threw her arms around Kypa's midsection, squeezing him tight.

Caught off-guard by this uncommon display of emotion, Kypa patted her back, trying to steady his trembling friend. "Easy," he soothed. "You are safe now."

As the words left his mouth, the ship shuddered once again. Kypa and Luna separated, each clinging to the handrails as the bridge wobbled beneath them.

An alarm sounded, and red emergency lights strobed throughout the cargo bay.

"Are we under attack?" Luna asked in a panic.

"Impossible," Kypa insisted, knowing they were in hyperspace.

The first thoughts to enter his mind were that some type of catastrophic mechanical failure had occurred, or perhaps the ship had struck debris in the hyperspace lane. While these were plausible theories, both scenarios were rare. His gut told him this was something else entirely.

The mothership shook again. Kypa and Luna exchanged knowing looks. This time, there was no mistaking the impact of disruptors against the ship's deflector shields. They were definitely under attack.

Below them, the obercai let out a deafening screech. Clearly agitated, the creature began lashing its tail and clawing at its handlers. Keeping the obercai at bay proved difficult. With their backs to the exit, the handlers worked in unison to fend off the beast's advances with the electrodes. All the while, the obercai was learning, testing their defenses for weaknesses.

Three additional Aiwans appeared at the far end of the bay and came running across the bridge. Kypa waved them over and pointed to the obercai.

"Get down there and help secure that creature at once!" he ordered.

Peering over the railing, the new arrivals saw the handlers in danger. They raced into action, disappearing into the adjacent corridor.

Kypa tapped Luna on the arm. "Come on; we must get to the bridge."

They sprinted out of the cargo bay and toward the ship's bow.

As they ran through the main corridor, another violent blast rocked the ship, causing an overhead conduit to explode and shower their path with white-hot sparks. Kypa and Luna pulled up short as cables and metal panels fell from the ceiling. The corridor went dark, and then the emergency lights flickered on.

"This way!" Kypa urged.

He ducked into a nearby stairwell and hurtled down a flight of stairs with Luna close behind. Exiting the stairwell, he paused and scanned the corridor in both directions. Sensing no danger, they continued toward the front of the ship.

Along the way, Kypa heard rumblings outside that indicated the space battle had intensified. The mothership's disruptor cannons thundered in succession to repel the attackers while the deflector shields were hammered by incoming salvos. Judging by the ferocity of the exchange, and the fact their cargo hold was empty, Kypa did not believe this was a pirate raid. Their attackers had come for blood. Royal blood.

Even more troubling was that their attackers knew exactly how to find them in hyperspace. Only a handful of people were privy to their entry point and route. This meant only one thing—there was a traitor onboard.

Suddenly, a wall panel exploded beside Kypa. The force of the blast threw him against the opposite bulkhead and knocked Luna backward off her feet.

Temporarily stunned and ears ringing, Luna rolled over onto all fours and picked herself up slowly. Coughing from the acrid smoke in the air, she crawled to Kypa's side and brushed off remnants of smoldering debris from his aquasuit.

"Are you injured?" she asked.

Dazed, Kypa blinked several times, shaking off the effects. As he rolled onto his back, a sharp pain erupted in his abdomen. Kypa winced, hissing between gritted teeth. A metal fragment protruded out of his suit just below his ribs. Green blood oozed from the wound.

Luna grimaced at the sight of Kypa's ghastly injury. She helped ease his head against the bulkhead. "You need a medic."

Eyes closed, Kypa nodded. "The stairwell ... get the medical kit."

"Try not to move," Luna said, getting to her feet. She then doubled-back up the corridor.

Kypa watched her depart then pulled his blood-stained hand from his abdomen. The wound looked nasty. Closing his eyes, he focused on taking slow, steady breaths. Luna would be back soon with something to close the wound and numb the pain ... he hoped.

As the battle raged outside, the mothership shuddered from the onslaught, knocking Luna off stride. She steadied herself against the bulkhead and continued along the corridor until reaching the stairwell. Ascending the stairs two at a time, she reached the mezzanine and removed the medical kit from the wall. Just as she started to head back, a faint call caught her attention.

Luna paused, unsure if her mind was playing tricks on her. She listened for a long-held breath. The voice sounded like it had come from the main level, one flight up. It was difficult to discern over the rumblings of the battle outside and her own heart pounding in her ears.

Feeling the need to hurry, Luna turned to leave. Then she heard the voice again. The call was unmistakable. After a split-second of indecision, Luna felt compelled to investigate. She ran up the next flight of steps. Reaching the main level, Luna looked up and down the smoke-filled corridor. There was no sign of anyone, so she ventured to the right, heading aft.

"Hello? Is anyone there?" she called out.

No reply.

Luna continued a little further. With her eyes and lungs burning from the smoke, she called out once more, "Can anyone hear me?" She coughed.

Still no reply.

Chiding herself for wasting time, Luna sprinted back to the stairwell. In the back of her mind, she feared her detour had put Kypa in greater danger.

Kypa sensed something was wrong. Luna should have been back by now. He tried reaching out to her with telepathy but failed to connect. She was either too far away, unconscious, or dead.

Pushing that grim thought out of his head, Kypa let out a breath of frustration. With each passing minute, he grew more impatient. There was nothing he could do for Luna and the rest of the crew while he was stuck here on the floor, unable to move.

"Prince Kypa!"

Kypa turned sharply to find Mena, a young crewmember from the bridge, rushing to his side.

"Mena, thank goodness."

"My Prince," she said, catching her breath. "The captain sent me—" Mena stopped mid-sentence and gasped at the bloody shard protruding from Kypa's abdomen.

Kypa ignored her reaction. "Are we under attack?"

His question went unanswered as Mena remained fixated on his wound. "Mena!"

She snapped back to his question. "Yes, sir. Sorry, sir. We were under attack," Mena clarified. "The enemy ship was destroyed."

Kypa considered this, shaking his head. "How bad are the damages?"

"Extensive, Your Highness. Shields are off-line. Propulsion is down to maneuvering thrusters only, and hull integrity in several sections has been compromised. The captain sent me to evacuate this level."

"Where are we now?" Kypa winced.

Mena grimaced with empathy. "We just exited hyperspace and are nearing our destination."

Kypa nodded. At least there was some good news. His thoughts jumped to Luna then the Reaper.

"Help me to my feet. We need to find Luna."

Kypa stood carefully, steeling himself against the excruciating pain. Once he was on his feet, Mena wrapped Kypa's arm around her neck.

"Luna went this way." Kypa gestured aft.

They took two steps before another massive explosion rocked the ship. Up ahead, the hull ruptured, and sudden depressurization whisked Kypa and Mena off their feet, dragging them down the corridor.

Clawing frantically for anything to latch on to, Kypa managed to grab a hold of a metal handle outside one of the ship's escape pods. Flailing about in mid-air like a kite in a storm, he looked over and spotted Mena clinging to a storage cabinet mounted on the wall. As the violent rush of air pulled them toward the cold vacuum of space, the cabinet lurched, and one corner detached from the wall.

"Mena!" Kypa shouted over the loud hiss of escaping air.

Mena had her claws dug into the cabinet, struggling to maintain a grip. Hearing Kypa's call, she looked to her left and saw him on the opposite side of the hall.

Pumped with adrenaline, Kypa looped his arm around the grab handle and hugged it tight. Extending his free hand, he yelled, "Take my hand!"

Sensing the cabinet was about to give way, Mena realized she had one shot at this. She retracted the claws in her left hand and extended her arm as far as it could reach.

Luna and Kypa touched fingertips, establishing a mental connection. Then, as if in slow motion, their eyes locked. In that fateful moment, Kypa experienced Mena's fear and helplessness as she felt the cabinet break free from the wall. Then, suddenly, she was gone. Mena's screams echoed in the corridor as she was swept through a gaping hole in the ship's hull and out into space.

"No!" Kypa cried out in horror.

His heart crumbled, but his own danger left him no time for sorrow. Still suspended in mid-air, Kypa realized the escape pod was his only hope for survival.

"Computer, open pod five!"

"Warning," the ship's main computer replied evenly. "Mating collar compromised. Seal integrity dropping."

"Override, on my authority!" Kypa yelled. "Do it now!"

The escape pod's hatch slid open.

Thinking fast, Kypa knew there was an identical grab handle on the opposite side of the wall inside the pod. Fighting against the howling wind, Kypa brought his knees up to his midsection, careful to protect his abdomen, which screamed with every movement.

Kypa then hooked the back of his foot inside the open hatchway. Using what semblance of leverage he had, Kypa swung his torso around in a lightning-fast maneuver and managed to grab the handle inside the pod.

Now straddling the hatchway, Kypa paused to catch his breath. The overexertion and the stabbing pain from his wound had zapped the last of his energy. But the end was in sight. With one final push, he would be safe inside the pod.

At the end of the corridor, the hull breach remained unsealed due to a blockage. A piece of metal debris had wedged itself at the base of the blast doors, preventing them from closing. Just as Kypa prepared to maneuver himself into the pod, the debris suddenly dislodged. A warning alarm sounded, and the blast doors slammed shut, allowing the cabin to pressurize.

The force of escaping air abruptly ceased, catching Kypa by surprise. He lost his grip and fell awkwardly into the pod, landing hard on his side.

Rolling onto his back, Kypa howled in agony. Without thinking, he wrapped his long fingers around the fragment protruding from his abdomen and angrily yanked it free. The pain was too much.

As his eyes rolled back in his head, the last thing he saw was the pod's hatch door closing.

Further up the corridor, Luna had been holding on for dear life in the stairwell when the chaos suddenly ended. The moment pressure was restored, Luna dropped face-first onto the floor.

Gathering herself, she slowly came to her feet. Her thoughts immediately turned to Kypa. Fearing the worst, she leapt down the stairs and landed by the open doorway. Entering the corridor, she found it deserted and littered with debris. Kypa was nowhere in sight.

Luna sprinted up the hall in search of her friend, daring to hope he was still alive. She passed the blood mark on the floor where she had last seen Kypa and continued to the end of the corridor. There, Luna reached the closed blast doors. Still no sign of him.

Backtracking, she ran to the control panel located outside pod five and activated the comm.

"Bridge, this is Luna."

A staticky reply followed. "Luna, this is Torga. Where are you?"

The sound of the captain's voice came as a welcomed relief. "Sub-Level One," she answered. "Is Prince Kypa with you?"

"Negative. I sent Mena to clear that level. Have you seen her?"

The mention of Mena gave Luna a glimmer of hope. Perhaps she had found Kypa and had helped him to safety.

Luna stepped away from the comm unit and called out to Mena at the top of her lungs. There was no response.

Returning to the comm, she replied, "No sign of them, Captain. I will keep looking."

In a passing glance, Luna noticed through the pod's window that the interior light was on. Curious, she peeked through the window. Her breath caught when she spotted Kypa lying on the floor, unconscious.

"Captain, I found the prince!" she reported. "He is inside pod five."

"Affirmative," Torga replied. He sounded relieved on that front, but they were far from out of danger. "Get in the—"

Torga's message cut out unexpectedly as an alarm sounded on the control panel. Luna jumped backward as the pod's blast door slid shut beside her, blocking access to it. She darted her eyes to the control panel where a warning message signaled the pod's mating collar was about to fail.

Luna lunged for the intercom. "Kypa, wake up!" she screamed.

Activating the internal viewer, she could see Kypa still on the floor, motionless.

Luna yelled again, but he remained unresponsive. Seconds later, the lifeboat jettisoned. Kypa was gone.

Luna pounded her fist on the wall, cursing to herself. If only she had found him a minute sooner.

The mothership then entered Earth's upper atmosphere. Jolted from the impact, Luna was thrown off her feet. She hit her head against the bulkhead, and everything went black.

Planet Earth
North Hamgyong Province, North Korea
30 December, 2355 Hours Local

Luna awoke with a gasp, finding herself facedown, wedged into a corner. Her eyes fluttered as she lifted her head then propped herself up on one elbow. She groaned. Every part of her body ached.

Forcing her eyes to adjust, she noticed the area was deathly quiet and still, a ghost ship. Main power appeared off-line as the eerie glow of the emergency lights provided scant illumination. Yet, even in the darkness, Luna could see the ship's dreadful state of disrepair.

Nearby, a bundle of power cables dangled from the ceiling. The frayed wires popped loudly, sending electrical sparks dancing across the floor. In that flash of light, Luna discovered the mothership was either listing to port or she had a concussion, perhaps both.

She winced. *What happened?*

Luna came to her feet and staggered against the force of gravity, making her way to the control panel beside pod five. Seeing the blast door was closed, it reminded her of Kypa being jettisoned in the lifeboat. She had to find him.

Thumbing the commlink button, she called the bridge, "Captain Torga, this is Luna. Come in."

No reply.

"Captain Torga, do you read me? This is Luna."

Still no answer.

Growing frustrated, she jabbed the button repeatedly. "Hello, hello! Is anyone there?"

Luna gave up, letting out an exasperated breath.

Pinching her forehead to relieve a growing headache, she ran a quick diagnostic. The ship was running on emergency power. Main systems were off-line, including the comms, which meant no distress beacon.

She checked their location. The mothership had failed to achieve orbit and crashed on the planet's surface.

"Well, at least we are on the right planet," Luna commented wryly. "Computer, locate pod five."

A map of Earth appeared on the screen, showing the mothership's location in proximity to pod five. Luna's shoulders sank. The distance between her and Kypa was considerable; they were separated by a massive ocean.

Knowing the prince was in grave danger, Luna searched for options. Judging by the mothership's current condition, the chances of getting airborne seemed unlikely, at least in the foreseeable future.

"I suppose I could swim," she thought aloud. It was doable but would take time, possibly weeks. Kypa could be dead before she reached him. Then it dawned on her.

The Reaper!

Hoping it was still airworthy, she headed for the cargo bay. Surely she would find someone along the way she could inform.

She made her way cautiously in the darkness to a nearby stairwell. Ascending the steps, Luna retrieved another medical kit from the wall. She had no idea what had happened to the first one. Continuing up to the main level, she found the corridor in shambles with collapsed ceiling beams and debris blocking her path.

"Luna?" a hoarse voice called.

Luna rounded sharply to find Captain Torga limping toward her. He looked battered and bruised with a deep gash on his forehead.

"Captain, thank goodness!" Seeing his condition, Luna opened the medical kit and started dressing his wounds. Torga did not resist.

"It is good to see you, Luna. I feared the worst." He searched the corridor behind her. "Where is Prince Kypa?"

"Jettisoned in pod five," she answered, making an effort to hold her voice steady. "He was seriously wounded. We need to find him."

Torga nodded thoughtfully, unsure at the moment just how they could accomplish such a feat. He also wanted to continue his search for survivors. He had discovered several bodies; Luna was the first live crew member he had encountered.

Luna read his expression. "Let me take the Reaper, Kypa's prototype vessel," she suggested. "I can rescue Kypa then return home and bring help."

"Good idea. Let us hope it is still in one piece. I—"

Torga paused, sensing movement behind him. He rounded slowly as a low hiss threatened from the shadows. The color drained from his face when he saw the obercai crouched before him.

Knowing his fate was sealed, Torga waved his arms above his head to make himself appear bigger. Then he turned his head sideways and yelled, "Luna, run!"

Wasting no time, the hulking beast attacked. The obercai pounced on Captain Torga, tackling him to the ground and knocking Luna against the bulkhead.

"Run!" the captain screamed as the beast tore into his chest.

Horrified, Luna fled in a panic. Barreling toward the front of the ship, she expected the obercai to be on her at any second.

Reaching a junction in the corridor, Luna paused. She could either continue forward to the bridge or turn left toward an exit leading outside.

Get off the ship! her mind screamed.

Luna made for the hatch door. Behind her, she could hear the beast's claws rattling on the grated metal floor as it thundered in pursuit.

"Computer, open the outer door!"

The ship's computer acknowledged, and the blast door slid upward. Natural light spilled into the area, along with a frigid blast of cold air and powdery snow that blanketed the ground outside.

Luna leapt from the ship. As soon as she was clear, she rounded to see the obercai overshoot the exit and skid to a halt inside.

"Computer, close the door!"

The obercai recovered, but it was too late to reach its prey before the heavy door screeched to a close and sealed shut.

Luna backpedaled, heart pounding in her chest. She listened to the beast as it clawed wildly on the opposite side of the door. Eventually, it gave up and moved on.

Oblivious to the blizzard conditions around her, Luna stared numbly at the black hull of the mothership. Gradually, her pulse slowed, and the bitter cold registered. Luna blinked back to reality. Shielding her face from the harsh winds, she circled in place, taking in her surroundings. Visibility was limited, but she noticed a thick forest behind her that could offer protection from the elements.

Then came a faint sound in the distance. It took Luna a moment to distinguish the mechanical noise over the howling winds. As the two North Korean Mi-24 attack helicopters approached, she realized the sound was not coming from nature.

This planet is inhabited!

In a moment of indecision, Luna considered reentering the ship and taking her chances with the obercai. However, the gruesome memory of Captain Torga's fate made her reconsider. Instead, she turned and ran for the forest.

The helicopters appeared moments later. They loitered overhead for several minutes, shining searchlights down on the mothership while Luna remained safely hidden in the tree line. She was huddled behind a large tree, shaking uncontrollably. Her aquasuit compensated for the freezing conditions and warmed her body, yet she could not stop shivering.

Luna took a deep breath to calm her nerves and formulate a plan. If a distress signal had not been sent, it would be quite some time before the mothership was considered overdue. A rescue seemed unlikely in the foreseeable future.

Then there was the Reaper. To get to it meant facing the obercai, and there was no way she was going back inside now. Guilt prodded her to try to warn the crew, but she remembered the comms were down. There was no way to broadcast a message from outside. Besides, for all Luna knew, she was the lone survivor.

Her only apparent recourse was to find Prince Kypa. She knew his general whereabouts, which was a start. With any luck, he was still alive and had called for help. Perhaps, by the time she reached him, a rescue ship might already be there. It was a slim hope, but enough to get her moving.

As the helicopters continued their reconnoiter, Luna stole away and began her trek through the wooded mountainside. The sooner she reached the ocean, the better. There was no telling what dangers lurked on the surface of this alien world.

1

TRIPLE FRONT

The Reaper
En route to Aiwa, three months later …

Dr. Neil Garrett entered the cockpit, stopping in the entry. "You know, these nano-suits may not leave much to the imagination," he remarked, "but man, they sure are comfortable."

Captain Ava Tan rotated her pilot's chair to find Neil modeling his new, form-fitting Aiwan attire and chuckled. "It's definitely you."

Having changed out of her North Korean uniform earlier, Ava agreed with Neil's assessment. The all-black nano-suit was more revealing than she preferred, conforming to her body from neck to toe. However, the nanites were silky to the touch, and the suit weighed next to nothing. But Ava's favorite feature was the padded feet with traction soles. They hit her arches just right, and for this Southern California girl, there was nothing more important than a comfortable pair of shoes.

Ava recentered her chair and turned her focus back to the head-up display. Outside, streams of fast-moving starlight raced past the windows.

Neil crossed the cockpit then sat on the two-seater bench in front of Ava, facing the bow of the ship. Looking over his shoulder, he asked with a devious grin, "So, have you tried it yet?"

"Tried what?" Ava replied distantly, not bothering to look away from her screen.

"You know … the suit," Neil hinted.

Clearly distracted by her readouts, Ava asked, "What about it?"

"The recycle feature …"

Ava's shoulders dropped. She turned to Neil with her eyebrow cocked. "Are you asking if I've relieved myself inside my suit?"

Neil nodded a little too eagerly, prompting Ava to roll her eyes at his juvenile question.

"Not that it's any of your business, but that would be a *no*," she replied. "Besides, that's just a last resort. All you have to do is hold it until you get back to the ship."

"Still," Neil persisted, "I'll give you all the money in my wallet if you test your suit first."

"Pass," Ava quickly shot him down. "Besides, your money's no good out here, anyway. Why don't *you* do it?" she dared. "I'll give you a cargo bay full of crystals if you deuce in your pants right now."

Neil cringed. "Gross. Now you're starting to sound like Colonel Nunez."

"Hans would do it," Ava countered.

Hans? Neil gave her an incredulous look. "Who's Hans?"

"Your *Star Wars* guy."

Neil guffawed. "You mean, Han? As in Han Solo?"

"Han, Hans, whatever." Ava shrugged with indifference. "He'd take that bet."

"No, he wouldn't." Neil laughed at the absurdity. "First off, this is wrong on so many levels. Second, maybe the Swedish version of my favorite *Star Wars* character would take your bet, but not *the* Han Solo."

"He would if Spock told him," Ava countered, suppressing a grin.

Neil stared at her, transfixed, not wanting to believe she could be serious. Then, as he realized she was jerking his chain, Ava broke out laughing.

"Ha, ha," Neil said sarcastically. "Nunez put you up to that, didn't she?"

"Actually, you can thank Dr. Landry for that one."

Neil nodded slowly, as if he were mentally adding his colleague, Dr. Rose Landry, to a make-believe retribution list. "Well, I know one person who's not getting a Christmas card this year."

Ava chuckled and went back to work.

Neil eyed her for a long moment then glanced around the cockpit, looking for something to do. Feeling like a third wheel, with no official responsibilities onboard, he let out a bored sigh.

"So, what are you working on?" he finally asked.

Ava motioned to the celestial map displayed on the HUD. "Just eyeing our path through hyperspace. We're still a few hours from our exit point."

"How can you possibly know what all that means?" Neil asked with a mix of curiosity and envy.

Ava shrugged. "I told you how Kypa revealed Garza's plans to me."

Neil nodded, recalling her telepathic episode with the Aiwan.

"He also shared extensive details about the Reaper. Somehow, all this makes sense to me now."

Lucky you, Neil thought. "What else did he share?"

Ava gestured to their surroundings. "This is it for the most part. He knew I needed to know more about the Reaper than just how to take off and land if I was going to help him escape from Groom Lake. As far as the ship goes, I feel I know it like the back of my hand. Everything else, I'm just as much in the dark as you."

That was not reassuring.

Neil sat back and imagined Aiwa, their destination, as Kypa had described it. The ringed world consisted of twelve moons, five underwater realms, and countless lifeforms no human had ever encountered. Being named Earth's ambassador to Aiwa was a dream come true. Yet, for all his theoretical work back on Earth, Dr. Neil Garrett, the astrophysicist, felt ill-prepared for what lay ahead.

"Are you worried?" he asked.

Her eyes still glued to the HUD, Ava replied flippantly, "Nah, the approach to Aiwa is pretty straightforward."

"No, I mean about visiting Aiwa ... encountering an alien civilization, and all that stuff," Neil clarified.

"Oh." Ava laughed at herself. "A little ... yeah. I mean, on one hand, we're returning Kypa home to his family and bringing a peace offering of much-needed crystals. That's got to go over well, right?" She paused, making a fair assumption. "Then again, we just went toe-to-toe with their best military commander and handed him his lunch. So, I'm guessing they might be a little sore about that."

"I am afraid that is the least of our worries," Kypa interjected.

Neil and Ava turned as Prince Kypa entered the cockpit.

"What do you mean?" Neil asked.

"Forgive me for eavesdropping," Kypa said then nodded a thanks as Neil and Ava waved dismissively. "You do raise a good point about Commodore Boa. We must be cautious around him, certainly. This may sound overly dramatic, but I am more concerned about the blue crystal powering the Reaper's core. It is quite possibly the most valuable commodity in the galaxy now."

Neil stood to face Kypa. Unused to not having pockets, he fidgeted with his hands before settling on crossing his arms. "You think we've got a target on our backs?" he asked.

Kypa sighed. "I am afraid so, Doctor."

This was not news to Ava. The moment she had defeated Commodore Boa's battlecruiser and witnessed the Reaper's full potential, she had realized they could never let their guard down. Every government, every entrepreneur, and every criminal mind would be vying to commandeer this vessel. And not just on Earth and Aiwa, but the rest of the galaxy, as well.

Fighting enemies on multiple fronts makes defense difficult, she mused, *and even harder to know who to trust.*

Neil pointed to two metal necklaces dangling from Kypa's hand. "What have you got there?"

The flimsy, metal hoops were less than one-sixteenth of an inch thick and roughly the diameter of a volleyball. Kypa handed one ring to each of them.

"These are additions to your nano-suits," Kypa replied. "I will explain in a moment. Now, if you would be so kind as to place these nano-rings over your heads and let them rest around your necks."

Ava and Neil complied. As soon as the rings settled around their necks, the nanites went to work, attaching themselves to the collars of their suits. Ava shuddered as the movement of the nanites tickled her neck.

"Very good." Kypa smiled with satisfaction. "The rings are now part of your suits."

"What are they for?" Ava asked.

"Protection," Kypa answered simply. "I've made similar devices for my family, and I thought they would serve you well. For starters, they can block all Aiwan telepathy. Your biosignatures were scanned when you put them on, and a neural link was established. Now you will be safe from any attempts to control your mind."

"Sweet," Ava remarked, twisting her head about to test the feel of the collar and suit.

"They can also generate a holographic helmet," Kypa explained. "Try it by giving your suit's AI a mental command to activate the helmet."

Ava went first. On command, a clear helmet formed from the neck and up over her head. It was nearly invisible to the human eye; only when the light hit the hologram projection at a certain angle could its presence be detected. And unlike the bulky helmets worn by NASA astronauts, this headgear fit snugly around Ava's head, giving her unhindered sightlines.

"Whoa," she marveled, rolling her head about. "It doesn't weigh a thing … and there's no echo. Neil, you gotta try it."

"Okay, here goes," he said, rubbing his hands together vigorously. Then he closed his eyes and scrunched his brow as he focused on giving his first mental command. As instructed, the helmet formed around his head.

Ava clapped, prompting Neil to open one eye first then the other. His face widened with delight at the sight of the HUD projected before him.

"This is so radical … and chic, I might add," he joked, tapping his finger against the invisible helmet. "This sure beats a tin foil hat."

Ava chuckled, but the joke was lost on Kypa.

"Each nano-suit has a standalone AI for you to interact with and customize individually," Kypa informed them. "Another benefit is its ability to translate any non-English communications for you, both incoming and outgoing dialogue."

To demonstrate, Kypa complimented Neil in Aiwan.

A slow grin formed on Neil's face as he listened to the phrase translated instantly to English. "Well, that's very kind of you to say, Kypa. Thank you for having me."

Neil's reply was then translated back to Kypa in Aiwan.

Kypa bowed his head in response.

"How cool is that?" Neil beamed. "An honest to goodness universal translator."

Eat your hearts out, Trekkies!

"The nano-rings also include a commlink," Kypa explained. "We will be able to communicate with one another and track each other's location at all times." Turning to Ava, he added, "You will even have constant contact with the Reaper."

"Does it include a remote starter for cold mornings?" Ava kidded. Seeing Kypa's blank expression, she waved it off. "Never mind. Bad joke. What else can these do?"

"The nano-suits work with or without the helmet to regulate your body temperature and recycle waste, similar to my aquasuit."

Neil and Ava exchanged looks, suppressing their grins.

"Likewise, you will not need your helmet on for the translator feature to work. However, you will need your helmet on for life support."

"Life support," Neil said. "Does it work in outer space?"

"Yes, for about six hours," Kypa answered. "While you are in the capital, you need not worry about wearing your helmet. Every underwater structure on Aiwa maintains an ambient pressure matching the planet's surface. You should be quite comfortable. Just remember to wear your helmet if you decide to step out for a swim. Otherwise, the hydrostatic pressures will crush you instantly."

"Duly noted." Ava nodded with a grin. "Anything else?"

"Yes, the helmet also includes an internal HUD, as you like to call it. You may toggle the holographic projection on and off to display whatever information you wish."

"Such as …?" Neil asked.

Kypa shrugged. "Basic readings, like temperature, navigation, biometrics … even archives on known civilizations. I thought this might aid your diplomatic efforts."

Neil brightened, considering the possibilities. Anything that made him more self-sufficient and less of a third wheel was welcomed news.

"Thanks, Kypa. I appreciate it."

Kypa dipped his chin. "My pleasure, Ambassador."

"Speaking of other civilizations," Ava started, "Boa mentioned Krunig's horde had returned. What did he mean by that?"

Kypa's cheerful demeanor turned serious. "Grawn Krunig," he replied. "His horde is just one faction within the Madreen Crime Syndicate, the galaxy's largest group of harvesters. He—we assume Krunig is a *he*—is brutal and tenacious. He is fixated on conquering Aiwa."

"You've never met him?" Ava asked.

Kypa shook his head. "We have received several bombastic threats from Krunig, but I have never crossed paths with him personally. Would you like to see him?"

Ava and Neil nodded in unison.

Kypa sent a mental command to the Reaper's main computer, calling up the latest image of Grawn Krunig. When it appeared on Ava's HUD, Kypa asked, "May I?"

Ava pulled back her hands. "Sure, go for it."

Grabbing the holographic image off her display, Kypa tossed it into the middle of the room so they could see their enemy at his full height.

Standing seven feet tall, Krunig wore the customary crimson armor of a Madreen Grawn, an underboss in charge of an assigned sector who reported directly to Grawn Supreme. His armor, uniquely designed to protect his body and identity, accentuated Krunig's ominous frame. He had two legs that were as thick as tree trunks and four arms. His two upper arms were longer and more muscular than the bottom pair, which had easy access to crisscrossing blade hilts attached to his chest plate.

But what made Krunig most intimidating was his facial features, or lack thereof. Hidden behind a sinister helmet, Krunig's appearance remained as mysterious as his background. Only a black, V-shaped optical lens that stretched from ear to ear—if he had ears—provided any visual clue as to his persona.

"Whoa," Ava muttered in mild surprise.

Kypa started the recording, and the crime lord suddenly came to life, pointing his finger right at Neil and Ava. They flinched.

"*I am coming for you, Loka,*" Krunig warned in a thundering voice. "*Soon, I will rain fire on the Five Realms, and you will pay for your resistance with every ounce of Aiwan blood!*"

The image froze with Krunig paused in a threatening pose.

Neil turned to Kypa, incredulous. "So much for veiled threats."

Kypa turned off the display. "Krunig's hit and run tactics over the years have taken their toll. Our defenses are weakening due to a diminishing supply of crystals."

"We can help with both," Ava insisted.

Kypa mustered a thin, appreciative smile, but his concern remained. Vanquishing one enemy did not mean their troubles would go away. In fact, he feared the Reaper would only draw more attention to Aiwa.

Ava read his reaction and understood. Krunig was the immediate threat, but like the mythical Hydra, when one head was cut off, two more appeared. The Madreen probably had others waiting in the wings to replace Krunig and, as Kypa alluded, harvesters were not their only enemy.

It was a lot to consider as Ava yawned heavily. Still recovering from her mission to North Korea, she had yet to catch up on sleep. As much as she hated to leave the discussion, fatigue was getting the best of her.

"Sorry, guys. Can we pick this up later? I need some sleep."

Kypa and Neil both nodded in understanding and shooed her away.

Ava retired to the main cabin. Sleepy-eyed, she fumbled in the darkness for the button on the wall panel to activate the hologram bunk. As soon as she pressed it, Ava realized a mental command would have accomplished the task much faster, but she was too tired to think straight.

Before climbing into bed, Ava opened a compartment where she stored her belongings. Inside, she retrieved the wool North Korean uniform jacket, given to her by General Vong Yong-hae, the man who had sacrificed his life for hers. Vong had paid the ultimate price to buy freedom for his daughter, Ji-eun, and her unborn baby.

Ava wondered how Ji-eun was faring in the United States, along with Min-jun, the ex-North Korean special forces operator who had led her into the country and had extracted Ji-eun. Looking around the Reaper, Ava appreciated their courage. If it were not for the three of them, none of this would be possible.

Retrieving the coat, Ava's brown, leather wallet fell out of her purse and onto the floor. It opened to a picture of Ava and her ex-fiancé, Mark Jordan. The photo captured them raising two pints of beer and smiling for the camera.

Ava remembered that day vividly. They had attended an outdoor music festival last summer, right before they had left for Djibouti … a lifetime ago.

She stared at Mark's image for a long while, studying every contour of his face. He had been ruggedly handsome and built of solid muscle; probably the most physically fit person she had ever known. She would give anything to have his thick arms wrapped around her right now.

Ava wiped her eyes with shaky fingers. Moments like these were bittersweet. She missed Mark fiercely, but he was gone, and she was on a different path now. Yet, seeing his photo evoked feelings of guilt. Her dreams had come true, while Mark's life had been cut short.

Closing her wallet, Ava put it back in her purse. She stowed her belongings in the compartment, all except the oversized uniform jacket. Ava then crawled onto the hologram bunk hovering three feet off the ground.

"Computer, kill the lights."

As the cabin dimmed, Ava closed her eyes and curled up under the jacket. The nano-suit provided all the warmth she needed but snuggling under a blanket—or the next best thing—always helped her sleep.

Ava drifted off to the distant murmur of Neil and Kypa talking in the background. The last thing she heard was Neil asking Kypa what he looked forward to most when he returned home.

"My family," Kypa answered without hesitation. "I was only supposed to be gone a short while. They must be quite worried."

"I'm sure they'll be very happy to see you."

Kypa forced a halfhearted smile. "They might be the only ones."

Neil gave him a curious look. It was out of character for Kypa to invite self-pity. "What are you talking about?"

The Aiwan sighed. "It never looks good when the leader of a failed expedition returns home alone. I lost many friends and colleagues." After a solemn pause, he added, "They had families, too, yet I survived."

"I'm sorry for your loss," Neil empathized, "but it wasn't your fault. You were attacked, right?"

"Yes, but I expect my father will not be so understanding."

"Why's that?" Neil inquired.

"The Reaper, for one," Kypa replied. "I built it in secret by stealing precious resources. Then I handed it over to a foreign race who used it against us."

"Well, there is that, I guess." Neil smiled. "But you and Ava were only trying to prevent a war."

"True. Although, I doubt Commodore Boa's description of the incident will be as generous."

"You're bringing back crystals, too," Neil pointed out. "That's got to count for something."

"It will help, but it is not a permanent solution."

Neil considered this for a moment. "I've been meaning to ask: why haven't you tried other natural resources, like solar or wind power?"

"We have," Kypa replied with a defeated tone. "Those technologies are easy targets on the planet's surface, as well as from orbit. Harvesting crystals remains our best option, but as you know, Aiwa's supply is diminishing quickly."

Neil tried to stay upbeat. "Well, like Ava said, if we can establish peaceful relations between Earth and Aiwa, perhaps we can use the Reaper to defeat Krunig *and* rebuild Aiwa. It's a win-win. Not even King Loka can argue with that."

Kypa wished it was that simple. "You do not know my father. Besides, it will be complicated. There are those in the High Court who do not want me as successor to the throne. There will be a trial, and I will be made to answer for my crimes."

"There's an old saying on Earth … *No prophet is accepted in his hometown.*"

"Luke chapter four, verse twenty-four," Kypa cited the biblical reference.

"That's the one," Neil affirmed, impressed by Kypa's recall. "I think humans and Aiwans are more alike than we know. If I'm given the chance to testify on your behalf, I will argue that you were acting in both of our people's best interests."

"Thank you. That is most kind."

Neil clapped Kypa on the shoulder. "That's what friends are for." He paused, thinking of home. "You know, when we left for Aiwa, I thought we drew the long straw. I can only imagine what the fallout from your visit is like back home."

2

FALLOUT

Planet Earth
The White House, Washington, D.C.

A screaming child and a barking dog shook President Fitzgerald and the First Lady out of their peaceful slumber. In unison, both parents shot bolt upright in bed, threw off the covers, and were out the bedroom door in seconds.

Candace crossed the hall into the West Room first. She pushed the girls' bedroom door open and flipped the light on. Lilly, their tuxedo Pittie, rushed to her feet, whimpering as if to warn her alpha that something was wrong with the children.

Sitting up in the twin bed to the left, Rebecca was curled against the headboard, crying. She was the youngest of the seven-year-old twins by fifteen minutes. Across from her, Sophie groaned in protest and pulled the blankets over her eyes.

Candance rushed to Becca's side and gently pulled her into an embrace. "Baby, what's wrong?"

"I had a bad dream," she sobbed, crawling into her mother's arms. "Monsters, Mommy."

Roger knelt on the floor to keep Lilly occupied. The First Dog nudged her snout repeatedly under his hand, demanding affection, and got it. As the

President petted her nonstop, Roger glanced at Sophie, who remained huddled under the covers, determined not to lose any sleep. Meanwhile, Candace held Becca close.

"There are no monsters here, baby," she calmly reassured her daughter. "It was just a bad dream."

"The aliens." Becca sniffled.

Candace passed a concerned look to her husband—Roger's cue to interject.

The President shuffled closer to Becca's bedside. He smiled soothingly and wiped a lone tear from her cheek. "Mommy's right, kiddo. Remember, we talked about this. Kypa used to be scared of us, too, but now we're friends."

"He's gone home to be with his family," Candace added.

"Are they coming back?" Becca asked with a pouty face.

Good question, the President thought grimly. They had not received a single word from Captain Tan, Dr. Garrett, or Prince Kypa since their departure. There was no telling if or when the Aiwans and other harvesters might return.

"I hope they do come back," Roger said cheerily. "I can't wait to learn more about Kypa and his people. He even has a daughter your age. You know, it's a very exciting time for all Americans—"

Becca yawned heavily, signaling to her father that his speech was best kept for registered voters.

With a nod to his wife, Roger backed away as Candace tucked Becca under the covers. With her favorite stuffed animal—Sleepy Bear—at her side, Becca then drifted off to sleep.

Relieved the crisis was over, the President stood and gave Lilly a quick neck scratch before stepping out into the hall.

Candace turned off the lights on her way out but kept the door slightly cracked. Out in the hall, the husband-and-wife team exchanged knuckle bumps. Then Candace moved in close and wrapped her arms around Roger's midsection.

"I have to admit," she whispered. "I have the same fears."

The President of the United States sighed heavily. "So do I, babe. We all do."

United Nations Headquarters, New York City, New York

The three-vehicle motorcade carrying Ambassador Haley Nichols and her protection detail arrived at the United Nations Headquarters to find a raucous crowd of protesters lining the streets. Squads of New York's finest, dressed in riot gear, were stationed out front to keep the mob at bay.

As the ambassador's vehicle approached the security blockade, Nichols peered out the window of her Cadillac SUV. She was both amused and shocked by the crowd. On one hand, those wanting peace with the Aiwans seemed to be decked out in every kind of science-fiction apparel imaginable. One man, who stood out, was dressed as Mork from Ork. His family—also in costume—toted signs that read, "*Nanu Nanu!*" Nichols gave a half-suppressed laugh. The man looked deathly serious in his homemade, red onesie.

Then there were those protestors who wanted nothing to do with the Aiwans whatsoever. This group's malevolence was palpable. Dressed in camouflage fatigues, they chanted hate-filled expletives, demanding the U.N. create an alien defense force to blow those commie-loving aliens back to the outer rim.

Nichols shook her head in disbelief. "You gotta love democracy," she murmured.

"Ma'am?" her twenty-five-year-old assistant, Sara, asked.

"Nothing." The ambassador waved dismissively. "How are we looking on time?"

"We're good. The session starts in twenty minutes … if we can get through this crowd, that is."

The motorcade crept through security then entered the underground parking structure. Nichols was in the middle vehicle.

On Sublevel One, her driver pulled up in front of an entrance that was guarded by two uniformed U.N. security officers. As soon as the vehicle came to a stop, Special Agent Williams of the Diplomatic Security Service hopped out of the front passenger door. Members of the ambassador's protection detail in the other vehicles also appeared, scanning the garage for threats.

"All clear," the agents reported.

Satisfied, Agent Williams opened the back door. Ambassador Nichols stepped out and made a beeline for the Conference Building's entrance, surrounded by her guards. Sara tried to keep up in her high heels.

Located in the Turtle Bay neighborhood of Manhattan, just a stone's throw from the East River, the United Nations Headquarters complex consisted of four main buildings—the Secretariat Building, the General Assembly, the Conference Building, and the Dag Hammarskjöld Library. Ambassador Nichols headed straight for the Security Council Chamber, located in the Conference Building.

As one of the six primary bodies of the United Nations, the Security Council was charged with ensuring international peace and security, including the power to establish peacekeeping operations, enact international sanctions, and authorize military action. All of which were on today's docket. This was the ambassador's second official meeting since being appointed by President Fitzgerald. She expected a lively debate.

Nichols and her entourage arrived at the chamber with five minutes to spare. Agent Williams opened the door; Nichols entered alone.

The Security Council Chamber was a high-ceiling room, furnished by Norway and designed by leading Norwegian architect, Arnstein Rynning Arneberg. The room was easily identified by its central horseshoe-shaped table. On the east wall, behind the table, was a large mural by Norwegian artist, Per Lasson Krohg. The mural was meant to symbolize the promise of future peace and individual freedom, a fitting theme for the day.

Nichols took her assigned seat. To her right was the ambassador from the United Kingdom. Belgium's ambassador was to her left. The other members of the Security Council were already seated.

Jean-Francois Garnier, the French ambassador, called the meeting to order.

Nichols eyed the council's agenda set out on a piece of paper in front of her. There was only one topic listed: creation of an alien defense force.

The White House, Washington, D.C.

President Fitzgerald watched the Security Council meeting on television with keen interest. Joining him in the Oval Office was his trusted think tank. Seated in the chair to his left was the Vice President, Cathy Harrington. Moving clockwise from her left, on the first couch, were Ernie Gutierrez, Chief of Staff; Ken Hreno, National Security Advisor; and Russ Franks, Secretary of Defense. Across from them on the opposite couch were Bill Nguyen, Secretary of State, and acting Chairman of the Joint Chiefs of Staff, Admiral Susan Donnelly. The only two people missing were his replacements for the Director of National Intelligence and Director of the Central Intelligence Agency. Both of his nominations, Guy Lannister and Maxine Ratliff, were on the Hill today in their first day of Senate confirmation hearings.

"They're not pulling any punches," Fitzgerald remarked, watching Ambassador Nichols skillfully navigate a barrage of questions regarding U.S. involvement in the events that had occurred at Groom Lake over the past week. It seemed every member of the U.N. Security Council had come to seek a pound of flesh.

And who could blame them? the President lamented.

The final death toll from the Aiwan skirmish had been significant. Seven astronauts had been lost aboard the International Space Station. Two hundred and six aviators from Russia, China, Japan, and the United States had been shot down over the Sea of Japan. Sixty-two sailors aboard the Russian, Akula-class submarine, *Gepard*, were missing somewhere near Guam, and an estimated two hundred North Korean soldiers—plus one Supreme Leader—had been killed by the fiery destruction of the Aiwan mothership. So far, the President's cover story regarding the events in North Hamgyong Province was holding up. For how long was yet to be seen.

Bill Nguyen leaned forward and turned toward the President. "Haley's tough as nails, sir. She knew it would be brutal today."

The President could not argue with Bill's assessment of Ambassador Nichols. He had recommended her for the post, after all. It was one of the best decisions of his presidency.

"What about security?" Fitzgerald asked.

"All's quiet on the home front, relatively speaking," Ernie replied, hoping not to jinx their good fortune. "FBI and Homeland have their ears to the ground, but so far, no hint of any credible domestic threats."

"The crowd certainly appears to be getting bigger outside," the Vice President remarked with concern.

"Yes, ma'am," Ernie agreed. "Knock on wood everyone continues to behave." He did not need to remind her there were four thousand National Guardsmen standing by in riot gear just in case the crowd got unruly.

Fitzgerald turned to his Secretary of Defense. "Russ?"

"Our forces remain at DEFCON-4, Mr. President. No immediate threats detected across the globe ... or from space," he added as an afterthought.

"Any insights from Garza and Sizemore?" the President asked. The last time he had seen either man was on closed-circuit television. They had been in orange jumpsuits, being interrogated at Groom Lake by military investigators.

"Both are playing hard to get, Mr. President," Russ replied. "Sizemore is demanding a full pardon in exchange for his testimony against Mathias."

That came as no surprise. "What about Garza?"

Russ shrugged. "Nothing, yet. Garza sees himself as a patriot. He believes he was acting in the best interest of the country and makes no apologies for it."

"God love him." Cathy smirked, glad the "former" general was gone. It was no secret she and Garza had not seen eye-to-eye on matters in the past, but it was his patronizing tone that rubbed her the wrong way. At first, she had thought it was deliberate to test her resolve, then the VP had concluded that it was just one of his many character defects.

"Keep me apprised," the President told Russ. "Where are we at with contingency plans?"

"Regarding the harvesters?" Russ clarified, and the President nodded. "We're working up various defensive measures and counterstrike proposals, sir. Our hope is that we don't have to go it alone and the Security Council agrees to an international coalition. A multilateral response is our best defense, considering any space-related threat we face will be technologically superior."

The President looked at Admiral Donnelly, who agreed.

"A lot is hinging on how things go today," Bill Nguyen, Secretary of State, chimed in. "Naturally, everyone is still processing what's gone down over the past week, and they're not happy we kept them in the dark. Regardless of how the world views us right now, we have to put up a united front if we hope to survive the harvester threat."

Fitzgerald thought for a moment just how difficult that would be. One of humanity's best qualities was its ability to band together in a crisis. Yet, every nation on Earth had deeply-rooted cultural, social, political, and economic differences that were not easily set aside for the sake of multilateralism. Each country had its own vision of how this should play out. Who was to say the United States' version trumped the others?

"Just keep working the backchannels to sway any lingering discord," Fitzgerald said.

"Yes, Mr. President."

As Fitzgerald and the group turned their attention back to the television, the volume of dissension at the United Nations rose sharply. Unfazed, Ambassador Nichols parried another round of blatant accusations.

United Nations Headquarters, New York City, New York

"What else is the United States not telling us?" the livid ambassador from Russia demanded. "How do we know your President is not hiding more of those creatures and planning to use their technology against the rest of us?"

Nichols remained even-keeled, resisting the urge to react. The allegation was preposterous, but Nichols knew if she were in his shoes, she would probably feel the same.

After he finished his tirade, a few council members seconded the notion. The U.S. ambassador allowed the room to grow silent before replying.

"Since the formation of this council, the United States has championed its cause without equal. From climate change and biodiversity to human trafficking and nuclear disarmament, my President and our country has stood unequivocally for peace and democracy, for all the peoples of Earth. I can assure you, without a doubt, there are no other alien lifeforms residing anywhere in the United States or its territories."

3

SEA HUNT

Planet Earth
North Pacific Ocean

Luna floated effortlessly below the ocean surface, allowing the current to carry her as she searched for Kypa in the general vicinity of his last known location. It had taken her almost a month to swim from North Korea. The journey had been long, but not as arduous as she had expected.

To her dismay, all of Luna's efforts so far had proven futile. For two weeks, she had methodically investigated the ocean floor surrounding Kauai and nearby atolls for any evidence of her friend. Thus far, there were no signs of him or his escape pod anywhere. Even attempts to communicate with the locals—primarily telepathic bottle-nosed dolphins—turned up little more than a vague recollection of a splashdown event that occurred about the same time the mothership had crashed. It was not much to go on, but at least it was something.

Luna scoured the area in question from sunup to sundown. Widening her search, she refused to quit, knowing Kypa would do the same for her. In fact, he *had* risked everything for her.

Many years ago, when her home in Cirros had been destroyed by massive undersea earthquakes, Kypa had championed aid relief for Luna and her fellow refugees when no one else would, including King Loka. Kypa's efforts continued to this day, and despite being in the minority, Luna considered him a prince worthy of the title. Kypa was also her closest friend and colleague. Continuing the search was the least she could do until more help arrived.

Luna popped her head above the ocean surface, riding the waves, and noticed the sun setting. The days were shorter on this world, which did not help her search. Still, she had been at it all day, and now her crystal blue eyes hung heavy. Her stomach growled something fierce, and she realized she had not eaten since the previous morning.

Venturing south, Luna headed back toward Johnston Atoll, a tiny island approximately seven hundred and fifty nautical miles from Kauai, Hawaii. The remote atoll made for a safe location to get some much-needed sleep. On the way, she planned to find a meal.

A twelve-foot tiger shark lurking in the area had the same idea. For the past twenty minutes, the thirteen-hundred-pound macropredator trailed Luna at a distance, sizing up its potential prey. With every smooth swing of its massive tail, the shark gradually inched closer. Careful not to scare its meal away, the shark's mid-range senses—vision and lateral line system—allowed it to hone in further on Luna. Neither sense detected vibrations in the water to indicate its prey was in distress or aware of danger. This heightened the shark's anticipation, but the hunter remained patient. Appearing uninterested, the shark's slow, monotonous approach was a ruse to lull its prey into a false sense of security.

Shadowing Luna from below, the shark suddenly launched its attack in a burst of speed toward the surface. When it was within inches of the kill, the shark opened its enormous jaws, baring rows of razor-sharp teeth, and rolled back its lifeless, black eyes.

Luna countered at the last second. Having been aware of the shark's presence for quite some time, she had wisely conserved energy and waited for her meal to come to her. As soon as the shark attacked, Luna rounded sharply in a graceful and elusive spin. The shark's jaws clamped down with enough force to crush every bone in Luna's body. Instead of flesh, however, it only caught a mouthful of seawater.

Luna's spin brought her under the shark. Extending her claw-like fingernails, she rammed both hands into the shark's belly.

The incisions stunned the shark. It panicked and tried bolting for safety, but the predator was now the prey.

Luna held on as she was dragged through the water at a high speed. Despite the shark's thrashing, she focused intently on making a mental connection with the shark. Once that was established, the shark began to slow. Its behavior became docile as Luna coaxed it into a quasi-vegetative state. The shark remained awake but unable to respond as Luna finished it off.

Using her claws, she began stabbing the shark's belly with ferocity. Her razor-sharp fingernails acted like ice picks, chipping away at the shark's thick skin. Luna was relentless. As dark red blood billowed like clouds in the surrounding water, the shark convulsed helplessly.

Once all life had drained from the fish, Luna began slicing the shark open, cutting her way toward the tail. She then disemboweled the shark, allowing the entrails to fall out of the shark's body cavity. Knowing the scent of blood would attract other predators, Luna wasted no time carving away a large section of meat for her dinner. She discarded the rest.

As the dead shark began its slow descent into the murky depths, Luna placed her meal in her mouth and swam away at top speed. Minutes later, she reached the sandy beach of Johnston Atoll. This remote island had been her base of operations for the past few days. From all previous visits, the atoll appeared deserted. Still, she approached cautiously, ever-mindful of land-dwelling threats.

Lifting her head above the water to see the shoreline, Luna scanned the island in both directions. Seeing no movement, she exited the water and crawled up the beach to a thicket of tall grass. From this location, she could see all the way to the other end of the island, including an abandoned airfield.

Allowing herself to relax, Luna turned to face the ocean. She sat cross-legged on the water's edge and tore off a mouthful of shark meat. Luna found the texture to be a bit tough for her liking, but the flavor was palatable.

As she chewed, Luna stared out at the fiery sunset in the distance. Bathing in the warm glow of fading sunlight, she soaked up the breathtaking hues of orange, purple, and red.

This is a beautiful world, she thought to herself. It reminded her of Aiwa … of home.

With each passing day, Aiwa seemed more and more out of her reach. The guilt of leaving her crewmates behind weighed heavily, as well. Searching for Kypa was her duty, but she regretted abandoning any survivors aboard the mothership, especially with an obercai running loose. Leaving the crash site had been the most difficult decision of her life. Yet, if Aiwa was to survive, they needed Kypa and his prototype vessel, the Reaper. That had been their whole reason for coming here.

As she continued eating, Luna promised herself that the death of Captain

Torga and the others would not be in vain. If she was the only survivor, she would find a way to make sure others knew of their sacrifice.

Stuffed to the gills—not that she had any—Luna tossed the remains of her meal back into the water for others to scavenge. Then she rolled onto her back and placed her hands behind her head, staring up at the stars. Sleep came quickly.

The next morning, Luna awoke with a start. She sat up sharply to find herself surrounded by dozens of hungry seagulls foraging the beachhead for food. Realizing they were not a threat, just an annoyance, Luna threw a handful of sand in their direction and watched them flap away, squawking in protest.

She yawned heavily and rubbed her tired eyes. What sleep she had managed had been restless, fraught with nightmares from the mothership's crash. Now she was awake, feeling groggy and sluggish.

Luna shaded her eyes from the rising sun and looked up and down the beach. It was still empty.

As the maddening chorus of seagulls continued, any hope of drifting back to sleep was lost. Even being able to enjoy the calming sound of the morning tide was ruined by the irritating birds. Rather than hang around listening to this racket, Luna decided to start her day. At least searching for Kypa gave her purpose and kept her mind off things.

She came to her feet and dusted the sand off her aquasuit. Wading into the surf, Luna dove forward in a graceful arc and disappeared under the water.

Twenty minutes later, a single-engine Cessna made a low-level flyover of the island. After circling Johnston Atoll twice to inspect the dilapidated runway, the tiny aircraft set down. Inside the cockpit, the pilot taxied to a rundown hangar—the remnants of a long-since abandoned United States Air Force base.

The aircraft came to a stop and the engine cut off. As the propeller wound down, the cockpit door opened, releasing the operatic vocals of "Bohemian Rhapsody" by Queen. Out stepped the fifty-nine-year-old pilot—a white man wearing a tattered fishing hat to cover his bald head, along with khaki Bermuda shorts and a colorful, Hawaiian-style camp shirt. In his hand, he carried a 1980's-era Sony Boombox blaring his favorite rock band.

"*Galileo! Galileo! Galileo, Figaro, magnifico-o-o-oh!*"

His off-key, high-pitched singing would have scared off any inhabitant within earshot, but Dr. Samuel Hullinger did not care. The entire island—all one point zero three miles of it—was his own private concert hall, and he loved singing as if no one could hear him … and no one could. Johnston Atoll was closed to the public.

Dr. Hullinger was one of the few who had special permission to visit the National Wildlife Refuge. Access required a Letter of Authorization from the United States Air Force and a Special Use Permit from the U.S. Fish and Wildlife Service. Neither of those were a problem for the marine biologist. His research funding came almost exclusively from Mathias Industries, and they had a way of circumventing red tape.

Switching off his tunes, Dr. Hullinger set his radio down on the tarmac and began unpacking the wheel chocks from the aircraft's storage compartment. Placing the blocks around the wheels, he then unloaded his gear. For this trip, Hullinger had packed light. He was only planning to stay a week.

Anxious to stretch his legs and get started, Hullinger put off setting up camp and decided to take a stroll around the island. He arrived at the beach and began searching for anything out of the ordinary that had washed ashore. Half a mile into his walk, the scientist located a large object floating in the water next to a decrepit jetty.

Hullinger's brow furrowed as he squinted at it from afar. His first guess was a carcass of some kind. Moving to the water's edge, it became evident the remains were definitely a tiger shark, judging by its distinctive markings. It had been a big one, too.

Despite having been picked clean by other fish, Hullinger could tell by the distance between the dorsal fin and the tail that the shark had been at least ten to twelve feet in length. Once he pulled it to shore, a more exact measurement could be taken.

Eyeing the water around the carcass, it appeared the feeding frenzy had ended, but one could never tell. Hullinger cautiously waded waist-high into the water, mindful of any dark shadows in the otherwise crystal-clear water. Seizing the tail, Hullinger dragged the carcass to shore.

Winded by the effort, he removed his hat and wiped the sweat from his brow. As he suspected, there was not much left of the bloated remains. Retrieving a pair of wire-rimmed spectacles from his shirt pocket, he knelt down beside his discovery.

"Let's see what we have here," Hullinger said then gagged from the stench.

Examining the shark from various angles, he found multiple peculiar gashes in its underbelly. The fish had been sliced open from the throat to its pelvic fins. When he looked inside the body cavity, Dr. Hullinger found most of the internal organs were missing.

"Damn poachers," he muttered bitterly.

He leaned in closer, taking particular interest in a large section of flesh that appeared to have been cut away. The edges were serrated, but not from the teeth of a larger predator. This looked like the work of a jagged blade, further evidence the shark had been gutted and used for chum, most likely.

Hullinger let out a sigh of frustration. Sharks were needed for a healthy ocean, not sports fishing. But there was nothing he could do about it now.

Dragging the carcass back into the water, he left the shark behind and continued his walk around the island. Hullinger made it a quarter mile further before stopping in his tracks. Looking down, he noticed a set of oversized footprints in the sand. He knelt to get a closer look. These were not human footprints.

He scanned the immediate area for more prints, but the trail led straight into the ocean. Hullinger retrieved his cell phone and opened up the camera app. With the rising tide, the footprints would soon be washed away. He set his pencil down beside each footprint to give it scale and snapped two dozen photos from different angles. The scientist then switched to his video recorder and began recording his observations. Whatever lifeform had ventured to this shore had to be tall, at least seven feet high, judging by its gait, and it had webbed feet.

A mental image of *The Creature from the Black Lagoon* popped into his head. Hullinger quickly dismissed it as ridiculous ... or was it? Then it dawned on him.

"Aliens."

Recalling the images he had seen on the news, the scientist figured Aiwan physiology closely resembled the evidence here. It was also reported that Prince Kypa only ate seafood.

"The shark ..." he remembered, whipping his head around in the direction of the carcass. It made total sense now, except Prince Kypa was no longer on Earth. He had returned to his homeworld.

"Could there be others?" Hullinger asked himself.

Suddenly, he became highly alert to his surroundings. Perhaps he was not alone on this island, after all. For a moment, he considered going back to the shark for further examination but thought better of it.

What if I had interrupted its meal? he considered. It might not take kindly to it a second time.

Hullinger now felt vulnerable out in the open. He decided to return to the plane. Maybe the lifeform would come back to its meal. If it did, he had binoculars and a telescope onboard to study it from afar. In the meantime, a discovery like this was too big to keep to himself. Hullinger decided to make a phone call.

Mathias Industries Research Vessel, *Billy Bones*

Approximately twenty-six hundred nautical miles to the west of Johnston Atoll, the world's most advanced deep sea research vessel, *Billy Bones*, held station over Challenger Deep. Riding the Western Pacific's still waters, *Billy Bones* was the pride of billionaire venture capitalist, Dr. M. Edmund Mathias.

Named after the fictional character in the Robert Louis Stevens' book, *Treasure Island*, *Billy Bones* was modeled after the United States Navy Ship, *Impeccable*. Stretching two hundred and eighty-one feet in length from stem to stern, this unique vessel used a twin-hull catamaran design known as SWATH— Small Waterplane Area Twin Hull—to maximize the ship's stability, even in high seas and at high speeds.

Originally, the Navy had planned five *Impeccable*-class ships, but only one was ever commissioned after the builder went bankrupt. Mathias had seized upon the opportunity, purchased the blueprints, and built a modified version to suit his company's deep-sea pursuits. Never in a million years could he have predicted how much that investment would pay off. Now he was sitting on the greatest treasure trove in history and had the perfect vessel to exploit it.

On the main deck, inside the ship's navigation room, Mathias hovered over a six-by-nine-foot table with a flat screen monitor set within. A team of deep-sea salvagers huddled along with him around the table, discussing enlarged images of the cavern within Challenger Deep where the magnetarite crystals were located.

"How much longer until the drones are ready?" Mathias asked impatiently.

"Within the hour," his chief engineer replied.

Below deck, a team had been working feverishly to retrofit four remotely operated vehicles with armatures strong enough to extract crystals. This was their first attempt at harvesting, and no one knew what to expect.

"Get it done," Mathias added. "I want *Profiteer* ready to launch by daybreak."

"Yes, sir," the engineer replied, making eye contact around the table with his team to ensure they shared a mutual understanding. "She'll be ready."

Profiteer was Mathias' manned, deep-sea submersible vehicle. It had full-ocean depth capability, meaning it could safely descend thirty-six thousand feet to the bottom of Challenger Deep. Three days earlier, Mathias had piloted the vehicle into the abyss himself and had located the crystal deposits.

Mathias grumbled inwardly. If only they had Aiwan technology, the site could have been harvested by now.

The side door opened, allowing a warm breeze to enter the room. All eyes turned in that direction, most hoping it was the boss's scantily-clad girlfriend. Instead, in walked Mr. Renzo, a stern-faced, Peruvian man in his mid-thirties. He was lean and fit with a dark complexion. His bowl-cut hairstyle was shaved above the ears to honor his Chachapoyan heritage—an ancient tribe from the cloud forests of the Andes.

Mr. Renzo wore an all-black Wing Chun martial arts suit for comfort and flexibility. A leather strap slung across his chest, secured a black leather carrying case to his back. It held a custom-built, two-piece, big bore blowgun—his weapon of choice.

An uneasy tension filled the air as soon as Mathias' "fixer" entered the room. Despite his youthful appearance, Mr. Renzo carried the quiet confidence of a dangerous man. The crew learned quickly not to challenge his authority.

Early in the voyage, a drunken crewman had become belligerent and picked a fight with Mr. Renzo. The Peruvian showed no mercy or remorse. Renzo made quick work of the man, crushing his windpipe before throwing him overboard without breaking a sweat. No further performance issues had been reported since the incident.

Mathias straightened as Mr. Renzo closed the door.

The Peruvian approached, holding his hand over the mouthpiece of a satellite phone. Renzo whispered into his boss's ear.

Mathias' eyebrows raised. "You gotta be shitting me?"

Mr. Renzo shook his head and held up the phone.

"Everybody out," he ordered, shooing his staff away.

As the door closed behind their hasty exit, Mathias snatched the phone out of Renzo's hand and asked, "Where's Johnston Atoll?"

"Near Kauai, sir."

Holding the phone absently, Mathias considered this. "That's where they recovered Kypa," he thought aloud. "That means the reports out of North Korea are true after all." A sinister grin spread across his face. He turned to Renzo. "Get your team together. Whoever or whatever it is, I want it captured alive."

"Yes, sir."

Mr. Renzo's tactical brain immediately went to work. His first thought was to black out the island and cut off all communication.

Mathias dismissed him with another glance. "I'm heading back to Peru. I want constant updates."

Mr. Renzo nodded then exited the room, leaving Mathias alone to ponder this unexpected but welcomed turn of events. Unconfirmed sightings of a mysterious creature spotted near North Korea's shoreline, coupled with the discovery of several large, webbed footprints, led to speculation that a second survivor of the Aiwan mothership might exist. This could be the confirmation he sought.

"Makes sense it would seek out Kypa," Mathias mused.

"Hello?" came the muffled sound of Dr. Hullinger's staticky voice on the phone.

Mathias snapped back to the moment, having forgotten all about the man on the other end of the line. He put the phone to his ear.

"Yes, this is Dr. Mathias. Who am I speaking with?"

Tongue-tied, the scientist replied, "This is Dr. Samuel Hullinger, sir. I'm calling from Johnston Atoll."

"Tell me what you've found, Dr. Hullinger," Mathias said with cautious optimism.

Hullinger went on to explain his theory and shared the photos he had taken. While the biologist had not visually confirmed the sighting of another Aiwan, this information sounded promising.

"Good work, Doctor. This is very exciting news. Have you told anyone else?"

"No, sir. Not yet."

Mathias breathed a sigh of relief. "Good. Let's keep it that way for now. I'm sending a team to assist. It is imperative that you do not attempt to make contact with the creature. We don't want to spook it. Wait until backup arrives, and then you can lead them to the area where you made the discovery."

"Roger that, sir. I—"

Suddenly, the line went dead.

"Hello? Hello?" Mathias asked, but there was no reply from Dr. Hullinger.

Mathias started to curse technology then realized this was Renzo's doing. He had blacked-out the island.

Damn, he's fast. Edmund grinned with satisfaction. *Now it's just a matter of bagging the prize.*

4

GRAWN KRUNIG

The Reaper

Neil entered the darkened confines of the main cabin, dreading the task before him. He approached Ava, who was sleeping soundly on her holographic bed. Knowing how much she needed the sleep, it pained him to have to wake her, but Kypa had said their hyperspace exit was nearing, and they had to get ready for whatever awaited them at Aiwa.

Neil gently jostled his friend. "Hey, Ava," he whispered. "Time to get up." Ava did not budge, so he tried rousing her again. "Hey, Suntan, rise and shine."

Ava stirred. Groaning, she opened her eyes partially to find a darkened silhouette standing over her. "Mark?" she mumbled.

Taken aback, Neil cleared his throat. "Uh, no," he stammered. "It's me, Neil. Kypa sent me to get you." He thumbed toward the cockpit.

Neil's words took a second to register, and then Ava sat up sharply on one elbow and brushed the bangs out of her face. "Where are we?" she asked in a panic.

Neil backpedaled slightly. "Whoa, easy there," he said, putting his hands out to slow her down. "Everything's good. Kypa asked me to come get you. We're nearing our hyperspace exit."

Ava looked past Neil and toward the cockpit. All appeared calm—no alarms or commotion—just the low hum of the Reaper's engines. Her shoulders dropped, and Ava exhaled heavily. A wave of exhaustion then hit her like a brick wall.

"Man, I was out," she confided, rubbing the sleep out of her eyes. "How long was I asleep?"

"A couple hours," Neil replied, hesitant to comment about her slip in calling him Mark. "Don't sweat it. You've got time to freshen up and grab some coffee."

Ava yawned heavily and gave him a thumbs-up. "Now you're talking."

Neil nodded then moved to the down ladder leading to the engineering section. As he started descending, he added, "Kypa says you got about twenty minutes."

"Roger that," she replied, yawning again. Ava rolled off the bed and put her feet on the floor. "Computer, lights."

The lights came on immediately to full illumination.

Ava winced, shielding her eyes. "Fifty percent," she corrected.

The lights dimmed to a softer glow.

"Thank you."

As soon as her eyes adjusted, Ava stowed her jacket in the storage compartment. She then deactivated the holographic bed and turned her attention to the food synthesizer. "Computer, double espresso."

A mug of the hot drink materialized before her.

Cupping the mug with both hands, she lifted the brew to her nose to savor the aroma. She smiled. "God, I love this ship."

Leaning against the bulkhead, Ava sipped her drink in glorious solitude. After a few minutes, she began to feel like herself again. Then her thoughts turned to Aiwa and the enormity of what lay ahead. It was time to get to work.

Finishing her drink, she set the mug back on the synthesizer. The mug dematerialized before her eyes, a dishwasher's wet dream.

As Ava started to leave, the ship's computer asked, "Did you enjoy your drink, Captain?"

Ava pulled up. Surprised by the question, she looked up at the ceiling with curiosity. "Beg pardon?"

"Did you enjoy your double espresso?" the computer repeated.

Amused, Ava replied, "Well, actually, I did. Thank you. It was a homerun in my book."

"Who are you talking to?" Neil asked.

Ava gasped. She rounded sharply to find Neil's head sticking up from the floor. Clutching her chest, she let out a heavy breath. "Jesus, don't sneak up on me like that."

"Sorry." Neil chuckled as he finished ascending the ladder. "I thought I heard voices."

Confused by what he meant, Ava then realized he was talking about her interaction with the ship's computer. "Oh." She laughed, embarrassed. "That was just me talking to the ship."

Neil grinned. "Recording your captain's log?"

"My what?"

"Your personal log," Neil replied matter-of-factly. "All starship captains do it." Reading Ava's blank expression, he knew the pop culture reference was lost on her. "Never mind." He waved it off as he made his way past her. "I'll let you get back to your girl talk."

Unamused, Ava shot him a look. On reflection, however, Neil's remark did make her wonder about the computer's identity. Even if it was not self-aware, the AI clearly had a personality. Ava was also getting tired of calling it "Computer" all the time.

Ava thought for a moment then the perfect name came to mind. "Computer, from now on, you will answer to the name Reggie. Got it?"

"Reggie" was in reference to her father's favorite baseball player. It was also the name of his favorite candy bar, Ava recalled fondly. Her dad had kept a sealed *Reggie!* bar in a display case with his other baseball memorabilia. She had not had the heart to throw it away after he had died. Someday, she would have to deal with the storage unit where it sat with all of his other possessions.

"Affirmative, Captain," Reggie acknowledged.

Ava started to leave but stopped short of the cockpit entry. "Computer," she called over her shoulder.

No reply.

"Reggie?"

"Yes, Captain."

Excellent! Ava beamed. "Nothing, Reggie. Carry on."

Ava entered the cockpit. "Guess what, chicken butts?" she said.

Kypa and Neil both turned toward her.

"From now on, the main computer will only answer to the name Reggie. Got it?"

"Uh, okay," Neil replied with a slight grin. Knowing the computer's voice was distinctly feminine, he asked, "Is that Reggie, as in Regina?"

"Jackson, actually," she clarified. "My dad was a big baseball fan." She took her seat in the pilot's chair as Neil and Kypa exchanged curious looks. "I know, it's a little quirky," Ava admitted, "but per tradition, Reggie's still a female."

"Why is that?" Neil asked. "I mean, why are ships always referred to as female?"

"It's because sailors view the ship as a goddess or motherly figure who protects them, protects her crew," Ava explained.

Neil nodded slowly, accepting her reasoning. Then he shrugged. "Reggie it is."

"Captain, we are nearing our hyperspace exit," Kypa reported.

"Copy that." Ava turned her attention to the HUD. "All right, since we don't know what kind of welcome awaits, let's be ready for anything."

With that, Ava assumed manual control of the Reaper by settling her hands and feet into the four orbs. A mental command later, power was increased to the shields and weapons.

Meanwhile, Kypa surprised Neil with a new configuration of their seats. The holographic bench they were using split apart into two separate, crescent-shaped chairs similar to Ava's.

Neil sat stiffly, unsure what to do with himself as the chair conformed to his body.

At the same time, Kypa's chair conformed to his body. Then the floor beneath his chair opened, and he was transported along a conveyor to the forward cockpit in the bow of the ship. There, Kypa could manipulate the ship's extractor tools, specifically the precision laser that served as a second turret.

"Kypa, you ready?" Ava asked.

"Standing by, Captain."

"Roger that," she confirmed, her eyes narrowed on the HUD as the countdown to their exit approached.

Moments later, in a flash of white light, the rapid streaks of blue light from the hyperspace tunnel suddenly vanished. The Reaper slowed automatically to sub-light speed as the ringed world of Aiwa loomed large in the main viewport.

Any relief the Reaper's crew might have felt at the sight of the blue-green planet was short-lived. Warning alarms erupted throughout the cockpit as soon as they emerged from hyperspace. They had arrived in the middle of a fierce space battle as dozens of Aiwan ships, cruisers, and gunships engaged in a massive fight high above Kypa's homeworld.

Ava swallowed hard. *My God, what have we walked into?*

"Captain, that is Commodore Boa's ship. He is in trouble," Kypa called.

Ava knew the commodore's battlecruiser all too well. She spotted it sandwiched between two enemy gunships, being hammered on both sides from heavy cannons. The scene was reminiscent of sea battles back on Earth in the age of sails, when opposing warships maneuvered side-by-side to fire cannons along their broadsides. Only these ships of the line were not using gunpowder and cannonballs. Brilliant explosions lit up the area as the unrelenting exchange intensified.

Ava shifted uneasily, knowing she was partially to blame for Boa's crippled state.

Meanwhile, Neil studied the battlefield on his personal HUD. He zoomed in on the outer hull of one of the larger enemy vessels. "Kypa, the marking on that ship, that's the symbol you drew at Groom Lake."

"Yes," Kypa affirmed. "That is the mark of the Madreen Crime Syndicate. They control the crystal trade, but I have never seen so many gathered in one location," he observed with concern. "It appears the various factions have allied against Aiwa."

"You sound surprised," Neil remarked, curious.

"Each faction operates independently and controls an assigned territory. A combined attack is unprecedented."

"An attack on one is an attack on all," Ava commented.

"It would seem so, Captain. Even with our shrinking supply of crystals, Aiwa remains a lucrative target. We possess more crystals than any other system … except for Earth, that is."

Ava scrutinized the Madreen fleet on her HUD, paying particular attention to their unique design. Compared to the streamlined hulls favored by the Aiwans, the Madreen ships looked more industrial in appearance. A distinctive dorsal stabilizer stood out, which ran from bow to stern and gave the harvester ships a menacing, shark-like appearance. Clearly, they had been built for intimidation and, judging by the beating Boa's crippled battlecruiser was taking, the Madreen had the firepower to back it up.

Kypa's jawline tightened as he watched. Even from a distance, it was evident the battle was not going well for the Aiwans.

He tapped the lead gunship on his HUD so it displayed for Ava and Neil to see.

"That is Krunig's ship," he pointed out. While the bulk of the fighting took place around Boa's battlecruiser, Krunig's warship held back at a safe distance, along with several large transports.

"What are those other ships waiting for?" Ava asked.

"Those are troop carriers," Kypa answered. "They must be planning a surface attack." A sensor flashed, catching his eye. "Boa's ship is being boarded."

"Not for long," Ava muttered. Charging the disruptors, she banked hard to starboard on an intercept course. "Contact Boa. Tell him to seal off that section, pronto."

Neil turned sharply to Ava with an incredulous look. "Wait, you're not thinking—"

"Hold on to something," she warned. Ava's eyes narrowed on her target as she throttled up the impulse engines. "It's time to pick a fight."

Aiwan Battlecruiser

Commodore Boa tripped over a dead crewman as he staggered across the smashed bridge. Wrapping his arms around a nearby handrail for stability, he pulled himself upright as his warship continued to shudder under the constant barrage of enemy fire.

Boa coughed violently in the thick layer of black smoke clouding the bridge. Rubbing his eyes, he surveyed the damage in the room. Despite fire-damaged workstations and frayed cables dangling from the ceiling, the crew stayed at their posts, while others tended the wounded.

Boa clutched his chest, struggling for air. His voice grated when he said, "Divert all power to weapons and shields!"

The dutiful helmsman spun around in his chair, fear evident on his face. "Shields are off-line, sir. And our weapons are not enough against the enemy's defenses."

Boa drifted his eyes downward, searching his mind for a tactic or maneuver that might somehow deliver his ship and crew from certain doom. In doing so, he spotted his first officer laying crumpled in a ball on the floor nearby. Her eyes were wide open, staring lifelessly at the ceiling. Boa's heart sank at the loss of such a brilliant and capable leader.

Today is not our day.

In his long and illustrious career, Commodore Boa had never lost a battle until just a few days earlier, back on Earth. Now, experiencing defeat for the second time in a week, the sad realization came to him—for all his years of military prowess, these two failures would define his legacy.

It was a bitter pill, made even more difficult to swallow since both defeats were in large part caused by Prince Kypa's betrayal. The damages the Reaper had inflicted on his battlecruiser near Earth had doomed him today against the Madreen, who had a distinct advantage in numbers and firepower. In a fair fight, Boa liked his odds against anyone, but even a commander with his skills could not win with both hands tied behind his back.

For a fleeting moment, self-pity crept into his psyche, and then a new alarm sounded.

"Commodore, we are being boarded!" the helmsman cried.

Boa had anticipated this move. Krunig was coming for his access codes. Without them, even if the Madreen defeated Aiwa's orbital defenses, they could not disable the shields protecting Aiwa's four major underwater cities. And, as long as those shields were up, attempting a siege was futile.

Straightening his uniform, Boa made his way to his command chair and opened a ship-wide channel. "All hands, this is your captain. The enemy is attempting to board our ship. Prepare to defend yourselves."

Four decks below, Aiwan foot soldiers took up defensive positions in the corridor outside the main airlock. The inner blast doors were engaged, but the shriek of overstressed metal on the opposite side signaled the Madreen fighters were forcing their way through the airlock.

The senior Aiwan officer, tasked with repelling the enemy boarding parties, strode up the corridor, quickly repositioning his defenses. When he reached the blast doors, he rounded to face his troops. With unwavering resolve, he gestured over his shoulder. "Whatever comes through that door, you stand your ground!"

Raising their weapons, the Aiwans readied themselves to meet the first wave of attackers head-on.

Their leader took his position up front, crouching inside a tiny nook that offered little protection. Time stood still as the Aiwans listened to the enemy cutting through the outer airlock. Suddenly, the control panel on the wall outside the blast doors exploded, and the double doors slid apart.

Weapons fire erupted before the first Madreen fighter had made it through the door. The Aiwans concentrated their fire in the center of the accessway, creating a wall of death the Madreen had to cross if they hoped to enter. To counter this tactic, two Madreen fighters, toting body-length energy shields, led a two-column procession, forcing their way aboard. They soon fell in battle but served their purpose as a wave of attackers entered the Aiwan battlecruiser.

Bodies from both sides began to pile up, and the smoke-filled corridor became a bloody free-for-all. Close-quarters fighting ensued as the Aiwans and Madreen engaged in savage hand-to-hand combat, using holographic swords, energy pikes and, as a last resort, their bare hands and claws.

Boa and the bridge crew watched with horror as the fight unfolded on the main viewer. Over the comms, they listened to a terrifying mix of battle cries and the dying screams of the fallen. The Aiwans fought gallantly but were clearly outnumbered and quickly overwhelmed by the pirate horde. Helpless to stop their advance, Boa knew it would not be long before the Madreen came for him. He and King Loka were the only ones with access to manually deactivate the dome shields protecting Aiwa's major underwater cities. Under no circumstances could those codes be compromised.

Realizing what he had to do, Boa stood to excuse himself to his ready room. He felt cowardly abandoning his crew in the heat of battle but taking his own life would save millions, at least in his mind.

"Sir, we are being hailed," the communications officer reported, confusion evident in his tone.

Assuming it was Krunig wanting to dictate terms of surrender, Boa replied gruffly, "Let Krunig eat static."

"The transmission is not from the Madreen." Rotating to face Boa, the officer's excitement faltered when he found the captain's chair vacated. His eyes darted about until he located Boa halfway to his ready room. "Sir," he called after him. "I think that is—"

"*Her,*" Boa seethed as the Reaper streaked past the main viewer.

As if this day could not get any worse, Boa watched the Reaper barrel roll between a pair of enemy warships, eluding fire. The tiny vessel then launched a barrage of disruptor fire against a nearby Madreen warship, penetrating its shields and slicing through its hull to rupture the engine core. The enemy ship exploded in a massive fireball.

Leaving destruction in its wake, the Reaper climbed up and away to line up for another attack run. In retaliation, several Madreen vessels targeted the Reaper with heavy cannons, but the spacecraft proved too elusive.

"Sir, I have Prince Kypa on the emergency channel," the comms officer reported. "He says to evacuate the main airlock and seal off that section immediately."

"What?" Boa scoffed at the absurdity. He was not about to sound retreat. Then Boa realized what Kypa might be scheming. It was a suicide run, but not for the Reaper and its crazy captain. "Do it!" he ordered, returning to his seat with a small ray of hope.

The comms officer called the senior-ranking commander leading the resistance down at the main airlock, but his attempts proved unsuccessful. As the fighting intensified, it became apparent no one could hear or respond amidst the chaos.

"Try the public address," Boa directed.

A ship-wide message was sent. However, none of the troops caught in the fighting reacted to the announcement.

Left with no choice, Boa gave the fateful order. "Seal that section."

"But, sir …" the comms officer started to object.

"Seal it now or we are *all* dead!"

The bridge crew watched with pained expressions as red lights began flashing in the corridor by the main airlock. Those Aiwans with the presence of mind to recognize what was happening broke off contact with the Madreen and retreated to safety. Others were not as fortunate. The heavy blast doors closed, trapping several Aiwans on the wrong side. They pounded on the door, demanding it be opened, only to be shot in the back or impaled from behind by the enemy.

The Reaper

"The airlock is sealed," Kypa reported.

"Get ready!" Ava replied.

The Reaper performed a Split-S maneuver, circling back between Boa's battlecruiser and the Madreen boarding ship.

Diverting extra power to the forward shields, Ava turned away as the Madreen ship opened fire. Squinting from the blinding barrage of flack pounding the Reaper's shields, Reggie compensated by polarizing the cockpit windows. It helped. Now Ava had a better line of sight and maneuvered into the narrow gap between Boa's battlecruiser and the Madreen ship.

Chewing on her bottom lip, Ava eased the throttle forward and skillfully rotated the Reaper on its z-axis to squeeze through the tight opening. She made a darting glance upward. The outer hull of Boa's ship was so close to the window that Ava could count every divot and scorch mark.

In the forward cockpit, Kypa lined up the crosshairs of the precision laser cannon. Normally, this tool was used to cut crystals out of ocean sediment. Today, however, he planned to sever the enemy's connection to Boa's ship.

With pinpoint accuracy, Kypa fired, carving into the boarding tube. Depressurization was instantaneous as the metal tube disintegrated. Warriors from both sides blew out into space, flailing and screaming.

Kypa watched the tragic scene unfold as the Reaper dove to avoid the debris and bodies. He had never killed before; this fateful decision had taken more lives than he could count. The Madreen must have had waves of fighters waiting in the wings to storm Boa's battlecruiser when the boarding tube collapsed.

Before they were clear, Kypa glimpsed several Aiwans mixed in with the dead. His mouth trembled. The naïve side of him had hoped only Madreen fighters would fall victim to their plan, but seeing his comrades floating amongst the deceased was unbearable.

Clutching his chest with one hand, Kypa reached out and touched the cockpit window. "Forgive me," he whispered.

The Reaper cleared both ships then went back on the offensive. Ava cycled her shield settings back to normal and targeted the nearest Madreen ship. Her assault proved unstoppable as the Madreen's shields collapsed under the strain of the Reaper's forward disruptors. Ava fired again, concentrating her weapons on the aft section. The barrage crippled the enemy's engines, which sputtered, then went dark. Ava peeled away from the scuttling warship, banking hard to port and leaving Aiwa's gravitational pull to finish it off.

Aiwan Battlecruiser

"Sir, core breach imminent on the Madreen ship," the helmsman called.

"Evasive maneuvers!" Boa coughed.

Relieved he still had access to his personal HUD, Boa called up a display that showed his ship's distance to the dying Madreen warship.

"Divert all power to the engines. We need to get clear!"

Watching on his screen, Boa grinned with satisfaction as the damaged Madreen warship collided with a passing corvette on its descent, taking out both vessels before the enemy warship's core could reach critical mass. Crisis averted, Boa then turned his attention to the Reaper.

Amazed by the tiny ship, he watched as the Reaper lined up for a strafing run against one of the Madreen's larger, capital ships. Its potent weapons made short work of the capital ship, carving through the hull from bow to stern. Successive explosions followed before the Madreen vessel erupted in a massive fireball and, through the fiery debris, emerged the Reaper, unscathed.

Madreen Command Ship

With his four hands clasped behind his back, Grawn Krunig stood on the bridge of his command ship in stunned disbelief. Staring out the main viewport, he watched helplessly as yet another ship in his fleet exploded before his eyes; the third victim of Aiwa's mystery savior.

Moments earlier, victory had been at hand. How quickly the tides had turned. Now his plan for conquering Aiwa was on the brink of disaster.

The unmarked, black vessel that had entered the fray, wreaking havoc on his fleet, was like an annoying insect buzzing in front of Krunig's face. Every attempt he made to swat the Reaper into oblivion was met with repeated failure.

Seated at a console, off to the side of the bridge, a Madreen science officer raised his hand nervously and reported, "Sir, I'm detecting a massive energy reading from the unknown vessel."

Vekka, Grawn Krunig's trusted advisor, approached and leaned over the science officer's shoulder to see for himself. He did a double-take. The tiny ship's energy output was off the charts and showing no signs of degradation, despite the heavy fighting.

"That cannot be right," Vekka concluded. "Run a diagnostic."

"I've run it twice, sir," the puzzled crewman reported. "The readings are accurate."

Vekka tried to make sense of the data and figure out how to explain the anomaly to his impatient boss. Krunig had killed for less, and Vekka preferred to keep his head.

Meanwhile, Krunig remained fixated on the Reaper as it destroyed two more Madreen gunships with relative ease.

The ultimate killing machine, he mused, admiring its indestructible lethality. The ship's design was uniquely un-Aiwan, leaving Krunig to ponder who this mystery ship belonged to and why they were allied to the Aiwans?

As Krunig chewed on this, he was driven to one conclusion.

I must have it!

Vekka approached tentatively from behind, triggering a proximity sensor inside Krunig's armor. The Madreen underboss cocked his head slightly, halting Vekka in his tracks.

Sensing more bad news, Krunig turned his attention back to the battle. "Report," he said calmly.

"My liege, it pains me to say this, but circumstances dictate we must withdraw our forces immediately."

Krunig had already reached the same conclusion.

Keeping his back to Vekka, he simply held out one of his oversized hands. Vekka stepped forward, producing a handheld device, then stepped back. Krunig activated the hologram projector. The Reaper appeared, along with the data from the science officer's scans. The facts were undeniable; the energy output of the tiny vessel far-surpassed that of his entire fleet combined.

Vekka bowed submissively. "Apologies, my lord. I cannot explain the anomaly at this time, but I promise we will figure it out."

The communications officer called out, "Sir, I'm receiving multiple hails from the fleet. They're demanding to speak with you."

Retreat was not in Krunig's DNA. However, in light of mounting losses, he had no choice. The hardest part was in knowing he would never get another chance like this. It had taken a lot of effort to persuade Grawn Supreme to sanction his plan, and even more concessions to get his peers to buy-in.

Now, with such a resounding defeat, Grawn Krunig stood to lose more than his credibility. It would not be enough to compensate the other Grawns for their lost ships, crews, and promised bounty. They would come for blood and challenge Krunig's claim on this territory … if his own crew did not beat them to it.

Krunig eyed the Reaper one last time on the battlefield, toying with his warships. The unknown ship had singlehandedly snatched victory from impending defeat, making a fool of him and the syndicate. Krunig turned to the hologram of the Reaper and crushed the device in his hand.

"Sound retreat," he ordered in a low, guttural tone.

Vekka relayed the order to the crew, who all jumped into action to recall what remained of the fleet and prepare for the jump to lightspeed.

As Vekka turned back to Krunig, the sound of broken glass crackled under his feet. He looked down to find the remnants of his pulverized projector on the floor.

"My lord, shall we …" He trailed off. Krunig was gone.

Looking toward the exit, Vekka caught a glimpse of the crime lord's backside as he departed without a word.

Hands clasped behind his back, Krunig strode off the bridge in deep thought then disappeared down the corridor, toward his private quarters.

Vekka swallowed hard, knowing there would be hell to pay for this debacle. He just hoped—as did the rest of the crew—not to be on the receiving end of Krunig's wrath.

Signaling one of his subordinates to clean up the mess on the floor, Vekka moved to the main viewport and watched as the fleet pulled back in full retreat. The last thing he saw before rocketing out of the system was the mysterious vessel that turned the battle in the Aiwan's favor. It had disengaged, allowing the enemy to withdraw without further bloodshed.

A noble quality, Vekka mused, *but a mistake, nonetheless.*

The fight was over ... for now.

5
FRIEND OR FOE

Planet Aiwa
The Reaper

Ava pointed the Reaper directly into the path of Boa's battlecruiser, similar to when she had confronted him near Earth days earlier. That time, she had wisely kept her distance just in case the prideful Aiwan commander decided not to leave Earth peacefully. A lot had changed since then, starting with Ava's confidence in the Reaper's capabilities.

Now, having soundly defeated Boa at Earth then saved his neck here at Aiwa—all in the same week—she could only imagine the swirl of emotions going through the commodore's head. Boa might lash out against her, but Ava doubted he would be that foolish. She held the upper hand, but pride made people behave irrationally, assuming that was a constant in the universe.

"Reggie, boost power to the forward shields," Ava commanded, just to be safe.

Still buckled in his chair, Kypa returned from the forward cockpit to join his friends.

Ava gestured to Boa's battlecruiser outside the main viewport. "You don't suppose Boa's holding a grudge, do you?"

"I would not want to be on the bridge at this moment," Kypa admitted.

"That's what I thought." Ava frowned. "How should we play this?"

Before Kypa could respond, a proximity alarm sounded. Ava checked her HUD; a small, unarmed personnel shuttle had departed the battlecruiser and approached. The pilot hailed the Reaper. Ava displayed the transmission on the HUD. An Aiwan female appeared. She had a fresh bandage above her left eye.

"I am Captain Tan of Earth," Ava announced, her words instantly translated to Aiwan. "With me is Prince Kypa, son of King Loka. We come in peace. Please state your intentions."

"My name is Commander Liera, acting first officer. I am unarmed." She spotted Kypa, and her face brightened. "Permission to come aboard."

"For what purpose?"

"Commodore Boa has sent me to discuss terms of our surrender."

Ava appeared nonplussed. "I can assure you there's no call for that. We are friends of Aiwa."

Relieved, Liera bowed her head in appreciation. "Thank you, Captain Tan. You have our ... *my* gratitude. Your heroism today will not be forgotten." She paused.

"But ..." Ava nudged.

Liera shifted uneasily in her chair. "I have instructions to bring Prince Kypa back with me."

Kypa stepped forward. "Commander, am I under arrest?"

"No, My Prince." Liera shook her head—at least to her knowledge. "Commodore Boa wishes to speak with you in private."

Ava muted the transmission as Kypa rounded to face her. With a raised eyebrow, she said, "It's your call."

Kypa shared Ava's skepticism. Commodore Boa had threatened him with charges of treason back on Earth, and once he left the safety of the Reaper, anything was possible. Kypa had dreaded this scenario the entire trip home, but he desperately wanted to see his family and talk sense into his father. Getting past Boa was the first hurdle.

"I will reason with Boa and try to arrange an audience with my father and the High Court, if need be."

Ava sensed uncertainty in Kypa's voice and demeanor but trusted her friend knew what he was doing. She nodded then unmuted the comms.

"Commander Liera, as a show of good faith, please tell Commodore Boa to lower his shields and weapons, and then you may proceed with docking."

Liera acknowledged, and the transmission ended.

Kypa started toward the main cabin to meet Liera at the docking collar. As he passed Ava, she raised her hand to stop him.

"Hey, if things go south in there, you call me. We've got your back."

Kypa forced a thin smile and placed his hand on her shoulder. "Remember what I said earlier … trust no one."

Feeling the weight of his words, Ava nodded.

As Kypa exited the cockpit, she turned to Neil. They exchanged looks, thinking the same thing.

So much for a warm welcome.

Moments later, the shuttle left with Kypa onboard. Returning to the battlecruiser, the spacecraft passed through an electronic containment field as it entered the ship's landing bay. Commander Liera lowered the four landing struts and eased the shuttle down onto the deck.

Kypa descended the boarding ramp alongside her.

Two stony-faced guards toting energy pikes were waiting at the bottom of the ramp. They wore military-issued aquasuits, similar to Liera's uniform, with a rank insignia on their collars. Kypa felt his chest tighten. He wondered if they were there to escort him with honor or to take him into custody.

Commodore Boa was noticeably absent, which did not bode well for the tone of their meeting. Refusing to personally welcome a member of the royal family aboard his ship was a blatant show of disrespect. Kypa did not put it past Boa to do such a thing, but he also considered that the commodore might be preoccupied coordinating the ship's damage control efforts.

Do not jump to conclusions, Kypa told himself as he glanced around the bay.

The area appeared relatively unscathed from the battle. Filled with Seekers, single-pilot starfighters, and other transports, Kypa noticed only a handful of service techs working in the area. The rest, he presumed, were quite literally fighting fires elsewhere.

Kypa approached the guards. They bowed respectfully then stepped aside without a word.

"This way." Liera gestured.

The guards fell in step behind them as Liera led Kypa out of the cavernous bay.

"How bad is the damage?" Kypa asked.

"Extensive"—Liera frowned—"but at least the ship is stable and holding orbit. We had hull breaches on levels two and six, which have been contained, but we lost twenty crewmembers with twice as many wounded. Many are still unaccounted for."

Kypa took a long, deep breath, thinking of how he had contributed to those numbers. Then he reminded himself that, if he had not intervened, more would have been lost.

"What about the rest of the fleet?" he asked.

"Last I heard, we lost seven ships … over two hundred souls," Liera reported sadly.

They arrived at a nearby lift and stepped inside.

"Bridge," she said as the doors closed behind them.

The lift started.

Seconds into the ride, Kypa felt the subtle inertia of the lift moving, which should not happen unless the ship's dampeners were mis-calibrated. Then the overhead lights flickered. Kypa looked upward, listening intently for audible cues as to the battlecruiser's space-worthiness. This helped to keep his mind off his meeting with Commodore Boa, at least somewhat. There was no love lost between the two, and something told him that was not going to change anytime soon.

For all of his brilliance as a military commander, Commodore Boa's effectiveness as a leader stemmed more from his rank and results than his ability to inspire the best in others. The no-nonsense commander had zero tolerance for those he judged as fools, Kypa being one of them. In the aftermath of Aiwa's catastrophic quakes, Boa—along with so many others—unjustly blamed Kypa for the disaster. After all, the prince had been responsible for Aiwa's harvesting efforts at the time. Yet, despite his warnings that overharvesting would destabilize Aiwa's core, the practice had continued, and millions had died as a result. Finally, harvesting had come to a halt.

Because of this rift, Boa refused to publicly endorse the king's son as a worthy successor. Without support from the military, Kypa's claim to the throne would be challenged, should that day ever come.

Kypa pushed those thoughts aside as the lift arrived at the bridge. Steeling himself, Kypa raised his chin. *You are a prince of Aiwa. Act like it.*

The doors slid open, and Liera gestured forward. All activity came to an abrupt pause as Kypa stepped onto the bridge. He scanned the shattered room, projecting both pride and sadness. Most of the crew seemed genuinely excited to see him, while others barely masked their contempt.

Empathizing with their losses, Kypa sighed heavily and dipped his chin slightly in a curt bow. "On behalf of King Loka and the Five Realms, I want to thank each of you for your brave service. You have defeated the harvester threat once again. Victory is yours." He paused, allowing his words to sink in. "Please accept my condolences for the loss of your crewmates. We will mourn their passings and honor their sacrifices."

An awkward silence followed. Finally, a female officer knelt in the center of the room.

"My Prince," she proclaimed.

Others nearby followed her example, and then the rest of the bridge joined in declaring their loyalty to the prince. They were alive only because of him, and if it had not been for Prince Kypa's mystery ship, Aiwa would now be part of a long, sad list of Grawn Krunig's conquests.

Kypa was taken aback by the crew's display of support; it was a first for him. He pulled in a deep breath then nodded with a satisfied smile. "Please, carry on."

Slowly, the crew went back to work.

Kypa followed Liera to Commodore Boa's ready room, stepping carefully over debris. They came to a single door near the front of the bridge. Liera tapped the call button.

The distant voice of Commodore Boa could be heard on the other side. "Enter."

Commander Liera stepped aside and bowed her head slightly. It would have been disrespectful to wish Prince Kypa good luck since he technically ranked higher than Boa in the chain of command, but she was certainly thinking it.

The door slid open, and Kypa entered alone.

Inside, Commodore Boa's ready room was devoid of permanent furnishings or decorations, which came as no surprise. Boa was not the sentimental type, nor was it the Aiwan way. Three of the four smooth, seamless metal walls were bare. Only the large window on the fourth wall offered anything of interest to the eye—an unobstructed view of Aiwa.

Boa's ready room did have two hologram daises similar to the Reaper's cockpit. One dais—currently occupied by Boa—projected a custom-fitted, high-backed chair with HUD display, which the commodore was currently using to review the status of his battle-damaged vessel. The second dais was situated directly across from Boa. It was configured with two less-comfortable-looking seats for visitors.

Remaining seated, Boa darted a glance in Kypa's direction then transferred his gaze back to the readouts. At that point, Kypa could no longer ignore Boa's insolence. When he had sent Commander Liera as his envoy, Kypa had said nothing, considering the circumstances. Again, when Boa had failed to greet him at the shuttle, Kypa had given him the benefit of the doubt. However, failing to stand in the presence of a member of the royal family was inexcusable.

Just as he was about to take the commodore to task, Boa took a curt breath and brushed the HUD aside. He stood and crossed the room. Kypa stiffened, but as Boa approached, he noticed the aging military leader limping and sporting a discolored bruise atop his head. His appearance disarmed Kypa. Pomp and circumstance now felt trite.

Facing one another, Boa eyed Kypa up and down firmly. The prince returned his withering look, unwavering. Looking into Boa's eyes, Kypa sensed the commodore's internal conflict—stubborn pride battling reluctant gratitude. In the end, duty compelled Boa to act. He surprised Kypa by lowering his head humbly.

"Welcome aboard, Prince Kypa."

Kypa looked down at Boa's bald head, speechless. He detected no gratitude or sincerity in Boa's voice, but at least it was something.

"Thank you, Commodore Boa. You and your brave crew have performed admirably. On behalf of my father—"

"Spare me your platitudes." Boa waved dismissively. "We both know who won this battle." Boa straightened to meet Kypa eye-to-eye. "I would not have needed rescuing in the first place had it not been for your infernal ship."

"The Reaper," Kypa corrected, "and it belongs to the humans, not me. You should thank them."

"Thank them?" Boa scoffed, his anger boiling. "We lost because of them!"

"You drew first blood," Kypa calmly pointed out. "Your unprovoked attack on their space station killed seven innocent people."

"They destroyed *your* ship and killed *your* crew!" Boa argued.

Kypa shook his head. "No, that is not what happened. My ship was attacked in hyperspace before reaching Earth. The humans had nothing to do with it."

"And yet, you alone survived …"

Kypa's nostrils flared. "What are you insinuating, Boa?"

Sensing he had struck a nerve, Boa smiled thinly. "I am merely stating a fact, My Prince."

"You will know all of the facts when I file my official report. Until then, know that my crew died trying to save our world, and if the humans had not helped me recover the Reaper, you would not be standing here now."

Boa huffed. "And what of this Reaper?" He stepped over to the window and pointed to the Reaper loitering off the battlecruiser's bow.

Kypa took notice of the tiny vessel, then looked past the Reaper to the blue-green planet in the background. It was the first time since returning that he could truly take in the sight of his majestic homeworld. The nearness of Maya and the children amplified his relief to finally be home.

"What about it?" Kypa asked.

"Sensor readings show it has an energy signature greater than the central core," Boa replied suspiciously.

Kypa gave the Reaper a cursory glance. He had hoped to reveal its ominous capabilities later to his father, but there was no hiding the presence of the blue crystal.

"The cargo hold is filled with crystals, a gift to Aiwa from the humans as a gesture of good will."

Boa shot him an irritated look. "Do I strike you as a fool?"

Kypa reacted rather sheepishly. "Of course not, Commodore."

"I had that ship outgunned a hundred-to-one, yet it made short work of this battlecruiser, dozens of Seekers, and most of Krunig's fleet. How?"

Kypa sighed. There was no sense keeping up the charade. "Very well, Commodore. The Reaper's engine core houses a single crystal of Maxixe Magnetarite."

Boa's eyes widened. "Impossible," he muttered, stepping closer to the window to lay eyes on the tiny ship.

"Now you understand why I went to Earth in secret. Once I detected Earth's abnormally high crystal readings, I knew it was only a matter of time before the rest of the galaxy discovered it as well. Our mission was to bring back enough crystals to turn the tide in the war once and for all."

Boa considered the possibilities. "Are there more blue crystals?"

Kypa shook his head. "Not to my knowledge. The humans helped me recover the one powering the Reaper, but we discovered rich deposits of other crystals," he pointed out. "Earth has more than Aiwa ever had, and the humans allowed me to bring enough back to buy us time against Krunig. They came here to form an alliance, Commodore, not to wage war."

"And yet, the presence of that ship puts Aiwa at even greater risk," Boa countered. "More harvesters will come once that crystal is detected, and our reserves are dangerously low. The king has initiated rolling blackouts to divert energy to each of the city shields, but we cannot hold out much longer."

"The humans can—"

"We do not need their help!" Boa spat in a rare show of emotion. He jabbed his finger at the Reaper. "That is our property. You had no right giving it to them," Boa declared then gestured back and forth between himself and Kypa. "We are fighting for our lives, and the survival of our race depends on us, not them!"

Chest heaving, Boa stared at Kypa with such ferocity the veins on his forehead pulsed. Every instinct wanted to reach out and strangle Kypa for being so naïve, and he might have done just that had Kypa's next words been the wrong ones.

Kypa squared his shoulders but wisely held his tongue. There was no point arguing the matter. Boa had made up his mind.

"What now?" Kypa asked.

The door to Boa's ready room opened suddenly, and two armed guards appeared in the opening. Kypa turned sharply and realized Boa must have summoned them telepathically.

Boa collected himself and straightened his uniform. Clearing his throat, he stated, "You have been summoned to appear before the High Court."

Kypa expected this—wanted it, actually—but the finality in Boa's voice gave him pause.

He gestured to the window. "And what of my friends?"

"I will deal with them soon enough."

6

BAGGING THE PRIZE

Planet Earth
Johnston Atoll, Pacific Ocean

Luna returned to her tiny island after another exhaustive day of searching for Kypa. Once again, she had nothing to show for her efforts, except a delicious dinner of local cuisine. Today's catch was a four-foot Yellowfin tuna, which she dragged to shore. Taking her customary seat on the edge of the beach, Luna enjoyed her meal in solitude while watching the golden sunset.

High above her, a drone quadcopter hovered in a stationary position, recording Luna's every move. Five hundred yards away in the abandoned airport hangar, Dr. Hullinger grinned from ear-to-ear. He was peeking over the shoulder of a formidable man dressed in all-black combat fatigues who held the drone's remote control. The man worked the control's three-axis gimbals with precision as the drone's Active Track 3.0 feature kept the camera locked on the Aiwan. It produced a picture-perfect, 4k image on a nearby tablet.

"Amazing," Hullinger remarked as Luna feasted. He pointed to the video. "Notice that he, or she, doesn't have any gills."

Out of the corner of the man's eye, he saw Hullinger's hand getting too close to the tablet. With lightning speed, he grabbed the doctor's hand and twisted his wrist.

"Ow. Sorry, sorry!" Hullinger howled.

"No touching," the man warned dangerously, his accent clearly German. He released the doctor's hand.

Stepping back and rubbing his sore wrist, the smile on Hullinger's face quickly faded with the grim realization that the twelve men sent by Dr. Mathias were not here for his benefit. In fact, they behaved like soldiers, not scientists. A chill ran down his spine.

The man in black swore under his breath. *Scientists.*

Having drawn the short end of the stick on this operation, he was stuck inside the hangar, listening to the annoying doctor's play-by-play commentary, while the rest of the mercenary team got to have all the fun outside. His patience with Dr. Hullinger was wearing thin. One more bonehead move, like touching his equipment, and there would be one less scientist in the world.

Returning to his surveillance, he leaned in close to the screen. The rest of the team had been in position for hours, waiting for the Aiwan to return. Now that the alien had finished its meal, he watched as it leaned back on one elbow, lounging on the beach. With its guard down and all the pieces in place, it was time to move in.

"Overwatch to Alpha-One," the man in black whispered into his headphone mic. "You are green to go. Repeat, green to go."

Downwind and concealed in high grass twenty yards behind Luna, Mr. Renzo clicked his mic twice, acknowledging the go-ahead signal. Adhering to strict noise discipline, Renzo then raised his hand, palm out, to ascertain if his team was ready. Down the line, encircling Luna's position, each of the mercenaries returned the "I am ready" hand signal.

Satisfied, Renzo nudged the merc crouched beside him. This man held a large animal net gun pressed into his shoulder. The bolt-action Remington 700 with full-length stock was loaded with .308 caliber blanks to launch a Dyneema net capable of entangling most targets. It was the preferred tactical net gun on game preserves for capturing and relocating animals. In aquacultures, this weapon was also used to protect beach-going swimmers from annoying fish and dangerous predators. Renzo had preplanned with his team that, as soon as the net was released, the rest of the team would move in. This would be the first field test on aliens.

Beside him, the net gunner took aim and fired. Immediately, the net expanded outward, carried by four rubber-padded corner-weights. It looked like a flying squirrel hurtling through the air.

Caught completely unaware, Luna spasmed wildly, tossing the remnants of her meal out of her hand just as the first net enveloped her. She let out an ear-splitting screech and tried to get to her feet when a second net wrapped around her.

Entangled in the netting, Luna darted her panicked eyes toward the ocean. Freedom was only three feet away, but she could not stand. Even crawling was impossible with the thick netting working against her.

The team of mercs moved in with rifles trained on the target. One soldier-for-hire carried a tranquilizer gun and fired, hitting Luna in the thigh. She cried out in agony, clutching her leg, and instinctively pulled the dart out of her flesh.

Luna swiveled her head back and forth rapidly as several dark shapes closed in on her from all sides. Baring her teeth, she hissed at the mercs and extended her razor-sharp fingernails, determined not to go down without a fight.

A second tranquilizer dart struck her in the buttocks. This one had an immediate effect.

Luna's surroundings began to spin and grow blurry, her muscles felt sluggish. She collapsed in the sand. Her eyes grew heavy as the will to fight escaped her. The last thing she saw before blacking out was a lone figure walking up beside her. He was dressed in all black clothing, but the Wing Chun-style outfit differentiated him from the military fatigues worn by the others.

Renzo approached and lifted his knit facemask. He crouched beside Luna, showing no outward fear, but wisely kept out of reach. On the flight over, he had read the CIA's top-secret reports on Prince Kypa and knew a great deal about an Aiwan's strengths and weaknesses, especially their telepathic abilities. He expected the same from this one.

A formidable foe, he admired.

Luna's eyes fell shut, and she drifted into unconsciousness.

The merc team gathered around, keeping their weapons trained on Luna as a precaution. Once they felt comfortable she was out, the team relaxed, raising the muzzles of their weapons skyward.

"Damn," one merc remarked at his first, up close view of an alien lifeform.

"That was easier than I thought," the team leader said as Renzo rose to his full height.

"Mm," Renzo agreed. He dusted the sand off his pants then snapped a few pictures with his satellite phone. As he turned to leave, Renzo told the team, "Get it ready for transport. And remember, no skin-to-skin contact. Wheels up in fifteen minutes."

"Roger that," the team leader acknowledged.

Just then, Dr. Hullinger arrived, panting heavily. "Pardon me," he wheezed out, shouldering his way between two mercs.

Seeing Luna curled in a fetal position under the netting, Hullinger's eyes widened with amazement. He dropped to his knees beside her and marveled at the Aiwan's olive-colored skin and red cranial markings. This was the biggest moment in his life.

Hullinger reached out to touch the Aiwan.

"No hands, Doc," the team leader warned.

Hullinger recoiled and laughed nervously. "You're right, of course. It's beautiful, though, don't you think? We're making hist—"

The doctor's speech cut off abruptly as a small dart struck him in the side of the neck. Hullinger reached up, thinking he had been stung by a bee, and was shocked to find the tiny projectile. He pulled out the poisoned dart, examined it, then looked up and discovered Mr. Renzo lowering his blowgun.

Confused, Hullinger asked, "Why?"

Renzo remained stone-faced, waiting for the poison to take effect.

Dr. Hullinger suddenly felt ill. His pale cheeks flushed, and then he began foaming at the mouth. Hullinger fell on his side and started to convulse as the merc team watched in silence. The doctor's arms and legs began twitching uncontrollably, kicking up sand, as he grunted in agony. Seconds later, the fit ended abruptly when his heart stopped. Dr. Hullinger's body went limp. He died with his mouth contorted in a rictus grin and his unseeing eyes staring up at the peaceful, twilit sky.

None of the mercs reacted. It was just business.

The team turned to Mr. Renzo, who was disassembling his blowgun. He casually stowed the weapon in its carrying case then slung it over his back.

"What do you want us to do with him, boss?" the team leader asked.

Renzo approached Dr. Hullinger and pried his hand open to retrieve the used dart. He placed it in a small carrying case kept in his shirt pocket. "Feed him to the fish but leave his plane and equipment alone. Make it look like he drowned."

"You got it, boss." To the others, the team leader said, "You heard the man. Bag the prize and dump the doc. We're out of here in fifteen mike."

Republic of Peru, South America

The Airbus ACJ319neo approached the coast of Peru, heading due east at an altitude of ten thousand feet. As the acting copilot of the world's most expensive private jet, Edmund Mathias sat up from behind his controls to get a better look at the bustling city of Lima.

It was a gorgeous late-February day in Peru's capital city. The country's warmest and wettest season was nearing an end, which meant the skies were normally overcast this time of year. Today was an exception. The sun was shining bright, and there was not a cloud in sight. Mathias took this as a good omen.

Since building his newest and largest research facility in South America a few years back, he had grown fond of Peru for more reasons than the climate. While the weather could be hit or miss, there was no shortage of cheap labor, and the value of the U.S. dollar to Peruvian Sol proved more than advantageous. Mathias Industries was enjoying its most profitable quarter to date, despite the negative press it was receiving back in the United States for the "misunderstanding" at Groom Lake.

With his human cloning efforts exposed, Mathias doubted he would be returning to the U.S. anytime soon. It was an unfortunate setback. On the bright side, with his political clout in Washington and the Congress of the Republic of Peru, any attempt to extradite him for violating the United Nations' Declaration on Human Cloning would be futile. Mathias had the best lawyers and politicians that money could buy.

Besides, it was no longer humans Mathias wanted to clone. If Mr. Renzo's mission to capture a second Aiwan proved successful, Mathias' cloning operations were about to take a giant leap forward. Soon, every government on the planet would be lining up to buy his alien-infused force enhancement serum. And that was only the beginning.

Mathias peered out the side window as the aircraft approached the small coastal city of Chancay. With a scant population of just over sixty-three thousand impoverished residents, Chancay struggled to survive in the 21st century. This was due, in large part, to its oil-polluted beaches and stunted economy. Only a few minor tourist attractions generated revenue, but that was all about to change with Mathias' Megapuerto de Chancay.

Thanks to Edmund and his Chinese investors, the Chancay Megaport would redefine the lines of maritime trade in the South Pacific. With a final investment of close to three billion USD, the megaport would open Peru to the world and solidify China's influence over Latin America, surpassing the United States as the continent's main economic partner.

To support the megaport, other major infrastructure projects were underway, including highways, tunnels, bridges, and even high-speed, transcontinental railway systems connecting Peru on the Pacific-side of South America to Brazil on the Atlantic side. The environmental impact to the Amazon River Basin was proving catastrophic yet, despite protests, construction continued. Soon, Peru would become the major economic center in this part of the world, and no one stood to benefit more than venture capitalist, Dr. M. Edmund Mathias.

Hedging his bets on the success of the megaport, Edmund set up a South American research facility to capitalize on this opportunity. It was a genius move. Labor and tax savings aside, his investments in key Peruvian lawmakers also provided Mathias more invaluable returns; most notably the protection from extradition. The Americans could not touch him down here, no matter what the treaty between the United States of America and the Republic of Peru stipulated. So, despite the bad press from Groom Lake, this project's windfall was sure to please his stockholders and keep him out of federal prison.

The aircraft continued east, past Lima for thirty minutes, and toward Satipo, a municipality in the mountainous Junin Region of Peru. As they neared the Mayor PNP Nancy Flores Paucar Airport, Mathias looked out at the vastness of the Amazon River Basin, the largest rainforest on Earth, and smiled with satisfaction.

Affectionately considered the "lungs of the planet" by environmentalists, Edmund had a different view of Amazonia. Where others saw an invaluable mosaic of ecosystems and vegetation types, he saw progress and dollar signs. Lots of them. And soon, massive highways and railroads would run through Amazonia, hauling his goods from his megaport.

Mathias grinned. *Life is good.*

As they neared the small airport, the voice of the air traffic controller drew him back to the present. Mathias confirmed the controller's instructions, received a thumbs-up from the pilot to his left, and started his final approach. He landed the aircraft five minutes later and taxied to a specially built hangar belonging to Mathias Industries.

Ariane Diaz, his lovely assistant, stood outside the hangar next to a bulletproof Cadillac Escalade. Standing beside her was the chauffeur, a middle-aged Peruvian man, dressed in a black suit and tie. With a Smith & Wesson M&P15 pistol slung across his chest, the chauffeur had been surveilling the area since their arrival. His eyes were always moving in search of potential threats.

Ms. Diaz, on the other hand, was dressed to kill, in a good way. Wearing an Italian-made, pink satin pant suit with a white silk top and patent-jeweled mules on her feet, Mathias' personal assistant had a knack for turning heads.

At thirty-four years old, this striking and brilliant professional could be in the C-suite at any major tech company if she wanted but turned them down to work for Mathias. Every minute of every day, she was always on. And, while her boss proved eccentric and difficult at times, Edmund never crossed the line of impropriety with her. He valued Ms. Diaz's services too much. He was also most generous to those loyal to him. Ms. Diaz had served him faithfully for five years. In another five, she could retire to a tropical island, earning fifteen percent on her stock options alone.

As soon as the aircraft came to a halt inside the hangar, a flight crew moved in to chock the wheels. When they signaled to Mathias the aircraft was secure, he shut down the engines.

The side passenger door opened, and one of Edmund's personal bodyguards—a stocky man the size of an NFL linebacker—was first to appear. He stopped in the opening and scanned the area. Satisfied, the guard led his boss to the awaiting SUV, shielding Mathias from the potential threat of corporate assassins.

Ms. Diaz greeted her boss with a smile. "Welcome back," she said. "Find anything?"

"Oh yeah," Mathias replied, grinning slyly.

The driver opened the back door while the ground crew finished loading the luggage in the back of the SUV. Edmund and Ms. Diaz climbed into the vehicle. As soon as the guard took his seat up front with the driver, the SUV rolled off the tarmac and headed for Mathias' private research facility nearby.

"Check this out," Mathias said as he fished an orange magnetarite crystal from his pants pocket, handing it to Ms. Diaz.

She marveled at the four-inch crystal glistening in the palm of her hand. "It's beautiful."

"Extracted this one a week ago. We found a cave full of them. It's enormous."

"This is what the aliens are after?"

"Mmhmm. And this is just one location. Imagine if there are more deposits hidden around the globe. We're sitting on Earth's next great natural resource."

"It'll put oil and gas out of business," Ms. Diaz remarked, holding it up to the light.

"And this is just the start." Mathias looked out the window as they exited the airport and onto a two-lane paved road. His vision for entering the intergalactic harvesting trade was coming along nicely, but he needed help. "Any word from Renzo?"

Ms. Diaz shook her head. "Not yet, but the investors began arriving this morning," she said, changing the subject. "They're waiting in the boardroom."

Mathias rolled his eyes. The timing of their emergency meeting could not have been worse, but not entirely unexpected. No doubt his investors were nervous after the debacle at Groom Lake, so it was Edmund's job to quell their fears with a dog and pony show.

Diaz returned the crystal, and Edmund tucked it back into his front pocket.

"Where are we on Groom Lake?"

"The Feds seized our hardware, but all of our research data has been recovered. Per your directive, IT initiated our fail-safe protocol. All of the hard drives will be wiped clean the first time the Feds try to boot those machines. They won't find anything."

"Any rumblings from our money friends?"

"They're worried, of course," she replied. "No one said as much to me, but from what I've gathered through our listening devices in the boardroom, there has been discussion of a hostile takeover."

Mathias raised an eyebrow and smirked. *Let them try.*

Just then, his encrypted cell phone vibrated. Edmund's face lit up. It was Mr. Renzo. He answered the call eagerly.

"Tell me you have good news."

"The mission was a success, sir," Mr. Renzo reported. "I'm sending you pictures now."

Edmund gave a fist-pump. "Good work, Renzo. I can't wait to see. Bring it here ASAP."

Renzo acknowledged, and then Mathias hung up.

Seconds later, the first images arrived on his phone. Edmund's mouth fell open at the sight of Luna tangled in the mesh netting. He scrolled through more images that showed the Aiwan free of the net and sprawled out on the island's asphalt tarmac with her hands and feet bound. She was wearing the same kind of suit that Kypa had worn when he had been found. Unfortunately, that material had been confiscated by the Feds.

Mathias grinned. Now he had his own aquasuit. *Eat your hearts out, Nike and Adidas.*

He leaned over and showed the images to Ms. Diaz. She muttered oohs and aahs as he flipped through each picture.

"Is it male or female?"

Edmund shrugged. "I'm not sure, but I know just the person who can find out."

7
HOMECOMING

Planet Aiwa
The Reaper

"Captain, incoming transmission from the Aiwan battlecruiser," Reggie reported.

Ava perked up. "Finally," she muttered. "Thanks, Reg. I've got it."

When Kypa appeared on Ava's HUD, she let out a breath of relief. "You okay?"

Before answering, Kypa gave a quick glance over his shoulder at the two guards flanking him. Turning to Ava, he replied, "I am fine for now. My father has summoned me to appear before the High Court. Commodore Boa requests that you follow my shuttle to the surface."

"Do I have his word—no hostilities?"

Kypa turned to Commodore Boa, who had been standing off-screen. Boa heard the translation and stepped in front of Kypa, forcing the prince to move aside.

"You have my word, Captain."

Ava dipped her chin appreciatively. "Thank you, Commodore Boa. I hope this—"

The transmission cut off abruptly from Boa's end.

Ava huffed. "He hung up on me ..."

Neil chuckled. "I'm beginning to see why he and Kypa don't get along."

"Yeah, me, too. What a jerk."

Moments later, a shuttle emerged from the battlecruiser's hangar bay and started its descent toward Aiwa. Ava switched to manual flight control, activating the four orbs around her hands and feet. She throttled forward, increasing power to the impulse engines, and fell in line behind the shuttlecraft.

As soon as the Reaper entered the ringed world's upper atmosphere, the friction between the air and the Reaper's shields generated a fiery display that engulfed the cockpit windows.

"It's like a blast furnace," Neil commented, trying to mask the tension in his voice. He had watched countless reentries from NASA missions, but there was nothing like experiencing it firsthand. Even with the inertial dampeners compensating for the turbulence, the ride was bumpy enough to keep his full attention.

"You definitely don't want to be outside right now," Ava said lightly, keeping a watchful eye on the HUD. Regardless of the Reaper's advanced capabilities, flying blind was never optimal.

Visibility soon returned, and Ava breathed easier once she visually reacquired the shuttle. It was right where it was supposed to be ... at least until it dipped into a thick layer of dark gray storm clouds.

Ava grimaced as distant flashes of lightning flickered under the cloud layer where they were heading. A blanket of mist soon appeared on the cockpit windows that gave way to large droplets of rain. Ava resituated in her chair. Things were about to get really interesting. As a precaution, she mentally activated the seat restraints for herself and Neil.

"Looks like we're in for rough weather," she warned.

Neil looked down as the holographic seat restraints formed across his chest and lap. He gripped his chair's armrests tighter, but it was little comfort as a deluge enveloped the ship.

The Reaper dove into the storm. Winds outside howled like the cries of wounded animals as visibility had once again been reduced to almost zero.

Ava remained cool at the flight controls. As they descended toward the surface, she monitored the shuttle's progress on her HUD. Every now and again, she caught glimpses of it through the forward window whenever a flash of lightning illuminated the skies.

In her head, Ava counted off the seconds between each lightning flash and the boom of thunder that followed. This was a game her mother had taught her as a small girl to help overcome her fear of storms. Now she loved thunderstorms, as long as she was safe indoors. High above Aiwa was a different story, and each time Ava counted off in her head, the gap between thunderclaps grew closer.

She glanced at the HUD's radar where the storm cell was displayed. They were flying directly into the red section depicting the worst of it. As best as she could tell, this storm front stretched for a thousand miles in every direction. There was no easy way around it.

Suddenly, a flash of white light filled the cockpit. Neil and Ava had no time to react as a powerful bolt of lightning struck the Reaper's forward shields, creating a blanket of static electricity that encased the ship. Both pilot and passenger were thrown sideways by the impact as the Reaper cartwheeled out of control toward the surface.

An alarm squawked as Ava's display flickered from the massive energy surge. Fortunately, this was not Ava's first rodeo. Back in her Air Force days, she had flown through storms like this many times in her HC-130. During one hop over the Sea of Japan, a lightning strike had destroyed the number three engine, nearly severing it from the wing. Ava's quick thinking and nerves of steel had enabled her to baby the crippled aircraft back to base.

She worked her magic once more. Still under power, Ava recovered from the spin and righted the ship, hardly breaking a sweat.

Silencing an alarm, she asked, "Reggie, damage report."

"No damages, Captain. All systems are functioning normal."

Checking the shields, Ava saw the lightning strike had zapped nearly five percent of the Reaper's strength. The blow had been more powerful than the attacks by Boa and Krunig combined. She breathed a sigh of relief as her resilient ship recovered and the shields steadily returned to full strength.

"Neil, you okay?" she asked.

He did not reply.

"Neil?"

Raising his hand, Neil said uneasily, "Uh, yeah … I'm here."

"You okay?"

"Uh-huh." Looking down at his lap, he added, "Good news, I think the suit works."

It took Ava a second to realize he meant the recycler that processed their waste. She made a face then guffawed. "TMI, Doc." She laughed. "And no, that doesn't count toward our bet."

The Reaper and shuttle passed through the storm without further incident. Dark clouds gave way to a sweeping jungle landscape with Aiwa's twin yellow suns setting on the horizon. The view was breathtaking, unlike anything Neil and Ava could have imagined.

First to catch the eye was a long range of jagged mountains that resembled dragon teeth poking through a thin layer of mist. Rainwater snaked down the mountainside in glistening streams that slithered into a wide, fast-moving river below. The river basin divided the mountains from the neighboring jungle and flowed south to feed a vast ocean visible in the distance.

Neil shook his head, imagining the diverse ecosystems within the untamed jungle below. Even from this altitude, he could make out bright-colored flora and fauna between thickets of gargantuan trees, some the size of skyscrapers. Covered in vines and broad leaves, they formed semi-closed canopies over the ground.

Neil grinned. "Man, every botanist on Earth would kill to be in our shoes." He checked his personal HUD and did a double-take. "Listen to this, it says Aiwa's Air Quality Index is almost zero."

"What does that mean?" Ava asked.

"There are hardly any pollutants in the air—no carbon monoxide, no particle pollution ... It's insane. On a good day," Neil continued, "the U.S. average is somewhere in the fifty to a hundred range, and that's considered a moderate health threat."

CAVU. Ava grinned inwardly. Flying conditions were perfect—ceiling and visibility unlimited.

Neil pointed to his display. "Man, I'm picking up massive life readings down there."

"Whoa, check that out!" Ava blurted, pointing straight ahead.

Neil looked up in time to see a flock of winged creatures taking flight from the trees below. They were featherless, with dark brown, leathery skin and two broad wings that stretched nearly thirty feet.

The creatures had long necks and small heads with hooked beaks for shredding prey into bite-size pieces. Two of their six limbs ran the length of the wings, similar to a Pterodactyl. It seemed as if they had stepped back in time one hundred million years to the Cretaceous Period.

Neil turned sharply to Ava with a boyish grin. "What if there are dinosaurs down there?"

The innocent remark sent a cold chill down Ava's spine. She recalled the piercing yellow eyes and blood-stained fangs of the obercai. The beast had wiped out Kypa's crew, bit the head off North Korea's Supreme Leader, and mauled to death his trusted commander, Colonel Wu. It would have done the same to Ava if she had been a slower runner.

Blinking back to reality, Ava repeated General Garza's cryptic warning when she had shared with him her dream of being a fighter pilot and flying against the best. "Be careful what you wish for."

"What do you mean?" Neil asked.

Ava shrugged. "Onboard the mothership back in North Korea, I came face-to-face with one of Aiwa's apex predators."

"An obercai?"

"Uh-huh. Trust me; you don't want to be anywhere near one of those things."

"You haven't said much about that mission," Neil said cautiously, trying to gauge Ava's willingness to share. "If you want to talk …"

Ava pressed her lips together in a thin line, considering the offer. "Maybe another time." She turned to her display and saw the shuttle descending. "Looks like we're getting close."

Their journey continued through a canyon of tall rock pillars topped with grass patches and trailing vines. When they emerged from the canyon, they passed over a sandy coastal strip that opened to a broad expanse of clear blue water. The Aiwan shuttle led them out to sea.

Moments later, the shuttle gradually descended toward the water and splashed down into the ocean. Ava followed, retracting the twin nacelles and pointing the Reaper's nose downward. Her ship sliced through the water like a torpedo, creating a screen of bubbles that soon gave way to a panorama of stunning undersea wildlife. Strange new species of fish and mammals scattered in response to the sudden appearance of both vessels, but sensing no danger, they soon settled back into the rhythm of their schools and pods.

"They look like fish on Earth," Neil remarked. "Only a whole lot bigger."

From goliath groupers and angelfish to sea trout the size of Ava's old car, they resembled distant cousins from Earth, with more exotic coloring, too.

"Look at that one and its massive flippers." Neil pointed to a slow-moving mammal that resembled a cross between a Brachiosaurus and a walrus.

They watched in awed silence as the massive creature glided effortlessly along the ocean current with its gigantic mouth open, snacking on krill and smaller fish.

"This is amazing," Neil said, grinning from ear-to-ear. "No one back home is going to believe this."

Both vessels continued their descent. As the sunlight from the surface dissipated, Ava activated the Reaper's external running lights. Ten minutes later, darkness gave way to the distant glow of a vast, underwater city. They were quickly approaching Supra, the capital of Eos, one of Aiwa's Five Realms.

Vibrant hues of purple, blue, and pink filled the Reaper's cockpit as they neared the capital. Transfixed by its beauty, Neil and Ava realized Kypa's description of the city had not done it justice. Supra's grandeur was beyond anything they could have imagined. The city's futuristic appearance was the antithesis of cyberpunk. Instead of a bleak and filthy industrial vibe with holographic billboards cluttering the skyline, Supra's design epitomized the three E's of architecture: efficiency, economy, and elegance. Each towering structure was designed with a cleverly simple and organic feel that was aesthetically pleasing to the eye while simultaneously serving a functional purpose. Each structure was stunning on its own and blended seamlessly with its surrounding neighbors to create a harmonious environment.

At the heart of Supra was a towering palace with a single spire pointing upward to the surface. Wrapping the spire from the ground up were clear, serpentine-like shafts, resembling tentacles that were used for transporting personnel and material to all levels.

Neil turned to Ava with a look similar to as if he was seeing fire for the first time. "It's like Disney World on steroids."

Ava chuckled until an unusual reading on the HUD caught her eye. "I'm detecting a massive energy reading on the far side of the city. Reggie, can you identify?"

"The energy source you are referring to is the central core, Captain," Reggie replied. "Powered by magnetarite crystals, the core provides clean energy to the entire city, as well as the other realms."

Neil raised his eyebrows. "One generator for all five realms."

"Affirmative, Dr. Garrett," Reggie replied. "The central core was designed this way for ease of defense."

"He who defends everything defends nothing," Ava quoted.

"What do you mean?" Neil asked.

"It's a quote from Frederick the Great," she explained. "It means protecting the core in one location is easier than doing it in five. That way, you don't have to spread your defenses too thin."

"So, if one realm falls, the others would not be affected by the loss," Neil reasoned.

Ava nodded. "Unless that realm is Eos," she added grimly.

To Reggie, she asked, "What other defenses are in place?"

"Each realm is encapsulated with a protective shield. Supra's shield has remained in place since Grawn Krunig's attack. However, this requires a great deal of energy and is only used sparingly. In addition to the shield, each realm has its own security force and every Aiwan must serve."

"Reminds me of Israel," Neil remarked.

"Mm," Ava considered. "I'm curious, Reg, where do the Aiwans build their starships?"

A map appeared on Ava's HUD, depicting the five realms. An area to the north was highlighted.

"All spacecraft are constructed and refitted at the shipyards in the realm of Dohrm."

"I hope they include that in the tour," Neil said.

Ava agreed but, judging by Commodore Boa's less-than-cordial attitude, it seemed unlikely they would get to see any of Aiwa's military infrastructure on this visit … unless it was in the stockade. That grim prospect reminded Ava she needed a contingency plan in case things went south with the Aiwans. The sight of Supra's central core sparked an idea.

Suddenly, the Reaper shuddered, and Ava felt the flight controls lock up. She darted a glance across the HUD, expecting a threat warning or cataclysmic equipment failure to appear.

"Reggie, what's happening?"

"Standard protocol, Captain. Central Control has locked onto the ship with a tractor beam. As visitors, the controller will pilot us through the dome shield to the palace's hangar bay."

"Tractor beams, cool," Neil geeked out.

"Captain, we are being instructed to modulate our shields and disengage manual flight controls," Reggie conveyed.

Leary, Ava complied. She adjusted their shields to match the frequency provided by the controller and relinquished control of the ship by removing her hands and feet from the four orbs. The tractor beam took over, and the Reaper continued along its present course toward the city center.

"Is it possible to break free of the tractor beam?" she asked. *In case we need to make a quick exit.*

"No, Captain," Reggie answered. "The tractor beam would need to be disabled at the source or destroyed to secure our release."

"Figures," Ava said dryly.

Not surprised, Neil turned to Ava. "You really need to watch *Star Wars*." This remark earned him a disapproving look. He raised his hands in surrender.

"Just saying."

Ava wondered if she was being overly paranoid. Yet, it was wise to be cautious. Kypa's warning about having a target on their backs had been percolating in her mind. If the Reaper was now the most coveted commodity in the galaxy, what was to stop the Aiwans from attempting to impound her ship and keep it for themselves?

It was not beyond reason to think they would demand their property back. No one could fault Kypa for using the humans to steal the Reaper to aid his escape. It was an act of desperation. Yet, despite Kypa's best intentions, Ava had to admit he had probably overstepped his authority by gifting the Reaper to her. Even if she had proven her worth, entrusting a human with such power was bound to create dissent.

She hoped offering King Loka a cargo bay full of crystals might influence his judgment, but Ava was not holding her breath. One shard of Maxixe Magnetarite was worth a helluva lot more than a tiny cargo bay full of orange crystals. As long as the blue crystal resided inside the Reaper, they were all at risk. For that reason alone, Ava's gut kept gnawing at her. She could not afford to be naïve.

Trust no one, Kypa had warned.

Ava took a calming breath as the Reaper passed through Supra's protective shield. Moments later, they made their final approach to the palace.

Boa's shuttle entered the hangar bay first and touched down. As the Reaper followed, Ava looked out the side window and noticed onlookers in the serpentine-like transport tubes draping the palace exterior. Male and female Aiwans of all ages stopped to gawk at the mysterious vessel entering the palace. Ava wondered if news had spread of the Reaper's exploits against Grawn Krunig.

Ava lowered the Reaper's three landing struts as it passed through the hangar bay's containment field. This energy barrier not only kept ocean water out, but it also evaporated all water from the Reaper's hull, drying the ship completely.

As if guided by an invisible hand, the Reaper set down gently on the deck beside the shuttle.

Neil turned to Ava. "Now what?"

Ava shrugged. "Beats me."

Outside, they noticed the shuttle's rear boarding ramp lower. Two guards exited the craft, followed by Kypa and Commodore Boa.

Ava frowned. "Kypa doesn't look so happy to be home."

"True, but at least he's not in shackles," Neil said lightly.

"Yet," Ava murmured.

They watched as Boa gave an instruction to Kypa, gesturing to the Reaper. Kypa nodded and approached the ship alone.

Ava leapt out of her chair and jogged to the down ladder to the engineering section. By the time Neil caught up with her, she was ready to open the outer hatch.

"Wait!" Neil exclaimed. "Don't forget your helmet."

Ava snatched her hand from the control panel. "I thought the city was pressurized, so we didn't need them?"

Neil shrugged. Erring on the side of caution, he activated his holographic helmet just in case.

"You're right. Better safe than sorry," Ava said. She gave a thought command to activate her helmet. "Okay, ready?"

Neil gave her a thumbs-up. "One small step for a man, right?"

Ava raised her eyebrows. "I'm impressed you quoted Neil Armstrong correctly."

"I better. My mom named me after him."

"Nice." Ava grinned. She then activated the button on the panel. The hatch opened while the ladder automatically lowered. Neil and Ava peered over the side and found Kypa looking up at them.

He waved. "Good, you remembered your helmets. Although, they will not be necessary. Please, climb down," Kypa instructed. "I assure you it is safe."

Ava gestured to the ladder. "After you, Mr. Ambassador."

Feeling the weight of his responsibility, Neil took a curt breath to calm his nerves then descended the ladder. Stepping onto the deck, he rounded to face Kypa and the others. His eyes settled on the armed guards first, gauging their demeanor. They were unreadable and silent, which was to be expected, and they kept their distance. Neither guard appeared in a hurry to arrest them.

Relieved, Neil gave a cursory glance at Kypa, wondering how his meeting went with Boa. Kypa's forced smile told him not to ask. He then turned to Commodore Boa. One look in his direction was enough to put Neil on alert. The commodore held his chin high, signaling a sense of superiority. His eyes narrowed, and his mouth pursed in an unmistakable expression of disdain for either Kypa, the humans, or the situation.

Probably all three, Neil surmised.

Undeterred, Neil faced Commodore Boa and bowed his head, maintaining eye contact. "My name is Dr. Neil Garrett, appointed ambassador for the peaceful nations of Earth. On behalf of my people, I bid you greetings."

His words were instantly translated to Aiwan.

Boa eyed Neil slowly, taking his measure. This was the first time he had seen a human male. His only prior encounter with the species involved Ava.

Exchanging pleasantries was not the commodore's forte. Boa bowed stiffly and replied, "Welcome to Aiwa, Dr. Neil Garrett of Earth. I am Commodore Boa, Commander of his majesty's royal fleet."

The translation was instantaneous. "Thank you." Neil smiled pleasantly. He started to say something humorous to lighten the mood when he noticed Boa's brow furrow. The Aiwan was looking past Neil, over his shoulder. Neil turned, following Boa's sightline to the Reaper's down ladder. It was empty.

Equally perplexed, Kypa approached the ladder. Not seeing Ava above, he called up to her, "Captain Tan?"

"Here!" Ava replied, unseen from above.

A moment of mystery followed, and then she appeared and started down. As soon as Ava stepped onto the deck, the ladder automatically retracted, and the hatch sealed.

Ava rounded on the group and smiled innocently. "Sorry, I—"

She stopped mid-sentence at the sight of Commodore Boa. Wearing his usual scowl, he fixed her with a formidable gaze that broke most others. Ava withstood the challenge, knowing she had bested him on the battlefield. An uncomfortable silence followed. Kypa and the others watched, waiting to see who would blink first. At last, Boa stepped forward with his hands clasped behind his back. Ava instinctively clenched her fists, ready to throw down.

Boa stopped short of invading Ava's personal space but still towered over her. If his intent was to use the height difference to project superiority, it was lost on Ava. She was not backing down. As Boa eyed her up and down, taking her measure, the feisty human raised an eyebrow, as if daring the Aiwan to make a move.

Boa *hmphed* then slowly averted his eyes and gestured to the exit. "This way. The High Court is waiting."

"Thank you, Commodore Boa," Neil interjected, hoping to break the tension. "Please, take us to your ... leader ..." He trailed off.

Boa led the way out, followed by the guards and Kypa. Ava and Neil exchanged looks then fell in behind the group.

Wrapping her arm around Neil's, Ava asked with a suppressed grin, "Take us to your leader, huh?"

Neil sighed heavily. "Don't you dare say a word to Rose or Nunez."

"Ha!" Ava chortled, elbowing Neil playfully before letting him go. "Your secret's safe with me."

Up ahead, Kypa kept to himself. The dread of facing his father showed as he caught himself fidgeting with his hands. He forced himself to stop, hoping Boa had not noticed.

Neil, on the other hand, could not mask his excitement. On the way out, they passed several Aiwans. Most kept their heads down to avoid attracting Boa's attention, but they stole furtive glances at Neil and Ava. Ambassador Garrett smiled and waved, but his friendly gesture was met with mixed expressions of confusion and fear by the Aiwans.

Next to him, Ava's uneasiness about leaving her ship grew with each step. Just before turning into a corridor to exit the hangar bay, she glanced fleetingly over her shoulder at the Reaper. A sinking feeling told her this might be the last time she saw Reggie.

8

THE HIGH COURT

Planet Aiwa
Supra, Realm of Eos

Commodore Boa led Kypa, Neil, and Ava to a nearby lift at the end of the corridor. The doors opened to reveal an enclosed elevator, similar to those on Earth; only, this one was taller to accommodate Aiwans, and it could move both horizontally and vertically.

Neil and Ava stepped inside first and instinctively turned to face the doors. Kypa and Boa followed, along with the guards.

"Grand Hall," Boa directed, and the lift began moving.

Crammed inside, Neil and Ava found themselves facing the guards. Standing toe-to-toe and too close for comfort, both felt small compared to the towering Aiwans. They avoided eye contact, for the most part, by looking at their feet. Meanwhile, the guards kept their eyes forward. They stared over Neil's and Ava's heads, focusing on nothing in particular but seeing everything peripherally.

Ava looked around and noticed Boa and Kypa facing one another on opposing sides of the lift. She caught Boa observing Kypa from afar, his eyes narrowed on the prince. Kypa seemed unaware of this, deep in thought.

Scrutinizing Boa closer, the Aiwan had not said a word to her since their stare down in the hangar bay. At first, Ava had brushed off his silence as pride. He was not the first alpha male she had encountered who had a hard time accepting failure—twice in one week had to be a serious blow to his ego. Thanking Ava for saving his life was probably too much to expect, but she could not help wondering what Boa thought of her.

Ava's train of thought was broken by a gentle nudge from Neil. She leaned in close so he could speak in her ear.

Grinning, Neil made a head bob behind them. "Check that out."

They rounded to face the window. Before them was the mind-blowing underwater city. As the lift carried them up and around the exterior of the palace's main spire, Neil and Ava enjoyed a spectacular, panoramic view of the entire capital. Even with several distant sections of the city noticeably blacked out to conserve energy, the sight was unmatched by anything on Earth.

"This place is amazing," Neil remarked as purple and orange hues illuminated the lift.

Ava agreed, but her thoughts still lingered on the tension between Boa and Kypa. Trying to avoid drawing attention to herself, Ava mentally deactivated her nano-ring's telepathy jammer. She then closed her eyes and attempted to make a connection.

"*Kypa!*"

Inches away, a faint echo tickled the back of Kypa's mind. His brow furrowed as he focused on the barely discernible mental tap.

Aiwan telepathy required practice and deep concentration. Above all, certain neural pathways in the brain had to be unlocked. Since Kypa and Ava had already established a mental connection, such communication was possible as long as Kypa initiated contact. For Ava to do so never seemed plausible because the human brain had appeared incapable until now.

Ava focused her thoughts again on his name.

As soon as Kypa recognized the mental call of Ava's voice, he gave a furtive glance in her direction. Still facing toward the window, Neil and Ava had their backs to him. Neil continued gawking at the cityscape, while he could see Ava had her eyes squeezed shut, focusing intently. Kypa pointed his gaze at the floor and responded to Ava telepathically.

"*Captain, I hear you.*"

Ava squeaked in surprise and cupped her hands over her mouth and nose.

Neil gave her a curious look, grinned, then returned to the view outside.

Calming herself, Ava casually dropped her hands to her sides.

"*Ava, I am here,*" Kypa called again.

"*You heard me,*" Ava whispered excitedly with her mind then realized it was completely unnecessary. No one but Kypa could hear her. "*How is this possible?*"

"*I do not know,*" Kypa replied, "*but try to relax your body as we communicate. We do not want to raise suspicion with Boa and the guards.*"

Ava nodded before she could stop herself. "*You seem cautious. What's wrong?*"

"*Boa definitely wants your ship,*" Kypa explained warily. "*He will press the High Court to have us arrested so he can seize the Reaper.*"

"*Let him try,*" Ava replied with an air of confidence and lifted her chin. Her lack of concern surprised Kypa. "*Besides, your father and the court will see the amazing technology you've developed. We can repair Aiwa with the Reaper and broker a partnership with Earth to trade for crystals.*"

Kypa frowned. "*I wish I had your optimism, but the situation is bigger than you and I. There are forces at work that want to discredit my father. Any hint of favoritism or leniency toward me will be viewed as weakness.*"

"*Heavy lies the head that wears the crown,*" Ava quoted Shakespeare.

Kypa considered her insightful words. He could relate better than most to the burden of leadership.

"*Behind every set of eyes in the High Court are differing visions of how Aiwa should be ruled,*" Kypa explained. "*I fear they will use this trial to advance their own agendas, not to seek justice.*"

The lift came to a stop. Kypa broke off their connection and Ava reactivated her nano-ring's jammer. Before following the others out of the lift, Ava and Kypa exchanged an uneasy look. Neither believed their audience with the court would be pleasant. Ava reached out and squeezed Kypa's hand to encourage her friend.

A small smile softened Kypa's jaw. "Thank you, Captain."

"C'mon; we got this," she assured him.

As they proceeded down a long corridor, Neil took in the ornate statues and various works of art lining the walls. A resonant harp-like music that reminded him of rolling tides played softly in the background. He was about to ask Kypa about it when they arrived at the Grand Hall.

Flanking the entrance to the High Court's chamber were two members of the Royal Guard. Tasked with protecting the royal family and heads of state, Royal Guards wore blue aquasuits with golden tentacles embroidered on their chests. The role was more than mere pageantry. Armed with custom energy pikes and shields, Royal Guards were the most highly-trained and disciplined warriors in the Five Realms.

As soon as the guards spotted Boa's approach, they retracted their crisscrossed pikes and snapped to attention.

Boa stopped in front of the tall doors. He glanced over his shoulder, ensuring Prince Kypa and the humans were ready. Boa then straightened his uniform and nodded to the guards to open the doors. He led the procession inside.

The Grand Hall of the High Court was an exquisite piece of architecture that honored Aiwa's long, rich history. Two oversized doors opened to a brightly lit, cathedral-style chamber with a vaulted ceiling and ivory-colored walls. Splitting the room down the middle was a glossy, black marble walkway with calm pools of water on either side. To the right and left were arched columns leading into recessed alcoves.

The center walkway led to a pavilion at the far end of the room. There, the court members awaited. They sat at two identical, crescent-shaped tables on either side with the king's oversized, gilded throne between them. Behind the pavilion, taking up the entire back wall of the hall, was an ominous statue of a legendary creature known as Gwaru. Carved out of ivory, the towering sculpture was a massive sea animal similar to a kraken, with a round body, bulging ruby eyes, and twelve, sucker-covered tentacles. Water flowed out of the sculpture's mouth to feed the narrow pools on either side of the central walkway.

Intrigued by the Gwaru's influence throughout the palace, Neil made a mental note to research the sea creature later. In the meantime, he took advantage of his helmet's HUD to familiarize himself with the court.

The High Court consisted of two males and two females. Each member was dressed in a sheer, golden robe and matching belt. None wore jewelry or makeup of any kind, not even a crown for King Loka.

Seated at the table to Loka's right was Lord Wahla, Warden of Dohrm, a middle-aged male of noble descent. His realm built the kingdom's subterranean transport ships and space-faring vessels, even Aiwa's intricate network of undersea, high-speed transport tubes. After the war against the harvesters had begun, Dohrm had become the epicenter for all military training and manufacturing.

Next to him, a serene female held herself poised with a studious countenance. Lord Cara represented the realm of Maeve, home of the Citadel for higher learning. Aiwa's best minds trained at the Citadel on matters scientific, medical, and historical before serving all of the realms as teachers and advisors.

Across from her, at the opposite table, was another female leader, leaning forward with fierce intensity. Lord Zefra, Warden of Fonn, represented Aiwa's largest realm. Fonn consisted mostly of small undersea settlements spread throughout a vast and untamed region known as the Outlands. This realm had a rich tradition of raising Aiwa's best hunters and, even without using telepathy, they had an uncanny ability to communicate with all sea creatures.

The seat next to her was unoccupied. It was reserved for the warden of Cirros, the kingdom that had been lost due to overharvesting the crystals needed for the war effort. Severe quakes had leveled Cirros' largest cities and destroyed many of the surrounding territories. Millions had perished, buried alive in the rubble of what remained. Most of the bodies had never been recovered, and those who had survived had taken refuge in other realms as displaced people. Their seat on the court was currently unfilled.

Rounding out the group was King Loka himself, who represented the realm of Eos. He was similar in build and markings to Kypa, yet he carried himself with a centering power that few could match, not even his son. Loka did not reflect a belief that the world revolved around him, but rather it was his sense of confidence, purpose, and well-being that gave him a supreme sense of balance. Even in these dark times, surrounded by chaos, Loka remained calm, cool, and collected. He was a rock, immovable in the face of a crisis or the passing and superficial.

The echo of the entrance doors opening interrupted the conversation the king was leading with the court. Glancing toward the sound, Loka brightened slightly at the sight of his son approaching. The king then trailed off as he narrowed his eyes on Neil and Ava.

Following the king's gaze, the other court members stopped talking, and a deafening silence filled the cavernous hall.

Commodore Boa led the group to the edge of the pavilion. He bowed and started to address the court but stopped short when Prince Kypa asserted his position as heir and stepped forward into the center of the pavilion, coming to stand before the throne.

Kypa bowed. "Greetings, My King and members of the High Court."

King Loka gripped the golden scepter in his hand tighter. As a father, he was torn between stepping down and embracing the son who he had believed to be dead or wringing his neck for insolence, perhaps both. Instead, Loka tapped the staff on the dais twice to call the court to order.

"Commodore Boa, step forward," Loka commanded in a deep voice.

Leaving Neil and Ava behind, Boa entered the pavilion with full military bearing—chest out, shoulders back, and chin held high. He stopped beside Kypa, standing shoulder to shoulder, and bowed humbly to the king.

"Report," Loka ordered.

"My King, as you are aware, the harvester threat has been put down. The enemy is in full retreat."

"Yes, a decisive victory. Well done, Commodore."

The king's sentiments were seconded by the court. However, Boa raised his hand, humbly objecting.

"The court honors me and our brave warriors, but in all fairness, this victory is not mine or theirs." He gestured to Kypa and the humans. "Prince Kypa and his … colleagues deserve the credit. They are the ones who should be commended."

All heads turned to the humans, showing expressions mixed with suspicion and disbelief.

Feeling the weight of their stares, Ava and Neil swallowed hard.

"Come forward," Loka commanded the humans.

Boa and Kypa stepped aside as Neil and Ava nervously entered the pavilion.

Clearing his throat, Kypa introduced his friends. "Your Grace, members of the High Court, allow me to introduce Dr. Neil Garrett, Earth's appointed ambassador to Aiwa."

Neil bowed.

"And this is Captain Ava Tan. It was her ship that engaged Krunig's forces, but she is also the one who rescued me and brought me home. I owe her my life. We all do."

King Loka stroked his jutted chin, thinking. "Do you concur with Commodore Boa's account?"

Kypa darted his eyes to Boa then nodded humbly. "Yes. Fighting alongside Commodore Boa's forces, our new emissaries from Earth turned the tide of the battle."

Loka's brow scrunched. He pursed his lips, straining to repeat the sound. "Yuurth?"

"Yes, Earth." Neil smiled. "If I may …" He stepped forward with his palms facing outward. "On behalf of the peaceful nations of Earth, we come before you as friends and wish to discuss an alliance against our shared enemy— harvesters."

His words were met with silence. The court members exchanged skeptical glances. Aiwa had no allies; they had never needed any.

"Friends, you say?" Boa scoffed.

Neil rounded on Boa, eyeing him up and down. "Yes," he declared. "Our actions today prove it."

Boa produced a palm-sized holoprojector and held it out for everyone to see. A projection of the Reaper appeared. "Behold their mighty warship,"

Boa announced. "More powerful than both our fleet and Krunig's. Now tell the king and this court how Earth came into possession of such a small yet powerful vessel."

Kypa steeled himself. "I built this ship," he announced.

"Built it yourself?" Boa clarified. He set the projector on the table then slowly began circling Kypa, Neil, and Ava with his hands clasped behind his back. "Where did you build this Reaper?"

"Off-world ... in my private lab," Kypa replied.

"Off-world? Where exactly?"

Kypa felt a lump in his throat. "Pria-12," he answered, referring to Aiwa's smallest and most-distant moon. "I am more than willing to grant access to the court so you may see it for yourselves."

"That is most kind, Prince Kypa," Boa feigned gratitude. "But to develop a warship off-world requires this court's permission."

"Mm," Kypa muttered, knowing it to be true.

"I did not hear that," Boa put his hand to his ear. "Please speak louder so the court can hear you."

"You are correct," Kypa answered, raising his voice.

"This is a law you broke not only to build your ship, but you broke it again by taking it to Earth, did you not?" he asked irritably, gesturing to the humans.

"That is correct."

"We will get to that in a moment," Boa promised. "Now, tell the court: how did you acquire the resources necessary to build this ship off-world?"

"I salvaged most of the materials from scrapyards in Dohrm ... some I had to purchase from off-world traders."

"And where did you acquire the credits to make said purchases?"

Kypa cleared his throat. "I had no credits. I bartered with crystals— shavings of crystals, actually—not full stones. I used them to purchase the parts I needed."

"So, you admit to misappropriating resources designated for the war effort," Boa accused.

"I—"

"Yes or no will suffice," Boa spoke over him.

"Yes, but I did it to save Aiwa," Kypa explained. "It was our only hope."

"The last time you took it upon yourself to save our planet, you caused massive quakes that destroyed the realm of Cirros. Millions perished."

Kypa shook his head. "No, that is not true. I warned this court about overmining, and those warnings were ignored. The resulting quakes were inevitable."

His hard truth struck a disapproving chord with the court. Despite their reaction, Kypa continued.

"I built the Reaper in secret because I knew I would never get your permission to do so. But it works," he explained, unable to contain the excitement and passion in his voice. "The Reaper has the ability to harvest crystals without damaging the core. We can resume full production *and* restore Cirros."

"It's true, Your Highness," Ava added. "I've seen it work."

"You will not speak unless spoken to," Boa rebuked.

Ava was taken aback. She flashed Boa an annoyed expression but held her tongue.

"Captain Tan is correct," Kypa addressed the court. "Their home, Earth, is ripe with large deposits of crystals. I discovered them shortly after I finished the Reaper prototype. That is why I set out for Earth without permission. I wanted to survey the find myself and verify the accuracy of my readings. Unfortunately, my ship was attacked in hyperspace and crashed."

"What happened to your crew?" Lord Cara from Maeve asked.

Kypa hesitated. An image of Luna popped into his head. "I am the only survivor," he answered somberly. "During the attack, there was a hull breach in my section. I was injured but managed to crawl into an escape pod. It launched automatically. When I regained consciousness, I found that I had been rescued by the humans. They helped me recover the Reaper."

Loka looked past his son to the humans. "Is this true?"

Neil and Ava looked at one another, trying to decide who would respond. Neil deferred to Ava. It was her mission, and she deserved the credit.

Ava stepped forward. "It is, Your Highness," she replied. "When I reached the crash site, I found the entire crew had perished. I managed to fly the Reaper to safety before the mothership's engine core erupted."

No sense telling them who made that happen, she thought wryly.

"A brave act, indeed," Boa countered.

To Kypa, he asked, "But, why did you entrust this task to her? Why not recover the Reaper yourself?"

"Humans have never encountered beings from off-world," Kypa explained. "They feared for my safety if my presence became public knowledge."

"Earth is made up of many independent nations," Neil added. "We do not always see things eye-to-eye. The crash site was in a dangerous area, ruled by a tyrant who wanted to use your technology against the rest of our world. Captain Tan risked her life to recover the Reaper before that happened."

"And instead of handing the Reaper over to its rightful owner, you kept it for yourself and attacked me," Boa charged.

Ava huffed. "You attacked us first," she countered. "All we wanted was to broker a peace agreement, but you wouldn't listen. You left me no choice. I had to defend myself."

"By attacking my ship, you crippled our defenses. Several Aiwans died today because of you."

Ava threw her hands on her hips. "Excuse me? I saved your life."

"And, in doing so, your infernal Reaper has invited every harvester in this sector to Aiwa."

"Silence!" Loka growled, startling everyone in attendance.

The bickering ended abruptly with Boa and Ava exchanging heated glares.

King Loka received a telepathic request from Lord Zefra, Warden of Fonn. The king turned to his counterpart. "Lord Zefra."

Judging from her age lines and skin tone, one might mistake the Aiwan leader to be as old as Boa. That was not the case for Lord Zefra. Raised in the rugged Outlands, she was a wrangler at heart and had both the calluses and bravado to go with it.

"Prince Kypa, you have not denied the charges Commodore Boa has brought against you," she pointed out.

"Lord Zefra, I deny causing the quakes that destroyed Cirros. As for misappropriating resources to build the Reaper and save our planet, yes, I am guilty. I did what this court refused to do," Kypa insisted. He paused to keep his voice from shaking. "I acted on behalf of all Aiwans. The quake that destroyed Cirros was not my fault, but I accepted the blame because it forced you to stop harvesting … at least for a time. If you decide to resume production," he warned, "I promise another disaster is inevitable. Whose realm will be next? Will it be yours, Lord Zefra?"

Not waiting for Zefra to reply, Kypa turned to his father. "Punish me if you must, but my conscience is clear. All I ask is the chance to demonstrate the Reaper's capability. We can rebuild Cirros *and* defeat the harvesters, I would stake my life on it."

His passionate plea resonated with the court.

After a pause, Lord Cara asked, "Is it true you are in possession of Maxixe Magnetarite?"

"Yes, the blue crystal exists," he confirmed. "However, it is not in my possession. The crystal came from Earth. Captain Tan harvested it; it belongs to her."

"Yet, the crystal resides inside the Reaper, Aiwan property," Boa argued.

"Not anymore," Kypa corrected. "I gifted the Reaper to Captain Tan, and it is bound to her and her alone. Captain Tan risked everything to save my life, including disobeying her superiors. I knew that if the Reaper harnessed the power of a blue crystal, it required a captain of impeccable character, someone who would use the Reaper to save lives, not take them." Kypa faced Ava and regarded her with pride. "She represents the best in all of us, Aiwans and humans. I cannot think of anyone more worthy of such responsibility than her."

Ava did not have to say, *Thank you*, nor did Kypa have to read her mind to see the gratitude on her face.

"Touching," Boa remarked with veiled sarcasm. "Nevertheless, it was not Prince Kypa's ship to give away. That is the king's property and should be returned immediately."

"No!" Kypa objected. "That crystal is Ava's property, not ours. However," he said approaching his father, "the humans have brought us a gift. The Reaper's cargo hold is full of crystals, enough to end the rolling blackouts and strengthen our defenses while we demonstrate the Reaper's potential." He gestured to Neil and Ava then looked into his father's eyes, imploring him to listen. "Please, they saved my life and this planet. If anything, gifting Ava the ship is fair compensation."

Before Boa could object, Neil interjected, projecting his voice with confidence. "King Loka, may I address the court?"

All eyes turned to Neil.

Loka eyed him briefly then nodded. "Granted."

Neil cleared his throat. "Thank you, Your Honor. Prince Kypa is correct; the leaders of Earth sent us to establish a peace accord with Aiwa. Both of our worlds are in peril. You have been fighting this war much longer than we have, but Earth will soon be on the front lines. The harvesters are coming for us. They will mine our planet down to the very last crystal and destroy our world in the process. But it doesn't have to be that way. There is time to save Aiwa and Earth if we work together." Neil paused to gauge his audience's reaction. It felt like a high stakes poker game. Now it was time to show his cards. "Earth has an abundance of crystals. More than enough for both of our needs, as I understand it. We would be willing to share these resources to aid in Aiwa's defense."

"And in return?" Loka asked.

"We are technologically inferior, that is no secret," Neil admitted candidly. "If the harvesters come, Earth is doomed. So, in exchange for crystals, we ask that you help us protect our world from the same invaders that threaten yours."

"Are you proposing we share our technology?" Boa scoffed.

Neil nodded.

"Ambassador Garrett, you just testified that the reason Captain Tan was sent to recover the Reaper was because your government feared other humans—tyrants, you called them—would use Aiwan technology against your own people. Who is to say your government will not turn against us?"

"That is not our intent," Neil promised. "What I said does not represent the majority of humans, either. We are imperfect beings. There are individuals who prey on the weak or seek power at the cost of hurting others, but most humans only want to live in peace … just like you and your families. We can both achieve this goal if we begin to trust one another and work together."

As the chamber fell silent, King Loka closed his eyes, and the other members of the court followed suit.

Neil and Ava looked about in confusion. It was as if they had fallen into a deep meditation.

"They are in conclave," Kypa whispered.

Ava glanced at Lord Zefra. She could see the Aiwan's bulbous eyes moving about under her eyelids as the court debated telepathically.

Turning away, Ava landed her gaze on Commodore Boa, who was watching her intently. The urge to call him out was unbearable, but Ava sensed that talking or, more accurately, shouting a four-letter expletive at him would be inappropriate during conclave. The commodore reminded her of General Garza, and now she could understand why Neil and Rose disliked the guy.

"Prince Kypa of Eos," King Loka said, startling Ava back to the present. The court had ended its silent debate. "Step forward," Loka commanded. "The court is ready to pronounce judgment."

Kypa approached his father and steeled himself.

"You have been found guilty of misappropriating wartime resources, a crime punishable by death. However, considering recent events, it is the court's decision to grant you clemency on the grounds that you fulfill your request to repair Aiwa's core. If you succeed, and we can safely resume harvesting operations without further damaging the planet, then you will receive a full pardon." He added with reservation, "But should you fail, you will be punished as the law dictates. Is this understood?"

Kypa breathed a sigh of relief. He bowed and replied, "Yes, My King. I will not let you down."

"Humans, step forward," Loka directed.

Neil and Ava approached tentatively.

Loka looked long at the humans while weighing the court's input. Lord Cara had sided with Boa, arguing the Reaper and the blue crystal were property of Aiwa and should be confiscated immediately. She had even gone so far as to suggest a mission to Earth was needed to forcibly harvest the remaining crystals without permission from the humans. Such a treasure trove could not fall into the hands of the Madreen Crime Syndicate or other harvesters. However, Loka and the wardens of Fonn and Dohrm argued to the contrary, reasoning that either course of action would compromise their ethical standards and make Aiwans no different than their enemies. Loka nodded once, as if to assure himself of the right decision.

"As ruler of the Five Realms, it is my decree that Aiwa accept your terms of peace."

Shocked, Boa spoke up, "My King, they cannot be trusted—"

Loka slammed his staff down hard in rebuke, his anger brimming, causing Boa to flinch.

Remembering his place, Boa stood silent, at attention.

The king held a fierce glare at his senior commander for a long moment then slowly transferred his gaze back to Neil and Ava.

"Your generous offer of crystals is accepted. This gesture of good will is a positive first step, one that I hope will begin to build a partnership founded on trust and friendship." Loka paused. "On a personal note, I also wish to convey my gratitude for saving my son's life and returning him to Aiwa. For that, I am eternally grateful."

Neil beamed. It was his first successful act of intergalactic diplomacy. Making prayer hands, he bowed in respect. "That is wonderful news. Thank you, King Loka, and members of the court."

The ever-so-brief moment of positivity was cut off at the knees when Ava felt compelled to address the elephant in the room. "And what about my ship … Your Highness?"

King Loka narrowed his eyes on the petite, human female.

"Ava," Neil whispered out of the corner of his mouth.

Ava ignored him and approached Loka. "As your son stated, the Reaper is bound to me. Now I am more than willing to help him rebuild Aiwa's core, but I want it to be clear that we are free to come and go as we please."

"This is preposterous," Boa said, incredulous. "Your Grace, please, give the word so I may reclaim Aiwa's property."

"Try it, and you'll regret it," Ava warned. "My ship is set to self-destruct if anyone attempts to confiscate my property, or if my crew should meet an untimely death."

Several court members gasped at her audacity.

Neil's shoulders dropped. They had been so close to ending on a high note, and now it was about to blow up, literally.

He smiled uncomfortably at Loka. Between gritted teeth, he muttered to Ava, "This isn't helping."

Ava shushed him, never taking her eyes off King Loka.

Loka looked down on Ava from his position of authority, unfazed by her threat. He knew good and well that if the Reaper's core detonated, the blast wave would not only destroy Supra, but most likely tear the entire planet apart, as well.

Cool under pressure, he eyed Ava for a long moment. The corner of his mouth creased upward ever so slightly, admiring her spunk. Admittedly, if their roles were reversed, he probably would have taken the same stance. Perhaps his son was right and there was more to these humans than met the eye.

Loka tapped his staff twice. The room hushed with anxious curiosity, awaiting the king's decree.

"We will honor Prince Kypa's judgment. The ship is yours, Captain Tan, as is the blue crystal."

Kypa, Neil, and Ava shared a collective sigh. Boa huffed but kept his bearing.

"My King," Kypa started, "with your permission, we will take our leave and begin preparations to repair Aiwa's core."

"How long will this process take?" Lord Zefra asked.

Kypa turned to face her. "The results will be immediate, my lord. Four rotations should suffice ... at least to demonstrate on a small scale that the Reaper works."

Zefra raised her eyebrow, skeptical of such claims.

"And where will you begin?" Lord Wahla inquired.

Kypa had the perfect location in mind. "Cirros, my lord. While we work on stabilizing the core, the crystals provided by Captain Tan and Ambassador Garrett can be used to fortify our defenses and put an end to the rolling blackouts."

No one objected.

"Then you may take your leave, Prince Kypa," Loka said. "Go, and may good fortune follow you."

For once, he did not add.

9

EKATOR

The Mishi Nebula

The Mishi Nebula was one place in the galaxy most travelers went out of their way to avoid. Shrouded in mystery, this gaseous, red cloud on the outer fringes of inhabited space was the equivalent to Earth's Bermuda Triangle.

Nicknamed Psi-Husaleth, which translated loosely to "Eater of the Lost," the Mishi Nebula earned a reputation for consuming unwary travelers. Some had tried their luck using the nebula as a faster route across this sector, while thrill-seeking others sought to debunk the nebula's mythos. In the end, no one ever made it out alive.

Of course, gossip and tall tales only added to the nebula's legend. In truth, the cloud did somehow wreak havoc on navigation instruments and protective shields. But the main cause behind the disappearances was piracy.

Chief amongst the scum and villainy who inhabited Psi-Husaleth was the crime lord, Grawn Krunig. His base of operations, Ekator, was an exclusive spaceport, dug out of a large asteroid drifting deep in the heart of the nebula. Here, the reclusive underboss of the Madreen Crime Syndicate ran his faction.

Relying on cutthroat tactics and keen business savvy, Grawn Krunig had established a lucrative enterprise that was feared throughout this sector, but it was his uncanny ability to snuff out challengers that kept him on top. This trait was as enigmatic as the nebula housing Ekator. Only his trusted advisor, Vekka, knew the secret to Krunig's longevity.

All of that was in jeopardy now. Despite the power and wealth accrued by his other seedy endeavors—gambling, drugs, slavery—Krunig's fixation on conquering Aiwa threatened to bring his reign to an end. Magnetarite was his most lucrative profit generator, and the crystal-rich planet of Aiwa presented an attractive revenue stream. But as the Aiwans defied him, prolonging the conflict and consuming the precious stores of energy crystals that remained, Krunig's single-minded quest for victory appeared to be driven more by blind obsession than simple greed.

Krunig's recent defeat at Aiwa compounded his problems. He had lost more than just ships and fighters; now, his credibility was at stake. Compensating the other Grawns for their losses would be costly, of course, but retreating to Ekator with his metaphorical tail between his legs made him appear weak. This invited ambitious contenders to challenge his leadership. It was nothing new in this line of work. However, two ships had already mutinied on the way home, and more were sure to follow. They would be dealt with soon enough. First, he had to placate Grawn Supreme and the rest of the Madreen governing body so he could begin the hunt for the mystery ship that promised to turn his fortunes around.

The doors to Krunig's private quarters slid open and he entered the darkened room alone. Soft, overhead lights activated automatically. As the doors closed behind him, a sensor inside Krunig's suit detected an unauthorized lifeform hidden behind a pillar to his right.

He snapped his head sideways, instinctively removing the hilts of two energy blades attached to his breastplate. The weapons hissed to life as soon as they were drawn, forming identical, crescent-shaped sickles.

Out of the darkness, a double-barreled weapon fired twice in succession. The first shot sent an energy bola—two power balls connected by a cable—whizzing through the air. Krunig skillfully sliced through the cable in mid-air and the power balls raced by, harmlessly smashing into the wall behind him. However, the second bola found its mark. Krunig was unable to react in time as the projectile hit him at the knees and instantly wrapped around his legs. The bola activated, energizing the cable connecting the two power balls and zapping Krunig with enough power to kill a large animal.

Krunig's armor saved him, but he lost his balance and fell backward onto his elbows. As the high-voltage current coursed through his suit, Krunig knew he only had precious seconds to free himself. If the bola did not kill him, his attacker certainly would.

Krunig spotted the assassin emerging from the shadows with a blaster in hand. With no time to waste, he sliced through the bola cable with his sickle. It short-circuited and fell to the floor as several blaster bolts exploded around him. Two shots managed to find their target and hit Krunig center mass. His armor held, but a warning alarm in his helmet told Krunig the integrity of his suit was failing fast.

Thinking quickly, Krunig raised his sickles, overlaying one over the other. Together, they generated a shield in the center of the ring. Krunig then pulled the sickles apart, elongating the shield. He brought one hand up to protect his head, while he dropped the other hand so the shield would stretch to protect his torso.

"Is that the best you can do, Zor-Zur?" Krunig taunted.

The two-headed assassin known as Zor-Zur continued forward, firing nonstop. As Krunig skillfully deflected the shots, Zor-Zur's frustration grew. His two heads were actually twin brothers who shared a humanoid body, each being a cyclops with a pig nose and pus-filled sores dotting their faces.

"Coward!" the head called Zor snarled. "You don't deserve to wear that armor."

His brother-head, Zur, snorted. "Yeah, it's time for new leadership."

In unison, Zor-Zur holstered their blasters. Then they drew separate butterfly swords from the scabbards on their belt and skillfully twirled the blades in their hands, readying for a fight.

Unfazed, Krunig called out, "Vekka, are you watching this?"

"Yes, m' lord," Krunig's trusty aid replied over a loudspeaker in the room. "They broke in shortly before you arrived, but as you directed, I let them be so you could make an example of them."

Zor-Zur halted, exchanging one-eyed looks of concern.

"Two heads and clearly these numbskulls have not thought this matter through," Krunig scoffed. "Explain to them how this works?"

"No rules," Zur declared.

"We fight, you die. Simple as that," Zor added.

"Not if you hope to lead this faction," Vekka corrected. "You see, now you are committed. There is no walking away. Even if you find a way to defeat Lord Krunig, the crew will kill you the moment you leave this chamber."

"Says you," Zor blustered.

"Says the syndicate," Vekka countered. "Grawn Krunig is the leader of this faction. That is the way it has always been and always shall be."

Zor-Zur's confidence faded. The two brothers wondered if this was some kind of ruse to make them lower their defenses.

Krunig spoke as he slowly circled Zor-Zur. "The Madreen only recognize Grawn Krunig as the leader of this faction, and this faceless suit of armor defines Grawn Krunig. No one has ever seen my face, nor do they know my true identity. The same was true for the Krunigs before me."

Zor and Zur exchanged an uncertain look. Neither knew how to respond. Learning that Grawn Krunig existed only as a nom de guerre, a persona passed along successively from one crime lord to the next, came as a shock.

Krunig continued to circle. "Let me break this down for you. Killing me requires you to assume the identity of Grawn Krunig. Otherwise, neither of you will ever set foot off Ekator."

"Now you're talking," Zor-Zur said dangerously. Each gripped their sword tighter and inched closer to Krunig.

Cocking his blades together to deactivate his shield, Krunig lowered his sickles. "Of course, two heads are not going to fit inside this suit, so that creates a problem."

Slow on the uptake, the dim-witted duo needed a moment to process the gist of Krunig's comment. Then Zor and Zur came to the same realization— one of them had to die.

What transpired next could only be described as a comical dance to the death. Zor and Zur turned on each other while Krunig and Vekka watched in amusement. The two-headed being clashed swords, each commanding their half of a shared body to overpower the other. Neither gained an advantage until they tripped and landed hard on the floor. With their faces only inches apart, the brothers snarled at one another, biting and cursing.

Krunig quickly grew bored of the stalemate. He had more important matters to tend to and decided it was time to end this challenge.

As Zor-Zur scuffled on the floor, Krunig approached with his sickles, ready to strike.

Out of the corner of his eye, Zor glimpsed Krunig move in for the kill. Terror gripped him in a vise.

Zur turned his head sharply, just in time to see Krunig raise the sickles.

"Fools," Krunig hissed.

His sickles then fell on both would-be assassins with guillotine-like precision, decapitating the brothers with such force that the sickles cracked the floor. A spray of purple blood showered Krunig's armor.

Straightening, Krunig deactivated his weapons and placed them back on his breastplate.

Vekka appeared at his side. The albino-skinned aide wore a crimson tunic that touched the floor, his long, gray hair pulled back tight in a single braid.

"Well done, m' lord."

"Make sure the crew sees you dispose of their body," Krunig said gruffly.

Vekka bowed then activated the commlink on his wrist, summoning the robotic cleaning crew. Sensing his boss wanted to be left alone, Vekka excused himself.

Krunig crossed the room in quiet reflection. He entered a side chamber, kept free from prying eyes, including Vekka. Inside, Krunig stepped up to an open decontamination unit. Raising his arms, six nozzles sprayed his armor from head to toe with a high-powered gas.

As he stood in the shower, alone with his thoughts, Krunig could not get the image of the mystery ship out of his head. Its design had a hint of Aiwan influence, but his sources in Dohrm and Eos would have reported its existence, had they known. No, this was something different, something truly unique.

Krunig grinned inwardly. *This is the future.*

What puzzled him more than anything was how such a tiny vessel packed such a powerful punch. It had carved through his fleet in minutes, without suffering a scratch. There was no defense against this superweapon. It was unstoppable.

"I must have it," Krunig muttered as the sprayers shut off.

His armor now sparkling clean, Krunig stepped clear into a prep area where he could undress. A long shower of his own would help clear his mind before he contacted Grawn Supreme.

As Krunig's suit of armor started to open, a chime signaled a visitor at the door. The suit immediately closed, and Krunig instinctively reached for his sickles.

"Yes," he replied cautiously.

"My liege," Vekka blurted. His agitation was uncharacteristic. "I bring important news."

Krunig accessed the surveillance system in his quarters and could see Vekka standing alone on the opposite side of the door. No other threats were detected.

Vekka stepped back, bowing slightly as Krunig appeared.

"What is it?" Krunig asked.

"The ship we encountered is, in fact, Aiwan. Our source in Eos says it was developed in secret by Prince Kypa."

"He survived?" Krunig growled.

"Yes, my lord," Vekka confirmed, casting a wary glance at his boss to gauge the likelihood of a sudden outburst. Two batches of bad news in one day never boded well for the messenger. "Kypa appeared before the High Court moments ago with his supposed rescuers."

"Explain."

Vekka cleared his throat. Unlike Krunig, he did not wear battle armor, so he felt quite vulnerable in moments like this. "Our attack on the prince's ship in hyperspace was effective but did not produce our desired result. Kypa's ship crashed, it seems, with the prince being the only survivor. His rescuers then helped him recover the prototype vessel that was used against us."

"A prototype? Does it have a name?"

"Reaper, my lord." Vekka shrugged.

"Reaper ..." Krunig mused. "What is its purpose? How is it so powerful?"

"Details are sketchy, my lord, but, apparently, this Reaper was built to harvest crystals without damaging the environment. Kypa claims it can even stabilize the planet core to rebuild those regions affected by the quakes."

Krunig scoffed at the idea but was pleased by the political turmoil it had caused. Since Kypa had been blamed for the disaster that had destroyed the Realm of Cirros, the prince's claim to the throne was in serious jeopardy. This had weakened King Loka's standing, as a result.

"Continue."

"Yes, my lord. Apparently, the mission Kypa set out on previously proved fruitful. The planet he sought out—Earth, I believe is its name—did indeed have crystals. A large quantity, I hear. In addition to bringing home a cargo-hold of orange crystals, he harvested one shard of Maxixe Magnetarite."

"What?" Krunig blurted, startling Vekka. "Are you sure?"

Vekka nodded vehemently.

Krunig considered the impossible odds of locating such a rare crystal. It all made sense now. Any ship powered by a blue crystal would be virtually indestructible and have enough firepower to destroy anything in its path. Oddly, this revelation made Krunig's earlier defeat easier to accept. He had never stood a chance against the Reaper.

"Where is this Earth?" he asked with urgency.

"I do not have the exact coordinates," Vekka replied, "but my source is trying to locate the system based on what we know of the hyperspace route Kypa used."

There was no need explaining to his boss that within a hyperspace tunnel were countless off-shoots. Kypa could have used any number of them. It would take some time to trace Earth's whereabouts unless one of their spies could provide its precise location.

"We must go there at once and stake our claim before others learn of this blue crystal," Krunig declared, believing there could be more just like it. "But first, I want this Reaper."

"That is another piece of intriguing information, my lord. Apparently, there was a matter of contention regarding who actually owned the ship. Prince Kypa gifted it to one of the Earth-dwellers who rescued him." Vekka searched his impeccable memory. "Captain Tan, if I recall. Loka and the court honored Kypa's gift to her. The Reaper is her property, and any attempt to steal it or kill her would result in the ship self-destructing."

"Mm," Krunig mused. "What do we know of these Earth-dwellers?"

"Very little, I'm afraid." Vekka retrieved a new handheld hologram projector. Images of Ava and Neil appeared that had been secretly captured in the palace's hangar bay. "Scrawny bunch," Vekka offered. "The smaller one, the female, is Captain Tan. She was piloting the Reaper when it attacked us. Reports say she also attacked Boa near Earth before he returned to Aiwa."

Krunig's mind drifted for a moment, back to the battle at Aiwa. "That would explain his weak defense. I thought his defeat came too easy." Thinking a moment longer, he asked, "So, Kypa simply handed over the most powerful warship in the galaxy?"

"It seems that way," Vekka replied, equally perplexed.

Krunig scoffed. "He is a bigger fool than I thought. Where is the ship now?"

"Inside the palace's main hangar."

Krunig began slowly pacing as the gears churned in his head. He had to act fast. All of his plans now hinged on obtaining the Reaper. The race to get to it first was already underway. Despite Loka's decree, Commodore Boa was no doubt scheming a way to claim the Reaper for himself. He would never let such a powerful weapon slip through his fingers. Boa would do everything in his power to make sure that ship did not go anywhere.

Getting to it will not be easy, Krunig mused.

Even if he could get a ground force past the orbital defenses and penetrate Supra's protective shield, the main hangar was heavily guarded. It would be impossible to overrun, even if he had the numbers. Then there was the safeguard put in place by Captain Tan to prevent anyone from stealing the Reaper.

"The female is the key," Krunig decided. "If we can separate her from the Aiwans, we can force her to hand over the Reaper."

Behind his faceless armor, Krunig imagined the blue crystal powering his personal gunship, or even one of his capital ships. Based on the effectiveness of the Reaper, a larger warship would be exponentially more powerful.

Vekka considered the strategy with some reservation. "A tricky gambit, my lord."

Krunig waved his hand dismissively. In his mind, he could see his plan coming to fruition. And if he could see it happen, he could make it happen.

Vekka bowed his head, submitting to the Grawn's judgment. Then he steered the conversation back to another important question.

"How will this impact your plans for Aiwa?"

The Reaper had disrupted Krunig's previous plans, as did the prodigal son's return. Kypa would complicate matters.

Or would he? Krunig corrected himself. The genesis of a new scheme began percolating in the back of his mind.

"We shall see," Krunig replied. "First, I must speak with Grawn Supreme. Anything else?"

"No, my lord. That is all for now."

"Well done, Vekka. Keep at it. I want to know more about the Reaper and these Earth-dwellers. In the meantime, locate Smythe and have him report to me immediately. I have a job for him."

"It will be done, my lord." Vekka bowed then made his exit, leaving Grawn Krunig to iron out the details of his final solution for Aiwa.

Planet Gomaiyus

Two light hours away, the party was just getting started in the Pleasure District. Located deep in the industrial sector of the Gomaiyan capital, the Pleasure District was a neon-soaked collection of dive bars, small-time casinos, and brothels—all controlled by the Madreen Crime Syndicate or, more precisely, Grawn Krunig. Since he also owned the local authorities, Gomaiyus' notorious Pleasure District was an inviting haven for the galaxy's most deviant minds and wanted criminals.

This is what brought the bounty hunter known as Smythe to the district. Wearing a black, worn-leather poncho, Smythe shouldered his way through the turbulent mob thronging the narrow street. Careful to avoid drawing attention, the bounty hunter kept his head down and twin antennas up as he smoothly sliced his way through the crowd. Pivoting at just the right time, he managed to avoid contact with every stumbling drunk and swaggering thug in his path.

Smythe was of average height and build for an insectoid species, and his hardened exoskeleton was covered with a thin layer of purplish, hairless skin. Hidden under his poncho's cowl, the bounty hunter's small, triangle-shaped head resembled a praying mantis with bulging, pale-yellow eyes and a lipless mouth pressed in a thin line. Smythe walked with a jerking rhythm on two legs with a pair of blasters holstered to each thigh. Under his poncho, two bandoliers crisscrossed his chest, loaded with ammunition. And clutched in his bony hands was a short-barrel, fast-repeating blaster rifle.

Techno-infused music blaring from inside a nearby cantina grew louder as Smythe approached. Two patrons stumbled outside in a brawling embrace. It was hard to tell if they were lovers or enemies—maybe both. The bounty hunter stepped aside, using the opportunity to steal a glance down a dead-end alley to his right. He had scoped out the cantina while his ship was still in orbit and knew there were only two means of egress—the front entrance and a side door leading into this alley.

Satisfied the alley remained clear, Smythe stepped through the cantina's arched entryway and was greeted by a rancid mix of body odor and cheap synthetic tobacco. He slouched through the crowd to the bar, where most patrons drank from jars of home-brewed hooch that was strong enough to flush out the hydraulic lines of a hyperdrive engine.

Behind the counter, a sultry femalien, wearing a red and yellow feathered robe, glided toward him. No words were exchanged. Smythe simply placed two credits on the counter: one for his typical shot of spiked guava juice and the second for information.

The barkeep scooped up the credits then stepped away to make Smythe's drink. One credit disappeared inside a hidden pocket in her dress. She dropped the second coin in a slot behind the counter that connected to a secure counting room in the basement.

When the barkeep returned to Smythe, she slid his drink toward him. Their eyes met for a split-second. As she wiped the counter in front of him, the barkeep made an almost indiscernible head bob over her right shoulder then moved away to serve the next patron.

Smythe grinned inwardly. *Money well spent.*

The bounty hunter nursed his drink for the next few minutes then gulped it down and set the glass back on the counter. Smythe straightened in his seat and signaled the barkeep for another round. In doing so, his antennas reached above the crowd. Smythe quickly pinpointed his marker—a portly, blue-skinned gambler named Ton-Walba, sitting at a card table along the back wall of the establishment.

Ton-Walba was on a hot streak, judging by the stack of credits piled in front of him.

Smythe channeled his focus to isolate the sounds, smells, and vibrations emanating from Ton-Walba's table.

"That's too rich for my blood," one player said in disgust. He threw his cards on the table, knocking over his chair as he stood and walked away.

Smythe held his focus on the dealer and the two remaining players at the table. Ton-Walba's opponent pushed his last credits into the pot. Even from a distance, Smythe picked up trace amounts of sweat forming on the player's upper lip.

He's bluffing, Smythe thought to himself.

Now it was Ton-Walba's turn. As Smythe waited for his quarry's next move, an unusual sound caught the bounty hunter's sharp attention. It was so faint that Smythe had missed it earlier. Now he could not unhear it.

Concentrating on the noise, he parsed out a recurring chirp with a distinct pattern to it. Based on sequence and signal duration, the bounty hunter realized it was a code. Ton-Walba was cheating.

"Very clever," Smythe muttered.

He scanned the crowd, looking for Ton-Walba's partner in crime. Smythe could not care less about their scheme. Cheating at a small-time game of cards was nothing compared to the debt Ton-Walba owed to Kaji Clan. Smythe's fee for bringing in Ton-Walba was probably twice what the card shark was clearing tonight.

It did not take long for the bounty hunter to locate Ton-Walba's partner. An insectoid seated behind Ton-Walba's opponent was the culprit. Like Smythe, it had antennae, but that was where the similarity ended. Small and gray, like an oversized locust, it perched casually on a stool, rubbing its antennas together to send signals to Ton-Walba's trained ears.

Knowing his opponent's hand, Ton-Walba confidently tossed his credits on the pot. "Call," he announced.

The dealer nodded then gestured to the other player to show his cards. Ton-Walba's opponent smiled nervously and displayed his hand. It was strong, but beatable.

With a smug grin, Ton-Walba fanned-out his cards and placed them on the table.

His opponent stared at the cards in disbelief. "That's ten hands in a row."

Ton-Walba shrugged. "What can I say, playing cards is like mating—everyone thinks they're the best, but most don't have a clue what they're doing."

He laughed heartily as he raked in the credits with his chubby, green arms.

Shamed and broke, his opponent cursed under his breath as he departed. Ton-Walba kept a close eye on him until any threat of retribution passed then made eye contact with his insectoid partner. He winked.

Ton-Walba waited several moments for a new game to pick up, but there were no takers. No one was foolish enough to challenge his streak of luck. Dismayed, Ton-Walba decided it was time to move on to another gambling establishment.

He signaled the dealer to cash him out.

The dealer scanned Ton-Walba's stack of winnings with a handheld device. He then turned the display toward Ton-Walba so he could see the final sum. Agreeing with the count, Ton-Walba went cheap on adding a tip for the dealer then pressed his thick thumb on the screen to transfer the winnings to his private account. Focused on the transaction, he did not notice a hooded figure exiting the cantina.

Two beeps on the dealer's device signaled the transfer was complete. Ton-Walba confirmed receiving the funds on his own device and smiled with satisfaction as he tucked it back into his pocket.

A good start, he thought, *and the night's still young.*

Standing, Ton-Walba scanned the crowd warily for anyone taking interest in his affairs. Sensing no one, he glanced in his partner's direction and found him already heading toward the front door. That was his cue to exit through the side door leading to the alley.

Ton-Walba made his way to the exit. There, he found the muscular bouncer on guard duty beside the door slouched in his chair, snoring loudly. Ton-Walba rolled his eyes. "Don't get up. I'll get it," he muttered sarcastically.

Opening the door, Ton-Walba poked his head cautiously into the alley. Careful to keep his lower body safely inside the cantina, he checked that the coast was clear. To his left was a solid wall. To the right, the narrow passage leading to main street was completely empty—no cargo containers or trash bins for would-be muggers to hide behind. In the distance, a few staggering drunks passed by the alley entrance, but they continued on singing a garbled tune.

Breathing a sigh of relief, Ton-Walba stepped out into the open-air alley. The cantina door slid shut behind him. In the stillness, he drew a palm-sized blaster as a precaution.

Before he could take another step, a web-like substance hit him square in the face.

Ton-Walba panicked and let out a muffled cry. Dropping the blaster, he whimpered as he frantically clawed at the webbing. Freeing his mouth, nose, and eyes, Ton-Walba wiped the sticky substance onto his trousers then scanned the area wildly, expecting another attack, but none came.

Remembering his blaster, Ton-Walba searched the darkness until his foot inadvertently brushed against the weapon. He crouched to snatch it up. Straightening, he then raised the blaster as a sudden bout of lightheadedness set him off balance.

Ton-Walba staggered backward, and the alley spun around him. He steadied himself against the door, keeping his weapon pointed at the shadows. Ton-Walba tried to shake off the effects, realizing the webbing must have been laced with some kind of paralytic toxin.

He tried the door, thinking to reenter the cantina from the alley. It was locked. His instincts screamed for him to run while he could still move, but his legs did not obey.

Then a pebble fell at his feet.

Sensing a presence above him, Ton-Walba looked up slowly. Above the door, a dark shape clung to the stone wall. Ton-Walba gasped and backpedaled slowly.

Before his marker could think to raise his blaster, Smythe leapt from his perch. He landed behind Ton-Walba and, with quick precision, disarmed him and tossed the blaster aside.

The effects of the toxin reached full potency. Ton-Walba's eyes rolled back in his head, and his knees buckled. Smythe caught the heavy-set gambler before he could hit the ground and wrapped Ton-Walba's arm around his shoulders. Propping him up, the bounty hunter walked his marker out of the alley and blended seamlessly into the sea of drunkards.

At the end of the street, a land speeder appeared. It was piloted by Gort, Smythe's partner. No words were exchanged as Smythe dumped Ton-Walba in the back seat. He then climbed in the passenger seat beside Gort, and they sped away toward the nearby docks where a twin-engine transport was waiting.

Unlike his insectoid partner, Gort had a frog-like head attached to a squat body. He was not a bounty hunter per se, at least not in the same rank as Smythe. He was an ace mechanic and skilled pilot who kept their unassuming transport running smoothly. When needed, he also had a knack for grand theft. Hence, the stolen speeder they currently occupied.

Reaching their ship, Gort parked the speeder in a deserted alley then quickly departed to prep for takeoff. Meanwhile, Smythe retrieved Ton-Walba from the back seat and dragged him toward the ship—a purpose-built freighter with a large cargo hold that was ideal for smuggling. The ship was nothing to look at on the outside, which was the whole point. Drawing attention was never a good thing in their line of work. The interior was no better, but neither of them cared. It served its purpose.

Reaching the base of the boarding ramp, Smythe's commlink chirped a familiar sound, one reserved for his best client. He released Ton-Walba, allowing him to flop to the ground. Smythe checked his commlink and confirmed the sender. There was no information or mention of payment in the signal. Those details would follow later on a secure channel. For now, all Smythe had to go on was a set of coordinates, and that was enough. The bounty hunter knew what had to be done next.

He looked down at Ton-Walba lying in a fetal position, a puddle of drool forming in the dirt where his mouth hung open. Then Smythe turned his commlink to a different channel. Seconds later, the holographic image of a scrawny, three-eyed creature appeared—his contact from Kaji Clan.

"Do you have him?"

"Yes," Smythe replied in his typical, raspy tone.

"Show me."

Smythe pointed his device at Ton-Walba's face.

"Yes, that's him," the triclops affirmed. "Good work as always, Smythe. Bring him here at once."

"First, transfer my payment," the bounty hunter insisted.

Taken aback, the three-eyed creature gently corrected Smythe, "You will be paid upon delivery, per our customary arrangement."

Smythe shook his head. "The bounty's to be paid, dead or alive. This one ain't going to make it," he decided.

"Wait, I can send someone to collect him."

"No time. Deal's a deal."

"What about his credit link? He owes us a lot of money."

Smythe crouched beside Ton-Walba and searched him. He found the gambler's personal banking device inside his trousers and showed the triclops.

"Make the transfer," Smythe repeated.

Frowning, the triclops reluctantly agreed. He knew his boss would have preferred to torture Ton-Walba a bit, but it was Smythe's call how he collected the bounty.

The transfer was made while the bounty hunter waited patiently. Smythe received confirmation moments later of a new deposit in his account for the agreed upon amount.

"Good. Our business is finished," Smythe said.

"Hold on. I want his credit link," the triclops insisted.

"The bounty said nothing about a credit link," Smythe pointed out. The triclops started to protest, but Smythe continued, "Luckily for you, I'm in a hurry for another job. What's it worth to you?"

The triclops narrowed his three eyes. For a split-second, he searched for ways to stiff the bounty hunter, but he knew Smythe had all the leverage. Plus, it was not good business. Even in the underworld, there was a code of conduct. Certain lines were not to be crossed. Doing so meant Smythe and every other bounty hunter in the galaxy would never work for Kaji Clan again.

"Ten thousand," the triclops offered.

"Twenty," Smythe countered.

"Fifteen and right of first refusal on the next job."

"Done," Smythe agreed. "Transfer the funds, and you'll have the device tomorrow. Cracking it is on you," he added.

Before the triclops could protest, Smythe ended the transmission. He placed his commlink back in his pouch just as Ton-Walba started to regain his senses.

The fog cleared enough for Ton-Walba to realize he was staring down the barrel of the bounty hunter's weapon. He raised his hands to shield his face and cried out, "No! Please, I can pay you!"

His plea fell on deaf ears as Smythe pulled the trigger, burning a hole through Ton-Walba's skull.

Just then, Gort descended the ramp. "What's taking so long?"

Smythe shouldered his rifle, unfazed by taking a life. "Change of plans. Krunig has a new job for us."

Gort looked at the smoldering hole in Ton-Walba's head. "Kaji Clan's good with that?"

"They are now."

Gort shrugged acceptance without further explanation. "I hope we got paid first."

"In full, and then some."

That was all that mattered to Gort. Besides, any job from Grawn Krunig paid triple their usual fee.

Smythe turned to his partner. "We're done here." He tossed him Ton-Walba's banking device as he started up the boarding ramp. "See if you can crack this. We keep half then send it to Hiromi. Have her deliver it to Kaji Clan as soon as possible."

"Where we heading?" Gort inquired, following Smythe up the ramp.

"Set a course for Aiwa."

10
FAMILY REUNION

Planet Aiwa
Realm of Eos

Kypa, Neil, and Ava were dismissed from the High Court. As they made the long walk back through the Grand Hall, they were confident they could deliver on their promise to rebuild the planet core, but Kypa knew they had gotten off easy. He had expected the court members, including the king, to side with Commodore Boa. The political climate before Kypa had left for Earth had been tenuous for his father. Now he felt responsible for making it even worse. He wondered what had swayed the court's decision.

Since the use of telepathy was forbidden to all but the court members during the session, Kypa had tried and failed to read them using his other senses. The hardest to read was his father. King Loka had been an enigma to Kypa all his life, and vice versa. Father and son were polar opposites and, ironically, not even telepathy could fix their communication problem. Now it seemed, if Kypa truly wanted to understand why his father had taken the risk to give him this second chance, he would have to muster the courage to ask.

Kypa pushed that thought aside. He had bigger issues to contend with, like saving this planet and the millions of Aiwans depending on him. It was his responsibility, regardless of politics or a personal death sentence looming over his head. As the doors to the Grand Hall opened into the corridor, Kypa resolved himself to fulfill this calling … somehow.

"Father!"

Kypa snapped out of his thoughts at the sound of his three children running to greet him. He dropped to his knees, and the children piled on, wrapping their arms around their father in a joyful tangle. Toma, his oldest son, held on to Kypa in a tight embrace, while his younger sisters, Arya and Fraya, spoke a mile a minute about everything that had happened while their father was away.

Kypa laughed, trying to take it all in. They had grown so much in his absence, especially Toma, who was nearly as tall as his father now. It was then that Kypa truly realized how much he missed his family. All that had happened over the past several months, the loneliness and fear, washed away in an instant.

Maya, his mate, stood a few feet away, grinning from ear-to-ear with tears streaming down her face. Kypa stood slowly, eyes locked on hers. It was like he was seeing her again for the first time.

Since the children would not let Kypa budge an inch, Maya laughed and wiped the joyful tears from her eyes. She then made her way to him and wrapped her long arms around his neck.

"I thought we lost you," she whispered.

Kypa squeezed her tight, choking back his own tears. "Never."

They affectionately buried their faces in each other's necks—the Aiwan equivalent to kissing—and connected telepathically.

"*Forgive me,*" she begged. "*When your ship was overdue, I feared the worst. I told your father where you had gone, and he dispatched Boa to find you.*"

This was news to Kypa. Thankfully, she had not been charged as an accessory to his crimes. "*Maya, you did the right thing. Thank you.*"

"*But Luna and your crew … is it true?*"

Maya could feel Kypa's pain as he acknowledged the hard truth. "*Yes, they are gone. We were attacked in hyperspace and crashed. I was the only survivor.*"

"*What about the court? What did your father say?*"

"*Shh,*" Kypa soothed. "*Everything is all right. I will tell you more later.*"

The unfamiliar and distant sound of Neil's voice distracted Maya. She broke her connection with Kypa and turned to find their youngest daughter, Fraya, staring up at the human while holding his hand.

"Fraya, no!" Maya blurted, fear evident in her voice. She rushed to separate the two and scooped the child up in her arms.

Neil stepped back, raising his hands in defense. "Sorry, I meant no harm."

Kypa intervened. He put an arm around Maya and smiled an apology to Neil. "Maya, the children are not in danger. These are my friends."

Maya looked from Neil to Ava suspiciously. Both humans showed their hands, palms out, and smiled innocently.

"Maya … children, this is Captain Ava Tan and Dr. Neil Garrett from planet Earth. They saved my life."

Maya turned sharply to Kypa with a look of surprise. "*Is this true?*" she asked, using telepathy.

Kypa nodded and smiled sheepishly.

Maya's expression softened. Trusting Kypa would tell her the details later, she took solace in knowing he was alive and home once again. For that, she was eternally grateful.

To Neil's surprise, Maya put Fraya down and approached him slowly, arms outstretched. Lamenting her knee-jerk reaction earlier, Maya knelt before Neil and gently took his hands in hers. She smiled warmly, regret and gratitude evident on her face.

"Neeil," she said softly in English.

Looking down into her deep blue eyes, Neil's heart melted. This was how he imagined first contact should be. "Hello, Maya." He smiled. "I've heard so much about you and your beautiful children. It's an honor to meet you."

Maya shook her head. "No, the honor is mine. Thank you for bringing Kypa back to us." She stood and took a step back, which was the green light Fraya had needed to rush to Neil's side and latch on to his leg. The little one's energetic attachment to Neil made everyone laugh.

"Actually," Neil corrected, "Ava deserves all the credit. She's the one who saved Kypa, not me."

When Maya turned to face her, Ava shrugged modestly. "It was a team effort."

"Neil is right," Kypa affirmed. "Ava risked her life for me on several occasions. If not for her, I would not be here."

Maya stepped closer to Ava and knelt, offering her hands. Ava accepted. Regarding one another genially, Maya then said, "A-va."

Ava grinned. "Hello, Maya. It's nice to meet you. I love your gown," she said, gesturing to Maya's scarlet, sheer gown that highlighted her body markings.

Maya dipped her chin in gratitude, then stood.

Ava turned to the two oldest children. "And you must be Toma and Arya. Your father hasn't stopped talking about either of you."

Arya smiled shyly, hiding behind her reserved brother, Toma. He was a younger version of his father, while Arya had traits of both parents. All three children wore similar, sheer gowns and belts, the traditional daily attire of most Aiwans.

As Kypa peeled Fraya away from Neil, Maya glimpsed an Aiwan couple passing by. They gave the humans an ill-favored look, whispering amongst themselves.

"Perhaps it is time we leave," she suggested. "You must be tired and hungry from your journey."

Everyone agreed, and the group made their way down the corridor. With a Royal Guard escort, the prince and his family naturally attracted attention. Ava's and Neil's presence drew even greater interest, ranging from morbid curiosity to downright disdain. This prompted Maya to speak up.

"Please forgive the stares," she said to Neil as they walked.

"You noticed, too?" he replied lightly, waving politely to passersby.

"Throughout our history, we have had little experience engaging off-worlders," she explained. "There was no need since very few ever visited Aiwa. Then, when the harvesters arrived, things changed. Suddenly, we were at war with various species we had never encountered before. You and Ava are the first non-Aiwans to ever visit the capital."

"Seriously?"

"Yes, few of our kind have ever encountered non-Aiwans so, naturally, they are curious and nervous."

Hearing this, Neil had a new appreciation for Kypa. Not only had he braved going off-world to acquire the tech he needed to build the Reaper, but the way he had handled himself on Earth was admirable, considering Aiwa's isolation.

As they continued, Neil and Maya kept talking to show the humans were not a threat. Kypa and Ava picked up on it, too, offering a friendly wave and kind greeting to passersby as the children kept them engaged. Arya, the middle child, educated Ava on the architecture and technology of the underwater city, while Toma showed a lot of interest in Earth and the Reaper. Fraya—adorable, high-energy, and unfiltered—interrupted her siblings constantly with her own fascinating facts and random questions, which Toma and Arya patiently endured.

They reached a private lift, reserved for the royal family, and piled inside. This lift had no stops and would take them directly to the top floor where Kypa and Maya shared a residence with the rest of the royal family. For this reason, the guards stayed behind.

As soon as the doors closed and they were underway, Kypa and Maya exhaled heavily.

"We must be gossip fodder for the entire city by now," he muttered with uncharacteristic annoyance.

"Let them talk," Maya said, taking his hand. "All that matters is you are home."

Neil admired their commitment to one another. "It must be hard with everyone always watching and judging you."

"Yes, but they are nothing like your paparazzi," Kypa replied with a wry smile.

Sad but true, Neil chuckled in agreement.

"Still, word of mouth is no doubt spreading of your presence in the capital."

"Will that be a problem?" Ava asked.

Before Kypa could reply, Maya discreetly squeezed his hand. Taking her cue, he realized the children did not need to hear such things.

"No, of course not," Kypa said dismissively, but Neil and Ava could tell from the look in his eyes that he was holding back the truth.

They arrived at the top floor, and the lift doors opened. There to greet them in the corridor was Kypa's mother and his younger sister. Dressed in matching golden sheer gowns that touched the floor, Queen Qora and Princess Seva carried themselves with regal grace, both dignified and stately.

Queen Qora was a striking female who stood out in a crowd, regardless of her title. While age lines around her eyes and mouth gave some indication to her years, the queen had lost none of her outer beauty. But it was her inner strength, love for her people, and devotion to family that inspired respect.

Standing beside her, Princess Seva closely resembled the queen, especially her soft, blue eyes. Seva was still in early adulthood, yet the likeness between mother and daughter was uncanny.

Kypa rushed to greet them. All etiquette aside, the trio hugged in a heartfelt embrace. They were quickly joined by Fraya and Arya. Neil and Ava followed Maya and Toma off the lift and quietly enjoyed watching the family's reunion.

"We heard about the others," Qora said softly. "I am so sorry for your loss."

Kypa was still coming to terms with it himself. Throughout his time on Earth, he had held out hope that other crewmembers aboard the mothership had survived. It was not until Ava had discovered their gruesome fate during her mission that he had begun to process the loss. The death of one crewmate, in particular, stung the most.

Kypa looked at his feet and lowered his voice. "Luna ... she did not make it."

The mention of her name evoked an overwhelming sense of guilt—a feeling that he had failed his close friend and colleague. Kypa remembered little about his last minutes aboard the mothership and had no clue about Luna's fate. He liked to think she died in the crash and not at the claws of the obercai.

The queen knew how much Luna meant to her son, to all of them, for that matter. Luna was practically family, having been one of Kypa's only friends growing up. She had come to live with them after the disaster in Cirros. Witnessing Kypa's grief, Qora wished she could take away the pain, but that was not in her power. Kypa had to deal with this loss in his own way and accept what he could not change. All Qora could do was empathize with her son and offer support.

She gently lifted Kypa's chin with a long finger and smiled warmly.

Kypa stole glances at her, fearful if he held her gaze too long, she would see the failure in him.

To the contrary, facing her son at arm's length, Qora beamed with pride and suggested, "It is up to you now, my son. Only you can truly honor their memory by proving their sacrifice was not in vain."

Qora's wise words were not what Kypa wanted but what he needed to hear. Focusing on his guilt would not take away his pain; instead, using his talents to pay tribute to his friends was the best way he could channel his grief for good.

Kypa knew she was right, again. He raised his chin and looked her in the eye. The unspoken exchange filled him with renewed purpose. Kypa then turned to his sister. He pressed his forehead gently against hers. No words were needed between the close-knit siblings.

When they separated, Seva wiped her eyes and gave a subtle nod in Neil and Ava's direction. "Are you going to introduce us to your guests?"

Forgetting himself, Kypa straightened and cleared his throat.

"Where are my manners?" he chided himself. Kypa gestured to his friends. "May I present Captain Ava Tan and Ambassador Neil Garrett of planet Earth. This is my mother, Queen Qora, and my sister, Princess Seva, of Eos."

Neil and Ava bowed.

"It is a pleasure to meet you both," Neil greeted. "We are honored to be guests in your home."

Qora's and Seva's formal demeanors had softened with their tearful reunion with Kypa. Trying to resume their stately postures with children clinging to them also proved difficult. Both recognized this, making for a light-hearted moment. To their credit, the queen and princess appeared completely at ease around the humans.

Neil and Ava had been under the watchful eye of capital security since stepping off the Reaper, studied carefully until deemed nonthreatening. Qora and Seva had been briefed in detail on their actions at Earth and against Krunig. In their eyes, Neil and Ava had earned Aiwa's gratitude and respect. Yet, one matter still needed to be addressed.

Qora stepped closer. "You saved my son's life."

"They did indeed," Kypa affirmed. "Ambassador Garrett and I met first. He rescued me from my escape pod and has become a dear friend."

Qora cradled Neil's hands in hers and bowed. "Thank you, Neil."

"And Ava," Kypa added, "she risked her life on several occasions to save mine. She is the bravest pilot I have ever met."

Princess Seva asked in her soft-spoken voice, "Saved you from who?"

"From those who wanted to keep Kypa from leaving," Ava replied as vaguely and diplomatically as she could, much to Neil's relief. "I didn't want to see him go, either, so I offered to give him a ride home," she said light-heartedly.

"And we are grateful, Captain Tan." Qora took Ava's tiny hands in hers, regarding her warmly. "Thank you for returning Kypa to us."

"It was my pleasure, ma'am." Ava winked at Kypa. "That son of yours is pretty special. I can see why you'd want him back."

Qora regarded her son with pride.

Meanwhile, Neil made a passing glance in Seva's direction and caught her stealing a look at him. Seva blushed and quickly turned away.

"Will you stay for a meal?" Maya asked the queen.

Qora crossed her hands in front of her and beamed at her grandchildren. "Nothing would please me more, but this is your night. Kypa has been away too long, and he needs to be with his family. Tomorrow, perhaps, we will organize a formal meal to officially welcome the delegates from Earth."

"We graciously accept, Your Highness," Neil replied. "And perhaps Captain Tan and I should follow your lead and return to our ship for the night."

Kypa started to protest but realized it was probably for the best. Besides giving him much-needed time alone with Maya and the children, he considered the limited meal options they had to offer their guests. The food synthesizer onboard the Reaper was better suited for their tastes for the time being.

"That is very thoughtful, thank you," Kypa said. "Take the lift down. The guards can show you back to the ship. If you need anything, you know how to reach me."

Ava nodded. "And tomorrow, we get to work."

"Yes," Kypa replied with relief. The thought of finally realizing his visionary purpose for the Reaper lifted his spirits. "I will see you first thing in the morning."

Neil and Ava took their leave. As soon as the lift doors closed and they were alone, both exhaled heavily.

Ava leaned back against the lift's tall window and closed her eyes. "What a day," she said, exhausted.

"I'm with you," Neil agreed, turning toward the window. "All things considered, I'd say we did pretty darn good."

"Me, too." Ava smiled wanly, resting her tired eyes. "I like Kypa's family."

"Yeah," Neil said, distracted by the view of the underwater city.

Warm hues of pink and purple filled the lift as Neil watched several Aiwans outside swimming about freely. Awestruck by their grace and speed, the experience reminded him of visiting the National Aquarium in Baltimore. Then he was struck with guilt, imagining how restricted Kypa must have felt swimming in that dinky-sized pool at Groom Lake and knowing Garza and the others were watching him like one of those paid dolphin exhibits at the zoo.

This was their home; gawking at them through a window suddenly felt wrong, like he was invading their privacy. He turned away.

Putting his back to the window, Neil sighed heavily. "I can't imagine us stepping into a worse scenario."

Ava raised an eyebrow but kept her tired eyes shut. "How so?"

Neil shrugged. "It didn't sink in until Kypa's judgment was announced earlier. I mean, we've not only walked into a war zone here, but our chief advocate is facing execution if we can't clear his name."

Ava waved dismissively. "Piece of cake. If we can survive today, we can get through anything."

"At least they didn't confiscate your ship."

Ava *hmphed*, opening her eyes. "That'll be the day. I don't trust Boa one iota."

Neil chuckled at her corny bravado as the lift came to a stop and the doors opened. Standing there to meet them were the same two guards from earlier. Neither guard was welcoming, and there was a moment when Neil and Ava both wondered if they would be detained.

"This way," the senior guard directed, escorting them back to the hangar bay.

Ten minutes later, Ava was relieved to find the Reaper right where she had left it, intact and seemingly untouched. Ever since leaving it unattended, she had fretted about the Aiwans—specifically Boa—snooping around her ship. Apparently, all that worry was for nothing.

"Ahh, home sweet home," Neil joked, stretching out his arms as they approached the Reaper.

Ava felt the same. She could not wait to get onboard and catch up on sleep. But, until they were safe and sound inside the Reaper, she would not rest easy.

Ava likened it to her military days. From the moment she would land on foreign soil to the time she shipped out, rule number one was to never let your guard down.

"Hold up a sec," Ava told Neil as they arrived at the ship. She conducted a walk around, looking for any foreign objects attached to the hull or signs of damage. "Sorry, force of habit," she told Neil as she circled back.

"What are you looking for?" he asked.

"Anything that doesn't belong," Ava replied. She then sent a mental command to Reggie. *"Status?"*

"All systems nominal, Captain," Reggie responded.

"Good. Are you detecting any threats?"

"Negative, Captain."

Satisfied, Ava gave a wary glance at the guards, who were watching her from afar. "Lower the boarding ladder," she instructed aloud.

Neil climbed aboard first. Ava followed, hurrying up the ladder, half-expecting the guards to seize her from behind while her back was turned.

Once onboard, Ava retracted the ladder and sealed the hatch. She then deactivated her helmet. "Reggie, deactivate security protocol *Ava-1*."

"What's that?" Neil asked, deactivating his helmet, as well.

"A fail-safe in case Boa made a play on my ship."

Neil admired her moxie. "So, you weren't bluffing back there."

Ava put her finger to her lips. "Actually, I was," she whispered with a wry grin. "Kypa's right; we've got targets on our backs, but I'm not about to risk blowing up my ship or Aiwa. I left instructions with Reggie that only you, me, and Kypa are allowed onboard. If anyone attempted unauthorized access, Reggie was supposed to lock the ship down and alert me."

Neil nodded approvingly. "Well played, Captain Tan."

Ava shrugged in mock modesty. "It's a gift. But don't tell anyone. I'll let Kypa know so he doesn't worry."

"Your secret is safe with me."

Heading out of the engineering section, they passed the open storage bin filled with sparkling, yellow and orange magnetarite crystals.

"Maybe when we hand these over, they'll start to trust us a little more," Neil remarked, ever the optimist.

"One can only hope," Ava sighed. However, a sinking feeling told her it was not going to be that simple.

"C'mon," Neil said, starting up the ladder to the main cabin. "I'll make us some dinner."

Ava followed. Reaching the top of the landing, she activated her hologram bed while Neil worked on meal prep.

Within seconds, a plate appeared with a savory bacon and cheddar cheeseburger and thick steak fries. Neil turned to offer it to Ava.

"Bon appétit, mon capitaine," he said with his best French accent.

Neil's shoulders dropped at the sight of Ava curled up on her bed, sound asleep. Then he grinned crookedly, knowing how she needed the rest.

Neil set the plate aside and retrieved the North Korean coat from the cabinet. He gently placed it over her.

Watching Ava for a long moment, Neil fondly recalled their chance encounter in the hangar at Hickam Air Force Base. It seemed like a lifetime ago. Despite almost knocking her out with the bathroom door, and the horror of spilling classified photos of Kypa on the floor in front of her, Neil remembered more than anything being caught off guard by Ava's beauty. Even now, as she slept with her hair draped over her face, Ava was radiant.

Remembering himself, Neil blinked back to the present. Embarrassed, he grabbed the plate of food on his way out and stopped at the cockpit entry. Before turning off the lights, he gave Ava one last look.

"Sleep tight," he whispered, hoping no nightmares disturbed her sleep. Ava deserved a bit of peace.

11

BLOWBACK

Planet Earth
Global Children's Relief Mission, Sanhe, China

It was the middle of the night when the GCRM staff and children under their care were startled awake by Chinese Army troops. In a coordinated assault, the soldiers kicked in the front and back doors to the building and stormed inside. Dragging the frightened staff out of bed, most of the young women were on a short-term mission trip and did not speak Chinese. They trembled in their nightclothes as the soldiers barked orders and pointed AK-47s in their faces.

"Yídòng! Yídòng!" the soldiers barked, directing the foreigners to the front room.

Stumbling into action, the GCRM workers quickly herded the crying children. As they did so, soldiers went to work searching the property.

Outside, a dozen troops with flashlights scoured every inch of the building, looking for contraband or any material that looked out of place for a relief organization, particularly weapons and spy-craft tools. The outdoor well was torn apart and inspected. Even the outhouses were searched.

Inside, the building was ransacked. Mattresses and pillows were ripped open with bayonets, Poly-fil stuffing flying everywhere. Food stores, including large bags of rice, were dumped upside down onto the kitchen floor and sifted through. Cabinets emptied. Luggage searched.

This building search was unlike any the Chinese Army had ever performed before. It was evident by their methodical and determined approach that this was not some kind of petulant scare tactic to feed the ego of the local commander, nor was it an attempt to extort bribes. No, there was fear and urgency in the eyes of the soldiers, and that meant this raid had been ordered from the top brass. Ordered with the expectation of producing results.

A Chinese officer with lieutenant colonel rank insignias on his shoulders entered through the front door. He carried a QSZ-92 semi-automatic pistol. Judging by his heated expression, he was bound and determined to find something—anything—to please his superiors.

He turned sharply to the GCRM workers and children huddled together in the corner.

The sight of a weapon and the feral look in the colonel's eyes startled the kids. Whimpering, they curled up closer into the arms of the equally-terrified staff.

Not seeing Ms. Aguri, the woman he thought ran the place, the colonel pointed his pistol at Arial, the supervisor in charge. She happened to be the closest worker to him. "Nǐ," he called, waving her to stand.

Arial did not speak Chinese but understood his demand. She peeled off the three children clinging to her and approached hesitantly.

"Xìngmíng?" he asked.

"I-I ... don't understand," Arial stammered.

The officer rolled his eyes. "Name?" he repeated, this time in English.

"Arial ... s-sir," she replied, unable to make eye contact.

The officer held up a piece of paper with two images on it. "Where?"

Arial looked at the pictures of Jessica Aguri and their fix-it man, Choi Min-jun. Her brow wrinkled, wondering what this could be about.

Her hesitation earned a sharp rebuke. "Where!" the officer snapped.

Arial jumped and replied quickly, "I don't know. Jessica left yesterday. She's been reassigned. Min-jun has been gone for a week. He had to take one of our employees home. She was sick."

The officer's English was not good. He only caught part of what she said but, judging by her apologetic tone, he could tell neither person he sought were on the premises.

Just then, someone called from the back of the house. The officer hurried to the kitchen where a soldier was standing inside a pantry. He looked down at an opening in the floor. One of the boards had been removed. The officer peered into the opening. It was empty.

"Jìxù xúnzhǎo!" he shouted. *Keep looking*!

Headquarters, Central Intelligence Agency
Langley, Virginia

Seven thousand miles away, CIA Agent Jessica Aguri sat in the back seat of a chauffeur-driven sedan, staring at the screen of her encrypted laptop. She had finished her last official report as Station Chief in Sanhe, China, on the plane before landing at Dulles. The commute to Langley gave her one more chance to double-check her work before submitting it to her boss, Brett Brenham, Deputy Director of the CIA's National Clandestine Service. The challenge she found in this particular write-up was separating fact from fiction or, more precisely, science fiction.

Jessica had hardly slept a wink since departing Sanhe thirty-six hours ago. She had been ordered back to Langley rather abruptly and without warning. At first, she had thought she might be in trouble after orchestrating the recent North Korean op to extract General Vong's daughter, Ji-eun, but when she had landed in Tokyo, Jessica had soon discovered that the metaphorical shit had hit the fan.

Having been in the field and essentially off the grid, Jessica had no way of knowing the events that had rocked the world over the past week. Her first clue that something was amiss came when she had stepped off the plane at Haneda Airport. Masses of awaiting passengers had been clustered around televisions, glued to the images and news reports on the screens.

Since Jessica had little time between flights, she had kept moving but managed to catch two words on the screen:

Alien Invasion!

Jessica had dismissed it as some kind of border crisis, of course. However, when she had passed a nearby newsstand, Agent Aguri had stopped dead in her tracks. Her mouth fell open. The headlines on all of the major newspapers and magazines read the same:

Extraterrestrials exist ... on Earth

Nuclear Explosion Rocks North Korea

International Space Station Destroyed by Aliens

As a senior U.S. intelligence officer, it was her job to stay abreast on current events, but this was insane. Never had she felt so out of touch and clueless in her life. Making it worse, she could not call Langley for confirmation. COMSEC protocols forbid it. So, like everyone else, Jessica's only recourse was to snatch up as many credible news sources as she could find during her layover and try to piece it all together before reaching Washington.

This turn of events prompted her to revisit her report. Knowing now what she did not know then, Jessica wanted to make sure she had not left anything out that could be pertinent to what was happening in the world, especially the Korean Peninsula. The timing of her last op and the death of Kim Sung-il could not be coincidental, but it was not her place to connect the two. Her mission had been strictly to get one person into North Korea and one person out. Nothing more, nothing less, and she had done that successfully.

Yet, as she read over her report, Jessica could not help but second-guess herself… again. Two days ago, during her regularly scheduled check-in, she had found one encrypted message in her inbox. It contained one simple codeword ordering her back to Langley for good. This had come as a complete surprise. She was being reassigned without explanation.

It also made for an awkward exit from Sanhe. She had known this day would come eventually, but leaving the children and GCRM staff behind had been harder than she had thought it would be. Jessica had grown attached to all of them, which was dangerous for everyone. Lots of tears had been shed, and Jessica had done her best to run down a list of things for the staff to remember. They had limited experience, but Arial had stepped up and would do just fine.

What's the worst that could happen? Jessica had thought as she had said goodbye to Sanhe.

That was thirty-six hours ago, and the world looked completely different now.

Satisfied with her report, Jessica shut down her machine and stowed it in her bag. Tapping her foot incessantly, she could not wait to get the lowdown from her boss.

Moments later, the driver pulled up to the front gate at CIA headquarters.

Two guards approached the government-plated, four-door sedan. One guard carried a long pole with an undercarriage mirror attached. He inspected the underside of the vehicle, while the other guard approached the driver's window.

Jessica's chauffeur produced his credentials and informed the guard he had one passenger. Knowing the routine, Jessica rolled down her window and held out her passport. The guard greeted her with a nod and checked the ID against her face. He then walked inside the guard shack and verified her in the employee database.

Satisfied, the guard returned to the vehicle and handed Jessica her passport.

At the same time, his partner finished the vehicle inspection. He nodded that all was clear, and the gate opened.

The sedan entered the restricted grounds of one of the world's most secretive communities. Situated nine miles from the White House, CIA headquarters encompassed two hundred and fifty-eight acres of wooded land right off the Potomac River. The campus was the brainchild of former director, Allen Dulles. Back in the late 1950s, Dulles had envisioned a college-like atmosphere where his intelligence officers could work. The original headquarters building had been completed in 1961 and was still utilized today. However, a new headquarters building, comprising two, six-story towers, had been introduced in 1991. Connected seamlessly via a tunnel, the old and new headquarters buildings now formed the George Bush Center for Intelligence, the world's largest spy complex.

Being back at Langley felt like returning home from college on winter break for Jessica. Here, she was with her people, and being back on the campus filled her with renewed vigor.

The sedan pulled up to the main entrance. Leaving the car running, the driver hopped out, opened Jessica's door for her, then retrieved her lone piece of luggage.

A bitter cold blast of frigid air stung Jessica's cheeks as she stepped out of the vehicle. Three inches of fresh snow covered the ground with a prevailing wind from the north that chilled her to the bone. That was one thing she did not miss about Virginia winters, but it sure beat the unbearable humidity in August.

Jessica shouldered her laptop bag and thanked the driver before pulling her mid-size suitcase behind her to the main doors. Inside, the warmth of the building was welcoming.

Approaching the security checkpoint, her somewhat disheveled appearance drew a few leery glances. Jessica ignored the stares. She was too tired to worry what some desk jockeys might think of her. Having been plucked out of the field and put on a red-eye flight, she had been on the go for more than a day. Running on fumes, what she really needed was a long, hot shower and a change of clothes. But first, Jessica wanted to hear directly from her boss how the world had gone to hell in a handbasket.

Jessica checked in at the security desk and was issued a temporary badge until she could produce her own. She passed through security and made her way to the Directorate of Operations.

Arriving at her work area, Jessica entered the security code on the door's keypad. A clicking sound signaled the door had unlocked, followed by a loud buzzer as soon as she opened the door to alert those inside of her entry. Jessica grinned, forgetting how much she had missed that sound.

That euphoric feeling quickly dissipated, however, as the mood in the office was grim. Jessica picked up on it immediately. Normally, the office was filled with frenzied activity. Not today. Most everyone was sheltering in their cubicles, keeping to themselves.

"Jesus, who died?" she muttered.

"Jessica?"

Agent Aguri turned sharply to find her friend, Sally Parker, approaching. Jessica lit up at the sight of a familiar face. The two exchanged a cordial hug.

"How long are you in town?" Sally asked.

"Not sure." Jessica frowned. "I was on my way to find out. So, how are you?"

"Just another day in paradise," Sally grumbled, clutching her empty coffee mug.

Jessica cringed. "That doesn't sound good."

"You heard about Sizemore, right?" Sally asked, inviting the drama. She was the office rumormonger and always had the lowdown on the latest gossip.

"No, what?"

Sally reacted with surprise. Peering past Jessica for eavesdroppers, she motioned her friend aside for a hushed discussion. "Rumor has it he's been arrested," Sally explained. "He might've been involved in the illegal cloning at Groom Lake."

"What?" Jessica hissed.

"It's all very hush-hush, but no one's seen him all week."

Jessica looked down for a moment, considering this unexpected news. She had read about the illegal cloning experiments at Groom Lake, but Sizemore had not been mentioned. However, he was most certainly aware of her North Korean op. Deputy Yao would have had to brief him in order to get the green light.

Jessica scratched her head. There was not enough information to connect her op with Groom Lake and all of the alien events.

"Did you hear about Garza and Drake?"

The question broke Jessica's train of thought. She hesitated, switching gears, then nodded affirmation. Jessica had read about the arrest of General Garza, the Chairman of the Joint Chiefs. In a seemingly unrelated story, Director of National Intelligence, Nancy Drake, had committed suicide the same day. Coincidence? Not in the eyes of the media.

Hollywood couldn't have written a script this juicy, Jessica mused.

The look on Jessica's face prompted Sally to ask, "Quite a shock, isn't it? Maybe that's why they called you in," she fished.

Jessica ignored the remark. Lifting herself on her tiptoes, she peered over the cubicles. "Is Brenham in?"

"I think so."

Jessica lowered herself. "I've gotta run. It was good to see you. We'll catch up later."

With that, Jessica walked away quickly, dragging her luggage behind her. Sally watched her friend with curiosity as Jessica made a beeline to the office of the Deputy Director of the National Clandestine Service. Once she lost sight of Jessica, Sally shrugged and entered the breakroom, armed with new gossip.

Moments later, Jessica arrived at her boss's office, slightly winded. She was greeted by a middle-aged woman seated behind a large desk. Her boss's executive assistant had worked for the agency for nearly thirty years and was harder to get past without an appointment than any Marine Corps sentry. Fortunately for Jessica, her boss had left instructions to make room on his calendar for Jessica the moment she arrived.

The executive assistant saw her coming and picked up the phone to inform the director. Hanging up just as Jessica arrived, she welcomed her with a pleasant smile. "Good morning, Agent Aguri. The director is expecting you. Please have a seat. He will be with you shortly." She gestured to a nearby couch in a sitting area.

Jessica parked her luggage and took a seat. Tapping her foot anxiously, she glanced down at the coffee table and spotted today's newspaper. The front-page headline read:

UN to Establish Earth Defense Taskforce

She started to reach for the paper when the office door opened. Jessica rose to her feet.

Her boss, Brett Brenham, appeared. Dressed in a dark blue suit and tie, Brenham wore his tailored outfit well for a single man in his late-fifties. A self-proclaimed exercise junky, he competed in triathlons to help manage the stress of his work and it showed.

"Jessica, welcome back," he greeted, offering a handshake.

Jessica shook it firmly. "Thank you, sir. It's nice to be back. Excuse my appearance; I came straight from the airport."

Brenham waved dismissively then gestured inside. "C'mon; we've got a lot to talk about."

Jessica reached for her luggage but hesitated, reluctant to bring it inside.

"I can keep that behind my desk, if you like," the executive assistant offered.

Jessica thanked her and handed it off.

Brenham waited patiently then closed the door behind them. Inside, the divine aroma of freshly brewed coffee filled her senses. Brenham crossed the room to a coffee bar on the far wall, passing two opposing, leather couches.

"Coffee? I've got some wonderful Highlander Grog here."

"Yes, please," Jessica answered, despite being past her quota for the day. "Black," she added.

"Coming right up. Have a seat."

Brenham poured two mugs. He then handed Jessica her drink before sitting on the couch opposite her.

Jessica sipped her drink and raised her eyebrows in delight. "Mm ... This is wonderful."

"Yeah." Brenham smiled, taking a drink. "You should try the Royal Kona blend. I get it from this little family-owned coffee shop in Nashville, Indiana. Great people. Luckily for me, they can ship it."

Jessica set her mug on the glass table between them and started in. "Sir, forgive me for being so blunt, but what the hell is going on?"

Brenham chuckled. "That seems to be the question of the day ... or week, I should say." He set his mug down on the table. "Where do you want to start?"

"You tell me." Jessica pulled out half a dozen newspapers and magazines from her bag and tossed them on the table. "When I landed in Tokyo, I found all this about aliens. Then I just heard about Sizemore, Drake, and Garza. This is crazy."

"That's the understatement of the century," Brenham quipped. "Truth be told, you were right in the thick of it all."

Jessica gave him a curious look. "Hoeryong?"

Brenham nodded. "Most of what I'm about to share is public knowledge, but the rest stays in here."

Jessica turned serious. "Understood."

"How much do you know about aliens?"

"Aliens? You mean real extraterrestrials?"

"That's right," her boss confirmed. "Two months ago, an alien spacecraft crashed inside North Korea. Our worst nightmare, right?" he said wryly. "Turns out, one survivor made it off the spacecraft. We pulled him out of the ocean off the coast of Kauai. His name is Kypa ... *Prince* Kypa, actually," Brenham corrected. "He's from the planet Aiwa, on the outer arm of the Milky Way."

Jessica slowly shook her head in disbelief.

"Kypa was moved to Groom Lake. There, we developed a way to communicate with him."

"That's amazing," Jessica uttered, finding it all difficult to imagine.

Brenham stood and retrieved a manila folder from his desk. He set it on the coffee table and pulled out a headshot of Kypa, handing it to Jessica. She had seen it already on the cover of *Newsweek*.

"The President shared this image with the nation earlier this week. Everyone knows."

"Fallout?"

"Oh, I haven't even gotten to the good stuff yet," he assured her. "Naturally, we could not have North Korea capitalizing on advanced alien tech. Everybody and their brother wanted access to the crash site, but Kim Sung-il dug in his heels. He expelled all foreign diplomats, including Russia and China, and promised all-out war if anyone even thought about crossing his borders."

Jessica forgot her coffee and hung on to every word.

"Any overt action against North Korea could've triggered World War III, or at least a major regional conflict," Brenham explained. "We couldn't have that. Fortunately, no one knew we had Kypa."

"Why?" Jessica wondered aloud. "I mean, why is he here?"

"Kypa came to Earth looking for some kind of power crystal." Brenham shrugged. "We're looking into that, but he says his ship was attacked by a rival force known as harvesters. That's what caused his ship to crash." He pulled out a second photo, this one a grainier image of the Reaper taken from CCTV footage outside Area S4. "This is a prototype vessel called the Reaper. It was designed to harvest crystals from the ocean floor."

Jessica's first thought at hearing the name, *Reaper*, evoked images of death, but in the context of farming and harvesting, it made perfect sense.

"Enter your friend, Samantha Ri. Or, should I say, Captain Ava Tan of the United States Air Force," Brenham explained.

Jessica's shocked reaction came as no surprise.

Her boss grinned with satisfaction. "Your op—which, by the way, you carried out exceptionally well—was part of a bigger mission to steal the Reaper in North Korea. Captain Tan succeeded and, in so doing, she blew up the Aiwan wreckage, along with Kim Sung-il."

Jessica gaped. She was ecstatic to hear that Ava was alive, and kudos to her for having the guts to carry out such a daring heist. But to kill North Korea's Supreme Leader along with it was freaking insane.

"The success of Captain Tan's mission was an operational coup for us, but things went downhill soon after," Brenham said with a heavy sigh. "She disobeyed orders, and instead of handing the ship over to us, she used the Reaper to break Kypa out of Groom Lake." He gestured to the photo.

Jessica's brow crinkled as she eyed the picture. "She give a reason why?"

Brenham took a drink. "Apparently, *former* CIA Director Sizemore and *former* Chairman of the Joint Chiefs, General Garza, were in cahoots with Mathias Industries to clone Kypa's DNA and reverse engineer the Aiwan technology."

Jessica nodded. This was the connection she had been missing.

"Kypa discovered they had no intention of ever letting him leave, so he convinced Captain Tan and two other scientists to help him escape."

"Did it work?" Jessica asked.

Brenham rolled his eyes. "Oh yeah. Their actions kicked off a geopolitical shitstorm." After a brief reflection, he added, "I have to admit, though, if it hadn't been for Captain Tan, we might be engaged in an intergalactic war right now."

"How so?"

"Kypa's people came looking for him," Brenham explained. "An Aiwan battlecruiser showed up and destroyed the International Space Station in retaliation for us blowing up their downed spacecraft in North Korea. A giant air battle ensued, and the Aiwans were handing us our lunch when Captain Tan used the Reaper to turn them away. Crisis averted, at least for now."

This was a lot to digest. There was so much more to this story than the press had discovered.

"Which brings us to you," Brenham switched gears.

Jessica's stomach tightened. She swallowed hard. "Yes, sir."

"We pulled you from Sanhe for your own safety," he explained, expecting Jessica to argue. He was surprised when she remained silent. "Tensions are still running very high in the Korean Peninsula. Kim Sung-il's sister, Sol-ju, has assumed power and has yet to stand down their forces. Our cover story may not hold much longer."

"Our cover story?"

"No one knows Captain Tan stole the Reaper. The President has led everyone to believe it was a second Aiwan survivor from the crashed mothership who helped Kypa escape. From what I understand, Russia and China aren't buying it, but they've agreed to play along and keep North Korea in check. That being said, it stands to reason that, eventually, what happened in North Korea could be traced back to GCRM. You're the only one who knows anything, so it's probably safer that you be reassigned."

"What about our asset, Min-jun, and the general's daughter?"

"They're safe. Both are in witness protection, somewhere outside Missoula, Montana, if memory serves."

That was the best news Jessica had heard all day. She could only imagine the culture shock Min-jun and Ji-eun must be going through, but anywhere was better than North Korea.

"What's next for me?"

"It's up to you, but I thought you could use a break. You've been in the field a long time."

Jessica fidgeted in her seat. A break from the field meant a desk job.

Brenham picked up on her lack of enthusiasm and, as Jessica started to object, he raised his hand. "Before you say anything, consider this. Director Sizemore is out, so a regime change is in the works."

"Who's going to take his place?"

"Maxine Ratliff is on the Hill as we speak, going through confirmation."

That came as welcomed news. The President could have easily looked outside the agency for Sizemore's replacement, yet he tapped Brenham's boss to lead instead.

"She's a good choice. She'll do right by us."

"I think so, too," Brenham agreed. "We've already spoken. Barring an unforeseen attempt to block her nomination, she's asked me to lead NCS."

"Wow, that's great. Congratulations."

"Thank you." Brenham leaned forward, steepled his fingers, and pointed to Jessica. "I want you to be my deputy."

Jessica's smile morphed to stunned disbelief. She swallowed hard. "I ..." she stammered.

"No need to answer me now," Brenham insisted. "Let it sink in on your way to Groom Lake."

A second curveball in as many seconds caused Jessica to do a double-take. "Sir?"

"Somebody needs to oversee the clusterfuck Sizemore created," he explained. "I can't go, so it needs to be someone I can trust."

Despite the weight of Jessica's physical and mental exhaustion pressing down on her, she squared her shoulders and nodded curtly.

"Yes, sir. I'm on it," she replied without hesitation.

"I knew I could count on you, Jessica. As for the promotion, you've certainly earned it. Your work in Sanhe notwithstanding, you have proven yourself to be an outstanding operative and damn fine leader. You're the perfect person to take over as deputy."

Jessica beamed inwardly. "Thank you, sir. It means a lot to hear you say that."

However, the mention of her last post dimmed the mood somewhat. For fear of showing emotional attachment, Jessica was reluctant to inquire further about the fate of GCRM, yet she had to ask. "What will become of Sanhe Station?"

"Humanitarian efforts will continue," he assured her, "but we'll hold off replacing you until things cool off a bit. North Korea is still a threat, and I don't see that changing anytime soon."

Knowing GCRM had a future in Sanhe came as a relief. Helping those impoverished children had been one of the most rewarding experiences of her life.

A knock came at the door. Brenham's executive assistant poked her head in. "Sir, Director Ratliff has been confirmed," she stated with an approving grin.

Brenham pumped his fist.

"Also, Senator Dayley is on line one," she continued.

"Perfect. Thanks, Jenn."

Brenham stood, cueing Jessica the meeting was over. She got to her feet, and they shook hands.

"One more thing," Brenham added. "We're taking a lot of heat from the Hill about all of this alien business, especially as it pertains to Mathias Industries. The man has deep pockets and lots of clout in this town." Brenham referred to the billionaire, Edmund Mathias. "Anything gleaned from Garza and Sizemore goes directly through me."

"You got it."

Tempted to accept Brenham's job offer on the spot, Jessica refrained. A promotion to Deputy Director was a dream come true, but she also did not want to appear overly eager. Hopefully, by the time she got up to speed at Groom Lake, Ratliff and Brenham would be settled into their new roles. Since more organizational changes were sure to follow, she could broach the subject with Brenham later, once the dust settled. Until then, she would bide her time.

Jessica collected her luggage and headed off to her cubicle. News had already spread that she was in the building, and many colleagues stopped her in the hall to say hello. It was good to see everyone and, naturally, there was speculation surrounding Jessica's private meeting with Brenham. She artfully quelled any rumors.

Arriving at her tiny cubicle, Jessica found it exactly as she had left it months ago; six months, to be exact. It did not feel that long, but the mold in her unwashed coffee mug was evidence it could have been longer.

Jessica set her luggage aside then unlocked the side drawer of her desk, retrieving her official CIA credentials. Eyeing the photo of *Agent* Aguri, Jessica smiled as she considered the title of Deputy Director of the National Clandestine Service.

You've come a long way, baby.

Reflecting on the fifteen years of hard work that had led to this achievement now seemed like a flash in the pan.

Tucking her belongings in her purse, Jessica picked up the handset on her desk phone to book her flight to Groom Lake. Pending promotion aside, she fluttered with nervous excitement for her first trip to the super-secret facility at Area S4. She had heard rumors about it and had always wanted to visit. Now she would get her chance.

12

TRANSFER COMPLETE

Planet Earth
Mayor PNP Nancy Flores Paucar Airport, Satipo, Peru

The ATR 42 cargo aircraft touched down just after sundown. Taxiing toward Mathias' private hangar, the twin-turboprop was the only aircraft operating at the small airfield. All other flights, inbound and outbound, had been canceled earlier in the day for reasons unknown to airport employees. They had been told to drop everything and go home without explanation, which usually meant a drug shipment of some kind was arriving or departing. None of the workers had questioned the order, especially since they had received their full day's wages.

Only the air traffic controller remained at his station in the tower. The silver-haired man fulfilled his duties with beads of nervous sweat dripping down the sides of his face. He had two armed thugs toting MGP 9mm sub-machine guns standing over him.

As soon as the aircraft was safely on the ground, one of the armed men nudged the controller's arm with the muzzle of his weapon and said, "Ahora lárgate de aquí." *Now get the hell out of here.*

The frightened controller did not need to be told twice. Without daring to look the men in the eyes, he bolted out of the tower, leaving his jacket and lunchbox behind.

Down on the flight line, the lone aircraft pulled up to an empty hangar. Four black SUVs awaited, along with an armored car similar to those used by banks. Members of Mathias' private security detail were already in position surrounding the hangar.

The aircraft came to a halt inside the building, and then both turboprops began to wind down. Mr. Renzo was first to exit the rear door of the aircraft. Although he had not slept in over forty-eight hours, Renzo looked fresh and alert.

A member of the ground team approached. He was an American, ex-Green Beret. "We've got the hangar secured, sir. The men are ready—locked, cocked, and ready to rock."

Renzo nodded. "Our guest is heavily sedated, but remind the men to use tasers only."

"You got it, boss."

"What about the route?" Renzo inquired.

"We've got every intersection and side road blocked off, just like you instructed."

It was probably overkill, but Mr. Renzo was not taking any chances. Peru had its share of criminal elements, and Mathias Industries had a target on its back. Security was taken seriously to protect the company from industrial espionage, organized crime, and a slew of small-time crooks looking for a big score. Even in this peasant community on the outer fringes of the Amazon, a blind squirrel could still get lucky and find a nut. One lapse in security was enough for Mathias' enemies to strike.

Edmund chose the jungle village of Satipo over Lima proper for one reason: isolation. Satipo was in close proximity to a remote airfield, the secluded villages were sparsely populated, and only a few unpaved roads led in or out. In fact, only one road led from the airfield to Mathias' private compound, where his state-of-the-art lab was located. Yet, even with these tactical advantages, Mr. Renzo was not about to risk losing his quarry so close to home.

He waved the armored car inside the hangar and directed the driver to back up to the aircraft's forward cargo door. As soon as the vehicle was in place, the ground team moved into position to receive the package. Renzo called the team inside the aircraft on a handheld radio and confirmed they were ready to start the transfer.

Taking a step back, he waved the ground team forward. A portable conveyor belt was brought in to connect the plane to the back of the armored car. As soon as it was in place, Renzo gave the order to proceed.

"Open the cargo door."

Unconscious on the aircraft's floor, Luna was stretched out on her back and secured to a gurney. Four, thick mesh straps across her chest, abdomen, thighs, and shins kept her in place, while her wrists and ankles were handcuffed for added measure.

Two men stood over her—one at Luna's head and the other at her feet. They raised the gurney and locked it in the upright position. Two more men flanking her sides anxiously held tasers at the ready. They were prepared to apply the highest degree of nonlethal force necessary to subdue their guest, but only Renzo could give the order to take Luna's life. That was reserved as a last-ditch option to prevent her escape.

Offloading went smoothly. Luna was rolled into the back of the armored car. The guards collapsed the gurney, keeping the Aiwan lying prone at floor level. The four guards then took seats on opposing benches inside—two on each side of Luna. Not taking any chances, the guards kept a constant watch for any hint she might be waking.

Renzo secured the door from the outside and bolted it with a heavy-duty padlock. He and the remaining guards then piled into the escort vehicles. Moments later, the caravan departed the airport.

The journey to Mathias' compound took less than ten minutes. Mr. Renzo rode in the lead vehicle. On his lap, a hand-held tablet fed him live aerial footage from four drones being controlled by operators in the trailing vehicles. Renzo's eyes never stopped moving, constantly jumping between the road ahead and the drone footage, watching for ambushes.

There were only two side roads along their route. Leveraging technology to his advantage, Renzo used the drones to check both roadblocks his team had put in place up ahead. This high-definition aerial coverage proved to be a wise investment, as did their deforestation efforts.

When construction of Mathias's new compound had begun, Renzo's first act had been to clear the thick forestry along the routes leading to the site. Now only fields of regularly mowed grass grew where trees once stood. Would-be ambushers had nowhere to hide, and the drones allowed him to see for miles around, giving him the tactical advantage.

Seeing well in advance that the roadblocks were clear, the caravan raced by both locations, kicking up a cloud of dust in its wake. The vehicles arrived at Mathias' compound moments later without incident.

Four guards with machine guns in hand stood outside the gated entrance.

Mr. Renzo called ahead and properly authenticated. The entrance opened, allowing the caravan inside without slowing. Once the last vehicle made it safely inside, the entrance was secured.

Edmund Mathias' high-tech, donut-shaped groundscraper rivaled Apple's headquarters in Cupertino, California, although on a much smaller scale. Surrounded by a high wall for security, the two-story, ring-shaped building housed over one thousand employees. The compound provided all of the amenities needed to keep the isolated workers happy. From lavish apartments and spas to a movie theater and restaurants, the compound had it all, including a beautiful courtyard in the center of the ring with a scenic walking path.

Nothing on the South American continent compared to this facility. Its ultra-modern design was a stark contrast to Lima's Spanish Colonial heritage, which rubbed many locals the wrong way. Mathias' facility was often compared to the controversy surrounding the design of the Louvre Museum in Paris. Many viewed it as a slap in the face to the country's rich traditions and culture. Environmentalists also cursed its location so close to Amazonia. Just like the Chancay Megaport project in Lima, Mathias' facility here in Satipo had caused irrevocable damage to the local ecosystems. Yet, those outcries only fell on the deaf ears of the politicians in Edmund's back pocket.

If Mr. Renzo cared about such things, he never expressed it. Despite his deeply rooted Chachapoyan heritage, he understood the ways of the world. It was no different now than when his ancestors had been ruled by the Incas. Wealth always bought power, and the powerful always ruled the weak.

That was how Renzo had come into the employ of Dr. M. Edmund Mathias. As one of Peru's lost children, abandoned by his family and scorned by society, Renzo had grown up on the harsh streets of Lima, stealing for food and sniffing glue to escape his miserable existence. But what he had lacked in resources, Renzo had made up for in resourcefulness. He had a talent for grifting, which had led him to his fateful encounter with Mathias.

Renzo, a scraggly thirteen-year-old at the time, had spotted Edmund standing outside a plush hotel in Lima, waiting for a ride to the airport. As the concierge helped other guests, an emboldened Renzo had seen an opportunity and seized it. Catching Mathias by surprise, Renzo had crouched in front of the unwitting American and had begun untying his dress shoes.

"Te ato los zapatos," Renzo had insisted.

"No, I don't want you to tie my shoes," Edmund had replied, perturbed.

He had tried to shoo the boy away, but Renzo was persistent. Finally realizing the only way to get rid of the grungy peasant was to give him a few sols, Edmund had set his briefcase down to retrieve his wallet. Renzo snatched the case and ran.

Unfortunately, he had not made it far. Betrayed by a passerby, Renzo had been cornered by the policía in a nearby alley. They despised his kind more than the locals. While Mathias' property had been returned, young Renzo had been beaten and jailed for his crime.

As it turned out, Edmund had been carrying the formula for a new drug to treat Crohn's Disease in his briefcase. He had just secured financing from his Peruvian investors to go public when the incident with Renzo had occurred. Through the experience, Edmund had realized he needed his own hired security and, with it, a fixer who could discreetly handle matters outside of the law.

With an eye for talent, Edmund had been impressed by the would-be thief. He had secured Renzo's release then had given him the one thing lacking most in his life—a path.

Renzo was all in. He owed Mathias a life debt. From that point on, he lived to serve Edmund. Food, shelter, clothing, and education had just been the start. Renzo had been groomed, not to be Mathias's heir apparent but his protector. Tapping into Renzo's street smarts and fighting instincts, Edmund had the boy trained in everything from Gracie Jiu-Jitsu and the art of war to counter-terrorism and corporate espionage. In-between, Renzo had become a well-refined student of social etiquette, excelling in all areas. Most importantly, he was loyal to Edmund, almost to a fanatical state. This combination of devotion and skill was rare, and Mathias had come to trust Renzo absolutely.

With the caravan now safely inside the compound, Renzo shifted gears to transfer the Aiwan from the armored car to a subterranean holding cell inside the facility. The vehicles pulled up to a large overhead door on the northeast corner of the building. It automatically opened, thanks to the security controller watching the convoy via CCTV. As soon as the vehicles were inside, the door closed. The escort vehicles then came to a stop with the armored car backing up to a loading dock.

Renzo's team quickly exited their vehicles and surrounded the armored car. He then gave the green light to off-load the Aiwan.

Luna's gurney was wheeled through the loading dock to a nearby freight elevator. Five guards, along with Renzo and Luna, crowded inside. Renzo punched the "S2" button for the lowest of the subterranean floors.

On the way down, Luna stirred slightly, causing the guards to flinch. Bringing their tasers to bear, Renzo raised his hand, ordering them to stand fast. He watched Luna closely, hoping the tranquilizer did not wear off before they could reach her cell.

The elevator bell chimed, and the doors opened. Wasting no time, the procession wheeled Luna down a well-lit, sterile corridor. Passing several doors, each with biometric access controls, the team arrived at a door simply marked "*S2-H*."

Renzo entered his access code on the wall-mounted panel then had his retina scanned. The door unlocked, and Renzo held the door open as Luna was wheeled inside. He scanned the room's interior, impressed that his boss had been able to construct a makeshift holding cell to his specifications on such short notice. The room—a converted hazardous materials laboratory—had been divided into two equal sections by a thick wall of transparent aluminum that ran from floor to ceiling. In the center of the divider was a heavy door with a slot for passing food back and forth.

For now, Luna would live on the opposite side of the divider, in a space reinforced with steel panels. No furnishings were provided, other than a metal chair bolted to the floor and a simple drain in the middle of the room for body waste.

As Luna was wheeled into her new living space, Renzo glanced to his right and noted a glass door leading to a neighboring laboratory. Inside, he spotted a team of scientists dressed in white lab coats, standing on temporary scaffolding overlooking a boulder-sized, mechanical object in the middle of the room.

A female scientist happened to look his way. Seeing Luna, her eyes flashed with excitement, and she called her colleagues over.

All work abruptly ceased in the neighboring lab and, in unison, the scientists broke their huddle. Those standing at ground level came to the door for a peek at the Aiwan. Others climbed off the scaffolding, revealing the damaged Aiwan Seeker Mathias' deep-sea salvage team had recovered off the coast of Isla Guadalupe.

Edmund had briefed Renzo on the recovered alien tech days ago. Recalling that conversation, this was the Seeker that had singlehandedly destroyed a Russian Akula-class attack submarine and countless coalition jet fighters over the Korean Peninsula before engaging the Reaper. According to classified reports, Captain Ava Tan had shot down five of these deadly drones. This one appeared to be the Seeker she had disabled with a well-timed landslide. The drone was mostly intact but damaged to the point it could no longer fly or, fingers crossed, be a threat. Enough had been recovered from the rubble for the scientists to examine the Seeker, and now, with a little help from their newly arrived Aiwan guest, they hoped to reverse engineer it.

Still unconscious, Luna was moved into the middle of her cell. The guards lowered the gurney to the floor then looked at Renzo expectantly. He made a curt nod to proceed. Luna's restraints were removed, and the guards hastily transferred her to the metal chair. She was then strapped down at her wrists, torso, and ankles.

"Clear the room," Renzo ordered as soon as they finished.

He was the last person out. Before securing the door, he eyed Luna from afar. Still unconscious, she sat propped up in the unforgiving chair by her restraints, head hung low. Renzo allowed himself an inward pat on the back. Mission accomplished.

Three floors up, Edmund Mathias stood at the head of a long conference table, addressing five of his wealthiest investors.

"There is no need to worry about the recent drop in share prices," Edmund assured them. "All our data from Groom Lake has been recovered, including the samples of alien DNA. Our Peruvian lab is up and running, and we have picked up our cloning research right where we left off."

"What about the Americans?" a middle-aged Chinese man asked.

Mathias waved dismissively. "Not a concern. Shutting down Groom Lake actually did us a favor. Here in Peru, we can work unhindered by meddling snoops. I assure you, Mathias Industries remains the leader in the tactical application of biological defense."

"The Americans represented a large market share," a female Russian oligarch remarked with concern.

"True," Mathias countered. "But, as soon as each of you convince your governments to place orders for our force enhancement serum, I suspect the Americans will have a change of heart."

Judging by the consensus of head nods, the group agreed with Edmund's assessment.

"Now, for the really good news." Mathias fished in his pocket and retrieved the orange magnetarite crystal harvested from Challenger Deep. He held it up between his thumb and index finger. "Behold the future of Mathias Industries."

Edmund gave the crystal to the closest attendee, a Saudi Arabian man wearing a traditional checkered red and white ghutra headdress and a long, white thobe shirt. He examined the polished crystal closely, appreciating its size and elegance. Yet, the sheikh did not see the company's future in rare jewels. As president of the world's leading integrated energy and chemicals enterprise, and the largest provider of crude oil, his interests revolved solely around the world's global energy markets. He passed the crystal to his neighbor, unimpressed, and asked, "Diamonds?"

"Not diamonds, my good friend. Magnetarite."

The sheikh's brow furrowed. "Mag—"

"—netarite, yes," Edmund finished as he began circling the room while the others passed the crystal around. "Magnetarite is a rare crystal that captures the energy of dying stars," he explained. "When harnessed correctly, a crystal this size can power a large city for decades with *zero* emissions."

The sheikh raised his eyebrow skeptically.

Having expected this reaction from the oil baron, Edmund picked up the television remote and turned on the television. "See for yourselves how powerful just one crystal can be."

Footage from the Reaper's encounter with Commodore Boa's battlecruiser played. The recording had been obtained off the internet, so the quality was grainy, but the images were undeniable. The sleek, black spacecraft plowed through a swarm of Aiwan Seekers then launched a powerful energy beam to knock out the battlecruiser's shields.

"Impressive display," a Colombian woman remarked, "but what you're proposing could put our oil, gas, and energy companies out of business."

"That is already happening," Edmund countered. "The Stone Age came to an end, not for a lack of stones. One day, the oil age will also end, but not for a lack of oil. The burning of fossil fuels is killing our planet. Consumers are demanding hybrid vehicles to reduce our carbon footprint. Meanwhile, the use of solar, wind, water, and nuclear power to generate electricity has had mixed results. There are pros and cons to each, but imagine a world where nations rent *our* technology to power their cities. We will have a monopoly."

Mathias displayed two charts, side-by-side, on the television. The one on the right projected the return on investment for a major city with more than one million citizens. Just by shutting down aging power plants and reducing the number of workers needed to maintain those facilities, the savings were in the hundreds of millions USD over the first ten years. Likewise, the chart on the left demonstrated the reliability of energy output from a crystal-powered generator compared to current technology. Again, there was no comparison.

"These crystals give new meaning to 'energy as a service,' my friends. And Earth represents only a fraction of the market," Mathias added with a devilish grin. "There is a brutal trade war taking place beyond our world. These crystals are the rarest and most precious commodity in the galaxy, and Earth has them in abundance. It is the reason why the Aiwans came here in the first place. They seek to harvest our crystals, to take them right out from under us, unless we jump their claim. I tell you, we are at the dawn of a new era—the crystal energy era—but we must act swiftly. When word gets out about Earth's crystal surplus, other harvesters will come and take our crystals by force."

"What would you have us do?" the Russian asked, knowing his country had suffered terrible losses at the hands of the Aiwans.

"Mass harvesting the crystals from Challenger Deep will be a costly venture. We need an influx of cash and room to work."

"Room to work?" a gray-haired, Asian Indian woman, dressed in a ten-thousand-dollar saree made of Chennai silks, asked.

"Yes, we need the Russian, Chinese, and American fleets to depart the area around Challenger Deep. Tensions remain high, and the last thing we need is more fighting to break out."

The Russian and Chinese members exchanged knowing looks. Patriotism and politics had no room at this table. They spoke only one language—profit. With a simple head bob, both agreed to have their country's fleets removed from the vicinity of the Mariana Trench. For them, it was a matter of one phone call.

"Excellent," Mathias said cheerily. "Shall we move on to purchase orders?"

A North Korean investor raised his hand. "The Democratic People's Republic of Korea wishes to be the first to place an order for your serum. But first, how do you plan to harvest the crystals at those depths?"

Mathias chuckled slightly. "Like I said, it won't be easy, but I've just acquired a valuable resource to expedite the process. I'm also bringing in an old colleague of mine who has firsthand knowledge of the Aiwans and worked directly with Prince Kypa."

A picture of Dr. Rose Landry appeared on the screen.

13

SECUESTRO

Planet Earth
Arbor Ridge, Georgia

Dr. Rose Landry shuffled into her bedroom, juggling a travel cup full of tea in one hand and a large handbag in the other. Taking a quick sip, she set her cup on the dresser and her bag at her feet. Opening the closet door, she cleared away a pile of clothes covering a heavy duty safe on the floor. She knelt and pressed her thumb against the safe's biometric fingerprint reader.

The safe unlocked without delay. Inside, Rose retrieved her trusty tablet, the one she had used to teach Kypa English. In turn, he had recorded much about Aiwan language, customs, and history. The Feds had allowed her to keep the device for ongoing research since she was now viewed as the government's resident expert on Aiwa.

Rose tucked the tablet in her handbag. As she started to close the safe, she spotted the wrist beacon, gifted to her by Kypa. Taking it out, Rose eyed the device with a heavy heart. To would-be burglars, the bracelet could be mistaken for a normal piece of jewelry, perhaps even a family heirloom. Nothing about the device shouted advanced alien tech or could be misconstrued as a high-dollar item at a pawn shop.

She had managed to keep the beacon a secret from the Feds and swore to herself it would remain in her home safe, never to be seen in public. Rose had no idea when she would ever have cause to use it. Certainly, Kypa did not intend for her to activate it on a whim, but it was tempting.

Rose missed her friends dearly. She could only imagine the adventures Kypa, Neil, and Ava were experiencing, and she was dying to hear all about them. Even more, Rose missed their comradery. After Groom Lake, the world seemed to turn upside down. All the talk was about alien invasions, and she had no one to confide in, other than Colonel Marlana Nunez.

Speaking of whom, Rose realized she would be late for her meeting with Marlana this morning if she did not get a move on.

She placed the beacon back in the safe and locked it. Resituating the pile of clothes to cover it up, Rose closed the closet, grabbed her tea, and headed out the door on her way to work.

The morning commute on westbound US-78 was unusually light this morning, which was a pleasant surprise. Traffic in and around the Atlanta area was some of the worst in the nation. Normally, it was bumper to bumper this time of day, with drivers honking their horns and dodging in and out of lanes just to move up a car or two, but traffic was moving steadily for a change. Rose's first day returning to the CDC after nearly two months away from the office was starting off better than expected.

Driving up from her home in nearby Arbor Ridge, Rose had begun her day by dropping off her two grandsons at daycare. Her daughter, Becky, could not get her car to start, and with her son-in-law already gone for work, "Memaw" had come to the rescue. Rose lived close by, and the daycare facility was on her way to work, so it was not an inconvenience. In truth, she had jumped at the chance. Rose had been having grandbaby withdrawal and had needed a fix.

Having just recently returned home from Groom Lake, she had discovered how much the boys had grown in her absence. Rose had not seen them since her Hawaiian vacation with the family had been cut short for a CDC emergency. Little had she known at the time that she was being sent to investigate Earth's first encounter with an alien lifeform, nor had Rose expected to be away from home for so long.

Fortunately, it had all worked out in the end, relatively speaking. Earth was still spinning, intergalactic war had been averted, and military intelligence had finally allowed Rose to return home. But to say the world had returned to normal was a stretch.

Listening to morning talk radio was proof of that. The never-ending media coverage of the alien encounter and speculation of an invasion only fanned the flames of public unrest. Rose feared a global panic would lead to mass hostilities and the eventual unraveling of society.

"Enough," she said in disgust, turning off the radio.

Admonishing herself for letting the media's fearmongering get to her, Rose took a calming breath, doing her best not to let so-called "alien pundits" ruin her day before it had even gotten started.

She drove the rest of the way in silence, making mental notes of projects and people she needed to check on. Judging by her inbox and calendar as of last night, this was going to be a maintenance day, filled with responding to emails and meeting with her team. If possible, Rose hoped to squeeze in time at the lab, but with her boss out of town on vacation, it fell on her to put out any fires.

Now inside Atlanta proper, Rose turned onto North Decatur Road and followed it to CDC Parkway. There, she stopped at the entry control point, flashed her ID card to the guard, and was allowed to pass. Two minutes later, she entered the east parking deck of the Edward R. Roybal Campus, home of the Centers for Disease Control and Prevention.

As Assistant Director for the Division of High-Consequence Pathogens and Pathology, Rose worked in CDC Building 21, a twelve-story office facility, housing the CDC's headquarters and emergency operations.

She parked and, a short walk later, passed through the turnstiles at the front entrance, making her way to the elevators.

Being back at work after such a long time away felt like the first day of school. It was exciting and invigorating, and yet, there was little that had changed in her absence.

She stepped off the elevator and entered the section for the National Center for Emerging and Zoonotic Infectious Diseases.

Snaking her way through rows of cubicles, Rose ran into a few colleagues who welcomed her back. No one knew exactly why she had been away so long, only that it was work-related and not an illness. It was challenging to keep her involvement at Groom Lake under wraps. Everything she had seen and heard was now classified but, judging by their knowing looks, her friends had connected the dots between her Hawaiian vacation and the sudden hush-hush field deployment. It did not take a rocket scientist, or a Doctor of Biomedical Sciences, to figure out Dr. Landry had some involvement in the alien encounter.

Rose skillfully deflected such inquiries, trying hard not to feed the rumor mill. She then made her way to her office. After checking in with her admin assistant, Angela, Rose sat at her desk and began unpacking her laptop.

A knock came at the door moments later. She looked up to find Angela standing in the opening with a cup of hot tea.

Rose smiled appreciatively and waved her in. "You're an angel."

Her assistant transferred the cup to Rose. "Just a reminder, you've got a Zoom call with a Colonel Nunez in five minutes." Her assistant had said the name as a question.

Rose checked her watch. Catching up with colleagues in the hallway had eaten up more time than she thought. "Thanks, Angela. Would you mind getting the door? I appreciate it."

Rose turned back to her machine, logged in, and opened her calendar. Sure enough, her meeting with Marlana was due to start in two minutes.

After connecting to the meeting, a sleepy-eyed Colonel Nunez appeared on the screen.

"There she is." Marlana yawned, brushing her dark, unkempt hair out of her face. She was still dressed in her pajamas.

Rose chuckled at her appearance. "Good morning, sunshine."

Nunez raised her coffee mug. "This is what I get for staying up late to help Hector with his campaign. We didn't get to bed until two."

Rose empathized. "What campaign?"

"Hector's decided to run for president of our HOA." Marlana rolled her eyes. "Says he's determined to fix the system."

An impish grin creased Rose's lips. "Fix the system, huh? Sounds like a man on a mission."

Nunez scoffed. "A rebel without a job is more like it. Retirement has him circling the drain, so I told him to make himself useful. Go figure."

"Ex-pilot, right?" Rose recalled, taking a sip of her tea. "What did he fly?"

"A mahogany desk," Marlana joked. "At the end, I mean. He flew A-10s most of his career."

"And now he's cooking you romantic dinners every night ...?"

Nunez guffawed. "Please. Lord knows I love the man to death, but he's no Casanova. Get this, the other night, I'm at the sink, washing dishes, and he tried to 'get me in the mood,'" she said, making air quotes. "Up to my elbows in dirty dishes, I hear him turn on the Righteous Brothers. Then he nuzzles up behind me and wants to start slow dancing. Like that ever worked with a Brillo pad in my hand. Anyway, Hector whispers in my ear, *Am I the best one you've ever had?*"

Rose shook her head, smiling as her friend continued the story.

"I said, *Yeah, all the other guys were nines and tens.*"

Tea nearly came out of Rose's nose from laughing. "You're awful."

Nunez grinned mischievously. "I try." She took a sip of coffee and switched gears. "So, how does it feel to be back in the office?"

Rose started to reply when a knock came at her door. "Hold on a sec; there's someone at the door," she told Nunez. "Come in."

Angela opened the door. "Sorry to disturb your meeting, but there's an urgent matter down in the lobby."

Rose's initial reaction was curious skepticism. "In the lobby? What is it?"

"Security says there's a man wanting to see you … a Dr. Cristiano Rojas," Angela read off a sticky note then shrugged. "He doesn't have an appointment."

"Did he say what it's about?"

Angela frowned. "Security said he has a Peruvian passport and government ID card. He's reluctant to share specifics but said it is a sensitive matter regarding the Amazon basin."

Rose frowned and let out a curt sigh. "Okay, tell security I'll be right down."

Angela nodded and closed the door.

Rose turned to Nunez. "Sorry about that. I gotta go."

"Duty calls. I get it." Nunez raised her mug. "I promised Neil I'd look in on you, so don't be a stranger."

"I won't. Oh, speaking of Dr. Garrett, he gave me a parting gift." Rose retrieved a Yoda action figure from her purse and held it up for Nunez to see.

"O-M-G," the colonel guffawed, squinting as she leaned toward the screen to eyeball the tiny toy. "Makes you wonder why he's still single," Nunez said dryly.

Rose shook her finger. "Now, now. To each their own." She arranged the toy prominently on her desk.

"Yeah, well, maybe he'll hook up with an Aiwan and make Yoda babies," Nunez suggested.

Rose shook her head, blushing. "Actually, I'm holding out hope for him and Ava."

"He could only be so lucky," Nunez agreed. "All right, I'll let you go. But I mean it, let's keep in touch. Who knows? Maybe next time we talk, I'll be first lady of the HOA."

"I'll have a special tiara made up just for you."

"Do it." Nunez gave her two enthusiastic thumbs-up. "I'll wear it to the meetings."

The two laughed together at Hector's expense then said their goodbyes and the meeting ended.

Taking one last sip of tea, Rose came to her feet and threw her suit jacket back on. Heading for the elevators, she adjusted her collar along the way.

A few minutes later, Rose stepped out of the elevator and approached the security desk by the main entrance. Scanning the lobby, she noticed a man in a brown tweed suit sitting by himself on a leather couch. From afar, she pegged him to be about her age, likely Peruvian in descent judging by his distinctive, high cheekbones, dark complexion, and charcoal black hair combed to the side.

The two made eye contact, and then the man stood as Rose passed through the turnstiles.

"Dr. Landry," the man greeted with a soft smile and a Spanish accent.

After shaking his clammy hand, Rose discreetly wiped her palm off on her trousers.

"My name is Dr. Cristiano Rojas." He produced a picture ID badge. "I represent CONCYTEC, Peru's National Council of Science, Technology and Technological Innovation."

Rose nodded, familiar with the organization, as she looked over his credentials. "Nice to meet you, Dr. Rojas. How can I help you?"

Reluctant to speak openly, Rojas gestured to the lobby furniture a few paces away from the constant traffic around the security desk. "Do you mind?"

The Peruvian's cautionary demeanor spiked Rose's curiosity.

She waited for Dr. Rojas to pick his seat on the couch then sat opposite him in a chair. Rojas scooted closer and leaned toward Rose.

"Thank you for seeing me, Dr. Landry. I apologize for showing up unannounced. The matter I wish to discuss is quite sensitive."

"I'm listening."

"Are you familiar with the Mashco-Piro?" Rojas asked.

"I am. They're one of the last uncontacted tribes on Earth."

"Correct." Rojas smiled, impressed by her knowledge. "They inhabit a protected region of the Amazon known as the Mashco-Piro Indigenous Reserve. However, over the past several years, this tribe has strayed out of the reserve with greater frequency. Their sporadic, and sometimes deadly, interactions with people in the surrounding areas have raised concerns about the tribe's future."

"I see." Rose nodded thoughtfully. "What did you have in mind?"

"Your work with lost tribes is well-documented, Dr. Landry. We were hoping you could come to Peru and help us communicate with the Mashco-Piro. We want to find an amicable solution for them and the nearby towns without any more bloodshed."

Rose empathized. "I'm flattered, but I'm afraid this isn't my area of expertise anymore. If there were signs of infectious disease, perhaps, but there are others more capable than me. Three or four names come to mind. I'd be happy to recommend—"

Rojas shook his head. "We really wanted it to be you."

Rose frowned, trying to soften the blow. "Sorry, this really isn't in my wheelhouse. And besides, this is my first day back in the office after a prolonged absence. I've got a lot of catching up to do. I hope you understand, but I'll have to decline. Like I said, I'd be happy to give you some names of very capable anthropologists."

Clearly disappointed, Dr. Rojas let out a sharp breath of frustration. "That will not be necessary." He stood and extended his hand, unexpectedly ending the meeting.

Somewhat taken aback, Rose followed his cue and came to her feet.

"Thank you for your time, Dr. Landry," he said with a forced smile. "Good day."

Rose accepted his handshake. "Sorry I couldn't be more …" She trailed off as Dr. Rojas departed rather abruptly.

She watched him exit through the front doors. Their brief encounter and his hasty exit left Rose scratching her head. She shrugged it off and returned to her office, thinking if this was the worst she had to deal with today, then she could count herself lucky.

Later that evening, Rose left work around seven o'clock. She checked in with her daughter on the drive home to see if she needed help in the morning. It turned out her car was still in the shop, so Rose happily volunteered to drive the boys to school.

After a quick stop at a drive-thru to pick up dinner, Rose pulled into the garage. She was anxious to get out of her work clothes, into some comfy sweats, and eat.

Closing the overhead garage door behind her, Rose entered the mud room by the kitchen and flipped the light switch. Nothing happened. She tried several times with no success.

"That can't be good." She frowned in the darkness.

Feeling her way into the kitchen, Rose set her oversized handbag and keys down on the counter. She then noticed the digital clocks on the microwave and stove were off, as well. Opening the fridge, it was dark inside, too.

She exhaled heavily. "Great."

Fortunately, Rose had not been to the grocery store since returning from Groom Lake, so there was not much that could spoil. However, everything in the freezer might be lost if the power did not return soon.

Setting her dinner on the counter, Rose retrieved a flashlight from the kitchen drawer then made her way to the bedroom. Oddly enough, the back bedroom lights were still working, which gave her hope the kitchen breakers had simply tripped.

Her mind shifted to the portable generator Joe kept in the garage. She had not used it since his passing. Hopefully, it would start if needed.

Returning to the kitchen, Rose stopped in the archway leading to the dining room. She flipped the light switch there, hoping to be surprised, but that room remained dark, as well. Rose huffed with disappointment and started for the garage to check the breaker box. All at once, a large man dressed in black reached out from the darkness and seized her from behind.

Rose gasped in terror, too frightened to scream. Her body jerked, and she inadvertently dropped the flashlight. It landed with a heavy *thump* on the floor. Then, before Rose could find her voice, the assailant cupped his gloved hand over her mouth with a cloth doused in chloroform.

Rose's eyes widened in panic as her muffled scream fell on deaf ears. She struggled, trying to free herself, but the intruder was too big and too strong. He held Rose close from behind, keeping her left arm pinned at her side while avoiding the harmless swats of her flailing right hand.

Rose could feel the chloroform beginning to take effect, her senses dulling.

Out of the corner of her eye, she saw movement to her left, indicating a second intruder. Rose struggled more as the assailant approached. It was not until Dr. Cristiano Rojas moved within inches of her face that she recognized the man.

Wearing an arrogant grin, Rojas waved his finger at Rose. "You should have accepted my offer, Dr. Landry. It didn't have to be like this."

Rose's eyelids grew heavy. As darkness closed in, seeing Rojas invoked a jolt of fury that gave her one last surge of adrenaline to free herself. Rose kicked Rojas square in the groin, catching him completely off-guard. He dropped to his knees in agony, cupping his crotch as Rose fought against the iron grip of the man holding her. But the drug eventually won. The room began to spin, and Rose's legs buckled. She collapsed in her abductor's arms, and he let her slide to the floor, unconscious.

"Perra estupida," Rojas spat, holding his throbbing groin. Cursing came easier in his native tongue.

He stood gingerly, using the kitchen table to brace himself. The other assailant watched him struggle. Smirking behind his mask, he offered Rojas no assistance.

The quiet assailant did not care much for Rojas. This was the first time they had been paired on a job together for Mathias. Being an actual scientist, Rojas was unaccustomed to getting his hands dirty, like his partner. And ever since Dr. Landry had rejected his offer, Rojas had grumbled all day about having to participate in her abduction. His quiet partner ignored him. However, it was satisfying to see Rojas brought to his knees by a sixty-year-old grandma.

Despite his misgivings toward Rojas, the assailant recognized he was not being paid to make friends. Let Rojas be the salesman—a bad one at that—and he could stick to being the hired muscle. So, while Rojas cursed about being bested by an old woman, the assailant went about his business zip-tying Rose's hands and feet with practiced precision.

Leaving Rose on the floor, the assailant removed the SIM card from Rose's phone. He then grabbed her handbag from atop the kitchen counter and tossed both items inside. Noting a tablet also in the bag, he considered leaving the device behind but thought it might raise suspicions.

After passing the handbag and uneaten takeout to Rojas, he lifted Rose's limp body over his shoulder and moved to the back door. Peering through the window, he found the backyard dark and quiet. Earlier, he had tripped the breakers to part of the house and shot out the lone streetlamp in the back alley using a Glock 9mm with a silencer. There was little chance now of being seen by anyone.

Outside, they followed a quaint path of paver stones to the back gate. A stolen Ford Bronco waited for them in the alley. The engine was running, with the third member of their team anxiously tapping the steering wheel, ready to leave.

Rojas peered up and down the darkened alley. With no sign of nosy neighbors, he turned to his partner and waved him forward. Rojas opened the tailgate. They placed Dr. Landry carefully inside and threw a black tarp over her.

With their business finished, Rojas shut the tailgate, and then both men climbed into the vehicle. The driver sped away, heading toward the Georgia-Florida state line.

Five hours later, Rose's abductors reached their destination. The Bronco pulled into the Jacksonville Executive at Craig Airport shortly before three o'clock in the morning. There, a twin-engine Cessna Citation X business jet awaited their arrival inside a single-bay hangar.

Rose was transferred to the aircraft by the driver and hired muscle as Rojas watched. They set her down inside on one of the comfy leather chairs and fastened her seat belt. Rojas took a seat facing their guest.

With their end of the bargain complete, Rojas handed the driver and hired muscle envelopes filled with cash. Neither bothered counting their fees. Saying nothing, they departed to find a location to dump their stolen vehicle.

The copilot then appeared from the cockpit and closed the side door for departure. He checked that Rose was buckled in. Seeing Rojas fastening his seat belt, the pilot did not bother covering emergency procedures.

"Prepare for departure," he said then returned to the cockpit.

Soon after, the Cessna's engines came to life. With only the aircraft's running lights to guide them, they taxied out of the hangar and proceeded to the runway. Minutes later, they were airborne.

Rojas glanced at Rose across from him. The dose of chloroform guaranteed she would remain unconscious for a couple more hours. That would afford him time for a quick nap. He leaned back in his chair with a satisfied grin on his face. Next stop: Satipo, Peru.

14
TOURING AIWA

Planet Aiwa
Supra, Realm of Eos

Ava's eyes snapped open as she jolted awake. Panting, she looked around the darkened cabin in a panic, instinctively clutching her chest. The soft glow of light bleeding in from the Reaper's cockpit provided enough illumination for her surroundings to register. Ava let out a long breath of relief. She was safe, aboard her ship.

Recalling her nightmare, vivid images of Ava's experience aboard the Aiwan mothership in North Korea still haunted her. She remembered the hair rising on the back of her neck when she had discovered the grisly remains of a half-eaten crewmember. Then came the deaths of Kim Sung-il and Colonel Wu, victims of the savage obercai. It was just after that, when Ava had fled the beast and could feel the obercai breathing down her neck, that she had woken in a cold sweat.

It was just a dream, she told herself. *You're alive.*

Still, getting the images out of her head would take time, and coffee— lots of it.

Putting her feet on the floor, Ava yawned heavily and rubbed the sleep from her eyes. She stood and noticed Neil asleep on the top bunk. Careful not to wake him, she crossed the cabin to the control panel on the wall by the cockpit. Before deactivating her bunk, Ava paused to clear her vision. Neil would not take kindly if she accidentally shut off both of their beds, though it would make a good prank someday.

"You okay?"

The sound of Neil's groggy voice in the darkness gave her a start. Ava rounded to find Dr. Garrett propped up on one elbow with a sleepy look on his face. Seeing him like that, up on the top bunk, reminded her of summer camp as a kid.

"Yeah, I'm good." Ava forced a thin, unconvincing smile. "Sorry if I woke you."

"It's all right," he said, yawning. "What time is it, anyway?"

Neil's yawn triggered one of her own. "I have no idea, but I need coffee."

Sleeping in a strange place made for a rough night, especially with the uncertainty surrounding their presence in the capital. But that was only part of the problem. Supra was like New York City—it never slept. Except for the areas of the city affected by the rolling blackouts, the capital remained lit up at all hours with unceasing activity. That included the comings and goings in the hangar bay. It seemed that every time Neil and Ava started to drift asleep, a foreign noise startled them awake.

Then there was the whole lack of natural light issue. At this depth, being unable to witness the position of Aiwa's suns, it made it impossible to gauge the time of day. Neil and Ava had felt it last night. Their bodies were still on Earth time, so their circadian rhythms told them when it was time to sleep. But the days were longer on Aiwa so keeping time with Earth did not make much sense. In truth, neither of them knew how or if Aiwans measured time. It would certainly take some getting used to. For now, they would have to rely on caffeine to be the great equalizer.

Neil climbed off his bunk, using a holographic ladder, and approached Ava as she synthesized a hot drink. He leaned against the bulkhead beside her and asked politely, "Do you want to talk about it?"

Ava gave him a curious sideways glance. "About what?"

"Your nightmares."

Her drink materialized. "It's no big deal," she dismissed, bringing the hot beverage to her lips and blowing on it.

"I hear you talking in your sleep," Neil said without sounding judgmental.

"Seriously?" Ava gave him a disbelieving look. "What did I say?"

Neil could sense she was playing coy with him. He started to reply but hesitated, reluctant he might say the wrong thing.

"Go on," Ava insisted with a raised eyebrow, as if daring him to say something silly just so she could refute it.

Neil looked her in the eyes. "All right … I've heard you calling out for Mark."

Ava's skeptic expression washed away. She swallowed the lump in her throat. An uneasy silence followed.

"I'm sorry, Ava," Neil apologized, regretting he brought it up. "I don't mean to upset you. I'm just worried, that's all." He paused then added, "It reminded me of the bad dreams you shared with me back at Groom Lake. The ones about Kypa, remember?"

Ava's first thought was to continue downplaying Neil's concerns but, deep down, she knew he was right. Nightmares had been a constant since Mark's death and had only gotten worse with everything that had happened in North Korea until now.

She moved to the steps leading up to the cockpit and sat. With her coffee cupped in both hands, Ava stared distantly for a long moment, gathering her thoughts.

Neil waited patiently in silence, giving her space.

"You're right," she said finally. She darted her eyes to Neil for his reaction. He smiled back warmly. Ava reverted back to staring at her feet.

"You miss him," Neil said. It was a statement, not a question.

Tears welled in Ava's eyes. She twisted her mouth, fighting to keep it together, and nodded.

Neil sat on his knees beside her and placed his hand on Ava's. She squeezed it tight, appreciating his support.

"You know, the irony of grief is that the person you need to talk to the most is the very person you lost."

Ava agreed wholeheartedly. However, this was not just about Mark. She felt embarrassed to elaborate, but who else could she confide in?

"It's not just that," she said on a sigh. "I'm reliving moments from North Korea. I can't get the images out of my head."

Neil repositioned, sitting cross-legged across from Ava. He gently took her coffee cup out of her hand and set it aside, triggering a curious look from Ava. Neil then took both of her hands in his.

"Listen to me," he said, squeezing her hands gently for emphasis. "You've been through a lot, Ava. You could be experiencing PTSD."

Post-traumatic stress disorder was nothing to be ashamed of and was not limited to combat soldiers. Certainly, witnessing any kind of traumatic event could trigger intense emotional and physical reactions, such as nightmares, anxiety, and depression. Ava had displayed some of the warning signs. And, with PTSD awareness gaining international attention, Neil knew enough not to ignore her symptoms.

Ava shook her head dismissively. "I'm just tired, that's all." She released her hands from him to wipe her eyes then retrieved her cup. "I've got all I need right here." She held up her coffee and smiled unconvincingly.

Neil frowned. "It's not that simple, Ava. Maybe if you shared what happened … just getting it off your chest and talking to someone could help."

Ava fidgeted uncomfortably, averting her eyes.

Neil resituated so she was forced to meet his gaze. "Talk to me," he implored. "C'mon, we're in this together. I'm putting all my faith in you out here. Now let me help you."

He watched Ava wavering then an idea struck him. Neil stood and walked to the food synthesizer. "Computer, er … rather, Reggie, two beers, please."

Identical pints of frothy brews appeared on the pad. Neil retrieved both glasses and returned to Ava.

She gave him a funny look and accepted the drink he offered, setting her coffee down. "What's this?"

"I promised you a beer when you got back. Remember?"

Ava searched her memory and recalled their conversation at Groom Lake the night before she had departed for North Korea. Neil had visited her room after hours, but his intentions had turned out to be honorable, despite Colonel Nunez's belief to the contrary. Even though they had been at odds on whether or not Ava should go to North Korea, Neil had promised to buy her a drink upon her return. It was time to settle up.

"Dude, it's way too early to be drinking." Ava chuckled. "I think," she added, uncertain if it was day or night.

Neil flashed her a Doubting-Thomas look. "Au contraire, mon frère," he rebutted. "It's five o'clock somewhere, right? Now, raise your glass."

Ava gave a chuckle and lifted her drink. "What shall we drink to?"

"To you, silly," Neil replied. He thought for a second then raised his glass. "To Ava, may you take everything in moderation, including moderation."

They tapped glasses then chugged their drinks, eyeing one another to see who could finish first or quit while trying. Neil won. He finished his drink with a loud gasp and wiped his mouth with the back of his hand. Ava was right behind him. With a big grin on her face, she raised her empty glass and belched long and loud enough to make Colonel Nunez proud.

"Good one," Neil praised.

Ava laughed and set her glass down, feeling the buzz from the synthetic alcohol. The belch also sparked a fond memory of North Korea, one of the few good experiences from her time there.

Neil picked up on her mood shift and asked, "What is it?"

Ava shook her head dismissively, but Neil insisted.

"Okay," she relented, starting to blush. "But you can't tell anyone. Promise?"

Neil scooched forward with eagerness. "Cross my heart and hope to die." He drew an X across his chest.

Ava laughed. The more she thought about it, the funnier it got.

"Well," she began, "on my way to the crash site in North Korea, I was in a car wreck."

Neil was taken aback. "Seriously?"

Ava nodded. "This isn't the funny part. My driver was actually killed, and I was knocked unconscious." She frowned.

Neil shook his head. "Ava, that's awful."

"I know, right?" she replied. "I woke up in a field hospital at the crash site on the morning of the launch. Guess who was there?"

Neil shrugged and waved her on to tell him.

"Kim Sung-il," Ava answered. "The Supreme Leader of the Democratic People's Republic of Korea."

Incredulous, Neil blurted, "Shut the front door!"

Ava shook her head. "I'm crappin' you negative. He was right there at the foot of my bed. Then the creepy bastard started to hit on me."

Neil recoiled, making a disgusted face. "What did you do?"

"Well, I had a concussion from the crash and, as he made his move, I started to feel nauseous. He was sitting right beside me, closer than you are right now, and my belly made this unholy gurgling sound."

Neil's curiosity morphed into a wide grin, as he could see where this was going. "Oh my God, you didn't."

"I did." Ava laughed. "It happened so fast. I blew chunks all over him."

Neil guffawed as he pictured the scene in his head. He opened and closed his mouth a couple times, trying to find the words. Finally, he asked, "What happened next?"

"The tent went silent. Everyone was so mortified that they didn't know how to react. I thought I was dead, and probably everyone else did, too. Kim just stared at me then stormed out of the tent."

"That is insane," Neil said, shaking his head and laughing.

"Yeah, that was when I met General Vong for the first time."

Ava's mood sobered at the mention of Vong's name. She had never expected, in the short time they had been together, that the two would bond the way they had, at least in her mind. There was the genuine respect they had shared for one another as warriors, and certainly the connection they felt being in combat together had also played a part in forging their bond, but it had gone beyond that. For a brief stint, even though they were not related by blood, they had shared a father-daughter moment. Vong had imagined walking with his daughter, arm-in-arm, while Ava had missed the company of the two most important men in her life—her father and fiancé. It was unfortunate that Vong did not get to experience the real thing with Ji-eun.

Neil gave her a curious look. "Was he your contact in North Korea?"

Ava blinked back to the present. She nodded, remembering Neil and Rose were not privy to all of the details of Operation Sundiver.

"You haven't said much else about your mission," Neil remarked.

Ava rolled her eyes. "Yeah, well, some of it, I'm trying really hard to forget."

"What was the highlight?"

Jessica Aguri, Choi Min-jun, and the Global Children's Relief Mission team came to mind. "I met some really good people over there." Her smile softened. "I hope they're safe."

Neil started to inquire further when both of their nano-rings beeped. They exchanged curious looks.

Ava tapped her collar. "This is Captain Tan."

"Good morning, Captain," Kypa replied. "I am outside with my sister and the children. May we come aboard?"

Ava stood and entered the cockpit. Peering outside, she located Kypa standing near the front of the ship. He was joined by Princess Seva, along with two of Kypa's children—his youngest daughter, Fraya, and son, Toma.

Fraya spotted Ava above and waved.

Ava waved back then held up one finger. "One second," she told Kypa.

Ava called over her shoulder to Neil, "We've got company."

"Who?" he asked.

"Kypa and his kids, as well as Princess—"

"Seva," Neil finished.

"That's the one, and it looks like a team of freight handlers, too," she added, noting a pair of Aiwan workers approaching the Reaper. They were driving single-person hovercrafts with large, empty bins in front for holding cargo. "I'm guessing they're here to unload the crystals. Chalk up Dr. Garrett's first diplomatic victory."

"As if there was any doubt," Neil quipped, playfully polishing his fingernails on his suit.

Ava rolled her eyes.

To the ship, she said, "Reggie, open the storage bay and drop the ladder."

"Yes, Captain," the computer replied.

Before leaving to greet their guests, Ava paused and patted Neil's shoulder. "Hey, thanks for the talk, and the beer," she said earnestly. "You were right; it helped."

Neil smiled. "Any time."

Making her way to the main cabin, Ava deactivated the hologram bunks just as little Fraya appeared. She had ascended the ladder fearlessly with her father trying to keep up. Wide-eyed and filled with excitement, a big grin stretched across her face at first sight of the humans, especially Neil. As soon as she stepped off the ladder, Fraya rushed to his side and wrapped her skinny arms around his leg.

"Well, good morning to you." Neil laughed, surprised by the affection.

Ava flashed him a look of amusement then transferred her gaze to Kypa. Noticing her friend had an extra skip to his step, Ava grinned. "Somebody looks happy to be home."

"It was a good night," Kypa replied, keeping the details of his reunion with Maya to himself.

Seeing his daughter clinging to Neil, Kypa frowned at Fraya's lack of respect for his personal space. "Fraya, come to me," he said, embarrassed, pointing to a spot beside him. "My apologies, Dr. Garrett. Fraya can be rather ..."

"Rambunctious?" Neil finished.

Kypa nodded vigorously with an expression that said, *You have no idea.*

"It's okay." Neil chuckled. "I wish my students were this happy to see me."

Fraya refused to budge, which earned her a disapproving look from her father. However, since Neil did not seem to mind, Kypa let it go.

Princess Seva and Toma soon arrived. With everyone crowded into the main cabin, they stood stiffly with their hands at their sides.

"Welcome aboard, Princess," Ava greeted, bowing.

Seva returned the gesture in kind.

Neil raised his hand in a slight wave. "Good morning."

Seva mimicked the wave, somewhat awkwardly, and replied with a tentative smile, "Greetings, Dr. Garrett. I hope your first night on Aiwa was pleasant."

"It was, thank you. I'm looking forward to seeing more of the capital today."

"That is why we are here," Kypa explained. "Seva has offered to escort Dr. Garrett around the capital while Ava, Toma, and I survey a location to begin reconstructing the core."

"Sounds good to me," Ava replied, "but we just woke up. Can we grab some breakfast and coffee first?"

Seva gave her a curious look. There was not a direct translation in Aiwan for either term.

"Coffee is a type of drink that Captain Tan is rather fond of," Kypa explained.

Seva nodded slowly.

"Fond is an understatement. It's more of a necessity, just below oxygen." She winked.

"I want to come, too," Fraya insisted, clinging tighter to Neil's leg.

"Not this time, little one," Kypa said, which earned him a pouty face from Fraya, but she decided not to press her luck.

Ava noticed Toma quietly admiring the Reaper's interior. "Toma, what do you think of your father's creation?"

Toma cracked a shy smile. "I like it very much."

Kypa's son reminded Ava of every lanky, socially-awkward teenage boy back on Earth, searching to find his identity. Despite a recent growth spurt that brought him nearly to Kypa's height, Toma was no longer a child but not yet an adult. Ava found his reserved yet polite demeanor charming.

"It is hard to believe such a small vessel could defeat all of Krunig's forces," Seva pointed out. "Very impressive."

Hearing another Aiwan praise his efforts brought a glint of pride to Kypa's eyes. He rarely received positive feedback, nor did he acknowledge his own accomplishments, even to himself. To hear it from his sister was most gratifying.

"Thank you. Actually, it was Captain Tan's skillful piloting that brought out the best in this ship," he deflected.

Ava waved dismissively. "Kypa, you're being modest. You deserve a heckuva lot more credit than that." She pointed to Kypa. "Your brother is brilliant. If it wasn't for him, our worlds would be at war with one another right now. Instead, we are now allies."

"At least, we hope to be," Kypa said, cautiously optimistic. "There is much work to be done."

That was a formidable understatement. The "work" included forging an alliance between Aiwa and Earth, defeating Krunig's horde in perpetuity, and rebuilding the planet's core. Kypa's life literally depended on the Reaper's ability to do all of this and prove his so-called crimes were in the best interest of Aiwa.

"Let us leave you to your coffee," Seva suggested, feeling guilty for the intrusion. "I will take Fraya back to her mother and meet Ambassador Garrett back here."

Neil started to reply, but Fraya interrupted.

"I want to go, too," she whined.

Kypa let out an exasperated sigh and approached his daughter, expecting a battle.

Smiling empathetically, Ava moved aside. Then she had a thought.

As Kypa tried to coax Fraya to obey, Ava opened the nearby storage cabinet. She rummaged through her bag and retrieved the toy F-22 fighter jet General Garza had gifted her back at Wright-Patterson AFB. Why Nunez had packed it was beyond her, but it would serve as a good distraction.

"Fraya," she said invitingly, "look at this."

Fraya quelled her tantrum the instant she caught sight of the toy. Fixated on the curious object, she released Neil and elbowed past her father to accept the toy from Ava. Fraya marveled at the packaging for a long moment, eyeing it from different angles.

"What is it?" she asked.

Crouching beside her, Ava pointed to the toy inside. "That is a replica of a ship we fly back on Earth … although it's not as sophisticated as the one your father built."

Ava helped her open the packaging and removed the die-cast metal aircraft. Fraya held it in her hands, rubbing the texture with her fingers. Finally, she clutched it against her chest and declared, "I love it!"

"Proof that if you put enough engine on something, even a brick can fly," Ava mocked Garza with a Southern drawl. Her humor escaped everyone in the room.

Looking up to her father, Fraya asked, "Can I keep it?"

Kypa hesitated, considering the ramifications, but his youngest could be persuasive. Fraya batted her big, blue eyes with a lost puppy look that her father had a hard time saying no to.

Ava did not make it any easier. She made pouty lips and begged, "Pleeease."

Kypa sighed. Left with little choice, he nodded approval.

Fraya made a gleeful sound then lunged forward and wrapped her arms around Ava's neck. Ava returned the hug. The unexpected show of affection was just what the doctor ordered.

When they separated, Princess Seva stepped in and herded Fraya down the ladder. "I will be back shortly."

The group said its goodbyes. Then Neil's stomach growled.

"Okay, I need to eat something," he declared. "Toma, do you want anything?"

He shook his head bashfully. "No, thank you." His eyes then darted toward the cockpit.

Ava picked up on his interest. "Do you want to see?" she asked, waving him over.

Toma smiled thinly and nodded, following her into the cockpit.

Meanwhile, Neil synthesized a plate of bacon and eggs, and a cup of orange juice.

Where were you in my college days? He sighed as the food appeared, filling the compartment with a delicious aroma that was sure to linger in the air filtration system for some time.

Unabashed, Neil dug in.

Kypa watched him eat. While he did not share Neil's enthusiasm for bacon and eggs, Kypa did entertain the thought of helping himself to a plate of raw squid. *Perhaps later*, he decided. Food was a low priority for him at the moment.

After a few moments, Kypa said, "I hope your tour of the capital goes smoothly."

The phrasing and tone of his words struck Neil as odd. "Should I be worried?" Neil asked with his mouth half-full of eggs.

Kypa sighed heavily, clearly grappling with something. After a long pause, he said at last, "I hope not. I fear for my family's safety. That includes you and Ava."

Neil swallowed and turned to face his friend. "What makes you say that?"

"One attempt has already been made on my life. I am confident that whoever was responsible is not pleased that I have returned. I am the heir to the throne … unless my father has me executed, that is," he added with a wry smile.

"Who do you think is behind it?"

Kypa shrugged. "My father has many enemies, both on Aiwa and abroad. Opposition to his rule has grown as the war continues."

"Back home, we have a saying. *You can't please all of the people all of the time.*"

"True. But there are groups who are unwilling to idly stand by and let the war drag out. The attack on me is proof of that."

"Are you thinking we should cancel today's tour?"

"No, appearances are important, especially if we hope to build an alliance between our worlds." Kypa crossed his arms. "I spoke with my sister last night, and she supports what we are trying to accomplish. She vowed to help our cause, which is why she offered to personally escort you around the capital."

"She's not scared?"

Kypa scoffed. "No, and that is what I am afraid of. Despite being mature beyond her years, Seva has a rebellious streak in her. Many will see the two of you together today and not take kindly to your presence … or perceived fraternization."

"Because I'm an off-worlder?"

"Yes. As I have said before, Aiwans are a proud race. We do not trust outsiders, which is why we have stayed secluded on Aiwa. Seva is different, though. She is a forward thinker and carries a great deal of influence, especially with our youth. Today is certain to create a stir, and I think she is relishing the opportunity to push society's boundaries yet again."

Neil chuckled and said facetiously, "Sounds like she'd make a great social media influencer on Earth." *Whatever the hell that means*, he did not add.

Kypa did not disagree. He put his hand on Neil's shoulder, his demeanor turning serious. "Be vigilant, my friend, and please watch out for my sister. There is no telling what forces may be at work in the shadows."

Neil took Kypa's message to heart.

After finishing breakfast, they joined Ava and Toma in the cockpit. Toma was sitting in the pilot's seat with Ava coaching him through the controls. He turned excitedly to his father, a look of joy Kypa rarely saw in his son.

"Captain Tan said I could fly the Reaper today. Can I?"

Ava winced. She had hoped to introduce the idea later, at a more opportune moment.

This, Kypa thought, *is what happens after months of being off-world and your family believes you to be dead*. Ava was not helping much, either, despite her best intentions. Kypa was at a disadvantage, and Toma and Fraya knew exactly how to press his buttons. How could he say no?

"Very well," Kypa allowed. "But after we are well away from the capital. Agreed?"

Toma nodded excitedly.

"Great, it's settled." Ava brushed her hands off. On her way out of the cockpit, she patted Kypa's shoulder, assuring him he made the right decision. "Now, who made bacon?"

Thirty minutes later, Seva returned to collect Neil. She was accompanied by two unpleasant-looking Royal Guards who carried energy pikes. Neil met her outside the ship.

"My brother insisted on the chaperones," Seva explained, bobbing her head toward the guards and sounding none too thrilled.

Neil eyed the elite warriors head to foot. Unlike Seva, he was more than happy to have them tagging along, even more so because of their physical presence. These Aiwan males were unlike Kypa and Toma. They were considerably bulkier, not Hulk-ish, but lean and strong, with the hardened physique of seasoned fighters.

One other nuance Neil picked up on was their head markings. Unlike Kypa and every other Aiwan he had encountered so far, the guards had blue markings instead of red on their face and crown. He found that distinction curious and filed it away to inquire about later.

Neil shrugged. "Better safe than sorry, right?"

Seva smiled pleasantly, although she inwardly disagreed. Sensing Kypa's influence had led to Neil's support for tighter security measures, she held her tongue and quickly changed the subject. "Shall we get started?"

The guards remained several paces behind as the princess led Neil out of the hangar. Behind them, the Reaper's nacelles whirred to life. Neil made a passing glance over his shoulder as the ship lifted off the hangar deck and raised its landing struts. He paused and waved, unsure if his friends had seen him before the Reaper sped away.

Seva watched Neil with curiosity. His earlier stance made her wonder just how far Kypa's influence reached. She could not read Neil's thoughts telepathically due to his nano-suit, but Seva was an excellent judge of character. Neil had a child-like innocence and naivety to him, which was understandable considering his inexperience in galactic affairs. Yet, Kypa spoke highly of him and trusted Neil with his life. She sensed there was more to Ambassador Garrett than met the eye. Peeling back the layers of her guest would be an intriguing endeavor.

15

WILD THING

Planet Earth
Satipo, Peru

Luna stirred in the darkness, moaning as the lingering effects of the sedatives gradually wore off. She awoke slowly and discovered every fiber of her being ached, most notably the muscles running up her spine and neck. Her head hung low, and she lifted it slowly, but the strain proved difficult. Luna grimaced from the effort, causing her eyes to flutter.

She sat back, thinking nothing of it at first. Together, the darkness and the solitude helped calm her throbbing head. Then the lights came on, sending a searing pain through her skull.

Wincing, Luna groaned angrily. She tried raising her hands to shield her face, but they would not budge. Puzzled, Luna tried again and again. With each attempt, her anxiety increased until she forced her eyes open and found herself sitting in the middle of a sterile room, strapped to a metal chair by thick, leather straps.

Full-scale panic ensued. Luna blinked rapidly to force her eyes to adjust to the light and bring her blurred surroundings into focus. Gritting her teeth and clenching her fists, she thrashed and pulled with all her might to free herself. But the bonds securing Luna to the chair by her wrists, ankles, and around her torso proved too strong and unforgiving.

Luna's futile struggle ended soon after, punctuated with a blood-curdling scream at the top of her lungs. Wild-eyed and chest heaving, she searched frantically for something, *anything*, to free herself.

How could you be so careless? she chastised herself.

Biting back her frustration, Luna sighed heavily. In a moment of weakness, self-pity began to creep in, but she quickly shook it off and steeled herself.

Focus! Luna prodded herself in an attempt to control her welling anxiety.

She started with a self-assessment. Scanning her body for injuries, she was relieved to find herself in relatively good shape. However, in a passing glance, she noticed a tiny bump in the pit of her elbow. The mark was the remnants of a healed wound. Her captors had drawn her blood.

Just then, an audible *click* caught her attention. Luna snapped her head sideways toward the door. Four guards entered the room in full riot gear, holding shields and taser batons. They formed a barrier, blocking the door should Luna attempt to escape.

Luna narrowed her eyes on the guards as her nails slowly extended.

"Jesus, it looks pissed," the guard in the middle said nervously.

"Easy," a second guard spoke to Luna. "We just want to talk."

The two guards on the edges cautiously began flanking Luna. Her eyes bounced back and forth between them, as if watching a tennis match. The tension in the room became palpable. Despite being weaponless and incapacitated, Luna could see she had struck fear in their eyes. They had no idea who or what they were dealing with.

Luna waited until the guards were within a few feet of her then lashed out suddenly, gnashing her teeth and hissing savagely. The guards jumped, causing one to fumble his baton. It clattered on the cement floor, forcing its owner to blurt an expletive as he hurried to recover it. When the guard resumed his position, he saw Luna sitting calmly in her chair, grinning with satisfaction. She retracted her claws, savoring a tiny victory.

Realizing she was toying with them, the guard shook his head, peeved. "Seriously? I nearly pissed my pants."

The guard directly in front of Luna was less forgiving and hated being publicly embarrassed. He drew back his baton and lunged at Luna, threatening to crack her skull. "C'mon, you alien freak!" he shouted, standing over her. "You wanna dance? Huh?"

Unflinching, Luna hissed defiantly in the guard's face.

"Enough!" Renzo barked, his commanding voice stifling the exchange.

The guard spun around to find his boss in the doorway. Distracted by Luna, he had been unaware that Mr. Renzo had entered the room. He lowered his baton without question then stepped away from Luna and bowed to Mr. Renzo apologetically.

With order restored, Renzo turned his attention to Luna. Their eyes met and, judging by her dangerous glare, he could tell she remembered him from the beach. *So much the better.*

"We good?"

Renzo turned to Mathias, who was standing in the doorway, and nodded.

Edmund entered the room wearing a finely tailored gray suit and colorful bowtie, as per usual. As Renzo closed the door behind him, Mathias straightened his silver cufflink.

Luna eyed him closely. While not physically intimidating, this person carried himself with the confidence of a man who knew he held all the power in the room.

She took a controlled breath, watching and waiting to see where this would lead.

Renzo whispered instructions in his boss's ear.

Nodding agreement with his fixer's counsel, Mathias transferred his gaze to Luna. His eyebrows raised in mild surprise to find the Aiwan's piercing glare locked on him. Unfazed, Edmund crossed his arms and began tapping his upper lip in thought.

"Okay, let's see if this works," Edmund started. He placed his arms at his sides and turned his palms facing outward. "Welcome to the planet Earth," he greeted. "My name is Edmund Mathias. I am your host."

Luna's brow furrowed with a quizzical look.

Seeing her confusion, Mathias chuckled. "That sounded ridiculous, didn't it?" He waved dismissively. "Never mind. You probably didn't understand a word I said, anyway. That will change soon enough. But first, I want you and I to get acquainted."

Luna moved her eyes back and forth amongst her captors.

Picking up on her anxiety, Edmund shooed the guards back. "Let's give her some space, shall we?"

The guards complied but kept their batons at the ready, just in case.

Luna relaxed somewhat but was clearly still on high alert.

Edmund then reached into his interior jacket pocket and retrieved several items. He stepped forward and held the first item up in front of Luna's face. It was an image on his phone. Her eyes opened wide at the sight of Kypa. The picture was taken at Groom Lake, and the headline read in bold letters, "*WE ARE NOT ALONE*"

In a moment of weakness, Luna's face softened with the elation of seeing her dear friend.

My prince, you survived!

"Kypa," Edmund offered, nodding agreeably. "I take it you know him."

Luna looked up from the image, meeting Edmund's gaze. Processing this new information, it took every ounce of restraint not to erupt in anger. After months of isolation, searching for Kypa, not knowing if he was dead or alive, this was the break she had been waiting for. She was too close now to be denied, but common sense prevailed. Her captors held the upper hand, and fighting would not help her cause. They wanted something from her; otherwise, she would already be dead.

Forcing herself to remain calm, Luna opened her hands and rolled her wrists as far as the restraints would allow to show her palms.

Edmund recognized her gesture of peace and smiled with satisfaction.

"Very good. See? We can be friends," he told the others.

Edmund then held up an image of Kypa's escape pod resting inside the hangar at the super-secret facility at Area S4. He had obtained the classified photo from one of his NSA contacts. Mathias tapped the photo.

Luna's eyes widened with recognition. That was definitely pod five from the mothership.

"Do you want to know where Kypa is?"

She had no clue what Edmund was asking, but his raised eyebrow seemed inviting. All she could think to do was nod and appear cooperative.

"Kypa is on his way back to Aiwa," Edmund continued, making a sweeping gesture with his hand skyward.

Luna furrowed her brow as she tried to decipher his meaning. Piecing together the image and gestures, she came to the gradual realization that Kypa had gone home and left her behind.

It cannot be. Her gaze drifted downward, refusing to accept this conclusion. *Kypa would never do that to me … unless he thinks I am already dead.*

The grim finality of this revelation felt like a sucker punch to the gut. Luna had been abandoned once again by her people. First, after Cirros was destroyed, and now on Earth. Her shoulders slumped as she contemplated the truth. She was truly alone. Worse yet, a prisoner on an alien world.

Did Kypa even come looking for me? she wondered with dismay.

Edmund could see by Luna's pained expression that she had swallowed the bait. Now it was time to reel her in.

He reached into his pants pocket and retrieved his magnetarite crystal, lifting the rare gem up to the light between his thumb and index finger. Dazzling hues of orange sparkled within the crystal, as if it was the heart of a miniature star.

Seeing the crystal snapped Luna out of her self-pity. It also confirmed Kypa's suspicion about a large deposit of crystals being on Earth, which offered her some consolation. This was what they had come for, which meant their friends had not died in vain. There was still hope for Aiwa. And, as much as she wanted to be angry for being left behind, deep down, she believed Kypa would have come for her if he had known she was still alive. That was one constant in the universe she could count on.

Luna was also relieved to know he was alive and heading home. She imagined the joy Maya and their children would feel when they saw Kypa again. At least one of their crew had survived to tell what had happened.

What if they do not come back for me?

Just as that dreadful thought crossed Luna's mind, Mathias pulled retrieved another photo. This one, also of Kypa, showed him standing in front of the window of his holding cell back at Groom Lake. In the foreground was the hand-drawn image of Aiwa and Earth crudely etched in fogged glass. Between the two planets was the hexagonal image representing harvesters. The photo was taken moments before Kypa had smeared his blood and Neil's on their respective homeworlds as a warning of the impending threat.

"Aiwa," Mathias pointed to the ringed world.

Luna nodded slowly.

Encouraged by this, Edmund pointed to the other planet and gestured to their surroundings. "Earth … here."

With that established, Mathias gestured back and forth between the two planets then did the same between the two of them. "You and me"—he held up the magnetarite again—"together, we can find more crystals. Yes?"

Luna got the gist and sneered. She had no intention of helping this stranger whatsoever. Magnetarite had brought her people nothing but trouble. The only reason she had even agreed to come to Earth was on the promise that whatever crystals they did harvest would be used to defeat Krunig and restore Cirros. Now this guy, whoever he was, wanted in on the action. No, thank you.

Eyeing Mathias up and down with disdain, it was evident he was no different than Grawn Krunig and all the cutthroat harvesters responsible for her people's plight. He reeked of greed, same as the others. And no matter how big Mathias thought he might be on *this* planet, it was nothing compared to the forces that would come and bleed Earth dry when the crystals were discovered.

Luna turned up her nose and looked away defiantly.

Edmund scoffed and asked Renzo, "Did she just turn me down?"

"Yes, sir. I believe so."

Edmund straightened, tugging on his shirt cuffs to mask a deep-welling anger bubbling to the surface. He was a man accustomed to getting what he wanted, and with time being of the essence, he was done with the niceties. Perhaps it was time to let his guards teach their guest a lesson in humility.

"You"—he pointed to the guard from earlier who had a score to settle—"show her what happens when I don't get what I want."

Happy to oblige, the guard set his shield down and approached Luna, anxiously tapping his stun baton in the palm of his hand. Standing over Luna, a sinister grin creased the guard's face as he thumbed the activator. Blue sparks of energy sizzled from the end of the device inches from her face.

Luna's heart hammered in her chest, but she refused to look away. Clenching her fists and gritting her teeth, she stared defiantly into the guard's eyes, determined not to give him the satisfaction of seeing her fear.

"Hold up," Edmund interjected, breaking the tension in the air. He sighed heavily. Luna had called his bluff. "On second thought, this is no way for me to treat a guest. Let's start over, shall we?"

The guard stood down. Disappointed, he took a step back.

Luna sneered, knowing she had won this round.

The perceived insult triggered the guard. Without thinking, he slapped Luna across the face with the back of his bare hand. It was the last mistake he would ever make. The connection was made.

Luna's eyes narrowed on the guard. Her upper lip curled as she channeled her telepathy on the center of his forehead.

The poor bastard realized his mistake a second too late. He had known not to touch Luna. Mr. Renzo had made that point clear, but a hot temper was usually a bad advisor.

It started with a dull tickle to his brain, followed by a stabbing pain. He suddenly cried out in agony, startling the others, who were oblivious to what was happening.

Dropping to his knees, the guard clutched his throbbing head with his free hand. But Luna was just getting started. The guard's eyes widened in horror as she commanded him to turn his stun baton on himself.

Shaking his head, unable to speak, the guard's face pleaded for mercy. Yet, he found no remorse in Luna's eyes.

His arm raised, as if it had a mind of its own. Whimpering, the guard gripped his baton firmly in one hand and jammed the electrode into his groin. A thirty-thousand-volt shock sent the guard convulsing onto the floor. His howls of agony echoed in the room, sparking sympathy pains in the groins of those watching.

All except Renzo.

Thinking quickly, he snatched the baton out of the second guard's hand and zapped Luna in the chest. The jolt temporarily severed her connection to the guard on the floor.

"Get him out of here!" Renzo commanded.

Edmund withdrew as the guards took their incapacitated colleague by the arms and dragged his limp body out of the room. Renzo was last to leave, keeping the baton trained on Luna, who remained slouched in her chair, equally spent by her punishment. He backed out of the room and closed the door behind him.

"What the hell just happened?" Edmund demanded as Renzo brushed past him.

Without responding, Renzo retrieved a poison dart from the carrying case behind his back. He knelt beside the debilitated guard and stuck him in the neck. The poison entered his bloodstream immediately. His body convulsed, and then foam dribbled out of the corner of his mouth. Death was instantaneous.

Seeing the life drain out of the guard's eyes, Renzo stood and placed the used dart back in its case.

"Dispose of that," he said callously.

The remaining guards did not ask questions as they hastily dragged the corpse down the hall. His body would be taken outside and dumped in the jungle.

Renzo turned to Mathias. Seeing his boss's shocked expression, he calmly explained, "A simple slap to the face was all the Aiwan needed to make a telepathic connection. The guard was compromised at that point, and too much of a risk to keep around."

Edmund could not care less about the guard. He was still trying to process Luna's uncanny abilities. "Just like that, she took control of him," he said in awe.

"She's very dangerous, sir. We must exercise extreme caution around her."

Mathias nodded thoughtfully. He turned to the window, eyeing the Aiwan slouched in her chair. She was the key to everything he had ever dreamed of achieving. Fortunately, the meeting was not a complete loss. He had witnessed firsthand how powerful Luna's telepathy could be. More importantly, her reaction to the news about Kypa had intrigued him. There might be some leverage there he could use.

To say this Aiwan was a fighter was an understatement. Edmund knew the type well. Breaking her physically was doable—his "unconventional" clinical methods had proven quite effective in this area—but employing them would not win Luna's heart and mind. Mathias had no need for a slave that cowered in his presence. He needed a partner who shared his vision and would be willing to channel all of her creative energies to that end.

Ruling out torture, at least for now, Edmund sought another angle. Pulling on Luna's heartstrings seemed the better route. She had responded to his mention of Kypa and Aiwa, which told him she was deeply loyal to both. If that trust were compromised, any feelings of abandonment and betrayal were low-hanging fruit to be plucked.

Unfortunately, after today's debacle, the Aiwan would be hard-pressed to trust him. But Rose was another matter. He checked his watch. The plane carrying his old boss and mentor was due to land any minute.

16

UNDERCURRENT

Planet Aiwa
Supra, Realm of Eos

Neil's guided tour of the capital began in the corridors of the palace's spiral tower. He had seen parts of the building on his way to the High Court the previous day, but that was in a hurried rush to meet with King Loka and the other court members. Today, there was time for Princess Seva to provide a more in-depth tour at a leisurely pace. She was also gracious enough to entertain his elementary-level questions, explain the nuances of Aiwan culture, and describe life at two thousand feet below the surface.

Seva led them back to the Grand Hall, where they discussed the history of Aiwa's democratic monarchy. This led to an informative discussion on civics and public policy, which Neil found quite fascinating and overwhelming at the same time. To help him absorb all of this new information, he chose to wear his holographic helmet. This allowed him to interact with Seva while discreetly sending neural commands to the HUD inside his helmet to explain details he was too embarrassed to ask about.

One such item he found perplexing was the lighting systems used to illuminate the city. Ever since their arrival, Neil had been mesmerized by the brilliant array of colors that brought Supra to life. But he soon discovered, as they walked the corridors, that the Aiwans did not use lightbulbs. He was amazed to learn that the city used a lighting system that combined the harnessed energy of magnetarite crystals with an organic, iridescent algae built into the construction of every building. From floor to ceiling, the energy from the crystals interacted with the algae to generate lights that varied in color, depending on the species of algae. Purple and blue hues dominated the cityscape, which provided ample lighting for most tasks. However, a special variant of algae that produced a soft, white glow was used in work areas requiring brighter illumination.

"This lighting system also serves a secondary purpose," Seva added. "We have found that certain hues deter a good number of ocean predators. When a sensor detects a predator near the city perimeter, the lights activate to turn it away without harming the animal. This allows us to move about outside with less risk to personal safety."

"That's very interesting. What about the shield?" Neil asked. "Doesn't it keep the predators out?"

Seva shook her head. "No, I am afraid not. The shields are designed to prevent energy weapons and fast-moving projectiles from entering the city. Swimmers, like you and I, and every other sea creature, can pass through the barrier unhindered if you move slow enough."

"That shouldn't be a problem for me," Neil quipped.

"Can you swim?" she asked.

"I can, but nothing like you, I'm sure," Neil admitted. "Back on Earth, I watched Kypa swim. He moved so fast and effortlessly. It was impressive."

Seva smiled with pride. Then she gestured to a nearby window. Outside, a group of a dozen Aiwan younglings were training with an adult. "Our children are taught from birth how to survive and fend for themselves."

Neil stepped up to the window and watched as the children chased their female instructor in a game of tag. Like a school of bluefish, they moved rhythmically as a unit in pursuit, but the adult was quicker. She led the younglings in a series of loops, rolls, and dives, always able to elude their touch.

It reminded Neil of his childhood, running around the neighborhood with his friends, playing games like Ghost in the Graveyard and Capture the Flag. As long as he was home before the streetlights came on, his mom let him play outdoors to his heart's content.

"Do you have children?" Seva asked.

"Me, no, but maybe someday," he hoped. "How about you?"

Seva shook her head, smiling wanly. "No … I had hoped to by now, but plans changed."

Neil gave her a curious look. Not wanting to pry, he remained silent, giving Seva room to say more if she felt comfortable.

"I was once betrothed to Prince Moorga of Cirros," Seva said distantly, picturing the dashing Cirran in her mind.

Neil turned to face her, intrigued by her story. "What happened?"

Seva took a long breath. "The quakes," she replied with a sadness to her voice. "Cirros was destroyed, and Moorga's family were all killed. Since my father had arranged the marriage to forge an alliance with Cirros, he canceled our engagement and promised me to another."

"What happened to—"

"Moorga?" Seva finished.

Neil nodded.

"Gone," she replied. "No one has seen or heard from him in years."

Neil considered this for a long moment then asked, "What about the other suitor?"

"Our wedding will be in the next rotation," Seva replied. "I am to marry Commander Rega of Fonn."

Her lack of enthusiasm made it clear how Seva felt on the matter.

"Well, I wish you both much happiness and many younglings." Neil smiled, gesturing to the swimmers.

As he turned his attention back to the game outside, Seva made a cursory glance over her shoulder at the two even-faced guards on their protection detail. The guards kept their distance, remaining ever vigilant.

"How is Kypa doing?" Seva asked without preamble. "My brother has not said much about his stay on Earth."

Neil continued watching the swimmers. "Happy to be home, I'm sure," Neil replied distractedly then ooh'd as one youngling nearly caught the adult.

"What do you know of the attempt on his life?"

The blunt question caught Neil off-guard. He rounded to face Seva with a concerned look. "You mean the attack in hyperspace?"

Seva nodded.

Neil shrugged. "I don't know much really. I don't think he does, either. Whoever attacked his ship caused it to crash on Earth. That's how we came to meet."

Seva considered this for a moment. "It saddens me that the rest of his crew did not survive, especially Luna," she said solemnly.

Neil gave her a curious look. "Luna?"

It was Seva's turn to act surprised. "Kypa did not mention her?"

Neil shook his head.

"Luna and Kypa were long-time colleagues and very close friends," she explained. "In fact, it was Luna who introduced my brother to Maya."

"Is that right?" Neil muttered, wondering to himself why someone so significant had never come up in their conversations. Come to think of it, Kypa had not mentioned any of the crewmembers aboard the mothership destroyed in North Korea.

Maybe he was protecting them?

That seemed like the logical explanation. Kypa had held a lot of personal information close to his chest until after he had escaped Groom Lake, including his royal lineage.

Turning his thoughts to the mothership, Neil recalled that macabre moment when Ava had reported how she had found corpses disemboweled by the obercai. At the time, Kypa had been apologetic for not warning her in advance. Apparently, it had slipped his mind. But, thinking back on it, Kypa had seemed to take the grisly news in stride. Instead of becoming grief-stricken over the loss of his crewmates, he had remained focused on guiding Ava to complete her mission.

Still, their loss, even after the mothership had been destroyed, was a subject Kypa refused to broach. Both Neil and Rose had offered their condolences, which Kypa had appreciated, but he had quickly steered the conversation elsewhere.

Perhaps he felt responsible for the death of his crew and could not bear the shame of discussing it openly, Neil considered. *Or perhaps it was something else altogether.*

He had to remind himself that Kypa was not human. Aiwans likely had an entirely different way of viewing death, and it was not his place to tell Kypa if or how he should grieve, so he let it go. Death and the afterlife—along with a million other questions—were topics Neil tucked in the back of his mind to discuss with Kypa at a later date.

"What can you tell me about Luna?"

Seva steered Neil away from the window, and they continued their chaperoned tour. The princess thought for a moment then replied, "Luna was also from the Realm of Cirros, but she was fortunate to survive. Pulled from the rubble, Luna had lost her entire family, like so many others. She was forced to evacuate and came to Eos with countless other refugees. My family took her in."

"How did she know Kypa?"

"As younglings, they trained together for many years at the Citadel in

Maeve. Both were prodigies. In fact, Luna was one of the few who could match wits with my brother. They became instant friends, inseparable for a time," Seva reminisced. "After graduation, Luna settled back in Cirros, and Kypa returned to the capital. Then the war intensified and the earthquakes started," she recounted somberly. "Their reunion was under most unfortunate circumstances."

Neil nodded thoughtfully.

"But that is in the past," Seva said, breaking the glum mood. "Kypa has returned to right a dreadful wrong. Repairing Aiwa's core is just the beginning."

"What do you mean?"

"Come and see for yourself."

Seva led Neil and their bodyguards into a nearby lift. They rode it down to the bottom floor. As they neared ground level, Neil sensed the guards growing increasingly anxious. Before the lift came to a stop, both guards positioned themselves in front of the door and readied their energy pikes.

The doors opened to a bustling lobby, filled with Aiwans differing in all shapes, sizes, and markings. As soon as Neil stepped out of the lift, a wave of silence fell over the crowd like falling dominoes.

Neil gulped and smiled uncomfortably.

Paying the crowd no mind, Seva led her guest to an adjacent transport tube with the guards positioning themselves between the princess and the crowd. They entered the empty transport and, as soon as the doors closed behind them, they departed the palace.

"That was awkward," Neil said lightly, relieved to be moving.

Seva appeared unfazed. "Please do not take it personally. Aiwans are naturally curious and suspicious of outsiders. We will not let any harm come to you."

"Kypa doesn't share your optimism."

"My brother does not know the people the way I do. You will be safe. Trust me."

Neil dropped the subject in favor of the awe-inspiring view of the city as they passed through Downtown Supra at high speed.

Seva pointed out several key locations, which included various government facilities, housing districts, and several centers for the performing arts. One clam-shaped amphitheater caught Neil's eye. His HUD told him it was a symphony center. It reminded him of the Hollywood Bowl in Los Angeles and sparked a brief bout of homesickness.

The yearning quickly passed as Neil thought of the congestion and overpopulation back on Earth. Supra was larger than New York City but did not suffer from the effects of a major metropolis filled to capacity. One thing Neil noticed right from the start was Supra's lack of consumerism. The city was devoid of annoying billboards and advertisements pushing citizens to buy crap they did not need. Likewise, there were no shops or restaurants, either. There was no need. Aiwans were simplistic and did not use currency. They did not believe in the accumulation of wealth, nor did they rely on the government to provide for their basic needs.

"Every citizen works for the betterment of themselves, their family, and society as a whole," Seva explained. "At least, that is how it should be."

When they reached what appeared to be the outskirts of the city, their transport entered a noticeably darker and more dilapidated section of Supra. Gone were the dazzling lights and beautifully-designed structures. Instead, this area consisted of tenement housing and rudimentary structures that were clearly intended to be temporary.

A shanty town? Neil thought. He looked to Seva for an explanation. His confusion was matched by her pained expression.

Seva gestured outside. "Behold the forgotten refugees of Cirros."

17

AMBUSH

Planet Aiwa
Realm of Eos

As Neil and Princess Seva toured the capital from within, the Reaper crew viewed it from above. Unaware of how traffic flowed, Ava opted to let Reggie fly at the outset. Standing beside Kypa and Toma, she watched as they climbed above the city and picked up speed before merging smoothly into the main commuter lanes.

Allowing Reggie to fly afforded Ava the opportunity to enjoy the splendor of Supra's skyline. Kypa and his son proudly pointed out several of the capital's main attractions, but one sight stood out from all the others: the central core.

At first glance, Ava thought it was some kind of gargantuan, glow-in-the-dark octopus attacking the city. Upon closer inspection, she realized this power station was not organic at all. It was mechanical, but the strange engineering design left her scratching her head.

The central core consisted of a round base resting on the ocean floor with a dozen long and lanky armatures extending upward, twenty stories in height. Always in motion, these pliable armatures waved effortlessly to the rhythm of the ocean current, similar to the arms and tentacles of one of Earth's rarest cephalopods, the bigfin squid.

Acting as control rods, the armatures harnessed energy from the crystal-powered reactor core buried deep underground. The energy traveled up from the reactor, along each of the twelve armatures, and out through dish-shaped emitters on the ends. Together, their combined output formed a dazzling lattice of golden beams high overhead that expanded over the city to create an impenetrable protective dome.

"So, each of the capital cities draws from the same reactor to power their shields?"

"Correct," Kypa replied. "Sharing energy is a more efficient use of our limited supply of crystals."

"Aren't you afraid the harvesters will cut those lines?"

"It is a danger," he admitted, "but the power conduits are buried deep underground with seismic sensors in place to warn us if there is an attack or unsanctioned drilling."

Ava frowned, thinking of home and how Russia attacked Ukraine. Of the many atrocities Russia committed, it tried choking the supply of energy to Europe to prevent NATO from interfering with its invasion. Europe was dependent on Russian gas the same way the outlying realms depended on Eos. It was not hard to imagine Fonn, Dohrm, and Maeve being unsettled by this arrangement.

"You said rolling blackouts are being used to conserve energy," Ava commented. "How do the other realms feel about that?"

"It is a tenuous subject," Kypa admitted. "They understand the necessity. We are at war, after all. But, like pups fighting for their mother's milk, no one wants to be left out."

"Well, hopefully the crystals we brought will do some good." Ava said, trying not to sound glum.

"They will. It buys us time to protect our people and lift the blackouts. And if the Reaper proves successful in rebuilding Cirros, we can repair the planet core and safely resume our own harvesting."

"But it's not a long-term solution to your energy problem."

"True, but perhaps yesterday's defeat will deter Krunig from ever returning. If we can move past this war, Aiwa can pursue maximizing the crystals we have and, if need be, broker a deal with Earth."

Again, the impossible prospect of trying to defend two worlds with one ship made Ava's stomach clinch. If Grawn Krunig and the other harvesters were smart, they would figure this out and coordinate a two-pronged attack on Earth and Aiwa.

That's what I'd do, she thought to herself.

Kypa did not have to read Ava's mind to know what she was thinking. He had reached the same conclusion, as did Commodore Boa, no doubt. The Reaper was the key to victory, at least for the foreseeable future. Kypa had no regrets about gifting the spacecraft to Ava, even after they had discovered the Maxixe Magnetarite. The powerful crystal belonged to Earth or, more precisely, to Ava, since she had found it in international waters. What troubled Kypa was the fact that she might have to choose between Earth and Aiwa at some point. This possibility remained unspoken, but like so many other things between Ava and Kypa, they were both thinking it.

Ava decided to change the subject. "Do we need to adjust our shields to exit the capital?"

"No, Captain," Kypa answered. "That is only necessary to keep unwanted vessels out of the capital. Ships are free to exit at will."

Ava nodded and took her seat in the pilot's chair. Kypa and Toma followed suit. Moments later, the Reaper departed the traffic lane, and Reggie banked to starboard. When they reached the shield, they passed through without incident and headed out toward the open sea.

Before long, the bright lights of the big city faded until the Reaper was cast in darkness. Taking the initiative, Reggie activated the exterior running lights and adjusted the sensors in the cockpit windows to enhance visibility. The crew could now see unhindered for miles in all directions.

"Thanks, Reggie," Ava said without thinking. She caught herself afterward, realizing this was the second time the ship's computer had the forethought to make a kind gesture on her behalf. Ava could not help but wonder if it was coincidence or something more. The idea of an artificial intelligence achieving sentience was a concept even a sci-fi-challenged person, such as herself, had contemplated.

Or perhaps she read your thoughts?

Ava considered this angle. It was one thing to give mental commands to Reggie to pilot the ship but having Ava's inner thoughts acted upon by an AI without her permission felt like a violation in the worst way.

But the nano-suit was supposed to prevent that, right?

"Kypa, how is it that my nano-suit can prevent Aiwans from using telepathy to read my thoughts, but Reggie can?"

Kypa rotated in his seat to face Ava. "Good question. The answer is simple; organic telepaths such as us"—he gestured to Toma—"can use their abilities to communicate freely with other telepaths or forcefully penetrate the minds of others to read and potentially manipulate their thoughts. Artificial intelligence is programmed to detect the crew's brainwaves and respond only to thoughts related to the ship's functions."

Ava searched her memory, wondering if her random thoughts had somehow been interpreted as commands by Reggie.

Kypa eyed her quizzically. "Is something wrong, Captain?"

In theory, based on the information Kypa had shared with her back at Groom Lake, Ava knew the answer to her next question but asked it, anyway. "Can Reggie plant ideas in our heads?"

The question took Kypa by surprise. His brow furrowed with concern. "No, Captain. That would require the ship's computer to achieve self-awareness."

"Then, what about me?" she considered. "Earlier, I was able to reach out to you with my mind. No human has ever done that, as far as I know. Is it possible your telepathic connection with me has somehow unlocked my brain?"

Kypa contemplated Ava's interesting hypothesis.

"I mean, what if my random thoughts are vulnerable now, and Reggie is receiving them without my knowledge?" To herself, Ava feared her brain might be like a laptop connected to the internet through an insecure Wi-Fi network. Anyone with the know-how might be able to hack into her thoughts.

Kypa tried to ease her concerns. "I am sure that is not the case," he soothed. "Your new telepathic ability is a fascinating development, and I will research it further, if you like."

"Please do." Ava laughed at herself for feeling so paranoid. "Sorry, it's just—"

She was interrupted by a warning alarm. Ava darted her eyes to the HUD. A large object was closing in fast on an intercept course. Instinctively, she thrust her hands and feet into the four orbs to assume manual control of the Reaper.

"Reggie, identify the inbound bogie!"

On the HUD appeared a massive eel-like creature slithering through the water toward them at a high rate of speed. The creature's fierce blue eyes glowed in the dark, and luminescent markings glimmered from head to tail.

"Warning: zemindar detected," Reggie said with calm urgency. "Recommend evasive maneuvers."

"Kypa?" Ava asked.

"Surface immediately!" Kypa blurted, fearing it was already too late. "Zemindar's feed off raw energy and can cripple a ship with an electromagnetic pulse. Our only hope is to get airborne."

That was all Ava needed to hear. "Hang on!"

She throttled up the impulse engines and pointed the nose skyward. The Reaper climbed, picking up speed and sending schools of exotic fish scattering in all directions to get out of the way. Checking the HUD, Ava eyed the zemindar and shook her head at the creature's closure rate. The cunning sea serpent was insanely fast and had adjusted course to cut them off before they reached the surface.

Chewing on her bottom lip, Ava could see the surface fast approaching but not fast enough. The zemindar was gaining on them. She pushed the Reaper to full impulse power, but it only made a slight difference. With the Reaper's nacelles retracted, the ship was much slower underwater than in air or space. The Reaper had no place to hide, and there were no obstacles in the predator's path to hinder its pursuit. For a second, Ava considered veering to port to buy some time then thought against it. Her high school math teacher's lesson on geodesics echoed in her head.

The shortest path between two points is a straight line, he had taught. *Learn it, you might need it someday.*

Ava inwardly cursed the man for being right. This was one math lesson that might actually save her life … or end it.

Outside the ship, the zemindar prepared to strike. Its glowing body markings increased in luminosity as it prepared to release its electromagnetic pulse.

Kypa saw this on his readout a split-second before an alarm sounded. There was no time to explain the danger to Ava. The Reaper approached the water's surface as the serpent opened its massive jaws to release its crippling emission.

Above the ocean surface, all was serene. Two of Aiwa's closest moons shone brightly in the clear midnight sky, and their moonlight glistened off the calm sea. A flock of seabirds slept on the crestless waves, oblivious to the approaching chaos.

Without warning, the Reaper suddenly breached the surface. It shot out of the water like a cannon, sending bird feathers in all directions.

The zemindar followed close behind, its gigantic head emerging above the water line. Jaws open, the serpent released its EMP into the air, but it had little effect on the Reaper. With no water to close the circuit, the pulse dissipated and proved ineffective against the Reaper's shields. Still, the zemindar would not be denied. From out of its gaping mouth shot an enormous pink tongue aimed at the Reaper.

Ava and the crew were flung forward in their seats by a sudden jolt. Checking the HUD, she blinked with surprise. The zemindar had latched on to the Reaper's stern with its sticky tongue and was attempting to reel the ship into its gullet.

"This is *not* how I thought today was going to go," Ava grumbled to herself.

Even so, she did not hesitate. Ava assessed the situation in a microsecond and made her decision. She extended the nacelles and throttled up in an attempt to gain speed and altitude.

The nacelles whined in protest.

You wanna a ride? Ava's lip twitched. *I'll give you a ride!*

Meanwhile, thousands of tiny receptors on the surface of the zemindar's tongue began absorbing energy from the Reaper, causing the lights and instruments in the cockpit to flicker.

The Reaper shuddered under the strain to stay airborne. Similar to an arm-wrestling match between equal opponents, predator and prey fought a battle of brute strength. At first, neither the Reaper nor the zemindar appeared to have the upper hand. Back and forth they struggled in a tug-of-war match to the death. The Reaper pushed desperately to gain altitude, while the zemindar relied on the sheer weight of gravity to prevent its meal from escaping.

Something had to give as the Reaper began to inexplicably lose power.

"Reggie, what's happening?" Ava asked, fighting the flight controls.

"The zemindar is absorbing our energy," Reggie reported. "At this rate, the ship will be pulled under in one minute, thirty-seven seconds."

Ava debated whether or not to kill the beast, if that was even possible. She hated taking its life. After all, the zemindar was only acting on its nature, but better it should perish than them, she concluded.

Ava targeted the serpent with the Reaper's rear disrupters.

"No!" Kypa yelled, catching her just in time. "Captain, wait! Our weapons are useless against the zemindar. It will only absorb the energy and grow stronger. We have to shut off the engines."

"Are you crazy?"

Kypa was asking himself that same question. His plan was unorthodox, but sound ... in theory.

"Trust me," he implored.

Despite Ava's misgivings, there was no time to argue. Kypa had not let her down yet, and she trusted his instincts.

"Okay, but whatever you're going to do, you better do it fast."

"We will only have one or two seconds at most. As soon as you shut off the engines, wait for the zemindar to relax its grip, then power up and make a short jump to sub-light speed."

She grinned at his gutsy call. "Okay, Reggie, you with me?"

"Course plotted, Captain. Awaiting your orders."

"Standby," Ava commanded. "Kypa, count us down."

Kypa's eyes bounced from one side of the HUD to the other as he worked on one final task while keeping a watchful eye on the beast. He finished in the nick of time and called out, "On my mark ... Three ... Two ... One—now!"

Ava cut the power just as Kypa dropped twin thermite canisters from the Reaper's underbelly. Both charges fell toward the creature's gaping mouth and detonated mid-air, creating two massive, sonic blasts.

The purpose of the thermite explosions was three-fold. First, the concussive blasts stunned the zemindar, causing it to recoil in defense with an ear-splitting wail. Second, with the Reaper powered down, there was nothing keeping the sea monster aloft. It began falling back to the ocean and pulling the Reaper down with it. Lastly, in that brief window of opportunity when the Reaper was powerless, the creature naturally turned its attention away from the dormant spacecraft to the new and greater surges of energy generated by the thermite explosions. This caused the zemindar to relax its hold on the Reaper before disappearing under the water.

Reggie took it from there. Without wasting a second, the Reaper made a quick jump to sub-light speed, pulling them free of the zemindar and into high orbit above Aiwa. It happened so fast that Ava needed a second to gather her wits.

"Reggie, we good?" she asked, now gazing at the blackness of space amongst a sea of stars.

"Yes, Captain. All systems operational," Reggie replied.

Toma turned around in his seat to face Ava. "Can we do that again?" he asked excitedly.

Ava chuckled. "Let's not and say we did."

Incredulous, she asked Kypa, "What possessed you to try that?"

Kypa rotated to face her and dipped his chin, appreciative of the compliment. "Zemindars are very dangerous and have insatiable appetites," he replied. "Normally, we would power down in a safe place and wait for the creature to pass, but it got the jump on us today. To be honest, I did not think my plan would work, but we had little choice."

Ava agreed. "Well, we're alive, and that's all that matters. Toma, your father has a very good habit of beating the odds," she praised. "You should be proud."

Father and son exchanged grins with Toma patting his father's shoulder. Kypa winked at Ava then rotated his seat to face forward.

Ava resituated. "Okay, crew, break's over," she announced. "Reggie, reset our course to Cirros. Time to get back to work."

18

MISSING PERSON

Planet Earth
Groom Lake, Nevada

Colonel Marlana Nunez stood at the kitchen counter, dunking a bag of Earl Grey into her steaming mug, when Technical Sergeant Bert Drummond entered the breakroom. She turned and smiled as he gave her a courteous wave from across the room.

"Good morning, ma'am."

"Hey, Bert," Nunez replied, tossing her trash in the nearby receptacle. "Shift change over?"

"Yes, ma'am. I am outta here," he said, sounding exhausted after a twelve-hour shift. Drummond retrieved his lunch bag from the refrigerator then moved to the water cooler to refill his bottle before heading back to base housing.

Marlana headed for the door. Before leaving, however, she stopped beside Drummond and leaned in. "So, get this. Two cannibals are eating a clown. One cannibal looks at the other and asks, *Does this taste funny to you?*"

A short laugh escaped Drummond before he could stop himself.

"Ha! Gotcha!" Nunez snickered in triumph.

Drummond shook his head as he screwed the cap back on his bottle. "With all due respect, ma'am, you've hit a new low."

"Ah, but it made you laugh," Nunez needled.

"Yeah, well, right now, I'm punch-drunk coming off three straight midnight shifts," Drummond countered. "I can't be held responsible for my actions."

"You saying I shouldn't quit my day job, Bert?"

Drummond shrugged with a *don't-ask, don't-tell* look on his face.

"Hey …" Nunez complained, feigning indignation. She then bobbed her head in the direction of the holding cells down the hall that were currently occupied by General Garza and former CIA Director Gary Sizemore. "Don't forget, I've court-martialed people for less."

Drummond knew she was kidding, but the reference to their VIP prisoners brought the conversation back to business at hand.

"Speaking of which," he said, "I meant to tell you Langley just sent out a new person to oversee the interrogation. Jessica Aguri is her name."

That name rang a bell, but Nunez could not place it. "Thanks, Bert. I'll take care of it. Enjoy your time off."

"Yes, ma'am. Call me if you need anything."

"Roger that," she replied, blowing on her tea.

They walked out together, going in opposite directions.

As Drummond made his way down the hall, Nunez called to him, "Sleep tight, Sarge. Don't let the clown-eating cannibals bite."

Drummond kept walking and gave her a thumbs-down.

Marlana *hmphed.* "No respect," she mumbled a Rodney Dangerfield impression.

Two minutes later, Marlana was back at her desk. She checked her calendar. A debrief with the Army Investigative Service, FBI, and CIA was scheduled this morning to bring her up to speed on the latest developments from Garza and Sizemore. Then there was Dr. Persons. He was back at work again, trying to reverse engineer the escape pod Kypa had left behind. She made a mental note to stop down by Hangar 17 to check on him.

The phone rang. Nunez recognized the Atlanta area code and smiled.

"Nunez," she answered.

"Colonel Marlana Nunez?"

Marlana's brow furrowed as she straightened in her seat. She expected Rose, but did not recognize the voice. It was a female, and it sounded like she was crying.

"Yes, this is Colonel Nunez. Who is this?"

"My name is Becky Anderson." The caller made an effort to compose herself. "I'm Rose Landry's daughter."

Nunez quickly searched her memory. "Becky, yes, your mom mentioned you. Is everything okay?" She could not tell if the girl was crying or simply had a cold.

"Have you talked to my mom lately?"

"A few days ago," Nunez answered. "Why?"

"We think something's happened to her." Becky's voice trembled. "We haven't heard from her since Monday."

One of Marlana's strengths was her ability to use levity to put others at ease, even though her politically-incorrect sense of humor tended to have more of a shock and awe effect than anything else. She knew when to turn it off and get serious. This was one of those times.

Colonel Nunez had only known Rose Landry for a short while, but one thing was certain about her friend—family came first. Rose's family was tight, and she would never forget to check in or go off-grid without anyone knowing her whereabouts.

Marlana grabbed a nearby pen and notepad. "Does Rose have any medical issues? Have you checked the hospitals?"

"Not that I know of," Becky replied. "We did call the hospitals, but nothing."

"What about the police?" Marlana asked with calm resolve.

"They're here now," Becky whispered, trying to hold it together. She paused to blow her nose. "Sorry."

"No need to apologize. Tell me how I can help."

"It doesn't look like a robbery," Becky said. "All of Mom's belongings are here, including her car, but her handbag and cell phone are missing. They've tried pinging it, but no luck."

"Credit cards?"

"No, they haven't been used. The police think she could have been abducted."

Nunez's face flushed with anger. *Who would do such a thing, and to Rose of all people?*

Dr. Rose Landry was a rare breed. Not only was she a brilliant scientist in her field, but she epitomized the term "servant leader." People naturally gravitated toward Rose because of her innate ability to uplift others with a gentle heart and kind words. Rose was special, and people would move mountains to follow her.

Nunez's mind instinctively jumped to a dark place, picturing a worst-case scenario. But hearing Becky cry on the other end of the line forced the colonel to push her own feelings of worry and anger aside to focus on finding Rose.

"Everything's going to be all right," she assured Becky. "We'll find your mom, okay?"

Becky struggled to speak. "There's more."

"What do you mean?"

"The power was out," Becky spoke choppily between sobs. "I mean, someone turned off the breakers in the kitchen."

Nunez's eyes darted back and forth, processing that information. It struck her the same as it had Becky—not good.

"When was the last time you spoke to her?"

"Monday night," Becky answered. "She called me on her drive home from work."

"Have the police talked to her co-workers?"

"Uh-huh."

"Good. Maybe that'll …" Nunez trailed off as she thought back to her video conference with Rose three days prior. Their meeting had been interrupted by Rose's secretary, something about an unscheduled visitor who had urgent business with Rose, but as hard as Nunez tried, she could not recall any specifics.

"Colonel, you there?"

Nunez snapped back to the present. "Yeah, sorry. I was just thinking back to my last conversation with your mom. Listen, give the police my name and number. I'd be happy to help in any way I can."

"Okay." Becky sniffled.

"Don't worry; we'll find her."

As soon as Nunez hung up, she was out the door and down the hall to her boss's office.

Brigadier General William "Buster" Dukes was sipping his coffee when his deputy barged into his office unannounced. He nearly dumped the coffee into his lap.

"Dammit, Nunez," the general cursed, trying to find a clear spot on his desk to set down his dripping mug.

"Sorry, sir." Nunez pulled some tissues from a nearby box and handed them to him. Dukes snatched them out of her hand with a scowl.

"Do you know why I'm such a good boss, Colonel?" Dukes asked as he wiped the bottom of his mug.

Nunez gave him a puzzled look. "I don't know, sir," she said thoughtfully. "Is it your stimulating staff meetings?"

Normally, Dukes was excellent at deflecting her unfiltered remarks, but he was in no mood to be trifled with today. Everyone from animal rights activists to bioethics groups were demanding access to his not-so-secret-anymore facility.

"No, I'm a good boss because I don't throw you in a cell every time you barge into my office unannounced. Now, what is it this time?"

"It's Dr. Landry, sir. She's gone missing."

Dukes stopped what he was doing. "Missing?"

"Uh-huh. The police are at her house right now. Her daughter says they haven't heard from Rose in three days."

"That doesn't sound like Dr. Landry."

"Not at all," Nunez agreed, taking a seat uninvited. "They think she might've been abducted. All of Rose's belongings are still at the house."

Dukes tossed the coffee-soaked tissues in the trash. Leaning back in his chair, he rubbed his chin as he considered this information. The general was a thoughtful yet decisive man who was not prone to wild speculation. Neither was Nunez. This was uncharacteristic behavior for her. She was always even-keeled and not one to be easily rattled, but this incident had clearly struck a nerve.

"What do you think happened?"

Nunez shrugged. In all honesty, she hadn't the faintest clue what could have happened to Dr. Landry. There was no evidence of a crime. Perhaps it was nothing. Maybe Rose ran off with a man to some tropical island. Lord knew she deserved it, but Nunez's gut told her otherwise. Disappearing without telling her family was out of character. Something bad had happened; Nunez felt it.

A knock on the door drew her attention from her reflection. Before she could share her thoughts with her boss, Dukes' civilian admin assistant poked her head inside his office.

"Sorry to interrupt, sir. There's an Agent Aguri from CIA here to see you."

"Thanks, Tracee. Send her in."

To Nunez, he said, "Maybe she should hear this, too?"

Nunez nodded.

They stood as Jessica entered the room. She wore a dark gray pantsuit and off-white blouse with a pair of loafers, a far cry from her usual GCRM attire back in Sanhe. Tracee closed the door behind her.

"Good morning, sir," Jessica greeted, offering a handshake. "Agent Aguri, CIA. I've been sent to oversee the interrogations of General Garza and Director Sizemore … former director, that is." She smiled.

"Nice to meet you, Agent Aguri." Dukes shook her hand. "Welcome to Groom Lake."

Dukes towered over Jessica. His giant hand practically swallowed hers up, making for an awkward exchange. Jessica played it off.

"Thank you, sir. It's nice to meet you."

Dukes gestured to Marlana. "This is my executive officer, Colonel Nunez."

Nunez smiled politely as they shook hands. She then changed seats and gestured for Jessica to join them.

"Your boss called ahead to let me know you were coming," Dukes explained. "Langley must surely be hopping these days."

Jessica raised her eyebrows at the understatement. "Indeed. Lots of changes happening."

"By the way, good work in Sanhe," Dukes said earnestly.

The remark was harmless but still gave Jessica pause. Having read the report on Operation Sundiver, she knew Dukes and Nunez were privy to her role in the top-secret mission, but it still made her cringe when others flippantly referenced her undercover operation with GCRM. Jessica nodded appreciatively.

"Have you talked to Garza or Sizemore yet?" Dukes inquired.

"Not yet. I've read your report and the statements from all of the witnesses. This has been a very messy affair," Jessica acknowledged. "Congratulations to both of you for uncovering their crimes."

"Actually, we have Prince Kypa and Captain Tan to thank for that. We were just acting on their intel."

"Still, it had to be a difficult call to make. Conspiracies this high up the chain of command create a challenging dilemma. You have to be damn sure you're right. What convinced you?"

"Neil and … Rose …" Nunez replied, trailing off at the mention of Rose, which sparked a memory of the last time Marlana had spoken to her friend.

Dukes and Aguri watched Nunez curiously, waiting for her to finish her thought. Finally, Dukes decided to continue.

"Doctors Landry and Garrett are reputable people, very down-to-earth," he explained. "Kypa confided in them, as well, and when their stories checked out, we acted on it."

"Hopefully, we can get Garza and Sizemore to talk more about Mathias's operations in Peru," Jessica said. "He has a large facility down there—"

"That's it!" Nunez blurted, snapping her fingers. She pointed to Dukes. "Peru. He said he was from Peru!"

Befuddled, Dukes asked, "Who's from Peru?"

"The man who met with Rose," Nunez answered. "We had a Zoom call a few days ago that was interrupted by Rose's secretary. She said a guy from Peru wanted to meet with Rose but didn't have an appointment."

Jessica looked from Dukes to Nunez in confusion. "I'm sorry. I'm not following."

"Dr. Landry ... Rose Landry," Nunez clarified. "You know she's missing, right?"

Jessica was taken aback. "No, I hadn't heard that."

"No one's seen or heard from her in three days. The police think she may have been abducted."

"Really?" A grave look of concern came over Jessica. "Have they filed a missing person's report?"

Nunez nodded. "The police are investigating, but it doesn't look good. All of her belongings were found at the house, including her car, but no trace of Rose."

Jessica reflected on this a moment then asked, "And what about this Peruvian man?"

Nunez shrugged. "I didn't get a look at him, but Rose's secretary said he had urgent business with Rose."

"Are you implying he may be connected to Mathias?"

"I don't know about that, but if the shoe fits ..." Nunez suggested.

"Assuming there's a connection," Dukes interjected, "what would Mathias want with Rose?"

"Good question," Nunez admitted. "I know they have a history. They used to work together, but that was a long time ago."

"In her statement, Rose mentioned running into Mathias here at Groom Lake," Jessica offered. "He even offered her a job, if I remember right. Rose turned him down. I got the impression she didn't care much for the guy."

"Rose knows all about Mathias's cloning experiments," Nunez added. "At least what was uncovered here."

"So does the CIA, FBI, and everyone else," Dukes pointed out. "Most of her knowledge was secondhand, anyway."

"I can't imagine Mathias would want to kill her," Nunez concluded. "He could've done that in her home. If he's behind Rose's disappearance, it would have to be for some other reason."

The trio considered this perspective, but after a few moments of silence, none of them could draw any rational conclusions.

"I'll report this and see what I can find out," Jessica said at last.

Even if it turned out to be just a home invasion, which she cringed to think, Jessica could not discard the fact that a key witness in an ongoing federal investigation had disappeared without a trace. And if Nunez was right about a Peruvian man coming to see her on the day of her disappearance, that was definitely a lead worth pursuing.

Changing the subject, Dukes asked, "What's next for our esteemed guests?"

Jessica gave him a noncommittal *we'll see* look.

Neither Garza nor Sizemore had been cooperative to this point. Being ex-CIA, Sizemore knew how the game was played. Hell, he practically wrote the book on the agency's interrogation methods. He could see through their tactics a mile away and was not about to self-incriminate or allow himself to be backed into a corner without certain written guarantees, starting with a full pardon.

On the other hand, General Garza's unwavering sense of duty was matched only by his altruistic ego. That gave interrogators something to work with. The key to gaining the general's cooperation was respectfully appealing to the former while casually stroking the latter. Yet, Garza was savvy in his own right. Calm and collected under pressure, he knew how to cover his six. The question was: who would cut a deal first? Jessica hoped recent intel on Mathias might get them talking.

"We'll definitely discuss Peru," Jessica assured Dukes. "Neither of them traveled to South America in recent months, at least not on our dime, but that's not to say they haven't been to Mathias's facility. We'll feel them out and see what they know."

"Are you going to ask them about Rose?"

"Only if they bring her up. We don't want to muddy the waters or offer up any free information, and we certainly don't want them using her as a bargaining chip. I'm going to leave Dr. Landry out of this for now until we know more about her disappearance."

Dukes and Nunez nodded agreement.

"Anything else for me?" Jessica asked.

Neither of them could think of anything more, so Jessica took her leave and shut the door behind her. Outside, a guard waited to escort her to the Area S4 side of Groom Lake.

Fifteen minutes later, Jessica arrived at Kypa's old quarters, which were now occupied by the disgraced general, Anthony Garza. A buzzer sounded as the door unlocked, and she entered. The guard remained in the hallway.

Inside the observation room, Jessica quickly got her lay of the land. Sound- and bulletproof glass separated her from Garza's new living space. She made a cursory glance in the general's direction then turned to the two sentries guarding the entrance to an antechamber leading into his room. Jessica approached and was greeted by the senior of the two Air Force security specialists. She lifted her ID badge for the guard to see.

"Good morning, ma'am," the guard said. He eyed her badge and nodded appreciatively.

"How's he doing?" she asked, thumbing in Garza's direction.

Airman Brixey replied, "Fine. No changes."

Jessica nodded, expecting as much. "He ask for anything?"

Brixey shook his head. "No, ma'am. Just a newspaper."

Turning to face Garza, Jessica peered through the thick glass and noted how far the general had fallen. Gone was Garza's crisp U.S. Army uniform with the four silver stars on the shoulder boards and rows of colorful chest ribbons that depicted his once-illustrious military career. Now the general wore a bright orange, prison jumpsuit with matching slippers. His high and tight haircut had begun to grow out and was complemented by a charcoal beard.

Despite his rugged appearance, Jessica did not get the impression Garza had let himself go. On the contrary, his jailers simply withheld the personal grooming care Garza was accustomed to. Federal custody had a way of doing that. Everything came at a price behind bars, and Garza's silence had earned him little favor, save for one luxury—a daily copy of the newspaper.

Garza was seated by himself at a metal table bolted to the floor, reading the latest news when Jessica arrived. The CIA had taken the lead on interrogating Garza and Sizemore while the Army Investigative Services and FBI conducted a joint investigation into their alleged crimes. This probe included the actions of the late director of the NSA, Nancy Drake.

The absence of agents in Garza's cell told Jessica they must be working on Sizemore at the moment. They had been going back and forth between the two prisoners since the arrests. Unfortunately, their efforts had proven unfruitful. Neither Garza nor Sizemore were cooperating, so it was still unclear just how deep the rabbit hole went regarding their treachery.

Jessica noted the fogged glass was activated. The general had no idea she was standing there, observing him, but he undoubtedly knew he was being watched at all times. Despite this, Garza casually went about reading his newspaper like it was a lazy Sunday morning.

Transcripts from previous interviews revealed he wholeheartedly believed his actions were in the best interest of the country. From Garza's point of view, he was just doing his duty, even if it meant violating a dozen laws and regulations. "Freedom's not free," he had been quoted saying.

"No, it's not," Jessica muttered to herself. "All right, let's do this." Jessica motioned to the guards that she was ready to go inside.

They opened the outer door and joined her inside the antechamber. As soon as it locked behind them, the inner door unlocked. Agent Aguri was first to enter.

Garza made a furtive glance in her direction then returned to his newspaper. Meanwhile, the guards took up stations at the interior door, remaining close enough to quickly subdue the prisoner, if needed.

"Good morning, General," Jessica said as she approached Garza. She sat diagonally from him and extended her hand. "My name is Agent Aguri, CIA."

Garza kept his eyes down, leaning over the paper. "One of Gary's kids?"

Jessica ignored the slight. "Not anymore," she replied evenly. "Will you answer a few questions for me?"

Silence followed as Garza continued reading. He then turned the page, straightened the newspaper, and continued. After a few seconds, Jessica could see she did not have the general's full attention. She gestured to the guards.

Airman Brixey stepped forward. "Excuse me, sir," he said politely as he removed the newspaper.

Garza exhaled heavily. He made no attempt to resist. Instead, he straightened in his seat and raised both hands as if to say, *Fine.*

"You can have it back after you've answered my questions," Jessica promised.

Garza folded his arms across this chest and stared back at her with a smug look. Then it dawned on him. "Aguri?" He searched his memory. "Jessica Aguri, right?"

Jessica pressed her lips together in a thin smile. "One in the same."

Garza looked Jessica up and down, as if reassessing his first impression of her. "You're a long way from Sanhe."

"So I've heard."

Garza nodded slowly. "You did good work over there. I'll give you that. Now, shall we cut to the chase?"

"Fair enough." Jessica reached into her bag and retrieved a document. She slid it across the table in front of Garza. "That's a presidential pardon. I—"

"Only have one?" Garza finished with a raised eyebrow. "Yeah, I know. Your colleagues already tried that tactic … unsuccessfully, I might add."

"If you don't want a pardon, you must want something. I can't imagine you'd want to stay down here anymore than Kypa had to."

Touché. Garza grinned.

Jessica pivoted to try a different approach. She reached back into her bag and retrieved several photos. She laid them out on the table. "These were taken yesterday at Mathias's research facility outside Lima, Peru. Anyone look familiar?"

Garza tried to appear uninterested. He kept his gaze fixed on Jessica.

Whether he was simply taking her measure or trying to demonstrate his superiority, Jessica did not know, nor did she care. She sat back, mirroring his body language by crossing her arms and met his gaze.

After a brief stare down, Garza's curiosity got the best of him. He slowly averted his eyes. Picking up the photos, Garza examined them one by one. He recognized many of the people in the photos, all were considered enemies of the United States and its allies.

Jessica noticed the general clenching his jaw. Of the dozens of images taken by surveillance drones, the ones laid out before Garza had been chosen for a reason—each included Edmund Mathias grinning broadly and chumming it up with Garza's adversaries.

"Quite a party," Jessica remarked.

Garza shrugged, feigning indifference.

"I'd say it's a who's who of America's enemies. FIS, MSS ... hell, even North Korea's Reconnaissance Bureau is buddying up to your pal, Edmund."

Garza took a controlled breath and calmly laid the photos down.

Jessica watched him keenly as the general began examining his fingernails.

"So, just like that, you turn a blind eye?"

"Not my fight anymore."

"I don't think you believe that for a second, sir. In fact, I think it's eating up your insides to see Mathias in bed with our enemies so soon after serving up you and Sizemore."

Garza did not respond.

"You know, I heard someone say, if given the choice between being a good soldier or a good person, choose to be a good person."

"Malarkey," Garza scoffed. "That way of thinking will get people killed, a lot of people ... good people," He trailed off.

"I agree," she seconded, relatively speaking. Jessica leaned forward. "You can still make a difference, General. We need to know what Mathias is doing in Peru."

"You already know what he's doing." Garza smiled slyly and tapped the photos.

Jessica shook her head. She needed to hear it from the horse's mouth. "What? Cloning?"

"Those investors you see in the photos want what I wanted," Garza replied snidely. "Force enhancement was the start, but I wanted more. I wanted a military force of cloned soldiers so I no longer had to sacrifice America's sons and daughters to fight other people's battles." Garza slid to the adjacent seat so he could face Jessica directly. Leaning in, he jabbed his finger repeatedly on the photos. "You made me out to be the villain when all I did was try to save lives, real lives," he said irritably. "Now you see our enemies lining up as Mathias's new buyers and, suddenly, it becomes a matter of national defense. A little hypocritical, don't you think?"

"I'm not here to judge you, sir. But I need you to tell me everything you know about Mathias's operations."

Garza *hmphed*. "You still don't get it, do you? You, the Russians, the Chinese … you're all missing the trees in the forest."

Jessica raised her eyebrow skeptically. "Enlighten me."

"For free?" Garza smirked. "Come now, Agent Aguri, even I'm not that stupid."

"I already offered you a full pardon."

"That's a start. I also want an honorable discharge with full retirement benefits, and an apology from the President."

How about a pony to go with it? Jessica scoffed inwardly. "*If* I can get you those things, what'll you give me in return?"

"I'll cooperate fully," he said, raising a three-fingered salute. "Scout's honor."

"You'll tell us everything about Mathias's force enhancement technology?"

Garza shook his head in disappointment. "Didn't you hear what I just said? Force enhancement and cloning is just his side hustle, I promise you."

"Meaning?"

"You need to think bigger, Agent Aguri. Much, much bigger. And it all starts in Peru."

19
DÉJÀ VU

Planet Earth
Satipo, Peru

Rose groaned in the darkness. Drifting in that transitional state of consciousness between wakefulness and sleep, her internal clock told her it was time to wake, but her body resisted. Her muscles felt lethargic and heavy, as if she was pinned to the mattress by an invisible force. Despite her desire to move, her arms and legs simply did not want to cooperate.

The warmth and comfort of the bed also begged her to stay put. Laying on her stomach, Rose ran her hand across the silk sheets. The smooth, luxurious texture of the fabric brought fond memories of weekend getaways with Joe. At first, Rose welcomed the thoughts, and then it registered that this was not her bed … and Joe had passed away five years ago.

Tipping toward consciousness, Rose urged herself to wake. She tried opening her eyes, but her eyelids felt as if they were glued shut.

Open your eyes now! she demanded of herself.

Vaguely alarmed, Rose could not understand why waking was so difficult. Then came the unsettling thought of being chemically incapacitated. This spurred Rose to try harder. She managed to open her eyes to slits, but a sliver of bright light peeking through the curtains made her wince. Stars danced behind her closed lids, and she felt the urge to drift back to sleep.

Rose, get up, dammit!

Growing agitated and more alert by the second, she managed to raise her hand up to shield her face as she opened her eyes once more. Rose blinked away the pain from the unwelcome light. Her body was no longer rebelling, but she felt groggy and weak.

She brushed her long, red hair out of her face and tried to locate a clock.

"It's almost noon," came a familiar and distinctly male voice in the darkness.

Jolted with adrenaline, Rose screamed as she sat up sharply and pulled the sheets up under her chin.

"Whoa, easy there," the stranger soothed. "You're safe." Seated in the far corner of the bedroom, the man flipped on a tall lamp beside him.

The light brought a sharp pain to Rose's already aching head. It took a moment before her eyes adjusted. She squinted with confusion.

"Edmund?"

"The one and only." Mathias smiled cheekily. "Sorry to frighten you, but you were sleeping so soundly that we didn't want to disturb you."

We? Rose thought.

That was when she glimpsed a second person in the room to her right— Mr. Renzo.

Rose stiffened in surprise then darted a glance toward the door, her only means of escape.

Renzo quelled any notion of fleeing. With his hands clasped in front of him, he calmly side-stepped once to his right, blocking the path to the door.

Recognizing a dangerous man when she saw one, Rose relented. Edmund was another matter.

She snapped her head back toward her former protégé. "What the hell is this?"

Edmund gestured to Rose with both hands outstretched. "You, Dr. Landry"—he then cupped his heart affectionately—"are my guest."

"*Your guest?*" Rose scoffed then flitted her eyes about the room. Judging by the high-end furnishings, she assumed she was in some plush hotel, probably one of Edmund's many properties. Rose turned back to him, incredulous. "You kidnapped me, you son of a bitch!"

Mathias cringed with feigned embarrassment. "You're right, you're right," he admitted. "That was an unfortunate ... misunderstanding."

"*Misunderstanding?*"

"I told Dr. Rojas to do whatever was necessary to convince you to come to Peru," Mathias explained calmly, trying to maintain civility. "I didn't mean it literally."

Peru? Suddenly, the fog began to clear as the events of the last few days came back to her.

"I am sorry, Rose," Edmund said earnestly. "Truly, I am, but I need you here."

"For what?" she snapped. "And quit calling me Rose. We're not friends."

Edmund frowned. "That hurts, Ro—Dr. Landry," he corrected dully. "Nevertheless, after I show you why I brought you here, you'll have a change of heart, I promise."

"Not likely," Rose remarked sourly.

Mathias smirked. Then he remembered Renzo. "Where are my manners? Dr. Landry, I want you to meet my most-trusted associate, Mr. Renzo."

Rose studied the stone-faced man, eyeing him up and down. His bowl-cut hairstyle and the Incan tattoos around his neck and wrists caught her attention.

Renzo politely tipped his chin in greeting. Rose said nothing.

Mathias slapped the top of his legs. "Well, then," he said, standing. "You should get cleaned up. Everything you need is in the bathroom. Clothes are hanging in the closet. My personal assistant, Ms. Diaz, took the liberty of selecting your wardrobe. I hope you approve. Mr. Renzo will wait outside. I'm sure you must be starving."

"This is crazy, Edmund. People are going to know I'm gone. My family will be looking for me."

Mathias waved dismissively. "Relax, as soon as you get cleaned up, you can let them know you're safe. I promise."

Now Rose looked utterly confused. *What kind of kidnapping is this?*

"I have your word?" she asked, suspicious.

"Of course. When you see why I brought you here, you'll be begging me to stay."

"I doubt that." Rose slowly shook her head, wondering how someone with so much potential could have fallen so far. "Your parents must be so disappointed."

"My parents?" Edmund laughed. "What is this, seventh grade? C'mon; don't be like that. Besides, we all have to carry our own water in hell, right?"

Rose scoffed at Edmund's cavalier attitude, convinced now more than ever that he was a complete psychopath.

As Edmund stood to open the curtains, she started to voice her opinion, but a sideways glance at Renzo made her rethink that move. His stern expression and the slight shake of the head served as a cold reminder not to test the limits of his patience, especially when it came to disrespecting his boss. Rose wisely held her tongue.

Meanwhile, golden rays of sunshine filled the room, with Amazonia visible in the distance.

Seeing the surprise on Rose's face, Edmund opened his arms wide and smiled. "Welcome to the jungle, Dr. Landry."

With that clever remark—one that he had been dying to use—Edmund started out of the room. "Now get cleaned up," he told his guest. "I've got an even bigger surprise waiting for you."

Mr. Renzo peeled away and followed his boss out of the room.

Rose waited until she heard the door close then climbed out of bed. Her muscles still felt heavy, but she moved quietly to the door and looked out the peephole. Not surprisingly, Renzo remained outside in the hall, keeping watch. The best she could tell, they were in a hotel or some sort of dormitory. Identical doors lined both sides of the hallway with an elevator and stairwell located at the far end.

Before turning away, Rose took a longer look at the tattoos on Renzo's neck. They were not Incan, as she had first thought. Upon closer inspection, the artwork was actually Chachapoyan, a hunter-gatherer tribe from the Andes Mountains. They were known as the "Warriors of the Clouds." Rose knew them from the movie, *Raiders of the Lost Ark*, her late-husband's favorite. Rumor had it that the fictional tribe depicted in the movie, the Hovitos, were based on the Chachapoyas. Rose doubted the real tribe ever hid a golden idol inside a secret temple filled with booby traps and bottomless pits, but it made for good entertainment.

Something else that caught her eye was the blow dart case slung on Mr. Renzo's back. It was not an odd fashion choice, she deduced, but rather a tool of the trade. Renzo was an assassin.

The realization sent a chill down her back.

She stared at the man with quiet intrigue for a long moment as he guarded the door with single-minded focus. Never did Renzo get distracted by checking his phone or pacing the area to pass the time. He stood in front of Rose's door, watching the hall and waiting.

What goes through the mind of a man like that? she wondered. *What compels such unwavering devotion?*

Realizing she was not going to find answers behind the door, Rose turned away and crossed the room to the window. That was when she passed a tall mirror and caught her reflection.

"What the …?" Rose stopped on a dime and noticed her attire—black silk pajamas with gold pinstripes.

Staring at herself in the mirror, she had no recollection of changing clothes or, for that matter, being changed by someone else. The latter thought gave her the willies, even more so if Edmund had seen her undressed.

Shaking that disturbing image out of her head, she moved to the window and took up a position behind the curtains. It was a beautiful, sunny day outside. Hardly a cloud was in the sky as a trio of blue and yellow macaws flew overhead.

Looking about, Rose discovered her room was on the second floor. Directly out her window was an immaculately manicured courtyard. Stone paths led to a large, rain curtain water fountain that drained into a shallow pool filled with bright orange Koi fish. Surrounding the fountain were marble benches situated under well-groomed shade trees.

Rose *hmphed*. Edmund had built her dream garden.

The courtyard had been unoccupied when a couple in lab coats appeared. They were talking incessantly, clearly excited about something. Rose waved her arms and slapped the thick glass, trying to get their attention, but it did not work. The passersby kept walking without so much as looking in her direction.

Discouraged, Rose turned her attention to the high wall surrounding the compound. Two armed sentries carrying MP4s appeared soon after, patrolling the perimeter.

"Jeez, you even have your own army," she grumbled.

On the opposite side of the wall was dense jungle in all directions. Amazonia.

Rose let out a heavy breath. Escaping in that direction was impossible. Even if she could get past the guards and the wall, her chances of surviving in the jungle with no supplies were slim to none. Despite her past field experience, she was no spring chicken. People disappeared in the jungle all the time. If disease did not kill her, the wildlife would.

Rose resituated several times to get a better view of her surroundings, even pressing her face against the glass, to no avail. It was a fixed window, so there was no way of opening it. Whether that was a security feature to keep "guests" in or simply a means to maximize energy efficiency was debatable. To Rose, it was a pain in the butt. She could not see much outside to judge the size of the compound or find any clues to reveal its purpose.

One thing was evident, Edmund had spared no expense in building this place. Everything about it was ultra-modern and high-tech, which was unusual for this part of the world. Whatever his deviant mind was scheming, it was clear

Mathias had invested a great deal of money to protect his interests from the outside world.

Turning away from the window, Rose noticed her handbag on the dresser. She quickly inventoried her belongings, noting everything was there, including her trusty tablet. All that was missing was her cell phone, which was disappointing. Rose removed her tablet and turned it on. To her surprise, it had been fully charged. She then opened the settings app and checked for a Wi-Fi signal.

"Figures." She frowned when no networks were detected.

Rose spent the next ten minutes searching her room for hidden cameras and listening devices. She scoured every nook and cranny but came up empty. If she was being watched, her captors had concealed their surveillance equipment well.

That was of little consolation. She was still being held against her will for reasons unknown.

And for how long? she wondered.

Until Rose understood what this was all about and why Mathias needed her so badly, the rest was just speculation. She could go mad trying to guess. Instead, she focused on what she could control, and that started with a shower.

Rose soon discovered that Edmund's affinity for nice things extended to the guest room's amenities. This facility—at least her guest suite—was five-star quality. The mini-fridge was stocked, the bathroom offered high-end toiletries, and on the nightstand was not one or two, but a bowl full of Andes Mints, her personal favorite.

Opening the closet, Rose's eyes widened at the rack of clothes hanging inside. Edmund's assistant had expensive taste, as well, along with a good eye for fashion. Next to her work clothes, which had been dry-cleaned and hung in a plastic garment bag, Rose had her choice of women's designer activewear, all in her size.

She went with a pair of brand-new olive-green pants and a loose-fitting, off-white, button-down blouse to match. The price tags were still on, probably to set her mind at ease that the clothes had not been previously worn by any other so-called guests. Altogether, the price of this outfit was more than she spent on groceries in three months.

Rose found undergarments in the dresser. She removed all of the tags with a small pair of safe scissors which, unfortunately, could not be used as a weapon, then climbed into the shower. It took her a moment to figure out how to work the multi-function shower panel, which boasted a rain shower and six body spray nozzles. It was bliss. She stood under the hot water for a good ten minutes, unmoving, and allowed the high-pressure shower heads to relax her back, shoulders, and neck. The steam also helped clear her head of the lingering effects of the sedative. Afterwards, she dressed and slid on a comfortable pair of walking shoes.

Feeling refreshed yet wary of what lay ahead, Rose left her handbag behind and made for the door.

As she reached for the door handle, Rose noticed her hand shaking. Clasping both hands together firmly, she took a deep breath then flexed her fingers several times to work the stress out.

Stay calm, Landry.

Opening the door, she found Renzo outside standing in the exact location where she saw him last.

"Everything to your liking, Doctor?" he asked politely.

Rose nodded uneasily.

"Good." Noticing her hands were empty, he gestured back inside the room. "If you don't mind, please bring your tablet device."

"Okay," Rose replied in a suspicious tone. "May I ask why?"

"You'll see," he replied simply.

Rose sighed and returned to her room to retrieve her device. She noted Renzo had toned-down his body language to be less intimidating. Still business-like, he sounded halfway cordial.

Stepping out of the room once again, Rose closed the door behind her and noticed the door had a keypad lock. "What's the code?" she asked.

"0516," Renzo replied. Rose's birthday. Another reminder that Edmund had done his homework. "This way."

Rose followed Renzo down a carpeted hallway and toward the elevator. The corridor was eerily quiet for this time of day.

Rose did not ask any questions or make small talk along the way. She used this time to examine her surroundings, noting each door they passed had a keypad lock on the outside, just like hers. Rose listened intently for the faint sound of a shower running or a hair dryer perhaps, but there were no signs of other occupants.

They reached the end of the hall, and Renzo called the elevator. As they waited in silence, staring patiently at the LED display above the elevator doors, Rose wanted to learn more about her escort.

"Are you Chachapoyan, by chance?"

Renzo acted impressed. "Top marks, Dr. Landry. How did you guess?"

"The tattoos."

"Ah," Renzo remarked, unabashed.

"So, you're native to this area," Rose inquired. "I'm curious how you came to work for a sleaze like Edmund."

"Careful, Doctor," Renzo warned.

Rose shrugged unapologetically. "Just making small talk," she said innocently.

Just then, the elevator arrived, and the doors opened. Rose entered first. As she passed Renzo, she swore she heard him say under his breath, "El silencio vale más que mil palabras." *My silence is worth a thousand words.*

The phrase stopped Rose in her tracks. Few understood the significance of the remark. Fewer still even cared. Renzo's statement was a street code shared by the so-called "lost children" of Peru. Whether he intended to reveal his secret or not, Renzo had identified himself as an orphan who had been abandoned by his parents, probably because they could not afford to raise him, and left to fend for himself on the streets.

Rose knew a part of Peruvian society had a callous view toward such outcasts, especially young boys. Rather than take pity on these discarded children and offer help, society wished them dead, especially the police. So, the children learned how to be invisible, only coming out for two things: food and drugs. Since begging openly was illegal, they were forced into prostitution or petty theft to fund their needs. If caught, they were thrown into police dungeons and beaten.

In this society, abandoned children had nothing and were given less. Their only object of value was their "truth," a mental diary they kept to themselves. None of the children ever talked about their truth with strangers. In fact, they would lie about their background to strangers to protect themselves. That was how the mantra, *My silence is worth a thousand words,* came about.

The fact Renzo muttered this phrase in Rose's presence was significant. Clearly, she was a stranger whom he did not trust.

So, why expose even a hint of his past?

It could have been a simple slip of the tongue, she reasoned, or even a cry for help, but those explanations seemed doubtful. Most likely, the way Renzo muttered it with disdain, directed at her—not to mention his chosen profession—signaled he was more than just a product of his environment. Rose got the sense Mr. Renzo was a sociopath, and a deadly one at that.

Renzo pressed the S2 button, and the elevator doors closed.

"Where are you taking me?" Rose asked as they started moving.

"You'll see," Renzo repeated, much to Rose's annoyance.

They rode in silence. Rose faced forward, focusing on watching the buttons on the control panel to track their descent. Moments later, they stopped, and the doors opened. For some reason, Rose felt a wave of relief as Renzo exited first. Maybe her instincts were warning her not to feel safe with him behind her.

She followed Renzo down an empty and sterile hallway lined with closed doors, each secured by biometric locks. It reminded her of Area S4 at Groom Lake.

Renzo led her to the far end of the corridor to a set of double doors. There, a retina scanner confirmed his identity and the doors unlocked.

"This way, Dr. Landry," he said, holding the door open.

Rose entered to find two labs, both sectioned-off by thick, glass partitions. Directly in front of her was a team of scientists in white lab coats, working on a large, round, mechanical object. Scaffolding had been erected around it to allow the researchers to conduct tests from all angles, using various equipment.

"What is that?" Rose asked curiously.

"An Aiwan Seeker," Renzo replied matter-of-factly.

"Aiwan? You mean it's alien tech?"

Renzo nodded as he closed the door behind them. "We recovered it off the coast of Baja, California. It was shot down by your friend, Captain Tan."

Rose clenched her jaw. The mention of Ava's name caused her cheeks to flush. Such information was highly classified, or supposed to be, she noted sourly. God only knew how Renzo had come into possession of it.

This served as a chilling reminder for Rose to take her own advice. Not too long ago, she had cautioned her colleague, Dr. Neil Garrett, to govern his passions around Garza and Sizemore. Mathias and his cronies were no different. They were powerful and dangerous men with deep pockets and far-reaching influence. Who knew what they were capable of?

"So, what do you want with me?" Rose asked point-blank. "I don't know anything about alien tech. I can barely change a flat tire."

Renzo cracked a mirthless smile. "Of course not, Doctor. We have something else in mind for you."

He led Rose to the left, where she could see a second room had been partitioned off from the lab with the Seeker. The room's glass windows were currently fogged to prevent passersby from seeing inside. Renzo stepped up to a control unit located on the wall and deactivated the privacy glass.

Rose turned and immediately spotted Edmund standing inside, but when she saw who he was talking to, her mouth dropped.

Kypa?

Rose blinked several times, fearing that her mind was either playing tricks on her or she was having lingering effects from the drug Edmund had used to sedate her. Either way, she could not believe she was really seeing an Aiwan here, of all places.

Still, something was amiss. Rose narrowed her eyes as she cautiously approached the glass. She homed in on the distinct markings on the Aiwan's head then realized the entire body structure looked different than she remembered. This Aiwan appeared slightly shorter with less muscle tone than Kypa.

Rose turned sharply to Renzo, confused and fearful. "That's not Kypa."

"Very observant, Dr. Landry. Again, top marks."

"A clone? Tell me you didn't clone him."

"No, not a clone," Renzo confirmed. He gestured to the Aiwan. "As you can see, Dr. Landry, Prince Kypa was not the only survivor from the crash in North Korea."

20

THE RUINS

Planet Aiwa

Twelve moons orbited the massive ringed world of Aiwa. The smallest and most distant of these natural satellites was a lifeless rock known as Pria-12. This moon resided on the outer fringes of Aiwa's gravitational field. And being so isolated, it also provided perfect concealment for those who were anxious to avoid drawing the attention of Aiwa's planetary defense force. The bounty hunters, Smythe and Gort, fit that bill.

Piloting their customized freighter, they exited hyperspace on the dark side of Pria-12. Adept at avoiding detection, they arrived without triggering Aiwa's deep space scanners. Yet, this bold tactic only bought them a short reprieve from prying eyes.

To slingshot past Aiwa's defenses and reach the planet's surface undetected, they needed a lot more moxie than usual. What they were about to attempt pushed the boundaries of their appetite for risk, but they had little choice. Krunig was not paying them by the hour. Their marker awaited on Aiwa, and they had never failed to deliver on a job.

Still, bounty hunters did not survive long in this business by cutting corners and making foolish mistakes. Smythe and Gort attributed their longevity to many factors, luck being the least of these. However, the success of this particular gambit required all the luck they could muster.

Smythe sat in the cockpit, making his calculations for their assault on Aiwa. If his numbers were off even a fraction, they were done. They would either jump too short and emerge directly in front of Aiwa's orbiting fleet or jump too far and crash into the planet. Either way, their day would be over before it started. Scratch two bounty hunters.

Jumping into that sweet spot behind Aiwa's defenses without crashing into the planet was the trick. Smythe triple-checked his calculations to be extra sure. Satisfied, he fed the coordinates into the ship's navigational computer.

He and his partner, Gort, were flying a twin-engine, light freighter. A faster, more agile spacecraft would have been better suited for what they were about to attempt but, in the end, this job required storage space over speed. A newer spacecraft would have also been better; this particular freighter was older than the two of them combined. She was not going to win any beauty contests, but at least she got the job done. It would be up to Smythe and Gort's ingenuity to see that they did not get caught.

"Here we go," Smythe said as soon as the computer signaled its readiness.

Seated next to him in the copilot's seat, Gort replied, "Ready, boss."

The freighter moved out of the moon's shadow and into open space. It was only exposed for a few seconds before making the jump to lightspeed. The vessel shot forward, rocketing past Aiwa's orbiting defenses and through its upper atmosphere, then it reappeared suddenly over a vast, sandy plain in one of Aiwa's desert regions.

Alive and cruising at a low altitude, Gort grinned with satisfaction. His partner had once again demonstrated his piloting proficiency by thwarting the Aiwan defenses.

"Nice work, boss."

"We're not safe yet," Smythe replied. Cautious of pursuers, he turned to Gort. "Any signs of—"

His inquiry was abruptly cut off as the freighter rocked violently, throwing the bounty hunters forward in their seats. Warning alarms erupted throughout the cockpit. Smythe and Gort righted themselves then quickly went to work diagnosing the situation.

Fighting to regain control of the ship, Smythe figured his stealthy maneuver had not been so sneaky after all. Assuming the Aiwans were onto them, the bounty hunter's mind immediately jumped to evasion mode. But if they hoped to escape their attacker, he needed the flight controls restored first.

"The stick is too heavy," he grunted. "It won't respond."

Gort's eyes flashed at what he was seeing on his sensors. "I think I know why," he said in disbelief.

Suddenly, an ear-splitting screech outside the ship gave them both pause. Smythe and Gort turned to one another with the same look of incredulity. This was not an Aiwan attack.

The main computer could not identify the species of the winged predator clamped onto their ship, but neither bounty hunter cared naming it at the moment. With its talons sunk into the ship's hull, the massive bird of prey had no intention of letting its meal get away.

"This is a first," Gort wise-cracked, although the edge in his voice betrayed his appearance of calm.

Smythe ignored the quip. "Divert everything to shields," he instructed coolly. "I'm going to try shaking it loose with an energy spike."

Gort was on it, agreeing with his partner's logic. "Go now."

On his dash, Smythe slid his index finger up the control panel to modulate the shields to maximum output. Outside, the predator let out an agonizing screech, and then the freighter shook violently back and forth. Clutching their seats, the bounty hunters held on for dear life. Seconds later, they found themselves toppling out of control toward the surface.

"We're free," Smythe said coolly. Ignoring the horizon spinning in circles out the forward viewport, he called to Gort, "Maximum thrusters!"

Gort channeled his focus and diverted power, as instructed. As soon as the energy transfer was complete, the starboard engine sputtered to life while the portside engine failed to ignite. A warning alarm confirmed the propulsion failure while the ship's computer repeated, "Pull up," as they dropped at terminal velocity. Smythe was too busy manipulating the flight controls to silence either of the annoying sounds.

Flying with one engine out tested the bounty hunter's piloting skills, but Smythe compensated with expert precision. The freighter leveled-off in the nick of time, avoiding impact so close to the surface that it kicked up a cloud of dust in its wake. Gaining altitude, Smythe silenced the alarms and calm was restored inside the cockpit.

"We clear?" Smythe asked, still grappling with the sluggish controls.

"Scopes are negative," Gort answered with relief.

"The stick is still too heavy," Smythe remarked. "I need to set her down."

This setback was unfortunate, but neither bounty hunter wasted energy complaining about what was out of their control. Focusing on a solution rather than blaming their circumstances was what made their partnership so effective.

On the edge of the desert plains, the bounty hunters came to a lattice-structured mountain range filled with numerous ridges and salt domes. Smythe located a large cave cut into the mountainside.

"That looks like a good place to hole-up and make repairs." Smythe pointed. "Can we fit?"

Gort quickly scanned the opening. "Won't be much headroom, but we should fit. I'm not reading any life signs," he added for good measure.

Smythe acknowledged with a grunt. Having now confirmed the stories of Aiwa's untamed environment firsthand, he figured that was enough excitement for one day.

Smythe slowed the crippled freighter, lowered the landing struts, and steered into the darkened cave. Scraping the walls a couple times in the process, he managed to pilot the ship safely into the shadows. When he went to land, the freighter dropped awkwardly on the portside. A pair of maneuvering thrusters had been damaged in the attack, causing the freighter to set down hard on the rock floor. The bounty hunter winced at the sound of the metal struts bending under the strain.

"That didn't sound good," Gort observed.

Smythe agreed as he powered down the main systems. "Go take a look and see what you can do. I'll contact Krunig."

Gort departed the cockpit, dutifully setting off to exact repairs. Meanwhile, Smythe stayed behind and opened a secure comm channel. It could only be used for a short while, or they risked having their transmission intercepted by the Aiwans.

A holographic image appeared on the console's projector pad between the pilot and copilot. Moments later, Grawn Krunig appeared.

"We made it," Smythe reported, withholding the details of their harrowing arrival.

"Excellent," the crime lord said. "Find a location to lay low for a couple days."

"Shouldn't be a problem," Smythe replied, welcoming the reprieve. "What's this about, anyway?" Krunig or not, he did not care much for unknowns.

"Your target is this ship. It is called the Reaper," Krunig explained as a hologram of the Reaper appeared. "Currently, it is docked in the city of Supra, the Aiwan capital of Eos. Your job is to capture this ship and bring it to me."

"Sounds simple enough."

"Not so. The Reaper is bound to its captain." Ava's holographic image replaced the Reaper. "Her name is Ava Tan, and she activated a fail-safe protocol that will self-destruct the ship should she meet an untimely demise."

Smythe scrutinized Ava's image and could not place her species. He made a mental note to search for it as soon as their transmission ended.

"So, I capture her and make her hand over the ship?"

Krunig's image returned. "Correct. You cannot kill her until she deactivates the security protocol. Understood?"

"Got it. How do I get into Eos? It has a shield, right?"

"No need. I will bring Captain Tan to you," Krunig said mysteriously. "Just be ready to move on my signal and snag her before the Aiwans do. Any questions?"

Smythe shook his head. He knew better than to ask clients about their business. Discretion was mutually understood.

"Very well. Good hunting."

The transmission ended, and Smythe sat back in his chair.

All this for one ship, he mused.

It was rare for Smythe to feel uneasy about a job, but this was not a normal errand. Tracking fugitives, collecting unpaid debts, and making the occasional smuggler's run was Krunig's usual appetite. This job had the makings of something bigger. He knew Krunig was holding back critical information, details that put the bounty hunters' lives at risk. But that was why Krunig paid them so handsomely. He knew he could count on Smythe and Gort because they always delivered.

That did not put Smythe's mind at ease. Despite his confidence in their abilities, a sinking feeling told the bounty hunter that he and Gort might have bitten off more than they could chew with this job.

Meanwhile, skimming above the calm sea at high velocity, the Reaper kicked up twin walls of water in its wake. After their heart-pounding experience with the zemindar, Ava had decided to continue their journey to Cirros above the water, at least for the time being. This far out at sea, it was unlikely they had any aerial predators to worry about, but one could never be too sure.

They traveled south for several minutes. Ava tracked their progress on the HUD. According to her readouts, they were now well inside Cirran territory. The location of Kypa's prospective worksite was nearly beneath them. It was time to go swimming.

"Okay, let's try this again," she told Kypa and Toma.

Retracting the nacelles, the Reaper gradually descended until the sleek spacecraft sliced into the ocean surface and disappeared under the waves. When the screen of bubbles cleared, the Reaper's crew once again found themselves submerged in a seemingly tranquil sea of beauty.

"Your worksite should be dead ahead," Ava remarked then cringed. She instantly regretted her choice of words but was relieved to see Kypa and Toma did not appear to catch it. At least, they did not let on as much.

The Reaper continued its descent. This time, Ava kept a close eye on the HUD's threat indicator. She was not about to get caught unaware twice in one day.

Diving into the murky depths. Ava reactivated the external running lights and adjusted the windows to enhance forward visibility.

A somber silence filled the cockpit. The weight of the moment did not escape them, including young Toma. They were not simply visiting the ruins of the so-called "forgotten realm." Cirros was a graveyard, a chilling reminder of how trying to do something good could go dreadfully wrong.

The Aiwans certainly had not intended to destroy Cirros with overharvesting, but that was the result of desperate people trying to save their world. It reminded Ava of J. Robert Oppenheimer, the father of the first atomic bomb. Oppenheimer had created a doomsday weapon to stop World War II, yet his experiment had inadvertently triggered an unending nuclear arms race.

And what about you?

Ava was surprised by the candor of her own psyche.

What about me?

She wrestled with the thought for a moment then eyed her hands and feet in the four orbs controlling the Reaper. Then it dawned on her that this ship was her atomic bomb. For all the good it could do, the Reaper could easily be perverted into a dreadful weapon. Being its captain came with a heavy burden of responsibility.

"There it is." Kypa pointed.

Ava looked up. Her eyes narrowed as she glimpsed the remains of a fallen city. Outside the forward viewport, they followed large cracks in the ocean floor that led to massive craters filled with toppled structures. The lifeless, moss-covered city looked as if it had been swallowed whole by the planet core.

The Reaper slowed.

Ava looked on in sadness. With a pained expression, she thought of all the innocent Aiwans who had died in the massive quakes. It must have been total chaos and fear. She imagined the apocalyptic scene and, for a split-second, could almost hear the screams of the dying.

Twisting her mouth to fight off tears, Ava shook off her emotions. They had a job to do. Even though they could not bring back the ones who had been lost, it was some consolation knowing that perhaps they could stabilize the region so the Cirrans who had survived could return and rebuild their true home one day.

Ava cleared her throat. "Did you have a spot in mind?"

"Yes, Captain. Continue on this heading. We are not far."

They continued on in silence. Passing over the ruins of the fallen metropolis, the Reaper's forward running lights cast eerie shadows over the abandoned structures.

"Odd. I'm not detecting many crystals," Ava thought aloud.

"Most were destroyed by the quakes," Kypa explained. "We salvaged what we could, but this region was decimated. The deposits were pulverized and reduced to dust."

Ava had no reply. Not only did the quakes claim millions of lives, but they also severely hampered Aiwa's defenses. She was tempted to ask what percentage of their mining operation was lost as a result then decided against it. Reopening an old wound would not do Kypa any good, especially with Toma present. His son had heard enough of his father's failings back in the capital. No need for more of it out here.

Ava straightened at the sight of a large crater up ahead. The cavernous hole in the planet's surface conjured images of Tycho Crater, one of the largest craters on the surface of Earth's moon. She knew this well.

Growing up, Ava and her father had been amateur astronomers. They used to climb onto the roof from her bedroom window late at night and stargaze through her father's old Meade 826 telescope. For hours on end, they would be out there, studying the galaxy until Mom caught them and made them come inside.

Good times. Ava grinned, having not thought about that old telescope in years.

"So, what do you think?" she asked.

Kypa stood and joined Ava. He pointed to several locations on her HUD.

"If you look close, you can still see the remnants of old harvesting efforts."

Ava enhanced the image on her display and leaned forward, squinting. The crater extended more than two miles down, which was deeper than any natural cave on Earth. Yet, still visible in the crater were the openings to a network of harvesting tunnels.

Based on the sheer number of excavation sites, it was not hard to imagine how overharvesting could have destabilized the entire region. Similar to the adverse effects of fracking back on Earth, removing mass quantities of sediment had created planar fractures in Aiwa's crust and upper mantle. The fractures had produced minor tectonic plates that had begun shifting. As a result, these shifts had triggered earthquakes of biblical proportions, impacting Cirros' capital city and surrounding areas.

Kypa called up a schematic of the old harvesting tunnels and had it overlayed on their current location. The resulting map resembled the veins in a body cavity x-ray.

"This main tunnel here leads to a large junction." He ran his finger along the display from the tunnel entrance to a large pocket of open space within the mountain of rock. "As you can see, several additional tunnels split-off from this junction. I must close all of those tunnels, then the junction, and work my way back to the main entrance. I will fill that in last," Kypa explained. "However, before I can start, I must stabilize the entrance and main tunnel. It is unsafe to enter, so I must repair these fractures along the crater wall first."

Ava exhaled. Back in her time at Area S4, Kypa had shared how the Reaper could extract crystals safely by filling in the leftover cavity with a synthesized gel, much like the food synthesizer she and Neil used for breakfast. The gel would then harden like a rock from geothermal heat produced deep within the planet core, thus stabilizing the affected area.

This ingenious terraforming concept reminded Ava of a *National Geographic* documentary she had watched on television not long ago. Massive land reclamation projects were underway on Earth involving the construction of artificial islands. Sand was dredged from the ocean floor and sprayed into a new location to create an island.

Such endeavors were nothing new—they dated back to prehistoric times. However, recent land reclamation projects in the South China Sea had heightened tensions between China and its neighbors. Currently, the Chinese were illegally building artificial islands in the territorial waters of several countries, like Vietnam, Taiwan, Malaysia, and the Philippines. To up the ante, China had also constructed military bases on those artificial islands to secure their influence in the region. Their audacity infuriated China's neighbors, heightening the risk of hostilities, and angered environmentalists due to the irreparable damage caused to living coral reefs in the area.

Kypa's terraforming process would have no such adverse effects on Cirros' natural environment. Wildlife would be undisturbed. And, if all went to plan, the Cirrans could return home with the assurance that their reconstruction efforts would be built on a solid foundation.

"I—" Kypa stopped mid-sentence when he felt a tap on his shoulder. He turned to find Toma standing behind him with a sheepish expression. "Yes, Toma, what is it?"

"I am hungry, Father. Can I go outside to hunt before you get started?"

Kypa's initial reaction was agitation, although he was exceptionally good at hiding it. The stress of the moment was getting to him. After all, his life did depend on the success of this experiment. Then Kypa caught himself. As he met his son's gaze, Kypa realized he could not squander this opportunity with Toma. When he was his son's age, Kypa would have loved to share an adventure like this with his father. Terraforming could wait.

Kypa chuckled and rubbed Toma's head. "Of course, you can go. Can I join you?"

Toma nodded vigorously.

"Captain?"

Ava shooed them away. "You boys go ahead. I've got some stuff to take care of here."

Neither Aiwan questioned her decision.

"We will be back shortly," Kypa said as he and Toma departed.

Moments later, Ava saw the indicator on the HUD that the lower hatch had been opened. Soon after, Kypa and Toma swam by the cockpit window and waved. Ava smiled and waved back. Once they were gone, she exhaled and lay back in her chair, closing her eyes.

Reggie dimmed the lights.

"Thanks, Reg." Ava smiled. "Wake me at the first sign of trouble."

"Yes, Captain."

Outside, Kypa and Toma enjoyed a leisurely swim. It was their first time out together in months. Kypa could not help but notice how much his son had grown while he had been away. A certain amount of guilt and shame came with that realization. Compared to the challenges Aiwa was facing, he had made family a lower priority. While on Earth, and here now with Toma, he realized how selfish he had been. Those other issues were certainly important, but not at the expense of Maya and the children. His work-life balance needed a course correction, starting now.

A large school of pin fish passed nearby. Father and son exchanged a look, and the hunt was on. Kypa prodded Toma to take the lead.

Toma grinned then narrowed his eyes as he took off in pursuit. Kypa followed. He deliberately lagged behind at first so he could watch Toma's strategy unfold but soon discovered keeping up was going to be a challenge. Toma had grown faster and stronger in his absence.

Sensing danger, the fish evaded Toma's pursuit. But, like a seasoned hunter, the young Aiwan anticipated their movements and herded them into a kill zone. Toma extended his fingernails and skewered two fish with either hand. Both fish squirmed in death throes before going limp.

Toma spun around and located Kypa. Gripping both fish, he raised his kills triumphantly overhead for his father to see.

"*Well done!*" Kypa called to him, using his telepathy. "*That was perfect!*"

Toma beamed. Pleasing his father meant more to him than the thrill of the hunt. He offered one fish to Kypa, who proudly accepted.

Kypa pulled the succulent fish off Toma's fingers and gestured to a nearby cliff overlooking the crater. There, they enjoyed a meal together while debriefing every move of the hunt. It was a moment neither of them would ever forget.

"*Did you hunt with your father?*" Toma asked.

"*Rarely,*" Kypa said with regret. "*But I wish we had done so more often.*"

He turned away, staring out at the ruins and reflecting on the relationship with his father that could have been. Blinking back to the moment, Kypa turned and realized Toma was waiting expectantly for his father to elaborate. Kypa sighed. He was never one to play the victim, so he decided not to air his frustrations about his father. Instead, Kypa realized that the father-son relationship he yearned for with Toma required more than occasionally hunting and playing games together. He needed to be more open with his son.

"*The war had begun when I was your age,*" he explained. "*There was little time for play.*"

Toma considered this thoughtfully. "*Do you think the war will ever end?*"

Kypa discarded the remains of his fish. "*It will, someday,*" he hoped. "*And when it does, I have a promise to keep with an old friend. We will rebuild all of this.*"

Toma read the sadness on his father's face. "*You mean Luna?*"

Kypa nodded solemnly.

"*I miss Luna, too,*" Toma admitted. He looked toward the Reaper parked in the distance. "*Ava reminds me of her.*"

Taken aback, Kypa considered the comparison. It had not occurred to him before, but now that he thought about it, Toma was right. Ava and Luna were very much alike—brave, tenacious, and loyal to a fault. The realization brought a smile to his face.

Toma turned to his father. "*I want to help you rebuild Cirros.*"

Kypa clapped his son's shoulder, beaming with pride. "*Nothing would mean more to me. Speaking of which, it is time to get started.*"

Both Aiwans prepared to swim back to the ship.

Before setting off, Toma turned to Kypa. "*Father?*"

"*Yes.*"

"*I like the humans very much, especially Ava,*" he confided. "*She makes me laugh.*"

Kypa chuckled. "*Me, too. We are lucky to have them as friends.*" He pushed off the ground then grinned slyly. "*Last one to the ship has to catch dinner!*"

Toma gladly accepted the challenge. Father and son sped away toward the Reaper, kicking fluidly through the water at high speed. This time, Kypa exerted his full strength to keep his son humble. He barely beat Toma back to the ship, and both shared a good laugh upon arrival.

After entering the Reaper, Toma hurried to the cockpit to tell Ava about their hunt. Kypa stayed behind to secure the hatch. Watching his son climb the ladder, Kypa made a promise to himself not to fall into the same patterns as his father. He could attest firsthand to the emotional damage an absentee parent—by choice—could cause a child. Kypa wanted none of that. He needed to be more involved with his family.

Quantity over quality, he resolved to himself.

This was the opposite approach his father took with him. Not that King Loka could be faulted. Kypa understood the heavy burdens his father carried, especially in wartime. Harboring any ill-will toward his father was unfair.

Kypa wrestled for a solution. As Aiwa continued its fight against the harvesters, Kypa knew he could not expect his father to change.

You need to stop waiting on him to seek reconciliation, Kypa told himself. *Go to him and meet him on his terms.*

With this revelation, Kypa felt as if a great weight had been lifted. The answer had always been in front of him, but it had taken until now, when he was ready to stop playing the victim, to see it. Now the challenge would be in finding the opportune moment to approach the king.

Returning to the cockpit, Kypa found his son standing in the darkness, dripping wet, watching the sea life pass outside the windows. Toma heard him approach, turned, and placed his finger to his mouth. He then gestured to Ava, who was fast asleep in her chair.

Kypa joined Toma and, together, they stood in silence, staring out at the Cirran ruins. The task before them was monumental, but with their renewed bond, both father and son felt unstoppable.

Ava woke with a start, gasping at the sight of the two Aiwan silhouettes standing nearby.

Kypa and Toma turned sharply.

It took Ava a split-second to recognize her surroundings. Then she relaxed and lay back, clutching her chest. "Dang, you and Neil need to quit sneaking up on me," she said, catching her breath.

"Apologies, Captain," Kypa said. "We did not mean to wake you."

"It's okay," Ava replied, forcing herself to sit up. "I've slept long enough." She yawned heavily. "How was your swim?"

Toma stepped forward with a look of excitement. "I caught two pin fish. Would you like me to catch you one?"

Ava chuckled groggily. "That's sweet, but no, thank you." Rubbing the sleep from her eyes, Ava rolled out of her chair and stood, stretching. "Reggie, illuminate the cockpit to fifty percent ... slowly, please."

The lights gradually rose.

Ava turned to Kypa. "So, what's the plan, Stan?"

Toma gave her a curious look. His father, though, had grown accustomed to the human's catch phrases and replied without missing a beat. Kypa began detailing his plan to reconstruct Cirros. She immediately picked up on his business-like tone. No more games; it was time to get to work.

Shaking off the cobwebs in her head, Ava listened intently, nodding understanding. When Kypa finished, she climbed back in her chair and powered up the ship. The Reaper lifted off and began its descent inside the crater.

"I must go alone from here," Kypa told Toma once they reached the bottom.

Toma did not object, which Kypa attributed to his son's desire to hang back with Ava and learn more about the Reaper. Kypa smiled thinly and started out of the cockpit.

"Be careful," Ava said as her friend departed.

"Always," Kypa replied over his shoulder.

Exiting the ship, Kypa swam beneath the Reaper's underbelly, toward the bow. There, he opened a hidden compartment. Interior lights flickered on. Inside the compartment was the Reaper's multi-function precision laser cannon. The cannon doubled as the main terraforming delivery system. When activated, the ingenious device converted seawater into a synthetic gel, creating artificial sediment that could be spread out over a large area. For today's experiment, Kypa was thinking on a smaller scale.

He retrieved a long, handheld device from a rack inside the compartment that resembled a particle thrower used in the movie, *Ghostbusters*. However, this tool was not connected to a proton pack. Instead, it was attached to the terraforming generator, via a long hose. This gave Kypa the mobility he needed to enter tight spaces and apply the synthetic gel in a more surgical fashion.

Kypa had spent years perfecting his invention. The terraformer had worked in every simulation. Now it was time to put theory into action.

He put on a headlamp and turned it on. Then Kypa set off for the first application site. He chose a long, narrow fracture in the crater wall. Filled with nervous anticipation, he activated the terraformer.

Instantly, he could feel the dispenser vibrate in his hands as artificial sediment found its way through the long hose. Then, like a fireman extinguishing a house fire, Kypa directed the output flow toward the base of the crevice. Filling the gap with orange goo, it immediately began to harden into artificial rock.

Kypa smiled at his invention. Once again, the Reaper had exceeded his expectations. Aiwa was now on the path to being made whole once again.

21

FIRST IMPRESSIONS

Planet Earth
Satipo, Peru

Mathias stepped out of the Aiwan's holding cell and struck a gangsta pose when he saw Dr. Landry approach. "Yo, yo!" he said, grinning smugly.

Rose rolled her eyes. *Yoyo brain is right*, she wanted to say.

Her initial shock of the Aiwan's presence had worn off, only to be replaced with revulsion. Rose's personal disdain for Edmund aside, the fact her former protégé had somehow captured an Aiwan and held it in captivity made her stomach churn.

"What have you done, Edmund?"

Mathias pointed to himself, surprised by her reproach. "*Me*? I rescued a stranded alien, just like you did with Kypa."

Rose shook her head, not buying it for a minute. She pointed to the Aiwan. "Who is that?"

Edmund shrugged. "I don't know, but I'm pretty sure it's a female. I can't say for sure because I wanted the aquasuit left intact."

Mentioning the classified term "aquasuit" did not escape Rose. Whether it was a slip of the tongue or not, it told her Edmund knew more about Kypa's incarceration at Groom Lake than he should. That peeved her to no end, but at least Edmund showed some semblance of restraint by allowing the Aiwan to continue wearing the aquasuit. That was more than she could say for Garza and Sizemore.

"Where did you find her?"

"Kauai … not far from Kypa's recovery site, actually."

"In a pod?"

"No, but I've had search teams combing the area, looking for one just in case. Nothing's turned up yet. I'm starting to think she swam all the way from North Korea."

"What makes you say that?" Rose did not discount the possibility. Swimming the Pacific was impossible for a human, but not for an Aiwan.

"There were several strange sightings around the Korean Peninsula after the mothership crashed. None of them panned out until weeks later. She must've been searching for Kypa when we found her."

"You mean, when you kidnapped her," Rose corrected, "like you did me."

Edmund rolled his eyes. "C'mon; let's not beat a dead horse. You're here now. Aren't you the least bit curious about her story?"

Rose hated to admit it, but Edmund was right. She wanted to know everything about Kypa's crewmate and, above all, advocate for her rights.

"Still, you could've at least asked."

Edmund growled in frustration. "I tried, remember? Besides, I couldn't have told you the truth even if I wanted to. It's too dangerous. Every government in the world will want a piece of our friend in there once they discover her existence."

"But she's safe here, right?" Rose raised her eyebrow. "Or are you planning to dissect her like you wanted to do with Kypa?"

Edmund raised his hands in defense. "Dissect? No. Study? Absolutely. But rest assured, Dr. Landry, I don't intend to harm my guest in any way, shape, or form."

"Does she know that?"

Edmund sighed. "No, but not for a lack of trying. We've had a tough go at communication. With Aiwan telepathy and all …" Edmund paused to gauge Rose's response. Judging by her incredulous look, he could not tell if she was genuinely impressed by his resourcefulness or thoroughly pissed he had such far-reaching influence. Probably the latter.

He waited for Rose to hurl an insult. When none came, he continued.

"I read your report from Groom Lake. I know all about Aiwan telepathy, and my people have gone to great lengths to avoid all physical contact. However, our guest has been uncooperative, to say the least. One of my guards learned that the hard way."

"Did she kill him?"

"No, but he won't be fathering children anytime soon." Edmund felt a phantom pain in his groin just thinking about it. "Since the guard was mentally compromised, I had him removed."

Rose could only imagine what that meant and decided not to ask for clarification.

Edmund thumbed toward the Aiwan's room. "It's safe to go inside. The partition is unbreakable. It's made of transparent aluminum, which is three times stronger than steel," he explained. "There's also a slot for transferring food and water without making physical contact, much like Kypa's setup at Groom Lake. I've got engineers working on building a bigger room that'll make our guest more comfortable."

This was all well and good, but Rose had heard enough. "So, what exactly do you need me for?" she asked impatiently.

"The work you and Dr. Garrett did with Kypa was remarkable. I want you to do the same with her." Edmund faced the Aiwan, watching her through the glass. He had a gleam in his eyes as he imagined the possibility of tapping into the Aiwan's knowledge. "Get her talking, Rose. Build rapport and gain her trust. I want us all to become friends." Then he added, "Allies."

"*Allies?*" Rose *hmphed*. "You just want to clone her so you can get filthy rich."

Mathias shrugged. No sense denying the truth. "Money is what makes the world go round." He gestured to their state-of-the-art surroundings. "It's what pays for this party."

"And betrays confidence …"

Edmund let out an exasperated breath. "Fair enough. I know you resent me for stealing Joe's research. It was a dick move; I admit it. I'm sorry, but we both know I took it further than he ever could."

Years of pent-up frustration erupted in Rose. She reacted sharply, getting in Edmund's face and jabbing her finger in his chest. "Don't you ever mention his name again," she warned between gritted teeth.

Renzo took a step forward to intervene, but Mathias waved him off.

Dr. M. Edmund Mathias had few regrets in life. Seeing the pain he had inflicted in Rose's eyes was one of them. Edmund measured his next words carefully.

"I'm sorry, Rose," he said earnestly. "You're right." He paused until Rose eased off and regained her composure. "Listen, I can't undo the past. And honestly, I wouldn't even if I could. Your husband's work helped thousands of people who suffered from a horrible disease, but it wasn't finished. I used the money to fund the cure, Rose."

She eyed him warily. "What are you talking about?"

"The cloning … we unlocked the cure for Crohn's."

Rose's stance softened.

"Joe's research was groundbreaking but still a decade away. Working here, unhindered, accelerated our progress."

Rose took that to mean there was no government oversight or ethics probes here in Peru to stand in the way of his unholy experiments. She folded her arms, waiting to be impressed.

"So, where is it? Why haven't you gone public?"

"There's no profit in a cure, Rose. You know that. Cancer, COVID, the common cold … Big Pharma has the cures, but pleasing their shareholders comes first."

"You disgust me," Rose sneered.

Edmund exhaled sharply. Rose's grudge was bigger than he had thought, and they were losing precious time.

He threw up his hands, conceding defeat. "Very well, what'll it take to put this behind us? Give me a number."

Rose scoffed. "You can't buy me off. No amount of money is going to bring Joe back."

"Let's be clear, I didn't kill Joe. But, if you'll let me, I can at least make some amends by helping your family."

Unconvinced, Rose decided to play along. "All right, fine. I want a billion dollars."

Edmund forced back the urge to laugh. Keeping a straight face, he said evenly, "I'm serious, Rose. Let's be reasonable. I was thinking twenty million, *and* you come work for me."

Rose shook her head emphatically. "Forget it."

"Don't be hasty, Rose. That much money could set up your grandchildren's grandchildren. At the very least, you could buy your daughter a new car."

The hairs on the back of Rose's neck stood up. "Have you been spying on my family?"

"My people are thorough, that's all." Edmund circled back to his offer. "Think about it, Rose. That's a lot of money on the table, and you get to work directly with another Aiwan."

Rose shook her head in disbelief. *I don't believe it. This is Groom Lake all over again, only worse.*

Veiled threats or not, Rose realized she had little choice but to cooperate. If she refused Edmund's offer or failed to deliver, it seemed likely she would be "removed," just like the guard who had the run-in with the Aiwan earlier. Her family could suffer the same fate, as well.

Rose steeled her nerves. "How do I know you're not going to kill me?"

Edmund guffawed. "C'mon, Rose. I don't want to kill you. Hell, if I wanted to hurt you, I could've done that back in Atlanta," he reminded her. "I need you. That's why I brought you here. No one knows the Aiwans better than you."

Taking Edmund at his word was a fool's gamble, but her choices were limited. If Edmund's offer was legit, her family would be set up for life. Plus, she would get a second chance to work with another Aiwan.

That was the dilemma. Legal or not, accepting Edmund's proposal felt dirty. Normally, she would simply reject his offer on principle, because he was a conniving little prick who would just as soon sell his mother to make a profit. But being on his payroll made her feel like she was accepting blood money.

Whose blood? she asked herself.

That was yet to be determined, but Rose trusted her instincts. For now, she had little choice but to play along. Her survival, as well as the lives of her family and this new Aiwan, depended on it.

Edmund sensed she was still on the fence, so he decided to throw caution to the wind.

"Would it help if you knew my end game?"

Rose was hesitant to reply. Perhaps the less she knew, the better.

"We're on the verge of unlocking Earth's newest and greatest energy source," he proceeded. "Forget about the cloning business. That is simply a means to fund other endeavors. The future of mankind is in magnetarite."

Rose was taken aback. "Crystals?"

"That's right." Edmund grinned devilishly. "Your pals, Kypa and Captain Tan, uncovered a treasure trove in Challenger Deep, and I want it. There's a cave of crystals just sitting there in international waters. Whoever claims that site first is sitting on the greatest source of wealth mankind has ever known."

Rose knew he was right and chided herself for not seeing this coming.

"The secret's out on this, Rose. China, Russia, the Middle East—America's enemies are lining up to be my investors because they know I'm the only one with the resources to mine the crystals. Mathias Industries is perfectly positioned to corner the market."

Rose chuckled. "You're forgetting one thing—harvesters."

Mathias grinned, surprised Rose had not figured it out yet. "That's why you're here. I know everything that happened in North Korea. After Captain Tan stole the Reaper—fitting name, by the way. Did you come up with that? Makes me think of that song by Blue Oyster Cult." Edmund hummed the tune then waved dismissively. "Anyway, when I learned of Kypa's purpose for coming to Earth, the ship's name made more sense. Then Captain Tan extracted one of these beauties from Challenger Deep." Mathias retrieved the orange crystal from his pocket and offered it to Rose.

She rolled the crystal around in her palm then held it up to the light. She knew of magnetarite from Kypa but had never seen one of the crystals in person. The gem sparkled like the sun.

"I removed that one from the same cave," Edmund said. "There are thousands more like it, just ripe for the taking."

"Ripe for harvesting, you mean?"

"Po-tay-toe, po-tah-toe," Edmund granted. "Point is, you're right; the harvesters are coming. Kypa promised as much, and when word gets out about these crystals, then every fortune-seeking prospector and trader in the galaxy will be knocking on our doorstep. We can't let that happen." He pointed to Luna. "The arrival of our friend in there was a godsend. Don't you see? She can help buy us some time."

Rose's brow furrowed. "What do you mean?"

"I need you to convince her to help me hide the crystals," Edmund explained.

"Hide them?"

"Yes, if we can somehow mask their presence, then any harvesters who come looking for the crystals won't find bupkis. They'll think the reports were bogus and move on."

"Just like that," Rose said facetiously, raising an eyebrow at Edmund's naivety. "That's an awfully big gamble. So, what's *your* endgame?"

Mathias grinned widely. "You know me, I'm an opportunist. Once we've harvested the crystals, I plan to enter the galactic crystal trade. Mathias Industries is going interstellar, baby."

Rose shook her head. "You're way out of your league, Edmund. We've both seen there's no defense against the harvesters. They'll destroy you—*us*, I should say—and take all of the crystals without batting an eye."

Mathias sighed with the patience of a knowing parent.

"Ye of little faith. I've got the harvesters covered," he said mysteriously. "All I need is a device to hide the crystals. Help me do that, and I promise your family will be rich beyond your wildest dreams."

"You'll let me leave whenever I want?" Rose could not believe she was actually considering this outlandish scheme.

"Absolutely … after you've signed a very lengthy and detailed NDA, of course."

Rose figured as much, although it was probably just for show. A bullet to the head was the only surefire way to guarantee her silence.

She nodded her agreement. "I want Joe publicly credited with the Crohn's research."

"Done," Edmund quickly agreed. "And the money?"

Rose swallowed hard. *Are you really doing this?*

As Dr. Landry grappled with her decision, Luna finished her meal, pretending to be uninterested in the conversation outside. In truth, she was watching the humans carefully, trying to read their body language.

Rose glanced in her direction. Making eye contact, Rose saw past the Aiwan's harsh exterior. They shared a brief connection, not telepathic, but a mutual understanding that, despite being complete strangers, their fates were intertwined.

"And what about her? Will you let her go if the Aiwans return for her?"

"Yes, or as soon as she finishes hiding the crystals." Edmund offered a handshake. "Deal?"

Leery, Rose eyed his hand, reluctant to accept but, deep down, knew what she had to do. Rose accepted.

"Don't make me regret this."

"You won't. I swear." Mathias crossed his heart. "What else?"

Rose wiped her tainted palm on her trouser. "You said I could call my family, and I need to check in at the office. Jesus, they're probably worried sick."

Edmund raised his finger in contention. "About that, like I said, you'll need to sign a non-disclosure agreement. It also requires you resign from the CDC effective immediately."

"No, I won't resign," Rose countered, "but I will request a leave of absence. Good enough?"

Edmund reluctantly agreed.

"You know this'll raise a lot of red flags," she warned.

Edmund's blasé reaction showed his lack of concern.

"One more thing," he added. "I'm allowing you to keep your tablet because it doesn't have internet access. You can call home shortly on one of our devices, too. But, just to be transparent, your conversation will be monitored to ensure my company is not mentioned, at all. You can't tell people what you're doing, who you're working for, or even what continent you're on. Understood?"

"I got it," Rose replied dryly, none too pleased to be spoken to like a child. "So, how exactly is this going to work?" She poked her thumb toward Renzo. "Will I be chaperoned everywhere I go?"

"No, you'll be free to move around the facility, like everyone else. In fact, how about I give you a tour?"

Rose glanced at the Aiwan. "Later, I want to get started with her."

"That's what I like to hear." Edmund rubbed his hands together excitedly. "I'll have the NDA amended to add Joe. Once it's signed, I'll have an off-shore account opened to transfer your money. Agreed?"

Rose nodded.

"Anything else?"

Rose lifted the tablet. "This is all I need, but some food would be nice."

Edmund snapped his fingers, remembering. "Of course. My bad. You want it sent down here?"

"That'll be fine … and tea," she emphasized.

"You got it." Elated, Edmund put his arm around Rose and squeezed her tight. "This is going to be just like old times."

Rose cringed as Edmund pinned her arms at her sides. She abruptly slid out of his grasp.

Mathias feigned rejection. "Not a hugger, eh?"

Rose forced a polite smile. "Good day, Edmund."

Smirking, he made a head bob to Renzo, signaling that it was time to leave.

As soon as they were gone, Rose blew out a breath of relief. "Thank God that's over."

Turning to the Aiwan, she thought back to her introduction to Kypa. At the time, she'd had no idea that telepathy played a big part in Kypa's quick assimilation of humanity's languages and customs. She was not ready to take that leap the second time around.

Despite any good intentions or moral high ground Kypa claimed the Aiwans adhered to, telepathy felt like a violation, especially since it was a one-way street. For the time being, she would have to rely on her trusty tablet to bridge the communication gap. With the English-Aiwan translation that Kypa had programmed, perhaps progress would come easier than expected.

Still, Rose had an uphill battle ahead. From the sounds of it, Mathias's men had destroyed any hope of establishing trust with the Aiwan.

Trust, she mused, grinning fondly. *You're starting to sound like Neil.*

Rose approached the door to Luna's room with all of the courage she could muster. She gave a nod to the guard to open the door.

"You want me in there with you, ma'am?"

"Thanks, but no. That won't be necessary." *I hope.*

The guard gave Rose a questioning look. He knew firsthand how cunning and lethal the Aiwan could be but held his tongue. "Just remember to keep your hands away from the door slot. Don't let it touch your skin," he instructed as he opened the door. "Holler if you need anything."

"Thank you," Rose replied as she stepped inside. The heavy door was closed behind her, followed by an audible *click* of the lock that echoed in the room.

Luna, Rose noticed, remained seated in the far corner of the room with her back against the wall. However, her eyes tracked Rose's every movement.

Approaching the clear partition, Rose tucked her tablet under her arm. She faced Luna and smiled to show her teeth then placed her palms facing outward to demonstrate her peaceful intentions.

Luna watched, unmoving.

Rather than try to talk gibberish through the partition, Rose sat on the floor in front of the slot for passing items back and forth. Not surprisingly, the Aiwan remained seated in the back corner.

Undeterred, Rose picked up the tablet and opened a custom application Kypa had built to translate English to Aiwan. It was a gift he had left behind as a good will gesture to help humans prepare for future encounters with Aiwans.

Rose turned up the volume then typed in the word, "*Welcome.*"

The resulting translation sounded like a cross between dolphin chatter and the clicking and popping of Taa, also known as !Xóõ, a rare language spoken in Botswana.

Luna recognized her native tongue immediately. She came to her feet and approached Rose cautiously with a fierce look of curiosity.

Seeing Luna's reaction, Rose waved her closer, inviting the Aiwan to join her on the floor. Luna accepted. Seated across from one another, Rose typed in a second message.

"My name is Rose," the device voiced.

Luna's brow furrowed. A tense moment passed. Rose watched with bated breath as Luna's mouth began to quiver, as if she was forming a reply.

"Rose," Luna uttered.

Rose nodded vigorously. "Yes, yes!" She pointed to herself. "I am Rose."

She then gestured to Luna. "And you are?"

Conflict was evident on Luna's face. Until now, she had assumed she was dealing with an inferior race and refused to cooperate with her captors. Rose was a game changer. She might be the only person who could provide the answers she sought.

A new strategy was needed, and Luna recognized she could no longer afford to be obstinate. She had to give a little to get a little.

Luna straightened. Gesturing to herself, she replied, "Luna."

Rose put her hand to her heart, wanting to cry. If only Kypa were here.

"Luna," she repeated with a warm smile.

Luna bowed her head in response.

Beaming, Rose mirrored the greeting. "Welcome to Earth, Luna."

Hours later, Mathias made his way down the hall to a private room that only he and one other person had access to. He entered the keypad combination, and the door unlocked. As expected, he found his fixer, Mr. Renzo, training inside the Chachapoyan's personal dojo.

Renzo's training room was sparsely furnished with a red sparring mat in the center of the room. Mounted on one wall was a floor to ceiling mirror, while a large mural of his idol, Roberto Puch Bezada, filled another wall. Bezada, an ex-convict, was regarded as the founder of the martial art known as Bakom (aka Vacón).

Renzo was an ardent student of Bakom. He and Bezada hailed from the same shantytown in the Lima district of Villa el Salvador. There, the Peruvian street fighting style of Bakom was widely practiced. Its core principle was to disrupt an opponent's balance then inflict as much injury as possible.

At the moment, Renzo was training vigorously with a custom-built, six-foot tall Wing Chun wooden training dummy in the corner of the room. Made of solid oak, the training dummy was secured to a flat, wooden base for stability. Three wooden pegs extended outward at upper torso height to practice head and neck strikes. Two additional red pads were wrapped around the dummy's center torso for hand and leg strikes, while a lower wooden armature at the base could be used to practice leg sweeps. Since Bakom relied on quick arm movements and strong legs to defeat opponents, this training dummy was the next best thing to a live opponent.

Mathias watched with amusement and intrigue as the Chachapoyan demonstrated his mastery of the martial art. Renzo's hands moved in a blur as he performed a flurry of strikes and blocks with fluidity and precision while mixing in additional leg kicks and sweeps that would surely inflict a great deal of damage to bone and flesh.

When Renzo paused, his face now dripping with sweat, he turned at the sound of clapping.

Edmund approached. "Very impressive."

Renzo responded with a *palm-holds-fist* salute, placing his right-handed fist against the palm of his left hand and bowing. This salute demonstrated how the fist is stronger than the palm, so the fist is restrained. In martial arts, it was considered a non-offensive sign of respect.

"I'd hate to be the other guy," Edmund joked as he eyed the well-used dummy. The wooden pegs were worn and splintering.

If Renzo found the joke humorous, he kept it to himself. This prompted Mathias to get down to business.

"Dr. Landry has decided to join us. She's with Luna right now."

"Luna?"

"Yeah, that's the Aiwan's name. Rose already has her talking."

Renzo was impressed.

"I have an NDA for her to sign. Once that's done, she'll be sending an email to her employer, requesting a leave of absence. Proof it before she sends it," he said, the mistrust clear in his voice.

"Understood," Renzo replied.

"Good. After that, let her use your encrypted phone to call home so her family knows she's safe. I'll be back later to give Dr. Landry a tour of the facility."

Renzo nodded, wiping sweat from his brow. "How long will she be staying, sir?"

Edmund grinned. "Indefinitely."

22
HERDING XIPOS

Planet Aiwa
Realm of Cirros

Ava covered her mouth and yawned heavily as the first day of reconstructing Aiwa's core wound down. Sitting in her pilot's chair, she watched Kypa on the HUD as he sealed the fractures surrounding one of the largest harvesting tunnels in the lower levels of the crater.

"I don't know how he does it," she muttered, marveling at her friend's stamina.

Kypa had spent all day manually dispensing the artificial sediment generated by the Reaper. A tedious, labor-intensive task, it required Zen-like calmness and focused concentration. He had only taken one break that Ava could recall yet had produced major results. With surgical precision, Kypa had sealed no less than a hundred cracks in the crater wall to stabilize the area. The question still to be answered was whether or not the artificial sediment would hold permanently. Initial stress tests appeared positive, but he would give it overnight to cure. If the sediment passed muster, Kypa could then move inside the main tunnel and begin work on a much larger scale, sealing off the deep arteries of mining shafts that had destabilized Aiwa's core and led to the catastrophic quakes.

Ava climbed out of her seat and stretched. After hours of prolonged sitting and staring at a screen, not to mention extroverting to keep Toma entertained, she was ready for some time alone. A run or, better yet, a swim, sounded inviting. Perhaps on the trip back to Supra, a detour to a sandy beach was in order.

Speaking of Toma, Ava realized she had not heard from him in a while. She headed aft in search of him but did not have to look far. She found Toma in the main cabin, sitting cross-legged on the floor. He was tucked in the corner with a long look on his face. Ava gave him a curious glance as she stepped up to the food synthesizer.

"Hey, you okay?"

Shoulders slouched, Toma replied halfheartedly, "Yes."

"That doesn't sound too convincing," Ava remarked.

To Reggie, she said, "Latte Supreme, unleaded, if you please."

A frothy, decaf caramel latte with soy milk materialized before her.

Rounding to face Toma, she blew over the top of her hot drink to help cool it. "Wanna talk about it?"

Toma shrugged.

Ava took this as a yes and sat on the floor across from him. She sipped from her cup, holding the silence until Toma was ready to talk. At first, he avoided eye contact, then Ava began sipping louder from her cup. Her slurps reached the point of being obnoxious before Toma cracked a smile.

"Do all humans drink that loud?"

Ava feigned surprise. "Oh, I'm sorry. Was I being loud?" She grinned.

Toma chuckled.

"So, what's going on?" Ava asked.

Toma sighed. "I have to return to the Citadel soon."

"Is that a bad thing?"

Toma hesitated then nodded in shame. "The other students mock me."

Ava nodded thoughtfully. "Children on Earth can be cruel, too. We call it bullying."

Knowing Kypa was still outside, Toma confided, "They taunt me because of my father," he whispered with bitterness. "I hate it."

"Your father is not responsible for what happened here."

"I know, but tell them that," Toma replied dourly.

"I'm sure it hasn't been easy for you, but soon, things will be different. Trust me. What we're doing here is making a difference."

Toma did not look convinced. He had to deal with the mockery on a daily basis, and not just with his peers. Adding salt to the wound was the fact his instructors often joined in and were just as cruel as the students.

"Have you told your father?"

Toma's face turned pale. "No, I cannot do that. And you cannot say anything," he said in a panic. "Promise?"

Ava raised her hands. "Okay, I promise." She let him calm down. "Is there anyone at the Citadel who can make them stop?"

Toma shook his head in defeat.

Ava thought for a moment. "Well, you can't keep all this bottled up inside."

"What can I do?" Toma replied, discouraged. "If I say anything, it will only get worse."

Ava shrugged. Before she knew it, she had channeled Colonel Nunez. "Then don't say anything. Give them the ole unicorn fist."

Toma's brow scrunched in confusion.

"I can't believe I'm showing you this, but what the heck." Ava made a fist and raised her middle finger. "This is called a unicorn fist, or sometimes known as flipping the bird on Earth."

Toma eyed her quizzically. "I do not understand."

"It's a vulgar gesture, a way of disrespecting someone nonverbally," she explained.

Toma brightened, liking the sound of that.

"No one on Aiwa knows its meaning except you, so it'll be your thing."

Toma gave it a try, balling his fist and raising his middle finger up in the air.

Ava chortled. "Good. You got it." She reached out to cover his hands and make him stop. "Now put that thing away before somebody gets hurt," she joked. "Remember, use it sparingly. And, if anyone asks what it means, just make something up. Tell them it means goodbye."

Toma grinned slyly. He was already picturing the first person he wanted to use it on.

Just then, his father appeared.

"Is everything all right?" Kypa asked.

"Yep," Ava replied, coming to her feet. "We were just talking, getting to know each other. What's up?"

Kypa rubbed his weary eyes. "I have reached a good stopping point for today."

"I can't believe how much you've accomplished. Good job."

"Thank you." Kypa bowed his head slightly, clearly exhausted.

Turning to Toma, he asked, "Ready to head back?"

Feeling like himself again, Toma nodded.

"What say we give Toma his first flying lesson?" Ava suggested.

Toma's face lit up. He leapt to his feet and looked eagerly to his father for approval.

Kypa grimaced. "Perhaps we have had enough excitement for one day."

"No, Father, please," he begged. "Just for a little while."

Kypa eyed Ava warily. "Are you sure about this?"

"Absolutely," Ava replied. "We spent all day going over the avionics. Time to put theory into action. Right?" She clapped Toma's shoulder.

He nodded vigorously.

"Besides, my father taught me how to drive when I was Toma's age. He'll do great."

Kypa sighed, too tired to debate the matter. He did not want to end such a good day on a sour note. "Very well. Just for a little while."

Toma beamed and raced into the cockpit to sit in the pilot's chair.

Ava turned to Kypa and patted his shoulder. "Not to worry. I charted a course back through Fonn to avoid any run-ins with zemindars."

Kypa nodded appreciatively. He followed Ava into the cockpit and took his place in the forward bench seat, while Ava stood at Toma's side. The holographic pilot's chair was just finishing its readjustment to fit Toma's frame.

"Okay, Reggie's going to get us underway, so just relax and feel how she eases the controls. Once we get out into the open waters, I'll let you take over."

Toma nodded briskly as the Reaper lifted off. They departed the ruins and turned north, heading toward the Realm of Fonn, Aiwa's underwater equivalent to the Great Plains on Earth. Moments later, they entered a broad expanse of open flatland.

Reggie continued on this heading a while longer then announced to the crew, "We have entered Fonn, Captain."

"Thanks, Reggie," Ava replied.

To Toma, she said, "Now place your hands and feet in the four orbs like we practiced."

Toma reached out, and the flight controls came to life.

"Good. Okay, don't make any sudden movements. We're going to take it nice and slow."

Toma nodded rigidly, trying not to move his limbs.

In front of him, Kypa interacted with his HUD. "Ava, I have notified Fonn authorities of our presence. We are clear to navigate."

"Good thinking," Ava replied, chiding herself inwardly for not considering that in advance.

Back to Toma, she said, "Okay, just try to relax. Can you feel the ship under you?"

Toma nodded.

"It took me a while to get the hang of it myself. Now use your right hand to gradually alter course."

"Which direction?" Toma asked nervously.

"You decide. You're the pilot."

The confidence boost worked. Toma shifted his hand slightly to the right while twisting his wrist. The Reaper banked slowly to starboard. A faint smile creased the young Aiwan's face. He centered the orb to right the ship, correcting their course to line up with the plotted route displayed on the HUD. Toma did this several times, banking right and left. With each maneuver, he pushed his comfort level further and grew more confident in the Reaper's responsiveness.

"All right, now let's open her up a bit," Ava said.

Using his left hand, Toma eased the throttle forward ever so gently. The Reaper accelerated, which was difficult to visualize out in the open with no seabed markers to judge speed and distance. However, at the rate in which they approached large schools of fish, which scattered at the last minute, it was evident they were traveling at a much higher rate of speed.

Suddenly, an alarm beeped on the HUD. Ava's eyes narrowed as she leaned forward to check the display. A large and fast-moving object was on an intercept course.

"Reggie, can you identify?"

"It is a herd of xipos, Captain."

"Xipos? Are they dangerous?"

"No, Captain," Kypa interjected. "Xipos are harmless creatures bred by the Fonn."

"I am also detecting multiple Aiwan lifeforms," Reggie stated.

"Those would be wranglers," Kypa explained. "They herd wild xipos by chasing them relentlessly until the creatures reach a state of complete exhaustion. This makes them easier to corral and lead back to Fonn's capital to be broken."

Ava imagined a high-speed horse drive of wild stallions. *Wow, this really is the Wild West.*

She patted Toma's shoulder. "Throttle back. I'd like to see this."

To Reggie, she added, "Put the stampede on the display."

A massive herd of xipos charged in the Reaper's direction. Whinnying in protest, the twin-tailed sea creatures with long-beaked snouts and burning red eyes stampeded to evade the Fonn wranglers.

"The herding serves two purposes," Kypa elaborated. "Xipos are work animals, so several times a year, the Fonn thin the herds to break in the next crop. It also serves as a rite of passage for adolescent Fonn's entering adulthood. Herding is quite dangerous, but every Fonn, male and female, must prove themselves out on the plains."

Ava found it all quite fascinating. She watched as the herd charged in their direction, disappeared down a ravine then reappearing on the other side.

"That is so cool," she observed. "Okay, Toma, time to resume course. You got it?"

Toma nodded with a look of confidence. "Yes, Captain."

The Reaper throttled up and continued home toward Eos, leaving behind the stampeding xipos. Once they were underway, Kypa and Ava exchanged looks. Both were thinking the same thing—Toma had a real knack for flying and, better yet, it had brought him out of his shell. Kypa flashed a proud grin. Ava winked in return, jokingly thinking to herself she better watch her back or the kid might angle for her job.

23

BOXCAR

Planet Earth
Groom Lake, Nevada

Situated in a room that felt no bigger than a large closet, Jessica Aguri sat at her temporary desk, reviewing the transcripts from recent discussions with Garza and Sizemore. Garza's demands made her chuckle. The man's gall had no bounds.

Jessica's encrypted cell phone rang. Seeing it was her boss, Director Brenham, she answered immediately.

"Agent Aguri."

"Good news. Dr. Landry is alive and well."

Jessica relaxed. "Well, that's good. Nothing sinister?"

"Nope. She called her daughter twenty minutes ago and explained that she had accepted a new consulting gig. I guess she had to leave town immediately."

"Just like that, huh?" Jessica replied, somewhat suspicious. "Where did she go?"

"Unknown," Brenham replied. "I guess she signed an NDA and couldn't reveal much. The FBI tried tracing the call in case it was a ransom demand, but it was unsuccessful."

"Huh …" Jessica said curtly. All this seemed odd, but having never met the woman, it was not for her to judge. "Well, I'm sure her family's relieved to know she's okay."

"Actually, I hear they're even more unsettled," Brenham shared. "Hold on a sec …" Silence filled the line as Brenham put Jessica on hold to take another call.

While her boss was away, Jessica could not help but wonder why Dr. Landry had not called earlier. Spotty cell service was one thing, but that she had not called her family before leaving seemed out of place for someone Nunez described as incredibly close to her family.

"Okay, I'm back. Get this," Brenham said in a conspiratorial tone. "I just got word that Dr. Landry requested a leave of absence from the CDC. Emailed it in."

"That must be some consulting gig…"

"Try twenty million dollars," Brenham said, incredulous. "She just received a deposit in an off-shore bank account."

Jessica's mouth fell open. Being a professional spy, she was forbidden to take on any side hustles due to the requirements for keeping her security clearance. Besides, who had the time? Perhaps a career in the private sector consulting for security firms was possible someday, but nothing paid anywhere close to what Dr. Landry was making.

"Who would pay her that much money?"

"Probably Big Pharma," Brenham speculated. "A scientist with her skills is worth a lot these days. Anyway, at least she's safe and no longer our concern." Brenham eyed his watch. Knowing he had another meeting to get to, he got to the real reason he had called. "Have you given more thought to my offer?"

Jessica straightened. "Yes, sir. I have, and I accept," she said proudly.

"That's good to hear, Jessica," Brenham said. "Congratulations, you earned it."

"Thank you, sir. I won't let you down."

"You won't," Brenham said confidently, although Jessica was not sure if he said it as a vote of confidence or a veiled threat.

Jessica hardly knew Brenham except by reputation. She had only been reporting to him for a short while, and save for their recent meeting at Langley, their paths had rarely crossed. That was why she was so surprised to be tapped for the Deputy Director role. Typically, a new appointee would bring along a trusted confidant, someone with a shared history and ideals. She and Brenham had little of the former, and the jury was still out on the latter. Which made her wonder: *why me?*

Brett Brenham was a well-respected operative in his own right. Like Jessica, he had cut his teeth in the field, gathering human intelligence across the globe and steadily rising through the ranks. His appointment as head of the National Clandestine Service came as no surprise. It was well-deserved.

The same could not be said for Jessica's promotion. This would set the office's rumor mill on fire. Not that she was undeserving. Jessica's career was unblemished, and she was coming off of a big win in Sanhe. Still, there were a couple of others in line for Deputy Director who many thought were being groomed for the position. Jessica's unexpected ascension would undoubtedly cause an uproar.

Perhaps that's the effect he's going for? Jessica thought. *Shake things up a bit.*

If that were the case, it was a side of Brenham that surprised even her. She knew the director to be a no-nonsense guy who expected results. Apparently, he saw something in her that she did not.

"Your promotion goes into effect immediately," Brenham continued. "You can move your stuff into your new office when you get back."

"Sounds good, sir. Is the coffee bar included?" she half-joked.

Brenham chuckled. "I'll see what I can do." Steering back to business, he asked, "What's the word on Garza and Sizemore?"

"They're both ready to cut deals," Jessica answered, sounding optimistic.

"What are they offering?"

"Sizemore obviously knows a great deal about us, beyond Mathias and Kypa. We can't let that get out. They both want full pardons and their pensions."

"Not surprising. What about Garza?"

"Get this, he wants a personal apology from the President."

Brenham scoffed. "That man's certainly got a brass set on him. He better have something good."

"According to him, we're 'missing the forest in the trees' when it comes to Mathias. Garza says we're not thinking big enough."

"Bigger than human cloning and force enhancement?"

"So he says, and he believes Peru is the key."

Brenham considered this. It was no secret that Mathias was pursuing human cloning. Groom Lake was proof of that; and sources in Russia, China, and elsewhere had confirmed he was shopping around a breakthrough force enhancement serum. Even a fool could see it had to involve Aiwan DNA. Kypa's blood and tissue samples had no doubt been removed from Groom Lake before it had been shut down, but Mathias's cloning technique was not perfected … yet. Every expert on the planet believed decoding Kypa's genome could take years, but it was possible. Mathias could then resume his illegal experiments and perhaps even create the kind of super soldier Garza had yearned for. It seemed that cloning for military purposes was no longer a question of if, but when.

However, that kind of research and development cost serious dough. Brenham eyed Edmund Mathias's psych profile sitting on his desk. He flipped it open and eyed a photo of the eccentric billionaire. Having read the report multiple times, Brenham heeded one bit of information gleaned by the agency's best profilers. Despite Mathias's age, the man was as shrewd as he was disciplined. History showed he did not spend his own money to fund his business pursuits. Investors with deep pockets did that for him. From the look of it, Mathias was already courting buyers willing to fork over the money to bring his cloning and force enhancement products to market.

Still, many questions remained. Where did Peru fit into all of this? What did Garza know that the agency did not? And what could be bigger than cloning and force enhancement?

Suddenly, it clicked in Jessica's mind. "You think Garza's referring to the crystals?"

"Possibly," Brenham replied. "But that's not anything we don't already know. Kypa's whole reason for coming to Earth was to seek them out. Hell, the President gifted Kypa a bunch before he left Earth. Maybe we're overlooking something here."

"I'll keep digging and see if Garza's just blowing smoke."

"Tell him he needs to give us something substantial," Brenham said. "I can't go to Ratliff or the President without actionable intel."

"Will do. Anything else?"

"Just keep pressing and see what you can come up with," Brenham replied. "Oh, wait, there is one other thing. CAPS says you're overdue for vacation. They want you to take some time off before transitioning to your new role. For once, I agree. I need you fresh before you return."

The CIA's Counseling and Psychological Services office were well-intentioned, but this was the first time in her career that Jessica had been ordered to take a vacation. Nevertheless, CAPS and Brenham were right. Taking a vacation had been stirring in Jessica's mind for a few days.

Although she would never admit it to her boss, Jessica was having withdrawals from GCRM and missed the children terribly. There was no way she could return to Sanhe, but taking some time to visit her nieces and nephews in Idaho was the next best thing.

Before ending the call, Jessica agreed to take some time off and return to Langley in a week. From there, she would dive headfirst into her new role as

Deputy Director of the National Clandestine Service. The thought was both exciting and scary as hell, but Jessica was never one to shy away from a challenge.

She stood from her desk and headed out of the room to go meet with Garza. Two steps down the hall, she remembered the update on Dr. Landry. In the swirl of emotions that had come with accepting her promotion, she had completely forgot about Rose. She checked her watch, hoping it was not too late to catch Colonel Nunez before the end of the business day.

The underground trek from Area S4 back to Area 51 took fifteen minutes. To her relief, Jessica found Nunez in her office with the door open. The colonel was sitting at her desk, huddled over her laptop, intently reading an email with her back to the door.

Jessica knocked, and Nunez jumped in her chair. She turned sharply to find the CIA agent standing in the doorway.

Nunez exhaled curtly, patting her heart. "Jesus, I almost peed my pants."

"Sorry." Jessica grinned. She gestured to Nunez's laptop. "You know you'll go blind if you keep doing that."

Nunez caught her drift and chuckled. "Yeah, if I had a dime for every time I said that to my husband …" She waved Jessica inside.

Jessica took a couple steps forward, remaining by the door. "Just thought you'd like to know that Dr. Landry is okay."

"Yeah, I just talked to her daughter, Becky." Nunez's eyebrows drew together. "What do you make of it?"

Jessica shrugged. "Not much, really. I heard she accepted a really well-paying consulting gig, but nobody knows for whom or where. Kinda struck me as odd, but I don't really know her."

"Tell me about it," Nunez replied, incredulous. "I mean, I don't know Rose all that well, either, but one thing I do know is that she loves her family more than anything. She would not just up and leave like this."

"Maybe she had a good reason," Jessica countered. *Like twenty million of them.* "Although, I've always had a problem with people who up and leave without giving notice, but that's just me."

Nunez's mouth dropped. "Rose resigned?"

"Took a leave of absence, actually, but you didn't hear that from me."

Nunez nodded distractedly as she considered this new information. After a long pause, she shook her head with a worrisome look. "There's definitely something fishy going on here."

"How so?"

Nunez hesitated before answering. She eyed Jessica, sizing her up, then decided to trust her gut. "Get the door."

Intrigued, Jessica closed the door then took a seat across from Nunez, expecting to hear juicy gossip. What she heard was completely unexpected.

"I think Rose was kidnapped," Nunez stated emphatically. "I think her phone call to her daughter was a cry for help."

"What do you mean?"

Nunez turned her laptop around for Jessica to see. "This is the email Becky sent me. Read it."

Jessica leaned forward. She squinted as she read the email twice. When she finished, Jessica sat back, shaking her head. "Who the heck is Boxcar Willie?"

"Right?" Nunez agreed. "I looked him up. He was a country music star who died more than twenty years ago."

Jessica struggled to make a connection.

Nunez elaborated. "During their phone conversation, Rose apologized to Becky for having to miss an upcoming concert. The thing is, they had tickets to see Willie Nelson, not this Boxcar Willie guy."

"Okay, so Rose made a mistake?"

"Not likely, I think this was intentional," Nunez explained, becoming more convinced by saying it aloud. "Hear me out. Two months ago, when we rescued Kypa off the coast of Hawaii, he was brought here to Groom Lake. Rose and Dr. Garrett were tasked by the President to make first contact."

Jessica nodded. She had read as much from the files.

Nunez continued, "Neil was the first to actually go inside the room with Kypa. Naturally, he was hesitant, so he asked Garza for a duress word in case he felt threatened. The duress word that day was Boxcar."

Jessica's eyebrows raised. *The plot thickens.*

She read the email once more then steepled her fingers under her chin, thinking. As she stared distantly at nothing in particular, Nunez watched her with quiet anticipation.

After a few moments, Jessica looked up at Nunez. "Becky's sure about all this?"

"Absolutely. Willie Nelson is Rose's favorite singer." Nunez opened the email attachment and pointed to the monitor. "See for yourself."

Becky had scanned their concert tickets. Plain as day, Rose had referenced the wrong singer. It would have been easy to chalk the mistake up to simple human error. After all, people made mistakes all the time, and no one could fault Rose for that. However, from what Nunez and others had to say about the woman, Rose Landry was not prone to such oversights. She was sharp as a tack and keenly observant.

Even more disturbing was the fact that the tickets were in Rose's name, and the concert was only two days away. If Willie Nelson was her favorite singer, she would have been bouncing off the walls to go see him, not cutting all ties with the world.

Then there was the large money transfer.

Sitting back in her chair, Jessica pursed her lips, thinking and weighing their options. For all intents and purposes, the investigation into Rose's disappearance was closed. She was no longer a missing person. And with no evidence of wrongdoing or ransom demands, they would be hard-pressed to prove she had been kidnapped. Still, her gut sided with Nunez. This was all too peculiar.

"There's something else." Jessica locked eyes with Nunez, weighing her next words carefully. "This stays between us."

Marlana nodded.

"Twenty million US dollars were transferred to an off-shore bank account this morning in Rose's name."

"What?" Nunez blurted then covered her mouth.

Jessica nodded affirmation.

Nunez sat back with a stunned look on her face.

"Listen, I don't know what all this means," Jessica admitted. "We don't have evidence of a crime and, frankly, it's completely plausible that Rose took a very lucrative consulting gig. More power to her, in my mind, but I have to admit something ain't right here. Let me take this back to my boss and see what he says. Maybe he'll let me dig around some more."

Nunez was still trying to reconcile how much money had been exchanged. She doubted Rose would have gotten involved in some kind of shady deal, but this was huge. There had to be a law being broken somewhere.

She nodded. "Thank you."

"Don't thank me yet," Jessica replied. "All we have are hunches."

Jessica was right, but that did not matter to Nunez. Rose was in trouble. That much, she was sure. Opening her desk drawer, she pulled out a five-by-seven photo and handed it to Jessica.

The photo included Nunez standing alongside President Fitzgerald, Prince Kypa, and the rest of the Operation Sundiver team. Ava Tan—aka Samantha Ri—stood beside Kypa. The Aiwan towered over the petite pilot. It brought a smile to Jessica's face.

Nunez tapped the photo. "That was taken right before Ava left for North

Korea. Rose is on the far right."

Jessica's focus narrowed on Dr. Landry with her long red hair and warm smile.

"She's one of us," Nunez emphasized.

Jessica nodded. Message received.

She handed back the photo. "I'll see what I can do."

Nunez accepted Jessica's word and put the memento away. Lightening the mood, she then said, "Since you're new here, how about dinner tonight?"

Jessica brightened. "Yeah, sure. That would be nice."

Nunez grinned, somewhat devilishly. "Great, I know just the place."

Rachel, Nevada

Later that evening, Jessica followed Nunez's directions and drove her rental car off the base, heading north on NV-375. This patch of interstate was affectionately known as Extraterrestrial Highway by the locals and every UFO hunter on the internet.

Jessica sensed something was up when she approached her destination. All of a sudden, she began seeing tons of RVs parked off a frontage road leading up to the restaurant.

"What the—"

In the front parking lot of the Little A'Le'Inn diner was a crude replica of the Reaper spacecraft. It was hoisted on the back of a rusted-out tow truck.

Jessica guffawed. "O-M-G." Then she grinned widely, looking forward to seeing inside the diner.

Jessica pulled onto the gravel lot and found an empty parking spot in front of the building. Before stepping out, her phone rang. It was Brenham.

"Agent—" she started to say then quickly corrected herself. "Deputy Director Aguri."

"It takes some getting used to, huh?" Brenham laughed.

Jessica's cheeks flushed. "Yes, sir. I'll have to work on it."

"No worries. I saw you called."

"Yes, sir. I know it's late there, so I'll make this quick. I'm not sure we should close the investigation into Dr. Rose Landry's disappearance."

"Why's that?"

"Do you know Colonel Marlana Nunez here at Groom Lake?" Jessica asked.

"Not personally, but I know of her involvement with Sundiver."

"This may be grasping at straws, sir, but we think Dr. Landry's phone call home may have been a cry for help."

"I don't understand."

"Well, aside from the fact she abruptly left town without telling anyone, suddenly took a leave of absence, *and* received a very hefty deposit in her bank account, Dr. Landry is also a Willie Nelson fan."

"Come again?" Brenham asked.

"Rose was supposed to go see her favorite singer, Willie Nelson, in concert this weekend with her daughter, Becky. However, when they spoke, Dr. Landry mentioned they were going to see someone else, an artist named Boxcar Willie." Jessica paused long enough to see if that name rang a bell. Her boss said nothing, so she continued, "Knowing her mom loved Willie Nelson so much, Rose's daughter found that error out of character, especially since Dr. Landry was the one who bought the tickets. But the real kicker came from Colonel Nunez. She's the one who realized Dr. Landry passed a duress word to her daughter."

"What duress word?"

"Boxcar, sir. That was the duress word used here at Groom Lake when first contact was made with Prince Kypa. Only Rose and Nunez would know that. Call me crazy, but something ain't right here."

"Mm," Brenham muttered, noncommittal. He thought for a moment as Jessica waited on the line in silence. Finally, he asked, "Conclusions?"

"Honestly, sir, I think this has Edmund Mathias written all over it. I've been giving this some thought, and we know Dr. Landry used to work with the guy. Also, the mystery man Rose met with the morning of her disappearance was from Peru. Mathias has a giant facility down there, and the shipments we confiscated leaving Groom Lake were intended for Lima."

"Coincidence, perhaps, but go ahead. What else?" Brenham prodded.

"That's it," Jessica admitted, slightly deflated. "I'm still working on his end game."

"Too bad the hard drives were wiped from the equipment we seized. If it wasn't for those identical twins and cloned dogs, we'd have nothing on Mathias." Brenham paused for a moment as he considered next steps. "Listen, you may be on to something here, but we have to tread lightly."

Jessica seemed taken aback. "How so?"

"The ink hasn't even dried on our new appointments, and that includes my boss, too. Mathias has friends in high places, both here and in Peru, so we need to pick our battles wisely."

"So, we do nothing?"

"I'm not saying that. We do our sworn duty to protect this country, but we do it smartly. That means we don't go sticking our necks out until we have rock-solid evidence."

Jessica rubbed her temples. A beer was sounding really good right about now.

"I hear you," she replied. "What about sending in a SOG team to observe Mathias in Peru?" SOG stood for Special Operations Group, a branch of the CIA's Special Activities Center. Similar to the Navy SEALs and the Army's Delta Force, SOG carried out clandestine paramilitary operations on behalf of the United States when the government did not want to be directly associated with a mission. Led by Deputy Yao, this was the same group that had organized Operation Sundiver.

"It may come to that, but not yet. Keep working Garza and see what he can offer, then we'll reevaluate. I can't take this up the chain until we have more to go on."

"All right," Jessica replied with mild disappointment. "I'll keep you posted."

They said goodbye, and then Jessica hung up. She let out a heavy breath. *I hate effing politics.*

Just then, a knock on the car window startled her. Jessica jumped at the sight of Nunez looming beside the vehicle, dressed in civvies.

Nunez grinned triumphantly. "Now we're even," she said, her voice muffled by the glass.

Jessica frowned as she stepped out of the vehicle. She was met by a brisk evening breeze.

Shouldering her purse, Jessica gave their surroundings a quick glance and raised her eyebrow. "Interesting choice of restaurants."

Nunez looked about. Even she was surprised by the size of the crowd. "Yeah, this place is no longer a secret. The van-lifers and UFO geeks have been flocking here ever since Ava made her not-so-subtle appearance." She gestured to the Reaper monument then pointed up the highway. "And right up there is where they confiscated Mathias's trucks carrying the clones."

Jessica recalled reading how a mob of people had blocked several of Mathias's trucks from exiting Groom Lake and, inadvertently, exposed the company's cloning operations. It was a lucky break for the feds and had made headlines around the world. The repercussions from the fallout were still being measured.

"We ate here the night before Ava left to meet up with you," Nunez said matter-of-factly.

"Oh yeah? Who's we?" Jessica asked as they headed for the entrance.

"Me, Ava, Rose, and Dr. Garrett."

"How'd you like working with him?"

"Who? Neil? Tall, dark, and handsome is cool, but funny gets a bedroom invite," Nunez joked.

The colonel's blunt humor caught Jessica by surprise.

"Seriously, he's a good guy. Very smart, *and* he surprised everyone by standing up to Garza and Sizemore. If it wasn't for Neil, we'd probably have nothing on Mathias."

"I want to talk to you about that," Jessica said grimly as they entered the diner.

Despite the full parking lot, there were several open tables inside. They were greeted by a friendly, gum-chewing waitress and seated in the back corner. Jessica was amazed by all of the old paraphernalia on the walls, not to mention the new Reaper and Prince Kypa-themed merchandise for sale.

"Looks like business is good," Nunez said to the waitress.

Margie, the waitress, rolled her eyes as she removed the pen from behind her ear to take their orders. "Tell me about it," she said, exasperated. "Don't get me wrong, we need the business, but I've been working doubles without a day off since the big air show."

Jessica and Nunez exchanged looks but said nothing.

"So, what's your favorite thing on the menu?" Jessica asked.

"Well, the Mystery Ship platter is new," Margie replied. "No one knows what the black spaceship is called, so we refer to it as the Mystery Ship, like in the Blues Image song. Anyway, the platter comes with a spicy brat, no bun, and corn on the cob. You see, we split the brat in half to make the wings of the spaceship and use toothpicks to pin it to the corn. That was my idea." She smiled as she chomped on her gum. "It also comes with a side of curly fries and mystery sauce for dipping."

Feeling adventurous, Jessica handed back her menu. "I'll go with that and a light beer on tap."

"Make that two," Nunez added.

"Coming right up," Margie said, departing for the kitchen.

Once she was out of earshot, Jessica leaned forward. "So, I talked to my boss."

Nunez bent closer. "And?" she asked in a hushed tone.

"I told him what we have so far, but he said it's not enough." Jessica shrugged. "Technically, he's right. There's no evidence of a crime being committed, at least as far as Rose's disappearance. He wants me to keep pushing Garza and Sizemore."

"Good luck with that," Nunez said dryly as their beers arrived.

Once Margie departed again, Jessica continued, "They're both wanting to cut deals, but I did some digging. As far as I can tell, neither has been to Mathias's site down in Peru … at least in an official capacity."

"Peru, huh?" Nunez pondered the idea in her head as she sipped her drink.

Jessica nodded, following suit. "I wanted to send in a surveillance team to see what they could find out, but my boss nixed it. With all that's happened recently, he doesn't want to stir things up during our first week on the job."

Nunez acted surprised. "You got a new job?"

"Yeah, Deputy Director, if you can believe that."

"Congratulations!" Nunez lifted her drink, and they tapped glasses.

"Thanks," Jessica said, downplaying her excitement. "That and five dollars might get me a cup of coffee."

Nunez could relate. She had carved out a successful career serving her country, and while she loved the military, she was not blind to its imperfections. Each branch had its own bureaucracies and headaches to contend with. At times, it was a thankless job, but Nunez accepted those challenges because wearing the uniform was never about getting stars on her shoulder boards or earning medals. And it certainly was not about making money. That was laughable. No, her reason for serving was the same as Jessica's, although in a different capacity. They served because their country called, and they had the courage to answer. Plain and simple.

"So, assuming Mathias is involved," Nunez continued, "what do you think he wants with Rose?"

"Good question. I keep going back to the man she met with on the day of her disappearance. You said he was from Peru."

"Uh-huh."

"I saw the security footage of their meeting," Jessica stated. "The man practically stormed out of the building. It was like Rose had offended him, but even she appeared shocked by his behavior."

"Whatever he wanted, you think Rose turned him down?"

Jessica nodded, thinking. The exchange appeared somewhat heated, but not reason enough to warrant kidnapping Rose, at least in her mind.

Jessica shrugged. "Perhaps Rose changed her mind and decided to go willingly." That was certainly in the realm of possibility, but neither of them wanted to believe it. "I wish we had audio, then we'd know what he wanted."

An air of frustration hung between them as neither could formulate a reasonable motive for Rose's presumed abduction.

Finally, Nunez broke the silence. "Screw it. I'll go," she said with an unexpected flash of devilry.

Jessica looked at her with a cocked eyebrow. "Go where?"

"Peru. I'll go," Nunez replied, as if it was a done deal. "I've been wanting to take some leave, anyway. I've got distant relatives in Brazil. Plus, I speak the language. Nobody will suspect me."

Jessica gave her an amusing look. "That's kind of you to offer, but we're not talking about a camping trip. This could be dangerous."

"I'm serious."

"So am I," Jessica said in earnest. "Mathias's facility is out in the middle of the jungle. It's super high-tech, and he has a small, private army protecting it. We need someone with SpecOps experience, but like I said—" Jessica stopped mid-sentence as a wild idea crossed her mind. She quickly discounted it.

"What?" Nunez coaxed her to complete the thought.

"Nothing." Jessica waved dismissively, thinking it foolish. "Just a bad idea."

"Those are the best kind. Tell me."

Jessica hesitated, telling herself to drop it, but something inside her was not so quick to dismiss the notion. "I know a guy," she said with a conspiratorial grin.

"A guy? Do tell," Nunez said as their food arrived.

Margie set both platters on the table. The corn-brat replicas of the Reaper made them laugh. Margie saw to it they had everything they needed then excused herself.

As Jessica dipped a French fry into her mystery sauce—chipotle mayo—she debated fueling this discussion any further. Common sense told her to drop it and never broach the subject again. Coordinating an unsanctioned surveillance operation on foreign soil was not only a direct violation of her boss's instructions, but it had Leavenworth written all over it. But who was she to tell Nunez where she could go on vacation.

"So?" Nunez prodded.

Jessica raised her eyes slowly to meet Nunez's. The look they exchanged sealed the deal.

Jessica leaned in and said with a hushed tone, "If we do this, you can't tell anyone. I can't even let our station chief in Lima know."

A shiver of excitement went up Nunez's spine. "Agreed. Now, who's the guy?"

Jessica checked for eavesdroppers before answering, "His name is Choi Min-jun. He's the North Korean defector who helped Ava sneak across the border."

Nunez nodded thoughtfully. "I remember him. Where is he now?"

"Montana. He's in witness protection with General Vong's daughter. Problem is, even if he agrees to go, he can barely speak English, let alone Spanish. He'd stick out like a sore thumb."

"Even more reason for me to go. My husband and I can help your boy get situated locally and handle the logistics. Then we'll hop over to Brazil to see my family while he does his recon. It's the perfect cover."

Nunez was right. If they timed it right, they could be in and out without anyone knowing. And, with any luck, maybe they could put eyes on Rose and turn up some clues about Mathias's intentions.

"I'm thinking two weeks, tops."

"Yeah." Nunez chewed on a fry. "I can't be gone any longer than that."

"Will your husband play along?"

Nunez smirked. "Are you kidding? Since Hector retired, he's been driving me up the friggin' wall. He'll jump at the chance to play secret agent."

Jessica could tell she was joking but had to be sure they were on the same page. "Marlana," she said gravely, "the less he knows, the better."

Turning serious, Nunez put her fears to rest. "You're right. We should come up with a cover story for your friend. Maybe we even fly separately."

Crap. Jessica frowned. "Those are both good ideas, but it just dawned on me. The CIA can't front the money for your trip. Nothing can trace back to the agency. That means we have to foot the bill."

"Not a biggie," Nunez said, unconcerned. "We're only talking a few nights in a hotel. The rest, we'll stay with family."

"I can pay cash for the plane tickets," Jessica offered.

"That works." Marlana sipped her beer.

Jessica's mind was already working on Min-jun's legend. Sending him in as a nature photographer was her first thought. That meant setting him up with a few cameras and lenses. She winced. This little enterprise was starting to add up.

"How long before you can leave?"

Nunez did not hesitate. "Our passports and immunizations are current. Let me clear it with General Dukes first, but we could probably leave in the next few days."

"Okay, that gives me time to make preparations and get out to Montana."

"Oh, I almost forgot." Nunez's face lit up, and she reached for her purse. She fished around inside and pulled out a silver necklace with a locket. "I was meaning to give this to you. Ava wanted Ji-eun to have it."

Jessica's mouth fell open. She recognized it immediately.

Cupping the necklace in her hands, Jessica opened the locket to see the photos of General Vong and his wife. Then she remembered the poison pin but found the tiny weapon was missing.

"How did Ava say it?" Nunez tried to recall back to the night the Reaper's crew departed Earth for Aiwa. "Oh yeah, she said she spent the dollar … on Kim Sung-il."

"What?" Jessica hissed.

Nunez nodded slowly up and down. "Said she used it on him before blowing up the mothership."

Jessica shook her head in disbelief. She had underestimated Ava greatly. A part of her wanted to call Brenham and share this, but eyeing the locket, she decided against it. It would mean more to Ji-eun if she gave it to her. Besides, as far as the agency was concerned, Kim was dead. End of story.

"Thank you. I'll pass it along."

Jessica pocketed the necklace in her purse. The two continued eating and, before long, their makeshift plan began to take shape. Feeling confident in their idea, or perhaps it was the liquid courage that came with two more rounds, Jessica and Nunez decided to call it a night. Each had a to-do list of tasks to complete in the coming days, but none more important than Jessica's recruitment of Min-jun. Everything hinged on the former SpecOps soldier's willingness to walk away from a new life and return to one filled with danger, uncertainty, and painful memories.

24

COMMON GROUND

Planet Earth
Satipo, Peru

Circumstances dictated Rose take a different course of action with Luna than she had with Kypa. Since Mathias had prohibited physical contact, Rose and Luna were forced to work on opposite sides of the glass partition. This protocol certainly hindered their progress. With no opportunity to connect telepathically—which no doubt aided Kypa's quick assimilation of Earth's languages and customs—Luna's education came slower than expected, but the Aiwan still proved to be a fast learner.

Rose was able to leave her tablet with Luna, which helped accelerate the learning curve. Like Kypa, Luna used the device to consume information at a rate Rose simply could not match. Her self-directed learning, coupled with her ability to store a high capacity of knowledge in long-term memory, made it possible to converse in English by the end of their second day together.

Luna's behavior had also changed dramatically since Rose's arrival. She no longer defended herself like a caged animal. Empowered with the information Rose shared, Luna felt strangely liberated by having a way to communicate with her captors. With each session, her relationship with Rose grew.

Sitting cross-legged in front of one another, Luna leaned in and asked politely, "Dr. Landry, please tell me about Kypa's time on Earth."

Reflecting fondly on Kypa, Rose began by simply saying, "I miss him."

Luna could see the sincerity on Dr. Landry's face and shared the sentiment.

"Shortly after the mothership went down," Rose continued, "we found Kypa in an escape pod, badly wounded. It was a miracle he survived."

"What did he remember?" Luna inquired.

"Not much. He knew your ship had been attacked but didn't know by whom. Honestly, we didn't spend much time talking about that. The trauma of the event pained him greatly, and he badly wanted to search for survivors."

Horrific scenes from the attack flashed in Luna's mind, forcing her to turn away.

Then it dawned on Rose. "Oh, my goodness, what was I thinking?" she said, covering her mouth. "Luna, please forgive me. I haven't even asked about you. You poor thing, you've been through so much." Without thinking, Rose placed her palm against the partition to offer support.

Luna took a moment to compose herself and refocus. Glancing warily at Rose's hand, she was reluctant at first to accept the invitation, but months of isolation got the better of her. Luna placed her palm up to Rose's and smiled appreciatively.

"Thank you, Doctor," Luna said. "It has been a long and lonely path to this point." She decided not to go into details. It was bad enough having to relive the nightmares every night in her sleep. "Please continue."

"Are you sure?" Rose asked, empathizing. "I'm here for you if you want to talk."

Luna removed her hand. "I appreciate that very much. Perhaps another time."

Respecting Luna's wishes, Rose placed her hands in her lap. She then regrouped mentally, thinking for a second where she had left off. "Well, let's see, Kypa learned about our world much the same way as you. A colleague and I began working one-on-one with him, exchanging information about Earth and Aiwa. To his credit, Kypa realized early on that the fate of our worlds is intertwined."

"What do you mean by that?"

"For one, we're facing a common enemy," Rose answered. "Harvesters."

Luna nodded thoughtfully. "We have been fighting them all of my life. I do not know a time without war," she reflected somberly. "Krunig is relentless."

Rose's eyebrows raised. "Krunig?"

Luna raised her gaze to meet Rose. "Grawn Krunig is the leader of a faction within the Madreen Crime Syndicate, the largest criminal organization in the galaxy. The Madreen rule the crystal trade, and Krunig's territory includes Aiwa."

Rose scribbled notes on a pad. "Kypa never mentioned Krunig or any other harvesters by name."

"There are too many to count." Luna sighed with resignation.

"And is it fair to say that Aiwa's military proliferation—to defend itself," Rose made a point to specify, "led to the overmining of crystals?"

Luna felt her cheeks flush. She took a controlled breath before answering. "Yes, overharvesting caused the quakes that destroyed Cirros, my home. I lost my entire family."

Rose's bottom lip quivered. "Luna, I'm so sorry for your loss."

Luna forced a meek smile, trying to brush it off. "That was a long time ago."

"Maybe we should stop for today?" Rose suggested, fearful of further aggravating any post-traumatic stress.

"No, please," Luna responded with a tinge of desperation in her voice. "As you said, talking does help. I want to continue."

Rose let out a heavy breath and smiled warmly. "Okay, but if I touch on something you don't want to talk about, just tell me."

Luna dipped her chin in gratitude.

"Let's see, we were talking about overharvesting. That's the reason you're here, right? Kypa hoped the crystals from Earth could help Aiwa's defenses. That's why he built the Reaper."

Luna seemed taken aback, surprised Kypa would share such information. "You know of the Reaper?"

Rose rolled her eyes. "Oh yeah. It caused quite a stir. Kypa played a key role in its recovery."

"Recovery? So, he made it back to our ship?"

"Not exactly," Rose answered with a crooked frown. "It's kinda complicated. Basically, your ship went down in a very hostile part of our world. That's why we couldn't search for survivors—the risk of starting a war was too great. This frustrated Kypa to no end because my people wouldn't allow him to leave. They wanted to keep his existence a secret." She paused to gauge Luna's reaction. Seeing none, Rose continued, "Kypa knew his best chance of rescuing any survivors and returning home was the Reaper, so he helped us send in a pilot to steal it."

Luna hung on to every word. "What happened?"

"Long story short, we succeeded. My friend, Ava, stole the Reaper and later helped Kypa escape captivity."

"Escape? Was he your prisoner?"

"Not mine," Rose was quick to defend. "There were a few people in my government who wanted to hold Kypa indefinitely."

"Mathias?"

"No, although …" Rose glanced over her shoulder then thought it wise to keep her opinions to herself. "Never mind. Anyway, myself and a few others were able to expose their intentions. Afterward, my friends, Ava and Neil, took Kypa back to Aiwa in the Reaper."

Rose's answers seemed to satisfy Luna. "What about the mothership? Did your friend, the pilot, find other survivors?"

Rose caught herself before mentioning the obercai. She softened and shook her head slowly. "Sorry, I'm afraid not."

Luna nodded solemnly.

Sensing the need to change the subject, Rose pivoted. "I'm impressed by your determination to search for Kypa. I can't imagine how hard it must've been to cross the ocean."

"Yes, it was very difficult," Luna admitted, although her journey felt like a distant memory now. "I had almost given up hope of finding my prince and resigned myself to a life alone on Earth."

Rose found Luna's reference to Kypa as "my prince" endearing. "How long have you and Kypa known each other?"

"A long time … since childhood," Luna recalled fondly. "We studied together at the Citadel, and when Cirros was destroyed by the quakes, Kypa and his family took me in. For that, I am eternally grateful."

"Kypa is very special, but so are you. He wouldn't have left if he knew you were alive, Luna. He'll be back, I promise." Rose pictured the beacon Kypa had given her, sitting in her safe at home. "Just hang in there."

Luna eyed her surroundings. "What will become of me here?"

"Mathias promised me you wouldn't be harmed," Rose assured her. "He needs your help."

Luna's brow furrowed. "My help?"

"He wants to hide the crystals on Earth," Rose explained. "He doesn't want them falling into the hands of any harvesters."

Luna considered the idea. "It is possible to cloak the crystals. Kypa and I worked on a similar technology not long ago. It would depend on the number of deposits and available technology."

"I'll let him know," Rose replied. "I'm sure he'll be eager to discuss it further with you."

"What will I get in return?"

Rose smiled thinly. *Attagirl!*

"He promised to release you."

Luna's demeanor changed in a heartbeat. She leaned toward the glass with a purpose-driven expression. "Please, tell him I want to get started immediately."

Sensing Luna's urgency, Rose realized their friendly chat was over. Now that a clear-cut path to her release was on the table, Luna was hell-bent on making it happen. Rose could not blame her for that but wanted to warn her not to trust Edmund.

Rose stood up. "I'll go tell him right now."

Filled with relief and hope, Luna stood and bowed. "Thank you, Dr. Landry. Your help is greatly appreciated."

Rose smiled warmly. "It's the least I can do. I'll be back shortly," she promised.

As Rose turned to leave, Luna called to her, "Rose?"

Hearing Luna call her by her first name took Rose by surprise. Up to this point, Luna had always referred to her formally. It stopped Rose in her tracks, and she turned sharply with a brightened expression.

"Yes, Luna?"

Luna hesitated, searching for the right words. "At first," she began, "I was very angry about being captured and confined here. Now ... now I am relieved."

Her choice of words struck Rose as odd. "Relieved?"

"Yes, if I had not been brought here, I would not have met you. I would not have learned about Kypa and our crew, either. At least I have some closure. For that, I am grateful."

Rose was not convinced Luna's presence here was a good thing but held her tongue. The walls had ears, and she could not openly speak her mind, at least not yet. Despite Edmund guaranteeing their safety, and fronting twenty million dollars, only a fool would trust him to keep his word. That much Rose had learned the hard way.

Brushing her red bangs out of her face, an epiphany struck Rose. She was never keen on the idea of Kypa reading her mind, especially after what had happened to Garza and Sizemore. That being said, Kypa and Ava had certainly made it work to their mutual benefit. In fact, their telepathic connection had probably saved both of their lives, not to mention the rest of the world.

Rose and Luna needed the same discreet bond. Unfortunately, physical contact to establish the connection was prohibited.

Perhaps a strand of hair would suffice? Rose mused.

Just then, a lunch cart appeared with Luna's next meal. Figuring it was worth a shot, Rose decided to throw caution to the wind.

"By the way," she said casually, "I probably need to update your tablet. If you don't mind, I'll bring it back after lunch."

Luna thought nothing of it and relinquished the device through the slot in the partition.

Rose tucked it under her arm. "I'll let Mathias know you're willing to help with the crystals. I'm sure he'll want to start talking specifics right away."

With that, Dr. Landry took her leave. She immediately made a beeline for the elevator, taking it to the second floor. As soon as the doors closed and the elevator began moving, Rose stole a glance at the security camera tucked in the upper corner. She averted her eyes and tried to act casual as she considered how to inconspicuously obtain a strand of hair. It seemed simple enough, but openly plucking one from her scalp would draw attention, so she decided to snatch one from her hairbrush instead.

The elevator doors opened, and Rose proceeded down the hall to her room. Several housekeeping carts carrying cleaning supplies and fresh towels lined the corridor as crews went about their duties. She stepped around one cart blocking half the hallway. As Rose passed, a short, middle-aged Peruvian woman appeared from a room to her right. They made eye contact.

Rose smiled with a friendly wave. Noticing the woman's name tag, she said cheerily, "Hola Camila."

The housekeeper brightened. "¡Hola, señora!"

Rose continued. Reaching her room, she unlocked the door and stepped inside. As Rose closed the door behind her, she gave a fleeting look back up the hall and caught the housekeeper staring at her. The woman hastily averted her eyes then retreated into a nearby room.

The incident left Rose unsettled. It was probable that the housekeeping staff was spying on her. Still, she could not show that she suspected as much. Doing her best to act nonchalant, Rose crossed to the bathroom. She set the tablet down by the sink then pretended to use the toilet.

To this point, Rose had made every attempt to block out the fact that Edmund was probably monitoring her every move. If not him, then one of his cronies for sure. Truth was she had become so comfortable here that she had not given much thought to hidden surveillance lately. But now that she was flirting with disaster, she had to assume zero privacy.

After pretending to go, Rose flushed and moved in front of the mirror to wash her hands. As she dried off, Rose leaned closer to her reflection and inspected her face from different angles. Then she acted as if she had found something wrong with her hair. Rose picked up her brush and ran it through her locks several times. Afterward, she bent over the trash can and went about removing the hair from her brush and threw it away ... all except a few strands subtly pinched between her thumb and index finger.

Rose exited the bathroom and collected the tablet, careful not to lose the hairs. Holding the tablet with her left hand, she swiped through the screens, giving the impression she was working. As she did so, Rose used her left thumb to discreetly tuck the hairs under the tablet's flexible, polycarbonate case.

It worked. The hairs were crammed inside and well-hidden.

Relieved to have that task complete, Rose finished her subterfuge by closing all of the open apps and locking the device. Heading out, she opened the bedroom door to leave.

Rose's face turned ghostly white, and she shrieked loudly, startled by the unexpected presence of Edmund and Mr. Renzo standing in her doorway.

25

QUID PRO QUO

Planet Earth
Satipo, Peru

Rose exhaled sharply, clutching her chest. "Jesus, you scared me."

"So jumpy," Edmund said with a crooked grin that belied any true remorse. "We didn't mean to startle you. Just stopping by to ask if you've had lunch?"

Rose darted her eyes between both men, gauging to see if she was in trouble. "Thank you, but I think I'll pass."

"You sure? Tuesdays are surf and turf ..." Edmund pressed.

A moment of awkward silence followed as Rose caught Renzo eyeing the tablet. "Actually, I was just updating Luna's speech app," she offered. "I was about to head back down to see her."

"Sounds like she won't be needing it much longer," Edmund remarked, pleased that they were finally getting somewhere with the Aiwan.

"Luna is progressing nicely," Rose replied. "In fact, I was meaning to speak with you. She's open to cutting a deal and helping you hide the crystals."

Edmund's face lit up. "You're kidding! That's awesome. Let's go see her!"

Something told Rose she was working herself out of a job. Despite her financial agreement with Mathias, as well as Edmund's assurances that she and her family were safe, Rose did not trust him one bit. He could renege on their deal at any time, which meant the clock was ticking to devise her own means of escape, should the need arise. With any luck, her conversation with Becky had raised a red flag. In the meantime, Luna might be her only ally. She needed time alone with the Aiwan to pass her the tablet and make the telepathic connection so they could talk in private.

"How about after lunch?" Rose suggested. "Luna is eating now."

Looking between Edmund and Renzo, Rose watched for any sign that her deferral had raised suspicion. There was a moment of disappointment on Mathias's face, which was none too surprising. However, it quickly passed, and he accepted her reasoning. The Chachapoyan was more difficult to read. Renzo wore his usual, impassive expression, which gave the impression he would just as soon kill you as hug you.

Turning to his boss, Renzo said, "We should discuss protocols before allowing the Aiwan access to the recovered tech."

Edmund nodded thoughtfully. "And for her trip to Challenger Deep," he added.

"Challenger Deep?" Rose scoffed. "You do that, and you might never see her again."

"Perhaps," Edmund granted, although the swagger in his voice said he believed otherwise. "You said it yourself, she wants to cut a deal. I'll make her an offer she can't refuse," he projected his best *Godfather* voice.

Rose understood his meaning and folded her arms, unamused.

Edmund rolled his eyes. "I'm kidding, Rose. Jeez, lighten up."

Rose let it go but saw an opportunity. "You know, if you really want to win her over, I have an idea."

"Oh yeah? Tell me."

"Move her topside," Rose answered. "Give Luna a room next to mine."

"Not with you?" Edmund suggested with a perverted grin.

"Uh, no," Rose kiboshed. "I think we both prefer to have our own space."

Edmund considered her idea but deferred to Renzo. "Your call."

"She's definitely a flight risk," Renzo stated the obvious. "We could install sensors on the windows in case she tries to break the glass and post additional guards in the hall."

Edmund slowly nodded as he considered the measures.

"What about going outside?" Rose advocated. "Luna needs fresh air and access to a pool. She must be getting tired of wearing that aquasuit all the time."

Renzo was less sympathetic to Luna's comfort, but Dr. Landry had a point. He turned to Mathias for his stamp of approval.

Edmund scratched his chin, thinking. Luna had demonstrated a propensity to lash out at her captors, and the mercs on Edmund's payroll were equally contentious. They already had itchy trigger fingers and would be hard-pressed to rely on nonlethal tasers to defend themselves, should Luna act out again.

Still, Edmund had to admit that Rose was right. Giving Luna a longer leash would earn him brownie points and no doubt improve her well-being. Perhaps that was enough to lure her into a false sense of security until he could find what really made the Aiwan tick. Once he knew her weakness, Edmund felt confident his knack for exploiting the vulnerabilities in others would open the door to securing Luna's services permanently.

"Can your men be trusted not to harm her?" Edmund pressed Renzo.

"If that is your decision, consider it done."

"Make it so. In exchange for Luna's services, I will guarantee her freedom if an Aiwan rescue ship arrives. In the meantime, we will move her to the room next to yours and grant her access—under guard, of course—to a pool and the grounds. I agree to these concessions as long as she agrees to behave and not touch anyone."

Renzo kept his misgivings to himself and departed to start preparations.

"Why don't you share the good news with our guest?" Edmund suggested to Rose. "I'll be down shortly to finalize the deal."

Rose's reaction was a mix of surprise and suspicion. "Don't you want to be there?"

"I want her to hear it from you first ... give her time to chew on the terms. If she's amenable, we can arrange unhindered access to the recovered Aiwan tech so she can get started."

"And what if she uses that technology to 'phone home,' as it were?"

Edmund shrugged, as if unconcerned, but Rose sensed it bothered him more than he let on.

"Honestly, there's not much I can do about it," he admitted shamelessly. "I'm trusting Luna will live up to her end of the bargain, and if a rescue ship comes for her, then so be it. Maybe she'll put in a good word for me."

Not likely, Rose thought.

She was not buying this façade for one minute. Edmund Mathias prided himself on never being less than ten steps ahead of the competition. To flippantly wish Luna bon voyage and let her just walk away was uncharacteristic. Edmund was definitely up to something.

"I'll pass your offer along," Rose said, stepping into the hallway.

Edmund retreated two paces to give her room.

Rose turned to close the door and could feel Edmund's eyes on her backside. She gave the door an extra tug, double-checking it was locked.

"Again, you have my thanks," Edmund said earnestly.

Rose rounded on him. Careful not to step in his BS, she replied matter-of-factly, "No thanks necessary. This is what you're paying me for, right?"

"True, but still, I'm glad you're here. Luna seems much happier, too."

"Let's hope it stays that way," Rose said, meeting Edmund's eyes. "Now, if you'll excuse me …" Rose flashed a polite smile and started down the hall with the tablet tucked under her arm.

At the elevator, she pressed the call button and waited, fighting the urge to look back and see if Edmund was watching her.

A bell chimed, and the elevator doors opened. Before entering, she quickly glanced back up the hallway. To her relief, Edmund was gone.

Rose stepped inside, pressed the button for Luna's floor, and waited for the doors to close. It felt like an eternity. At any moment, she expected Renzo to appear out of nowhere and seize the tablet.

As soon as the doors closed, Rose checked the device. A loop of one hair strand poked out from under the plastic case, making her heart leap. She discreetly tucked it back in place using her thumb then leaned against the side of the elevator. Breathing a sigh of relief, Rose closed her eyes to collect herself.

Landry, what are you doing?

Ten minutes later, Rose surrendered her tablet to the guard standing outside Luna's quarters. Her heart rate quickened, triggering memories of the first time she had used a fake ID in college to sneak into bars. She expected the guard to give her a suspicious look, much like the bouncer had, but perhaps grandmothers did not warrant the same scrutiny as a young coed.

The guard gave the device a haphazard glance then returned it to Rose without a second thought. He then politely opened the door.

Rose thanked him as she entered.

Inside, she found Luna sitting on the floor, anxiously awaiting word if Mathias had accepted her terms. She straightened as Dr. Landry approached.

Noticing that Luna's empty food tray had been passed through the partition to her side, Rose set it aside on the nearby cart to be cleaned up later. She then sat across from Luna.

"How was lunch?"

"Delicious, thank you. I can see why Kypa enjoyed your local cuisine so much."

"Yes, he was rather fond of squid." Rose chuckled, recalling Kypa's voracious appetite. She turned the tablet around so Luna could see the screen and rested it on the floor. "I changed a few settings," she explained.

Rose made casual conversation while swiping through multiple screens with her free hand. All the while, she worked the edge of the tablet's case up with her opposite thumb to reveal the hair tucked underneath.

Luna picked up on Rose's subtleties. Ignoring the tablet lesson, the Aiwan's bulbous eyes narrowed, zeroing in on what the doctor was trying to show her. Spotting the hairs, Luna's eyes widened. She gave Rose an odd look, expecting some kind of cue or explanation, but the scientist remained stone-faced.

"You can review these updates later," Rose said as she slid the tablet through the partition opening.

Their eyes met for an instant, and an unspoken understanding was reached. Luna accepted the device and set it aside without further comment.

"I spoke to Mathias," Rose continued without missing a beat. "He's very excited to hear that you're willing to help him hide the crystals. In exchange for your help, he says you are free to leave whenever a rescue ship returns to Earth. Also, he agreed to move you to a new room with access to a pool, *and* you get to walk the grounds outside. All he asks is that you make no physical contact with the staff. That's a deal breaker."

Edmund's last request regarding no physical contact evoked a devious grin from Luna, and rightfully so. Now his men knew better than to mess with her.

"Fair enough," Luna acquiesced. "What would he say if I wanted to leave right now?"

Before Rose could answer, the exterior door opened. Rose twisted her torso to find Edmund entering alone. "Speak of the devil," she muttered.

Edmund approached, wearing a shit-eating grin. He waved to Luna behind the glass. "Hey, partner!"

Luna stood and customarily dipped her chin politely. "Greetings, Dr. Mathias."

"*Pshaw.*" He waved dismissively. "Please, call me Edmund."

Rose interjected, "Luna was just asking if she was free to leave right now if she wanted."

"Of course, you both are," Edmund replied as if that fact was never in doubt. "Although, I would caution against it, Luna. I'm sure, by now, Dr. Landry has explained to you the chaos that is happening around the world since Kypa's arrival. Humanity was unprepared to meet inhabitants from other planets. It's crazy out there. You're much safer here."

"If I agree to help you …"

"You can stay regardless," Edmund assured her. "I mean that, Luna. You are my guest, but make no bones about it, one way or another, I'm going to harvest all of the crystals on Earth. Your help would certainly expedite the process. Off-world harvesters are coming. Kypa was sure of it. But if we work together, both of our worlds can benefit."

Luna agreed.

"Is it possible to hide the crystals from scanners?" Edmund asked point-blank.

Luna nodded slowly, having given it some thought. "With the right materials, I believe I can build a small-scale cloaking device. Its effectiveness would depend on the size of the site, of course."

"There is only one site that I'm aware of," Mathias stated. "I've been there and can show you pictures. Is there a way of detecting other deposits?"

Luna sighed heavily, wishing she had access to lab equipment back on Aiwa. "Again, it will depend on available resources. Dr. Landry said that you have recovered pieces of Aiwan technology?"

"We have. I'd like to show them to you, but first, did Dr. Landry share with you my terms?"

"She has," Luna replied. "In exchange for my help cloaking the crystals, you will provide me with a new room, access to a pool, and freedom to walk the grounds."

"Chaperoned," Edmund clarified. "And no physical contact with any of my staff. In return, you have my word no harm will come to you while you are my guest."

"How many crystals do I get to keep?"

"We split the find 50-50," Edmund proposed. "You keep half of everything we harvest."

Luna considered his offer. After a brief pause, she nodded agreement. "Your terms are reasonable. I agree."

Edmund rubbed his hands together like a greedy banker. "Excellent. I'll need a day or two to work out the details on your new accommodations. As for your freedom of movement, naturally, we need to develop trust. Will you consent to wearing gloves to cover your hands when others are around?"

"I will."

"Wonderful." Edmund could hardly contain his joy. He looked over his shoulder and caught the guard's attention. Mathias gave him a thumbs-up.

The guard nodded then spoke into his radio, alerting the rest of the

264 | TODD HOSEA

security team.

To Luna, Edmund said, "Okay, next door is the lab where we keep the recovered Aiwan technology. If you're ready, I'll take you over."

Luna grabbed the tablet and smiled. "Let us begin."

26
ILLUMINATION

Planet Aiwa
Supra, Realm of Eos

"So, how's it going in Cirros?" Neil asked with a mouthful of toothpaste.

"Really well, actually," Ava replied. She sat on the step leading into the cockpit, brushing her wet hair. "Kypa's making a lot of progress with the terraforming."

It was day three on Aiwa, and their stay aboard the Reaper had begun to feel like an extended camping trip in a high-tech RV. Sharing a common living space—a tiny one at that—had taken some getting used to. Neither had seriously considered their living arrangements before setting off from Earth, but Neil and Ava were falling into an amicable routine. They had yet to get on each other's nerves; at least, neither had voiced any displeasure. However, their tiptoeing around each other in the tight confines of the Reaper had begun to wear off the novelty of their space adventure.

A hot shower helped.

Technically, their nano-suits were capable of keeping their bodies clean and hydrated, but a hot shower was one creature comfort that Ava cherished almost as much as coffee. To help in this area, Kypa had made some special modifications last night during their return from Cirros. As if he did not have enough on his mind, he was kind enough to rig a wet bath down in the engineering section.

Ava had pulled rank this morning and used the new shower first. After another restless night of sleep, standing under a high pressure flow of steaming, hot water had felt therapeutic.

Meanwhile, Neil finished brushing his teeth. After a quick rinse and spit, he placed his used cup of gray water in the synthesizer. Once it was gone, he stowed his toiletries back in his bag in the storage compartment. He then took the liberty to convert their bunk beds into a quaint, holographic dinette set so they could enjoy breakfast together.

Ava continued to brush out her tangles. "What's on your docket today, Mr. Ambassador?"

Neil thought for a moment. Their days had been long and draining, leaving little time at night for them to debrief. For him, after a full day of extroverting and meeting with various Aiwan officials, the only thing on Neil's mind when the Reaper returned each day was to climb onto his bunk and crash.

"Well, I'm meeting with Lord Zefra of Fonn this morning," he replied matter-of-factly. "She's taking me to watch a training exercise with the Royal Guard."

"That sounds cool," Ava said, wishing she could be there to watch.

"It sure beats all of the diplomatic stuff," he replied with a sigh. "Don't get me wrong; it's all very interesting, and the Aiwans are starting to warm up to me, but—"

"But what?"

"But they're *really* starting to warm up to me," Neil said half-joking. "I can't get a word in edgewise with some of them. They mean well—I know—and I love the cultural exchange, but a few of them have no qualms trying to curry favor before we negotiate a trade deal."

"Oh yeah?" Ava asked as she tied her hair back in a ponytail. "What did you tell them?"

"Nothing, really. I just listened." Neil shrugged. "Kypa told me not to commit to anything until he's done in Cirros. Then he promised to help guide me in the treaty talks."

Ava considered this and agreed. "He's probably right. From the sounds of it, Kypa's preliminary work in Cirros should be finished in the next day or two."

"Then what? Do we head back home?"

"Probably," Ava replied. "I'm sure everyone back on Earth is anxious to hear about our adventure, but I'd like to see some of the capital first. All I've seen since we arrived was the inside of this ship." She looked at the ceiling. "No offense, Reggie."

Always present, Reggie replied, "None taken, Captain."

Ava grinned as Neil turned to the synthesizer and ordered two chocolate vanilla creme Pop-Tarts and a tall glass of ice-cold milk. His food materialized before him, toasted just the way he liked it.

Biting into the first frosted pastry, Neil closed his eyes and nodded. "Oh yeah," he spoke with his mouth full, savoring every morsel. "I swear, this ship is like Wonka's factory."

Ava chuckled then came to her feet and stowed the brush with her belongings. Next, she ordered a veggie omelet and coffee before joining Neil at the table.

"Kypa sure seems happy to be home," Neil remarked as he finished off the Pop-Tart and washed it down.

"Wouldn't you?" Ava replied, cutting into her eggs. "Distance makes the heart grow fonder, right?"

"I suppose," Neil granted.

A silence followed as both continued eating.

Ava reflected on Neil's assessment and agreed. Having spent the most time with Kypa recently, she saw a change in their friend, as well. He seemed to have a different outlook on fatherhood since returning from Earth.

Sensing Neil had more to say on the topic, Ava finished a bite and asked, "Is something wrong?"

Neil thought for a moment then shrugged it off. "Nah, I was concerned about his state of mind. I mean, he does have a death sentence hanging over his head. I was just worried, that's all."

"Honestly, I think he sees his innocence as a foregone conclusion. The terraforming is working, so why give any energy to his enemies?"

"Good point." Neil finished his drink. "So, what do you do while Kypa's working outside the ship?"

"Toma's tagged along each day, so he's taken me cave diving," Ava replied, lifting her eyebrows.

"What?" Neil feigned jealousy.

"It's kinda fun, actually, but kinda scary, too. After our run-in with the zemindar, you never know what predators might be lurking about."

"I'm swimming with a different kind of shark," Neil joked at the expense of his Aiwan diplomatic peers. "Wanna trade?"

"No, thanks," Ava rejected unequivocally. "The President appointed you, remember?"

"Lucky me," Neil replied with a hint of sarcasm. "Although ..." He stood and retrieved two items from his bag. "Check these out ... gifts from the realms of Dohrm and Maeve."

Neil set two small objects on the table. The first was an ivory-colored gem with a symbol carved in the center.

"I can't remember the name of it, but that symbol represents the search for infinite wisdom," Neil explained. "Lord Cara gave it to me. She's from Maeve. That's where the Citadel resides, the Aiwan center for knowledge."

Ava nodded, impressed. She picked up the stone and eyed it from different angles. "I feel smarter already."

"Right?" Neil played along. "Try balancing it on your head, then you'll look really smart," he dared.

"Uh-huh," she replied dryly. Ava handed back the stone. "Toma goes to the Citadel," she remarked, frowning. "Says he gets bullied a lot because of his father."

Neil sighed. "That's tough. Here I thought bullying was just a human flaw."

"I guess not." Ava picked up the second object and gave it a curious look. The six-inch cylindrical tube was made of a lightweight alloy with eight small holes drilled into the shaft, four each on opposing sides. "What's this?"

"It's a fertility flute," Neil replied, trying to keep a straight face.

Mortified, Ava immediately put it down on the table and recoiled her hands.

Neil laughed heartily. "Apparently, they make more than ships in Dohrm," he quipped.

Ava made a face then chuckled.

"This could be why Kypa's so happy to be home. It's mating season."

Ava nearly spit her coffee on Neil. "You think that's why he needed our help to steal this ship? Kypa wanted to get home in time to get laid?" She laughed.

Neil raised his hands, as if not to judge. "Hey, I can't fault him for having priorities."

Ava shook her head, grinning. She pictured Mark Jordan, recalling fondly how he always got a silly grin on his face before they made love. It was like Christmas morning, and he could not wait to open his gifts.

That reminder sobered Ava's mood, but it was interrupted by Reggie.

"Captain, Prince Kypa is approaching."

"Shoot-dang, it's that time already?" Ava said to herself. "Drop the ladder for him, would you, Reg?"

"Yes, Captain."

Ava came to her feet and finished off her coffee as Neil stowed the trinkets. He then cleared the table and deactivated the hologram dinette. Ava added her mug to his pile of dishes at the last second before they disappeared.

Kypa arrived moments later, climbing up the steps. "Good morning, my friends."

Neil and Ava greeted him in unison. Both picked up on Kypa's cheerful disposition and grinned inwardly.

"Ready for another productive day?" Ava asked.

"Indeed," Kypa replied. "Although, we will have to cut the day short. This evening, the crystals you provided are being put to use. My father plans to lift the rolling blackouts and has asked that we attend an unveiling as the capital returns to full power."

Ava elbowed Neil and smiled. This was encouraging news on the diplomatic front.

"Absolutely, we wouldn't miss it," she replied for both of them.

"Good. It is settled," Kypa said. "Oh, and Neil, Lord Zefra's escorts are waiting for you at the hangar entrance. I did not want their presence with me to alarm you, so I had them keep their distance."

"Much obliged, sir," Neil replied. "Well, I guess that's my cue to skidoo," he said lightly, checking his pockets to make sure he had not forgotten anything. Then he remembered his nano-suit did not have pockets. Neil chuckled and started for the ladder. "You kids have fun without me."

"Always," Ava called to him as he disappeared below deck.

To Kypa, she asked, "Are we waiting for Toma?"

Kypa shook his head. "No, he has to prepare for his return to the Citadel. We will see him tonight."

Ava considered mentioning Toma's troubles at the Citadel but thought better of it, remembering her promise to his son. Toma wanted to handle it himself.

"Sounds like a plan," she said dismissively. "Shall we get going?"

Kypa nodded and followed Ava to the cockpit.

Once they were at their stations, Ava called for clearance to depart. Permission was granted without delay, and the Reaper lifted off. Feeling more comfortable navigating the capital's traffic, Ava steered the ship out of the city and headed back to Cirros.

Meanwhile, Neil met up with his escorts—two impressive-looking warriors of the king's Royal Guard. Neil followed them to the lift that took him up to the main concourse. There to greet him was Lord Zefra, Warden of Fonn.

Dressed in a green, sheer robe that matched her piercing eyes, Zefra dipped her chin regally. "Greetings, Ambassador Garrett."

Neil mirrored her welcome. "Greetings to you, Lord Zefra. Thank you for taking time out of your busy schedule to meet with me today."

"Walk with me," she said, gesturing to her right.

Zefra's no-nonsense approach caught Neil off-guard, but it was also a welcome change compared to his dealings with the other heads of state. He fell in step beside her.

As they proceeded down the corridor at a leisurely pace, Neil was taken by Lord Zefra's reserved cordialness. He soon discovered she was not prone to idle chit-chat. She had a habit of carefully considering each word and speaking with unabashed directness.

"You wish to present trade terms to King Loka, yes?"

"That's the plan," Neil replied. As soon as the words left his mouth, he regretted the tone they implied and decided to backtrack. "Actually, I'm not here to present terms. My hope is that we can reach an agreement that is amicable to both sides. I want us to negotiate in good faith."

"Mm," Zefra muttered. "Have others tried to impose their terms on you?"

"Yes, although some have been more direct than others." Neil chuckled. "But I have remained neutral on the subject. I don't plan to formally address any terms until Prince Kypa is fully exonerated. He will act as our intermediary."

"I see," Zefra replied. She walked with her hands clasped behind her back. "And you feel Prince Kypa can act impartially?"

"Absolutely. From what I know of Kypa, Aiwa and its people come first to him. That I have no doubt," Neil attested. "I'm not naïve enough to see the conflict of interest, but I believe in Kypa. I trust he will do right by both of us. Whether or not we all want to admit it, Earth and Aiwa need each other … at least for the time being. We're facing a common enemy, and together we are much stronger."

Zefra concurred. "Inspiring words, Ambassador. But how can we be certain humans are trustworthy?"

Neil smiled. "You know, my mother used to say, *Don't trust everything you see. Even salt looks like sugar*," he said lightly.

Lord Zefra said nothing, prompting Neil to give a furtive glance in her direction. Judging by Zefra's scrunched brow, his attempt at humor had crashed and burned.

"Never mind." Neil waved dismissively. "I guess what I'm trying to say is that we're both looking for reasons to trust one another. We made the first move by returning Prince Kypa safely and gifting you crystals. Surely, that is enough to start us down the path of friendship."

"Indeed," Zefra granted.

They continued down a long corridor lined with large windows that ran from floor to ceiling. Walking in silence, Neil marveled at the exotic fish swimming by as Lord Zefra mulled on his remarks.

He was about to ask a follow-up question when Zefra veered to a set of double doors to their right. The two Royal Guards in their detail hustled to reach the entrance first and open the doors.

Zefra stopped and turned to Neil. "I sense that your words are sincere, Ambassador. As you are aware, these are dangerous times, and trust is something we take very seriously. It must be earned, not purchased."

"I agree," Neil replied.

"Good. That is why I have brought you here." She gestured inside.

Neil followed Lord Zefra through the doors to a unique training facility. Directly ahead was a dome-shaped enclosure filled with seawater and contained by an invisible energy field. Within the dome, Aiwan warriors sparred with energy pikes and shields. The scene conjured images of Roman gladiators practicing hand-to-hand combat for upcoming tournaments in the Colosseum.

Curious about the physics of the enclosure, Neil approached the invisible barrier. Fearful if he touched the energy field he might get zapped or cause it to start leaking, he kept his distance while peering toward the ceiling. As warriors battled underwater less than six feet to his left, Neil could see additional Aiwans entering the dome from above.

"It's open at the top," he observed, resituating for a better look.

"Correct," Zefra replied. "The Royal Guards use this facility for subterranean combat training."

"And to weed-out candidates," came an unfamiliar voice.

Neil rounded sharply to find a daunting male warrior standing beside Lord Zefra. He held an energy pike in one hand. Strapped to his forearm was a device that, when activated, generated a personal shield.

The Aiwan's stealthy arrival surprised Neil almost as much as his physical presence. Besides being tall, lean, and muscular, the warrior sported unique markings on his head. Unlike those on Kypa and his family, which were a turquoise blue, this Aiwan's dark green markings matched those of Lord Zefra.

"Ambassador Garrett, this is my son, Rega, Commander of the Royal

Guard." Gesturing to Neil, she added, "This is Ambassador Garrett of planet Earth."

Rega? It took Neil a second to place the name, then he recalled his conversation a few days earlier with Princess Seva. Commander Rega was her betrothed.

"It's an honor to meet you, Commander," Neil replied. "Congratulations on your engagement to Princess Seva."

Commander Rega gave Neil a once-over then dipped his chin politely but never took his eyes off the human.

"You are aware of the arrangement between our two houses," Lord Zefra remarked, finding it curious the human was current on such matters. "Tell me, what do you think of the match?"

Nonplussed, Neil stammered a reply. "I, uh, think Rega is a lucky man … *Aiwan,*" he corrected with a smile. "Your union is scheduled for the next rotation, if I recall."

Rega nodded.

"If tradition allows, I would be honored to attend."

"Of course, Ambassador," Zefra interjected on her son's behalf. "The entire kingdom will gather here in Supra for the ceremony. You are most welcome to attend."

"Thank you," Neil said. "If you don't mind me asking, does marrying the princess affect your standing with the Royal Guard?"

"I am required to resign my commission, if that is what you mean," Rega answered evenly.

Neil got the impression Zefra's son was none-too-pleased by this requirement. *Or was it at the king's behest?* he wondered.

"I see." Neil nodded. "Who will be taking your place?"

Commander Rega pointed behind Neil. "Major Gora will be my replacement."

Neil rounded to the training dome. As four warriors took turns lunging, parrying, and riposting with their pikes, Major Gora swam off to the side observing. He intervened when necessary to correct their techniques and tactics. Neil marveled at the warriors' fighting skills.

"Thank you, Rega. We have taken enough of your time," Lord Zefra said, cueing her son to take his leave.

Rega bowed dutifully then departed.

Zefra watched him walk away, regarding him proudly. "My son will be exchanging one title for another, Ambassador," she continued. "That is why I wanted to introduce you. You see, Royal Guards must swear strict loyalty to the crown—no mates, no offspring while serving. It is a special calling that requires great sacrifice and devotion."

"It must have been a difficult decision for your son to resign his commission, especially during times of war," Neil remarked.

Zefra sighed. "It took some convincing," she admitted. "Rega is not a politician, nor does he strive to be king. If anyone was ever meant to be a Royal Guard, it was him. But sometimes we must make personal sacrifices for the greater good."

"You mean a union between Fonn and Eos?"

"Yes. This war has taken a great toll on Aiwa," Zefra explained. "With the five realms essentially reduced to four, our once noble society has begun to lose its way. King Loka sensed as much. That is why he betrothed the princess to my son."

In the back of his mind, Neil considered the impact that military backing had on the crown. Based on Lord Zefra's point of view, the influence her son and Commodore Boa had on public perception of the king reached further than Neil had anticipated. He assumed that Aiwa, an advanced society, had moved beyond the need for military support to maintain government stability and was focused more on good governance.

Is Aiwa's government really that fragile? he wondered. Judging by the air of Zefra's comments, perhaps Aiwan society was unraveling faster than Kypa had led him to believe.

"Well," Neil began, still gathering his thoughts, "let's hope an alliance between Earth and Aiwa can bring a quick end to the war, and your son and soon-to-be daughter-in-law can begin their lives together in peace."

Lord Zefra smiled thinly and continued walking.

During the remainder of their time together, she made no attempt to illicit favor or sway Neil's opinion. Zefra asked pointed questions about Earth, wanting to learn more about humans and their need for Aiwa's protection. Neil fielded her questions admirably, sparking deeper conversations as they strolled the palace.

When they parted company thirty minutes later, both diplomats walked away with a greater sense of mutual admiration. Neil had every reason to feel intimidated by the leader of the Fonn, but to her credit, Lord Zefra showed patience and understanding with her human counterpart. In the end, it seemed the foundation was in place to begin good faith negotiations for a future trade agreement.

The two guards led Ambassador Garrett back to the lift that led to the royal family's residence. Alone with his thoughts, Lord Zefra's words ruminated in Neil's mind, "*Trust must be earned, not purchased.*"

Taking those words to heart, Neil realized it was not a coincidence that they had run into Zefra's son, Commander Rega, on their tour. Nor was it by accident that the meeting had taken place beside the training dome for the Royal Guard—the epitome of service and devotion in Aiwan culture. Neil took all of this to mean one thing: if Earth and Aiwa were to be allies, their relationship had to be based on more than the exchange of Magnetarite.

For the remainder of the day, Neil spent time with Maya and Seva. With Toma leaving for the Citadel soon, preparations were made for his return to school. Afterward, Seva took Neil on a trip to the serpentine-like central core. There, he witnessed firsthand as the crystals from Earth were prepped for integration into the core's main power grid.

They returned to the palace afterward, where Ava and Kypa, along with his entire family, were waiting. Little Fraya ran to Neil, clinging to his leg all the way down the hall. No sooner had they arrived did Kypa turn them around.

"Come," Kypa said with excitement, herding his family toward the lift. "It is almost time for the special light show."

Arya and Fraya jumped for joy and raced to the lift. The adults followed, along with Toma, who nonchalantly made sure he was next to Ava.

"Helmets on," Kypa reminded his friends. "And if you are willing, deactivate your nano-ring's telepathy jamming so we can communicate underwater."

Neil and Ava agreed. Filled with nervous excitement, they activated their hologram helmets as seawater began entering the lift. By the time they reached the top of the palace spire, the lift was flooded and pressurized.

"*Ready?*" Kypa asked.

Ava nodded vigorously. Neil appeared hesitant. This was his first venture into the open ocean, let alone at crush depth.

Kypa opened the door. Fraya and Arya burst outside, anxious to play. Maya, Seva, Toma, and Kypa followed with Neil and Ava lagging behind. Neil half-expected to implode, but, as promised, their nano-suits compensated for the conditions. Neither felt a twinge of discomfort.

Treading water in the opening, Kypa waved them out. "*Join us!*"

"After you, Mr. Ambassador." Ava gestured, speaking over their commlink.

"Nuh-uh, Captain. You get to go first this time," Neil insisted.

Ava playfully punched Neil's arm then accepted Kypa's hand. He helped her outside as Neil brought up the rear.

Out in the open, both humans were transfixed by the spectacular, overhead view of the city. It was a surreal feeling to be floating above the underwater skyscrapers and not experience the fear of height or falling.

Around them, the children chased one another playfully, while Maya and Seva carved fluidly through the water like ballerinas dancing across a stage. Their elegance was matched only by their sheer enjoyment of being outside in their element. This sparked an idea for Ava, who was already growing tired of treading water. With a simple thought command, the buoyancy in her suit increased while the feet of her nano-suit reshaped to form diving fins.

"Hey Neil, check these out," she called to him.

Neil's trepid expression morphed to a broad smile. "Bloody good! How did you—"

"Just a simple thought command." She grinned. "Increase your suit's buoyancy fifteen percent. That helps, too."

Neil succeeded on both counts. Now feeling more attuned with his environment, he joined the children's game of tag. However, even with the aid of his nano-suit, Neil could not keep up with them. It did not matter. The children laughed and played, much to the enjoyment of the adults who watched.

Their game continued for several minutes until King Loka and Queen Qora arrived. They were accompanied by Commander Rega and Major Gora.

Kypa's mood sobered at the sight of his father. Floating beside him, Maya noticed his wide grin fade.

"*What is it?*" She followed his eyes to the open lift and understood why.

Before she could say anything, Kypa swam to his parents. Princess Seva followed.

"*Father … Mother.*" Kypa bowed his head, being more formal than necessary.

His parents replied cordially, but the awkwardness between father and son was evident.

Thankfully, Fraya and Arya broke the tension. Ignoring all etiquette, the children appeared suddenly and thrust themselves onto their grandparents, catching the king and queen by surprise. The girls wrapped their tiny arms around the legs of Loka and Qora, drawing their laughter. This injection of humor seemed to relax everyone.

As the rest of the family gathered around, Neil and Ava hung back to give them space. They watched the reunion with enjoyment until Kypa insisted they join them.

It was then that Queen Qora picked up on Seva stealing glances at her betrothed, Commander Rega. Remaining at his post by the lift, Rega treaded water in place while holding his shield and pike at the ready. Qora reached out to Loka, bringing this to his attention.

Slow on the uptake, Loka realized she was correct, as usual. He turned to Rega. "*At ease, Commander. You will be family soon. Please, join us.*"

"*Yes, sir,*" Rega answered dutifully. He exchanged looks with Major Gora, his soon-to-be-replacement as head of the Royal Guard, ensuring he had overwatch covered.

Gora gave him a head bob, urging him to go.

Mixing in with the family, Rega was welcomed by Seva and the others.

Fraternizing with the royal family came difficult for the seasoned warrior. He could not shed his military bearing completely, but politely exchanged greetings and was introduced to Ava. Small talk followed as the family tried to put Rega at ease.

Moments later, Rega received a signal that the central core was ready to begin. Informing the king, Loka gave the command to proceed then gathered the family around. They looked to the south, at the darkened region of the capital currently affected by the blackouts. Suddenly, that area lit up with the warm glow of purple and orange hues. The family oohed and aahed. Seeing Supra fully illuminated for the first time in years brought elation and relief.

Kypa retrieved a hologram projector from his belt and activated the device. He held it up so the entire family could see. On display were three live feeds from the capitals of Fonn, Maeve, and Dohrm. They, too, were celebrating the end of the blackouts.

Neil swam over and gave Kypa a congratulatory clap on the shoulder.

Kypa beamed, taken in by the moment. "*Let us hope this is the dawn of a new era for both our worlds.*" Neil nodded agreement.

As the children returned to playing, Kypa transferred his gaze to his father to gauge his reaction. Their eyes met and, in a rare display of emotion, King Loka smiled proudly and nodded approval. No words were exchanged as Kypa felt his cheeks flush. The king then departed with his guards in tow.

Queen Qora smiled warmly at her son, knowing how much this meant to Kypa. She then joined Loka in the lift.

Kypa watched the doors close, quietly savoring the much-needed affirmation from his father. As soon as they were gone, Arya touched his arm.

"*Tag, you are it!*" she announced, then swam away.

Kypa turned to see his family and friends spread out, eagerly awaiting his response. With the capital fully illuminated in the background, Kypa beamed inwardly, grateful to be surrounded by those he cherished most in life.

Counting himself lucky, Kypa laughed and declared, "*Game on!*" as he joined his family.

27

RECALLED

Planet Earth
Missoula, Montana

It was two hours into her first trip to a Walmart Supercenter and Vong Ji-eun—aka Samantha Ri from Bakersfield, California—was nowhere close to leaving the store. What began as a simple run to pick up some toiletries had turned into a full-fledged shopping spree, compliments of the United States government.

Wide-eyed and speechless, Ji-eun had covered the length of the store at least twice, visiting every aisle. Top to bottom, she closely examined nearly every item on the shelves and took great pride in greeting every single person along the way. Her favorite location was the baby aisle. Well into her second trimester with her baby bump now showing, Ji-eun was fascinated by all of the ways Americans showered their infants with "stuff."

Never far behind was her burly FBI handler, Agent Boyd McDonnell, who was a career man scheduled to retire in six months. Ji-eun's fellow North Korean expatriate, Choi Min-jun—now known as Pei Wang—brought up the rear, pushing a full cart along with McDonnell. Both men were dressed in local attire that included blue jeans, hiking shoes, camouflage hunting jackets, and matching John Deere ball caps. McDonnell towered over Min-jun and, together, they resembled Big and Little Enos Burdette in the movie *Smokey and the Bandit.*

In addition to their matching outfits, the unlikely pair also shared a long look of boredom. Not wanting to spoil Ji-eun's fun, they hid their malcontent as best they could. Slowly but surely, they crept along in Ji-eun's wake, pretending to share her enjoyment of American culture.

One area of the store did catch Min-jun's attention. It was a section filled with newly arrived, alien-themed merchandise. From T-shirts and hats to all sorts of wall hangings and toys, Prince Kypa's image, and that of the Reaper, were plastered everywhere. Min-jun had no idea what to make of it at first, then Agent McDonnell explained the recent events in North Korea.

Shocked by this news, Min-jun's thoughts jumped to the young woman whom he had helped cross the border to switch identities with Ji-eun.

It cannot be a coincidence, he surmised with grave concern.

Min-jun kept his thoughts to himself. He dared not discuss it publicly with Agent McDonnell, let alone in a crowded department store. To his knowledge, their likable chaperone did not appear to know who Min-jun and Ji-eun were in real life. Later perhaps, he would share this news with Ji-eun when they were alone.

Thirty minutes later, the trio exited the store, pushing four shopping carts full of new items to fill Ji-eun's nursery. Agent McDonnell's SUV was packed solid by the time they finished loading. They drove away, satisfied they had done more than enough damage for one day.

"Anybody hungry?" McDonnell asked.

Ji-eun sat in the front passenger seat. She turned to him with an excited grin on her face, still on an emotional high from her shopping spree. "Oh, yes. Please."

She then twisted around to face Min-jun, who was sitting in back, quietly keeping to himself. "Min-jun—sorry—*Pei*," she corrected. "Are you hungry?"

Min-jun looked completely unenthused. He was sandwiched against the door with his arms pinned to his sides by plastic bags filled with boxes of baby wipes and diapers. The ex-member of the Korean People's Army Special Operation Force nodded patiently with a simple, "Yes." *Anything to get out of this car*, he did not add.

Ignoring his plight, Ji-eun clapped happily. "He says yes."

"Great," Agent McDonnell said. He grinned. "I saw a place earlier that looked interesting."

The trio made their way through town along Mullan Road, which ran parallel to the Clark Fork River. It was a cold and dreary day with overcast skies and five inches of fresh snow on the ground, yet nothing could dampen Ji-eun's spirits. This was their first outing since arriving in Missoula. She had her face glued to the window, taking everything in. The way of life and the scenic beauty was vastly different from the bleakness of Hoeryong.

Made popular by the movie, *A River Runs Through It*, Missoula nestled in the heart of the Northern Rockies where five valleys converged. It was known as the "Garden City" for its lush, green landscape and dense forestry, making it the perfect getaway for nature lovers.

The city also hosted a robust music scene. One bar in particular, Annie's Axes, had caught Agent McDonnell's attention earlier when they had entered town. The sign outside boasted loud music, sharp axes, and cheap beer. What could possibly go wrong?

Happy hour was already underway when they arrived at the two-story establishment. As they stepped out of the car, every note of Dwight Yoakam singing "Fast as You" could be heard loud and clear.

Min-jun casually surveyed the parking lot out of habit then followed Agent McDonnell and Ji-eun inside. The moment they walked through the doors, sensory overload triggered all of Min-jun's defenses. It was the wildest and loudest environment he had ever experienced.

"Hi folks!" a busty, young woman behind the hostess stand greeted. "Welcome to Annie's Axes."

Seeing the hostess nearly popping out of her low-cut tank top, Min-jun looked away with embarrassment, while McDonnell stepped forward to request a table. Meanwhile, Ji-eun was frozen in place with culture shock. Staring down at them from behind the hostess was the stuffed head of an enormous bull moose mounted on the wall. The wide-eyed and open-mouthed expression on the animal's long face was disturbing enough, but the throwing axe impaled in its skull right between its fuzzy, six-point antlers was over the top.

Ji-eun and Min-jun exchanged uneasy looks as the hostess grabbed three menus.

"Right this way." She smiled, gesturing for them to follow.

Inside the crowded dining area, they made their way to an empty table with a window view. The trio drew several curious glances from patrons. McDonnell paid the gawkers no mind, while Ji-eun smiled awkwardly and bowed to each table as they passed. Again, Min-jun brought up the rear.

Even-faced and ever-vigilant, he took in their surroundings as he might a battlefield. Between the loud music, crying babies, and movement all around, he found himself wishing he was back at the Tumen River, crossing a deadly minefield. Anywhere but here.

Before reaching their table, a raucous group gathered near the bar caught Min-jun's attention. Even over the music, they could be heard cheering loudly, high-fiving, and raising their beers in celebration. Min-jun dismissed them as a nonthreat and sat beside Ji-eun while the hostess handed out menus.

"Your server will be with you shortly," she said before departing.

Ji-eun and Min-jun followed McDonnell's lead and began perusing the menu, even though they had no idea what they were looking at. Flaming Hot Buffalo Wings, Jalapeño Poppers, and something called Rocky Mountain Oysters were some of the options that begged explanation.

When Ji-eun asked about the oysters, McDonnell laughed. "It's not seafood at all. Some people call them tendergroins, or Cowboy Caviar." He delicately explained the oysters were actually bull testes dipped in a special hot sauce labeled "Great Balls of Fire." Her wide-eyed reaction was priceless. Even Min-jun smiled.

Ji-eun turned to her counterpart and spoke in his ear. Back and forth in rapid-Korean, they questioned American cuisine and McDonnell's choice of restaurants.

The server showed up moments later with water and utensils. The two Koreans ordered blackened chicken salads while McDonnell went with the wings. As soon as the server stepped away, Min-jun turned to Ji-eun and asked a question in Korean. She then leaned across the table to McDonnell.

"Pei has to go to the bathroom."

"Okay," McDonnel said. He peered over the crowd and found the restroom sign at the far side of the restaurant. "Over there."

Min-jun followed the direction he was pointing. To his dismay, the restrooms were situated past the bar, near the three axe throwing lanes where the rowdy group was gathered. Min-jun bowed then stood and carefully made his way toward the men's room. McDonnell kept an eye on him as he navigated around several rambunctious children whose parents allowed them to run amuck between tables.

Min-jun did his best to mind his own business. Keeping his head down and eyes up, he humbly stepped aside for the busy servers and passing patrons, bowing to each along the way. However, despite his best efforts, trouble found him in the form of a six-foot-four man weighing somewhere in the neighborhood of two hundred and eighty pounds.

Nicknamed "Bull," the big guy had just thrown the winning axe to defeat his opponent. As he stepped out of his throwing lane to cheers from the crowd, Bull spotted Min-jun approaching and sneered.

"Hey, check this out." He pointed in Min-jun's direction. Then Bull stepped around two of his buddies in time to block the Asian's path.

Min-jun pulled up. He quickly eyed the large man head to toe then smiled politely before attempting to step around Bull. Each attempt was purposely thwarted. At first, Min-jun found their miscommunication comical, but he soon realized Bull was intentionally forbidding him to pass.

"Looks like we got ourselves one of those aliens from on TV," Bull announced. "An *illegal* alien, that is."

The crowd erupted in laughter as they gathered around Min-jun. One scrawny, half-drunk guy snatched Min-jun's ball cap while he was not looking and tossed it to a glossy-eyed girl. She put it on and modeled it for the crowd, much to their approval.

Min-jun let it go. Keeping his cool, he remained focused on Bull, the instigator. Min-jun was dwarfed in comparison to the man. The first thing he noticed about Bull was the belt buckle partially covered by his sagging beer belly. Polished silver and engraved with a bull rider, to Min-jun, it looked to be the size of a dinner plate. He had never seen anything like it. Then, when Min-jun looked upward to meet Bull's gaze, he noticed the big guy's tattoos that were visible because Bull's shirt sleeves had been ripped off. On each of his sizable arms—though they lacked muscle definition—were matching tattoos of two Old West-style six-shooters. Underneath the artwork was written, "*The Gun Show.*"

Bull belched loudly then blew it out of the side of his mouth. "You lost, my friend? Maybe fall off the boat or something?"

The drunken crowd laughed again, egging Bull on.

Min-jun ignored the remark and said nothing. Knowing he was surrounded and outnumbered, Min-jun simply shook his head. Smiling politely, he tried moving around Bull once again, but the large man was not having it. He put his large hand on Min-jun's chest to stop him. Min-jun halted and shot Bull a reproachful glare.

"Don't leave yet," Bull taunted. "The fun's just starting."

"Bull, leave him be," a middle-aged woman called from behind the bar as she wiped down the countertop.

Bull waved at her dismissively. He then clapped his hand on Min-jun's shoulder and bent over to hear better. "You speak English?"

Min-jun nodded.

"What's your name?"

Min-jun made a cursory glance at Bull's oversized hand resting on his shoulder then replied patiently, "Pei Wang."

Bull scoffed. "Wang, huh?" He looked Min-jun up and down, grinning. "Like Wanger?" he teased, winking at his buddies. "Or better yet, I'll call you Wangman. You can be my sidekick."

Bull turned around to face the crowd and announced, "Listen up, everyone! Meet my new sidekick, Wangman!"

Rowdy laughter ensued as the crowd raised their drinks, tapped their bottles, and chorused, "Wangman! Wangman! Wangman!"

Unamused, Min-jun lowered his shoulder to free himself of Bull's big hand. But when he tried to leave, two biker dudes blocked his path to the restroom. With their no-nonsense expressions and arms folded across their chests, Bull's leather-clad friends made it clear to Min-jun that he had not been excused.

Suddenly, Min-jun felt Bull's large hand on the back of his neck.

"Not so fast, Wangman," he said, pulling Min-jun back toward him.

Min-jun clenched his fists, expecting a brawl. Instead, Bull pulled him close and wrapped his thick arm around Min-jun's shoulders.

"C'mon, Wangman. Let's see how good you are at throwing an axe."

The crowd made room as Bull steered Min-jun toward the middle of three axe throwing lanes. Standing in the back of the lane was a referee wearing a black and white striped shirt. Seeing Bull approach, he smirked then removed two axes from a regulation-sized *World Axe Throwing League* target mounted on the back wall.

Min-jun stole a glance at the target as the referee approached. Stenciled on the round, wooden target were five concentric rings, and in the center was a red bullseye. He assumed the object of the game was the same as archery.

The referee handed Bull both axes.

Bull held out one axe in front of Min-jun. The second rested at his side. "You ever use one of these?" he asked. Before Min-jun could respond, Bull said, "Sure, you have, living in the jungle and all. My grandad fought in Ia Drang Valley. He said VC-types preferred machetes, but you'll get the hang of it."

Min-jun clenched his jaw. Despite his limited English, he deduced that Bull's racist remark was in reference to the Viet Cong. Min-jun was well-versed in military history, particularly the military tactics from the Vietnam War. It was required reading for North Korean soldiers. Nevertheless, he was not Vietnamese. Min-jun considered explaining this fact to Bull but thought better of it. It would only fall on deaf ears, anyway.

"Okay, Wangman, the game is simple," Bull said, raising the axe in his right hand and pointing down range. "Aim for the red bullseye. If your axe lands inside the outer ring, you get one point. For every ring you land closer to the center, you get an extra point. The bullseye is worth six points. Got it?"

Min-jun raised his hands and shook his head. "Me not play."

"Nonsense," Bull asserted, pushing the axe toward Min-jun. "I insist."

Min-jun met Bull's gaze as a brief battle of wills ensued. The last thing Min-jun wanted was to escalate the situation and put Ji-eun and Agent McDonnell in harm's way. In the end, he thought it best to play along, endure the ridicule, and hope for the best.

Reluctantly, Min-jun relented and accepted the axe.

"Wise man," Bull remarked. "Now step back, and I'll demonstrate."

Bull stepped into the throwing lane. The crowd fell silent as the referee moved out of the way. Taking a carefree approach, Bull purposely situated himself in a lackadaisical stance. He then raised the axe in his right hand, took aim, and effortlessly tossed it. The axe's metal head landed in the third ring, exactly where Bull had intended. The crowd oohed.

Turning to Min-jun, Bull shrugged innocently. "You see? Piece of cake. Now you try."

Min-jun let out an exasperated breath and stepped up to the throwing line, twelve feet from the target. Feeling the balance of the axe in his hand, Min-jun squared himself then let the axe fly. It hit with a loud *thump* inside the ring second-closest to the center but failed to embed in the wood. The axe fell to the ground for zero points.

The crowd aahed in disappointment.

"Too bad, so sad, Wangman. You had me, though," Bull praised, patting Min-jun's back. "If the blade stuck, you would've won." As the referee retrieved the axes, Bull said, "Now we throw for real. Whoever hits closest to the bullseye wins. Agreed?"

Min-jun nodded then eyed the target quizzically. "How much for blue dots?"

Bull followed Min-jun's eyes and chuckled. "Those are called *kill shots*," he explained, referring to the two blue dots near the top of the target, just inside the outermost ring. "They're worth eight points, but don't worry about those. Focus on the bullseye; it's easier."

The referee returned with both axes and handed one to each player. Bull stepped up to the line. As he was about to throw, he paused and feigned an aha moment. He turned sharply to Min-jun.

"Hey, Wangman. I've got an idea. How about a friendly wager?" Bull pulled a wad of cash out of his pocket consisting of his day's winnings. He raised it in the air for the group to see and handed it to the referee. "I'll bet you all this cash that I can outscore you. I'll even throw it blindfolded."

Min-jun got the gist of his meaning and shook his head. "No, thank you."

"C'mon, Wangman. I'll make it even easier. You get points wherever your axe hits, even if it doesn't stick."

Min-jun considered the offer. Agent McDonnell had given him a small stipend, but Min-jun had no idea what it was worth.

"Do you have any money on you?"

Min-jun sensed Bull was trying to con him. Even in North Korea, soldiers played cards to pass the time, and most were bad at bluffing.

Thinking once again of Ji-eun, Min-jun decided to play along. He retrieved fifteen dollars from his pocket, raised it in the air, and handed it to the referee.

"My man!" Bull grinned, smelling blood in the water. He retrieved a bandana from his pocket and handed it to the referee. Once Bull resituated at the line, the referee blindfolded him.

"Okay, Wangman. Watch and learn."

As the local axe throwing champion for three year's running, Bull approached this throw much more methodically the second time. He squared his body on the target and situated his feet in a stationary ball-style stance. Calming his breathing, he would rely on muscle memory to guide his throw. Bull raised the axe, held his breath, and threw it. The axe landed perfectly in the bullseye, much to the crowd's enjoyment.

Bull lifted his blindfold. Seeing his perfect throw, he pumped his fist then rounded on the crowd, soaking up their applause.

"Now you, Wangman," Bull said, waving Min-jun forward.

"Wangman! Wangman! Wangman!" the crowd chanted.

Min-jun ignored them and stepped up to the line. He set his feet and raised his axe, but just as he was about to throw, Bull grabbed his throwing arm by the wrist.

"Hold on, hold on." He sounded apologetic. "It ain't fair to have such a little guy throw such a big axe." Bull unsheathed two identical, SOG five-inch, fixed-blade knives from behind his back. One in each hand, he tossed the blades over in his palms then offered them to Min-jun, handles-first. "Here, these are more your size," he prodded. "Two throws to outscore me."

Min-jun eyed the knives then looked up to meet Bull's gaze. He wanted to wipe the big guy's smug grin right off his face.

Min-jun accepted, exchanging the axe for both knives.

Without a word, he stepped coolly up to the line as the crowd continued chanting his name. Keeping his back to them, Min-jun balanced one blade after the other on his index finger. They were identical. He guessed both weighed seven ounces, maybe a hair more. Both knives were made of high-quality steel. Engraved on each blade was "S35VN," which signified it as a heat-treated steel that carried a hardness rating around 60 HRC. In all, a high quality tactical survival knife, similar to what he had worked with in SpecOps.

Min-jun gripped the first knife by the tip of the blade then, in a flash, threw it at the upper-right kill shot. The blade cartwheeled in the air and embedded deep in the center of the blue dot. Before the crowd could react, Min-jun took the second knife in hand and hit the left kill shot center mass.

The crowd fell silent.

The contest was over so fast that it took the onlookers a moment to realize what had happened. Even Bull could not believe his eyes. He just stood there, mouth open with a Whisky Tango Foxtrot expression. Finally, someone in the back of the crowd acknowledged the remarkable shots.

"Daaamn!"

Others in the crowd followed suit, echoing the sentiment. Despite their earlier insults, the impossible throws won them over. There was clapping and many stepped forward to pat Min-jun on the shoulder. All except Bull.

As the referee approached Min-jun with the winnings, Bull's lip curled in disgust. He reached with one hand to block the referee.

"Nuh-uh, I wanna go again. He cheated."

"He didn't cheat, Bull. He won fair and square," the referee said.

"Wangman didn't call kill shots," Bull argued.

The referee paused, realizing Bull was right on a technicality. He looked at Min-jun and sighed. "Sorry, sir, but Bull's right. You're supposed to call it first."

Min-jun shrugged indifference. In his former life, he had won many bets in the field by wagering in knife games like this. He had given it up when he had gone to work for GCRM, but it was nice to know he still had it.

With a satisfactory grin, Min-jun offered Bull a handshake. "Keep the money."

Bull looked at his opponent's hand in disgust and *hmphed*. He then snatched the cash out of the referee's hand and elbowed his way through the crowd.

Min-jun watched Bull depart. He received more congratulatory pats on the back from the crowd, and even had his ball cap returned. As the crowd dispersed, Min-jun made his way to the restroom. No sooner had he finished at the urinal did the door to the men's room open. Bull entered with his two biker buddies—one a scrawny redhead with freckles and a mullet, the other a morbidly obese dude with more chins than a Chinese phone book.

Bull got right up in Min-jun's business as his friends blocked the door.

"You made me look bad," he fumed.

"Kick his ass, Bull," the redhead jeered.

Bull grabbed Min-jun by the shirt and drew back his fist. Just then, the toilet flushed and out of the stall stepped Sheriff Whitaker.

The face of each bully turned ashen. Bull abruptly released Min-jun and pulled his hands away while his friends made for the door.

The sheriff eyed Bull and shook his head in disappointment. "Can't a guy even have five minutes of peace without you crayon eaters muckin' things up?"

"It's not what you think—"

The sheriff raised his hand, stifling Bull's excuse as he stepped between them to get to the sink. Whitaker did not look up as he washed and rinsed his hands in silence.

Meanwhile, Bull pointed a finger at Min-jun, threatening him to keep his mouth shut.

Sheriff Whitaker finished. He snatched a few paper towels from the dispenser and began drying his hands. "You been drinking?" he asked Bull then tossed the towels in the trash.

Bull lowered his head like a petulant child. "A little. Not much."

"Not smart for someone in your position, wouldn't you say?"

Staring at his feet, Bull shrugged. "Maybe ... yes."

"Drinking's a violation of your parole. So is gambling."

"Yes, sir," Bull said sullenly. "Sorry, sir."

"Don't apologize to me," the sheriff replied. "Say it to him and hope he doesn't decide to press charges."

"Yes, sir." Bull lifted his head to meet Min-jun's gaze. "Sorry for making fun back there. I didn't mean nothin' by it," he lied. "It won't happen again."

Bull handed Min-jun his money back. He accepted and bowed formally, closing the matter in his mind.

"It better not," the sheriff warned him. "Now get your ass home."

Bull did not have to be told twice and exited hastily.

The sheriff turned to Min-jun. "You okay, friend?"

Again, Min-jun bowed out of respect. "Yes. Thank you, sir."

Whitaker eyed him curiously. "Passing through?"

Min-jun shook his head. "No, I just arrive from Seoul with my wife." He smiled genially, reciting his new legend without skipping a beat.

"I see. Well, watch yourself around here," Whitaker warned. "We got a lot of good ole boys who like to drink and have way too much free time on their hands. If anyone gives you trouble, just come and see me."

Min-jun thanked him then followed the sheriff out of the restroom. With the axe throwing crowd now dispersed, Agent McDonnell spotted Min-jun with the sheriff across the dining room and panicked. As soon as they went their separate ways, he breathed a sigh of relief.

"Problem?" he asked Min-jun as soon as he returned to the table.

"No. He welcome us to town. That is all."

McDonnell sensed it was more than that but let sleeping dogs lie.

Just then, their food arrived, and they ate their meals in relative peace. Afterward, McDonnell drove them home on the outskirts of town.

Ji-eun and Min-jun shared a two-story home off I-93. Their cozy, turn of the 20th century farmhouse was situated far from prying eyes on twenty acres of open land. And, while the exterior needed a power wash and a fresh coat of paint, this government safehouse offered the perfect cover.

They had agreed to pose as husband and wife until their new identities in the FBI's Witness Protection Program were finalized. Not that they had much say in the matter, but sticking together made the most sense for the time being. Both were still coming to grips with starting a new life in a foreign country. And with Ji-eun's pregnancy progressing, Min-jun was more than happy to help around the house and run errands.

In truth, in the few weeks since their arrival in-country, they had become fast friends. With no one else to talk to, they had little choice but to confide in one another. Their favorite part of the day had been watching the sunset.

Draped in the shadows of Blue Mountain, their rustic home included an inviting front porch with his and her rocking chairs. Ji-eun and Min-jun had begun a daily ritual of enjoying a simmering cup of tea while quietly watching the sunset over the nearby, snow-crested peaks.

Another unexpected perk was Buford, a five-year-old Bluetick Coonhound who had taken up residence in the pole barn behind the house. Buford and Ji-eun had bonded immediately. She had never owned a pet before and found the canine adorable. Now the dog faithfully remained at her side wherever Ji-eun went and made the quick transition to being an indoor dog.

Turning onto the gravel driveway, Agent McDonnell slowed at the sight of a dark blue Toyota sedan parked in front of the house.

"Who is it?" Min-jun asked, sensing the agent's caution.

McDonnel eyed the mystery vehicle. "I don't know. I wasn't expecting visitors." He noted the sedan's out-of-state license plate; there were no markings to indicate it was a government vehicle. If he had to hazard a guess, it looked like a rental, which could mean anything.

A woman appeared at the back of the house and approached the vehicle. McDonnell shifted the SUV into park but left the engine running. Out of habit, he unsnapped the strap on his holster as he reached for the door.

Min-jun smiled widely. "Miss Jessica."

McDonnell paused. "You know her?"

Without answering, Min-jun hopped out of the SUV and ran to see his friend.

"I guess that's a yes," McDonnell muttered.

It was rare for Min-jun to show emotion, but Jessica Aguri was the closest thing he had to family. She had saved his life in more ways than one. And after leaving Sanhe, China, Min-jun had figured he would never see her again.

They embraced in a warm hug and held it for a long moment. When they separated, the tears welling in Min-jun's eyes mirrored Jessica's.

Jessica laughed with embarrassment, wiping her eyes. "So, how are you? You look good."

Min-jun hesitated. "Things are good. We are finding our way," he said, gesturing to the SUV.

Jessica turned to find Ji-eun approaching. Recognizing Jessica from GCRM, the two hugged as if they were long-lost friends.

"It's so good to see you," Jessica said, stepping back and admiring Ji-eun's American apparel. "Look at you, fitting right in, I see."

Ji-eun blushed, placing a hand on her pregnant belly. "Thanks to you, Miss Jessica."

Jessica waved dismissively. Extracting Ji-eun from North Korea was ancient history in her mind. "How's the baby?"

"Very good," Ji-eun beamed. "I am starting to feel it move."

"Aw," Jessica melted. "That's wonderful. Boy or a girl?"

Ji-eun raised her eyebrows with a look mixed with excitement and nervousness. "I find out next week."

"Any thoughts on names?"

Ji-eun was about to answer when Agent McDonnell interjected, "No offense, but I'm feeling a little left out here."

Slightly embarrassed, Jessica retrieved her wallet and displayed her credentials. "Sorry, I'm Deputy Director Aguri, CIA."

Her title caught McDonnell by surprise. He gave her ID a cursory glance and nodded. "Thank you, ma'am. I'm Special Agent in Charge, Boyd McDonnell, FBI."

"Nice to meet you," Jessica replied, exchanging handshakes.

"We went to Walmart," Ji-eun announced with excitement.

"Oh dear." Jessica could imagine, picking up on Min-jun's drop in enthusiasm.

Ji-eun gestured toward the house. "Come inside where it's warm, and I tell you all about it."

Elated to have another female to talk to, Ji-eun linked her arm through Jessica's and led her toward the house. Min-jun and McDonnell began unloading the vehicle.

Inside, Buford greeted them happily, wagging his tail and spinning in circles. The girls slipped off their shoes at the front door then headed to the kitchen so Ji-eun could start boiling water. After some small talk to catch up, Jessica retrieved the locket from her coat pocket.

"I brought you something."

The sight of the silver necklace took Ji-eun by surprise. She gave Jessica a quizzical look and tried to refuse the gift, but Jessica insisted.

"It's a locket," Jessica explained. "Open it."

Ji-eun popped it open. She gasped at the sight of her parents and covered her mouth. Tears rolled down her face, and Ji-eun reached out for Jessica. Words could not express her gratitude. She sobbed in her friend's arms for a long moment, shaking from the deep-welling emotions that had been bottled up in the weeks since her defection.

Cradling the necklace in her hands, she asked, "Where did you get this?"

Jessica peered down the hall to make sure McDonnell was out of earshot. "Remember Samantha?"

Ji-eun nodded, recalling the young woman she swapped identities with before leaving North Korea. She had not seen or heard anything about the mystery woman since.

"She was with your father when he passed," Jessica explained. "She wanted you to know that he died saving her life."

And ours, Ji-eun thought, rubbing her belly.

Jessica held Ji-eun close to comfort her. "Your father loved you very much."

Sniffling, Ji-eun retrieved a tissue and cleaned herself up. She then regarded the image of General Vong Yong-hae for a long moment. He stood proud, with full military bearing, his shoulders back and chest out. She had never known her father to smile much. Even in this image, he looked so serious and reserved. Their relationship had suffered due to his military career, but things had changed with the passing of Ji-eun's mother and husband. In their absence, her father had made an effort to reconnect with her, and they had grown close. Now, looking into his eyes, she could see a love and kindness that had escaped her before.

Ji-eun clutched the treasure to her chest and whispered with heartfelt gratitude, "Gamsahabnida." *Thank you.*

Just then, Agent McDonnell entered the kitchen, breaking the mood of the moment. "Sorry, I didn't mean to interrupt."

Embarrassed, Ji-eun wiped away her tears and returned to the stove as the kettle started to whistle.

"No, we're good," Jessica said. She looked down the hall and caught a glimpse of Min-jun stepping into the front room, carrying shopping bags. "If you'll excuse me, I need to speak to Min in private."

Jessica made her way to the front of the house. She found Min-jun with his back to her, situating Ji-eun's recent purchases against the wall so no one tripped over them.

"Looks like you did some damage today," she remarked.

Min-jun did not act surprised. He had heard Jessica coming down the hall by her footsteps, one benefit of a rickety old house. He straightened and faced her with an exhausted look on his face. Clearly, Min-jun had not taken to American consumerism like Ji-eun. He offered her a seat in an old but comfortable recliner.

"No, thanks," Jessica declined. "Actually, I was hoping we could step outside for a moment. There's something I wanted to talk to you about."

Min-jun's interest was piqued. He had seen that look in Jessica's eyes before, every time she came to him with a new black bag job. Without a word, he nodded.

They grabbed their coats and stepped outside. Min-jun led her at a hurried pace to the dilapidated barn behind the house so they could escape the biting wind.

Inside, Jessica eyed the empty horse stalls and sagging roof. The barn was probably older than her, she surmised. One strong gust might bring the whole thing down, yet it remained, standing the test of time. She regarded Min-jun in a similar light. They broke the mold with him.

"So, how's the transition?" Jessica asked, shivering.

"I am fine," Min-jun replied evenly.

Jessica gave him a look. "That didn't sound convincing."

Min-jun shrugged. He did not want to burden her with his problems. Jessica had done so much for him already, but she was the only person on the planet he could truly confide in.

"Ji-eun is a nice person," he said sincerely. "We are becoming friends."

"That's good to hear." Jessica rubbed her arms vigorously. "Listen, I have a job, if you're interested. Like the old days. A friend of ours might be in trouble, and I need someone on the ground to do some recon."

"Who?"

"Actually, neither of us have ever met her. Remember Samantha Ri?"

Min-jun expressed a look of concern.

"Don't worry; it's not her, but someone close to her."

Jessica went on to explain who Samantha Ri really was and how the three of them had played an integral part in stealing the Reaper. Min-jun reacted with surprise, having read about the massive explosion in North Korea that had killed the Supreme Leader, Kim Sung-il. He had guessed Samantha was involved in the incident somehow but had chosen not to inquire further about the subject with his American hosts. Instead, Min-jun had taken solace in knowing he had helped end the reign of the despot who had been responsible for killing his family.

Jessica added that Dr. Rose Landry had been crucial to the success of Samantha's mission, and that she might have been kidnapped. "We think she's being held against her will in South America."

Min-jun nodded thoughtfully, digesting this new information. His logical response was, "Why me?"

"This has to be off the books, my friend. The CIA won't sanction a mission unless we have confirmation she is actually being held against her will. But my gut says there's something more to this. Mathias is hiding something. I need to know what."

Min-jun glanced through an opening in the barn's rotted slats and toward the farmhouse. "What about Ji-eun?"

Jessica frowned. She had not considered how this might affect her. "Unfortunately, I can't stay, but I'll call her each day while you're gone."

That seemed to pacify Min-jun.

"I leave now?" he confirmed.

Jessica nodded. "You won't be going alone. You'll meet up with a friend of mine, Colonel Marlana Nunez of the United States Air Force. She, too, was involved in our last mission and is a close friend of Dr. Landry's. She and her husband will meet you in Peru and help with any logistics. They speak the language and can get you anything you need."

That was welcomed news. "No extraction?"

"Nope, just in and out, simple recon. If we can produce evidence, then I can push it up the chain and get approval for additional assets."

Min-jun weighed his decision. He felt some guilt for leaving Ji-eun, but she would be in good hands. The mission itself seemed pretty straight forward. Shadow recon was his bread and butter, and truthfully, he was growing restless. He needed a taste of action, especially after his encounter with Bull earlier.

So much of his new life had been out of his control the last few weeks. A little dose of his former self might be just what he needed to close that chapter once and for all.

"Okay. I do it."

"Thanks, Min. It means a lot. I promise I'll have you back in a week, no worse for wear."

28
RECKONING

Planet Aiwa

Kypa's day of reckoning had arrived. The king's royal yacht had departed Supra earlier in the day and now made its way at high speed toward the Realm of Cirros. Flanking the ship on all sides was a quartet of ever-vigilant drone Seekers.

Ava, Neil, and Princess Seva were seated with Kypa in an observation lounge. Down the hall, the members of the High Court occupied a larger room where they would decide Kypa's fate after inspecting his terraforming efforts.

Being surrounded by friends and family helped, but Kypa was visibly on edge. Throughout the journey, he found himself unable to sit still, pacing the room and incessantly fidgeting with his hands. The others attempted to distract him with small talk and jokes, but it had no lasting effect. As soon as the conversation paused, Kypa was back at it. Ava, Neil, and Seva could only be present with him and let him cope in his own way.

A bell chimed. Kypa stopped pacing and turned as the lounge door slid open. Standing in the entrance was Commodore Boa.

All eyes turned to the stern commander whose gaze always narrowed whenever he looked at Kypa. Reading the disquiet on the prince's face, Boa made no attempt to put him at ease. He simply stated, "The king has summoned you. Follow me."

Kypa swallowed hard. He started out of the room and gave a passing glance at Ava.

She gave him a reassuring wink. "You got this."

They walked in silence as Boa led Kypa down the hall to the king's private chambers. A pair of Royal Guards stood watch by the door. The senior of the two nodded at their approach, clearly expecting them. Snapping to attention, the guard pressed a button on the wall panel, notifying the king his visitors had arrived.

Inside, King Loka stood alone in front of a large window, staring aimlessly as Aiwa's undersea beauty passed by unnoticed. Lost in his thoughts, Loka had dreaded this moment ever since Kypa had returned from Earth. No parent should ever have to endure losing a child, neither should they have to judge their fate. Unfortunately for him, this difficult task fell upon Loka the king, not Loka the father.

The sound of the door chime startled Loka back to the present. He rounded on the door. "Enter," he bellowed.

Prince Kypa entered first, followed by Commodore Boa.

Kypa looked about, unsure what to make of this summons. None of the other court members were present. "You wanted to see me, Father."

"Yes, Kypa. Come in," he said, waving him forward.

To Boa, he added, "Thank you, Commodore. That will be all."

Boa bowed, uncharacteristically quiet about what lay ahead for the prince.

An awkward silence followed as soon as father and son were alone.

Loka regarded Kypa, clearly struggling to find the words to explain why he had called for him. Despite being considered by many as one of the greatest rulers in Aiwa's history, Loka had yet to master how to have a normal conversation with his own son.

Kypa sensed his father's discomfort. It was nothing new. Since childhood, he and his father often struggled to connect on any level. The two practically spoke different languages when it came to simple conversations, let alone expressing emotions. However, Kypa had sensed something was off more than usual when he had entered the room. Gone was his father's charismatic presence—the bigger than life aura that people naturally gravitated toward. Instead, Kypa found his father tentative and unsure of himself, which was cause for concern.

"Is something wrong, Father?"

Kypa's display of empathy came as a dagger to his father's heart. Here they were, on their way to decide whether his son lived or died, and the prince cared more about his father's well-being than his own. Loka's eyes moistened.

His son approached, eyeing his father up and down for signs of malady. "Are you unwell? Should I call a medic?"

"No, no, that will not be necessary," Loka assured him. "What I am suffering from cannot be cured with medicine."

Kypa tilted his head slightly, trying to make sense of his father's behavior. "I do not understand."

Loka took a deep breath. "I allowed Boa to spy on you at Cirros," he stated without preamble. Then he gave his son a wary glance, as if expecting him to bristle. Kypa did not.

For Kypa, news of Boa's spying was not all that surprising. He had expected the High Court to watch his every move, considering the circumstances. However, Kypa found it disturbing that he had not picked up on Boa's monitoring during his terraforming work. This was the second time he had failed in this regard. The first had occurred while secretly building the Reaper off-world. Kypa had taken extra precautions to ensure his efforts went unnoticed. Yet, somehow, he had been discovered, which had led to the attack in hyperspace that had caused him to crash on Earth. He filed away this troubling thought for later contemplation.

"Then you know the Reaper works," Kypa stated simply.

"Indeed," Loka acknowledged, an open admission that surprised Kypa. Yet, his father's pained expression persisted. Something told him this was not the reason he had been summoned.

"Is there anything else, Father?"

Loka had expected his son to be angry for spying on him. Instead, Kypa's calm, if not flippant, acceptance of this news caught him off-guard. Normally, their conversations turned heated, culminating in an exchange that both sides regretted. Not this time. With that excuse removed, Loka was now forced to say what was really on his heart.

The king cleared his throat. "This is not easy for me, Kypa. I do not know why it has always been difficult for us to get along. That is my fault," he admitted with soulful eyes. "I know the reconstruction work you have completed has far-exceeded all expectations. The technology you have developed with this Reaper vessel will indeed save our planet."

Kypa's aquasuit could not quell the goosebumps triggered by his father's generous words. Compliments from Loka were as rare as a blue crystal.

"You are to be commended for your service, not condemned," the king added. "What happened to Cirros was not your fault. It was mine. I drove us to overmine the crystals, and I agreed to let Boa spy on you. I ignored my conscience, and both Cirros and you, my son, paid the price for my stubbornness."

"Father, I—"

Loka raised his hand so he could finish.

"Kypa, you risked everything, including your life, to make things right. You did not deserve to bear this burden alone or be mistreated by me, Boa, or anyone else."

Well, duh, was the human expression that came to mind, but Kypa respectfully held his tongue.

King Loka approached his son, shame written all over his face. "Today, you will be exonerated once and for all, but that is not why I am asking for your forgiveness."

Kypa searched his father's anguished expression, still unclear where this was leading.

"The footage Boa supplied included you and Toma together." Loka struggled to meet Kypa's gaze. "You are a good father, Kypa. I see now how badly I failed you."

A chill went up Kypa's spine.

Loka put both hands on Kypa's upper arms, the first physical contact they had shared in years. "Forgive me." His voice trembled.

Kypa felt a lifetime of buried emotions rise to the surface. Although many of them were painful, he was able to let them go at that moment. He had never seen his father so vulnerable and penitent. It was a breakthrough that deserved respect and compassion.

"You are too hard on yourself," Kypa said generously. "You are the king, you have duties—"

"No, I am your father first," Loka insisted, refusing to take the easy way out that Kypa offered. "I should have been first to come to your defense. I should have been there for you growing up. I—"

Without thinking, Kypa lurched forward and wrapped his arms around his father, pinning the king's arms to his sides. Kypa held Loka tightly, a gesture that took his father by surprise and left him unsure what to do with his hands. Public displays of affection were not the Aiwan way, but Kypa did not care. He had picked up a thing or two from his time on Earth, and hugging—thanks to Rose Landry—was one action he intended to make a habit.

He embraced his father like never before, burying his head against his father's chest.

Loka eventually took his cue and awkwardly mimicked the gesture by wrapping his arms around his son. They held each other for a long moment, neither in a hurry for it to end. Without using telepathy, father and son conveyed the depths of their love for one another in a way that was long overdue.

When they separated, both chuckled with embarrassment.

"What is next?" Kypa asked.

His father took on a determined look. "As soon as we clear your name, we will end this war—"

"No, I meant for the two of us," Kypa interrupted with a sheepish grin.

"Oh." Loka paused then laughed at his own expense. Switching hats between king and father was going to take some practice. "Let us get through today. Then we can take it one step at a time."

"I would like that very much," Kypa agreed.

With that settled, Loka returned to the business at hand. "Now I need your counsel. Tell me about these humans. How serious are they about a trade agreement?"

"Very serious," Kypa assured him. "First and foremost, they need protection against harvesters and are willing to pay us handsomely for it. But they could also benefit from our technology. They are killing their oceans and atmosphere with pollutants. They need to learn how to take care of their planet."

"Mm," Loka said, stroking his jutted chin. "Can they be trusted?"

"I believe so, but humans are no different than any other species. You get the bad with the good."

King Loka considered his son's insight. This was just the break he needed to turn the tide of the war. "I am appointing you our ambassador to Earth."

Kypa bowed humbly. "You honor me, Father. And what of the Reaper? Boa still insists it is Aiwan property."

"I will talk with him before we return to Supra. The ship belongs to the humans now, as does the blue crystal powering it."

Kypa took a breath of relief. "Thank you, Father."

Just then, the yacht slowed and the king's commlink chirped.

"Yes?" Loka replied.

It was Boa. "My King, we have arrived at Cirros."

Loka and Kypa exchanged looks of optimism.

"Very good, Commodore. Gather the inspection team at the main airlock. I will personally lead them down to verify Prince Kypa's work."

"Your Majesty, perhaps it is best to leave this task to the engineers," Boa suggested. "There is a danger, sir."

Loka scoffed. "Nonsense. We will be down and back in no time." He turned to Kypa and clapped his son's shoulder. "Besides, this will be a day long remembered, and I want to be part of it."

Minutes later, Loka and Kypa arrived at the main airlock where they were met by Lord Zefra of Fonn and the wardens of Maeve and Dohrm. With them were two engineers—one male and one female—who would conduct the official inspection of Kypa's work.

Standing off to the side by the airlock were three members of the Royal Guard. Led by Commander Rega, Lord Zefra's son, he was joined by Major Gora, his second-in-command, and a junior officer named Nica. Each of the warriors held an energy pike in one hand with a personal shield that could be activated by a device worn on their forearm. Rounding out the group was Commodore Boa, who greeted the king when Loka and Kypa arrived then politely stepped aside.

Seeing everyone was present, King Loka addressed the wardens, "Will you be joining us?"

All three declined graciously, much to Kypa's disappointment. Since they were to judge his fate, he wanted them to be present to see the result of his efforts with their own eyes. Still, he understood their reluctance. It was not about Boa's security warning; it was politics. This trial by fire was unprecedented, especially for a member of the royal family. A failed inspection essentially condemned the prince to death, a sentence that would be carried out immediately. It was clear they wanted to distance themselves from that possibility.

Downplaying their fears, Loka shrugged indifference. "So be it. And you, Commodore Boa?"

"No, My Lord." He nodded graciously. "I trust the engineers will provide an impartial inspection."

"Very well," Loka said, not surprised. Boa already knew Kypa's terraforming had been successful. The prince's exoneration was all but assured. "Then let us get on with it and put this nasty business behind us."

Both the king and prince removed their golden robes and handed them off to an attendant. Aquasuits were not necessary, but utility belts with handheld lights were distributed by Rega. Once the group was ready, Gora opened the inner airlock door to the pressure chamber, and the group of seven entered.

Gora sealed the door behind them, and then the cramped room began filling with seawater from the floor up. The submersion process took less than a minute. As soon as the chamber pressurized, a green light above the outer door turned on, signaling it was safe to exit the ship.

Major Gora opened the outer door and peered down into the massive crater below. Then he scanned the immediate area. Satisfied, Gora signaled Commander Rega. who disembarked the yacht with him to conduct a quick sweep of their surroundings.

Rega returned moments later, appearing in the doorway. "*It is clear,*" he told the group using telepathy.

Backpedaling, Commander Rega made room for King Loka and the others to exit. Lieutenant Nica brought up the rear and closed the door behind them.

"*Lights,*" Rega instructed.

Once everyone had their lights on, he signaled Kypa to lead the way. It was his show now.

They descended rapidly into the depths of the crater, slicing through the water with fluidity and grace. Still a strong swimmer for his age, King Loka glided beside Kypa as the others in the group fell in behind them.

Silence followed out of respect for the lost souls in this region, yet Loka recognized the importance of sharing this moment with Kypa. It was just swimming, but it marked a major shift in their relationship—the healing had begun.

"*It has been too long since we swam together,*" he said to Kypa.

Kypa turned his head sideways and nodded with a rare smile.

"*I realize now that I should have spent more time with you,*" Loka shared, regretting his past. "*A father's best gift to his children is his time.*"

"*I agree,*" Kypa replied. "*But do not beat yourself up. Let us make the most of our time ahead.*"

Loka smiled at his son, proud of the adult he had become.

Kypa led them to the side wall. Pulling up, he turned to the group and projected his thoughts to all of them. "*Before we proceed inside the old harvesting tunnels, I wanted to point out the many areas where I had to use the Reaper's terraforming technology to stabilize this crater.*" He pointed to the discolored veins in the rock wall that were filled with artificial sediment.

The two engineers swam closer to the wall to scan the veins with handheld sensors. After a long moment examining the readings, the engineers turned to one another and nodded with approval.

"*The artificial sediment appears stable,*" the senior engineer reported. "*We will need to examine a larger sample before rendering final judgment.*"

"*Yes, of course,*" Loka agreed, trying to mask the fact the outcome had already been decided in his mind.

He turned to Kypa with a knowing nod. "*Lead on, son.*"

Encouraged by the positive first readings, Kypa led the group deeper into the crater. They reached the entrance to the main tunnel where he had been working the past week with Ava and Toma. He paused outside.

"*This tunnel leads to a central junction then splits off into several shafts,*" he explained. "*In case we get separated or you get turned around, this is your primary means of egress.*"

The group nodded acknowledgement, and then Kypa led them inside.

They proceeded down the long tunnel, swimming single-file. When they reached the junction, Kypa stopped once more until everyone caught up. The space was large enough for all of them to fit comfortably inside.

"*Here are the five primary shafts used by our Cirran brethren to harvest crystals in this region. I have completely sealed-off the two shafts on the far left.*" Kypa pointed to the discolored sections of the wall where openings used to be. "*Your scans will show those shafts are now filled with artificial sediment and completely stable.*"

The senior engineer raised his hand with a confused look. "*My Prince, how did you get the Reaper inside to fill the shafts?*"

Kypa grinned, picturing a tiny Reaper in his mind. "*The Reaper can do many things, but shrinking to fit through that tunnel is not one of them.*"

Loka chuckled, which lightened the group's mood.

"*In truth, I used extension hoses to seal those shafts manually. It was labor-intensive and slower than I would have liked, so my next order of business will be to devise a more efficient, manual-delivery system. The good news is that I can use the Reaper to fill in the crater outside much more quickly.*"

Impressed, the two engineers had to admit that Kypa's terraforming technology was revolutionary.

They swam to the first sealed shaft and began scanning the integrity of the artificial wall.

As the engineers went about their task, Rega swam to check the unfinished shafts on the right. He shined his light down the darkened paths, making security sweeps, while Kypa led his father toward the entrance of the center shaft.

"*Work will begin on this shaft next,*" Kypa explained. "*I am starting to find my rhythm and—*"

The sound of blaster fire startled the group, causing the engineers to drop their equipment. All eyes turned to the entrance and found Major Gora with his energy pike extended, a thin line of vapor wafted from the tip of his weapon. Beside him, Lieutenant Nica sank to the floor, slumped over dead with a sizable hole in his back.

Commander Rega darted his eyes from Nica to Gora in disbelief. Realizing Gora's betrayal, Rega reacted a split-second too late. Before he could activate his shield, Gora turned his weapon on his former commander and fired. Rega was struck in the chest and blown backward against the wall.

Time seemed to stand still during the exchange. Everything had happened so fast that Loka and the others could not believe their eyes.

The king was first to put it together. He instinctively positioned himself in front of Kypa and raised his hands.

"*Stay where you are!*" Major Gora barked.

Kypa and the engineers slowly raised their hands, hearts pounding in their chests.

"*Gora, what is this about?*" Loka said, irritation sparking through his anxiety. "*What do you want?*"

"*What do I want?*" Gora scoffed, aiming his pike at Loka, center mass. "*Look around! You caused all of this. You robbed us of our homes, our families, our dignity ... then you abandoned us and made us outcasts!*"

King Loka had never known Gora was Cirran. His heart sank. "*We are here to correct that dreadful mistake, Gora. Please, this is not the answer.*"

"*You say that now when death is staring you in the face, but all this*"—he gestured to their surroundings—"*this is nothing more than a farce. A cheap attempt to save your son's life, so you can go back to your comfortable palace, ignoring our struggles. But mark my words,*" Gora declared, aiming his pike at Loka's face, "*a new order is rising, and you will not live to see it.*"

Suddenly, a blaster bolt struck Gora in the arm, causing him to drop his weapon. The force of the blow spun him around. Clutching his wound, he turned sharply to find Commander Rega aiming his pike at his former comrade-in-arms. Rega had him dead to rights, but the commander's chest wound proved fatal. Grimacing, Rega's eyes glazed over in a lifeless stare. Before his life was extinguished, he loosed one last shot that missed Gora by inches, exploding harmlessly in the wall behind him.

Gora ducked, but the distraction allowed the engineers time to tackle him from behind. They grappled with Gora, overpowering the injured warrior and pinning his arms.

Realizing he had no way out, Gora chose to die a martyr. He managed to free a thermite charge from his utility belt.

Seeing the explosive, Loka rounded sharply on Kypa. Their eyes met in a flash. Loka appeared frantic, but not for himself—for his son. Without hesitation, the king tackled Kypa around the waist then kicked as hard as he could to carry his son into the open shaft behind them.

They made it a few body lengths into the passage when the thermite charge detonated. The explosion generated a massive bubble of hot energy that instantly vaporized Gora and the others. A violent shock wave obliterated the junction, collapsing the chamber and filling it with rock and debris. Meanwhile, Loka and Kypa were catapulted deeper into the shaft, cart-wheeling head over heels in a high-speed surge of hot seawater and sediment.

With their arms and legs flailing about, father and son were bounced off the rock walls, knocking them both unconscious. Their wild ride continued nearly a mile until the energy wave began to dissipate. Kypa and Loka slowed, floating motionless and face-down in the shaft.

29

JETTISONED

Planet Aiwa
Realm of Cirros

Ava turned away from the window, wringing her hands nervously. "Oh, I hate all this waiting," she complained.

Neil shared her concern but tried to be supportive. "It'll be fine. Kypa said the Reaper's terraforming worked to perfection, right?"

"It did, but I won't relax until they officially absolve him of all charges."

Standing regally in the middle of the room, Princess Seva observed the humans with curiosity. "You both care very deeply for my brother." It was a statement, not a question.

"Of course, he's our friend," Neil replied. "You know, he doesn't deserve to be treated so badly. He's only trying to make things better."

"Amen," Ava seconded.

Seva sighed. "I agree. It was not his fault—what happened to Cirros. His effort to restore this once great kingdom is admirable. If you look closely, over there"—she pointed out the window—"you can see the remnants of the old palace."

Neil and Ava followed the direction of Seva's outstretched hand and peered outside toward the darkened ruins. Obscured by a carpet of algae, coral, and other plants, Cirros' fallen center of power had been reduced to nothing more than a pile of rubble. Adding to the sad picture was a fallen statue depicting a Cirran worker holding up a crystal while surrounded by Aiwans representing the other realms. This collapsed effigy, situated amidst the capital's fallen spires and towers, had once captured Cirros at the height of its glory.

The irony of harvester statues collapsing on themselves did not escape Neil or Ava, but neither dared mention it. No sense adding salt to the wound.

After a moment of quiet reflection, Neil turned to Seva. "If—or rather, *when*, I should say—Cirros is rebuilt, who is in line to rule?"

"You were right the first time," Seva corrected, thoroughly convinced Cirros would never be restored. "Despite my brother's best intentions, there are forces at work who adamantly oppose Cirros' recovery. They would rather see this territory annexed into the other realms."

"But what about Moorga or someone else stepping up to lead?"

"Who's Moorga?" Ava asked.

Seva exhaled heavily. "Prince Moorga, my former betrothed."

Mention of Seva having an old flame piqued Ava's interest. Hoping for more juicy details, she inquired further. "Where is he now?"

The image of Moorga, a dashing Aiwan prince, filled Seva's mind with fond memories. But the moment was fleeting. Composing herself, Seva snapped back to the present and stiffened. "Moorga is gone," she replied evenly. "His family's line is broken."

Ava was about to ask a follow-up question when an unmistakable rumble resonated throughout the ship.

"Did you guys feel that?" Neil asked.

No sooner had the words left his mouth did an alarm begin wailing throughout the corridors. He turned to the window and could no longer see down into the crater. The area was filled with a thick cloud of debris.

"Jesus …" he muttered. "Hey, I think there might've been an explosion in the crater."

Ava rushed to his side. Confirming his suspicion, she said grimly, "This can't be good."

"We should contact the bridge." Seva said, making her way to the control panel beside the entrance. Inches from the door, the unmistakable sound of blasters outside in the corridor stopped her in her tracks.

Neil and Ava exchanged looks.

"What the hell was that?" Ava asked.

They rushed across the room to Seva's side as she activated the display on the wall panel. On the other side of the door, they watched a bloody firefight involving Aiwan guards at both ends of the corridor.

Neil could not believe his eyes. "Why are they fighting each other?"

Seva shot him an incredulous look. "Is it not obvious? This is a coup, and if we stay, we die. We must leave the ship now!"

"And go where?" Ava argued, activating her helmet. "Kypa and your father might need our help. We should find out what's happening first."

The princess began working feverishly to encrypt the door lock to buy them some time. "No," she insisted. "We must go to the surface. That is our best chance for survival."

"I've got a better idea," Ava suggested.

She activated her commlink. "Reggie, come in. It's me, Captain Tan."

No reply.

"Reggie, do you read me?" Ava tried again.

Still, nothing.

"Shit, I can't get through."

"They must be jamming our communications," Seva deduced. The breadth of this coordinated attack was becoming more evident. "Whoever is behind this could be moving on the capital, as well."

Seeing Ava activate her helmet, Neil did likewise. "You think it's Krunig?"

Before Seva could answer, the shooting outside suddenly ceased. A brief moment of eerie silence followed. Seva checked the display. The corridor was littered with bodies, and then a fighter appeared. He looked straight into the camera then raised his weapon and fired. Seva's display went dark.

She quickly moved to the door. Putting her ear against it, Seva listened intently for a long moment. On the opposite side, she could hear muffled voices. Then a loud pop on the opposite side of the door gave her a start. A high-pitched sizzling sound followed. Seva stepped back as a small red dot appeared on her side of the door and began expanding into a white-hot glow.

"Move!" Seva cried.

She tackled Neil and Ava, forcing them to the floor just as the enemy cut their way through the door. Showers of sparks burst into the room then started climbing upward as the enemy began carving out a makeshift opening.

Picking herself up, Ava said in a panic, "Barricade the door!"

"No time," Seva refuted. She helped Neil to his feet. "We must get to the escape pods."

Ava and Neil looked about in confusion.

"This way. Hurry!"

Seva led them to the back corner of the room. Next to the lounge's large observation window was a single door with a small, oval-shaped window.

Ava had noticed the door earlier and had assumed it was a storage closet. To her surprise, it led to a room with four oblong escape pods standing upright on launch pads aimed at the ceiling. Each pod was designed to fit one adult Aiwan.

Seva motioned Neil and Ava inside.

Seeing the pods, Neil pulled up at the doorway. "Hang on. Are you sure about this?"

Exasperated, Seva nudged him forward. "Yes. Now, hurry."

Neil eyed his four options indecisively. "Which one?"

"Any will do. Go!"

Neil chose the pod on the far left. Ava took the one next to him.

"Face outward with your backs to the pod," Seva instructed.

Neil and Ava climbed aboard their pods tentatively and nestled themselves against padded cushions that lined the cramped interiors.

"Like this?" Neil asked.

"Yes, good," Seva replied. "Keep your hands at your sides and try to relax."

Easy for you to say, Neil thought as his heart pounded in his chest.

Suddenly, another loud pop caught Seva's attention. She turned sharply to find the enemy had made quick work of the door. They were nearly finished cutting their way inside.

Realizing there was no time to prepare her pod, Seva was faced with the decision to either save the humans or risk all three of them being captured. She chose to help Neil and Ava escape.

Working feverishly, she activated a pair of ceiling-mounted emitters above both pods. Two separate beams of blue light scanned Neil and Ava from head to toe, gathering their vitals. The system then calculated appropriate life support levels for their short rides to the surface.

As soon as the scan was complete, automatic restraints appeared across their chests and thighs, pinning them snugly in place. Clear canopies on both pods then slid upward from the base of the unit and sealed shut, enclosing them like cocoons.

Seeing Seva still in the doorway, Ava sensed something was wrong.

"Seva, c'mon!"

"Listen closely," Seva explained hastily. "I programmed the pods to take you to the surface. When you reach the beach, stay inside the pod. Do not venture into the jungle. It is too dangerous. We will come for you."

"What about you?" Ava asked, her voice muffled behind the canopy.

The cutaway piece from the lounge door suddenly crashed to the floor. Startled, the princess turned sharply to find enemy soldiers entering the lounge through the opening. Without hesitation, Seva lunged at the control panel and activated the launch sequence. The door next to her sealed shut, and the launch room began filling with seawater.

Ava and Neil protested, but their calls were drowned by the sound of the thrusters situated at the base of each pod rumbling to life. Their concern heightened to anxiety as a beeping sound signaled a ten-second countdown to launch.

Neil cringed. "Oh, I have a bad feeling about this."

Next to him, Ava's attention turned from the rising water back to Seva. Through the door's tiny window, she could see the princess had her hands raised, then Seva moved away. She was replaced by a male Aiwan, someone Ava had never seen before. He peeked through the window where Seva had once stood and made eye contact with Ava. Then she lost sight of him as water washed over the canopy.

"Seva!" Ava called, fighting her restraints unsuccessfully.

On the final beep, room pressurization was complete. The ceiling hatches above both pods slid opened.

Neil squeezed his eyes shut as his pod jettisoned. Ava followed right after him. She screamed a colorful expletive as her pod shot out of the launcher with a loud *whoosh*!

Outside the yacht, both pods cleared the ship amidst a screen of bubbles. The thrusters then ignited, rocketing Neil and Ava toward the surface like Trident missiles. Luckily, remnants of the murky cloud of sediment from the earlier explosion masked their escape.

Streaking toward the surface, the pods emerged from the cloud, sending startled schools of fish scattering in all directions. Teeth-rattling, their high-velocity ascent paled in comparison to the Reaper's smooth ride. Fortunately, Neil and Ava's nano-suits compensated for the g-forces and pressure changes but offered little in the way of calming their fears.

Neil kept his eyes closed and fists clenched the entire time as he muttered, "Please don't let me die. Please don't let me die."

Ava handled the rocky ride much better. She'd had her share of bumpy rides flying C-130s. Still, she wanted out of the pod just as much as Neil did, but for other reasons. Never one to run from a fight or leave a man behind, Ava felt helpless on both fronts, strapped inside the pod. She also knew that escaping the king's yacht was not the end of the danger. Rather, it was just the beginning.

Fearing whoever attacked the royal family might be after them now, Ava expected to be killed or captured at any moment. Either that or become an easy meal for one of Aiwa's many ocean-dwelling predators. She and Neil were sitting ducks in these unarmed, automated lifeboats.

Moments later, the pods reached a depth where sunlight pierced the blackness of the deep sea. Soon after, their underwater surroundings came into view. Ava looked out at a large pod of whale-like creatures swimming carefree in the distance, oblivious to her plight.

"Computer, activate HUD," she directed, her voice echoing inside the claustrophobic tube. The helmet projection appeared. "Show me our course heading."

Displayed before her was a map of their intended route, along with readouts showing their speed, direction, and ocean depth. At this rate, they would reach landfall within minutes.

The pods then altered course. Instead of a steep climb, their trajectory began to slowly level off until both pods skimmed just below the water's surface. Lying flat on their backs now, the two hapless passengers found themselves staring up at a red-orange sky. Welcoming beams of sunlight glistened through the water as it washed over their canopies.

Neil and Ava's harrowing journey ended moments later as the pods reached the shore and beached themselves, skidding to a halt in the sand.

"Neil, you there?" Ava called, using the commlink in her nano-suit.

"I'm here," he replied, relief evident in his voice. "My pod stopped. I think I made it to the beach."

"Me, too. You all right?"

"Yeah, I'm good, just … lying here," he said, unable to move.

Ava lifted her head for a look-see, but her helmet bumped the canopy. Forced to stare up at the fast-moving clouds directly overhead, she fussed with her unforgiving restraints, trying to get comfortable. It was no use. The more Ava tried to relax, the antsier she became. All the while, Princess Seva's last words echoed in her mind.

Stay in the pods. We will come for you.

"Screw it," Ava said at last, huffing in frustration. "Computer, remove restraints and open the canopy."

The restraints retracted as the canopy slid open. Just like that, Ava was free. She wasted no time climbing out of the pod but stumbled in the process. Landing precariously on the white sand, Ava cursed as she sprang to her feet, expecting danger. She spun in a tight circle but found no threats on the empty beach. They were safe, at least for the moment.

Placing her hands on her hips, Ava let out a breath of relief as she surveyed the area. The pods had landed in a crescent-shaped alcove. With the ocean to her back, heavy rock formations to the right and left formed natural barriers—great for cover and concealment, she noted. Straight ahead, the beach extended to the edge of a thick, tropical jungle filled with giant palm trees, vines, and ferns of varying sizes and species.

Ava spotted Neil's pod closer to the surf, ten yards away. His canopy was still closed, so she made her way to him.

Still tucked inside the pod with his arms pinned at his sides, Neil looked up to find Ava standing over him, grinning. He wiggled his fingers in greeting.

Ava chuckled. "Are you going to stay in there forever?"

"Seva said we should stay in the pods," came his muffled reply. "It's safer."

Ava scanned their surroundings once again. "Maybe, but who knows what or who we're up against? I'm not going to hang out here just waiting to be picked up."

Neil pictured one of the Pterodactyl-like creatures he spotted a week earlier swooping down and carrying them away to be fed to a nest full of younglings. "But—"

"You do what you want," Ava said then walked away, leaving Neil to ponder his fate.

She made it ten paces before hearing his canopy open. With a thin smile on her face, Ava turned and watched Neil carefully climb out of his pod. He nearly made the same mistake as she had done but caught himself before faceplanting in the sand.

Catching up to her, Neil asked, "So, what do you think happened back there?"

Ava shook her head. "I wish I knew, but it can't be good." She activated her commlink. "Reggie, come in. Do you read me? Reggie?"

Out of habit, Ava put her hands to her ears to block out the sound of the crashing waves nearby, but her holographic helmet interfered. Feeling silly for trying, Ava realized she could use the technology to her advantage. "Computer, silence all background noise."

Suddenly, the ambient noises from the ocean, wind, jungle, and even Neil were silenced.

"Yes, Captain, I read you," Reggie replied.

Ava's shoulders dropped, breathing a sigh of relief. "Thank God. Are you okay?"

"Affirmative, all systems nominal."

"Good. Listen, Dr. Garrett and I are stranded on the surface," Ava explained. "I need you to come pick us up."

"Standby," Reggie replied. "I will request authorization for immediate departure."

As Ava waited patiently, "Raindrops Keep Fallin' on my Head" by B.J. Thomas began playing softly inside her helmet. The music surprised Ava at first then elicited a chuckle.

Seconds later, Reggie returned. "Captain, authorization to leave has been denied. All traffic in and out of the capital is grounded until further notice."

Ava swore under her breath then let out an exhaustive sigh. "Copy that. Keep trying and notify me as soon as clearance is granted. Understood?"

"Yes, Captain."

"By the way, what prompted you to play the music?"

"I detected stress in your voice," Reggie replied. "Muzak on Earth was created to help ease the fears of elevator patrons. I thought the calming music would help you relax."

Wow! Ava mused. "That was very thoughtful. Thanks, Reggie."

"My pleasure, Captain."

"Listen, just hold tight until we sort things out," Ava added. "If you hear from Kypa or Seva, let me know ASAP."

Reggie confirmed the order, and then Ava ended the transmission. Next, she tried reaching Kypa and Seva herself but failed on both fronts.

Ava huffed with frustration and deactivated the noise canceling feature. She rounded on Neil, who had his hands clasped atop his head with a pained expression on his face, trying to make sense of their predicament.

"We're stranded, aren't we?"

"Looks that way … at least for now." Ava grimaced. Patting Neil on the back, she added cheerily, "Look on the bright side, you always wanted to explore an alien planet."

Neil flashed her an unamused look. "Not what I had in mind."

Ava frowned crookedly. "Yeah, me neither."

Her SERE training came to mind. Ava located Aiwa's twin suns descending toward the distant horizon. "Our first order of business is survival—food, water, and shelter. Computer, how long before sunset?"

The HUD inside her helmet displayed a graphic showing the arching path of both suns, along with other weather readouts that included wind speed and direction, precipitation, and air quality.

"Thirty-two minutes and fifty-five seconds," came the reply.

Ava frowned. "That doesn't leave us much time. We're awfully exposed here. I suggest we get off the beach and find shelter."

"Seva warned us to steer clear of the jungle," Neil reminded her. "Kypa said the same thing back at Groom Lake. Lots of predators."

"I don't think we have much of a choice," Ava reasoned. "I figure, if we stick to the coastline as much as possible, we can avoid any trouble."

"Why don't we just stay here? We can use the pods for protection."

Ava shook her head. "We have to expect that whoever's responsible for the attack will come for us, too."

"Why's that?"

"The Reaper," she said evenly. "If that was a coup back there, God only knows who's in charge now. They'll want Reggie's blue crystal, and they need us to get it."

"You mean, you," Neil grumbled, feeling expendable.

Ava did not respond. A mild look of surprise passed over her as a thought dawned on her. She took a few paces up the beachhead, scrutinizing their location more closely. Ava then closed her eyes as if forcing herself to recall a distant memory.

Neil gave her a curious look. "What are you doing?"

"I know this place," she muttered. Then it came to her. Ava rounded on Neil with an incredulous grin. "This is Kypa's beach."

Neil stared back blankly.

"Remember the nightmares I had before leaving for North Korea? It was right here," Ava explained. "This is where Kypa always brought his family. The children were playing in the water over there"—she trailed off—"right before the planet tore itself apart."

"How could you have possibly known about this place?"

"I didn't know it at the time, but Kypa was sharing this vision with me telepathically. He had to find out whether I could be trusted."

Again, a twinge of jealousy flashed across Neil's mind, but he kept it to himself. The fact Kypa had not confided in him the way he had with Ava never sat well with him. It was childish, he knew, but it stung, nonetheless. After all, he was the one who had made first contact with the Aiwan.

Neil changed the subject. "C'mon, if we're going to do this, we should get these pods out of sight."

Ava failed to pick up on Neil's hurt. She was still processing the fact that they were standing in the same location where Kypa's nightmarish visions had taken place. Recalling the scene vividly, Ava remembered the cries of terror from Kypa's family and the godforsaken sound of Aiwa's core disintegrating around them. Yet, here they were, on the undisturbed beach with a lazy tide rolling in. Kypa's fears never became reality, thanks in large part to the success of Operation Sundiver.

Or did they? she pondered, considering the explosion inside the crater.

Ava's thoughts drifted to Kypa and his father, wondering if they were safe.

"A little help?" Neil grunted.

Ava turned to find Neil struggling to push his pod into the surf. Agreeing with his logic, she joined him. Together, they moved the open pod off the beach. Catching their breaths, they watched in silence as the pod's compartment slowly filled with seawater then disappeared under the waves.

Daylight expired by the time they had finished sinking the second pod. The binary stars floating along the horizon now gave way to nightfall.

Neil and Ava ventured off the beach to the nearby rock formations. There, they found a small nook overlooking the ocean that offered some semblance of protection, at least for one of them. The tiny space was too small for both of them to fit inside, so Ava offered to take the first watch. As Neil nestled into a fetal position behind her, she sat cross-legged on a rocky ledge, facing the moonlit water.

The jungle soon came alive, teeming with the sounds of animals, birds, and insects who created a loud concert mixed with chirping, buzzing, and thrumming.

Ava stared up at the stars and moons, mesmerized by the beauty of this alien world. Aiwa's planetary ring was especially breathtaking. In the celestial light, the clarity of its blue, white, and gray bands was even more pronounced.

Her stargazing ended abruptly with the bellowing roar of a distant predator. Shivers ran down Ava's spine, prompting her to activate the proximity sensor in her nano-suit. It would alert her if anyone or anything entered the area.

"Okay, that was terrifying," Neil remarked dryly, unable to mask his concern.

"Yeah," Ava replied. She cocked her head sideways. "Whatever it was, it sounded far away."

"Let's hope it stays that way," Neil muttered. A gap of silence followed, and then he sighed heavily. "I hope Kypa is okay."

"Me, too," Ava dared to hope. Inwardly, she knew the chances of Kypa and his father surviving the explosion seemed unlikely.

Then there was the coup. Had it been successful? It ate at her—not knowing what had happened or who was responsible. Being separated from Reggie made it worse. They were alone, cut-off, and with no way of getting home.

"What are we going to do?" Neil asked, resting his head in the crook of his elbow.

Ava sighed. "I don't know. Try to get some sleep. Something tells me we're going to need it."

One hundred and sixty kilometers away, sporadic flashes of bright-blue light illuminated the cavern walls where Smythe and Gort were holed up to make repairs. Perched atop their ship, Smythe held a pair of protective goggles up to his bug eyes as he continued welding the freighter's damaged port-side engine.

Sparks popped and crackled while he worked, then the commlink on his belt vibrated. The bounty hunter stopped what he was doing and set down his equipment.

"Yes?"

"Incoming transmission on the secure channel," Gort replied. "I think this is the call we've been waiting for." He sounded hopeful. The sooner they finished this job and got off this godforsaken planet, the better. But they were not going anywhere until they got the propulsion system up and running.

"I'm on my way," Smythe said.

Leaving his welding torch and goggles behind, he returned to the cockpit and took his seat beside his partner. Smythe then hit the receive button on his console. As expected, the transmission only contained a set of coordinates and a short message: *Urgent. Expect resistance.*

Smythe tapped the display, triggering a hologram of Aiwa to appear. The precise location of the coordinates showed an alcove on a beach. He then tapped a second command, and a red line appeared, mapping the most-direct route to the beach from their current location.

Grunting in disgust, Smythe looked at the distance with dismay. There was no way their ship could fly in its current state, which meant he had to either walk—which would take too long—or use the sled. Judging by the urgency in Krunig's message, it looked like he had little choice.

Smythe ended the transmission. "Time to go to work. Looks like I'm taking the sled."

Gort raised his eyebrow and snorted. He knew how much Smythe hated using the sled, but they had acquired it as a backup for just this type of situation.

"The engine is almost finished," Smythe added. "I left the torch up there for you."

"I'll get right on it," Gort replied as he followed Smythe aft. "The landing strut needs serious attention."

"Do your best, but be ready to leave at a moment's notice. Something tells me this job might require a quick getaway."

Gort agreed and watched as Smythe retrieved his sniper rifle from a closet and slung it on his back. He then unstrapped a long, surfboard-like contraption from the wall. Gort watched with amusement as his partner carried the gravity sled down the ramp and set it on the ground outside.

Smythe tapped a button on the sled's dashboard, and it came to life. The sled rose to knee-height beside the bounty hunter and remained in hover mode. Smythe then tapped a button on a device strapped to his forearm to transfer the beach's coordinates to the sled.

Next came the fun part. Smythe grumbled to himself as he straddled the single-rider, light transport. Lying flat on his stomach, he situated himself on the board. The sled was long enough to fit his entire insectoid frame.

As soon as he gripped the two-hand controllers near his head, a clear, protective canopy appeared over Smythe's head. An internal head-up display turned on and showed the route to the beach where he would intercept the humans.

"Why is it you get all the fun?" Gort quipped.

Smythe ignored the remark. "Just be ready for my signal."

With that, the bounty hunter throttled forward and exited the cave, heading toward the jungle. He had a lot of distance to cover. Smythe just hoped he could reach the humans before the Aiwans did.

30

UNSANCTIONED

Planet Earth
Jorge Chavez International Airport, Lima, Peru

Marlana and Hector Nunez touched down in Lima an hour before Min-jun's arrival. After passing through customs, they collected their luggage and found an empty bench near baggage claim. This location gave them an unhindered sightline of the down escalator that Min-jun would have to use to get to their designated meeting spot. To pass the time, they played their favorite people-watching games like *How drunk is that toddler?* and *Is that person schizophrenic or just listening to a Bluetooth headset?*

As their rendezvous time neared, Hector confirmed Min-jun's flight had arrived. Turning serious, they scanned the crowd, trying not to appear too obvious in the process. Jessica had provided an old photo of her colleague, but having never met the man, Marlana and Hector were sure the Asian would stick out in this largely Latino crowd.

It was not long before Hector spotted Min-jun at the top of the escalator. He had a camera bag slung over his shoulder and wore a Nikon ball cap.

"That's gotta be him," he said to his wife, "coming down now."

Marlana glanced in that direction and located Min-jun. They made eye contact and exchanged knowing looks.

"Yeah, that's him."

Marlana stood and started collecting her luggage. Hector did the same as Min-jun approached.

"Mr. Wang?" Hector greeted.

Min-jun nodded and said, "Hello."

"Hi, we're the Nunezes. I'm Hector"—he extended a handshake—"and this is my wife, Marlana."

Min-jun adjusted his backpack to shake hands with both of them. "Please, call me Pei." He bowed.

Dressed in denim blue jeans with a maroon Polo underneath a dark blue windbreaker, Min-jun's appearance had come a long way since his days of extracting defectors from North Korea. Ji-eun and Jessica had helped clean him up with a wardrobe and hairstyle makeover. The same could not be said for Hector Nunez.

The fifty-two-year-old retired Air Force major—turned amateur method actor/spy—was taking his role as an unsuspecting tourist quite seriously. Despite his wife's fashion objections, Hector had stepped off the plane sporting peach-colored slacks and a tropic-patterned, button-down camp shirt, plastered with toucans. Covering his balding head was a newly-purchased, straw Fedora. Thankfully, he had remembered to remove the price tag. All he was missing now was a classic Polaroid slung around his neck.

After the introductions, there was a moment of awkwardness as the trio exchanged looks, wondering what to do next. Marlana broke the silence.

"Hector, why don't you arrange some transportation?"

"Sure thing." he replied, making his way to a nearby taxi stand outside.

"I get my bag." Min-jun pointed to the carousel.

Marlana stayed behind with their luggage. Minutes later, Min-jun had collected his suitcase and followed Marlana outside.

A warm and welcoming breeze greeted them. It was a beautiful morning in Peru's capital. The sun was shining, and the temperature was a comfortable seventy-four degrees Fahrenheit.

They spotted Hector at the taxi stand, chatting with a friendly-looking young man. He waved them over.

"This is Paolo," Hector said. "He speaks fluent English and has agreed to take us to Satipo."

"¡Hola!" Paolo smiled and exchanged handshakes excitedly. He was a wiry young man in his early twenties with unkempt, charcoal black hair.

After their introductions, Paolo took the initiative to collect everyone's luggage, all except Min-jun's camera bag. He politely declined, opting to keep his delicate equipment up front with him. Paolo understood and shrugged it off, taking no offense.

Leading them to his 2004 Nissan Sentra, Paolo opened the back door for Marlana before loading the baggage in the trunk. It was evident he was going above and beyond to curry favor. Long distance fares in Peru were primo, especially if American tourists were involved. Their destination, Satipo, was twelve hours away by car, which allowed Paolo to negotiate a ridiculously high rate with Hector. Add in a generous tip, and it was as if Paolo had won the lottery.

He finished loading the luggage in the trunk. Meanwhile, Hector decided to sit up front to keep Paolo company but also to draw attention away from Min-jun as much as possible. He sat quietly in back with Marlana.

Climbing behind the wheel, Paolo turned to his passengers with a big smile. "¡Vámanos!"

And so, they were off, departing the airport and heading north out of the city on Peru's central highway, known as National Route 22.

The first hour of the trip was a tense affair, filled with nerve-racking traffic. They soon learned that driving in Lima was not for the faint-hearted. Peru's capital had the third-worst traffic congestion in the world, and it was on full display this morning. Getting out of the city proved challenging, even with Paolo's aggressive driving style. Hector had his ass cheeks puckered the entire time.

On the bright side, the congestion afforded Paolo an opportunity to double as their tour guide. Despite having family in São Paulo, the Nunezes had never been to Peru, so they enjoyed listening as Paolo proved quite knowledgeable and proud of his hometown.

"Over there is the Saint Francis Monastery." Paolo pointed out the window. "Many tourists go there. We cannot see it from here, but I can take you to it if you like. It has a beautiful library, and the catacombs are quite spooky." He grinned. "You can even light candles and pray for blessings from the Apostle Jude."

His passengers declined the offer, but it did not stop Paolo from trying to stretch out the fare a little longer with other stops along the way.

"Here, you see the Acho Bullring," Paolo continued. "There are no bullfights today, but you can see the historic architecture dating back to 1766. Lima's annual bullfighting festival is *magnifico*. You should come back for it."

Being an animal lover, Marlana was not too keen on this tradition.

Paolo tried to convince her otherwise. He argued that La Fiesta Brava—The Bullfight—was not the cruel and savage sport some believed it to be.

"It is a tradition that dates back thousands of years, a profound ballet between man and beast."

Marlana raised her eyebrow. "Does the bull know that?"

Paolo shifted in his seat, smiling nervously at her in the rearview mirror. "Ernest Hemingway wrote that Toro Bravo—a Spanish Fighting Bull—is to the domestic bull what a wolf is to your pet dog. Toro Bravo is a breed apart. He is majestic, revered by everyone."

"Uh-huh," Marlana replied, unconvinced.

"Señora, have you ever been to a bullfight?"

Marlana shook her head.

"Imagine sitting in the stands, waiting, when suddenly, the trumpet sounds. You get chills up your spine. Then the arena erupts as Toro Bravo, a half-ton brute of horned fury, explodes onto the scene, ready to destroy anyone in sight."

Marlana raised her eyebrow. "Then he dies for sport."

Paolo shook his head. "Bullfighting is a sport in the same sense as gymnastics and figure skating," he tactfully disagreed. "It is about the art, the method, not the accomplishment. The torero is an artist who engages Toro Bravo's violent nature and transforms it into a complicated and intimate dance to celebrate life."

"But the bull never wins."

Paolo shook his finger. "Not true. Toreros have died, and the average bullfighter receives his last rites at least six times in his career … just ask my cousin, Alejandro."

Marlana was not swayed, so Paolo wisely changed the subject.

Meanwhile, Min-jun stared out the window, marveling at the bustling city. Lima was drastically different from Pyongyang, and even Missoula, for that matter. The city was alive in a way he had never experienced before, evoking all of his senses. As Paolo continued talking incessantly about his beloved country, Min-jun sat back and allowed a soft, warm breeze to blow on his face as he took in his foreign surroundings.

Who would've thought such a place existed? he directed his thoughts to his wife, Binna.

She had been gone now for ten years, but Min-jun spoke to her often. They had dreamed of a new life together with their son, Seo-jun, far removed from the oppressive Kim regime. Sadly, it never came to pass. Still, Min-jun kept their memories alive by sharing his experiences with them in moments of private contemplation.

Their trek continued out of the city, following Route 22. Paolo explained they would stop for the night in the city of Tarma, six hours away. Situated in the Andes Mountains of Central Peru, Tarma was the halfway point to Satipo, their final destination.

Paolo made good time, thanks in large part to unseasonably fair weather and the fact the roads were paved. They stopped once at a roadside diner to stretch their legs and eat lunch. Min-jun and the others allowed Paolo to order for them. It was Min-jun's first taste of Peruvian cuisine, so Paolo recommended his favorite dish—Arroz Con Pollo, coupled with Inca Kola, Peru's national soda. The combination was well-received by all three of them. Soon after, they were underway again and reached Tarma in the late afternoon.

Founded as Santa Ana de la Ribera de Tarma—now shortened to simply Tarma—the town's latest census estimated the local population to be at just over forty-seven thousand residents. Nicknamed the "City of Flowers" and "Pearl of the Andes," this sprawling town was situated within a fertile valley in the Junin Region, east of Lima. Its scenic beauty, along with nearby ruins, caves, and waterfalls, were the main draws for Tarma's primary economic resource—tourism.

"It's pretty," Hector observed as they entered town.

"Sí, but most people don't know Tarma has a dark secret."

"Oh yeah?" Hector remarked, intrigued.

Marlana leaned forward between the front seats to hear better.

"Sí, Tarma is considered the gateway to jungle colonization … very controversial in these parts."

"What do you mean?"

"Peru's largest cement manufacturer is located here in Tarma," Paolo replied, speaking over his shoulder. "They pave the roads through the Amazon."

"Terrific," Marlana grumbled as she sat back and folded her arms.

Paolo darted his eyes to the rearview mirror. He could see her frustration. "Permanent roads are only part of the problem, I'm afraid. Deforestation is mainly caused by logging, cattle ranching, and gold mining."

"Logging for houses?" Hector asked.

Paolo shook his head. This was a popular misnomer. "No, logging to produce food containers, like takeout pizza boxes. Many American fast food chains are accomplices."

"You're kidding," Hector sounded surprised. His two favorite meals—

hamburgers and pizza—were contributing to climate change.

This downer filled the car with silence as the group quietly mulled Paolo's remarks while passing a large cement manufacturing plant.

They entered Tarma and snaked their way through the narrow streets, past the crowded town square. Plaza de Armas de Tarma and the Catedral de Santa Ana stood out to Hector and Marlana. These two buildings were the tallest in town and exemplified classic Spanish architecture. They also drew the largest crowds. Flanked by artisan booths and other tourist shops, the plaza and cathedral were a must-see for visitors.

Minutes later, Paolo turned onto a driveway leading to a quaint, three-star-rated hotel. The building's yellow stucco walls and arched entryways highlighted its Colonial-style construction.

"This looks nice," Hector remarked, taking in the property's well-manicured lawn. "I love the cobblestone walking paths."

"Sí," Paolo said then pointed to their right. "Those walls are espaliered with Cantua buxifolia, Peru's national flower." Paolo quickly glanced at Marlana and grinned. Even she was taken in by the beauty of the place.

The driveway connected to a roundabout leading to the front entrance. Paolo brought the car to a stop under an awning where two valets awaited. One opened the passenger-side car doors and welcomed the guests warmly. The second valet went to work unloading the trunk.

Before Marlana and the others were led inside, Paolo explained he would be staying elsewhere to fit his budget. No one seemed to mind, but Hector insisted he join them later for dinner. Paolo happily accepted.

Heading inside, they found the hotel lobby's decor flashed elegance and cultural pride. Its checkered black and white marble floor caught everyone's eye. The simple pattern complemented the ornately crafted, wooden furniture and accent tables situated around the spacious entry. Topping off the look and feel were replicas of Incan pottery and colorful wall hangings.

Hector took the lead and checked them in, while Marlana and Min-jun quietly perused the lobby. Afterward, a female concierge led them to their rooms on the first floor. Min-jun was staying across the hall from the Nunezes, which he appreciated after sharing a long ride in a compact car.

After a thirty-minute siesta to freshen up, they rendezvoused in the lobby before heading into town to pick up supplies for Min-jun.

"How's the room?" Hector asked as they exited the lobby.

"Very nice and clean," Min-jun replied. "Thank you."

"Don't thank me yet," Hector quipped. "Watch out for spiders. We found a big hairy one in the shower."

That tidbit dampened Min-jun's mood but served as a reminder he was not here on vacation. He had a job to do, which was the first order of business before dinner. Min-jun needed extra gear to get him through the week once he parted ways with the Nunezes in Satipo. It was better to shop here in Tarma, he reasoned, than to draw unwanted attention to themselves when they reached their destination.

Before leaving the hotel, the concierge had directed them to a trekking supply store in town that was popular with the tourists. It was less than a ten-minute walk. There, they stocked up on lightweight, non-perishable foods that would require no cooking during Min-jun's jungle recon. Other supplies included an olive-colored rain poncho, KA-BAR hunting knife, machete, matches, a flashlight, and a good supply of tablets to purify drinking water.

After their shopping spree, the trio headed back to the hotel where they found Paolo waiting in the lobby. Min-jun dropped off his gear, and then the group headed back into town for dinner. They ate at a lovely outdoor restaurant, enjoying wine and a delicious order of Lomo Saltado, a popular dish of stir fried beef. For dessert, they opted for fresh Picarones.

"Can I get you anything else?" the waiter asked.

Hector lifted their empty wine bottle and raised an inviting eyebrow to his wife.

Marlana nodded approvingly.

"One more, por favor."

The waiter nodded then departed with the empty bottle.

Marlana smiled at her husband. "I love you."

Hector eyed her with a wry smile. "Is that the wine talking?"

"That's me talking to the wine," Marlana clarified, eliciting a chuckle from Paolo.

Min-jun remained relatively quiet throughout the meal. He made small talk when asked a direct question, but mostly sat and listened. After dinner, when the group called it an evening, he returned to his hotel room, fully stuffed. He could not remember ever eating so much.

In North Korea and China, food was too scarce to be gluttonous, but here, the portions had been overly generous, and the food too flavorful to stop eating. Laying on the bed, unable to move, Min-jun figured he deserved this one indulgence. After all, he would be living off the jungle and protein bars for the next week.

Sleep came quickly. Min-jun slept soundly for the first time since leaving

Sanhe, and the half-grin on his face spoke to his comfort in what lay ahead. Min-jun, the shadow warrior, was returning to what he knew best.

The next morning, the Nunezes met up with Min-jun bright and early. After a light breakfast, they loaded up in Paolo's car for the remaining leg of their journey. Cutting through habitats at different altitudes along the way, they experienced a wide range of plants and animals on the road to Satipo. Most notably, Paolo spotted a stunning Black-and-Chestnut Eagle.

By the time they reached the small town of Satipo, their winding trip up, down, and around the Andes Mountains had reached a highest elevation gain of ten thousand feet in Tarma then back down to two thousand feet in Satipo. Breathing came easier at this altitude; they felt the difference as soon as they exited the car outside their hotel near the main square.

Looking about, Hector and Marlana exchanged uneasy looks. Unlike Tarma, Satipo had a totally different vibe to it. Gone was the festive atmosphere and ornate decorations. Judging by the dilapidated state of the local buildings, including their hotel, something told them the online reviews of this place were drastically overrated.

Across the street was a brothel attached to a rundown cantina. Two local drunks lay passed out on the wooden sidewalk by the front door. Catty-corner to the hotel, they spotted several cars parked on the street corner with half a dozen seedy-looking hombres watching them with keen interest.

"Not too late to turn back," Hector muttered to his wife.

Marlana was thinking the same thing. There was definitely an air of criminality wafting about the area. However, despite her misgivings, Marlana reminded herself this was not about them. Jessica said Mathias's lab was here in Satipo, and if Rose was in trouble, this is where they needed to start looking.

"Stay sharp." She patted her husband's shoulder comfortingly.

To Min-jun, she said "C'mon, Pei; let's check in."

Hector remained outside, keeping a leery eye on the hombres as he discreetly settled up with Paolo.

"Gracias, señor." Paolo smiled, quickly pocketing the cash.

Hector shook his hand. "Adiós, amigo. See you in a week."

As Paolo climbed back in his car to start his return trip, Hector joined the others inside. It turned out the lobby was as bad as the exterior, only with more flies. There was no point in complaining as Marlana handed them their keys. Best to suck it up and get the clock started. The sooner this was all over, the better.

Their reservations were for an entire week, even though the Nunezes were scheduled to fly to São Paulo in two days to visit family. The plan was for them to stay the first two nights to ensure Min-jun was situated then return at the end of the week. If, at any time, Min-jun felt the mission was FUBAR—effed up beyond all recognition—he was free to bug out and return to the hotel until Hector and Marlana returned.

Minutes later, Min-jun opened the door to his room and grimaced at the sight of his lodging. Compared to the hotel back in Tarma, he thought it might be safer taking his chances out in the jungle. Even by North Korea living standards, this place was a dump. Fortunately, he did not have to stay here long. In fact, Min-jun reevaluated their plan and decided to leave for Mathias's compound tonight after sundown.

31

SECRETS IN THE DARK

Planet Earth
Satipo, Peru

It was the middle of the night and Edmund Mathias sat alone in the darkness of his private suite, lounging on a leather sectional. Nursing a glass of his favorite cognac—five thousand dollar a bottle—he watched video feeds on two flat panel televisions mounted on the wall above his fireplace. One screen displayed a live feed from Luna's new bedroom, just down the hall. A similar feed existed in Dr. Landry's bedroom, but tonight, Edmund used the second monitor to replay Rose's earlier interviews with Luna.

As Edmund listened to their discussion, he glanced at Luna sleeping soundly on the floor where a king-size bed used to be. The finest bedding had been offered to the Aiwan, but Luna had politely declined, preferring the hard floor with the heat turned up. Seeing this as one less security concern to worry about, Renzo had no qualms removing the bed, along with the blankets and pillows.

Edmund shrugged indifference as he drained his glass and started sucking on an ice cube. Watching the Aiwan closely, he picked up on Luna's erratic sleep, tonight being worse than others. Perhaps her new sleeping arrangements were to blame, he considered. Certainly, Luna's current predicament wreaked some degree of havoc on her subconscious, as well, but Edmund hoped to peel back her layers and uncover a deeper inner struggle, one that could be manipulated. He was still searching for that elusive hook that would convince Luna to be his long-term business partner rather than settle for a short-term marriage of convenience. She was the key to not only dominating the harvester trade, but her expertise could no doubt be exploited to benefit Mathias Industries in so many other areas, as well.

While listening to the conversation between Rose and Luna, Edmund zoomed in on the Aiwan's sleeping face. Her eyes were moving under the lids. Such rapid eye movement was indicative of a sleep disorder, one where a person physically acted out vivid, perhaps even unpleasant, dreams with sudden movements and vocalizations.

Edmund increased the volume in Luna's bedroom in hopes of recording her talking in her sleep. So far, all he had captured were a few unintelligible sounds but, judging by her rapid eye movement, she was definitely worked up about something.

Mathias raised his glass in a toast to Luna. "Let your dreams be your wings, my dear."

Behind him in the adjacent bedroom, Edmund's voluptuous girlfriend, Deanna, rolled over lazily in her silk sheets. She reached for her sugar daddy in the darkness, blindly searching Edmund's side of the bed, only to find it empty. Curious about his absence, she lifted her head, brushed her long, blonde locks out of her face, and made a groggy scan of the surroundings.

Noticing the televisions on in the living room, Deanna spotted the back of Edmund's head as he sat on the couch. She groaned in frustration. This was the third night in a row she had found him awake in the middle of the night, spying on the female alien when he should be in bed with her.

Deanna threw the covers off and crawled out of bed. She shuffled sleepy-eyed into the living room, wearing a black, sheer teddy that left nothing to the imagination. Approaching Edmund from behind, Deanna leaned over the back of the couch and ran her hands under his silk nightshirt.

She pouted. "Eddie, come back to bed."

The caress of her hands across his chest came as a welcomed surprise. Deanna's timing was perfect. There was little happening on either screen and, with the stress mounting to stake his claim on Challenger Deep, Edmund decided he needed a release. He lowered his glass and closed his eyes, allowing Deanna to carry out her sole purpose for being in his life.

"Come to bed," she whispered in his ear then nibbled on the lobe.

Edmund smiled. *Sold!*

He tossed the remote aside and set his drink on the table as he stood. As he rounded the couch, heading for bed, Deanna slipped off her lingerie. The garments fell to her ankles. She opened her arms, inviting Edmund to take her.

He paused, admiring all her glory with a horny grin on his face. Moments like this reminded Edmund how much he loved being filthy rich. Back when he had been a struggling grad student, a girl like this would have never given him the time of day. Funny how money changed all that. Now he had unlimited access to gorgeous women, all at his disposal and ready to give him whatever he wanted, whenever he wanted.

Edmund scooped Deanna off her feet, cupping her buttocks. As they started toward the bedroom, he heard Luna mention the destruction of her home in Cirros. Edmund stopped on a dime and turned sharply to the television. In doing so, he abruptly released Deanna. She nearly fell to the floor but got her feet underneath her just in time.

"Hey!" she complained.

"Shh," Edmund hissed, racing back around the couch to get closer to the television.

Rebuffed and forgotten, Deanna made a pouty lip and snatched her teddy off the floor. She then turned on her heels and stomped to the bathroom naked, slamming the door behind her.

Edmund tuned her out. Enamored by Luna's tragic story, he knew immediately he was onto something. He returned to the couch, Deanna now a distant afterthought.

Edmund listened intently, hanging onto every word as Luna described the chaos of Aiwa's massive earthquakes, the loss of her family, and the displacement of thousands of fellow Cirrans.

Glancing at Luna asleep on the adjacent screen, he muttered. "No wonder you're having a hard time sleeping."

His empathy, if any, was short-lived. Watching Luna's distressed slumber, he knew refugees rarely fled happy pasts. This was the angle he had been seeking.

While Edmund watched his screens, Rose and Luna were in the midst of their first telepathic connection. Having their bedrooms in close proximity made the task easier on Luna, though it still required effort that could be easily misconstrued as restless sleep.

Rose tossed and turned, as well. Having her mind accessed by another being was unsettling, but her subconscious acclimated quickly. Unlike the blank construct Kypa had provided Ava at Groom Lake, Rose found herself standing on a precipice with Luna overlooking a magnificent underwater kingdom.

"*What is this place?*" Rose asked, marveling at the breathtaking landscape.

"*This is my home, Cirros, before the quakes,*" Luna explained. "*That is the capital.*"

Rose took in the breadth of the stunning subterranean metropolis. The warm glow of iridescent algae illuminated the city's spires, conjuring childhood memories of Emerald City from *The Wizard of Oz.*

As if that was not enough to take in, a large, nonthreatening mammal resembling a walrus swam by. Rose reached out and gently stroked the imaginary animal's blubbery belly, grinning in childlike wonder.

"*It's magnificent,*" Rose said, imagining what Neil and Ava must be experiencing. She turned to Luna and asked, "*Is this how Kypa communicated with Ava?*"

"*Yes,*" Luna replied. "*I wanted you to see the beauty of my home before the quakes destroyed this entire region.*"

Rose frowned with empathy. There were no words to convey her condolences.

Not seeking Rose's sympathy, Luna steepled her long fingers under her jutted chin. "*Kypa took a great risk exposing his abilities to your friend, Ava.*"

Rose nodded. "*Ava was his only chance, and she was willing to risk her life for him. Perhaps that's why he did it. They needed each other.*"

"*Garnering such trust in a short amount of time is commendable,*" Luna observed. "*You took a similar leap of faith by making our connection possible.*"

"*Yeah, well, don't make me regret it.*" Rose smiled crookedly. "*This mind-sharing stuff really creeps me out.*"

"*I understand. You can trust me, Rose,*" Luna promised.

"*I know. Something tells me we're going to need each other if we hope to make it out of here.*"

"*You could not be more right,*" Luna replied gravely. "*I gleaned information from the guard who struck me. He was privy to Mathias's cloning operations, including the fact DNA samples were taken from Kypa and myself.*"

"*I know. He plans to use that technology to fund his harvesting efforts,*" Rose offered.

Luna shook her head with disappointment. "*Mathias is no different from other harvesters. He will stop at nothing to monopolize Earth's resources.*" She paused then looked Rose in the eyes. "*I can use that against him.*"

Rose raised her eyebrows. "*Oh yeah? How so?*"

"I will build the cloaking device he requested and, in doing so, I will lull him into a false sense of security. At some point, he is bound to slip up and make himself vulnerable to my telepathic abilities. I will use that opportunity to our advantage."

"Escape?" Rose asked.

"Perhaps, but we have nowhere to escape to at present. Mathias is right; it is not safe for me out in public. From what little I have gathered, the presence of my people on Earth has caused a great disruption to your society."

Rose nodded, picturing media reports of angry protesters in front of the White House and around the globe.

"I am better off staying here until an Aiwan rescue ship arrives."

"I have a way of contacting Kypa … a beacon."

Luna's mouth opened in surprise. She inched close to Rose. *"Please, tell me."*

"Kypa gave it to me before he left," Rose explained. *"Nobody else knows about it. He said it was for emergencies."*

"This would certainly qualify," Luna said lightly, her first attempt at humor. *"We must send word to him immediately."*

Rose grimaced. *"I don't think Edmund will ever let us leave this place."*

"Me, certainly not, but you, perhaps."

"Edmund only wants me around to keep you happy, especially now that he can communicate freely with you," Rose hated to admit. *"And Renzo scares the hell out of me. Watch out for him."*

"We must both be cautious and never let on that we are meeting like this."

Rose nodded earnestly.

"If you are freed, Rose, would you be willing to contact Kypa for me?"

"Absolutely. You deserve to be free. I want to help you return home."

Luna's eyes softened as she smiled warmly. *"Now I can see why Kypa trusted Ava,"* she said, taking Rose's hands in hers and squeezing gently. *"Perhaps this is enough for one night. Do you feel comfortable continuing these meetings?"*

"I do," Rose answered, realizing her fear of being brainwashed was all for naught. *"How about we can keep our daytime sessions strictly academic?"*

"Very well." Luna bowed her head. *"I will leave you now. Until tomorrow, Rose. Sleep well."*

Rose waved goodbye as Luna faded to darkness. Then she peacefully returned to deep sleep.

32

CAVING

Planet Aiwa
Realm of Cirros

Kypa slowly regained consciousness. Opening his eyes gradually, he found himself underwater and immersed in darkness. Panicked, Kypa yelped, his voice muffled by a high-pitched ringing in his ears. He then kicked upward and struck his head on the mineshaft's low ceiling. Stars danced in front of his eyes as the concussive hit sent a searing pain through his already aching skull.

Calm yourself. He winced, nursing his tender head. *You are alive. Now think.*

Recalling the explosion that had sent him hurtling down the shaft, Kypa began groping blindly in the darkness to find the side walls and get his bearings. Then his heart nearly skipped a beat.

Father!

Reaching out with telepathy, Kypa called frantically to King Loka. *"Father, can you hear me? It is Kypa. Please, answer me!"*

There was no reply, and Kypa got no sense of his father's presence nearby. Thinking quickly, he tried calling for help on his commlink but found the device had been damaged from the blast. Kypa growled in frustration, then a grim thought crossed his mind.

What if everyone onboard the king's yacht was dead?

Still shocked by Major Gora's treachery, Kypa wondered if this was an isolated terrorist attack or part of a larger coup to topple his father's regime.

And if Gora had turned, who else might be involved in this conspiracy?

Kypa's thoughts turned to his family. In a rush of panic, he realized they were in danger, too. He had to warn them … if it was not already too late.

Reining in his emotions, Kypa knew losing his head in this environment would kill him just as quickly as an assassin. He could not help his family until he escaped this mine, so the first order of business was to find his father and locate an exit. Unfortunately, he would have to do both without his sight. Kypa had lost his handheld light during the explosion, forcing him to grope his way blindly through the giant maze of intersecting shafts, chambers, and passages. On the bright side, he had a pretty clear recollection of the mine's schematic, despite his throbbing headache, but he still needed a landmark to figure out which direction was out.

"*Kypa …*"

The weak call of his father's voice stopped Kypa cold. He snapped his head sideways, listening intently. "*Father, I hear you. Are you safe?*"

"*Ceiling … collapsed,*" Loka muttered.

Even through telepathy, Kypa could tell his father was in great pain.

"*Buried in rocks,*" his father continued. "*My leg is broken.*"

"*Stay awake, Father. Let our connection guide me to you.*"

Loka grunted. "*Hurry …*"

Kypa closed his eyes, forcing himself to relax. He then pictured complete blackness in his mind's eye. Focusing on that void was a technique he used to help himself fall asleep when his restless mind refused to slow down. It also worked to accentuate telepathic connections. Like pointing a satellite dish at the right latitude in the night sky, embracing the emptiness allowed Kypa to narrow the focus of his echolocation to isolate his father's biosignature.

There you are! Kypa breathed a sigh of relief.

Reversing course, he made haste and began feeling his way through the darkness.

Back aboard the king's yacht, the lift's doors opened to reveal Commodore Boa surrounded by four guards in his protection detail. They were met by Captain Roka, one of Boa's up-and-coming young officers. Behind Roka, scattered about the corridor, were the remnants of the attack on Princess Seva. It was a tragic scene; the bloody corpses of dead Aiwans were strewn about on the floor outside the observation lounge.

Roka waved Boa forward and bowed. Even though the fighting had ended, danger still loomed. Boa's guards fanned out with their blasters drawn.

Boa surveyed the carnage with a clenched jaw. Closer to the lounge entrance, he noticed a team of Aiwan investigators using handheld devices to scan the crime scene. Meanwhile, medics treated the wounded.

"Report," Boa said with cold authority.

"This was a well-coordinated attack, sir. While the assault occurred outside, the insurgents inside the ship moved against the princess. To her credit, she managed to barricade herself inside the lounge." He pointed to the damaged door with a large hole cut in the center. "Reinforcements reached her in time and put down the attackers. The princess is in her quarters now. I posted two guards as a precaution."

Boa nodded approval. "The other wardens are safe, as well. Reach out to their security heads and see if they need anything."

"Yes, sir."

"Any idea who is behind this?" Boa asked.

"No one has claimed responsibility. We are gathering evidence and tagging the corpses we believe to be part of the insurrection. Unfortunately, none survived, so it could be some time before we learn their motive."

Boa glimpsed the bloodied field dressing on Roka's arm. "Are you all right, Captain?"

Roka eyed his wound and shrugged it off. "I will be fine. Thank you, sir. I wish I could say the same for them." He gestured to the fallen. "We lost good soldiers today."

Boa sighed, sharing his frustration. He patted Roka's shoulder as a minor comfort. Just then, Boa's commlink chirped. He removed the device from his belt. "Yes?"

"Sir, this is Areda," the ship's captain replied. "The rescue team has reached the tunnel leading to the king's last location. It was blocked by a landslide, but they expect to enter shortly."

"Any signs of life?"

"Negative, sir, but that could be due to interference from all of the debris." Areda's grim tone did not sound hopeful.

Boa considered this. After a brief pause, he said, "Understood. Call in reinforcements to help with the search. I am returning to the bridge now."

Boa ended the transmission and turned to Roka. "Continue your investigation, Captain. I want regular updates."

"Yes, sir." Roka bowed and went back to work.

Boa turned to leave when a troubling reminder halted him in his tracks. He looked about the crime scene with a furrowed brow. Not finding what he was looking for amongst the corpses, he called Roka over. "Captain."

"Yes, sir?"

"Where are the humans?"

Surprised by the question, Roka stammered a reply. "Gone, sir," he answered matter-of-factly.

"Gone where?"

"To the surface, sir. They fled in escape pods during the attack. My apologies, I thought you knew."

Boa's olive cheeks flushed as he clenched his fists. This could not be a coincidence.

I warned the court this would happen, Boa seethed, *but they refused to listen*!

Then, a dreadful thought came to mind: the Reaper's failsafe protocol. Assuming Captain Tan's threat to self-destruct the ship was legitimate, the capital, and all of Aiwa for that matter, were at risk if anything happened to her.

Rounding sharply, the commodore returned to the lift without another word. His protection detail joined him. They rode straight to the bridge. There, Captain Areda called the room to attention as soon as Boa entered.

"As you were." Boa waved dismissively.

Areda approached. "Sir, the rescue team has entered the tunnel. We should have a status update shortly."

Boa acknowledged with a curt nod. "What about the humans?"

"Sir?"

Boa looked incredulous. "The humans … they escaped in pods during the attack. Where are they now?"

Rather than make an excuse, Areda turned to his science officer. "Locate the pods."

The science officer went to work at her terminal and quickly responded. "No sign of them, sir."

"How can that be?" Boa interjected.

"They may not have made it to the surface, sir."

The science officer was not wrong. Insurrectionists, or any number of sea-dwelling predators, could have taken out the escape pods. However, since the planet had not been torn apart yet by the Reaper's "supposed" failsafe protocol, he had to assume the humans were still alive.

"Keep searching," he insisted. "I want the humans found."

"Right away, sir."

Areda turned to his weapons officer seated at a nearby station. "Launch a spread of Seekers immediately. Program the drones to search for the missing pods as well as the humans' biosignatures. Do it now!"

The weapons officer jumped into action. His mental connection to the ship's computer sped up the process.

"Launching Seekers now, sir," he announced.

Boa moved in front of the main viewer with his hands clasped behind his back. Seconds later, six Seekers raced by, on their way to the surface to locate Neil and Ava. He expected the humans would be found rather quickly but cautioned himself against underestimating their abilities.

"Sir, what do you want the Seekers to do once the humans are found?" Areda asked.

Without Kypa or the court to interfere, Boa knew he could do with them as he pleased. Ridding himself of the humans once and for all would certainly feel good, but until he could confirm if Captain Tan's threat to self-destruct the Reaper was real, he had to exercise extreme caution for the sake of all Aiwans.

"No harm must come to the humans. Pin them down and dispatch a ground team to retrieve them."

"Yes, sir," Areda replied. He made a simple hand gesture to his first officer who set off to organize the extraction team.

Seated behind Captain Areda, the communications officer received an incoming transmission from the search and rescue team. "Sir, the search team has reached the site of the explosion."

Deep inside the crater, a pair of Aiwan search and rescue divers arrived at the king's last known location, only to find an impassable pile of rocks standing in their way. Debris from the cave-in was stacked floor to ceiling, and sensors indicated it would take time to excavate.

Scanning the area, the team leader shook his head in dismay. "*I am not reading any life signs,*" he told his partner.

Beside him, the other diver shined a light along the wall and ceiling, examining the discoloration of the rock surface. "*What do you make of this?*"

The team leader joined him and, upon closer inspection, did a double-take. There were no horizontal lines indicating sedimentary strata or layers. It was as if the walls had been painted a solid, warm beige.

He reached out and ran his hand along the wall. Giving his partner a peculiar look, the leader said, "*It is as smooth as glass.*" He then pounded the wall with the ball of his fist. "*Solid, too.*"

"*Have you ever seen anything like this?*" his partner asked, unsettled.

Sizing up the tunnel blockage and the foreboding task ahead of them, the leader shook his head and sighed. Nothing about this place felt right. "*Go get the others,*" he instructed. "*We have a lot of work ahead of us.*"

Kypa continued blindly through the darkness until catching sight of a soft glow of white light in the distance. He knew instantly it had to be his father.

"*I see you!*" he called out. "*Hold on!*"

Tearing off into a full-on swim sprint, Kypa used the light as a beacon to guide him to his father. The light grew brighter as he neared, as did Kypa's hopes. He had never wanted to be with his father more than now.

Kypa reached a large pile of rubble partially blocking the passage. He found Loka completely buried, save for his exposed hand protruding from the rocks. In his hand, Loka clutched the light.

"*Father, I am here,*" Kypa said, gently taking the light from his father and squeezing Loka's hand.

"*Kypa …*" Loka replied weakly.

"*Hold on,*" Kypa urged. "*I will get you out.*"

He raised the lantern and surveyed the structural integrity of the surrounding area. Despite the urge to frantically dig out his father, Kypa feared further cave-ins if he went about it sloppily. Exercising patience, he began to methodically remove stones and stack them off to the side until his father's bloodied face was revealed.

Loka's eyes opened to slits, squinting from the light. "*I knew you would come,*" he said, creasing a smile.

"*Save your energy,*" Kypa replied. "*I will get us out of here.*"

Just how he planned to accomplish such a feat was still up in the air. The king was lucky to be alive, but for how long was yet to be seen. Loka had a sizable gash on the crown of his head. and there was still a broken leg to contend with, amongst other yet-to-be-diagnosed injuries.

Kypa finished removing the remaining debris until his father's whole body was floating free. As his father predicted, Loka's right leg was broken. Kypa could tell from its unnatural contortion.

"*Do not move,*" Kypa instructed then ever-so-gently felt around Loka's torso to gauge the extent of his injuries.

"*I am detecting several broken ribs, and your abdomen is bloated, which could signal internal bleeding.*"

Loka winced. "*Yes, I am detecting that, too.*"

336 | TODD HOSEA

Kypa looked at his father, who flashed him a wry grin. They both chuckled, which triggered sharp pains in Loka's side. The king gritted his teeth, grimacing.

"*Easy,*" Kypa soothed.

Sensing his son's empathy and desire to help, Loka eyed Kypa through new lenses. It was as if he was seeing him for the first time. "*It is good to see you smile.*"

Kypa squeezed his father's hand. A lifetime of distance between father and son had been bridged in the last hour. Whatever differences they had in the past seemed inconsequential now. But their time was running out. Loka coughed, and a spittle of green blood floated from the corner of his mouth, surprising them both.

"*Can you swim?*" Kypa asked.

"*You go on without me,*" Loka insisted. "*Get to the ship and warn the others.*"

"*Nonsense, I am not leaving you here.*"

Kypa took the light and shined it up the corridor opposite from whence he came. "*I believe that is the way back to the junction. Stay here while I check it out.*"

"*If you insist,*" Loka replied with a shade of dry humor as his eyes grew heavy.

"*Father, you must stay awake,*" Kypa insisted. "*No sleeping.*"

Loka forced his eyes open to his son's satisfaction.

"*Good. Now hang on. I will be right back.*"

Kypa set off, swimming as fast as he could while holding out the light to illuminate his path. Still, it took him longer to reach the junction than expected. The blast wave had carried them far. And, to his dismay, the shaft was completely blocked before he could reach the junction. There was no way to get through to the main tunnel leading back to the ship.

Assessing the mine's schematic from memory, Kypa decided against venturing down the cross-sections that led to the other shafts. It was highly likely they had also collapsed, so there was no sense tempting fate. At least he knew the way he had come was open and, with any luck, it would stay that way until they reached the nearest emergency exit.

Kypa returned to Loka and found his father clinging to consciousness, holding his tender ribs in quiet suffering. He frowned, uncertain how his father would manage the pain during the difficult journey ahead.

"*That direction is blocked.*" Kypa reported. "*We will have to find another way out.*"

Loka closed his eyes and nodded, resolving himself to endure whatever needed to happen next.

Kypa considered different angles to try and support his father then shook his head in defeat. There was no easy way to approach it. This was going to hurt like hell.

"*Ready?*"

Loka nodded vigorously, mustering the strength to move.

Kypa took his father by his upper arm and shoulder, turning his body gently toward the way out. The king gritted his teeth in agony as a searing pain coursed through his body. Kypa ignored his father's cries and moved quickly to wrap Loka's arm around his neck. For added stability, he grabbed the back of his father's utility belt to keep him steady as they swam.

"*Good. The worst part is over,*" Kypa said, trying to sound upbeat. "*You hold the light. I'll drive.*"

Loka nodded with a pained expression. He held the light at his side as Kypa began flutter kicking. Together, they set off deeper into the shaft. Slowly but surely, father and son made their way forward into the unknown, hoping beyond hope that somewhere in the darkness ahead they might find a path to freedom.

33

GROUNDED

Planet Aiwa
Realm of Cirros

Rescue efforts intensified as more than a dozen Aiwan vessels arrived in Cirros. With hundreds of divers in the water scouring every inch of the crater and surrounding area, the search for King Loka and Prince Kypa now included resources from each of the four realms.

News of the attempted coup cast a pall over rescue efforts. Investigators kept details under tight wraps, fueling accusations and rumors about who was responsible for the attack on the royal family. Naturally, this led to quiet discussions about the transition of power in the event of regicide. By law, if Kypa was also dead, the crown would be passed to the king's daughter, Princess Seva. While it was still too soon to speak of it openly, closed door debates were underway to challenge this edict, should it come to pass.

Despite being approached by several potential challengers, Commodore Boa avoided declaring his allegiance to anyone other than the king. He knew the weight of his position, but to speak on the matter before knowing the status of King Loka and Prince Kypa was not only inappropriate, it could also incite a civil war.

Instead, Boa focused on more pressing matters. He had to get to the bottom of who was responsible for the attack, and yet, finding the humans was also of paramount concern. Deactivating the Reaper's failsafe protocol notwithstanding, Boa needed the humans in custody long enough to seize their ship. They possessed the most powerful warship the universe had ever seen, a power they were unfit to wield, at least in his mind.

For now, the Reaper was grounded. All traffic in and out of Supra had been halted due to the coup, so the ship was going nowhere unless it forced its way out.

However, Boa was aware of several departure requests made on the Reaper's behalf. This confirmed the humans were still alive. But Boa could not risk them reuniting with their ship. He knew if the humans made it back to the Reaper, they would leave Aiwa behind in a heartbeat. Any hope of securing the ship as property of the Aiwan government would be lost. And worse yet, with the Reaper running free in the cosmos, it still presented a grave threat to Aiwa should it fall into the hands of their enemies. Boa had no choice but to devise a way to permanently separate the ship from Captain Tan.

The last person to have seen the humans alive was Princess Seva. Boa made his way to her quarters, ready to tactfully question the king's young daughter. In the lift on the way down, Boa contemplated his next move. He knew he had to tread lightly with the princess, especially in the absence of Queen Qora. Upsetting Seva in this time of grief and uncertainty was unwise, both in terms of conducting his investigation and gaining her trust as the potential heir to the throne. Boa was stern by nature, so empathy and consolation were not his strong suits. Yet, he would need both in the coming minutes.

Exiting the lift with his protection detail, Boa approached the two sentries posted outside Seva's private quarters. Both warriors snapped to attention and moved aside in unison. Boa pressed the call button on the wall panel to announce his arrival.

"Enter," came the distant voice of the princess.

Inside, Boa found Seva standing alone in front of a large window. She rounded as he entered.

Boa dropped to one knee, bowed his head, and held it. This formal display of loyalty caught Seva by surprise. The commodore had never shown her this level of respect. It was reserved for her father or, as she discovered, the person soon to be named as the head of state.

Boa's etiquette set the tone for their meeting.

Seva straightened and lifted her chin as she approached. She placed her hand atop Boa's shoulder, as was the custom, and acknowledged his pledge.

As Seva stepped back, Boa raised his eyes and stood. "Princess, our search efforts continue. It will be some time before our rescue team can safely access the last known location of your father and brother."

"And my betrothed," she added.

"Yes, of course," Boa affirmed, kicking himself for the oversight.

Seva considered this thoughtfully. "Thank you, Commodore. My father has always held you in the highest regard. I know everyone is doing their best to find them."

Boa inclined his head slightly. It was more of a gracious nod than a bow. "I offer the same service to you, Princess, which is why I am here. Is this a good time for us to speak?"

"Yes, Commodore. What is it?" Seva replied, welcoming the distraction. She gestured to the couch, and they sat on opposite ends, facing one another.

Boa cleared his throat. He had mentally practiced his delivery but looking into Seva's anguished eyes made him reconsider. Despite having grown into adulthood, Seva was still a child in Boa's eyes. She had never been meant to rule. Although she was quite intelligent in her own right and demonstrated exceptional leadership potential, Seva was young and inexperienced in the ways of governing. Her role in the monarchy had been predestined. She was to secure an alliance through marriage to help keep the Five Realms unified. That had been her father's intention.

"My Princess," Boa began delicately, struggling not to appear callous, "these are perilous times. I must find out who is responsible for this attack, and in the absence of your father and brother, you are now acting Warden of Eos and the rightful heir to the throne."

Seva appeared daunted by the prospect of becoming sovereign.

Boa sensed her feeling of overwhelm and flashed a thin yet empathic smile to set her mind at ease. "You are not alone, Princess. I will protect you, I swear, but you must tell me everything you know about today's attack."

"Yes, of course, but I am afraid I may not be of much help."

"Tell me about the humans," Boa said directly.

Seva gave him a peculiar look. "What do you mean?"

"As I understand it, you and Dr. Garrett spent time together in the capital." Boa paused for confirmation.

Seva nodded.

"Did he say anything to you indicating malice against our people? Did you notice anything unusual about his behavior leading up to the attack?"

Thinking for a moment, the princess shook her head. "No, not that I can recall. He was most cordial."

"Yet the humans fled during the attack."

"At my behest," Seva clarified. "I helped them escape." She searched Boa's face for approval, but the commodore's level expression gave her no such affirmation.

"May I ask why?" Boa inquired.

"Everything happened so fast," Seva explained, suddenly feeling defensive. "We did not know who was attacking or why. All I could think was to get off the ship, but they broke in before I could get to a pod. I acted to save the humans."

Sensing Seva's agitation, Boa backed off and spoke in a calming tone. "That showed courage and quick thinking," he praised. After a pause, Boa asked, "Do you know where they went?"

"To the surface," Seva answered. "I told them to wait on the beach until help arrived."

"I see," Boa considered. "We have dispatched Seekers to locate Ambassador Garrett and Captain Tan and bring them back immediately. You may not be aware, but if any harm should come to them it is possible their ship could self-destruct and destroy the capital, along with most of Aiwa."

Seva was taken aback. "No, I was not aware," she remarked, now feeling responsible for jeopardizing the safety of all Aiwans. "Had I known—"

"It is not your fault," Boa assured her. "We will find them and deal with this matter so that no harm comes to our people."

"Thank you, Commodore."

"In the meantime," Boa added, "if you think of anything else, no matter how minute, please bring it directly to me."

Seva nodded earnestly. "I will."

Satisfied, Boa stood to leave. "Thank you for your time, Princess." He bowed and started for the door.

"Commodore?" Seva called to him.

Boa paused and turned. "Yes, Princess?"

"W-What will become of me now?" she fretted.

Seeing the childlike innocence on Seva's face, the commodore softened. He exhaled heavily. "It will depend on our rescue efforts. For your protection, I can make arrangements for you to return to Supra. You will be safe with the rest of your family in a secure location. As for the transition of power, that will be determined by the High Court. But let us not get ahead of ourselves. I intend to find your father and brother, and Commander Rega, alive."

He refrained from adding that, if King Loka and Prince Kypa were truly dead, there would surely be challengers to Seva's claim to the throne. After a customary mourning period across the Five Realms, rivals would no doubt begin lining up at the palace steps, seeking the seat of power.

They are probably securing allies at this very moment, Boa mused.

All of that would play out in the days ahead. For now, there was no sense burdening Seva with more than she could handle.

Taking his leave, Boa turned his thoughts back to the investigation and his search for Neil and Ava. His gut told him it was unlikely the humans played any part in the king's death but finding them was his top priority. The fate of Aiwa depended on it.

34

ALPHA TEST

Planet Earth
Satipo, Peru

Rose kept to herself as she looked through the window into Luna's personal laboratory. Beside her, Edmund, Renzo, Ms. Diaz, and several of Mathias's best scientists watched anxiously as Luna made final preparations to test her newly constructed cloaking device.

Excitement filled the air as the group waited for the show to begin. Up until a month ago, no one in attendance had imagined cloaking was possible outside of a science fiction movie. Several of the scientists hypothesized—rather loudly—how the Aiwan's device might work, yet none of them really had a clue. It was just a conceited attempt to impress Edmund.

Bored by their chatter, Rose tried tuning them out as best she could. If she were carrying any coins, she probably would have sounded like a piggy bank the way her hands fidgeted ceaselessly in her pockets, but not Luna. The Aiwan appeared unflappable, going about her business with quiet precision, confident in her abilities.

Inside the lab, Luna stood at a sterile, metal table, hunched over a device no bigger than a standard microwave oven. She was alone in the room, per Renzo's new security protocols. No one was allowed near her. In fact, since

Luna's work had begun on the cloaking device, all research previously being carried out on the recovered Aiwan tech had ceased. That lab had been handed over to Luna, and her work was the only work that mattered for the time being. The other scientists were merely spectators, watching and learning from afar as Luna disassembled the damaged Seeker and pieced together a cloaking device from the scraps.

Looking up, Luna eyed the crowd gathered outside. She gave a nod to Mathias, who activated the intercom on the wall.

"Ready?" he asked, grinning widely.

Beside him, Renzo's jaw clenched. Unlike the others who were excited to witness history unfold, his anxiety stemmed from the unknown. For all he knew, Luna had built a weapon of mass destruction or a means to call in an invasion force.

"Yes," Luna replied in a business-like tone.

"Before you begin, can you explain what you've built?"

"Of course." She rested her hand on the device, like an infomercial spokesperson. "For starters, let me differentiate between cloaking an object and scrambling its signal. Scrambling a signal, like a ship's engine exhaust, electronic signature, or other traits, does not hide the signal output. Rather, it jumbles the signal to the point where sensors misread it to be something other than what it really is. However, a cloaking device, or invisibility shield as some call it, is a form of stealth technology used to selectively bend light in order to render an object completely invisible to the electromagnetic spectrum, as well as most sensors.

"Cloaking devices are very rare, mostly due to cost," Luna explained. "The other major drawback for starships involves the inability to fire weapons or use advanced navigation systems while cloaked. In combat, warships cannot afford to sacrifice firepower, speed, and other vital systems. However, this will not be an issue with stationary crystals laying at the bottom of the ocean. Cloaking the crystals is a viable option."

Luna started to share how her own research into nanotechnology might someday solve the combat issues but caught herself. It had been so long since she had worked in a lab and been surrounded by knowledge-seeking scientists that she got carried away. Besides, her research had been theoretical and never made it to practical application.

"Wow, that is amazing," Mathias gushed. "I'm sure the team has a ton of questions, but we don't want to hold you up. Let's see your device in action."

"Very well. Without getting into the details, I will simply say that this device is essentially a low-energy projector. For today's test, when I activate the device, the light around any object in a ten-foot radius will be deflected to make it appear as if it did not exist, rendering it invisible. Allow me to demonstrate."

Luna shot a cursory glance at Rose, who flashed her a nervous smile and a thumbs-up. She then activated the device. The sides opened to reveal a glass cylinder that glowed a soft white. The audience gasped in stunned amazement. Everything in the room around the device suddenly disappeared right before their eyes, including Luna.

The group clapped with excitement, all except Renzo. Misconstruing the experiment as an escape attempt, his heart leapt when the Aiwan disappeared. He started toward the door to the lab, ready to sound the alarm, when Luna reappeared suddenly. She stepped out of the beam's path, unaware of Renzo's fears.

"As you can see," she pointed out, "the device cloaks everything in the vicinity, including the device itself, from outsiders. When we move to beta testing at Challenger Deep, I will expand the range to ensure the entire site is amply cloaked. My only concern at this point is making sure the device can withstand the extreme underwater pressures."

Truly moved by Luna's craftsmanship, Edmund applauded her efforts, even clutching his heart endearingly. He then thumbed the intercom. "*I saw the angel in the marble and carved until I set him free,*" he quoted Michelangelo. As if on cue, the other scientists echoed the sentiment. "Bravo, Luna," Edmund continued. "You are indeed an artist. All of the pieces were right there in front of us, but only you could turn it into a masterpiece."

Luna bowed graciously.

Around Mathias, the smiles on the faces of the scientists slowly faded as they realized the slight directed toward them.

"Shall we make plans to field test the unit?"

"I need to conduct additional integrity tests," Luna replied. "Barring any setbacks, I believe the device will be ready soon."

"Excellent. Again, good work, Luna."

Edmund silenced the intercom and turned to Renzo. Before he could speak, his fixer assured him all preparations had already been made.

"Perfect, we leave for Challenger Deep as soon as she's ready."

USS *Ronald Reagan* Carrier Strike Group

Admiral Clancy entered the combat information center with a purpose, displaying his typical gruff expression. As usual, he found the CIC dark, crowded, and cold, but the room was hopping with activity. Technicians manning various radars, electronic warfare systems, and status boards were collecting, evaluating, and rapidly disseminating pertinent tactical information to command and control stations throughout the ship.

Ever since the encounter with the Aiwans, the CIC had been working overtime. Tensions between the United States, Russia, and China in the Pacific remained tenuous, at best. At the forefront of the crisis was the recovery of a Russian Akula-class submarine sunk by an Aiwan Seeker near Guam. At least that was what the Russian's wanted the world to believe.

In truth, due to the extreme depths where the sub had gone down, recovery was impossible. The sub's hull would have been crushed to the size of a soda can, leaving no chance for survivors. However, the situation afforded the Russians a convenient excuse to linger in the area, gathering intel on the Americans, who in turn were spying on Mathias Industries' deep-sea salvage ship, *Billy Bones*.

China, Japan, and South Korea also had vessels patrolling in *Ronald Reagan's* area of operations. With so many surface ships and submersibles crowding the Western Pacific, Clancy's carrier strike group was forced to remain at a high state of readiness, pushing his sailors to the brink.

Clancy located the CIC Watch Officer, Commander Remley, on the opposite side of the room. He weaved his way through the crowd to reach Remley's side. "What've you got, Robbie?"

"They're buggin' out, sir. All of them." The incredulity in Remley's voice spoke to the man's mix of confusion and surprise.

"Who's bugging out?"

"The Russians and Chinese, sir. It's the damnedest thing. They departed the area at exactly the same time ... as if on cue."

"What about the other contacts?"

"Japanese and South Korean vessels followed. We're not detecting *any* surface or submersed combat vessels within a two hundred and fifty mile radius."

Clancy removed his *CVN-76*-embroidered baseball cap and scratched his balding head in confusion. This move made no sense. Having one country pull out was plausible, but all of them at once required an act of God. To achieve this level of coordination required something, or someone, capable of moving mountains. Only one person came to mind.

"What about Mathias's ship?"

"No changes," Remley replied. "We've continued reconnaissance flights, but our drone images show no activity on the deck of his ship. It's as if they're waiting for something."

Clancy was taken aback. "Waiting for what?"

Remley shrugged. "We're still working on that, sir."

"I don't like this one bit," Clancy grumbled, putting his hat back on. "Any updates from HQ?"

Remley shook his head.

The admiral exhaled in frustration. Thus far, the Office of Naval Intelligence remained mum on the subject. On the bright side, his carrier group had not been ordered out of the area. Not yet at least.

That's saying something, Admiral Clancy mused, a testament to the President he had voted for.

The White House, Washington, D.C.

"Seriously?" President Fitzgerald asked. Seated behind the *Resolute* desk in the Oval Office, he looked back and forth between his two top intelligence officers with incredulity. "My phone's been ringing off the hook all morning from nearly two dozen members of Congress—and their mothers—asking me to remove *Ronald Reagan* from Challenger Deep. Now you're telling me the Russians and Chinese are doing the same? Are Mathias's pockets really this deep?"

"If he is behind this move, sir, we've grossly underestimated his reach," Maxine Ratliff, newly appointed Director of the Central Intelligence Agency, replied.

Seated on her right was Guy Lannister, acting Director of National Intelligence. Both he and Ratliff had been thrown into the deep end their first week on the job, thanks to the failings of their predecessors, Nancy Drake and Gary Sizemore.

"I'm afraid she's right, Mr. President," Lannister concurred. "Since the events at Groom Lake, we've made satellite flyovers of Mathias's facility in Peru. Everyone from international arms dealers to high-powered investors have been seen entering the facility in recent visits, including agents from Russia, China, and North Korea."

"What's he up to?" the President asked pointedly.

"Our intel doesn't support any conclusions yet, but we know he ran a 'force enhancement' division at Groom Lake. That's where he housed the cloning operation that Garza funded."

Picturing his former Chairman of the Joint Chiefs of Staff in an orange prison jumpsuit, Fitzgerald asked, "Is he talking?"

"No, sir," Director Ratliff answered. "Garza and Sizemore are both wanting immunity from prosecution and other concessions before they'll cooperate."

"So, I've heard," Fitzgerald commented wryly, referring to the formal apology Garza had demanded. "Do we have anyone on the inside?"

Despite being new, neither Lannister nor Ratliff had been born yesterday. Both looked to the President's watchdog, Chief of Staff, Ernie Gutierrez, for approval to fully brief the Commander in Chief.

Ernie shook his head, indicating they should answer the question yes or no, but they could not give away any further information to ensure the President retained plausible deniability.

Ratliff cleared her throat. "Yes, sir, we do."

Fitzgerald understood the game and deferred to Ernie's judgment. "I see. Well, when do you hope to have concrete intel explaining what the hell Mathias is up to?"

"Hopefully soon, Mr. President." Lannister made no promises. "Mathias's facility is top-notch, with the best security money can buy. We know little about the inner workings, but we'll keep at it."

"It's taking everything we have to keep the world from unraveling around us," Fitzgerald grumbled. "With the threat of alien invasion looming, the last thing we need is having this rogue billionaire in bed with the enemy."

"Clearly, he's interested in the crystals," Ernie chimed in, circling back to Challenger Deep. "How he managed to singlehandedly pull four countries from the area isn't as important as why."

"At least having Russia and China out of the area deescalates the situation," Lannister remarked.

"Maybe that's the point," Ratliff speculated. "His ship"—she opened a manila folder on her lap to check her file—"*Billy Bones*, is a deep sea salvage ship, one of only a few capable of working in those depths. If he's planning to harvest crystals on his own, it stands to reason he needs us out of the way."

Makes sense, Fitzgerald mused. "But how does this relate to cloning?"

Blank expressions were exchanged around the room, much to the President's frustration.

"All right, get back to it," Fitzgerald cued the meeting was over. "Let me know when you have something."

As soon as they were gone, the President opened a side drawer in his desk where he kept a bag of black jellybeans.

"If Candace finds out ..." Ernie warned.

"Which she won't as long as you keep your mouth shut," Fitzgerald warned, knowing his chief of staff was right. The First Lady was on a health kick and would toss his candy stash if she discovered it.

He popped a handful in his mouth.

Ernie chuckled at the sight of the President. His cheeks were stuffed as if he was storing nuts for winter. "I have to side with her on this one. Those things are disgusting. But don't worry; your secret's safe with me."

Fitzgerald washed the candy down with a glass of water. Leaning back in his chair, he sighed heavily. "This business with Mathias is getting out of hand."

"No matter how dirty he is, the Peruvian government will never allow us to carry out covert ops against him," Ernie stated. "Mathias lines too many of their pockets."

"We can't allow him to go unchecked," Fitzgerald countered, knowing what Ernie would say next.

Ernie raised his eyebrow. "Do you want to be reelected or not?"

The President tossed his pen onto the desk in frustration. "Damn the election, Ernie. We took oaths, and I intend to live up to my end."

Ernie smiled thinly. "Just checking to make sure we're still on the same page." He closed his planner, knowing the President's next appointment was waiting. "Rest assured, Mr. President, when the time comes, I'll make sure we have all of our options on the table."

"I knew I could count on you, Ernie," Fitzgerald said earnestly.

Ernie stood then retreated to his office, leaving the President alone with his thoughts.

It seemed each day his administration was facing a new defining moment, and there was no rest on the horizon.

"Dammit," he muttered, opening the side drawer for another handful of licorice.

35

SHADOW RECON

Planet Earth
Satipo, Peru

Marlana huffed and slammed her paperback novel down at her side.

"¡Por el Amor de Dios!" she muttered angrily, directing her frustration at Hector. She loved her husband dearly, but tonight's snoring was over the top.

Forced to sleep with the window cracked only exasperated Hector's sleep apnea. Still, hearing him drone away was like listening to a hog calling.

Sitting up in bed, Marlana eyed Hector impatiently. He snorted again, loud enough to be heard over the thunderstorm currently wreaking havoc outside. She nudged him with her elbow, hoping her husband would resituate and somehow clear his nasal passages.

It had no effect. Hector continued sawing logs, oblivious to his wife's frazzled mental state.

For a brief moment, Marlana jokingly entertained thoughts of smothering Hector in his sleep. She figured her odds of getting off scot-free were fifty-fifty, probably better in this area of the world. All she needed was a sympathetic female judge with a husband who also snored. Case closed.

"For better or for worse, my ass," she grumbled and threw off the covers.

Resolving herself to the fact that only one of them would sleep well tonight,

Marlana looked around their bleak hotel room for any kind of distraction. Their half-star accommodations had no television or radio, and it was impossible to concentrate on her book. Still wide awake, she decided to check on Min-jun instead. Dressed in sweats and T-shirt, she threw on her zip-up hoodie rather than bother with a bra and was soon out the door.

Min-jun's room was across the hall. Putting her ear to his door, Marlana listened intently for movement inside but heard nothing. Looking down, she noticed light coming from his room under the door. She knocked lightly.

Still not a peep inside, but she caught a shadow move on the other side of the door. Marlana backed away hastily.

"Yes?" came Min-jun's voice.

"It's me—Marlana," she whispered.

The creaky door opened slightly. Min-jun peeked through the opening, bracing himself behind the door in case someone tried to barge in. Seeing Marlana in her night clothes, he eyed her up and down suspiciously.

"Problem?"

"No." Marlana waved dismissively. She then thumbed toward her room. "Hector's snoring so loud I can't sleep. I thought I'd check on you."

Min-jun opened the door wide enough to stick his head out and steal a glance up and down the hallway. Seeing she was alone, his posture relaxed. He opened the door fully then bowed and welcomed her inside.

As Marlana entered, Min-jun checked the hallway once more for good measure before closing the door behind him.

Inside, Marlana could not help but notice Min-jun's attire. Rather than being dressed for bed, he was decked out in night camouflage gear. His backpack rested under the windowsill.

"Going somewhere?"

"Yes," Min-jun replied. He sat on the bed and began lacing up his boots. "Less chance of being seen in storm. I leave now."

Marlana gave him a peculiar look. "You sure? It's pretty nasty out there."

Min-jun nodded. "I go. Better than hanging around here."

"I can't argue with that," she said dryly.

Marlana eyed him curiously as he continued lacing his boots. She knew Min-jun had been ex-North Korean special forces prior to being recruited by the CIA. Night ops, particularly infiltration and exfiltration missions, were his specialty. From what Jessica had told her, Choi Min-jun was a badass operator, but at five-foot-six and a buck-fifty soaking wet, she marveled at how such a dangerous asset could come in such a small package.

How many had made the fatal mistake of underestimating him? she wondered. Marlana had no intention of making the list.

"Do you have everything you need?"

"Yes." Min-jun nodded. "I be back in seven days."

"Got it. Hector and I fly out the day after tomorrow. We'll be back to get you next Friday."

Min-jun finished with his boots. Next, he stood and pulled a black poncho over his head. After a final room check, he turned to Marlana expectantly.

A tad slow on the uptake, it took a second for Marlana to realize that was her cue to leave.

"Oh, right. I'll just get going." She smiled sheepishly, thumbing toward the door.

Marlana started to leave but stopped short of the door and rounded toward Min-jun. "Can I ask a favor?"

Min-jun shrugged.

"Do you mind if I sleep in here while you're gone?"

Taken aback, Min-jun chuckled. Hector's snoring must be pretty bad. "Be my guest," he said, gesturing to the unused bed. He figured she was footing the bill for it, anyway.

"Thank you. You're a life-saver." Marlana then shooed him away jokingly. "Now go find Rose."

Min-jun nodded then gestured toward the door. "Lights."

"Got it." Marlana flipped the switch, casting the room into darkness.

A flash of lightning outside illuminated Min-jun's silhouette by the window.

"After I go, you close window," he whispered.

"Sure thing," Marlana whispered back.

As Mrs. Nunez felt her way in the darkness to his side, Min-jun parted the curtain slightly and peered out the window. To his relief, the storm showed no signs of letting up. Only a fool would go out in weather like this, so being spotted by the average local seemed unlikely. However, he had to assume Satipo's criminal elements had eyes everywhere.

Jessica had warned him before leaving that this area was a hotbed for drug traffickers and remnants of the defunct terrorist group, *Sendero Luminoso* (Shining Path). With Peru being the second largest producer of coca leaf in the world, it only stood to reason that organized crime had a heavy presence in this area. Growing coca was not a crime in Peru, but processing it was. So, Peruvian drug traffickers, known as firmas, would collect the coca leaves from farmers. They would then transport the leaves to international groups—namely the Colombian and Mexican drug cartels—outside of Peru where the product was processed into coca paste or cocaine.

Min-jun had no interest in the firmas' business. However, he was concerned about how they protected their interests. If this area was as dangerous as Jessica had warned, he expected the firmas would have made their presence known. Yet, in what little he had seen of Satipo, there were no signs of armed henchmen lurking about menacing the locals. That was not to say they were not watching.

It reminded Min-jun of North Korea. Regardless of how much caution and attention to detail he put into an op, it only took one person to sound the alarm. So, despite the seeming lack of high-tech surveillance systems or armed goons patrolling the streets, Min-jun had to assume the firmas paid the locals to be their eyes and ears. This meant that, even with the weather and time of day in his favor, getting from the hotel to the jungle unnoticed would require stealth.

From behind the curtain, Min-jun eyed the clearing directly behind the building. Fifty yards of open ground led to the edge of the jungle at the opposite end. Earlier, before sundown, he had picked his entry point and burned the image in his mind.

Three factors would determine his success: speed, timing, and nature. Min-jun figured he had to make the crossing in under ten seconds. That was slow, even for an NFL lineman, but taking into consideration the weight of his gear, the unfamiliar terrain, the adverse weather, and the fact he was no spring chicken, Min-jun knew if he took longer than ten seconds, he risked being caught out in the open when the next flash of lightning lit up the area. The clearing offered no cover or concealment, so he would be completely exposed and at the mercy of anyone who happened to be looking in that direction. Timing his sprint was crucial.

Undeterred, Min-jun felt confident in his abilities. To help him prepare, he had spent the last two hours going through his pre-mission routine, consisting of a yoga workout and hydration to get his mind and body in sync. Now it was just a matter of execution.

Min-jun turned to Marlana. "Okay, I go," he said in a hushed tone. "No noise."

"Got it," she whispered.

Min-jun slid the window up slowly and quietly. A gust of wind and rain pelted his face as he placed his backpack on the ground outside. Being on the first floor certainly helped. He then climbed outside feetfirst.

As Marlana closed the window behind him, Min-jun remained crouched under the windowsill, rain pattering off his poncho. He hoisted his waterproof backpack over his shoulders and clipped the buckles across his chest and abdomen. Taking two quick breaths to open his lungs, Min-jun then waited for his opportunity.

Suddenly, lightning danced across the skies in a forked display. Min-jun dipped his chin and closed his eyes. This technique not only saved his night vision, but in case anyone happened to catch a glimpse of his silhouette, Min-jun appeared as no more than a dark, huddled mass against the hotel's exterior.

As soon as the area returned to darkness, Min-jun reacquired his jungle entry point. He then took off at a sprint as the area shook from a loud clap of thunder. The run came easier than anticipated. His legs felt fresh, and the altitude had little effect on his breathing. Even the ground worked in his favor. Despite being saturated, the open field was mostly flat and still offered firm footing. In the off chance a flash of lightning caught him out in the open, Min-jun knew he could hit the deck in a pinch and land on relatively soft ground.

He covered the distance in eight seconds. As soon as he reached the fringes of the jungle, the sky lit up once again. Min-jun jumped through high grass then slowed until he found a tree to hide behind.

Putting his back against the trunk, he paused to catch his breath. Another loud crack of thunder followed. He waited on high alert until the rumbling subsided. As his breathing calmed, it became evident after a long moment that if anyone had seen him, the alarm would have sounded by now.

Confident the coast was clear, Min-jun retrieved his machete and set out into Amazonia to begin his reconnoiter. It was a three-mile hike to Mathias's compound. Sticking to the edge of the jungle made his task somewhat easier. With every lightning flash, Min-jun ducked for cover behind a tree and took the opportunity to get the lay of the land. Each time, he remained in place, unmoving until his night vision returned, and then he resumed his trek. He followed this routine for the next hour, moving quietly through the brush at a brisk pace, ever vigilant of his surroundings. Firmas were not the only predators in these parts.

Min-jun made good time. It was not long before the glow of perimeter lights was visible in the distance. He finished his hike in just over an hour and soon had eyes on Mathias's facility. Min-jun stopped behind a tall tree that offered some reprieve from the rain.

Eyeballing the facility at three hundred yards out, he could not help but wonder why a multi-billion-dollar corporation would build a state-of-the-art facility in the middle of the jungle ... in cartel-controlled country, no less.

Profit, he surmised. That was the simple answer. It always came down to money.

Min-jun was not interested in Mathias's business any more than he cared about the firmas. All that mattered to him was finding Rose, and in order to ascertain her status, he needed to get closer to the compound, a lot closer. He suspected the facility had the best high-tech security money could buy. Seismic and laser sensor motion detectors could operate under all conditions, day or night, so each step toward the facility increased Min-jun's risk of tripping some type of perimeter surveillance system.

Just how close he could get without sounding the alarm monopolized Min-jun's thoughts as he continued forward.

Taking advantage of natural cover, he leap-frogged from tree to tree, hiding behind the trunks. He doubted Mathias had sensors going into the jungle fringes where wildlife could easily trip them. However, trail cameras could be an issue. They were cheap, reliable, and could see in the dark. In fact, Mathias could be watching Min-jun right now, and he would not know until it was too late.

Pushing that unsettling thought aside, Min-jun made a mental note to survey the area for cameras as soon as the sun came up. In the meantime, he continued on. When the facility was within one hundred yards, he decided not to press his luck any further. The circular compound loomed large in front of him and, from this distance, he had a clear line of sight.

Part of the intel brief provided by Jessica had included an article on the compound's grand opening. Mathias had hosted a media extravaganza to show the world his new research facility. The article had included pictures inside the compound, as well as aerial photos showing the various buildings within the enclosed grounds.

The images had proven immeasurably helpful, especially since they were labeled. Min-jun knew exactly where he was in relation to the two-story employee housing. With any luck, Rose was being held there. All that stood in his way was the perimeter wall. To see over that meant he had to find higher ground.

Min-jun eyed his surroundings and found a thick tree with a branch system perfect for setting up an improvised, elevated roost. The worst of the storm appeared to have passed, now just a distant rumble. As a light rain continued, Min-jun sheathed his machete and stowed it in his backpack before climbing the tree. Straddling a crook, he allowed his legs to dangle freely and maintain circulation. Min-jun then located a nearby branch which served as a convenient hook to hang his backpack.

Unpacking his gear came next. Min-jun retrieved his brand-new Sony A7S III digital camera and attached an AF-S NIKKOR 200-500mm super telephoto zoom lens. Combat photography was not his forte, but the *Photography for Dummies* book Jessica had thrown in the cart on their pre-trip shopping excursion had helped pass the time on the plane ride over. Now Min-jun knew enough about his new toys to be dangerous. All he had to do was sit tight, stay vigilant, and hope for the money shot.

36

TOPSIDE

Ava stripped out of her flight suit, bursting with excitement. The red dress she had ordered online had arrived at her PSC box earlier that morning, just in time for the squadron's holiday party later that evening. As Mark waited outside her barrack's door, she slipped the dress over her head, hoping to God it fit.

Stepping in front of the wall mirror, she smoothed out the velvety material and examined her reflection closely from various angles. The knee-length dress fit perfectly and complemented her figure with the right balance of elegance and sexiness.

"Nice." She smiled approvingly.

Hiding behind the door, she cracked it open enough to speak to her boyfriend, who was patiently waiting in the hall. "Okay, close your eyes."

Captain Mark Jordan played along. "Eyes are closed," he assured her.

Ava poked her head around the door to make sure he was telling the truth then took his hand. "No peeking," she insisted, guiding him blindly through the door. Once Mark was in the room, Ava shut the door behind him. "Not yet."

Mark chuckled from the building anticipation.

Ava stepped in front of him. Taking a nervous breath, she straightened her dress one last time then struck a pose. "Okay, what do you think?"

Mark opened his eyes slowly. Seeing Ava before him, his playful grin slowly faded.

Unable to read his reaction, Ava suddenly felt self-conscious. "You don't like it?"

"No." Mark gaped as he eyed her from head to toe. "I love it. Ava, you're … stunning."

Ava's eyes sparkled triumph, but then a flash of self-doubt prompted another glance in the mirror. "You think?"

"Oh yeah," Mark said in his bedroom voice.

With Ava facing the full-length mirror, Mark stood behind her. He placed his hands on her tiny waist, and the handsome couple stared at their reflection together, grinning with satisfaction. Then Mark slowly began to slide his hands lower.

Ava eyed his crooked grin, the one he always got right before they turned up the heat.

Mark started kissing her neck gently, making Ava's skin tingle.

"Don't even think about it, Jordan," she warned, her willpower fading fast.

"My dear Captain Tan, what on Earth do you mean?" he whispered, lifting her ponytail to softly peck the base of her neck. "I happen to be an officer *and* a gentleman."

"Uh-huh." Ava giggled. "C'mon; I've got a flight to catch. You'll have to wait until tonight to unwrap your Christmas present."

With a heavy sigh, Mark relented. He rested his chin on Ava's shoulder and eyed her in the mirror for a long moment.

Ava gave him a curious look. "What are you thinking?"

"I'm trying to burn this image of you in my head. This moment, right here, is one I want to keep forever."

Ava melted. Mark was reserved when it came to expressing matters of the heart, but when inspiration hit him, man, oh man, he knew how to speak her love language.

She rounded and wrapped her arms around Mark's midsection. Burying her face against his chest, Ava closed her eyes and squeezed him tight, knowing this was the only man she ever wanted.

But her internal clock was ticking. Ava opened her eyes and saw her flight suit calling to her on the bed. She frowned and gave Mark's behind a playful squeeze. "Sorry, babe. We'll continue this later."

"It's a date, Suntan," Mark promised, returning the favor as she stepped away.

As Ava crossed the room, she pulled the dress over her head and laid it out on the bed. Wearing nothing but a bra and panties, Mark watched her from afar, burning more images into his long-term memory.

"So, where are you heading?" he asked.

"A liquor run to Thumrait," Ava replied, her disappointment evident in her tone.

Mark knew she was frustrated with her assignment. Their TDY to Camp Lemonnier had yet to prove satisfying for her and her flight crew.

"Be careful what you wish for," he warned.

Ava pulled on her flight suit and zipped it up. "Famous last words, right?"

Mark shrugged. "All I'm saying is that, in this part of the world, danger will find you—no need to go looking for it. Your chance will come," he assured her, although he dreaded it inwardly. "When it does, you and your team will kick ass. I'd bet my life on it."

Ava smiled for the vote of confidence. "What about you?"

"I better go check in, but I've got a last-minute gift to pick up first," he said mysteriously.

Ava raised her eyebrow, hoping for a hint, but Mark remained stone-faced. Then her watch alarm began beeping. She tried to silence it, but the alarm persisted and only grew louder.

Planet Aiwa

Ava awoke with a start. Lying on her side, she lifted her head off the ground and realized she had been dreaming of Mark again. She relaxed then rolled over onto her stomach to find herself teetering on a cliff's edge. Ava gasped at the sight of the twenty-foot drop with rolling white waves crashing against a dark, rocky beach below. She hastily backpedaled in a panic until her back touched the rock wall behind her.

Heart pounding, Ava turned to her left to find Neil nestled inside a darkened nook, still sound asleep. She relaxed as the familiarity of her surroundings returned.

It was then that the alarm beeping inside her helmet registered. Looking out at Aiwa's moons glistening off the ocean, she activated her personal HUD to see what it meant.

"Jesus!" she blurted as her proximity alarm detected six fast-moving objects approaching from out at sea. "Computer, identify."

"Aiwan hunter-killer drones," came the reply. "Model XP-11A. Also known as—"

"Seekers," Ava finished with dread in her voice.

"You say something?" Neil asked groggily.

Ava got to her feet and grabbed Neil by the arm, unceremoniously dragging him out of his hole. "Move your ass, we got company!"

A surge of adrenaline cleared Neil's cobwebs. He came to his feet and spotted the running lights of the inbound bogies in the distance. "What are they?"

When Ava did not reply, Neil turned to find her gone. He spun around and located Ava scrambling over the rocks, heading back toward the beach.

"Hey, wait up!"

Neil enjoyed rock climbing at the gym, but that was in a brightly lit room, wearing a fall protection harness and trusting that, if he fell, a comfortable pad would cushion the impact. Here, in the middle of the night, one false move on the slippery, jagged rocks could end his day rather painfully.

Scrambling on all fours, he made quick work of the obstacles without incident. As he neared the beach, he looked up and saw Ava urging him on impatiently.

"Don't wait for me!"

Ava took his words to heart and headed off the beach, racing toward the edge of the jungle. Unaware of what dangers lay beyond, she jumped blindly into a line of elephant grass.

Neil was right behind, catching a glimpse of Ava in the moonlight before she disappeared into the tall brush. He followed in the same spot. On his first step into the thicket, his feet became entangled in the undergrowth. Neil did a faceplant and landed hard on his hands and knees.

"Sonuvabitch!" he cursed under his breath.

Nursing his pride more than his bruised knees, Neil picked himself up and continued trekking forward. It was so dark that he could barely see his hand in front of his face.

Pushing aside the tall grass, he called out in a hushed tone, "Ava?"

"Neil?" she replied.

Neil halted. Ava sounded close. "Here," he whispered.

A brief, tense moment passed before Ava emerged suddenly through the wall of grass. Neil was relieved to see her, but there was no time for happy reunions.

"Turn off your HUD," she hissed. "It'll give our position away."

Neil did as he was told. Ava then took him by the hand. Channeling her friend, Min-jun, she whispered, "Follow me. No noise."

Meanwhile, the Seekers approached the beach at high velocity, flying in a single-file formation. They slowed in unison just short of the beachhead then fanned out horizontally, forming a skirmish line one hundred yards apart. The center drone then emitted a red beam of light downward. It squelched and beeped, communicating in its robotic language that the missing escape pods had been located.

A series of additional sounds followed, then each of the remaining Seekers activated their own crimson search beams. In unison, the drones approached the coastline to begin their search for the humans.

The drone at the beach remained. Inching up the foreshore, the Seeker began scanning the surrounding area in a methodical grid pattern. It was not long before the drone detected Neil and Ava's footprints in the sand, which triggered several high to low foghorn-like sounds, as if it were excited by its discovery.

Hovering above the sand, the Seeker followed the tracks to the nearby rock formations. There, it scanned every nook and cranny, altering its vision modes between thermal, night, and fusion settings. The Seeker found no signs of the humans. This prompted the drone to turn its attention back to the beach. There, it acquired two new sets of footprints leading into the jungle.

Running hand-in-hand, Ava led Neil hastily through what seemed to be a never-ending wall of high grass. Navigating the thicket proved more time-consuming than expected, and between the rustle of grass and cracking of twigs under their feet, she was sure the Seekers would pounce on them at any moment. Still, Ava forged ahead. Unwilling to slow down and check their six, she was determined to put as much distance between them and the beach as possible.

Just then, they emerged from the elephant grass. Before them was a vast rainforest of vine-laden trees, coupled with a low fog blanketing the jungle floor. Visibility was reduced to less than thirty yards as the jungle's four-layered canopy blocked out most of the light from Aiwa's twelve moons. That suited Ava just fine, if they were evading human or Aiwan eyes, but she doubted it would affect the Seekers. Still, there was more cover and concealment options before them than behind, which was better than being exposed on the beach.

She started for the nearest trees, only to be jerked backward by Neil. Without saying a word, he pointed to the Seeker's crimson search beam approaching their position from the right.

Thinking quickly, Ava located a large tree twenty yards in front of them that could hide them both. That was when she spotted a second search beam out of the corner of her eye. It was approaching fast from the left, both beams converging on their location.

Ava quickly did the math in her head. Judging by the approach speed of both beams, she knew they could not cross the distance to the tree in time. With no place to hide, Ava conceded the inevitable; there was no outrunning the deadly drones.

Her nano-suit took over from there.

Reading Ava's mental assessment of the threats, her suit reacted by creating a hood of nanites that crawled upward from her neckline to envelop her head.

Neil watched helplessly as Ava gasped before her face shield was completely covered.

Neil darted his eyes about his mummified friend. "Ava?"

"Neil, hide!" came Ava's muffled reply.

Taken aback, Neil scoffed. *Hide where?*

No sooner had he finished the thought did his suit go to work. The nanites cocooned Neil just as the Seeker's twin search beams crisscrossed over him and Ava. Back and forth, the red beams passed, sweeping the area for any sign of the humans.

Cast in complete darkness, Neil and Ava remained unmoving and deathly quiet. Holding their collective breaths, they feared being discovered by the Seekers more than their claustrophobic encasing. That soon changed as the need for oxygen became unbearable.

Neil was first to test his suit. He tried breathing in through his nostrils and quickly discovered he still had oxygen supplied through his holographic helmet. Relaxing, he began slowly inhaling through his nose and exhaling out his mouth to fight off the urge to hyperventilate. Ava held out a little longer but soon relented and came to the same realization.

After a few tense minutes waiting for the Seekers to either blow them to smithereens or demand their surrender, Neil and Ava discovered their suits had somehow camouflaged their biosignatures. Outside, they could hear a Seeker hovering nearby while a distinctive electronic hum accompanied each pass of its search beams. Yet, nothing happened.

Moments later, the Seeker ended its search of this grid location. Unable to proceed deeper into the jungle, the drone reported back to its controller then departed the area.

Neil and Ava waited a few moments longer, uncertain if the coast was clear. In this mode, their HUDs were off-line, which left them literally in the dark. As the seconds ticked away with no sign of the Seeker's presence, Ava decided to test her hunch that the drone had moved on.

"Computer, deactivate my concealment thingy."

The nanites covering her head retracted into her neckline. With her vision restored, Ava cringed, expecting a Seeker attack.

None came.

As her eyes adjusted to the sparse lighting, she spun in a tight circle, looking for the drone. It was nowhere in sight.

Ava breathed a sigh of relief. Next to her, Neil was still enveloped with nanites. She put her hand on his arm. He flinched.

"It's okay." Ava chuckled. "The coast is clear."

Neil's shoulders dropped, and he retracted the nanites. Overjoyed to have the microscopic robots off his face, he was even happier to find Ava at his side, safe and sound.

"Where'd they go?" he whispered.

Ava shrugged, equally perplexed. "Beats me, but I'm guessin' they'll be back."

"I wonder who sent them," Neil remarked, dreading the answer.

"Who knows?" Ava replied dourly as she scanned their surroundings. "I don't know about you, but I'm not going back until we know more about what we're up against."

Neil agreed, but surviving in the wild did not sound too appealing, either. He extended his arms out in front of him, eyeing his nano-suit fondly. "Did you know these suits could protect us like that?"

"No, but thank goodness for Kypa's foresight. I thought we were goners."

"Me, too. Remind me to read the owner's manual when we get back," he joked, earning a grin from Ava. "What now?"

Their reprieve from danger was short-lived as the foreign sounds of the jungle returned. The noise began quietly at first then rose to a cacophony of constant cries, howls, and whistles—none of which sounded friendly.

"We need to find a safe place to hole up," Ava suggested. Against her better judgment, she activated her HUD. "Computer, project a topographical map of the surrounding area."

A holographic display was projected outside her helmet for her and Neil to see. Ava zeroed in on the coastline.

"Look here, if we stick to the coast, we have a better chance of avoiding any land predators. This waterfall looks promising." Ava pointed to a wide river that flowed over a steep, vertical drop. The plunge pool at the base of the waterfall fed directly into the ocean. Using both hands, she zoomed in on the image, panned up and down, and then pinpointed a potential location. "Yep, right there. There's an undercut behind the falls with a cave. That'd be a good spot to make camp until we can find out more."

Neil nodded agreement.

"Computer, plot a route along the coastline to this location."

A red line from their current position to the waterfall appeared.

Neil frowned. "Looks like a full-day hike, at least."

Ava nodded thoughtfully. "Not ideal, but it's the best we can do for now. Computer, send this route to Dr. Garrett."

A microsecond later, Neil received the route.

"In case we get separated, rendezvous at this location."

Neil nodded.

"We have to assume they can track us if we're not cocooned. That means no helmets. We should stay off the comms and only use the HUD if you need to get your bearings."

"Got it," Neil affirmed.

"Computer, is it safe to remove our helmets?" Ava asked.

"Affirmative," came the reply.

Neil and Ava exchanged looks. Neither wanted to be the guinea pig.

"Rock, paper, scissors?" Ava suggested.

"No, I'll do it," Neil volunteered with reluctance. "If anything happens to you, neither of us is going home."

He had a point, but that was assuming they ever saw the Reaper again.

Neil cleared his throat. "Okay, here goes nothing."

He deactivated his helmet. The holographic shield collapsed into the nano-collar around his neck. His first physical contact with Aiwan air came from the gentle touch of a soft, warm breeze against his face.

A wide grin creased his face as he closed his eyes. Forgetting himself for a moment, Neil inhaled deeply, filling his lungs with fresh air for the first time in over a week. The scent reminded him of his mom's greenhouse—a combination of moisture, vegetation, soil, and decay.

That is the smell of life, his mother would say.

Neil suddenly shot his eyes open with a look of terror. Clutching his throat for air, he dropped to his knees and rasped, "Can't ... breathe!"

Ava rolled her eyes, not fooled. "Nice try, NASA boy."

Neil frowned and ended his charade. "You're no fun," he grumbled.

Ava offered her hand, helping Neil to his feet. "C'mon; we've got a long walk ahead."

A short time later, an Aiwan drop ship arrived at the beach and came to a hover just offshore. A compartment in its underbelly then opened and a tractor beam projected downward to the sea. The sunken escape pods used by Neil and Ava were plucked from their watery graves and hauled up to the cruiser's cargo hold.

Up on the bridge, the ship's captain sat in his command chair, anxiously awaiting an update. His commlink beeped.

"Report," he said impatiently.

"Both pods are empty, sir," his first officer replied. "Neither appears damaged."

"The humans must have sunk them on purpose," the captain deduced, suspicion evident in his tone. "Send down the search party. I want them found."

"Yes, sir."

Moments later, down in the cargo bay, the same tractor beam used to bring the pods up to the ship was reversed to project down to the beach. This time, it carried two fireteams of Aiwan shoretroopers to the surface.

Affectionately referred to as "riding the lightning," each soldier landed feetfirst on the sand, one after the other, until both teams reached the beach. As soon as all eight shoretroopers were safely on the ground, the beam retracted. The patrol ship then departed to assist in the search along the coastline, unwittingly heading in the opposite direction as Neil and Ava.

Meanwhile, the shoretroopers exited the beach. Dressed in aquasuits and toting assault rifles, both squads formed into two tactical columns then headed into the jungle. Moving in opposite directions, the game was afoot to see which team could capture the humans first.

37

JUNGLE PURSUIT

Planet Aiwa

Hidden behind an outcropping of tall grass along the shoreline, the bounty hunter, Smythe, curled his lip in frustration as he watched the Aiwan troopers come ashore. Having been forced to abandon his gravity sled due to the jungle's impassable terrain, he had reached the coordinates provided by Krunig moments too late. The Aiwans had beaten him to the scene, and from the looks of it, the humans had fled into the jungle before they had arrived.

At least they are not in custody already, Smythe thought to himself as he peered through the scope of his sniper rifle.

The bounty hunter lined up the crosshairs on one of the Aiwan fireteam leaders and adjusted the rangefinder. Factoring in windage, elevation, time of travel, and the target's movement, a kill shot from this distance would be tricky, but not impossible.

Smythe resisted the urge, resting his finger on the trigger guard. No sense revealing himself to the Aiwans. The element of surprise was in his favor, and he planned to keep it that way for as long as possible.

Not much of a landing party, he mused, eyeing the eight soldiers.

The fact the Aiwans sent such a small force ashore meant they did not perceive the humans to be much of a threat. And they probably did not expect there would be other interested parties joining the hunt.

Even better. Smythe smiled thinly.

His mood brightened momentarily, and then a spectacular lance of lightning slashed across the night sky. It was followed by a reverberating thunderclap, resounding and deep. Looking to the south, the bounty hunter noticed an ominous stormfront approaching.

Smythe sighed. "Figures."

He scanned the beachhead once more through his scope. The soldiers had split into two squads before entering the jungle, and their drop ship was now just a speck in the distance. Yet, it was not the Aiwan soldiers Smythe worried about; it was the Seekers. He had managed to avoid one earlier but expected others were probably scouring the area, searching for the humans as well.

Smythe knew the deadly drones by reputation. They were known to be relentless and hard to kill. The last thing he needed was to draw their attention. This meant he had to go off the grid to hunt down the humans, which was a reasonable trade-off. Even though it would take him longer without the aid of technology, he still held the upper hand. Smythe's tracking abilities and keen senses gave him the advantage over the Aiwans.

Low-crawling backward behind a tree, Smythe slung his rifle over his shoulder and pulled the cowl over his head just as thick drops of rain began to fall. He retrieved his commlink, the chronometer display indicating sunrise was still a few hours away. Time enough to get a jump on the Aiwans and make up for lost time.

"Gort," he called, "pick up."

"Here, boss," his partner replied.

"Things are getting interesting," Smythe reported. "I just missed them. Turns out the ship's captain isn't alone. I counted two humans."

"Who's the other one?"

"Not sure. I think it's a male," Smythe guessed. Since Krunig had not mentioned him, the bounty hunter figured Neil was expendable. "They arrived in escape pods and fled into the jungle before the Aiwans and I arrived." Smythe rounded toward the jungle to check his six. "By the way, be on the lookout for Seeker drones. I managed to avoid one on the way in."

"Copy that. Did they take the pods?"

"Affirmative," Smythe replied, dashing his partner's hopes.

Gort huffed. "That Aiwan tech could've fetched us a hefty sum."

"Maybe next time. How are the repairs coming?"

"Engine repairs are finished," Gort said matter-of-factly. "We're back in business."

"Good. Stay sharp," Smythe warned. "I'm going silent for a while. Be ready to move on my signal."

"Affirmative."

Smythe ended the transmission then returned the commlink to his belt. As he set off into the jungle, a cold grin creased the bounty hunter's mouth.

Let the hunt begin.

38

LOST AND FOUND

Planet Aiwa
Realm of Cirros

Finding a way out of the collapsed tunnel proved more difficult than Kypa had imagined. The effort required to swim while carrying his injured father had slowed them down considerably. Adding to the challenge, Loka dropped the light repeatedly as he drifted in and out of consciousness. This forced Kypa to stop and retrieve it, making their trek through the darkened passage even more arduous and exhausting.

Many of the human expletives he had learned on Earth came to mind along the way, but Kypa did not complain. Despite his burning muscles and splitting headache, he had to remain positive if either of them hoped to survive.

Loka reached out to Kypa once again using telepathy. *"I remember your first hunt,"* he said weakly.

The out-of-the-blue remark caught Kypa by surprise. He thought back to this coming-of-age-moment in his childhood. *"Yes,"* Kypa replied, none-too-proud. *"Hunting has never been one of my talents, but that was a special day. As the victor, I got to choose my prize."*

Loka grimaced as he chuckled. *"Not many children would have chosen a tour of the royal archives over a trip into orbit, but you did."*

Kypa reflected fondly on that choice. Visiting the Citadel had cemented his decision to pursue a life in science, one he had never regretted.

"*I was fortunate to happen upon a Ganchu fish before anyone else,*" he recalled. "*All of the other children had gone in the opposite direction, certain they would find one beyond the barrier reef. But I took your advice and searched the lagoon. And there it was, trapped in an alcove just waiting to be caught.*"

Loka was noticeably quiet on the subject, prompting Kypa to give him a curious look. Then it dawned on him how the kill had come so easily.

Kypa pulled up. "*It was you?*"

Loka did not reply immediately, nor did he deny the allegation. His eyes glossed over, picturing the scene in his mind with a warm grin on his face.

"*You should have seen the excitement on your face,*" Loka recounted. He then turned to his son, meeting Kypa's gaze. "*I knew how much you wanted to please me, but you were so little. I did not want you to be embarrassed in front of the other children, so I arranged for the Ganchu to be there.*"

Kypa's brow furrowed. "*Did the others know?*"

Loka shook his head emphatically. "*No, your grandfather took that secret to the afterlife.*"

"*You cheated on my behalf?*"

Loka averted his eyes and lowered his head in shame. "*It was my idea,*" he confessed. "*Please do not blame your grandfather. I made him do it.*"

"*Blame you?*" Kypa gently rested his head against his father's. "*I want to thank you.*"

Taken aback, Loka looked bewildered. "*You are not mad?*"

Kypa shook his head. "*No.*" He chuckled. "*If it had not been for the two of you, for what you did, I would not be who I am today ... and I am happy with who I have become.*"

"*So am I, Kypa, so am I.*" Loka beamed with pride. "*You will make a fine king.*"

Loka grimaced and began coughing uncontrollably. When it subsided, he spat blood.

Kypa eyed his weakened father. He could see the king's health was deteriorating rapidly—Loka's skin looked pale, and his breathing had grown shallow.

"*Hang on,*" Kypa urged his father. "*There was an exit around here somewhere,*" he recalled.

Forging ahead, Kypa pushed himself beyond exhaustion. Using every ounce of energy he could muster, he continued on, refusing to stop. Several minutes passed in silence, save for Kypa grunting from exertion.

Finally, Loka reached out to his son. "*Kypa,*" he said feebly. "*Make it right.*"

Sensing his father's lifeforce fading, Kypa finally stopped. Thoroughly spent, he sank to the ground and dropped to his knees, cradling Loka in his arms. "*Father.*"

Loka lifted his heavy eyes to look at his son one last time. "*Make it right, Kypa … for Cirros … for Aiwa.*"

With those dying words, Loka slowly closed his eyes, and his head rolled to the side.

"*Father, open your eyes,*" Kypa insisted. He tried jostling his father awake, yet Loka remained unresponsive.

"*Please, do not leave me,*" Kypa's mental voice trembled as he checked frantically for a pulse but found no signs of life.

Kypa's chest tightened as he searched Loka's tranquil face. He then pulled his father close and held him tight, sobbing. Overcome with emotional and physical exhaustion, Kypa howled in grief, passing out as the sound of his anguish echoed in the darkened passage.

Fifty yards away, outside the shaft's emergency exit, an Aiwan rescue diver heard Kypa's tormented cry. He turned sharply to his partner. "*Did you hear that?*"

"*What?*" his partner replied.

Unaware of the shaft's existence due to a pile of collapsed rock blocking the exit, the two divers continued treading water nearby, listening intently.

"*I swear I heard something.*"

Insisting his mind was not playing tricks on him, the lead diver swam closer to the rock wall. Shining his light about, he noticed the discoloration of the rocks piled nearby. They appeared to have been recently sheared off from the wall above. He began removing several stones, many covered in moss on only one side. The diver continued until he cleared a small opening and a faint light appeared through the rubble. He peered inside.

"*I see a light!*" the diver exclaimed, waving his partner over.

Together, the two began removing rocks until the lead diver was able to shimmy his way inside the shaft. He shined his light up ahead and spotted two bodies floating motionless in the darkened tunnel.

The lead diver turned to his partner, raising two long fingers. "*Two bodies. Both appear unresponsive. Call it in. I am going inside!*"

As the lead diver entered the shaft, his partner attached a beacon to the exterior wall so other rescue divers and search ships could zero in on their location. He then went to work clearing out more rocks so the bodies could be extracted.

Meanwhile, the lead diver had reached King Loka. Immediately, he could tell from the king's skin tone that the situation was dire. His fears were confirmed as soon as he checked the king's vitals. A profound sense of loss overcame him, but being a seasoned rescue worker, he pushed those feelings aside to focus on the other victim.

Turning to Prince Kypa, the diver was relieved to find a pulse. It was weak, but Kypa was alive.

Wasting no time, the diver rolled Kypa over onto his back. Using his hand to cradle the prince's neck, the diver grabbed Kypa by his utility belt and swam for the exit.

By the time they reached the opening, the diver's partner had cleared away enough rubble to exit safely. Outside, the entire area was now lit up with powerful searchlights. Kypa was carefully extracted and transferred to a rescue ship.

Before returning for King Loka, the lead diver relayed the unfortunate news of the sovereign's passing. His partner joined him inside the shaft and, together, they respectfully placed Loka inside a body bag. As they turned to leave, the lead diver noticed a handheld light resting on the floor, the same device that had been used by Kypa and his father to find their way out. He watched in passing as the light dimmed, its power fading fast. Then the light flickered and was extinguished, casting the area into darkness.

Supra, Realm of Eos

Three hours later, Kypa awoke to find himself floating horizontally inside a rejuvenation chamber. As his head cleared, he was aware of several medical staff hovering over him.

A female Aiwan medical technician leaned in. Nearly pressing her face to the glass, she smiled with relief. "He is awake," she reported.

Inside the recovery tube, the technician's voice sounded garbled and distant to Kypa. He tried to speak but could not make a sound. The fluid used to heal his body allowed him to breathe normally but not talk.

A wave of panic rushed over him, made worse by the claustrophobic confines of the chamber. With his arms and legs immobilized, Kypa rapped his knuckles on the glass.

The female technician stepped aside, and Maya appeared. Kypa relaxed the moment they locked eyes.

Kypa reached out to her telepathically. "*Where am I?*"

"*The capital,*" Maya replied soothingly. "*You are safe here, in the palace.*"

Peripheral movement caught Kypa's attention. He turned to his right to find his mother, Queen Qora, standing at his side, showing relief and sadness.

"*What happened?*"

Maya started to answer but paused at the queen's prompting. Kypa looked expectantly at his mother. Her usual, unflappable demeanor never wavered, but seeing her mouth tremble told him something was dreadfully wrong.

"*Where is Father?*"

Qora lowered her head, unable to meet Kypa's gaze. Maya wrapped her arm around the queen for comfort and held her for a long moment.

Steeling herself, Qora tempered her emotions and spoke calmly to Kypa. "*My son, the attackers have been put down. The five realms are secure, and our family is safe. But … I am afraid your father has succumbed to his injuries.*"

Kypa's expression slackened. His eyes drifted from his mother, and he began staring distantly at the ceiling. His memory slowly returned, and he relived each moment from the attack in the mineshaft to when his father had died in his arms. This profound loss, along with the assault on their very way of life, triggered a deep-welling anger. Trapped in the tight confines of the healing chamber, Kypa began pounding his fists on the side walls.

"*Let me out!*" he demanded.

Kypa's outburst startled his family. They stepped aside, deferring to the chief medical officer in the back of the room. Qora motioned him forward.

Standing over Kypa, the medical officer gave him a reassuring smile. "*Easy,*" he said in a calm voice, trying to soothe his patient.

It helped. Kypa's rabid expression relaxed somewhat, and he stopped banging on the side of the chamber.

Satisfied, the chief medical officer turned his attention to the nearby readout displaying Kypa's vitals.

"*The healing process is not complete,*" he explained to Kypa. "*If I let you out now, you will feel worse than when we found you. Nausea, vomiting, muscle fatigue—*"

"*Just do it,*" Kypa interrupted, ignoring the warning.

Against his better judgment, the physician relented and signaled his staff to release him. Moments later, the healing fluid in the recovery chamber began pumping out through ducts in the floor. As soon as the fluid level receded enough for Kypa's head to be free, he inhaled deeply, which triggered a coughing fit to clear his lungs.

The tube's glass covering then opened, and Kypa was assisted out of the chamber. A wave of vertigo forced him to take a seat on the chamber's edge. As he waited for the room to stop spinning, one of the nurses provided a thermal blanket to help Kypa retain body heat.

After a brief pause, Kypa insisted he was fine and carefully came to his feet. He took one step toward Maya before his knees buckled. Kypa collapsed to the floor and began retching violently. The medical staff reacted immediately to assist, but Maya pushed between them to be at her mate's side. She knelt beside Kypa, resituating his blanket, and wrapped her arms around him.

Kypa's dry-heaving subsided, only to be replaced with deep sobbing. Qora then threw aside her stately demeanor and joined her son on the floor. Together, the three of them wept as a family.

His body shaking uncontrollably, Kypa swore in a trembling voice as tears streaked down his face, "I tried to save him," he said, hoarsely.

Qora clutched Kypa's arm tighter and rested her head against his. "It was not your fault," she assured him. "You did all you could for him."

Out of respect for the grieving family, the medical team discreetly made their exit. The chief medical officer was last to leave. On his way out, he was approached by two Royal Guards, who appeared in the doorway unexpectedly.

The physician raised his hand to stop them from entering. "Can I help you?"

"Prince Kypa has been summoned to appear before the High Court," the senior guard stated. "We have orders to escort him to the Grand Hall for questioning."

"Questioning?" the physician scoffed. "It will have to wait. The prince is in no condition to be moved."

The arrival of the guards caught the royal family's attention. Overhearing the peculiar summons, and considering the timing, Kypa wiped the tears from his face and composed himself.

"Guard," he called. "On whose authority am I being summoned?"

"The Warden of Eos, My Prince," the guard replied evenly. "Princess Seva."

Ekator

Grawn Krunig sat alone in his quarters, staring blankly out a large viewport, deep in thought. Outside, robotic cargo transporters whizzed past, delivering contraband to and from the remnants of his fleet anchored at the port. In the background sprawled the vast, red-orange expanse of the Mishi Nebula.

Krunig gave neither his ships nor the nebula any attention. His mind remained elsewhere, on the not-too-distant world of Aiwa.

A door chime signaled he had a visitor.

"Enter," Krunig called from over his shoulder.

His faithful advisor, Vekka, entered from a side door. "My lord, Grawn Supreme demands you make contact."

"Mm," Krunig muttered, surprised it had taken this long to hear from his boss after the failed assault on Aiwa. "Any updates?"

Vekka cleared his throat. "Yes, my lord. Our source on Aiwa confirmed that King Loka is dead. Apparently, there was an explosion that claimed Major Gora's life, but he managed to carry out his mission. Loka's body was recovered, along with Prince Kypa who, unfortunately, survived the blast."

With his back still to Vekka, Krunig clenched his fists in anger. For the second time, Prince Kypa had eluded death by his hand. Fighting the urge to smash the console on his armrest, Krunig took a controlled breath.

Swallowing hard, Vekka continued his report, "Our source says Prince Kypa is due to be interrogated by the High Court. He has not been ruled out as a suspect in the king's death."

At least that is something, Krunig ruminated.

He relaxed the tension in his hands, much to Vekka's relief.

"See what you can do to pad those beliefs," Krunig charged. "It should not be hard considering Boa's well-known disdain for the prince. What about succession?"

"According to tradition, Princess Seva has been appointed Warden of Eos until her brother's situation is resolved."

This was just the news Krunig had expected. However, even if the king's firstborn and heir to the throne was somehow found culpable for Loka's death, there would always be a cloud over whoever sat on the Aiwan throne as long as Prince Kypa lived.

"What about the ship?"

"The Reaper, sir, is currently under lockdown in Supra. Boa will not allow it to leave."

"And the …"

"Humans?" Vekka offered.

Krunig grunted.

"Topside, sir. The bounty hunters are in pursuit, as are Boa's ground teams. It seems it is a race to see who finds the humans first."

"Boa wants them for the same reason I do," Krunig reasoned. "The blue crystal harbored in the Reaper is the key to winning this war."

"Our source says there are even more crystals on the humans' homeworld, Earth."

"So much the better." Krunig grinned behind his mask. "As soon as I have the Reaper, I will take control of Aiwa and then lay siege to Earth."

"Very good, sir," Vekka said agreeably. "And what of Grawn Supreme, my lord?"

Krunig sighed. Even he had a boss to appease … for now.

But the stars are aligning, Krunig mused with satisfaction. *Soon, I will bow to no one.*

"That is all for now, Vekka." Krunig waved flippantly. "Leave me."

Vekka bowed and made his exit. Krunig waited until he heard the door close behind him then accessed a secure channel on the deep space communication network. He waited patiently until Grawn Supreme, head of the Madreen Crime Syndicate, appeared as a life-size hologram projecting from the floor.

Like the other Grawns, the supreme leader's true identity remained shrouded in mystery behind a faceless suit of armor.

Krunig pressed his fist to his chest. "Greetings, Grawn Supreme."

The crime boss mirrored the hand gesture out of respect but dispensed with other pleasantries and cut straight to the point. "Report."

"My lord, the first phase of our plan is complete. King Loka is dead."

"Mm … and his son?"

"Kypa survived," Krunig admitted begrudgingly. "Nevertheless, it will work in our favor. Aiwa is in mourning and public support for Prince Kypa is at an all-time low. They are vulnerable."

Grawn Supreme sighed heavily. "I've supported this endeavor on the hopes of future profits, Grawn Krunig, but losses continue to mount. Aiwa's crystal reserves are nearly exhausted. Perhaps it is time to move on."

"But we are so close, and this ship—the Reaper—changes everything," Krunig countered.

"I am tired of excuses," the supreme leader retorted. "I had to move mountains to convince the other Grawns to help you take Aiwa. Your defeat dealt them a crushing blow in soldiers and materiel. They're demanding your head on a platter, and I'm considering giving it to them."

It was no veiled threat. Both crime lords had a long history together, but despite their mentor-mentee relationship, no one was irreplaceable in the eyes of the syndicate.

"The battle was won until this Reaper entered the fight," Krunig insisted, suppressing his frustration. "I tell you; it is the key to our future."

"*Our* future?" Grawn Supreme needled. "Sometimes, I question if your motives are still aligned with the syndicate."

Krunig bowed his head submissively. "They are aligned, my lord. I swear."

"Tread lightly," the supreme leader warned. "If you aspire to one day lead this organization, you must never allow your personal feelings to interfere with business."

Krunig tempered his emotions. "I hear you, and I thank you for the wise counsel."

Grawn Supreme paused to allow the air to clear then asked, "What news from your bounty hunters?"

News travels fast, Krunig thought, yet it came as no surprise that his boss was aware of Smythe and Gort's involvement. Grawn Supreme's web of spies spanned the cosmos, and he most assuredly had agents inside Ekator.

"They are tracking the humans on the planet's surface," Krunig reported. No sense denying the bounty hunters were brought in out of desperation. "We will get to them before the Aiwans. Once they are captured, I will force the ship's captain to relinquish control of the Reaper over to me."

"And what of the crystals on their homeworld?"

"Earth," Krunig offered, masking his dismay that the supreme leader was aware of this development, also. "My sources say it has the largest deposits ever recorded, and they are untapped."

"Then, why aren't we moving on it?" Grawn Supreme erupted, pounding his fist.

Krunig dipped his chin, accepting the verbal lashing. In truth, their losses suffered at the hands of the Reaper had depleted the syndicate's fleet. They, too, were vulnerable—at least for the time being—and could not risk diverting additional forces away from territories under their control to stake a new claim on Earth.

"Once we have control of the Reaper, we can take Aiwa and Earth with ease," Krunig promised. "Our enemies will not dare stand against us when they witness its destructive power."

"You have two days to deliver this Reaper to me, Grawn Krunig," the supreme leader said. "If this ship is as potent a weapon as you say, then all will be forgiven."

There was no need to spell out what would happen if Krunig failed.

"As you wish, my lord."

Krunig clenched his fist to his chest in farewell, and the transmission ended. Once the hologram disappeared, he let out a quick breath, relieved to have that irritating conversation over.

"Forgiveness?" he scoffed. "I do not need your forgiveness," Krunig muttered petulantly to himself as he came to his feet. Clasping his hands behind his back, he took in the expanse of the nebula and relished in the fact that soon he would no longer have to hide inside this cloud.

39

FOLLOW THE WATER

Planet Aiwa

With no sign of the Aiwans, and the storm now a distant rumble, Neil and Ava were on the move. Keeping the ocean to their right, Ava led the way through the outer fringes of the jungle before it opened up to a clearing. Ever vigilant to threats, she relied mostly on her SERE training to guide them. This was of little consequence, considering their alien environment. At least on Earth, if she was ever shot down in enemy territory, Ava would have some frame of reference, thanks to her pre-mission briefings. Here, everything was foreign and considered hostile, which had her on edge.

Neil, on the other hand, seemed oblivious to the danger as he continually lagged behind, enamored by Aiwa's exotic ecosystems. He was an exoplanet scientist; his life's dream had become a reality the moment he had set foot on Aiwa. Despite being marooned in the deadly jungle, he counted himself the luckiest guy in the world—make that, the universe—and he could not wipe the childlike grin off his face.

Neil's meandering did not sit well with Ava. She had understood at first, but it had grown tiresome after a while and only slowed them down.

Stopping once again to make sure she had not lost sight of him, Ava turned around and let out an exasperated breath. Neil was thirty yards behind, with his

380 | TODO HOSEA

head down, picking apart some type of seedling.

Planting her hands on her hips, Ava called to him, "You comin' or what?"

"That's what she said!" Neil hollered back without skipping a beat.

Ava mustered a tired chuckle. "Funny," she conceded. "I've got another one for you. Ever hear the one about the three tomatoes?"

Neil tossed the seedling aside and approached with a curious look on his face. "What about the three tomatoes?"

"Okay, so three tomatoes are walking in the forest—a papa tomato, a mama tomato, and a baby tomato," she began. "The baby tomato keeps getting distracted by his surroundings and starts lagging behind. Each time, the papa tomato has to go back and get him. Finally, he gets so upset that he goes over to the baby tomato, smashes him with his fist, and says, 'Ketchup!'"

Neil's shoulders dropped, and he shook his head with disappointment. "Ha, ha," he laughed, dully.

"Moral of the story, Dr. Garrett—keep up or get left behind." For good measure, she flicked the tip of Neil's nose unexpectedly so he would not forget.

"Ow, that hurt!" Neil recoiled, cupping his nose.

"Good. Let that be a lesson to you," Ava warned then continued on.

"You sound like Mrs. Littlejohn, my fourth-grade teacher," Neil said nasally, flexing his nostrils until the sting subsided. "She used to speak to me like that."

"A lot of good it did, I see," Ava replied over her shoulder.

Neil laughed, knowing she was right. No one had ever crossed Mrs. Littlejohn.

He trotted to catch up, and they continued on for several minutes. As the morning sun began to climb above the horizon, the temperature also started to rise.

Ava's stomach growled. "I'm starving."

"Me, too," Neil replied. "I've had 'Hungry Like the Wolf' running through my head for the past hour."

"Yeah?" Ava grinned. "How about a 'Cheeseburger in Paradise?'"

"Ooo, good one." Neil pictured a greasy bacon cheeseburger. "Maybe some 'Red Red Wine' to go with it?"

"Now you're talking," Ava played along. "Actually, I'm more of a 'One Bourbon, One Scotch, One Beer' kinda girl."

"Gotta love George Thorogood," Neil remarked, thinking of home. After a moment of reflection, he admitted, "I sure do miss Reggie's cooking."

"Yeah, me, too," Ava replied, her spirit sobered. "C'mon; let's forage for something to eat."

"We should look for water, too," Neil suggested.

"A drink of ice-cold water sounds awesome," Ava agreed. "But our suits should keep us hydrated."

"It's not that," Neil said, running his hand over his stubbly beard. "If you want to find life, follow the water."

As if on cue, the roar of a large animal stopped them in their tracks.

"Or it finds you," he added grimly.

Ava pulled Neil to the ground and whispered, "That sounded close."

Seekers be damned, Neil activated his helmet. Ava did not object. His helmet's AI came to life as the mystery animal let out another blood-curdling roar.

"Computer, identify the source of that animal noise."

On his HUD, the AI displayed a massive carnivore. Neil could not believe his eyes. The creature closely resembled a Tyrannosaurus Rex, at least by the shape of its head and scrawny forelimbs. But that was where the similarities ended. This beast—which towered twenty-five feet in height—had four massive hind legs and a long sweeping tail covered with spikes that ran up the spine to its head. Short, white fur with red spots covered the creature's body, matching its beady red eyes.

"A spotted krakadon," Neil read aloud. "Apex predator … not good. It's three klicks to the south. We must be in its nesting grounds."

"It sounds pissed," Ava said nervously then activated her helmet. "I'm calling Reggie."

As she tried to reach her ship, Neil led Ava by the hand, away from the krakadon. They reached the end of the clearing and ventured back into the shadows of the thick jungle canopy. There, Neil scanned their surroundings.

"Computer, locate the nearest fresh water source." On the HUD, a stream appeared half a klick away. "Okay, good. Now find any nonpoisonous fruits and vegetables between here and there."

The AI pinpointed several locations and displayed the Aiwan scientific name for each specimen.

Pleased with himself, Neil deactivated his helmet and turned to Ava. "Any luck?"

Ava shook her head in frustration. "Reggie's still grounded."

Reminding herself they were still being hunted by others, besides the krakadon, she followed Neil's lead and deactivated her helmet.

"We'll try again later," Neil assured her. "C'mon; there's water and food up ahead. If we keep moving north, we can steer clear of the krakadon's turf."

Six klicks away, a four-person Aiwan fireteam moved in a diamond formation through the jungle. They, too, had heard the krakadon but were undeterred in their relentless pursuit of the humans.

"Hold it," the communications officer, bringing up the rear, called out. She was eyeing a handheld tracking device.

Lieutenant Poda, the fireteam's leader, was on point and halted the squad. Each member hastily crouched, disappearing under the cover of the surrounding foliage. Both shoretroopers on the flanks provided overwatch as Poda moved to the rear of the formation.

"I think I have them, sir," she reported.

"Show me," Poda replied.

The comm officer held out her device. "The signal was brief, but it was definitely two lifeforms, both human."

Poda nodded agreement. "Looks like they are following the coastline." This brought a thin smile to his face. This was going to be easier than he thought.

"Shall I call it in?" the comm officer asked.

Nodding, Poda said, "Redirect Captain Acova's team to move in from the rear. We will flank the humans and try to cut them off here." He pointed to a kill zone where they could intercept Neil and Ava before they reached the waterfall. "They are somehow masking their signal, so I do not want to scare them off. Tell command to pull the Seekers back and have our transport hold position. We will call for extraction as soon as we have them in custody."

"Yes, sir."

As the comm officer carried out the order, Poda pulled in the other two squad members and explained his plan. He had just started to speak when an unexpected splatter sound from behind caught his attention. Poda turned to find his comm officer dropping to her knees with half of her skull missing.

It took a second for the horror to register and realize they were under attack.

As the comm officer flopped to the ground, Poda lifted his eyes, speechless. Just as the recoil of the first shot reached his location, a second blaster round appeared out of nowhere. The blast hit Poda center mass, ripping a hole in his chest and knocking him backward off his feet.

Instinctively dropping to the ground, the remaining two members of their team looked to one another in a panic. They had no idea who or how many opposing forces they were facing, only that staying put was a death sentence.

"On me," the Aiwan on the right flank directed.

Low crawling away from the direction of fire, the shoretroopers exited the area as fast as they could in hopes of finding better cover and concealment.

Little did they know that Smythe, the bounty hunter, was one step ahead.

He retrieved a custom-made device from his belt—a baseball-shaped mechanism that fit into the ball of his hand. Smythe then activated the device and released it into the air. It took flight and began mapping the ground between the bounty hunter and the fleeing soldiers.

On his wrist-tracker, Smythe waited until the aerial mapper located the low-crawling Aiwans. The bounty hunter locked in on their body signatures then wasted no time switching the settings on his weapon. Smythe targeted the general location of the Aiwans and lofted two incendiary rounds into the air. The projectiles arced skyward. As soon as the targets were acquired, both rounds homed-in. The shoretroopers had no chance.

Seconds later, Smythe watched with satisfaction as the jungle erupted in a fireball.

Once the smoke cleared, the aerial mapper provided images of the Aiwans' charred remains spread throughout the area. Confirming all four kills, Smythe recalled the device and returned it to his belt. He then approached the first dead Aiwan, the comm officer. Prying the tracking device from her hands, the bounty hunter checked the last reading. The humans were moving along the coastline. It was a safe bet the Aiwans had reported it, which meant the clock was working against him now. As soon as this squad failed to report in, others would come looking for them.

Smythe tossed the device and eyed the sky. Morning sunlight peeked through the canopy above. By his measure, if all went to plan, the humans would be in his custody by mid-afternoon. Then things would start to get dicey. He had yet to figure out how Krunig planned to get the Aiwans to hand over the Reaper. And even if they did, how did he expect the ship's captain to go along with it? She had to deactivate the failsafe protocol without blowing them all to bits.

There was only one thing that the bounty hunter hated more than being in the dark, and that was having to rely on others. With the exception of his trusted partner, Gort, Smythe preferred to work alone, and for good reason. He controlled the risk.

The notion of being in control sparked a thought.

Why does Krunig and the Aiwans want the Reaper so badly? he wondered. *Does it hold a different meaning or value to either party?*

Krunig and the Aiwans had been fighting for many years; that was no secret. Their war revolved around crystals, and crystals ruled the galaxy. Following this train of thought, Smythe concluded that the Reaper had to represent the one thing both sides coveted most—power. The Aiwans possessed it, and Krunig wanted it. It was that simple.

So, how powerful is this Reaper? the bounty hunter mused as he made for the coastline.

That was the question. The more Smythe considered it, the more he began to rethink his terms with Krunig. Perhaps there was opportunity afoot. Once he had the Reaper, the humans were expendable. Then he was free to renegotiate with Krunig … or the highest bidder.

40

MONEY SHOT

Planet Earth
Satipo, Peru

Nature called after Min-jun had been perched in the tree for two hours. After finishing his business, he stretched his legs then climbed back into the Amazonian cedar tree. To his left was a large, open field that provided unhindered sight lines to both Mathias's facility and the only access road leading in or out. On the right was nothing but jungle for approximately two point three million square miles.

Min-jun retrieved his camera hanging from a nearby branch. It was wrapped in a black, rainproof poncho built specifically for his long-lens camera. This would protect it from the elements but also ensured any light from the camera's LED screen remained hidden. The cover also prevented moon- or sunlight from reflecting off the camera lens and compromising his position.

Placing the camera strap around his neck, Min-jun then pulled the hood of his own poncho over his head. Satisfied, he flipped the "*on*" switch and raised the camera to eye level to snap a few pictures before sunrise.

"Ji-Ral," he cursed under his breath, realizing he had left the lens cap on.

Feeling silly, Min-jun removed the cap and allowed it to dangle from its leash. He then took a deep breath to refocus. If that was the worst part of his day, he would count himself lucky.

Settling into his nook, Min-jun raised the camera once more, aimed it at the compound, and began testing various zoom settings.

With the exception of the exterior perimeter lights, the facility remained dark, which made it difficult to spot the silhouettes of armed soldiers patrolling the high wall. Min-jun counted five men in all, each with H&K MP5 submachine guns tucked against their chests.

Serious firepower for a research facility, he noted.

The more Min-jun thought about it, five men patrolling a facility that large seemed inadequate. Granted, he might not have eyes on all the soldiers lurking about, but it appeared there were gaps in security that could allow a team of shadow warriors to infiltrate the facility.

This thought conjured happy memories of his past life as a North Korean special forces operator. He missed his men, not the regime, and recalled the day he made the fateful decision to leave that life behind to defect with his wife and son. Min-jun never regretted that choice, despite losing both families in the process.

Shaking those thoughts out of his mind, he returned to the task at hand. The goal of his reconnaissance was to locate Dr. Landry.

From his shirt pocket, Min-jun retrieved a photo of Rose that had been given to him by Jessica before leaving the States. He had already committed her likeness to memory but eyed it once more for good measure. At least, that was what he liked to tell himself. In truth, Min-jun was drawn to Rose's picture. Something about her tranquil beauty and warm smile brought him comfort.

It also served as a reminder that his mission had real purpose beyond doing a favor for Jessica. Dr. Landry looked like a good person, and the world needed all the good people it could get. So, if his skills could be put to use to help Rose return safely to her family, then it was worth the risk.

Min-jun tucked the photo back in his pocket. Sitting back against the tree trunk, he held his camera at the ready, staring distantly at the second floor of the compound where Jessica suspected Dr. Landry was being held. If he managed to photograph Rose, the images were to be uploaded to a handheld, tactical SATCOM radio in his backpack. He could then transmit the encrypted files via satellite directly to Langley and call it a day.

If only it were that easy, Min-jun thought humorously.

Years of fieldwork told him otherwise. Missions rarely went exactly to plan, so adapting to change was not just a given; it was a necessity. The key was to keep a calm head when the proverbial shit hit the fan.

Min-jun was reminded of this as he allowed the camera to dangle around his neck. He then reached into his backpack for a breakfast bar and a swig from his canteen. As he leaned back against the tree trunk, chewing his food in solitude, Min-jun listened to the myriad of sounds emanating from the jungle. From trilling insects to chirping birds, he found it all quite soothing but remained ever vigilant. The jungle was alive, and since every noise was completely foreign to him, it made separating wildlife from manmade sounds tricky, at best. Still, this was the closest he had ever come to a rainforest. Amazonia was the polar opposite to North Korea, and he found it to his liking.

Finishing his breakfast, Min-jun tucked the wrapper in his backpack. He downed more water and made a mental note to refill his canteen during the next rain.

Min-jun gave a haphazard glance at the facility. A second-floor light was now on, catching his attention. From this distance, there was no way of knowing if it was an office, bedroom, or something else entirely, but it piqued his interest.

Min-jun sat up and lifted his camera to eye level. Zooming in tight enough to keep the lighted room and its neighbors in frame, he rested his finger on the shutter-release button and waited. Min-jun dared to hope that today might be one of the rare exceptions when everything actually went according to plan.

Luna sat on the floor of her room with the light on and reached out to Dr. Landry telepathically. "*Rose, are you awake?*"

It took a few attempts to rouse Rose, but on the third try, her eyes fluttered. Rose rolled over in bed and squinted at the clock. It was still early. Too early. "I'm here," she grumbled out loud.

"*Rose?*"

Rose's eyes shot open, realizing it was Luna in her head. "*Oh, sorry,*" she corrected, this time formulating her reply nonverbally. "*Good morning.*"

"*Good morning,*" Luna replied. "*I apologize for disturbing you so early, but I have urgent news.*"

Laying in the darkness, Rose propped herself up on one elbow and wiped the sleep from her eyes. "*What's up?*" She yawned.

In the neighboring room, Luna came to her feet and began pacing. "*I just learned I am leaving this morning. Mathias is taking me to field test the cloaking device.*"

Rose sighed heavily. "*Well, I can't say this is a complete surprise. We all knew this was coming. Are you okay?*"

"*Yes. I can take care of myself,*" Luna assured Rose as she moved to the window and opened the drapes. Peering outside, she could see dawn glimmering on the horizon.

"*I know you can, but I still worry. It's in my DNA,*" Rose admitted. "*What do you need from me?*"

"*Nothing at the moment,*" Luna answered, looking about at the empty courtyard below. "*I may be unable to check in on you while I am away.*"

"*How long will you be gone?*" Rose asked.

"*One week, says Edmund, maybe less depending on how well the test goes.*"

Rose frowned, unsure of Edmund's intentions once Luna's mission was complete. Despite their financial agreement, Rose did not trust him to simply let her go.

"*Is something the matter?*" Luna inquired.

Summoning her courage, Rose pushed aside her grim thoughts. "*I'm fine. Do what you need to do, and I'll see you as soon as you get back.*"

Luna could tell Rose was not being completely forthcoming but respected her space and did not pry into her mind to search for what might really be bothering her.

A knock at Luna's door broke her train of thought. She turned away from the window and crossed the room. Peering through the peephole, she said to Rose, "*They are here. I must go now. Take care until I return.*"

Luna severed their connection.

Rose immediately threw off the covers and hurried to her door. Pressing her ear against it, she could hear the muffled conversation between Edmund and Luna. She then watched through the peephole as the guards placed Luna in handcuffs. They were wearing protective clothing to cover their skin, she noticed. Luna was then led down the hall.

Rose watched them reach the end of the hallway and disappear into the elevator. Dreading the prospect of never seeing her Aiwan friend again, Rose whispered a prayer for luck and turned away from the door.

Meanwhile, Min-jun sat back against the tree, flabbergasted. His mouth hung open slightly, but he could not find the words to describe what he had just witnessed.

An alien!

He recalled images of Prince Kypa in the newspaper and plastered on merchandise displays in Walmart but never did he expect this mission would take a turn like this.

Min-jun sat up and feverishly went about scrolling through the photos on his camera. There had to be at least one hundred images, probably more. The moment the alien had appeared in front of the window, he had begun shooting, as if his camera was a fully automatic rifle.

Blowing out a breath of relief, Min-jun grinned in disbelief at the clear images of the Aiwan peeking through the drapes.

Miss Jessica will freak when she sees this!

Glancing back at the window, the light in the Aiwan's room had turned off. Min-jun frowned. Yet, his disappointment was short-lived. He knew he had struck gold.

The light in the adjacent room turned on, catching him by surprise. Cursing under his breath, Min-jun fumbled with the camera and changed the settings so he could shoot more pictures. He then hastily raised the camera to his eye and spied the silhouette of a person passing back and forth in front of the window. With the sheer drapes drawn, he could not get a positive ID but was convinced it was a woman judging by her petite figure.

Min-jun expended a few more shots, the camera's internal shutter clicking away. Assuming Mathias had noise sensors blanketing the perimeter, he cringed with each photo. Unfortunately, the camera was not rigged for noise discipline, so for someone like him trying to avoid detection, every click sounded louder than it actually was. That was the risk he had to take, but something told him he would not be in this tree much longer, anyway.

Little did he know that his presence was indeed being tracked or, more precisely, *smelled* through the flicking tongue of a nearby green anaconda. Stretching nearly fifteen feet in length, the full-sized adult female slithered slowly and methodically through the tall grass toward Min-jun, pausing occasionally to use the chemical receptors in its forked tongue to hone-in on the location of its prey.

Meanwhile, Min-jun held his breath as the curtains finally opened. Snapping away on his camera, he recognized Dr. Landry immediately and smiled. Rose was alive and well. At least, it seemed that way considering her silk pajamas.

After a moment, though, Min-jun realized something was amiss. He watched as Rose peered out the window with a fierce look of concern. Ignoring the view around her, she searched the area intensely for something … or someone.

The alien? Min-jun wondered.

Just then, the main gate opened, and a convoy of three vehicles exited the facility. Sandwiched between two black SUVs was an armored car, which struck Min-jun as odd. He had never seen a bank car before. Assuming it was a military-grade vehicle, the lack of windows and gun turrets made him question its usefulness … unless the intent was to keep passengers from getting out rather than breaking in.

They must be moving the alien, he surmised. *Is that why Rose looked so worried?*

For what it was worth, Min-jun snapped several photos of the convoy as they passed. Once he lost sight of them, he turned his attention back to Rose's window. To his dismay, her bedroom light was off. She was gone.

A moment of indecision followed. Part of him wanted to dig deeper and ascertain Rose's status, but the soldier inside of him told Min-jun to stick to the mission. He was not here to rescue Rose; his job was to locate her and provide proof of life. Those objectives had been met, and then some. It was time to report his findings.

Min-jun grabbed the custom-built satellite phone from his backpack and connected it via USB to his camera. Knowing he could not upload all of his photos, he cherry-picked the best ones of Rose, the Aiwan, and the convoy. Min-jun then dialed a predetermined number on the phone. The call was received, followed by three short beeps and one long tone. After the latter, Min-jun punched in a six-digit code, and the rest was automatic. The images on the camera he selected began uploading to a CIA-controlled satellite. Then they would be forwarded to Deputy Director Jessica Aguri at Langley.

Exhaling with relief that his part of the mission was over, Min-jun eyed the morning sky beginning to peek over the tree line. It looked to be the start of a beautiful day.

As the upload continued, he considered his return trek to the hotel. The Nunezes would no doubt be surprised to see him back so soon, and he could only imagine their reaction to seeing Rose and the alien. He could not wait to show them his amateur photos.

Min-jun eyed the progress meter on the phone's display. The upload crept along slowly, currently at twenty-five percent complete. Tapping his foot impatiently against the tree, Min-jun feared, at this rate, he might be here all day.

Suddenly, he felt a sharp, searing pain in his calf. Min-jun screamed into the air through gritted teeth then looked down to clutch his aching lower leg. Staring up at him were the lidless eyes of the green anaconda, its four rows of teeth sunk into the meaty part of his calf.

Min-jun's eyes opened wide in terror. He had never seen a snake so large. Before he could react, the mammoth reptile pulled him from the tree. Min-jun landed hard, momentarily disoriented as the anaconda went to work coiling itself around him.

Feeling no pain from the sudden rush of adrenaline, Min-jun's fight or flight instinct kicked in. He had seconds before the snake wrapped him up in a death grip. If that happened, it was all over. The snake would slowly constrict him until Min-jun could no longer breathe, and then he would eventually suffocate. Then came the worst part, as soon as the snake sensed all the fight had left him, even if he were still clinging to life, the anaconda would swallow him whole.

Thinking fast, Min-jun rolled over on his stomach and tried to crawl away on all fours, but the snake would not have it. Sinking its teeth in deeper, the anaconda doubled its efforts. With lightning speed, the predator slithered its massive body up to Min-jun's waist to halt his escape. The snake then rolled him over, wrapping itself up closer to his chest.

Meanwhile, inside the security control room at Mathias's compound, a panel of ground sensor alarms erupted. Two sleepy-eyed Peruvian guards monitoring a wall of closed-circuit television screens jolted upright in their chairs. Both floundered for a second, trying to clear their heads and figure out which alarms were going off.

"¿Qué es eso?" one guard asked the other with urgency. *What is it?*

The second guard silenced the alarms. Realizing it had originated from a perimeter sensor outside the compound, he then manipulated the control pad on his desk to rotate the nearest external camera for a look-see. What the guards witnessed on the monitor sent shivers up their spines.

Having grown up in this area, both guards were familiar with the danger of anacondas. It was common for an unsuspecting goat or a curious dog to meet its demise in the belly of such snakes, but never had they seen man versus snake in a gruesome battle to the death.

The guard sounded the alarm as his coworker made the sign of the cross on his body and whispered a prayer for the victim. Together, they watched with pained expressions and morbid curiosity as nature took its course.

Oblivious to the alarms in the distance, Min-jun knew he had only one shot. With his left arm pinned against his side, he reached behind his back with his free hand for his KA-BAR. He wrapped his fingers around the hilt just as the snake rolled him over like a rag doll and squeezed tighter.

Min-jun grimaced. He could feel his lungs constricting. It was just a matter of time before all breath escaped him.

Gripping the knife, Min-jun made a feeble attempt to stab the snake. The blade sliced into the anaconda's thick skin, causing the snake to reflexively clamp its jaws down harder. Min-jun cried out, and while he exhaled, the massive reptile seized the opportunity to squeeze him tighter.

Min-jun dropped the knife. As his last hope of escape slipped from his fingers, he could no longer draw a breath. His mouth opened and closed like a fish out of water, suffocating. Helpless to escape his fate, Min-jun stared wide-eyed through a gap in the snake's coiled body as darkness began to close in around him.

Then a splash of blood showered on his face. The unmistakable sound of a high-velocity round striking flesh registered somewhere in the deep recesses of Min-jun's mind, but it was the searing pain that followed that jolted him back to the moment.

The snake had instinctively bit down on Min-jun's lower leg when the sniper's first round missed wide, blowing a giant hole in the anaconda's body. Readjusting his scope for windage, the shooter on the compound's perimeter wall took aim once more and fired again. This time, the round found its mark. The anaconda went limp and relaxed its grip, leaving Min-jun a contorted mess draped in its bloody carcass.

Gasping for air, Min-jun filled his lungs with deep inhales. Once he had his wits about him, he realized the snake was dead and frantically wriggled his way free of the tangled heap. Crawling on all fours, Min-jun made it a few feet away then turned back to make sure he was truly safe. That was when he saw the snake's massive head split in half by the sniper's shot. It was as dead as dead could be.

Min-jun collapsed on his back in the grass, thoroughly exhausted. Facing toward the sky, he stared up at the heavens, shocked to still be alive. This was the closest he had ever come to death.

In the background, perimeter alarms echoed in the distance, and he could hear the sound of Mathias's security teams rushing to the scene. A part of him screamed to get up and run, but Min-jun could not muster the strength to do so. He passed out just as the guards arrived in a pickup truck and leapt out of the bed.

"Son of a mother trucker," one guard said with amazement as he approached. Keeping his weapon trained on the snake just in case, the guard guffawed at the size of the reptile. "Jesus, that thing could've eaten him whole!"

Two of his buddies crowded around him and gawked at the lifeless snake.

Meanwhile, a fourth guard crouched beside Min-jun and checked his pulse.

"I'll be damned, this poor sap is still alive."

"What the eff is he doing out here?" the first guard wondered aloud.

"Beats me," his buddy replied, "but he's one lucky S.O.B." The sentiment was shared by the others.

"Hey, check this out!" a fifth guard called.

All eyes turned to a burly man who had meandered closer to the trees. He held Min-jun's camera up for them to see then began scrolling through the images stored on the memory card.

"What've you got?"

The burly guard held up the camera and shook his head. "Looks like we caught ourselves a spy."

Mr. Renzo's phone rang just as the convoy reached the Satipo airport. "¿Sí?" he answered.

Sitting in the front passenger seat, he listened intently to the remarkable events that had just transpired back at the facility. Mathias and Ms. Diaz sat in the back of the SUV and could tell immediately something was wrong.

They approached the company's private hangar and parked next to the awaiting cargo aircraft. As soon as the vehicle was in park, the chauffeur hopped out and opened the back door on Diaz's side. Renzo raised his hand, signaling them to wait.

"Affirmative," Renzo said in English. "Take him to the empty storage room on level one and keep it quiet. I'm on my way."

Renzo ended the call and turned around in his seat.

"What is it?" Edmund asked.

"We've got trouble, sir. A man was caught outside the compound, taking pictures of Dr. Landry and the Aiwan."

"Who?"

"Don't know yet. They didn't find any ID on him, but they did recover a photo of Dr. Landry in his pocket."

"Interesting," Edmund mused, considering the ramifications.

"Apparently, the man was attacked by an anaconda and set off the perimeter alarms. One of our snipers took out the snake from two hundred yards," Renzo explained, impressed by the shooter's skill.

Taken aback, Edmund tried to imagine a man wrestling an anaconda.

"My guys think he's a spook," Renzo said. "I should head back and take care of this."

Mathias preferred to have his best man with him as they transported Luna halfway across the world to Challenger Deep. However, this disconcerting news deserved immediate attention.

"Do it," Edmund said. "You can meet up with us later."

"Yes, sir."

With that, Mathias and Ms. Diaz climbed out of the vehicle to oversee Luna's transfer to the aircraft.

The driver unloaded their bags then climbed back behind the wheel. Before the SUV sped away, Ms. Diaz caught a glimpse of Renzo. The Chachapoyan's normally stern expression seemed fiercer, if that was possible. She pitied the soul who had stumbled into his playground.

41

BANDITOS

Planet Earth
Satipo, Peru

Marlana Nunez barely slept a wink all night. As hard as she tried, she could not turn off her brain. Ever since Min-jun departed on his mission, her thoughts dwelled on a man whom she had only just met but felt responsible for, nonetheless. He was part of their team, and she worried for his safety no different than for herself, Rose, and Hector.

Future-tripping only added to Marlana's restlessness. Eager for news on Rose, a million what-if scenarios bounced around in her head, causing her to toss and turn for hours on end while Hector sawed logs in the other room.

Morning came at last. As golden rays of sunlight peeked through an opening in the tattered curtains, Marlana'd had enough of staring wide-eyed at the ceiling and decided to return to her room. Giving up on any notion of sleep, she huffed in frustration and threw off the covers. They had a full day to kill in Satipo before flying out the next day to Brazil, and she could not lay still another moment.

Returning to her room, Marlana deliberately made noise when she entered to stir Hector out of his slumber. It worked. Her husband woke to the sound of his heavy-footed wife moving about the room on the creaky floor. Squinting from the morning sun in his face, he rolled over and found Marlana sliding on a pair of denim jeans.

"What's up?" he yawned out and resituated his head on the pillow.

"Can't sleep," Marlana replied with an anxious voice. "I'm going for coffee."

"Not alone you're not," Hector replied, speaking with his eyes shut. "It's not safe."

Marlana zipped up her fly. "Keeping me from my morning coffee is more dangerous than any banditos."

Hector opened one eye and found Marlana giving him a warning look. Knowing his wife was stubborn enough to go without him, he blew out a heavy breath. "All right, wait for me."

Rolling out of bed, Hector straightened, exposing a strip of his bare belly as he stretched. He sauntered past his wife on the way to the bathroom.

Marlana patted his bottom. "I knew I loved you for a reason."

"Mm, remember that later when I hit you up for vacation sex."

Five minutes later, the Nunezes were dressed and ready to leave. Hector grabbed their room key off the nightstand and stopped short of the door.

"Should we invite our friend?"

Marlana cringed and put her finger to her lips, drawing a curious look from her husband. She leaned up on her tiptoes to whisper in his ear, "He's already gone."

Surprised, Hector mouthed, "*Seriously?*"

Marlana nodded then stepped back. "Better let him sleep," she added, purposely louder than normal in case anyone might be listening.

"You say so." Hector shrugged. "¡Vamonos!"

Hector unlatched the door, and then all hell broke loose. Two masked gunmen forced their way inside, catching the Nunezes by surprise. When the gunmen barged in, the door hit Hector in the head, knocking him backward. Seeing stars, Hector lost his footing and stumbled to the floor as Marlana screamed.

The first gunman through the door was on top of Hector in a heartbeat. Holding a silencer-mounted pistol to Hector's head, he screamed, "¡No te muevas!" *Don't move!*

Hector froze, too stunned to speak.

Meanwhile, the second gunman pointed an identical weapon at Marlana's terrified face. She held her hands up, trembling.

With the room secure, both gunmen retrieved black hoods from their jacket pockets and handed one to Hector and Marlana.

"¡Póntelo!"

"Do as they say," Hector told his wife.

Shaking uncontrollably, Marlana cooperated and placed the hood over her head. Hector did likewise. Then he was made to roll over so they could zip-tie his wrists behind his back. He could hear them doing the same to his wife. Hector was helped to his feet. Both he and Marlana were led out of the room and down the hall to the lobby. There, the man at the front desk ignored the hostages being ushered out of the building. He wisely kept his head down and went about his business, praying the gunmen left without further incident.

Outside, Hector and Marlana were placed into the bed of an old pickup truck and forced to lay on their stomachs. One gunman remained in the back to keep a watchful eye on the hostages. A second gunman closed the tailgate then climbed behind the wheel. He pulled off his mask before starting up the vehicle, and they were soon underway.

"Marlana, can you hear me?" Hector grunted, testing his restraints. They did not give an inch.

"I'm here," she answered, fear evident in her voice.

"You hurt?"

"No," Marlana replied. "What do they want with us?"

"I don't know. Try to stay calm."

The guard kicked Hector's foot. "¡Silencio!"

Five minutes later, on the outskirts of town, the pickup truck pulled onto a dirt road that led into the foothills. The ride was bumpy, tossing around the hostages in back, but Hector and Marlana remained quiet. Shrouded in darkness under their hoods, they feared any noise might be their last.

Finally, the vehicle slowed to the sound of squeaky brakes and came to a stop in front of a luxurious home surrounded by palm trees. The tailgate was lowered, and the guards unceremoniously dragged the Nunezes out of the truck bed and marched them into the house.

Inside, they were greeted by a refreshing breeze from the home's air conditioner. The Nunezes were then steered through a hallway toward the back of the house to a staircase leading down to a basement. Raucous laughter and jeering in Spanish could be heard from the top of the stairs and grew louder as they descended the creaking steps.

Images of an underground fight club or, worse, a torture room, entered Hector's mind. Having watched several documentaries on the drug trade, his best hope was that this was a simple kidnapping. He and his wife would be ransomed, and once paid, they would be released unharmed. But if Hector and

Marlana were viewed as enemies, they could expect to be tortured extensively then killed and dumped on a roadside.

Hector prayed silently to himself as they reached the bottom of the steps. The gunmen pushed them blindly forward, triggering a frightened whimper from Marlana under her shroud.

Noticing the arrival of the Americans, a hush fell over the large group gathered in the basement. It was then that Hector heard the most peculiar sound.

Pac-Man?

The hoods were removed, and the Nunezes found themselves standing in a semi-darkened basement with a dozen hardened men staring back at them in silence. Each of their captors wore either a shoulder holster with their preferred handgun or carried a snub-nosed machine gun slung over their shoulder. The group stood around a couch in the center of the room where an older man sat holding a video game controller. He paid no heed to the new arrivals and continued playing.

Relieved to see her husband, Marlana leaned against Hector. With their hands still bound behind their backs, this was the only solace they could offer one another.

She and her husband exchanged looks. Scared and utterly confused, they remained silent while keeping a leery eye on the game player. The vibe in the room indicated he was in charge.

The man on the couch was of average build and height, and he looked to be in his late sixties. His thick, black hair was speckled with gray and touched his shoulders. Wearing off-white Bermuda shorts and a colorful, red camp shirt, the dark-complected man remained laser-focused on his game.

Hector followed the man's eyes and slowly turned to the large flat-panel television on his right. Sure enough, their "host" was playing *Pac-Man* or, more precisely, *Ms. Pac-Man*. While the player continued his game, navigating Ms. Pac-Man through the maze, eating pellets, and avoiding ghosts, Hector scanned the room.

Instead of a dank, musty-smelling dungeon wreaking of blood, sweat, and death, they were standing in the most luxurious game room Hector had ever seen. To one side, the room boasted a saloon-style bar stocked with beer taps and an ample supply of international liquors. The custom-made bar was carved out of Peruvian black walnut and included four leather bar stools to match.

Panning around the room, Hector counted a dozen pinball machines and stand-up arcade games, including *Stargate*, his childhood favorite. A pool table, ping pong, and pop-a-shot game rounded out the entertainment options. And if that was not enough, one could simply walk outside onto the decorative, tiled deck and take a dip in the pool.

An agonizing groan resounded throughout the basement, startling Hector's attention back to his captors. Several watchers were comforting the man on the couch as he pointed to the television screen with a look of contempt and frustration. Game over.

"¡Esos bastardos fantasmas!" he cursed those cheating ghosts.

His subordinates echoed the sentiment, with one overzealous chap waving his pistol at the screen and making boisterous threats.

Tossing his game controller on the coffee table in disgust, the man in charge sank back into the couch, closed his eyes, and sighed heavily. Then came the unmistakable sound of a female voice as Marlana cleared her throat to get the man's attention. His eyes shot open in surprise, and he located the Nunezes.

"¿Qué es esto?" he admonished the two gunmen holding Hector and Marlana. Coming to his feet, he gestured to their bound hands. "Where are your manners? These are my guests."

Both gunmen apologized and hastily cut the zip-ties off with switchblades.

"¡Déjanos!" their boss ordered, shooing all of his men out of the room.

As they shuffled out, he turned to Hector and Marlana, steepled his fingers under his nose and bowed humbly. "I apologize if you have been mistreated in any way. My men can be a little overzealous at times. Eager to please, if you know what I mean."

"W-Who are you?" Marlana asked pointedly.

"My name is Eduardo Salazar. This is my home … Welcome."

The Nunezes exchanged looks of confusion, and then Hector took Marlana's hand in his and asked, "What exactly do you want with us, Mr. Salazar?"

"What indeed?" Salazar pondered aloud as he crossed the room and moved behind the bar. "You see, tourists come to Satipo all year round and, for the most part, we leave them alone to enjoy our beautiful country and spend their tourist dollars. It's good for them; it's good for us." Salazar smiled vastly and opened his arms wide, gesturing to his magnificent home. His mood then turned serious. "But nothing—and I mean nothing—happens in this town without me knowing. ¿Comprendes?"

Hector and Marlana nodded vigorously.

"Good, then you can appreciate my concern when I heard about your Asian friend sneaking out of your hotel in the middle of the night."

Marlana swallowed hard but held her tongue.

"It seems your friend—who stands out like a sore thumb, I might add—

has found himself in quite a pickle."

"What've you done with him?" Marlana demanded.

Hector squeezed her hand as a reminder to tread lightly.

"Yo no, mi amiga," Salazar replied, holding up his hands in defense. "Your friend was captured outside Mathias Industries this morning. And, I hate to say it," he added, shaking his head with pity, "but right now, I'm betting your friend wishes he had stayed in his room last night, if you catch my drift."

Salazar read his guest's expressions as it dawned on them that Min-jun was serious trouble, probably being tortured and interrogated. Message received, Salazar went about setting out three crystal champagne glasses on the countertop.

"Please, join me." He gestured to the bar stools.

Hector and Marlana were hesitant at first but acquiesced. As they took their seats, Salazar opened a bottle of Bricco Riella Moscato D'Asti, his favorite sweet wine. He filled each glass halfway then topped them off with freshly squeezed orange juice.

Before their host could raise a glass in a toast, Marlana grabbed the closest mimosa and gulped down the drink to calm her nerves.

Caught off-guard, Salazar and Hector both watched in silent amusement.

Salazar placed a glass in front of Hector and raised his own drink. "¡Salud!"

Not wanting to upset his host, Hector returned the toast, and they drank together.

"Aaah," Salazar exhaled with enjoyment. "Mother's milk, yes?"

Hector shared the sentiment. Circumstances notwithstanding, the drink was fabulous.

Setting his glass aside, Salazar poured a second round for Marlana. This time, she waved her hand to keep the Moscato flowing until he had filled her glass to the brim, foregoing the orange juice altogether.

Salazar glanced at Hector, who shrugged with a thin smile. It was then he noticed the clock and frowned.

"Look at my manners," Salazar chastised himself. "You must be starving. My chef makes the best humitas in all of Peru. You must try it."

Hector and Marlana nodded assent.

Using a direct line from behind the bar, Salazar called the kitchen and ordered breakfast for three. As soon as he hung up, he gestured to the patio.

"Come; let's eat outside, and we can discuss business."

They followed their host to the back patio and sat around a circular, two-piece sectional with a round table in the center that doubled as a footrest. Constructed of wicker rattan with plush cushions, the outdoor furniture was large enough to seat ten people.

Hector and Marlana sat across from Salazar and watched in silence as their host closed his eyes and sunned his face, basking in the warmth of the morning light. They continued nursing their drinks while waiting for Salazar to speak. For a moment, it appeared as if he had fallen asleep. Then his eyes popped open. Seemingly refreshed and clear of purpose, he leaned forward and addressed the Nunezes with a deep look of concern.

"I know why you are here, my friends, but I fear your Asian friend's recklessness has put all of us in a very difficult position."

Both Hector and Marlana fumbled for a reply, looking to one another for a plausible cover story. Marlana spoke first.

"How so, Mr. Salazar?"

"I told your people three weeks ago when Mathias's aircraft first arrived that I could get you the answers you seek," he answered, somewhat annoyed. "Do you not believe me? There was no cause for sending in your man. I know what, or rather *who*, Mathias brought in."

"Dr. Landry?" Marlana offered.

Salazar recoiled sharply. "Who?"

"Dr. Rose Landry of the CDC," Marlana clarified. "Mathias kidnapped her, right?"

Salazar gave them a curious look. "I don't know anything about that," he confessed, "but now that you mention it, my people did say something about a new scientist in the facility … a redhead." Salazar grinned and nodded at Hector, who smiled back politely.

Marlana gave her husband a stone-cold look, prompting Hector to clear his throat and take a well-timed sip of his drink.

"I'm talking about the alien," Salazar clarified. He started sucking his teeth in the most annoying fashion then added flippantly, "Like the one on television who made friends with your President."

Marlana's mouth dropped. "You mean, Kypa? He's here?"

Salazar nodded.

"That's impossible."

Salazar shrugged as he fished his cell phone out of his short's pocket. He scrolled through several photos of his children then handed the phone to Marlana. "See for yourself."

She reached across the table and examined the image while Hector peered over her shoulder. Marlana noticed instantly it was not Kypa, but someone else. Then it dawned on her why Rose was here. It made perfect sense. Mathias had

402 | TODD HOSEA

captured an Aiwan, and no one on the planet knew more about them than her.

A million questions flooded Marlana's mind. Who was this Aiwan? How did Mathias get his hands on him or her? More importantly, what was happening to Rose and Min-jun?

Before she could respond, Hector sat on the edge of his seat and said, "Clearly, there has been some miscommunication with our people, Mr. Salazar. Who exactly is your contact?"

Salazar sighed heavily, dumbfounded by their disorganization. "How can you not know? You're the CIA," he said, exasperated. "Ratliff. My handler is Maxine Ratliff, your new director."

42

PENTAPODS

Planet Aiwa

Forced back into the thick of the Aiwan jungle by necessity, Neil and Ava stopped to forage for food and take a quick breather. Standing atop a fallen log, Neil reached again for a plump, blue-colored fruit dangling at his fingertips. With every failed attempt, his language grew more colorful.

"Hurry up," Ava prodded, standing with her back to him and keeping a nervous eye out for any land predators or Aiwan soldiers.

"I'm trying," Neil grunted, lifting himself onto his tiptoes. "A ladder would sure help."

Ava made a cursory glance over her shoulder at Neil. Seeing he had the fruit almost in his grasp, she turned back to her watch when a slithering movement at her feet caught her attention. Ava looked down in time to catch sight of a giant, yellow and black-striped centipede crawling over her foot. The insect was close to twelve inches long with at least thirty sets of legs.

Ava blurted something indiscernible and hopped clear, startling Neil. In a wave of panic, he lost his balance and jumped free of the log, landing on his feet in the nearby brush.

"What?" he asked, frantically scanning their surroundings for something awful.

Totally creeped out, Ava flapped her hands to shake out the heebie-jeebies. She then pointed to the insect as it disappeared innocently into the log.

Neil's shoulders dropped. "Seriously? You did fight an obercai, right?"

"Sorry." Ava frowned crookedly, feeling silly. "It caught me by surprise, that's all."

Neil chuckled, knowing he probably would have reacted the same way. "Hey, check this out." He smiled proudly as he held up the softball-sized fruit he had snatched from the branch. Neil tossed his prize to Ava.

She examined it, gently squeezing the plump fruit to see if it felt ripe. "Bravo, Dr. Garrett."

"That makes me a harvester, right?"

"I wouldn't say that too loudly in these parts," Ava warned and tossed it back.

"Point taken," Neil agreed. "Don't you want some?"

"I'm good, thanks," Ava politely declined.

Neil scoffed at her reluctance. "It's perfectly safe."

"I'm sure it is. Knock yourself out," Ava said, patting his shoulder as she went back to scanning for threats.

"Suit yourself." Neil shrugged. "More for me."

Undeterred, he took a big bite out of the juicy fruit. Sweetness flooded his mouth and dripped down his chin.

"Oh my gosh, this is amazing," he said with a mouthful. "You gotta try this."

Neil swallowed and offered it to Ava. She was about to take it but recoiled her hand and stared back at him with a mortified look.

Reading her expression, Neil became concerned. "What?"

"Your mouth and teeth ... they're blue." She grinned.

Neil covered his mouth. "Seriously?" he mumbled.

Ava nodded then burst out laughing. "You look hungry, like the Smurf!"

Neil panicked and began spitting on the ground. The sight of his blue saliva made him whimper, and he began vigorously scrubbing his teeth with his finger.

Ava snorted, which caused her to laugh even more.

"Don't laugh," Neil fretted. "What if it's permanent?"

"Relax, Brainy, it's not that bad," Ava consoled. "Why don't you try the creek?"

Neil jumped at the idea and made a beeline to the nearby water source. Ava sauntered behind, still chuckling. She found Neil moments later, crouched beside a narrow stream. He was slurping water from his hands, gurgling, and spitting in a repeated cycle.

Ava joined him, crouching on the bank's edge. The taste of cool water was refreshing. They had been on the move all day and, despite being rehydrated by their protective nano-suits, a drink of fresh water invigorated them both.

"Better?" Neil asked, grinning wide like a chimpanzee to show his teeth.

Ava forced back a laugh. "Yes, much better."

Relieved, Neil came to his feet and offered his hand to Ava. Just as she reached up, the grass beside them rustled. Before they could react, a pinkish tentacle sprang forward and wrapped around Neil's calf. In unison, he and Ava looked down at his leg then their eyes met and both thought the same thing—*Oh shit*!

Neil suddenly came off his feet as the mysterious creature let out a high-pitched squeal and took off running, dragging him in its wake.

"Neil!" Ava screamed.

She started after him when, out of nowhere, a blue stun bolt hit Ava square in the chest. Her suit's protective shield and helmet automatically activated a split-second before the blast knocked her backward off her feet. She landed flat on her back in the creek.

With a steady stream of water coursing over her body, Ava lay dazed in the creek. Looking up at blurred rays of sunlight peeking through the trees high above, the view was strangely peaceful, but the moment was short-lived.

Move or die! Ava's inner voice yelled.

Blinking back to reality, Ava shook off the gut-punch effect from the blast. She then rolled over onto her stomach and picked herself up. Staying low, Ava ran clumsily through the water to the opposite side of the creek.

As she reached the bank, a second stun blast hit her in the back and threw her forward. Ava landed hard in the brush, nearly knocking the wind out of her. Now in full panic mode, she scrambled on her hands and knees, crawling as fast as she could through the brush, searching desperately for cover and concealment.

She found refuge behind a thick tree nearby. Putting her back against the trunk, Ava came to her feet. Catching her breath, she activated her commlink. "Neil, do you read me?"

After a moment's pause, Neil replied, but his transmission was choppy and indiscernible.

"Hold on. I'm coming!" Ava promised.

Keeping her back to the tree, she peered slowly over her shoulder, hoping to lay eyes on whoever was shooting at her. As soon as she poked her head out, Smythe fired another round. It came flying in from thirty yards away. Ava ducked just in time, and the stun bolt missed her head by inches.

Cursing under her breath, Ava did not stop to question who or why. All she cared about was finding Neil, and every second wasted here was time lost helping her friend.

Ava's eyes darted frantically about the area, searching for options. Her best chance was to move deeper into the jungle then attempt to flank Neil. It would take longer to reach him that way, but at least she could move under cover.

Taking two quick breaths, Ava psyched herself up to run.

Whatever you do, don't fall. Recalling not one but two painful mishaps that had occurred while crossing the border into North Korea, she remembered how nimble Min-jun had been on his feet. He had made it look so easy.

"Screw it!"

Throwing caution to the wind, Ava launched herself and ran as fast as she could to the closest tree. Mindful to pick up her feet, she carved her way through the brush, expecting at any moment to be gunned down from behind. She made it without incident.

Chest heaving, Ava planted her back against the trunk. She paused long enough to listen for the recoil of the shooter's rifle. Hearing nothing over the sound of her heart pounding in her ears, Ava started off again. This time, she had the good sense to run bent over. Mixing up her silhouette made for a harder target to acquire. No sense making the shooter's job any easier.

Feeling fleet of foot, Ava ran deeper and deeper into the jungle. Leap-frogging from one tree to the next, she cared not for what dangers lay ahead, just the one behind her. All Ava could think to do was put as much distance between herself and the shooter as possible.

Her plan worked. At least, it seemed that way. By the time Ava stopped behind another tree to catch her breath, the shooter had gone quiet. Now, standing chest-high in foliage, which was not saying much considering her short stature, Ava activated her HUD.

"Computer, locate Dr. Garrett."

A topographical map appeared before her with a red dot indicating Neil's location. He was moving fast, no doubt still being dragged by whatever creature had grabbed him.

Where is it taking him? Ava wondered. Although, deep down, she feared the answer to her question. Neil was to be the main course in some predator's next meal unless she got to him fast.

Meanwhile, Neil continued his wild ride, dragged on his stomach through the brush by an unseen force. Clawing desperately at the ground for anything to latch onto, he knew he had to free himself before the creature stopped to feed.

Grabbing nothing but weeds and air, Neil rolled over onto his back. Shielding his face from the grass rushing by, he only caught glimpses of the tentacled creature from behind. It was black, stout, and ran close to the ground. And despite Neil's one-hundred-and-eighty-five-pound frame, the creature tore effortlessly through the rugged terrain, unhindered by the extra weight.

Neil grunted as he pulled himself upright and reached for his lower leg. A slimy tentacle was wrapped tightly around his calf. He grabbed at it, trying to free himself. In response, the creature squeezed tighter, cutting off the circulation in Neil's leg.

Grimacing as he clutched his leg, Neil looked up just in time to see a fallen log blocking their path up ahead. The creature ducked underneath without slowing. Thinking fast, Neil flattened himself at the last second and watched as he narrowly slid under the obstacle. Breathing a sigh of relief to still have his head attached, Neil wondered when this hell ride would end.

His answer came moments later. The creature dragged Neil into the center of a muddy clearing and stopped. Battered and bruised, Neil sat up and saw the five-legged creature—a pentapod—for the first time. It resembled a giant rhinoceros beetle with a shiny black shell, two eyes on stalks, and long, stringy legs ending in crab-like pincers. The slimy tentacle wrapped around Neil's leg suddenly released and retracted into the pentapod's hind end like the slurping of a wet noodle.

"Oh God," Neil gagged, vomiting in his mouth.

The pentapod then rounded on Neil and opened its circular mouth, revealing multiple rows of needle-like teeth.

Fear ran down Neil's spine as the pentapod let out a screeching hiss. Suddenly, the muddy pit came to life around him as a dozen pentapods surfaced. Neil found himself surrounded.

In a panic, he quickly rolled over and struggled to get to his feet. Slipping and sliding, he could find no traction as the swarm moved in for the kill.

Then, all of a sudden, everything stopped. Covered in grime and muck from head to toe, Neil was too frantic to realize something was amiss. It was not until the pentapods in front of him began burying themselves again in the mud that he paused.

Neil looked about, stunned to find the creatures were gone. For a fleeting second, he thought they were going to attack him from underneath then came the impact tremor. Earlier, in Neil's haste to find footing, he had not felt the ground shaking under him. The pentapods knew differently and had gone to ground in fear of what was coming.

Neil froze as the thundering footsteps drew closer. He snapped his head sideways at the sound of nearby trees snapping and collapsing. Something big was approaching, and in that moment, Dr. Garrett regretted telling Ava he hoped Aiwa had dinosaurs.

His worst fear came to life as the massive krakadon appeared. The towering, six-legged predator with white fur and red spots emerged from the tree line and let out a blood-curdling roar that echoed throughout the jungle.

Neil turned ghostly white, his heart pounding in his chest. He dared not move, hoping everything he had learned in Hollywood movies about a dinosaur's poor eyesight was correct. No such luck.

The krakadon spotted Neil on all fours in the muddy clearing. Opening its enormous jaws, the predator launched its attack and came stampeding across the field.

Neil whimpered as he tried to flee, but the mud made it impossible to move. Crawling in place, he heard the krakadon's thundering footfalls draw closer. Just as the monster was on top of him, Neil rolled over on his back and raised his arms in futile defense.

"No!" he cried out.

To his surprise, Neil's nano-suit read his thoughts and went to work creating a defense against the threat. Pinning his arms to his sides, the suit generated a hard-shelled sarcophagus around his body just as the krakadon chomped down. The dinosaur immediately recoiled. This was not the food it had expected.

Equally shocked, Neil opened his eyes to find himself encased in darkness. Realizing what had happened, and the fact he was not dinosaur food, he let out a joyous yell.

However, his victory cry was quickly stifled. The krakadon did not give up so easily.

It began testing the strength of his nano-suit by chomping at Neil then pressing him into the mud with its clawed feet. Each time, it met with frustration.

Finally, after another ear-splitting roar, the krakadon took Neil in its mouth, shook him violently, then tossed him in the air. Cartwheeling out of control, Neil landed high in a tree then bounced off what seemed like every branch on his way down. He hit the ground hard.

The last thing he heard before drifting into blackness was the angry roar of the krakadon and what sounded like blaster fire.

Ava was in a full-on sprint as she approached Neil's position. Then she heard the earth-shattering roar of the krakadon, followed by the unexpected sound of blaster fire. She pulled up behind a tree to catch her breath and assess the situation. Placing her hands on her hips, chest heaving, Ava checked her six. There was no sign of the shooter.

"Neil, come in. It's Ava," she called over the commlink in a hushed tone. "Do you read me?"

Her friend did not respond. Ava tried again and got nothing. She cursed under her breath.

"Computer, show me Dr. Garrett's location."

"Subject not found," the AI replied.

"What do you mean, not found? Check again," she hissed.

"Life signs not detected," the AI stated evenly.

Ava's chest tightened as a wave of sadness came over her. In stunned disbelief, she put her back against a tree, trying to process the unthinkable.

Suddenly, a Shuriken-style throwing star appeared out of nowhere. The five-bladed, handheld weapon sliced through the air and found its mark in the tree beside Ava's head. It landed with a loud *thunk*, missing her right ear by an inch.

Jolted back to the moment, Ava cocked her head sideways only to have her face shield tap against the metal weapon embedded in the tree. Her eyes opened wide in terror as she got an up-close view at its alien craftsmanship.

Run! her brain screamed.

With Ava's will to live being stronger than her need to grieve, she had no choice but to abandon Neil. As she ran, something about the shooter's tactics struck her as odd. Whoever was chasing her had not been pushing her toward the direction of the blaster fire. Instead, the shooter had been doing the opposite, trying to lead her away from it.

This would explain the use of a throwing star instead of a blaster, she reasoned. *It was much quieter.*

For the first time, Ava entertained the possibility that she was being hunted by two enemies—three if she counted Aiwa's land predators.

Ava chided herself for being so naïve. *You have to be smarter than this, Suntan.*

With that much-needed gut check, Ava deactivated her helmet once again to go off-grid. She then pushed on through the jungle, running harder than she ever had before.

Moments later, Smythe retrieved his throwing star from the tree. He brushed off the splinters and deactivated the weapon. The five, razor-sharp points retracted, leaving only a disc that fit into the palm of the bounty hunter's hand. Smythe placed the device back on his belt then scanned the area.

His quarry had revealed her position by using her comms. Now Captain Tan had gone dark once again but, judging by her tracks, Smythe knew exactly where she was heading—a dead end.

Turning his attention to the Aiwans, Smythe detected four shoretroopers up ahead, along with one large apex predator that seemed to be keeping them occupied.

So much the better, Smythe mused with satisfaction.

The arrival of the second fireteam was not unexpected. Having taken out one unit earlier, the second team had no doubt been diverted to their last known location when the first team had missed their scheduled check-in.

At least the Aiwans did not send a Seeker, Smythe thought, counting himself lucky.

But this raised the stakes. It was dumb luck the Aiwans had found the human male first. Now it was just a matter of time before this entire area was saturated with search teams looking for the female.

Smythe checked his scanner once more, confirming Captain Tan had truly gone off-grid.

Wise move, he granted. *But it won't save you next time*, Smythe promised as he broke into a sprint to pursue.

Ava slowed, forced to a walker's pace by several low-hanging vines hindering her path. Pushing the thick ropes of vegetation aside, she ducked and side-stepped the obstacles while pressing on. All the while, Ava knew she had to start doubling back to the original course she and Neil had set out on. If she ever hoped the good guys—whoever that was at this point—would find and rescue her, she had to reach the waterfall before sunset. At the least, that location offered excellent cover and concealment to hole-up for the night while she tried to call for help.

As she cleared the annoying vines, Ava could see the tree line thinning up ahead. With it came the welcome sight of bright sunshine. Unlike the thick canopy that cast the jungle floor into constant twilight, the warm glow of Aiwa's twin suns shining through encouraged her not to give up.

Ignoring the stitch in her side, Ava quickened her pace. Moments later, she emerged from the jungle and came skidding an abrupt halt on the edge of a steep cliff. Momentum nearly carried her over the side, but she pulled up in time, aided by a strong thermal updraft that blew her backward.

"You gotta be kidding me," Ava said between breaths as she backpedaled. "My luck can't be this bad."

She slowly stepped forward, peering warily over the cliff's edge and into the valley below. Feeling the warm breeze blow against her face, Ava eyed the drop-off. There was no way to free climb down the sheer rock face, and any notion of jumping the chasm was ridiculous. Even if she tried, she knew it was not the fall that would kill her …

"It's the sudden stop," she said wryly, finishing an overused pilot's joke.

Looking to her right and left, Ava searched for a way around, but either direction ended with rock walls. Her only options were in front or behind her. Rounding toward the jungle, she hid behind a tree and decided to tempt fate once again by activating her helmet.

"Computer, show me any approaching lifeforms."

Sure enough, Smythe appeared on her HUD. He was less than two hundred yards out and closing fast. Ava zoomed in on the bounty hunter's image to get a closer view of who she was up against. To her surprise, her pursuer was not Aiwan but rather a giant insect in human form.

She cringed. "What the hell is that?"

Rather than sticking around to find out, Ava returned to the task at hand. Time was running out, and she needed a solution. Returning to the jungle made the most sense, but it was only a matter of time before she was caught by her pursuer or eaten by some predator. Never had she missed Reggie more than now.

Her shoulders slumped. *If only I had wings.*

Ava dismissed the notion at first, but then a radical idea began to percolate.

"Computer, can this nano-suit reconfigure into a wingsuit?"

"Unable to compute," came the reply. "Restate question."

Imagining a wingsuit in her mind, Ava knelt and hastily drew a picture in the dirt of a stick figure with wings below its arms and between its legs. Grinning inwardly, Ava realized her idea gave new meaning to the term *winging it*.

"Like this." She pointed to the ground. "I want to glide over the gorge riding a thermal updraft. Is that possible?"

After a brief pause to calculate the science of her scheme, the AI displayed a projected flight path across the gorge. Seeing the sharp undulations created by thermal up- and downdrafts, Ava realized she was in for the rollercoaster ride of her life. Success basically came down to adding and subtracting lift at just the right time, much like her old flying days in her HC-130. Back then, she had used the wing flaps to climb and descend. Here, it would be her arms and legs.

"Okay, I can do this," she psyched herself up.

Displayed next to the projected path on Ava's HUD was her probability of success. Based on current conditions, the AI calculated an 11% chance of safely reaching the opposite side of the gorge if Ava attempted the feat manually. Her odds improved to 64% with AI assistance, plus or minus ten percent depending on the stability of the updraft needed to create the requisite lift.

Ava grimaced, having expected better odds. This discouraging news forced her to reconsider doubling back into the jungle. With any luck, she could lose whoever was hunting her and locate Neil, if he was still alive.

Smythe nixed that idea as a blaster bolt whizzed past Ava's head. She ducked instinctively, realizing her only way out was forward.

"Computer, make the change," she ordered. "Configure the wingsuit and prepare to auto-pilot my flight over the gorge."

Instantly, Ava's nano-suit began to change shape. She likened the sensation to when the Reaper's holographic pilot's chair adjusted to her body type. Nunez would approve, she thought with a grin.

Seconds later, Ava's tight-fitting nano-suit ballooned into a full-blown wingsuit. She eyed her new get-up but had no time to inspect it as Smythe fired another round that struck a nearby tree, showering her with sparks and splinters.

"Ready?" she asked the AI.

"Calculations complete. You may proceed."

"This is crazy, this is crazy," Ava repeated, flapping her arms to calm her nerves and muster the courage to venture forward. Another laser blast struck nearby. "Screw it," she said, eyes ablaze with determination. "Sixty-five percent will have to do."

With that, Ava waddled as fast as she could toward the cliff's edge with her arms and legs outstretched. Just as she leapt blindly over the side, Ava screamed, "CAVU!"

A blast of warm air grabbed her instantly and vaulted Ava skyward. Flailing her arms and legs about wildly, trying to right herself, the AI took over automatically. Forcing Ava's arms and legs outward, she resembled a flying squirrel as the computer flattened her body into a prone position. This action stabilized Ava's flight and allowed her to ride the updraft above the treetops.

Shocked to still be alive, the realization that she was flying made Ava laugh. *It's working!*

Grinning from ear-to-ear, Ava took in the spectacular view of the valley below. It was incredible. She could see for miles around, thanks to a cloudless, blue sky. However, the exhilaration was short-lived as the AI gradually adjusted the angle of Ava's arms from ninety-degrees to one-hundred-and-twenty-degrees. Leaving her legs spread apart, the adjustment caused Ava to drop headfirst into the center of the gorge.

At this point, she was just a passenger. All was going according to plan until Ava hit a vortex of swirling gusts where the updraft met a downdraft. Caught unaware, Ava was tossed ass over teakettle out of control until she was fully inside the downdraft and plunging rapidly.

Ava screamed as the rush of the canyon walls passed by her on both sides.

"Extending arms to ninety-degrees," the AI said evenly.

Unable to control her limbs, Ava's arms were forced back to the original prone position, which slowed her descent, but she kept falling, nonetheless. However, this maneuver did propel her forward across the gorge. Then, as soon as she hit the next invisible vortex, Ava rocketed skyward in another updraft.

The AI compensated for the sudden lift, making micro-adjustments to the placement of Ava's arms and legs until she stabilized. Reaching the treetops again, the AI adjusted Ava's arms to begin a controlled descent and subsequent landing on the opposite side of the gorge.

Smythe arrived on scene to catch the tail end of the show. Impressed by what transpired, he watched as Ava gradually floated downward toward the cliff's edge opposite him. Unshouldering his rifle, the bounty hunter then lined up his gun sight on Ava.

For a snapshot in time, Ava thought everything was under control. She pictured herself landing gracefully on her feet like a parachutist, but the AI had other plans. As Ava gradually approached the opposite ledge headfirst, the AI abruptly forced Ava's arms to her sides. Picking up speed, Ava dove out of the updraft then lost all lift. She dropped from the sky like a sack of potatoes.

Ava landed hard on her stomach, right at the cliff's edge. With her legs dangling over the side of the drop-off, she dug her fingers into the ground, clinging for dear life. In a frenzy, Ava used her feet to search blindly for a perch. After several attempts, she managed to locate a crevice wide enough to wedge her toes inside. This provided much-needed leverage so she could catch her breath and collect herself.

After climbing to safety, Ava crawled away from the ledge and collapsed on her back. Staring up at the sky, she could not help but laugh. By all accounts, she should be a pancake at the bottom of the gorge, yet she had somehow survived.

Ava lay there for several breaths, unwilling to move. But the clicking sound from Smythe charging his rifle had her rolling onto her side. Across the gorge, she spotted the bounty hunter, and her heart leapt. Looking down the barrel of Smythe's weapon, Ava knew he had her dead to rights. One pull of the trigger, and it was lights out.

Shakily coming to her feet, Ava mentally commanded the AI to return her nano-suit to its original setting. As her wingsuit reconfigured to her body shape, Ava raised her hands in surrender. She was tempted to run despite knowing her adversary could gun her down before she reached the jungle, but curiosity stayed Ava's desire to flee. The creature staring at her through a sniper's scope was her only link to the outside. She wanted to know who was behind the attack on the Aiwans and what was her role in all of this.

As seconds ticked by, Ava began to wonder why the hunter had not killed her already. Then it dawned on her. The creature needed her alive, needed her so she could hand over the Reaper.

Ava slowly dropped her arms. "Can't kill me, can you?" she called over the whistling updraft.

Smythe remained unmoving, his finger resting on the trigger. Unable to translate the human's native tongue, the bounty hunter could not comprehend her words, but the meaning was clear. They were at a standoff and both knew it.

Keeping his weapon trained on Ava, Smythe surveyed the area. He sneered at the realization he would have to backtrack and find another way around. Turning his attention back to the human, the bounty hunter considered firing another stun blast, but that seemed futile considering Ava's protective suit. Besides, even if it worked, he did not want her eaten by scavengers in the time it took him to reach her.

Lowering his rifle, Smythe conceded temporary defeat.

Ava jabbed her unicorn fist at him in defiance and yelled, "You're never getting my ship!"

Smythe did not reply. Keeping his eyes locked on Ava with cold calculation, the bounty hunter shouldered his weapon. They stared at one another for a long moment. Then Ava swallowed hard as a thin smile creased the insectoid's mouth. Its sinister grin sent a shiver up her spine. Ava knew exactly what her opponent was thinking.

You can run, but you cannot hide.

43

MONGREL

Planet Earth
Groom Lake, Nevada

Jessica Aguri walked down the hallway in a foul mood. After spending the past four hours in the interrogation room with ex-Chairman of the Joint Chiefs of Staff, General Garza, she was ready for a stiff drink. Once again, the brash military man had played coy in his knowledge of Edmund Mathias's operations. Since a plea bargain was yet to be finalized, Garza kept his cards close to his chest. Yet, he had made a point to dangle just enough carrots in front of Jessica to keep her coming back for more.

Five minutes of waterboarding would do the trick, she half-joked to herself while forcing a smile at a passing colleague.

Adding to her tension, Jessica had yet to hear from the Nunezes and Min-jun. She had no idea whether their so-called "working" vacation was turning up any actionable intel on Dr. Landry. Which reminded her, she still needed to call Ji-eun to check up on her.

Nearing the end of the hall, Jessica slowed at the sound of voices coming from her temporary office. She paused just shy of the door and listened. Then her eyebrows arched at the unmistakable voice of her boss, Brett Brenham.

It was uncharacteristic for Brenham to make an unannounced visit but, considering the high profile prisoners being held just down the hall, it was not surprising. Jessica actually welcomed his presence. Perhaps Brenham could make headway with Garza and Sizemore so they could get down to business.

Then came a female voice, one that Jessica did not recognize.

Curious to see who Brenham was talking to, Jessica straightened her blouse, mustered a calm smile, and entered her office. She halted midway through the door at the sight of new CIA Director, Maxine Ratliff, who was seated at Jessica's desk as if she belonged there.

Ratliff's conversation with Brenham abruptly ceased and both turned to Jessica. An uneasy silence filled the gap between them.

This can't be good, Jessica thought grimly.

"Director Ratliff … Director Brenham," she greeted, "this is a nice surprise."

Ratliff stood as Jessica stepped forward and extended her hand.

"Deputy Aguri," Ratliff said as firmly as her handshake. "Join us."

Jessica turned to grab the door and made a passing glance at Brenham. If her boss's underlying expression of disappointment did not confirm Jessica's fears, his first question did.

"Are you running an unsanctioned op in Peru?" Brenham asked as soon as the door closed.

Jessica fumbled to reply but nothing came out of her mouth.

Brenham shook his head. "Your stunned silence is very reassuring," he said with disgust. "Jesus, Jessica, how could you be so stupid?"

Director Ratliff kept silent. With her fingers steepled under her chin, she watched and listened as Brenham grilled Jessica.

He had every reason to be livid. The Director of the CIA's National Clandestine Service had personally vouched for Jessica to be his number two, yet here she was, less than a week on the job, and she had already gone off the reservation.

As Brenham chewed her a new one, Jessica wisely kept her mouth shut and accepted the verbal lashing. This was not how she had thought her day would go. Former CIA Director, Gary Sizemore, had agreed to a full immunity deal the day prior in exchange for his cooperation. It was a big win for Jessica. And, she had assumed once Garza learned of this, he would be tripping over himself, begging for a similar deal. That had not been the case. Now this. Her boss and his superior had flown all the way across the country to confront her in person. Jessica's career dissipation light was blinking before her eyes.

When Brenham finally stopped to take a breath, Jessica chose her words carefully.

"I know you're pissed, and I'm sorry I didn't run this past you first, but all I did was ask a friend to do some minor recon on Mathias's facility. That's it. Nothing illegal."

"Oh, that's it, she says," Brenham scoffed, making air quotes. "And by *friend* do you mean Choi Min-jun, the ex-North Korean special forces operator who happens to be an accomplice in the assassination of Kim Sung-il? *And*, who is supposed to be secretly under the protective custody of the United States government?"

Putting it that way made her feel like a reckless amateur. Looking at her feet, Jessica nodded sheepishly.

"And that's not all. You dragged others into this, too," Brenham fumed. "Colonel Marlana Nunez and her husband, Hector, are also involved."

Jessica sighed heavily. As far as screw-ups went, this had to be one for the record books.

"How did you know?" she was afraid to ask.

"We have a source in Peru who told us Min-jun was compromised."

Jessica looked up sharply. "Compromised? What are you talking about?"

"Oh, you didn't hear? Mathias's private army found him snooping around outside the facility in Satipo. He's in their custody now."

Jessica's eyes darted back and forth between her superiors, hoping this was some sort of joke, but she found no humor in their expressions.

"And the Nunezes?"

Brenham deferred to Ratliff.

Trying to inject some semblance of calm and professionalism, the CIA's new director gestured to an empty seat. Jessica sat as Brenham collected himself.

Dressed in a light-charcoal pantsuit and cream-colored blouse, the middle-aged head of the world's largest spy agency wore her silver hair cut short in back with long bangs for easy maintenance. Her stylish yet professional appearance epitomized the look of today's female power executive, and God help anyone who misjudged her keen fashion sense for weakness.

In truth, Maxine Ratliff cut her teeth in the field as a successful operative and station chief. Dubbed "Mad Max" for her road warrior mentality and willingness to travel anywhere in the world to take on the toughest assignments, Director Ratliff could be best described as an assertive careerist with unwavering devotion to her country. She never lacked confidence but kept her ego in check whenever it came down to trusting the eyes on the ground.

Ratliff leaned forward, resting her elbows on Jessica's desk. "You're not the only one interested in Mathias's dealings in Peru," she said calmly. "You know we've had him under surveillance since long before the events at Groom Lake. Same goes for my predecessor. We knew Garza and Sizemore were in cahoots with Mathias for some time but didn't know how deep the rabbit hole went until recently."

Jessica looked to Brenham, incredulous.

He nodded affirmation.

"Mathias is selling his cloning technology to the highest bidder," Ratliff explained, "thanks in large part to off-the-books funding arranged by Garza and Sizemore. Now that they're out of the picture, and with Mathias's force enhancement serum close to going to market, he's got all of our enemies lining up, ready to accept their first shipment."

Jessica nodded slowly, considering this new information. She had gleaned most of it already from satellite photos of arms dealers visiting Mathias's compound in Peru, along with Garza's admissions.

"But that's only the tip of the iceberg," Ratliff continued. She bent over and pulled a classified file folder from the briefcase at her feet. She retrieved a black and white photo from inside then slid it across the desk to Jessica. "Look familiar?"

Jessica gaped at the sight of Luna standing next to Edmund Mathias and Dr. Rose Landry. She gave Luna and Mathias a quick once-over but fixated on Rose. The good doctor appeared safe and healthy, if not chummy with her supposed abductor.

"That was taken three days ago," Ratliff offered. "Now you know why Dr. Landry took an abrupt leave of absence and received such a large sum of money. Mathias needed her to get to the Aiwan."

"I thought he went home ..."

"He did," Brenham chimed in. "That's not Prince Kypa; it's someone else."

Jessica looked at the photo again. "Who is it?"

"That's what we were working on before your unsanctioned op," Brenham needled, still unable to let go of his deputy's lapse in judgment.

Jessica sighed. "Listen, I take full responsibility for this, but we needed visual proof that Dr. Landry was okay. She was part of Sundiver, and all of the signs said she was under duress."

"She may well be," Ratliff conceded. "That's why there's a SEAL rescue team standing by, waiting for the green light to go in and get her."

Jessica perked up with a hopeful grin. "Seriously?"

"The plan was to extract the Aiwan and Dr. Landry, but now that's on hold," Ratliff explained. Seeing Jessica cringe, the director put up her hand. "Relax, it's not because of you. Mathias moved the Aiwan this morning, right before he captured your friend, Min-jun. We don't know yet where the Aiwan was taken, but we believe it's to Challenger Deep."

"Why there, if you don't mind me asking?"

"Energy crystals," Brenham answered. "They're sitting at the bottom of the Pacific. That's why the Aiwans came here in the first place. Mathias is one of a few people on the planet with the resources to harvest these crystals. Our guess is he wants to get to them before anyone else, and the Aiwan is the key. Hence the need for Dr. Landry's services. She has experience with Prince Kypa, and Mathias is probably using her to get to this Aiwan, too."

"What about Min-jun?"

"When Mathias learns who he is—*and he will*—Min-jun's a dead man," Ratliff predicted. "He'll likely be sent back to North Korea to answer for his crimes, and after being tortured mercilessly, they will kill him in the most gruesome manner imaginable. And that's just the beginning." Ratliff paused, noticing Jessica's hollowed expression as she pictured poor Min-jun's fate. "Deputy Aguri, are you with me?"

Jessica blinked back to the present. "Yes, ma'am. Sorry."

"Once Mathias learns we're on to him, that Aiwan is gone baby gone. We'll never see it again. So, that's one problem. Then there's the North Koreans." Ratliff sighed. "Once they learn the truth behind Kim Sung-il's death and tie Min-jun to us, they'll be looking to retaliate."

"What can we do?" Jessica asked.

"Simple, we get Min-jun out, along with Dr. Landry," Brenham replied matter-of-factly.

"Simple, he says," Ratliff chuckled, thumbing at Jessica's boss. "I'll be sure to tell the President that."

"Do you have an extraction plan?" Jessica inquired.

"We do, for what it's worth, but it involves an asset currently on Peru's most wanted list. His name is Eduardo Salazar, code-named Mongrel, and rightfully so. He's a former senior leader of Shining Path, a fanatical Maoist guerilla group that terrorized Peru back in the eighties and nineties. Fortunately, Shining Path never came to power, and even though it lingers on, Salazar disassociated himself from the group. He moved on to drug trafficking and other lucrative endeavors."

Jessica made a face, trying to piece everything together. "So, Mathias isn't holding the Nunezes; it's this Mongrel?"

"Correct," Ratliff affirmed. "He's been our eyes on the ground for some time now. In fact, he controls the union that supplied the workers who built Mathias's compound, so Salazar knows that facility inside and out. He even has custodial staff on Mathias's payroll. That's where the photo originated.

"Mathias is taking over Satipo and pushing out all of the criminal elements," Ratliff stated. "Salazar knows his days are numbered and wants out of Peru … fast. If the federales don't get him first, Mathias will, once he finds out who Min-jun was traveling with."

"Arrangements are being made by Salazar to send the Nunezes home," Brenham said. "As long as they keep their mouths shut, they'll be all right."

Jessica steeled herself, waiting for the hammer to fall on her. If they did not fire her or demand her resignation, she was certainly looking at a sizable demotion.

Sensing this, Ratliff tried to put her mind at ease. "We'll discuss your future at another time. For now, no more rogue agent crap. Got it?"

Jessica nodded fervently, which satisfied the director for now.

To Brenham, Ratliff said, "I'll give you two a moment."

Ratliff stood and exited to the hallway. As soon as the door closed, Jessica jumped into another apology. Brenham raised his hand to stop her.

"Consider this your one and only mulligan. I'm not going to beat a dead horse. You screwed up, and you know it. Did you learn anything?"

Jessica's entire body relaxed as she exhaled heavily. "I did, for sure. I shouldn't have acted without your approval. It won't happen again."

"I know," he said earnestly. "Let's just hope we can get to your friends before it's too late."

"Speaking of which," Jessica said, perplexed, "I don't know how they could've caught Min-jun. He's the best."

"You know as well as I that anything can go wrong in the field," Brenham conceded. "No op ever goes to plan, but this one takes the cake."

"How so?"

Brenham could not help but laugh at the absurdity of it. "Salazar said Min-jun was attacked by a snake—a big one, apparently—right after he uploaded images of the Aiwan and Dr. Landry." Brenham handed her Min-jun's photos of Luna and Rose, each standing alone in front of their bedroom windows at Mathias's compound. Jessica did not bother asking how Brenham had gotten his hands on them.

"In the life or death struggle," Brenham continued, "Min-jun somehow triggered the facility's perimeter sensors. It saved his life. Your friend was this close to being eaten alive if it hadn't been for one of Mathias's sharpshooters."

Jessica's heart sank, thinking of poor Min-jun. *What are the odds?* she wondered. At least he was alive … for now.

Changing the subject, she asked, "What's next?"

"The director and I have a video conference scheduled here shortly to brief the President, then it's back to Washington." Brenham stood and straightened his suit jacket. "By the way, any progress with Garza and Sizemore?"

"Sizemore took the deal," she reported, her victory somewhat deflated. "Garza's still holding out for a personal apology."

"Garza," Brenham scoffed. "What a piece of work."

"You wanna take a crack at him?"

"Nah, you got this. Let me know when he comes around."

Jessica stood to see him out. "Sure thing, boss."

Reaching for the door, Brenham stopped short and turned to Jessica. "On second thought, if the President green light's this extraction, it'll go down real soon." With a slight grin, he said, "Might not be a bad idea to have you fly back with us and watch the op unfold in real-time."

Jessica read her boss's sly expression. With Sizemore talking, having her away meant leaving Garza isolated to sweat Jessica's next move.

She nodded agreeably. "Let me grab my stuff."

44
FEAR UP

Planet Earth
Satipo, Peru

Four hours earlier, Min-jun's semi-conscious body had been carried off the field outside Mathias's compound. Using a two-person crutch technique, the guards whisked the supposed industrial spy to a pickup truck that delivered him inside. There, he was taken to an unused section of the facility, far removed from the eyes and ears of the workers who were just starting the morning shift.

With his feet dragging behind him, Min-jun was hauled to the end of a long, narrow hallway. Reaching an unfinished storage room, the guards carried their prisoner inside and turned on the single lightbulb dangling from the ceiling.

In the center of the room were two folding chairs facing one another. Between them sat an empty paint bucket that had been turned upside-down and used as a makeshift card table, evidenced by an open deck from a recent game. Next to the cards were two Styrofoam coffee cups and a leftover candy wrapper.

The lead guard collected the trash into the bucket and set it against the wall, along with one of the chairs. Min-jun was then dumped onto the remaining chair in the middle of the room.

Mr. Renzo arrived from the airport moments later to find the half-dead man now with his wrists zip-tied with heavy-duty cuffs behind his back. Renzo eyed Min-jun up and down with a cold, hard look.

"ID?"

"Nothing on him but this." The guard handed Renzo a wrinkled picture of Dr. Landry, along with an article about the grand opening of Mathias's Satipo facility.

Renzo pocketed the items then readied his cell phone. "Hold his head up."

The nearest guard grabbed the prisoner by the hair and lifted his head. Still exhausted from his near-death encounter with the snake, Min-jun opened his heavy eyes slightly. He winced at the stinging pain of the overhead light.

Renzo snapped several photos from different angles. Satisfied, he stepped back and texted the images to Ms. Diaz with a simple message, "*ID ASAP.*"

To this point, Min-jun had made no attempt to thwart his captors. The anaconda had drained most of the fight from him, but the overhead light sparked a surge of adrenaline. He raged against his bonds to free himself. Renzo and the guards merely watched his futile effort, unamused.

Min-jun eventually abandoned his struggle. Chest heaving and sweat dripping down his face, he looked about the room like a caged tiger sizing up his captors.

One man stood out from the rest. Unlike the others who were dressed in black military fatigues and matching Polos sporting the Mathias Industries logo, this man had a style all his own. He wore a white shirt underneath a dark blue Tangzhuang jacket with matching pants. Min-jun recognized the traditional martial arts attire, but the long carrying case slung behind the man's back was a mystery.

A sword, perhaps? Maybe a bow?

One thing was clear—this man had authority. The guards watching over Min-jun seemed to be waiting for their leader to act, but the man in charge did not appear to be in a hurry. As Renzo scrolled through the images on the prisoner's confiscated camera, Min-jun debated whether or not to address him directly.

Having seen enough, Renzo shut off the camera and handed it to one of the guards. He then turned to face Min-jun.

"Who are you and why are you here?"

Min-jun cleared his dry throat. "My name is Pei Wang," he said hoarsely, trying to appear meek. "I am nature photographer."

"Nature photographer?" Renzo scoffed. "Judging by the images on your camera, Mr. Wang, I would say you are more of a Peeping Tom. I didn't see any nature photos on your storage card, just a lot of pictures of this facility and our staff in their bedroom windows."

"Please, I do nothing wrong, just take pictures," Min-jun insisted.

"For whom?"

"I am freelance photographer. I sell my pictures to wildlife magazines and websites—"

"Wildlife?" Renzo interrupted. "You got an up close look at our wildlife today, didn't you?"

His men laughed.

"Perhaps you should consider another line of work, Mr. Wang," Renzo said lightly. "If it wasn't for us, right now, you'd be slowly digesting in the stomach of a big snake."

Min-jun dropped his chin and nodded sheepishly.

"We saved your life, Mr. Wang; the least you can do is give us the courtesy of being honest."

"But I tell you the truth," Min-jun argued. "I just take photos, nothing more. Please, I leave and not come back."

"You're not going anywhere until we get to the bottom of this," Renzo assured him. "Now tell me, who are you working for?"

As Min-jun started reciting his cover story again, Renzo sighed heavily and cut him off. "Stop. I don't have time for games, Mr. Wang, or whoever you are, so let's cut to the chase. Come clean right now, and you can save yourself a lot of discomfort, or we do this the hard way."

Min-jun knew there was no point carrying on this charade and decided to conserve his energy. His day was about to go from really bad to much worse. It was just a question of how long he could hold out.

Min-jun erased the panic-stricken expression he conjured as part of his ruse. Picking a spot on the wall to channel his focus, his eyes glossed over with numbed defiance, expecting his interrogators to "fear up," meaning they would start using unconventional, if not illegal, coercion tactics to expedite his confession.

North Korea's secret police were masters at this game. In a country ruled by fear and paranoia, Min-jun had been conditioned from an early age that silence and submission were key to survival. His safety, and that of his family, had depended on strict discipline. One careless remark could lead to a life sentence in a labor camp or death by summary execution.

Such was the fate of his parents, although it had not been their fault they got arrested by Kim's regime. Min-jun's mother and father had the misfortune of crossing paths in Downtown Pyongyang with a high-ranking party member who had been looking to make an example of someone. Unjustly accused of being from the lowest level of North Korea's socio-economic caste system, Min-jun's parents had been seized in broad daylight by the Ministry of State Security and hauled away to labor camps without due process. Min-jun had never seen or heard from them again. But, rather than voicing his dissent and risking the safety of his wife and son, he had chosen a different path.

Now, ten years after his defection, Min-jun's life had come full-circle. He realized it was only a matter of time before his captors discovered his true identity. When they did, he doubted they would kill him here. They would probably ship him back to North Korea for a fate worse than death.

In that moment of clarity, Min-jun pictured his entire family gathered together in his parents' garden. It was a pristine day with the sun shining down. They were smiling and laughing, with his beautiful, young wife, Binna, waving to him.

Yearning desperately to be reunited with the love of his life, Min-jun imagined himself holding Binna once again and playing with their son, Seo-jun.

Today would be a good day to die.

But there was business to take care of first. Thinking of his friends—Ji-eun, Jessica, and the Nunezes—Min-jun steeled himself. To die with honor meant adhering to the same vow of silence he had once made to his family. But now, it extended to his friends.

Renzo sensed his prisoner's attitude shift, confirming his suspicion that Min-jun was not who he claimed to be. The question now was whether or not he could break his prisoner before Ms. Dias confirmed his true identity, a challenge he relished.

"Long ago, my people were enemies with a tribe called the Jivaroa," Renzo said, casually circling Min-jun. "The Jivaroa were headshrinkers, you see. Very dangerous. They believed that removing the head of an enemy and shrinking it would harness the enemy's spirit and compel him to serve the Jivaroa. Thus, the enemy's soul was prevented from avenging his death."

Renzo waved dismissively. "Of course, I don't believe in such spiritual nonsense. If I wanted you dead, I would've left you to the snake. No, I need you alive and talking, my friend. So, I ask myself: how best to achieve this end? Have you ever heard of El Guiso?"

Min-jun remained stone-faced and silent.

Renzo smirked. "El Guiso means *The Stew* in Spanish. It is a torture technique used by the Mexican drug cartels. You see, they will dip their enemy in a large pot or barrel of boiling liquids until they talk. Sometimes, they will even douse a prisoner with gasoline, and if they refuse to speak, the cartel sets them on fire."

Renzo searched Min-jun's face for any signs of heightened fear but found none. Not surprised, he continued.

"Both methods are crude but effective." Renzo stood in front of Min-jun and leaned in close, face-to-face. "Problem is, there's never a barrel of gasoline around when you need one. So, we shall try another way."

Movement by the door caught Min-jun's attention. He turned his head slightly to see a pair of guards arrive, each carrying two, one-gallon jugs of tap water. Before Min-jun could react, one of the guards behind him placed a black cloth hood over his face and forced his head backward. Now facing the ceiling, Min-jun took a deep breath and closed his mouth instinctively just as his captors began pouring water slowly but steadily over his mouth and nose.

Recalling his military training, Min-jun knew waterboarding relied on three elements: air, water, and fear. The intent was to coerce the subject into talking, not kill him, although death was certainly possible since they were essentially drowning him.

With his mouth closed, water still found its way through the fabric and into Min-jun's nostrils, trickling down to his lungs and creating the overpowering sensation of drowning.

Min-jun held his breath for as long as possible but inevitably gave in. Inhaling through his mouth and nose, water washed down his throat, causing him to gag and choke. But that was not the worst part. Inhaling acted like a suction, bringing the damp cloth in tight over his mouth and nostrils. Panic set in as Min-jun could not differentiate between inhaling and exhaling. Either way, the drowning sensation became inescapable.

Just as Min-jun reached the cusp of suffocating, his captors sat him up and removed the damp hood. Retching fluid, Min-jun coughed hoarsely while trying desperately to fill his lungs with air at the same time. It took him several moments to recover, but as soon as he caught his breath, the process started over.

Gurgling and squirming as the waterboarding continued, Min-jun panicked at the hands of his captors who showed no mercy. They only stopped after emptying the first water jug. At that point, the guards sat the prisoner up and removed the hood once more.

Renzo stood off to the side, waiting patiently as Min-jun vomited. He showed no sympathy. This was just business, after all.

Gesturing to one of the guards, Renzo clenched his fist then raised one finger. The burly brute gave a sinister grin.

"Yes, sir," he replied, all too eager to oblige.

Stepping forward, the guard began cracking his knuckles for Min-jun to see.

Min-jun raised his eyes and sensed what was coming. Unable to move, he winced as the guard reared back his fist and threw the first punch. Min-jun absorbed every ounce of the crushing blow to his face. As soon as the punch landed, he heard his nasal bone snap, followed by a wave of sharp pain that resonated throughout his skull. The room started spinning. Yet, except for a repressed grunt from the initial strike, Min-jun held his tongue, not giving his captors any satisfaction.

The guard sneered as a stream of blood ran down Min-jun's face. He looked to Renzo, who gave a head bob to continue working the prisoner over.

One blow after another, the guard used Min-jun's face as a punching bag.

By the time Renzo interceded, the prisoner's eyes were nearly swollen shut. He pulled Min-jun's head up by the hair and lifted each eyelid to check that the pupils were dilated. Min-jun's eyes rolled deliriously back in his head.

"Good thing we took your picture first," Renzo joked, eyeing Min-jun's battered face. "Now is the time to say something, my friend. Anything?"

After gagging on the salty taste of his own blood, Min-jun's mouth moved slightly as he struggled to form a word.

"Yes?" Renzo leaned closer, turning his ear toward the prisoner.

Min-jun whispered hoarsely, "Snake fight better."

Renzo clenched his jaw, irritated by the prisoner's defiance.

The guard who had inflicted the damage stepped forward, ready to continue the beating, but Renzo waved him off as his phone rang. Seeing it was Ms. Diaz, he picked up immediately.

"His name is Choi Min-jun," she began. "North Korean special forces. At least, he used to be."

Renzo nodded. Ms. Diaz's resourcefulness had come through once again. However, news of his prisoner's affiliation with the Democratic People's Republic of Korea did catch him off-guard. Renzo had pegged Min-jun to be former military—*South* Korean, perhaps—but he had never crossed paths with a North Korean operator.

"RGB?" Renzo inquired, referring to the Reconnaissance General Bureau, North Korea's primary foreign intelligence service.

"Oddly, no," Diaz answered. "Turns out, your boy went AWOL ten years ago and was believed to have defected with his wife and son. His military dossier is impressive, but he's been working for an international aid organization in

South China, called Global Children's Relief Mission. A facial recognition scan pulled his image off their website, so I did some digging. GCRM looks legit from the outside, helping impoverished children with food, shelter, health care—yada, yada, yada—but my guess is it must be a CIA front."

"Mm." Renzo pursed his lips. "Where in China?"

"Right on North Korea's northern border, across the Tumen River. Funny thing is, I've also got airport security footage of him leaving China on the very day the alien spacecraft blew up last month … and he wasn't alone. We've also ID'd Vong Ji-eun. She's the daughter of General Vong Yong-hae, former head of the North Korean military. He reportedly died at the crash site, along with his daughter."

"This guy helped her defect?"

"Better yet," Edmund chimed in on speaker phone, "he's probably the one who helped the American pilot cross the border and swap places with the general's daughter. The North Koreans are going to go ape shit over this."

Renzo considered this. "Anything else?"

"Nada for now," Diaz replied. "I just emailed you his personnel file, but I'll keep digging."

"Good work," Renzo said.

To Edmund, he asked, "What do you want me to do with him, sir?"

"Find out everything he knows, but don't kill him. He's too valuable now. We need him alive."

"Affirmative. And Dr. Landry?"

Thirty thousand feet in the air, Edmund Mathias sat in one of the jump seats near the front of the aircraft. He looked aft, where Luna sat isolated in the back of the cargo section. Next to her was Edmund's crown jewel, the prototype cloaking device.

As the Aiwan stared out the window, unaware of Edmund's eyes on her, he considered Luna's relationship with Rose. For all intents and purposes, Dr. Landry's work was complete. Luna was now fluent and able to communicate on her own. More importantly, she had built the cloaking device.

Edmund sighed heavily. He knew this day would come eventually. Retracting the twenty million dollar money transfer to Rose's bank account was easy enough, but killing his mentor turned out to be harder than he had thought. Besides, she might still be of some use.

"Leave her be for now," Mathias replied. "Keep me posted if anything new turns up."

Renzo acknowledged, and Edmund nodded to Ms. Diaz, who ended the call.

"Oh-ho, we've got Fitzgerald by the balls now," Mathias said with a devious grin. "I'm going to blackmail the President against North Korea, China, and the Russians. Hell, throw in the rest of the world, for that matter." He laughed. "Fitzgerald's world is about to come crashing down on him if he tries to interfere with my plans."

45
BOLD FORTRESS

Planet Earth
Groom Lake, Nevada

Sitting around a rectangular table in the Blackbird conference room, CIA Director Ratliff and Director of the National Clandestine Service, Brett Brenham, awaited President Fitzgerald to start their impromptu meeting. Having already authenticated to establish the encrypted connection, they sat in silence, facing a wall-mounted television that displayed the Seal of the President of the United States emblem.

Staring blankly at nothing in particular, lost in his thoughts, Brenham drummed his fingers anxiously on the table.

"You good?" Ratliff asked with her eyebrow cocked.

He did not respond.

"Brett?"

Brenham snapped back to the present. "Pardon?" he replied.

Ratliff stared pointedly at his tapping fingers, and Brenham hastily flattened his hand on the table and smiled ruefully.

"Sorry."

"Worried about Aguri?"

Brenham exhaled. "It's that obvious?"

"Uh-huh. Let me do the talking," Ratliff said. It was not a request. "I expect the President's going to address the elephant in the room right off the bat."

"I'm sorry for this," Brenham said sincerely. "You didn't deserve to be put in this position, especially your first month on the job."

Ratliff shrugged it off. One did not rise to her position without thick skin.

"We'll see how it plays out. The President's a fair man, but Jessica's fate depends on the success of the mission."

"She made a mistake, but she's one of my best."

"*Our* best," Ratliff corrected with a wry grin. "Besides, I can't fault her initiative. Eagles don't flock after all; they soar."

Brenham liked the analogy. "True, but they do lay an egg from time to time … just saying."

"We've all been there, Brett, including you and me. Mind you, I'm not condoning what she did, but you picked her as your deputy for a reason, just like I picked you. She'll learn from this, and if the op goes to plan, her mistake will be forgotten. The key is keeping the President focused on the op and not her."

Brenham agreed. He appreciated Ratliff's support for Jessica and, by extension, him. It was not the start either of them wanted, but the director was right; everything hinged on successfully extracting Dr. Landry and Choi Min-jun from Mathias's custody.

Just then, the television came to life, and President Fitzgerald appeared. He was seated in the PEOC, the President's emergency operations center, surrounded by his national security council.

"Maxine, welcome," President Fitzgerald greeted. "This was unexpected."

"Thank you, Mr. President," she replied. "My apologies, but we have a critical situation to brief you on. Before I begin, I want to introduce Brett Brenham, my new Director of NCS."

"Congratulations, Director Brenham," the President said. "Your boss holds you in high regard."

Brett was unaware the two had spoken about his appointment but appeared to take it in stride. "Thank you, sir."

Ratliff cut to the chase. "Mr. President, we have a new development regarding Mathias Industries, and it's not good."

"What's Edmund up to now?" Fitzgerald asked in a wary voice.

"Sir, we have confirmation he is holding an Aiwan hostage."

Ernie Gutierrez nearly choked on his coffee as the other members inside the PEOC reacted with equal surprise, including the President.

"What?" Fitzgerald leaned forward in his chair. "How is this even possible?"

432 | TODO HOSEA

Ratliff shared her laptop screen, showing an image of Luna in her holding cell, along with Dr. Rose Landry and Edmund Mathias.

Fitzgerald squinted as he scrutinized the image. Immediately, he could tell something was off based on the Aiwan's physique and body markings. "That's not Prince Kypa?"

"No, sir. We believe it's a second Aiwan."

"A second? Where did it come from?"

"Better yet, how many more are there?" Russ Franks asked, raising the notion of an invasion force.

"We don't know," Ratliff replied frankly. "To date, there has been no extraterrestrial activity spotted by our deep space surveillance systems. All we have at this time is confirmation of the Aiwan in this image. The photo was obtained inside Mathias's research facility near Lima, Peru."

"Peru?" Fitzgerald shook his head in disbelief. "Assuming that Aiwan was on the mothership, how did it get from North Korea to Peru ... undetected?"

"Yes, sir," Ratliff replied, unfazed by the grilling. "Our theory is that this second Aiwan survived the crash in North Korea. There was no sign of a second escape pod landing, so we believe it must have exited the mothership before it was destroyed. Since news of Kypa went public, we've received thousands of reports of alien sightings."

"I can only imagine," Vice President Harrington said under her breath, referring to the growing crowd of alien conspiracy theorists gathered outside the White House lawn each day.

"Some of those sightings came from North Korean intercepts," Ratliff continued. "Nothing panned out until now. Obviously, Mathias got the jump on us and brought the Aiwan to Peru on or around February 25th."

"That woman looks familiar." The President pointed at Rose on the screen. Ratliff's jaw stiffened. *Here it comes.*

"Yes, sir. That is Dr. Rose Landry of the CDC."

"CDC?" Fitzgerald searched his memory. "Wait a second, I met her at Groom Lake."

"Yes, sir. Dr. Landry was part of Operation Sundiver."

Fitzgerald raised his voice. "Well, what the hell is she doing helping Mathias?"

"Dr. Landry disappeared from her home three weeks ago. Her family reported her missing. We believe she was kidnapped by Mathias and taken to Peru for the sole purpose of establishing contact with this second Aiwan, just like she did with Prince Kypa."

The President turned to Ernie with an incredulous look.

"Neither one of them looks to be in distress," the White House Chief of Staff observed, although the armed guard standing watch in the background of the picture made him wonder.

"That's where things start to get complicated, sir," Ratliff began tentatively. "We know Dr. Landry did not leave the country on a commercial aircraft and, to the best of our knowledge, she did not fly out on any of Mathias's personal planes. We also know that she and Mathias have a history."

"What do you mean?"

"Mathias was her protégé many years ago, but Dr. Landry's late husband accused him of stealing research, which ultimately funded his startup of Mathias Industries."

"I don't follow," Fitzgerald admitted.

Ratliff cleared her throat. "Shortly after Dr. Landry disappeared, a twenty million dollar deposit was made in a Cayman Island bank account in her name. At the same time, she requested a leave of absence from the CDC."

The President steepled his fingers under his chin, processing this turn of events.

"You think Dr. Landry sold out?" Ken Hreno, National Security Advisor, inquired.

Before Ratliff could answer, Admiral Donnelly reminded the group, "She's definitely a security risk. Dr. Landry knows everything about Sundiver."

"Not everything, Admiral," Brenham responded. "Dr. Landry and her colleague, Dr. Neil Garrett, were only privy to Kypa's existence and our intent to steal the Reaper. She doesn't know the details of the ground operation."

"Nevertheless, she is a key witness," Fitzgerald agreed with Donnelly. "If Dr. Landry talks, and we're found culpable, there's no telling how the North Koreans will respond."

There was consensus around the table, and it was not just the North Koreans they feared. Each member of the NSC pictured themselves testifying before congress.

"I'm afraid there's more, sir," Ratliff offered reluctantly. She could sense Brenham stiffen. The CIA director displayed the images obtained by Min-jun. "These images were taken yesterday outside Mathias's facility in Peru."

Fitzgerald and the others stared at three images on the screen. The first photo captured the armored car and several SUVs leaving Mathias's compound, while the other two showed Luna and Rose standing in their bedroom windows.

"We believe Mathias moved the Aiwan this morning," Ratliff explained. "We tracked this convoy to the local airport and one of Mathias's private hangars. A cargo transport departed soon after, heading to Guam. We believe Mathias is taking the Aiwan to Challenger Deep."

Seeing where this was going, Fitzgerald sighed heavily. "He wants the crystals."

"Yes, sir."

Russ Franks pulled no punches. "Greedy bastard. He's inviting a whole lotta hurt if any harvesters show up."

"I couldn't agree more," Guy Lannister, the new Director of National Intelligence, said. "Even if Mathias successfully harvests the crystals, where can he hope to hide them? Kypa said he detected the crystals from deep space. We have to assume other harvesters can, as well."

"They can. In fact, I'd wager Mathias is counting on it," the President said with disdain. "He's up to something big, and the Chinese and Russians are in on it, too. They've cleared him a path to Challenger Deep, and my constituents are pressuring me to pull the *Reagan* strike group from the area. We need to know Mathias's endgame."

Silence fell over the room as expectant looks were exchanged around the table. Finally, the Vice President spoke.

"I'm curious why Mathias didn't take Dr. Landry with him?"

Harrington's question caught the group flat-footed. With all the talk focused on Mathias, the Aiwan, and crystals, Rose had become an afterthought … except to Ratliff and Brenham, who remained deliberately reserved.

"We don't know," the CIA Director admitted. "Assuming Dr. Landry served her purpose, it's logical to assume the second Aiwan has assimilated our language and customs by now. Perhaps Mathias no longer needs Dr. Landry's help."

"Considering the fact she knows just as much about his operations as ours, that would make Dr. Landry a liability. And, if Mathias is planning to off her," Ernie speculated, "it makes sense he doesn't want the Aiwan to know, at least not yet. That wouldn't bode well for their new relationship."

Several members at the table agreed with Ernie's assessment. Some even went so far as to voice their support for allowing Mathias to kill Dr. Landry and solve their security problem for them.

"What is their relationship?" Admiral Donnelly posed to the group. "And what could Mathias possibly offer of value to this Aiwan?"

Watching from afar, Ratliff eyed the President's think tank on the screen as they pondered these questions. She read the frustration on their faces and shared their annoyance. One man had the world's greatest superpowers by the balls, and they all knew it. And, without more information, it was futile to even speculate on Mathias's grand scheme. Ratliff was reluctant to further aggravate the situation, but duty compelled her to be fully transparent.

Ratliff sighed. "Mr. President, there's one other matter."

The room fell silent as Fitzgerald transferred his gaze to her.

"Sir, one of our operatives was captured while surveilling Mathias's compound. He's currently a prisoner inside the facility."

The President exhaled heavily. *And the hits just keep on coming.*

He turned to Ernie, seated to his left. "Can we negotiate a release for Dr. Landry and Maxine's operative?"

Ernie raised his eyebrow with a knowing look. "You realize what Mathias will want in return?"

Fitzgerald scrubbed his hand over his face. "He'll want *Reagan* out of Guam so we can't interfere with his plans."

"Correct," Ernie replied. "And even if he agrees, Mathias won't release our people until he's done harvesting the crystals in Challenger Deep."

Fitzgerald looked around the table. "I don't see any choice. Besides, it's not like Mathias can do anything with the crystals right now, anyway."

Ernie concurred, and several others around the table nodded consensus.

"Mr. President?"

All eyes turned to Ratliff on the television.

She stiffened, readying for the hammer to fall. "The operative in custody was directly involved in Sundiver. In fact, he was our asset in China who helped Captain Tan infiltrate North Korea, and he exfiltrated General Vong's daughter out of the country."

The President's puzzled eyes narrowed as he tried connecting the dots. "I don't understand. What the hell is our Chinese asset doing in Peru?"

"To be accurate, sir, he's North Korean," Ratliff gently corrected.

"Thank you for clarifying," Fitzgerald said testily. "Now answer my question."

Guy Lannister swiveled his seat to face the screen. "Mr. Choi is supposed to be in protective custody …"

Ratliff felt her chest tighten. There was no easy way to sugarcoat this mess. Just as she opened her mouth to reply, Brenham beat her to the punch.

"I take full responsibility, sir."

Ratliff's cheeks reddened as she forced back the urge to override her subordinate. Brenham's eagerness to jump on a grenade was premature, but to contradict him in front of the President made them both look bad. Under the table, Ratliff discreetly grabbed Brenham's forearm to reel him back.

"Enlighten me," the President said with cold reserve.

Knowing his career rested on his next words, Brenham swallowed hard. "Sir, the truth is Dr. Landry's family feared for her safety and reached out to my deputy for help. They were convinced Dr. Landry had been kidnapped and, long story short, they acted on their own to arrange a private trip to Peru to obtain evidence of Dr. Landry's captivity."

"Our people committed no crimes, Mr. President," Ratliff pointed out. "Impulsive and reckless, yes, but not illegal."

"Yet, Mr. Choi and Dr. Landry hold our fate in their hands," Ernie rebutted, looking to the President to roll some heads.

The White House Chief of Staff did not have to mention the word "impeachment," but that was what everyone was thinking. And that was just for starters. Criminal charges and prison sentences could be on the table, not to mention the fact Kim Sung-il's older sister now ruled North Korea. If she ever got wind of the truth behind her brother's untimely death, she would look to retaliate directly against the United States or its allies in the Korean Peninsula.

"Obviously, we can't let that happen," Fitzgerald decided. "What are our options?"

This was the opening Ratliff had hoped for. "Sir, we have a snatch and grab operation standing by, ready to go."

"Snatch and grab?" the President raised an eyebrow. "Will it piss off one of the wealthiest and most powerful men on the planet, not to mention half of Washington?"

Ratliff hesitated then went for it. "Yes, sir, it will."

"Good, because I'm not about to let Mathias blackmail this administration. Proceed, Director Ratliff."

The President's remark came as a welcomed vote of confidence, which elicited a thin smile from Ratliff. Putting her predecessor's failure and Deputy Aguri's antics in the rearview mirror, she saw an opportunity to restore the Commander in Chief's faith in the agency.

"Normally, this type of op would be handled as a joint mission using Delta operators and a contingent from the FBI's Hostage Rescue Team," she began, "but due to the circumstances, Operation Bold Fortress will utilize local assets already on the ground in Peru to extract Dr. Landry and Mr. Choi. We will then use a SEAL team to exfiltrate the hostages out of the country."

"What about the Aiwan?" Lannister asked.

"We don't know if or when we will see the Aiwan again," Ratliff replied, "but our sources reported that Mathias took at least a dozen of his private security forces with him when he and the Aiwan departed yesterday. That makes the facility low-manned and vulnerable. Plus, with the Aiwan gone, we think he'll be less inclined to expect a rescue attempt of Dr. Landry and Mr. Choi."

Lannister nodded agreement with Ratliff's logic, as did others around the table. Sensing no objections, she shared a recent satellite image of Mathias's circular facility.

"Here, you can see Mathias's compound." Using her mouse, Ratliff began highlighting various locations in and around the facility. "We believe Dr. Landry and most of the staff reside in this part of the facility on the second floor. The research labs are all subterranean," she explained then pointed to the field outside the compound. "Mr. Choi was captured here then moved to this unused section of the building near the main entrance."

"There's a wall around the entire compound. How do you plan to get in?" Russ Franks asked.

"Our primary asset employs workers with access to the facility. They have been spying on Mathias's dealings for some time now."

"Dare we ask who your asset is?" Fitzgerald inquired.

"His name is Eduardo Salazar, code-named Mongrel. He's a former member of Shining Path, an extremist terrorist group that wreaked havoc on the Peruvian government some forty years ago, but those days are behind him. Now Salazar has his hands in everything from coffee and construction to cocaine and other contraband. He actually built Mathias's compound, and many of his laborers still work inside the facility as custodians and general contractors. In fact, they are the ones who supplied the images of the Aiwan standing with Mathias and Dr. Landry. Salazar is confident he can get our people out without a shot being fired."

Ratliff paused for questions and rebuttals. Receiving neither, she continued with growing confidence.

"Once outside the compound, we'll have a SAD team pick up the two hostages by helicopter. They'll fly south through Bolivia then head out to sea and land on the *George Washington*."

"What's a SAD team?" the Vice President asked, fuzzy on the acronym.

"Special Activities Division," Ratliff answered, referring to the CIA's covert operations branch.

"We have two groups within SAD; one is responsible for carrying out tactical paramilitary operations while the second focuses on covert political action. Bold Fortress will be a CIA-led operation with JSOC coordinating the special mission units."

The special mission units Ratliff referred to included members of the Navy's SEAL Team Four and the Army's 160th Special Operations Aviation Regiment (SOAR). Nicknamed "Night Stalkers," SOAR was an elite aviation unit dedicated to flying special forces operators on the most secretive missions around the globe. For Bold Fortress, their task would be to fly the SEALs in and out of Peruvian airspace undetected, with coordination from Joint Special Operations Command and a ground controller from the CIA.

Ratliff cleared her throat. "For legal reasons—just as we did in Abbottabad to capture Osama bin Laden—both the SEAL and SOAR team members will be temporarily reclassified as civilians and transferred to the control of the CIA. Acting as a SAD team, they will fly to the open field where Mr. Choi was captured, pick up the hostages, and fly out."

"What about resistance?" Admiral Donnelly asked.

"Mathias's men will be heavily armed, but like I said, the facility will be undermanned when we arrive. Plus, Salazar will create a distraction inside the compound to draw attention away from our people."

"What kind of distraction?"

"A fire in a mechanical room," Brenham answered. "One of Salazar's men works on the facility's HVAC system. He'll have access to the room."

"So, what's Salazar's angle in all this?" Russ Franks asked skeptically. "He must want something in return."

"Asylum," Ratliff replied matter-of-factly. "He wants out of Peru and to retire peacefully and anonymously … preferably in Florida, he says."

"You trust him?" the President asked.

"I trust he can deliver Dr. Landry and Mr. Choi, sir. Like I said, he's provided valuable intel to us in the past, and he's motivated for this operation to succeed."

Fitzgerald turned to Ernie with a raised eyebrow. "Blowback?"

The White House Chief of Staff let out a heavy breath. "As long as everything goes to plan, all we have to worry about is wrinkling Mathias's feathers. He'll bitch and moan through his channels, but we can deal with it. And just like in Pakistan when we got bin Laden, Peru won't put up a stink since we're not acting directly against them." He paused briefly then added with a cautionary tone, "However—"

Fitzgerald held up his hand. "I know, if things do go south, we can kiss reelection goodbye." Ernie nodded. The President turned to Ratliff. "How soon can you begin?"

"Tomorrow morning, sir. Oh-three hundred hours, to be precise. The *G-Dub* is currently passing the southern cone of South America enroute to Japan and can be in position by nightfall. Likewise, the SOAR team already has two stealth-equipped helicopters onboard the carrier, ready to go. All we need, Mr. President, is your approval to fly the SEAL team in from Little Creek."

"Jesus, that's a tight window," Russ Franks remarked, considering the flight time to get from Joint Expeditionary Base Little Creek-Fort Story in Virginia Beach down to Peru.

"We can make it work," Admiral Donnelly assured the council. "SEAL Team Four can be deployed within the hour. All we have to do is point them where to fight."

Fitzgerald looked around the table. "Any objections to a hostage rescue?"

No one dissented.

To Ratliff and Brenham, the President said, "Very well, let's get this right. Operation Bold Fortress is a go. Godspeed, you two … and Maxine, I want updates."

"Yes, sir. Thank you, sir." Ratliff clicked the button to leave the meeting.

As soon as the screen went blank, Brenham breathed a sigh of relief. "That went better than expected."

"We're not out of this yet," Ratliff cautioned as she dialed the number to Lima station from memory. "Now all of our necks depend on the success of this mission."

The phone rang twice before being picked up by an automated security system. Three beeps followed. Ratliff said her first and last name, waited for three more beeps, then entered a six-digit authenticator on the keypad.

"Secure," an automated voice stated, confirming the line was encrypted. The call then rang through to the CIA station chief in Lima, Peru.

A man answered right away as if he had been sitting by his phone, anxiously awaiting her call. "Wiggins."

Ratliff recognized his voice. "Paul, it's Maxine."

"Yes, ma'am. How'd it go?"

"Bold Fortress is a go for tonight, oh-three hundred hours," she replied.

"Jesus, that was fast." Wiggins sounded surprised, but it was a testament to his new boss/longtime colleague's persuasiveness.

"Yeah, if anything, this President is decisive."

Lima Station Chief, Paul Wiggins, had been monitoring Dr. Landry's presence at Mathias's facility since assuming this role from none other than his predecessor, Maxine Ratliff. Since her departure to take over as the agency's director, Wiggins had been working with his new asset, Eduardo Salazar, to gather HUMINT (human intelligence) inside the facility. Their efforts had paid off with the astonishing photo of Luna, standing alongside Mathias and Dr. Landry. Then came recent confirmation of Choi Min-jun's capture less than twenty-four hours ago.

The level of trust between Wiggins and Ratliff was evident in his ability to keep all of this information absolutely confidential while Maxine approached the President. Both were old-school operators, driven by the mission instead of career ladders. He did not debate who was responsible for the mistake of sending Min-jun on an unsanctioned recon op, and he did not question Ratliff's decision to protect Jessica Aguri.

For her part, Ratliff had full confidence in Wiggins' ability to carry out the snatch and grab operation. Hostage rescues were nothing new in Latin America, and he had extensive experience in such matters as a former SAD operator back in the day, albeit never with the stakes this high. Wiggins also knew Mathias's facility inside and out, so he was the logical choice.

"How fast can you get to Satipo?" Ratliff asked.

Wiggins thought for a second. "One hour, maybe less depending on wind direction."

"Then you'd better get moving," Ratliff said. "JSOC has the mission units inbound. You'll be their eyes and ears on the ground, designated call-sign, Zephyr. The ground team will be designated call-sign, Condor. Overwatch is Bishop."

"Condor and Bishop," Wiggins repeated, jotting it down on a notepad. "I'll call you as soon as we're clear."

"Thanks, Paul. Good hunting."

46

EXONERATION

Planet Aiwa
Supra, Realm of Eos

Answering his summons to appear before the High Court, Kypa rode a hover chair through the palace corridors to the Grand Hall. Now wearing his customary golden robe, the prince was still weak from exhaustion and injuries from the explosion. His mother, Queen Qora, and his mate, Maya, both walked beside him as people stopped to stare. Their protection detail included two Royal Guards—one in front and one bringing up the rear—who cut through the crowd to ensure they arrived without delay.

Qora could not fault the crowd's curiosity. News of King Loka's passing had sent shockwaves throughout the Five Realms. All of Aiwa shared in their mourning and offered condolences to the royal family. Truly touched by the outpouring of support, the queen acknowledged each and every one of their kind gestures. Dealing with the rumor mongers, however, was another matter.

On a normal day, Qora was impervious to such childish behavior, but today, she was in no mood to tolerate the few passersby who cast suspicious glances in their direction and whispered falsehoods. She snuffed out their mutterings with a reproachful glare.

Maya chose to keep to herself, although the deep look of concern on her face betrayed her thoughts. She was worried for her husband, and the mystery behind this summons had her future-tripping on matters out of her control.

Meanwhile, Kypa channeled his focus on the unsavory task ahead. Being summoned by his younger sister, Princess Seva, was unexpected. Although, on further reflection, it made perfect sense. In the absence of both him and the king, the role of Warden of Eos fell onto her. It was the timing that concerned Kypa. With this summons occurring right on the heels of their father's death, it raised several red flags. First and foremost was Kypa's fear that someone was pulling his sister's strings.

We shall find out soon enough, he thought, fighting back a bout of lingering nausea.

They rounded a corner to find a large crowd had gathered in front of the Grand Hall.

"Hold up," Kypa ordered the guards.

He turned to Maya in a panic. "Where are Neil and Ava?"

With all that had happened, he had completely forgotten about his human friends.

Maya crouched to eye-level. Cradling Kypa's hand, she said with a heavy heart, "They are missing. During the attack, Seva helped them escape to the surface. No one has seen or heard from them since."

"No ..." Kypa muttered. He knew the dangers they would encounter alone in the wild, with no means to protect themselves. "We must find them," he urged.

"Not to worry," his mother quelled. "Boa sent search teams to bring them back."

"Boa?" Kypa's brow furrowed in suspicion. This played right into the commodore's hands. "And what of the Reaper?"

"It is in lockdown," Qora answered, sounding surprised. "No one is allowed near the ship."

Kypa darted his eyes about, processing this news.

At least the Reaper has not fallen into enemy hands, he mused.

It made sense Boa would not want to let the ship out of his sight, but Kypa needed Reggie's help to find his friends.

"Step aside," Kypa ordered the guard leading their procession.

The guard obeyed, and Kypa accelerated forward in his hover chair. He made a beeline to the nearby entrance to the Grand Hall, with Maya, Qora, and the guards nearly jogging to keep up. They made their way through the crowd and approached a pair of sentries posted outside the Grand Hall. They crisscrossed their energy pikes to block entry.

"Well, are you going to allow us in?" Queen Qora snapped.

"Apologies, My Queen," one sentry replied, bowing. "By order of the High Court, only Prince Kypa may enter."

Qora scoffed.

Before she could rebuke the sentry, Kypa raised his hand to quell her protest.

"It is all right, Mother," he assured her. "I will handle this."

Kypa rose slowly from his chair. Fearing he might lose his balance, Maya stood poised to catch him should he fall. Kypa steadied himself, then straightened his robe in a courtly manner.

He turned to his mate. "How do I look?"

"Like your father's son," Maya affirmed with a proud smile. "Now show them you are the rightful heir to the throne."

Turning to his mother, Kypa gave her an assuring nod. He then approached the guards. "I am ready."

Retracting their pikes, the sentries opened the doors. Kypa entered alone.

Inside, he paused in the hall's narthex, waiting for the doors to close behind him. Once they shut, the cavernous room was filled with an ominous silence, save for the calming sound of water flowing from the mouth of Gwaru's statue in the distance.

Kypa swept his gaze around the Grand Hall, contemplating it in a new light. Then he drifted his eyes to the pavilion where the members of the High Court were already gathered, each seated around opposing, crescent-shaped tables. Not surprisingly, they were joined by Commodore Boa, who stood with his hands clasped behind his back.

Looking past the court members, Kypa eyed King Loka's vacant throne. His father's last words echoed in his mind: *Make it right, Kypa.*

At the sound of the prince's arrival, all eyes turned toward the entrance.

Kypa inhaled deeply to calm his nerves, let it out slowly, and then whispered, "Give me the strength, Father."

Holding his chin high, Kypa strode confidently up the black marble walkway between the two identical pools of water. As he approached the pavilion, Kypa studied each court member to gauge their moods, particularly Lord Zefra, Warden of Fonn. Her peers from the realms of Dohrm and Maeve kept their usual, unreadable expressions, but neither of them had recently lost a son in the attack. The sting of losing King Loka and Commander Rega on the same day remained fresh, and Prince Kypa—current criminal charges notwithstanding—served as a painful reminder of those losses. He wondered

444 | TODD HOSEA

how impartial Lord Zefra could be in the matter of judging his fate.

Kypa then turned his attention to his sister, Princess Seva. For a moment, Kypa's eyes deceived him. He felt he was looking at his mother. Sitting straight-backed beside Lord Wahla of Dohrm, Seva looked as if she had matured ten rotations overnight. Her regal posture and stately demeanor would make their mother proud.

Seva met her brother's gaze with reservation, although an ever-so-faint smile creased her mouth to show she was happy to see him. Kypa thought to reach out to his sister telepathically but resisted the urge. Such a gesture by someone awaiting judgment was forbidden and could put Seva in a dangerous position, if discovered. For such a tenuous proceeding, with the eyes of the Five Realms watching, any inkling of bias favoring her brother could trigger riots and possibly civil war.

Kypa was well aware of this and only made a passing glance in Seva's direction before stopping short of the pavilion.

"Greetings, members of the High Court," he said, recognizing the group with a courteous head bow. "It is good to be with you once again."

Each member nodded in return.

Kypa then turned to his accuser, Commodore Boa, and acknowledged him respectfully. Boa responded in kind, offering an empathetic bow for Kypa's recent loss instead of his usual scowl.

As Kypa shifted to face the court, Lord Zefra's eyes narrowed, and her mouth pursed as she considered the defendant's haggard appearance. "Prince Kypa, are you fit to stand before this court?"

Kypa smiled tiredly. "I am, Lord Zefra. Thank you. And before we proceed, please accept my sincere condolences on the loss of your son. Commander Rega died courageously. He sacrificed himself to save me and my father."

All eyes turned to Lord Zefra.

Suppressing her pain, she considered Kypa's words and nodded appreciatively.

"This court has convened at Commodore Boa's request," Lord Wahla continued. "Charges are still pending against you, Prince Kypa, for the theft of Aiwan resources and unlawful departure from the planet, which resulted in the deaths of your crew."

Kypa swallowed hard.

"Furthermore, Commodore Boa has been tasked with investigating the attack on the royal family. In light of this, he has petitioned the court to allow him direct access to your mind."

Stunned by this unprecedented move, Kypa nearly lost his composure. "I must protest," he rebutted. "Is my verbal testimony not enough?"

"Normally, yes," Wahla answered truthfully, "but as you well know, regicide is a very serious charge, even more so considering the fact our late king was your father. For the sake of time and public order, it is imperative that we resolve this matter expediently and impartially. Would you agree?"

Kypa hesitated. Considering his current physical state, he feared not having the endurance to maintain his mental focus during the procedure. Without being able to compartmentalize his mind, Kypa risked giving Boa free reign to all of his thoughts or, worse, being susceptible to implanted ideas.

An open book, as Dr. Garrett would say.

But Lord Wahla had a point; the political fallout from this trial could have far-reaching implications. Kypa's cooperation benefited Aiwa as a whole more than himself. Besides, there was one advantage to granting Boa access to his memories: he could see the truth firsthand. Kypa's memories provided him with the perfect alibi.

"You have my consent," Kypa stated.

"Then it is decided," Wahla replied. "Commodore Boa, you may proceed."

Boa stepped toward Kypa. Facing one another, their eyes met in a long-awaited showdown. Kypa steeled himself, mentally preparing for the fight ahead. Yet, he did not see resentment in Boa's grayish-blue eyes. Kypa sensed conflict within the aging commander.

Dropping his gaze, Boa paused for a moment, thinking. He then turned to address the court.

"Members of the High Court, before I begin, it is my duty to report that, before the attack on the royal family, my staff personally inspected Prince Kypa's work reconstructing Cirros. Their findings were later confirmed by data recorders recovered at the crime scene following the explosion. The evidence is clear that the Reaper performed exactly how Prince Kypa predicted. He fulfilled the obligations set forth by this court, and I humbly request that the previous charges of theft and unlawful travel be dropped."

Shocked by this bombshell admission, Lord Wahla asked, "You are sure of this?"

"I am, your grace," Boa replied. "I consider these charges separate from my investigation into the assassination of King Loka."

Lord Wahla looked at his colleagues. No one objected to Boa's remarks or saw the need to debate the matter further. "Very well, Commodore Boa. We shall take your findings under advisement. Do you wish to proceed?"

"I do," Boa replied.

Wahla gestured toward Kypa. "You may begin."

Boa turned to Kypa. "Relax your defenses and allow our minds to join."

Kypa inhaled deeply then let it out slowly as he closed his eyes. Relaxing his shoulders, Kypa held out his hands and began taking short, controlled breaths to slow his heartbeat.

Boa took Kypa's hands and mirrored his meditative state. Their telepathic connection was immediate.

Flashes of Kypa's memories raced in front of Boa faster than a hyperspace tunnel. From the prince's childhood recollections with family and classmates to recent encounters aboard the ill-fated mothership, Boa sifted through the influx of images and conversations seeking evidence pertaining to the assassination of King Loka.

One astonishing revelation came when Boa glimpsed Kypa trying to escape Area S4 on Earth and being forced to take control of four human minds, including Garza and Sizemore. Boa did not know either man, but judging from Garza's military uniform, this added credence to Kypa's earlier testimony that a certain few on Earth wanted to keep the Reaper for themselves.

Moving on, Boa's continued attempts to pierce the protected segments of Kypa's psyche were skillfully parried by the prince. Kypa had no intention of revealing his most-prized secrets, especially anything to compromise the Reaper. But his strength was waning, and Boa could sense it.

As the court members watched in silence, they witnessed the exchange between Kypa and Boa intensify. With tense brows and rapid eye movements under their lids, the opponents battled with dogged determination in a game of cat and mouse.

Finally, after many dead ends, Boa discovered a memory of Kypa and his father together aboard his yacht prior to inspecting the terraforming site in Cirros.

"I know the reconstruction work you have completed has far-exceeded all expectations, Loka said proudly to Kypa. *The technology you have developed with this Reaper vessel will save our planet. You are to be commended for your service, not condemned. What happened to Cirros was not your fault. It was the result of my own stubbornness. You risked everything, including your life, to make things right. You do not deserve to be treated the way you have, not by me, Boa, or anyone else."*

This affirmed the king's decision to exonerate his son of all charges.

Next, Kypa revealed the moment when Major Gora betrayed them inside the harvesting tunnel. Starting with the shooting of Commander Rega, Boa watched Gora recite his shocking manifesto.

"No," Boa muttered loud enough for the court members to hear.

Boa experienced the memory as if it were his own. He felt the chaos that ensued as Commander Rega fought with his last ounce of life to try to stop Gora, buying time for Loka to save Kypa. An explosion had followed, and Boa rocked on his heels as father and son were blown down the shaft by the shockwave, cart-wheeling out of control. Then Kypa's memory faded to black as he was rendered unconscious.

The last memory shared was that of King Loka's final moments, cradled in his son's arms.

"Make it right, Kypa ... for Cirros ... for Aiwa."

With those dying words, Loka slowly closed his eyes for the last time. A wave of loss and grief washed over Boa as he witnessed the memory. A single tear slid down his cheek.

This proved beyond a shadow of a doubt that Kypa was just as much a victim as his father. And for all of the years he had blamed Kypa for Aiwa's problems, Boa finally accepted the prince's innocence for what had happened to Cirros.

Boa slowly opened his eyes. He removed his hands from Kypa's and brushed the tear from his cheek.

Standing opposite Boa, Kypa opened his eyes at the same time. They exchanged a look of mutual understanding; their tenuous past was behind them now. Kypa smiled thinly, and then his legs faltered, but he caught himself.

Stepping back, Kypa wiped his nose. Seeing dark green blood smeared on the back of his hand, he looked to Boa, confused. Then his eyes rolled back, and he collapsed.

Lord Zefra and Princess Seva gasped as Boa reached out and caught Kypa before he hit the black marble floor.

Laying Kypa gently on his back, Boa called out, "Send for a medic! Our Prince needs help!"

47

RUN TO GROUND

Planet Aiwa

Ava finally had to stop running long enough to catch her breath. Planting her hands on her hips, she paced in a tight circle, breathing hard and stretching the nagging stitch in her side. All the while, she kept her eyes and ears open for not just the insectoid hunter on her tail, but every other predator in the jungle wanting to make a meal of her.

"Man, I'd kill for a smoothie," she said between breaths, wiping the chronic sweat from her brow.

With the heat from Aiwa's twin suns beating down, and the jungle's high humidity, Ava found the surface conditions downright unbearable. Even with her nano-suit working overtime to keep her hydrated, being unable to use her helmet made breathing the thick air difficult. The stifling conditions also forced her to take frequent breaks, sweating buckets at each stop. The temptation to activate her helmet was torture. One quick blast of A/C, even for just a few seconds, would be exhilarating. But Ava knew better. She could not risk giving away her position.

On the bright side, one unintended benefit of all this open-air-running was sweating off a nagging caffeine headache, which had lingered all day. Skipping coffee came with a price, but now that the withdrawal effects had passed, Ava realized she had missed more than just sipping her morning brew in the Reaper's cockpit.

She thought of her ship and her friends. Not knowing their status made staying off the grid even more frustrating.

As her breathing normalized, Ava knew she would not find any answers standing here. Before setting off once again, she noticed a fallen tree branch at her feet. Intrigued, Ava picked it up. The stick was as tall as her and solid, no signs of decay.

She eyed it up and down then started picking off sprouting twigs and leaves to make the stick relatively smooth from top to bottom. It would do little to protect her against a blaster or large predator, but having something in her hands gave her some semblance of security. It also reminded her of home.

Growing up, Ava and her friends used to play in the woods from sunup to sundown during summer vacation. It was the best time of her life, and the first order of business had always been to find a good stick. Such a treasure could entertain for hours.

This stick certainly had potential. Ava weighed it in her hands, admiring the balance. It felt just right. She tested its sturdiness as a trekking pole and smiled with satisfaction.

Setting out once again for the coastal waterfalls, she hoped to find Neil there, waiting for her. Ava knew the odds were slim. The last thing she remembered was her friend being dragged away, his panicked call for help echoing in her ears.

Still, she held out hope that Neil was alive. The same went for Kypa. Her efforts to reach him had gone unanswered, which made sense for a number of reasons, especially in the aftermath of a coup d'état. Bottom line: Ava refused to believe she had lost both members of her crew in less than two days. Until their status could be verified, she considered them missing in action—assumed alive without comms. Her most pressing dilemma was when to try again to reestablish contact.

Ava could only assume that whoever controlled the capital was also keeping her ship grounded, but this did not explain why the Aiwans were not pursuing her. Since their encounter with the Seeker on the beach, there had been no sign of a rescue party. Heck, even Boa would be a welcome sight at this point.

Ava found their absence troubling. She had expected teams of ground troops and scout ships to be combing the area until she and Neil were found. Yet, since the beach, the Aiwans had seemingly disappeared.

Were they called off? she wondered.

That would explain the mystery hunter, who was clearly not Aiwan. Ava suspected he had to be a hired gun brought in from off-world. Kypa had once said that no other civilized races lived on land due to the hostile environment—she now understood why—but maybe he was mistaken.

Assuming her instincts were right, Ava wondered who was behind all this. Carrying out the assassination of King Loka was a gutsy move that required impeccable timing. Only someone with internal knowledge of the king's schedule, and who had a plan ready to act on a moment's notice, could have pulled off such a feat.

"There can't be too many people who fit that description," Ava thought aloud as she trekked onward through the high grass.

Was separating me from the Reaper also part of that plan?

The hunter had appeared shortly after she and Neil had arrived at the beach. That could not be a coincidence. So, either one of King Loka's Aiwan rivals had led the coup and now sought the Reaper, or an outsider had orchestrated the attack—Grawn Krunig, perhaps—using someone on the inside.

A traitor, Ava mused. *But who?*

Being a stranger in a strange land had a distinct disadvantage. Ignorant to Aiwa's political establishment, Ava had no clue who had alliances with whom, or who could be remotely capable of carrying out high treason. All she knew for certain was that she had to do something. Being on the sidelines had gotten her nowhere. It was time to go on the offensive.

Just then, a distant roar shook Ava back to reality. Her skin pebbled with goosebumps, prompting her to pick up the pace.

She settled into a light jog, even more eager to reach the sanctity of the waterfalls. Her objective was close. With any luck, the insectoid hunter had been unable to pick up her trail again and she could soon find a safe place to take refuge for a while.

An hour passed before Ava slowed once again to a fast walk. Given her profuse sweat loss from the neck up, she found her nano-suit simply could not keep her hydrated. The cramps persisted, and her legs had grown heavy and weak.

Losing focus, Ava tripped over a tree root and nearly did a face-plant. Stumbling forward, she caught herself in the nick of time.

"Come on, Suntan," she chided herself. "Pick up your feet."

Adding insult to injury, Ava's headache had also returned. Every step seemed to reverberate up her spine and pound her skull. She licked her pasty lips and tried to blink the burning sweat out of her eyes. Recognizing the signs of severe dehydration, Ava knew that, unless she found a freshwater source soon, she risked collapsing on the jungle floor. Her only other choice was to activate her helmet so her suit could properly recycle her bodily fluids. That meant compromising her location.

Ava mustered a few more steps when a wave of lightheadedness hit. She staggered, suddenly feeling shaky and chilled. Collapsing against a nearby tree for support, she felt the ground lurch beneath her. Feeling faint, Ava knew she had reached her limit.

"Screw it," she said defiantly, figuring if the jungle or the hunter were going to kill her, then at least she could face it with a clear head.

Ava reached for the nano-ring around her neck to activate her helmet but stopped short as a distant rumble caught her attention. Holding her breath, she listened intently.

A thin smile creased her face. This California girl recognized the unmistakable sound of water pounding against rock a mile away.

With a surge of adrenaline, Ava pushed herself off the tree and trudged through the jungle as the waterfall called to her.

The thundering sound grew louder with each step until Ava emerged from the wilderness and stepped onto an empty, white-sand beach. Fighting back tears of relief, Ava drank in the sight of the blue ocean stretching to the horizon on her right. Aiwa's twin suns glistened off the pristine water. Directly ahead was an arched, rocky alcove. She felt certain the waterfall was on the opposite side.

Ava bent over, supporting herself with her hands on her knees, and took a moment to catch her breath before setting off again.

As she ventured up the beach, the low tide fizzed under her feet as she splashed through puddles. She soon passed through the cool shadows of the stone archway. It felt invigorating. Rounding a bend, Ava found the towering waterfall where a fast-moving river spilled over a high cliff and dropped some three hundred feet through a veil of mist at the base of the mountain. The waterfall drained into a large pool with tributaries that fed into the ocean.

Ava tilted her head back, feeling the refreshing mist on her face. "Hallelujah," she said wearily.

Despite her insatiable craving for the freshwater, Ava's body was not cooperating. Slow and steady, she used her trusty walking stick to balance herself as she approached the large plunge pool at the base of the waterfall. When she got there, Ava set down her stick and climbed carefully on all fours onto a flat rock near the water's edge.

At this point, she had no choice but to activate her helmet. Throwing caution to the wind, Ava tapped the nano-ring to bring it to life. The hologram enveloped her head, and a blast of cool air washed over her like a walk-in freezer.

Ava sighed luxuriously. "That's what I'm talking about."

Her suit immediately went to work capturing Ava's perspiration and recycling it. Beads of sweat from her clammy skin and saturated hair suddenly evaporated. Within seconds, Ava started to feel herself again, but not fast enough.

"Computer, analyze this water source. Is it safe to drink?"

"Affirmative," came the even reply.

Ava did not have to be told twice. She deactivated her helmet, but as she reached down to cup the water in her hands, she pulled back sharply. At the last second, it dawned on her there was no telling what dangers might be lurking beneath the surface if she disturbed the water.

"Dammit," she cursed, having to delay gratification a little while longer. Activating her helmet once again, she asked testily, "Computer, scan for threats under the water."

There were none.

Removing her helmet once again, Ava splashed her face and slurped handfuls of the purest water she had ever tasted. It felt so refreshing that she laughed. Ava doused herself for several minutes, careful not to drink too much, too fast.

Once she had her fill, Ava activated her helmet once more. Another welcome blast of A/C felt energizing. Getting to her feet, she surveyed her surroundings. There was no sign of Neil.

"Computer, locate Dr. Garrett," she asked.

"Scans negative," came the reply.

Ava frowned crookedly. After several attempts to reach her friends on the commlink, she gave up in frustration.

Deactivating her helmet for now, Ava resisted the urge to call out to Neil verbally. No sense ringing the dinner bell. She was exposed here, out in the open, and decided it was time to find shelter.

Her best option was the spot she and Neil had chosen earlier—a cave nestled halfway up the cliff face, hidden behind the waterfall. She quickly mapped out a route to boulder her way up the rocky slope.

The hike began with moderate difficulty but became gradually more treacherous. She had to abandon her stick as the rocks closer to the waterfall were covered with a slimy film that made it nearly impossible to traverse. Ava measured each movement carefully, methodically climbing higher while staving off the fear of falling.

Don't look down, she repeated in her head.

Ava soon reached an outcropping and discovered a narrow path leading behind the waterfall to the cave entrance. With the rush of falling water to her right, Ava put her back against the mountainside. From this perch, she could see for miles around, but dared not to steal a glance down the thirty-story drop.

Keeping her back tight against the wall, Ava carefully side-stepped to her left. Using her hand to feel her way forward, she reached a small opening carved into the mountain.

Standing at the cave entrance, Ava cautiously peered inside. The karst cave had a dome ceiling and was about twice the size of Kypa's old quarters back at Groom Lake. Thanks to a small opening in the ceiling, there was enough natural sunlight to show the cave was empty.

Her shoulders dropped. "Dammit, Neil, where are you?"

Venturing inside, Ava was hit by a powerful, musty-smelling odor. Crinkling her nose, she looked up at the moss-covered stalagmites hanging from the ceiling. They were the largest she had ever seen. Recalling her junior high Earth Science class, Ava estimated the cone-shaped columns must have taken hundreds of thousands of years to form, if not longer.

Walking the perimeter, Ava scanned for animal droppings, leftover carcasses, and other signs of occupancy. Ava hated bats, especially, so it came as a welcome relief to find none. As she circled back to the entrance, Ava felt confident in her choice of spots. Now the question was whether or not to risk contacting her friends again.

The rumble in her stomach decided for her. Save for some berries she and Neil had foraged that morning, Ava had not eaten anything substantial in over a day. There was still plenty of daylight out but venturing back into the jungle was not worth a handful of berries. Recalling her SERE training, she knew grass was an edible source of Vitamin C and some insects had more protein than a T-bone steak. The vegetation growing along the cliffside probably had both. With no other options, Ava decided it was better than nothing.

She took one step toward the mouth of the cave and froze in terror. Smythe blocked the exit.

Recognizing the insectoid hunter, she shrieked instinctively and retreated two steps backward. With the echo of her scream reverberating in the cave, Ava's fight or flight instinct kicked in. Abandoning caution, she charged the bounty hunter in an attempt to force her way past.

Smythe proved too powerful for the five-foot-nothing human. He grabbed Ava by the neck in a chokehold and lifted her off the ground. Gasping, Ava kicked wildly and tried to pry herself free of the bounty hunter's death grip. She had no effect.

Ava's feeble struggle was nothing more than an annoyance, but Smythe admired her spunk. This marker had proven more elusive than most, which was a nice change of pace. However, business was business, and Smythe was ready to conclude his affairs and get off this rock.

With her face starting to turn blue, Ava's fight began to leave her. Smythe lifted her higher, eyeing her face from different angles, then spotted the nano-ring around her neck. Recalling instructions from his contact on how to deactivate the device, the bounty hunter tapped in a sequence on the ring near Ava's clavicle. The nano-ring beeped three times then detached from the rest of her suit.

Smythe released his grip, and Ava fell to the ground, clutching her throat for air.

The bounty hunter leaned down and lifted the ring over her head then placed it inside a pocket in his cowl.

"What do you want?" Ava coughed out, rubbing her neck.

The bounty hunter did not understand what she had said, nor did he care. Smythe kept his weapon trained on Ava as he stepped back toward the cave entrance. He activated his commlink.

"Gort, it's me."

"I'm here, boss," Gort replied.

"I've got the female. Get ready to move," Smythe instructed. "On my signal, meet me at these coordinates."

"Affirmative," his trusty partner replied, equally relieved this job was coming to an end.

"Bounce my transmission through to Krunig," Smythe added.

"Sure thing. Stand by."

Ava listened to their interaction but, without her nano-ring, it all sounded like alien gibberish, punctuated by random clicks and grunts.

Keeping a wary eye on his prisoner, Smythe's transmission was boosted and encrypted by Gort through their ship's comm system.

Grawn Krunig answered immediately. "Do you have her?" he asked, the hope in his voice undeniable.

"I do. She's right here," Smythe affirmed. He eyed Ava, still wondering what was so important about this creature and her mystery ship. "Now it's up to you."

"Perfect. Standby to take possession of the Reaper."

"And Prince Kypa?"

"Same as before … kill him on sight."

48

NIGHT STALKERS

Planet Earth
USS *George Washington*
210 miles off the coast of Peru

A night landing aboard an aircraft carrier is the very definition of insanity. Unlike commercial aircraft pilots, who have the luxury of landing on a stationary airstrip about ten thousand feet in length, aircraft carrier pilots are required to perform what amounts to a controlled crash on a moving postage stamp in the middle of blackness. To help guide them safely on deck was the responsibility of the ship's Landing Signal Officers.

Tonight, standing on the flight deck of the USS *George Washington*, a team of three LSO's watched with cold authority as a Grumman C-2 twin-engine, cargo aircraft made its final approach. They were stationed at the LSO Platform located on the port side of the Nimitz-class, nuclear-powered aircraft carrier. Situated behind a wind deflector, the LSO's evaluated the aircraft's centerline and angle of approach. Any deviations were immediately radioed to the pilot and assigned a point value for later evaluation of the pilot's performance.

With the C-2 now "in the groove," meaning it was less than twenty seconds from touchdown, the Controlling LSO keyed the mic on her large, noise-canceling headphones.

"You're at three-quarters of a mile, Starman. Call the ball."

"Starman-221, Greyhound ball, five-point-seven," the pilot replied over the radio.

The Controlling LSO translated the pilot's response. Starman-221 identified the pilot's call-sign and the number on the side of the aircraft. Greyhound referred to the type of aircraft being flown. Calling "ball"—short for "meatball"—was the pilot's way of confirming he sighted the round, orange light on the flight deck's Fresnel Lens Optical Landing System. It was the pilot's responsibility to note the orange ball's relation to the green horizontal datum lights, which indicated if the pilot was high, low, or on the correct angle of approach. Last in the pilot's response was his fuel status—the number of remaining gallons.

Noting this information, and satisfied no deviations needed correction, the Controlling LSO clicked the handheld switch box in her hand. "Roger Ball," she replied, meaning the aircraft was cleared to land.

Twenty seconds later, the Grumman C-2 touched down on the flight deck. Its tailhook snagged the arresting wire system successfully, bringing the aircraft to an abrupt halt. In the back of the plane, the four members of SEAL Team Four let out a collective sigh of relief.

As flight deck personnel pulled the aircraft out of the landing strip and chocked it down on the flight deck, the SEAL team began gathering their gear to exit the plane. Dressed in civvies, each of the frogmen was anxious to breathe fresh air. Their long hop had originated at Joint Expeditionary Base Little Creek-Fort Story, a Naval site located on Virginia's Atlantic shore. Twelve hours and two mid-air refuelings later, their long, loud, and bumpy ride had finally concluded.

First to exit the aircraft was the fire team's leader, Lieutenant Commander Micah Diamond. A seasoned veteran with combat experience in several theaters around the world, he was into his second year as SEAL Team Four's leader.

Second out the door was Master Chief Petty Officer Ortiz. As the highest-ranking enlisted member on the team, Ortiz served as Commander Diamond's chief advisor. Behind him were Petty Officers Stringer and Croll. The latter, being the last man out, began tossing the team's gear out the aircraft's side door and into the waiting arms of the master chief.

Meanwhile, a flight deck officer leaned into a strong crosswind as he approached the aircraft. He located Commander Diamond and popped a crisp salute. Since it was pointless to try to talk over the noise on the flight deck, he pointed to a side door leading inside the *G-Dub's* conning tower. Standing by the door was Navy Lieutenant Harmon, a junior intelligence officer dressed in the traditional brown daily service uniform. Seeing the deck officer point in his direction, Harmon waved the SEAL team over.

Commander Diamond nodded, shaking the deck officer's hand, then hoisted his assigned gear and signaled the others to follow. Lieutenant Harmon then greeted them at the door and led the team below deck. With the booming sound of afterburners reverberating through the ship's hull as air operations resumed, the SEAL team snaked their way through the carrier's lower levels until arriving at a small briefing room.

Inside the room were six members of the United States Army's 160th Special Operations Aviation Regiment. Four members of this group were the pilots, each wearing the rank of Warrant Officer. For Operation Bold Fortress, they were tasked with flying the MH-60M helicopters carrying Diamond's team, along with two Army door gunners.

As soon as Diamond entered, the SOAR team jumped to their feet and called the room to attention.

"Ten-hut!" Warrant Officer Brewster announced.

Diamond immediately recognized him and the other pilots from previous missions. "As you were. Good to see some familiar faces." He extended a hearty handshake to Brewster.

Brewster accepted. "Hey, we fly, you buy. Right, sir?"

Diamond chuckled. "You rotorheads are drinking away my retirement savings."

Brewster feigned innocence and quickly changed the subject. "Sir, you know the usual suspects: Hernandez, Bellamy, and Jones," he said, pointing to the other pilots. "Rogers and Siskel here will be manning the door guns."

More introductions and handshakes were exchanged as the remaining members of the SEAL team entered.

After a brief bout of ribbing between service branches, Diamond had the group take their seats in folding chairs around a cramped, rectangular table bolted to the floor. Lieutenant Harmon took his cue to leave so the classified briefing could begin.

"What do you know of Operation Bold Fortress?" Diamond asked as soon as Harmon closed the door behind him.

As the senior-ranking officer, Brewster replied, "Pretty straight forward, sir. A hostage rescue in the town of Satipo, Peru. It's an unauthorized incursion, so we need to fly below radar. Once the snatch and grab is complete, we exit through Bolivia and return to the ole flattop. Easy-peasy."

"Aren't they all?" Chief Ortiz muttered with his trademark sarcasm.

His remark garnered a few chuckles from the group, including Diamond. Nothing was easy when it came to special operations, and this group was too experienced and too good at their chosen profession to believe otherwise. Hence Commander Diamond's operating philosophy: *Plans are useless, but planning is indispensable.*

"All right, let's go over the mission brief," Diamond began as he retrieved a file folder from his backpack. He checked his wristwatch against the clock on the wall. "It's twenty-one thirty right now. Mission go is zero three hundred. Where are we at with the choppers?"

"Fueled and prepped, sir," Brewster answered. "Me and Hernandez will fly the first bird. We'll be designated call sign, Condor, with Rogers in back as the door gunner. We'll be the ones putting down on deck, so whoever's grabbing the hostages will need to go with us."

Diamond nodded.

Brewster then pointed to Bellamy, Jones, and Siskel. "You three will fly overwatch. Call sign, Bishop. Got it?"

"Yes, sir," they confirmed in unison.

Commander Diamond made quick notes in his file then turned to his SEAL team. "We'll go in with Condor to grab the hostages. Stringer, you'll help Dr. Landry onboard, and I'll provide cover."

Stringer nodded.

To Ortiz, Diamond added, "You and Croll will assist Mr. Choi."

Both gave curt nods with no questions.

"Keep in mind," Diamond continued, "we're also picking up two additional ground assets, so it's going to be tight onboard."

Next, he unfolded a large satellite photo onto the table. Everyone leaned in close.

"All right, let's go through this," Diamond said, surveying the layout. "Our CIA contact on the ground—call sign, Zephyr—has two assets working inside the compound. The first asset is male. He goes by the name Lalo. Lalo's responsible for creating a distraction inside this mechanical room on the east side of the facility." Diamond tapped his finger at the exact location on the photo. To the pilots, he made a sweeping gesture with his hand from the bottom of the photo upward. "We'll approach from the south. Condor will set down in this field here."

The Army pilots scrutinized the plan. Three concerns weighed on their mind: physical hazards, downwash, and weight. Searching the photo, they saw no signs of power lines, telephone poles, or obstructions, like trees, that would hinder their approach, landing, and takeoff.

Also on their mind was a vertical flight phenomenon known as "settling with power." Believed to be the cause of the SOAR helicopter crash that occurred during the Osama bin Laden raid, "settling with power" occurs when a helicopter descends too quickly and is unable to settle to the ground properly. The rapid descent is caused when the chopper's rotors cannot get enough lift due to the turbulent air created by its own downwash. Landing in an open field would help decrease this risk.

Overall, their chief concern was weight. In the bin Laden raid, the helicopter that crashed was a radar-evading variant of the MH-60 Black Hawk—similar to the current "Mike" variant of the Black Hawk to be used on this mission. The problem with adding stealth characteristics to a helicopter is that it made the aircraft considerably heavier. In fact, the bin Laden chopper that crashed had flown at its maximum gross weight. Coupled with the "settling with power" issue, hindsight proved these two factors created the perfect storm that caused the crash.

Brewster grimaced inwardly. His chopper would be facing similar conditions when fully loaded, carrying eleven people. He looked forward to flying the Bell V-280 *Valor*, the next generation of long-range assault aircraft to replace the aging Black Hawks. The V-280 promised highly responsive maneuverability, enhanced low-speed and off-axis hover capabilities, and level acceleration and braking. It was every attack recon aviator's dream, but until the Black Hawk's replacement went into service, there was no sense dreaming about what could be. The SOAR team had to make do with the tools at their disposal.

"As soon as the fire alarm goes off," Diamond continued, "Lalo will grab Mr. Choi. Meanwhile, a second asset, Camila, will pull Dr. Landry from her bedroom. Lalo and Camila will then lead the hostages out this emergency exit door on the south side of the perimeter wall … right to us."

"Like I said, easy-peasy," Brewster quipped.

Diamond raised a skeptical eyebrow. "Let's hope you're right."

"What do they have in the way of firepower?" Petty Officer Stringer asked.

"Intel says about half the hired security personnel on site recently pulled out. Those remaining, or at least a good number of them, will have to help fight the fire in the mechanical room. That'll thin their ranks and hopefully divert their attention away from us," Diamond said with optimism. "But, to answer your question, there's nothing in the file to suggest they have weaponry heavier than standard machine guns and small arms." Even as he said it, Diamond questioned the accuracy of the intel. "Take that for what it's worth. All I know is that this guy Mathias has money to burn. He takes his security seriously, so you can bet his people will come to the party, ready to dance."

"Timing and speed are critical," Ortiz added.

"Affirmative. We need to time this perfectly. At precisely zero three hundred, we have to be on the ground and ready to help the hostages evac."

"That means we should be airborne and enroute by zero two hundred," Brewster stated.

"Copy that."

"What about the hostages?" Ortiz asked. "What kind of condition are they in?"

Diamond flipped through his folder and found the legends for Rose and Min-jun, including recent photos, which he passed around.

"Dr. Landry is a sixty-year-old woman," Diamond read aloud. "The other hostage, Mr. Choi, is male, early forties. He's a CIA spook that went and got himself captured. Says here, he may not be in good shape, probably tortured. Be ready to carry him out, if needed."

"What about Lalo and Camila?" Croll asked.

"Unknown." Diamond shrugged. "All we have on them are photocopies of their company badges. Who knows what kind of shape they're in? So be ready for anything."

"Sir, what about the rules of engagement?" one of the Army door gunners inquired.

"Don't shoot unless fired upon," Diamond stressed. "There are civilian workers inside, so let's avoid any collateral damage. I want in and out before they know we're there."

The gunner nodded. Although, in the back of his mind, he knew getting in and out cleanly was more of an aspiration than a real possibility. Even if things went perfectly to plan, both helicopters were most vulnerable to enemy fire when Condor set down to round up the hostages. In crude ops-speak, that was when the metal meets the meat.

"Any other questions?" Diamond asked, looking around the table.

No one spoke up.

He then pulled a stack of papers from his folder and passed them out. "Okay, you know the drill. Each of you needs to sign your discharge paperwork and leave me your dog tags." Checking his watch, he added, "We've got less than five hours to wheels up. Get some rest, eat a hot meal, and unwind a bit. Meet back here at zero one hundred. SEALs, stay behind for equipment checks."

"Aye, aye," the group chorused.

Satipo, Peru

The twin-engine Beechcraft Baron G58, carrying Lima Station Chief, Paul Wiggins, touched down at the Satipo airport shortly before sundown. After taxiing to the lone terminal, the small aircraft approached the end of the building where a dust-covered, white Toyota Land Cruiser was parked. Standing in front of the SUV were two Peruvian men with AK-47s slung over their shoulders.

Wiggins peered out the windshield and eyed the armed pair warily. "That must be my ride," he muttered grimly.

Out of habit, the pilot, a Peruvian man in his mid-forties, did not respond. He recognized cartel henchmen when he saw them and wisely minded his own business.

Swinging the aircraft around in a tight circle, he pointed the Beechcraft's nose away from the building, facing the taxiway. As soon as the plane came to a stop, the pilot shut off the engines. He then climbed out of his seat and opened the fuselage's side exit door.

As the pilot went about chocking the wheels, Wiggins grabbed his backpack and exited the aircraft. He approached the gunmen with his empty hands displayed.

No words were exchanged as one of Salazar's men gestured to Wiggins' backpack.

"Por favor," the gunman said politely.

Wiggins obliged. As his bag was searched, the second gunman signaled him to turn around. Wiggins did so without complaint and was patted down.

Satisfied that the gringo was unarmed, the gunmen returned his bag with a courteous nod and opened the passenger-side rear door.

"Gracias," Wiggins said. Taking his seat, he waited as Salazar's men climbed into the vehicle; one settled in back to his left and the other behind the wheel.

As the SUV sped away, Wiggins stared out the side window in silence, contemplating the mission ahead. All things considered, he felt fairly relaxed, but the night was still young. A lot had to go right and much of it depended on Eduardo Salazar, aka Mongrel.

Over the course of Wiggins' career, he had been in some of the darkest places on Earth, surrounded by the most ruthless scum imaginable. At least in this case, he knew Salazar was desperate. He needed Wiggins' help to leave Peru and start a new life with his family in the United States. That future depended on Salazar's ability to deliver Dr. Landry and Mr. Choi.

Ten minutes later, the SUV arrived at Salazar's home. The vehicle pulled up to the front entrance where two more gunmen awaited. One approached the SUV and opened Wiggins' door.

"Sígueme," he instructed. *Follow me.*

Wiggins nodded and followed him up the front steps. Inside the lavish home, the Lima Station Chief paused in the foyer. Several suitcases and Disney-themed backpacks were stacked beside the front door. Beethoven's "Ode to Joy" played softly in the background.

Curious, Wiggins followed his escort past the main living room and down a hallway laid with polished, hardwood floors. With each step, the sound of distant voices grew louder until they arrived at a set of wooden barn-style doors. When the gunman slid the doors open, Wiggins blinked in surprise. Seated around a rectangular, solid oak dinner table was a large group of people. From the looks of it, they had finished their meal and the adults were engaged in lively discussions while several children laughed and teased one another.

For a moment, the CIA operative thought he was at the wrong house. Then he spotted Eduardo Salazar at the far end of the table. They made eye contact, and Salazar beamed at the sight of his longtime acquaintance, now CIA handler. He waved Wiggins inside like an old friend, drawing everyone's attention. The raucous activity around the table quieted to a low murmur as all eyes turned to the new arrival.

Salazar wiped his mouth with a cloth napkin and stood. He crossed the room and greeted Wiggins with a hearty handshake, followed by a hug.

"It is good to see you, my friend," Salazar said in English. "Please, join us."

Suddenly the center of attention, Wiggins stepped forward a few paces. This was his first visit to Mongrel's home, and he had never met the man's family before.

Salazar wrapped his arm around Wiggins' shoulders and presented him to the group. "Everyone, this is the man I told you about. This is our dear friend, Mr. Wiggins."

Wiggins looked to his right and spotted Hector and Marlana Nunez seated at the table. They looked relieved he had finally arrived. But before Wiggins could formally introduce himself to the Americans, Salazar's plump wife and elderly mother came to their feet and rounded the table. Both Peruvian women held their hands to their mouths, literally trembling, on the verge of tears as they approached him.

Wiggins was at a loss for words as Salazar's wife took his hands in hers.

"May the Lord bless you, Mr. Wiggins, and all of your family," she said with heartfelt gratitude. Beside her, Salazar's mother made the sign of the cross on her chest.

Before Wiggins could reply, four children joined in and wrapped their tiny arms around his legs and waist. One child, a little boy no more than five years old, smiled up at Wiggins. Missing his two front teeth, the boy declared, "¡Quiero ir a Disneylandía!"

Unable to move, Wiggins forced an uneasy smile. "You want to go to Disney, huh? Okay …"

Salazar enjoyed the moment. Then, sensing his handler's discomfort, came to Wiggins' rescue. Clapping his hands, he called out his two oldest children, "Javi, Anna, sal de aquí."

Their father's command to leave elicited a few moans and groans, but the children reluctantly obeyed once their mother and grandmother got involved. The room quieted as soon as Salazar's family departed.

At the end of the table, Hector and Marlana stood. Both had cleaned up after moving out of the hotel. They approached, and Hector extended a handshake.

"Hello, Mr. Wiggins. I'm Hector Nunez. This is my wife, Marlana."

Wiggins shook hands cordially with both. "It's nice to meet you."

Marlana made a face. "I'm almost afraid to ask, but how much trouble are we in?"

Wiggins chuckled. "As far as I know, none, but the night is still young," he said lightly.

This was welcomed news to the Nunezes.

Turning to Salazar, Wiggins said, "We have a lot to discuss."

"Sí, sí, of course," Salazar agreed, his demeanor turning businesslike. He checked his watch. "Ay, caramba! Look at the time."

With an urgency in his step, Salazar made his way down the hall and announced to his family it was time to depart for the airport. The children erupted with joy, bouncing up and down, then running to the front door to grab their belongings. Salazar's wife and mother, who moments ago had shared the children's excitement for what lay ahead, now appeared less enthusiastic. Both knew Eduardo had unfinished business with the Americans. Their trip to freedom had a price.

Salazar led both women to the front door and said his goodbyes. His men—believing the family was only leaving on vacation—assisted with the luggage.

Of course, it had to be this way to guarantee the safety of Salazar's family. The hardest part of this ruse was in knowing that, as soon as the dust settled from this evening's raid on Mathias's compound, Salazar's involvement was bound to be discovered. So, his family had to leave now. The same went for his workers, Lalo and Camila. They would depart on the choppers tonight, and when Mathias learned of their involvement, the hammer would fall on Salazar's remaining men.

It was also to be expected that the power vacuum created by Salazar's absence would invite a cartel war to seize his territory. His men would then have to pick sides, and those who chose poorly would not survive.

Salazar pushed this unpleasantness out of his mind and tried to face his men as if it was business as usual. He kissed each of his children, telling them he would see them in the morning. His wife and mother played along, carrying on as if this was all part of their agenda. The family then loaded up in an SUV and headed for the Satipo airport. There, they would take Eduardo's plane to Lima before flying commercial to the United States.

Salazar waved goodbye. As soon as the SUV was out of sight, he returned to the dining room.

"My apologies," he said, closing the double doors behind him. "Now, shall we get started?"

For the next ten minutes, Wiggins explained Operation Bold Fortress. This was the first the Nunezes had heard of the CIA's plan. They listened intently, not interrupting until Wiggins finished.

"Sounds like a plan," Hector said. "What can we do?"

Wiggins suppressed a grin, appreciating the retiree's gung-ho attitude. "You two will stay here. As soon as the hostages have been successfully extracted, Eduardo and I will come back here to pick you up. Then we'll drive to Chile. I'll explain the rest later."

Hector and Marlana exchanged looks. They did not have any say in the matter but took solace in knowing someone was looking out for Rose and Min-jun.

A polite knock on the door drew the group's attention, stifling their conversation. Acting casual, Salazar crossed the room and opened the doors. Standing in the doorway, one of his men apologized for interrupting the meeting. He then spoke softly to Salazar so his voice did not carry.

"What is Lalo doing here?" Salazar asked, perplexed.

"He has urgent news," the gunman said in Spanish. "He insisted he talk with you."

Sensing this could not be good, Salazar nodded. "Very well. Send him in," he allowed.

Once the gunman departed, Salazar shot a concerned look over his shoulder at Wiggins.

"Everything okay?"

"We'll know in a minute," Salazar replied. His voice did not sound optimistic.

Seconds later, a tall and thin Peruvian man arrived. He had long, charcoal black hair tucked under a ballcap with the Mathias Industries logo stitched on the front. As soon as Lalo came face-to-face with Salazar, he abruptly removed his ball cap and bowed his head.

"Lalo, what's wrong?" Salazar asked. "You should be getting ready for work."

Clutching his hat, Lalo's eyes darted past Salazar before he replied. Seeing the group in the background, he lowered his voice. "Sí, señor Salazar. Disculpeme." *My apologies.* Unable to look his boss in the eyes, Lalo then mustered the courage to share the bad news.

Two sentences in, Salazar snarled in frustration and raised his fists in the air. Lalo cowered.

It took Salazar a moment to compose himself. Then, with a heavy breath, he opened his hands and patted Lalo on the shoulder.

"Gracias, Lalo. You did right by coming to me," Salazar said then told him to wait outside for a moment.

Lalo bowed obediently and stepped out into the hallway.

Salazar turned to Wiggins and the Nunezes. "That was Lalo, my man inside the compound who was supposed to help us tonight."

"What do you mean, supposed to?" Marlana asked.

"He says my other worker, Camila, has the COVID. She is very ill and cannot work tonight." He sighed. "I'm sorry."

"We'll have to abort," Wiggins decided.

"Wait a second," Hector objected. "Can't you find someone else? We've still got Lalo. He can get Min-jun. All we need is someone to bring Rose out, right?"

"I'll do it," Marlana volunteered.

Hector scoffed. "I didn't mean you. Eduardo's got people." He gestured to Salazar. "Don't you?"

Salazar shook his head, frowning. "My housekeepers all work the morning shift. Camila had special permission to work a midnight shift so she could inventory supplies while everyone was gone."

"See, it has to be me," Marlana argued.

"No, I forbid it," Hector insisted. "It's too dangerous."

"So was flying A-10s, but I never stopped you," his wife countered. Rounding on her husband, Marlana looked into his eyes and could see the fear Hector had of losing her, but her resolve was unwavering. "These are our friends," she reasoned. "We have to help them, and it has to be tonight. Besides, do you think Rose would actually go willingly with a total stranger? What if she refuses? That'll cost us precious time."

"She's got a point," Wiggins agreed. "I hadn't thought of that."

Hector considered this, even agreed with their logic, but hated it, nonetheless. There had to be another way.

Sensing his continued reluctance, Marlana gently redirected her husband's focus onto her. "Listen to me; I can do this," she assured him. "You know I can BS my way around better than anyone."

"What about security?" Hector questioned. "How will you get past the guards?"

"I have a guy who makes excellent forgeries," Salazar replied. "If we can get Camila's badge, he can put your picture on it. No one will know, I assure you."

Hector looked to Wiggins, who nodded support. He turned to his wife and could see by the look on her face that her mind was made up. "No heroics. Agreed?"

Marlana rolled her eyes. "I suppose," she said playfully. "We go in, grab Rose and Min-jun, then get the hell out."

Hector nodded. "Okay, I agree on one condition. I'm going, too."

Marlana's mouth dropped. For once, she was speechless.

Hector turned to Wiggins and Salazar. "No way I'm staying behind by myself. I want to ride with you guys."

Salazar and Wiggins exchanged looks. Neither objected. All eyes then turned to Marlana.

She let out a heavy breath. "Okay, Rambo. Don't get yourself killed." She then pecked him on the lips.

It was settled. Wiggins turned to Salazar. "Eduardo, get working on her badge. I need to phone this in."

49

THE EXCHANGE

Planet Aiwa
Supra, Realm of Eos

Kypa jerked awake to find himself once again in a healing chamber. After collapsing in front of the High Court, he had been rushed to the medical ward and placed in an induced coma. This time, when his eyes opened to find Maya standing over him, she was not as forgiving as before.

"What happened?" he reached out to her telepathically, his head still foggy.

"You nearly died!" she screamed with both her mind and her voice as tears ran down her cheeks.

Kypa's face softened. *"Forgive me, Maya. I did what needed to be done."*

Embarrassed at her outburst, Maya wiped her face. She understood his character better than anyone and knew he would take any risk for the sake of his people. Her relief to see him awake was stronger than her anger. She placed her hand on the chamber cover to show her support.

"I am almost afraid to ask, but did it work?" Kypa said.

"See for yourself," Maya replied.

A medical technician stepped forward and drained the chamber. As soon as the cover opened, Kypa sat up and blinked in surprise. Crowding inside the room was his entire family, along with Queen Qora and Commodore Boa.

Aided by the medical staff, Kypa stepped out and put his feet on the floor. He stood, feeling like his old self again. The healing chamber had done its work.

Fraya, Arya, and Toma rushed to their father's side and wrapped him with tight hugs.

Kypa looked at the court members. "I do not understand. Am I under arrest?"

Commodore Boa stepped forward. "No, My Prince. You have been exonerated of all charges. As we speak, the High Court is in conclave, debating your right to succession."

Kypa was speechless. Standing in the middle of the room, dripping wet with his children clinging to him, he could not express his relief. Finally having that ugly business behind him came as welcome news. Now came the daunting responsibility of leading Aiwa, should he be officially recognized as king.

"Well, say something," came a familiar voice as a medic handed him a towel.

Kypa turned sharply to find Dr. Garrett standing off to the side, now clean from his muddy encounter with the krakadon.

"Neil," he said, visibly relieved to see his friend.

Neil crossed the room, and they exchanged a heartfelt embrace.

"Thank God you're alive. When the attack happened, we feared the worst," Neil admitted. "I'm so sorry for the loss of your father."

Kypa nodded somberly. He then stepped back and eyed Neil up and down. Noting the scratches on his face and dark circles under his eyes, Kypa asked, "Are you all right? Colonel Nunez would say you look like hell."

Neil chuckled warily. "She would say that, huh? Actually, I'm fine. I had a little run-in with a krakadon, but your nano-suit sure saved me. Then Boa's troops picked me up and brought me here for questioning."

Kypa's eyes widened at the mention of a krakadon then narrowed at the thought of his friend being interrogated by Boa.

"You were treated well?"

"Yeah, yeah." Neil waved dismissively. "No harm, no foul."

Kypa looked past Neil with concern. "Where is Ava?"

Neil shook his head in frustration. "No one knows," he said gravely. "We got separated, and my comms were jammed as soon as I was picked up. I haven't been able to reach her since they let me go."

Boa stood and approached. "I have Seekers and ground teams out looking for her as we speak," he reported. This news did little to settle Kypa and Neil's fears. "My Prince," Boa added, coming to the position of attention. "Forgive my timing, but duty compels me to resign my command."

Taken aback, Kypa turned to face Boa as the commodore began removing the rank insignia from his uniform. "Boa, what is this?"

Regretting his past behavior, Boa bowed his head in shame. "I have failed you, My Prince. I am not fit to lead. My conduct and treatment of you in the past deserves to be punished. I accept full responsibility for my actions."

Kypa was speechless at first as he considered Boa's reasoning. Then he asked, "At my trial, you knew my father intended to clear me of all charges, yet you petitioned to join minds, anyway. Why?"

"Because I am a stubborn, old fool," Boa growled with embarrassment. "It was selfish, I know, but I needed to find the truth, and I could only do that by seeing through your eyes. As you know, I lost everything in Cirros … my family, my home. Like so many others, I needed an outlet for my pain, to cast blame. I wanted to hate you." Boa's voice shook. He paused to compose himself. "Then I saw the miracle of the Reaper and realized how it could repair our world and heal our people. And when our minds joined, I witnessed firsthand your courageous effort to save your father. It was at that moment I knew the depth of my failure." Boa raised his eyes to meet Kypa's. "By birthright, you are heir to the throne, but I needed to see you as a leader worth following. I see now that you will make a fine and noble king."

Boa eyed the rank insignia in his palm, an emblem of his life's work. He sighed heavily then offered it to Kypa.

Weighing Boa's heartfelt admission, Kypa appreciated the commodore's candor. Despite all the years of misjudgment, Kypa had a deep respect for Boa's military prowess and his loyalty to King Loka.

Taking the rank insignia from Boa's hand, Kypa firmly pinned it back on his uniform. "Aiwa's healing begins now," Kypa stated, clapping Boa on the shoulder. "And we will need our best commander if we are to defeat Krunig once and for all."

Humbled by this vote of confidence, Boa's face brightened with a flash of gratitude then he quickly returned to his old, stern self. "I am ready to serve, My Prince. Perhaps our first order of business should be to move the Reaper out of the city."

"Why is that, Commodore?"

"Captain Tan's failsafe protocol," Boa reminded him. "If any harm comes to her, the ship could self-destruct … it would destroy the planet."

"No, it won't," Neil said matter-of-factly, causing all eyes to turn to him. "Ava was just bluffing. She only said that so you'd stay away from her ship." He grinned innocently.

Boa, for one, did not find it amusing.

"Neil is correct," Kypa added. "Ava confirmed it with me while we were working in Cirros. She never had any intention of risking Aiwa's safety."

"That's right," Neil seconded. "The only protocol she activated was for the Reaper to shut down if anyone attempted unauthorized access."

Boa moved to a nearby terminal and brought up a camera feed showing the Reaper parked in the hangar bay. Kypa and the others crowded around him for a look-see. Even little Fraya joined in, elbowing her way through the grownups to Boa's side and taking hold of his hand. This earned her a look from Boa, but he softened and allowed it, unable to resist her charm.

"You see, safe and sound, right where Ava left it," Neil remarked.

Just then, Boa's commlink chimed.

"Yes?" he answered.

"Commodore Boa, this is Captain Ranga in the command center. We are receiving an urgent deep space transmission. It is Grawn Krunig, sir. He demands to speak with you."

A stunned moment of silence followed until Kypa broke it. "Maya, please take the children out,"

Maya agreed and quickly rounded up the children with minimal protests. As soon as they were gone, Kypa then nodded for Boa to respond.

"Send it to the medical bay," Boa instructed.

Seconds later, the hologram projector on the floor behind them came to life. Kypa, Boa, and the others rounded to find a life-size image of Grawn Krunig standing before them. He stood eye-to-eye with his Aiwan adversaries.

Boa narrowed his eyes on their armor-clad enemy, instinctively balling his hands into fists. "Krunig," he seethed.

"Commodore Boa," Krunig said in mock civility. "We meet again. Too bad it is not on the battlefield."

"What do you want?"

"I have Captain Tan," Krunig stated, hoping to draw a reaction.

Boa kept his composure, but Neil did not.

"What've you done with Ava?" he blurted.

Turning his attention to Neil, Krunig gave the human a once-over. The height disparity between Neil and the other Aiwans notwithstanding, Krunig found him to be unremarkable.

Krunig *hmphed*. "You must be the other human … the *expendable* one," he sneered. "Yet, I must say that, despite your inferiority as a race, both you and Captain Tan proved quite elusive. My bounty hunter figured you for dead."

Neil ignored the slight. "Where's Ava?"

Krunig held out his holographic hand. In his palm was a miniature hologram projector. It came to life, displaying Ava on her knees with a blaster held to her head. "She is safe, but for how long depends on you."

Boa and the others moved aside as Kypa stepped forward.

"Grawn Krunig, this is Prince Kypa."

"*Prince* Kypa," Krunig repeated, as if the words were acid in his blood. "Not yet crowned, I take it? Perhaps soon," he taunted. "You can thank me for that."

Ignoring the bait, Kypa continued, "I demand you return Captain Tan at once, unharmed."

"You are not in a position to demand anything, but here are my terms. You, Prince Kypa, will personally deliver the ship known as the Reaper to a location of my choosing. You will come alone," Krunig emphasized. "Any sign of additional troops, and your beloved Captain Tan is dead ... as is the rest of your planet, if you know what I mean."

Boa and Kypa exchanged knowing looks—a trap.

Kypa thought for a moment, then replied, "I will agree to your terms if you agree to free Captain Tan, *unharmed*, and promise the syndicate will never return to Aiwa."

"You have my word," Krunig lied. "But no tricks. Deliver the Reaper to me or watch Captain Tan and the rest of your loyal subjects perish."

"Understood," Kypa replied.

"Stand by to receive my coordinates."

The hologram disappeared. Behind them, a beeping signal indicated another incoming transmission. Boa checked the readout.

"Here are the coordinates for the exchange. It is here on Aiwa." He sounded surprised.

Kypa recognized the location immediately. It was close to the private beach where he had taken his family so often.

"What now?" Neil asked grimly. "You know it's a trap, right?"

"Yes, but we must do as Krunig says. He claimed responsibility for the attack on my father, and I have no doubt he will do the same to Ava," Kypa reasoned. "However, Krunig did say something intriguing. Somehow, he knows about the Reaper's failsafe protocol, and he thinks it is active. We might be able to use that to our advantage when I make the exchange."

"I must protest," Boa interjected. "Forgive my bluntness, but we cannot hand over such a weapon to our enemy. Krunig will turn right around and use it against us. We cannot sacrifice millions of innocent lives just to save one ... no offense." He gave Neil a courteous nod.

Neil wanted to argue to the contrary but, deep down, he knew Boa was right. No matter how they spun it, relinquishing the Reaper to Krunig was a death sentence for Aiwa.

"I will not allow that to happen," Kypa assured him. "I will do everything in my power to protect Aiwa. Please, trust me," he said on his way out of the medical bay.

"Kypa, where are you going?" Neil asked.

"To see my family. I will meet you in the hangar bay." With that, Kypa departed and made his way to his private residence.

When he arrived, the doors opened, and he found Maya there to greet him. She threw her long arms around his neck and held him tight.

As Maya pulled away from Kypa, she could tell something was wrong. "What is it?"

"Ava has been captured by Krunig," Kypa explained, unable to mask the dread in his voice. "She is being held for ransom on the surface by one of his bounty hunters."

"We have to help her," Toma blurted, catching his parents by surprise.

Kypa turned sharply to find his son standing in the adjacent corridor. Aware of Toma's fondness for Ava, he tried to calm his fears.

"We will not abandon Ava. I promise."

"What does Krunig want?" Maya asked.

"He agreed to return Ava safely and leave Aiwa permanently if we hand over the Reaper."

"Not Reggie," Toma fretted.

Kypa noticed his son fidgeting with his hands, a nonverbal cue Toma displayed whenever he grew nervous or agitated. This made what he had to say next even harder.

"There is more," Kypa added somberly. "Krunig insisted that *I* deliver the Reaper when the exchange for Ava is made."

Kypa could see Maya's eyes begin to water as she shook her head, disapproving.

Meanwhile, Toma crossed the room to his father. "Let me go with you," he implored. "I can help you get Ava back."

Toma's devotion to Ava was admirable. His heart was in the right place, but this was not his fight.

"I am sorry, Toma," Kypa replied, looking his son in the eye. "Krunig's instructions were clear. I must go alone, or they will kill Ava."

"But I could go in a separate ship ..." Toma persisted.

Kypa shook his head to end the discussion. Knowing Ava was running out of time, he turned to Maya to say his goodbyes. Then he felt Toma grab him by the arm.

"Listen to me," Toma insisted. "I can help."

Kypa's own stress and fears manifested themselves in a quick burst of anger. "I said no, Toma! Now drop it!"

His father's stern rebuke sent chills down Toma's spine. Kypa had never raised his voice in such a manner. The sting of such rejection shook him to the core. Stepping back slowly, tears welled in Toma's eyes as his pain turned to anger. With no place to channel his rage, Toma stormed out of the room, toward the front door.

Realizing his mistake, Kypa pursued. "Toma, come back," he said with sorrow.

At the front door, Toma rounded on his father and raised his unicorn fist in defiance. Kypa recognized the profane human gesture. It stopped him dead in his tracks. Toma had never shown such disrespect. Before Kypa could call him on it, Toma was gone.

Maya came to Kypa's side and wrapped her arm around his. They sighed in unison. The joy of parenting.

"I cannot leave this way," Kypa said, still staring at the door.

"I will talk with him," Maya soothed. She gently directed Kypa's attention to her, and they touched foreheads. "*You must focus on Ava now*," Maya told him telepathically.

"*I would give anything not to go*," Kypa swore.

Maya smiled warmly. "*I know. That is why we love you.*"

Kypa closed his eyes, savoring their connection for a long moment. Then duty called. Rather than prolonging their goodbyes any further, Kypa squeezed Maya's hand and made for the exit.

As the doors slid open, Kypa turned to his mate. "I will be back soon, I promise."

Down in the hangar bay, Commodore Boa, Queen Qora, and Princess Seva stood talking on the flight deck, looking none-to-pleased at being kept in the dark about Kypa's plan to rescue Ava. Meanwhile, Neil stood inside the Reaper's cockpit, watching them anxiously and wondering what he could possibly do to help. Kypa arrived on the flight deck soon after.

Neil could tell Boa and Kypa's family were imploring him not to leave. Qora made an impassioned plea that seemed to fall on deaf ears. Kypa had made up his mind, however, and nothing they said would change it.

Tilting her chin up, Qora crossed her arms in frustration and began strumming her long fingers. They exchanged a few choice words, then Neil watched her depart, clearly displeased with her son's stubbornness.

Boa's body language did not give any clue to his feelings. He bowed to Kypa dutifully then set off with his own set of orders to carry out. That left Kypa and Seva, who started walking together toward the Reaper's boarding ladder.

Neil headed toward the main cabin and climbed down to the engineering section. He arrived just in time to meet Kypa and his sister.

Kypa cut straight to the chase. "No matter what happens to me or Ava, we cannot allow the blue crystal to fall into enemy hands. Agreed?"

Neil and Seva nodded.

"Good. My plan is simple. I must swap out crystals," Kypa explained. "Neil, with your permission, I would like to entrust the blue crystal with Seva. She can take it to the royal vault where it will be protected while I am away. When I return with Ava, it will go back into the Reaper."

"Makes sense," Neil said, "but won't the bounty hunter scan the ship and know the crystal is missing?"

"It is a risk," Kypa granted. "I may be able to fool him with a false energy signature to buy us time. With any luck, the bounty hunter will not know the difference."

"What'll this do to Reggie?"

Kypa glanced warily at the blue crystal hovering nearby inside its containment field. "The ship has gone through this process before, only in reverse. The recalibration should go much faster this time." *In theory*, he did not add.

Neil inhaled nervously. "You say so."

Kypa moved to the nearby terminal. As soon as he accessed the ship's energy management system, Reggie abruptly locked him out.

Kypa recoiled his hands. "Reggie, what happened?"

"Prince Kypa, you are attempting to remove my energy source from the engine core."

"That is correct. I am replacing it with the original crystal."

"May I ask why?"

Kypa found the question curious. "What do you mean?"

"Exchanging crystals would result in a decreased energy output that would negatively affect every major system. It would make me … less."

Taken aback, Kypa was stunned by Reggie's profound statement. He looked to the others, lost for words. Neil and Seva were equally shocked.

Kypa stammered a reply, "How does that make you feel?"

After a brief pause, Reggie replied, "I do not understand. Please rephrase the question."

The scientist and engineer inside him wanted to pursue Reggie's train of thought to its logical conclusion, but pressed for time, Kypa knew this would have to wait.

"I understand your hesitation, but it is necessary to help Captain Tan. She is in danger."

"How will exchanging crystals help her?"

Good question, Kypa admitted. "The person holding her hostage wants your blue crystal in return. We cannot allow that to happen, so I need to swap crystals. May I proceed?"

After a millisecond pause, Reggie released access to Kypa. "You may continue."

"Thank you, Reggie. I promise I will put it back as soon as Captain Tan returns."

Kypa powered-down the ship and went to work swapping the crystals. As soon as the blue crystal was safely removed, Kypa handed it to his sister.

Seva cupped the rare crystal in her hands. She marveled at its beauty as the overhead lights glistened within the perfect blue gem.

"It is magnificent." She smiled.

"Indeed," Kypa agreed. He retrieved an oily rag from a storage compartment and handed it to Seva. She wrapped the crystal inside. "Now, off to the vault you go. Keep it safe. No one must know about it."

Seva nodded fervently.

"One more thing …" Kypa hesitated to mention. "With the court in conclave, I left instructions with Boa; you will remain Warden of Eos in my stead."

Seva understood the weight of his words. There was no need to say more.

She approached her brother, and they gently pressed foreheads in a heartfelt goodbye. At that moment, it dawned on Kypa that, with all of the chaos of recent events, he and his sister had not had time to mourn their father's death together. That would have to be corrected on his return.

"Father would be proud of you," he offered as a consolation. "As am I."

Seva patted his hand affectionately then departed.

Neil watched her leave then stepped up. "What can I do?"

"Go upstairs to the galley and retrieve the extra aquasuit."

"Got it." Without question, Neil hustled up the ladder.

Left to himself, Kypa rounded on his workstation and continued the crystal transfer. After reinserting the Reaper's original orange crystal, he activated the containment field still operating on reserve power. Satisfied the engine core was stable, Kypa brought the ship's main systems back online. The calibration was instantaneous.

He nodded approvingly. "Now, Reggie, can you create a false engine signature that emulates the blue crystal?"

"To a degree," Reggie replied. "By diverting all power to propulsion and decreasing the integrity of the core's containment field, it is possible to generate a false signature, but it is not recommended."

"How similar would the signatures be?"

"A nine-point-eight percent increase in power yield," Reggie answered.

Kypa sighed. He had hoped for a much higher output to trick the bounty hunter. Knowing the difference was minimal, he decided that risking a core breach was not worth the gamble.

"Never mind. We will just have to hope the bounty hunter does not know the difference. Maintain the ship's current power distribution and prepare for lift-off."

Neil returned, carrying the aquasuit. "What should I do with this?"

"Put it on," Kypa replied. "I need to borrow your nano-suit."

As soon as they swapped outfits, it was time to part ways. Not surprising, Neil made one last plea to tag along, but Kypa's mind was made up. He had a plan for the exchange, and it required going alone.

Trusting that whatever his friend had in mind was in everyone's best interest, Neil extended a handshake. "Good luck up there. Knock 'em dead … I mean that, literally."

Kypa forced a nervous smile. "Thank you, Neil. I will do my best."

Taking his cue, Neil climbed down the access ladder to depart the ship. After sealing the hatch, Kypa made his way to the cockpit. He sat in the pilot's chair and waited as the seat automatically conformed to his profile. The four orbs then appeared at his hands and feet, and the HUD came online before him.

Kypa took a calming breath then opened a channel and called for permission to depart the hangar bay. The controller's response was immediate; his request was approved.

Bringing the Reaper's impulse engines online, Kypa activated the maneuvering thrusters and lifted off the flight deck. He then rotated toward the hangar exit and throttled forward.

The Reaper departed the capital and headed for the surface. Smiling inwardly, Kypa realized this was the first time he had been behind the controls of his prototype since its trial runs. The Reaper had performed flawlessly in real-world conditions. From two major battles to terraforming Cirros, the ship turned out to be everything he could have hoped for and more. This made the task at hand even harder as Kypa changed course to rendezvous with Krunig' bounty hunter.

Meanwhile, up on the planet's surface, Smythe and Ava climbed down the slippery rock face to the base of the waterfall. Reaching the beachhead, the bounty hunter gestured with his blaster for Ava to drop to her knees. She reluctantly complied after learning the bruising consequences of several small acts of defiance along the way. The bounty hunter then bound Ava's hands behind her back.

Smythe's commlink chirped.

"Talk to me," he said to his partner, Gort.

"Inbound ship heading your way."

"Is it alone?"

"Looks to be," Gort said cautiously, expecting an ambush.

"ETA?"

"Twenty seconds," Gort replied.

Smythe shaded his eyes and scanned the ocean. Sure enough, he spotted the Reaper coming in hot, cruising at a low-level just above the water. "I see it. Get ready."

"Standing by, boss."

Smythe fastened the commlink to his belt then crouched behind Ava. Pointing his blaster to her head, they waited as the little black speck on the horizon quickly grew larger.

Ava brightened at the sight of her ship. Then it dawned on her what was about to go down.

"Oh, hell no," she protested, trying to stand up.

Smythe quickly quelled her objection. He struck Ava with a chop to the base of her neck. The blow stunned Ava momentarily, and she collapsed onto the sand.

Just then, the Reaper arrived and came to a hover at the water's edge, facing Smythe. A drastically lopsided standoff ensued.

Kypa was tempted to target the bounty hunter with the Reaper's forward cannons. One simple command to pull the trigger, and the insectoid would be dust. Both knew it, but Smythe did not back down. Positioning Ava as a human shield, he kept his blaster trained at her head, daring the Aiwan to take his best shot.

Kypa blinked first, unwilling to risk Ava.

The Reaper inched forward enough to clear the low tide then dropped its landing gear. Kicking up sand, the ship set down on the beach.

As the Reaper powered down, Smythe called Gort, "Start your run. Copy?"

"Roger that. I'm on my way," his partner replied, eager to finally collect their prize.

Smythe pushed Ava down on her side. With her hands still bound behind her back, she glared up at the bounty hunter, her eyes burning with rage. Smythe *hmphed*. He then turned his attention to the Reaper as the underbelly hatch opened, and the ladder descended.

Kypa appeared seconds later. As he climbed down, he kept his eyes on the bounty hunter. Smythe's cowl kept his facial features hidden, despite a stiff breeze coming off the ocean. Kypa did not know who he was up against, but Reggie's approach scan had told him the creature under the hood was an insectoid—a dangerous creature even without a blaster in hand.

Seeing Kypa, Ava called out to him in warning, "Kypa, go! Don't—"

Before she could finish, Smythe grabbed her by the back of the head and pushed her face into the sand. Ignoring her muffled cries, Smythe kept the pressure applied as Ava struggled against the bounty hunter's strong grip.

Kypa leapt off the ladder. When his feet hit the sand, he rushed to Ava's aid with his hands raised high. "Stop! I have what you want!" he said in Basic.

"That's far enough," Smythe hissed, juggling his attention between controlling Ava and keeping his weapon trained on Kypa.

Kypa halted. "I am unarmed," he declared. "Please, let her go. That was the deal."

Smythe kept Ava's face buried a few seconds longer to show who was in control then released her. Ava lifted her head and rolled over onto her back, gasping for air. Her face was covered with sand, and she began coughing hoarsely.

As soon as she recovered, Ava spit sand out of her mouth and glowered at Smythe. "You just made the list, bughead."

Smythe ignored her.

"I held up my end of the bargain," Kypa stated. "You can have the ship. Now let her go."

Ava balled her fists in the sand. "Don't do this, Kypa," she pleaded. "He'll kill us both."

Smythe pressed his blaster against Ava's cheek to quiet her. To Kypa, he said, "Tell her to deactivate the ship's failsafe protocol. Do it, or I shoot her and we all die."

"There is no need," Kypa explained as he slowly inched closer, hands raised. "The protocol is turned off."

Smythe waved the blaster in disagreement. "I don't believe you."

"Listen for yourself," Kypa replied. On his wrist, he wore a commlink. He hailed Reggie on a secure channel. "What is the status of Captain Tan's failsafe protocol?"

Reggie's response echoed over the sound of crashing waves. "Failsafe protocol currently off-line."

Kypa outstretched his arms. "Satisfied?"

Smythe narrowed his beady eyes. He suspected a trick of some kind.

Just then, Gort showed up. He brought the freighter to a hover with the ship's disruptors aimed at the defenseless Reaper.

"Gort, how we looking?"

"Ready when you are," his partner reported.

Smythe smiled thinly under his cowl. "Commence with capture."

Ava watched with dismay as the freighter repositioned over the Reaper and opened its underbelly cargo bay doors. She knew at that moment, if she did not act fast, Reggie might be lost forever.

With the bounty hunter distracted, Ava saw an opening. She took a quick, controlled breath, then kicked Smythe in the face as hard as she could. The blow caught Smythe by surprise, square under the chin. It was enough to stun him for a nanosecond, allowing Ava to roll over on her knees and straighten.

"Kypa, run!"

Before she could get to her feet, Ava felt the bounty hunter grab her by the ponytail and yank her back sharply. Smythe then emitted a weblike substance from a silk-secreting pore in the center of his palm. The shot hit Ava in the face, covering her mouth and nose. Her eyes widened in panic, and she screamed a muffled cry. Ava struggled, but with her hands still bound, she had no recourse as the paralytic quickly took hold. Within seconds, Ava's eyes rolled back in her head, and she fell to the sand, unconscious.

"What did you do to her?" Kypa demanded.

"She's alive," Smythe replied, coming to his feet. "But don't worry, she won't be your concern much longer."

Keeping his weapon trained on Kypa, Smythe stole a glance at Gort's progress. The Reaper was being hoisted into the freighter's underbelly. The bay doors then closed, and the freighter set down on the beach where Reggie used to be parked.

Smythe waited until the blowing sand cleared, then approached Kypa with his weapon outstretched. Time to finish the job.

Kypa swallowed hard, taking two steps backward. "We had a deal," he said nervously.

Smythe chuckled. "Krunig told me you'd say that. Famous last words for the likes of you."

Without further ado, Smythe fired. The blast hit Kypa center mass and threw him backward off his feet. He landed precariously on his back with his arms and legs sprawled about in the sand.

The bounty hunter stepped forward to admire his work. Looking down at the Aiwan's still form, the smoldering scorch mark on Kypa's chest was undeniable. Smythe holstered his weapon then raised his commlink to record the image as proof of death for Krunig.

Then something peculiar caught his eye—the absence of blood. Upon closer inspection, Smythe discovered Kypa was wearing two layers of clothing. Only the outer layer had been burned through.

"Impossible," he muttered.

Suddenly, blaster fire erupted on the beach as several shots zipped past Smythe's head. He turned sharply to his left and spotted four Aiwan shoretroopers emerging from the jungle. The bounty hunter rounded on the troopers and returned fire.

On the ground beside him, Kypa's bulbous blue eyes shot open. He let out a loud, guttural gasp. It took him an instant to gather his bearings. Then, seeing Smythe engaged in the firefight, Kypa rolled over onto all fours and stood. Gaining his feet, he extended his razor-sharp claws and lunged at the bounty hunter. Attacking him from behind, Kypa sank his claws into the insectoid's ribs.

Smythe howled in agony, seething through gritted teeth.

Kypa let him have it. Gritting his teeth, he began stabbing his claws into the bounty hunter repeatedly, with blind fury. But it was not enough to take him down. Smythe shook himself loose and swung his blaster around, catching Kypa in the face. The force of the blow sent blood spewing from Kypa's mouth. He dropped to his knees, disoriented.

With the shoretroopers advancing, Smythe realized he had to make a choice: try to finish off Prince Kypa and test his luck against the soldiers, or grab Captain Tan and retreat with his prize. Smythe chose the latter. He was still leery of any failsafe protocols, and since he was yet to discover why the ship was so valuable to both sides, he decided to take a hostage as well.

Holstering his weapon, Smythe rushed to Ava. Grimacing from the pain in his sides, he did not slow down as he lifted the petite human over his shoulder. Moving with a purpose, the bounty hunter carried Ava to the freighter's boarding ramp and disappeared inside the ship. Smythe closed the ramp behind him.

In a futile attempt to thwart their escape, the shoretroopers continued firing on the freighter, but it was not enough to cause significant damage.

Inside the freighter, Smythe called to Gort, "Get us out of here!"

The freighter's engines rumbled with power as it lifted off the beach, creating a swirling sandstorm in its wake. By the time the shoretroopers reached Kypa, the ship had raised its landing gear and was heading skyward.

"My Prince, are you all right?" asked Captain Acova, the ranking shoretrooper. He helped Kypa to his feet.

Kypa nodded, rubbing his sore jaw. He looked up in time to see the freighter disappear into the clouds. A sense of dread came over him. His plan had failed. Now the Reaper was gone, and Ava along with it.

50

SNATCH AND GRAB

Planet Earth
Satipo, Peru

Peering through a pair of long binoculars, Lima Station Chief, Paul Wiggins, patiently scanned the perimeter of Mathias's compound. Seated next to him in the darkened Land Cruiser, Eduardo Salazar picked and sucked at his teeth. Wiggins said nothing, trying to block the annoying sounds from his mind while inwardly counting down the minutes for their midnight stakeout to end.

Hector Nunez watched the time for different reasons. In the back of the SUV, seated behind Wiggins, he tapped his foot impatiently. Marlana and Lalo had entered the facility four hours earlier without raising any suspicions at the front gate. It had been touch and go for a moment when it appeared the gate guard scrutinized his wife's fake ID badge longer than usual, but she was eventually waved through.

With those two safely inside, Operation Bold Fortress was on track.

No alarms had sounded since their arrival. In fact, the facility remained dark and still, with only the occasional guard spotted atop the perimeter wall, making rounds.

At this point, Lalo and Marlana were expected to do nothing more than act normal. Upon entry, they parted company. Lalo went to work in the mechanical rooms, while Marlana played her part as a housekeeper, taking inventory.

For appearances' sake, she visited every storage closet in the residential section of the facility. Using a checklist and clipboard, she documented all of the cleaning supplies on hand. Taking this task to heart—either because of her OCD or the fact that it helped calm her nerves—Marlana ensured an accurate count rather than pencil-whipping the numbers. All the while, she kept her eyes on the clock. At exactly zero two-fifty-five hours, Lalo would trigger a fire inside a mechanical room on the far side of the facility. Once the fire alarms sounded, it was her job to collect Rose and escort her to the rendezvous point where Lalo and Min-jun would be waiting. Then, like the rest of the staff, they would exit the compound amidst the chaos.

Hector checked his watch for the umpteenth time. Three minutes to show time. All hell was about to break loose, and Marlana would be in the thick of it. The helpless feeling in the pit of his stomach grew with each passing minute. Sitting idle in the back of the car became unbearable.

"I need some air," he announced.

"Stay in the vehicle," Wiggins said with authority, keeping the binoculars trained on the compound. "Nobody gets out. Noise and light discipline, remember?"

Hector let out a heavy breath then wiped his sweaty palms on his pants.

Wiggins's satellite radio crackled.

"Zephyr, this is Condor," SEAL Team Leader, Commander Diamond, called. "Come in, Zephyr. Over."

Wiggins snatched his radio. "Condor, this is Zephyr. I read you loud and clear. Over."

"Copy that. We're in position, standing by."

"Roger, Condor. Hold position."

A breathless tension filled the air. Hector and Salazar raised their binoculars, zooming in on the east side of the facility, waiting for the fireworks to begin.

Wiggins checked his watch. "Okay, moment of truth."

Meanwhile, inside the facility, Marlana occupied a small closet on the second floor of the employee housing. Pacing in a tight circle, she abandoned her inventory and wrung her hands anxiously, mindful not to trip over a nearby mop and bucket on the floor.

She had been inside this closet, killing time for twenty minutes, only a stone's throw away from Rose's room. Ten steps, and Marlana could knock on her friend's door, but prudence dictated restraint. Salazar had warned her Dr.

Landry's room was being watched. In fact, everything and everyone inside the facility was under constant surveillance. Mathias trusted no one.

Marlana checked her watch; Lalo's diversion should happen in sixty seconds. Blowing out sharply to calm her nerves, she started reciting their escape route.

Earlier, Salazar had sketched a crude rendition of the layout using a drawing pad and crayons borrowed from his children. Marlana had committed it to memory.

She had hoped to walk the route as soon as they arrived at the compound, but Wiggins had nixed the idea since it might raise suspicion. Anything out of the ordinary could invite unwanted attention from the guards. So, Marlana stuck to the plan, conducting her inventory and waiting for the clock to wind down.

As the seconds waned, Marlana moved to the door and rested her hand on the knob. Heart pounding in her chest, Lalo came to mind. The lanky, unassuming guy seemed nice enough. They had no time beforehand to get to know one another, so she had no idea why Lalo would risk his life to aid their cause. For all she knew, he owed Salazar, and it was time to pay his debt.

What stuck in Marlana's mind was Lalo's last words to her before they had parted company. When asked how she would know his diversion had started, Lalo had replied with a sly grin, "Todo el mundo lo sabrá." *Everyone will know.*

On the far side of the compound, Lalo's confidence had not wavered. His only reservation at this point was the risk of creating too much shock and awe. A devout Catholic, Lalo preferred not to kill anyone—starting with himself— but if his mayhem helped his boss while simultaneously destroying the unholy activities taking place in the subterranean cloning labs, then so much the better.

For the past twenty minutes, he had worked diligently on staging a chemical storage room to explode. His primary catalysts were flammable materials stored in lockers and cages spread throughout the room, each segregated within fireproof closets. From gas cylinders and propane tanks to an assortment of paint cans and thinners, every combustible material in this secure storage room could blow up in a heartbeat with the right heat source and a little ingenuity.

Since he could not bring explosives into the facility, Lalo had to improvise a heat source using a timed detonation circuit he had copied off YouTube. Borrowing a kitchen timer from the employee dining room, he wired the timer to a nine-volt battery and a palm-sized circuit board designed to amplify the voltage. The circuit board, smuggled into the compound inside his metal lunchbox, was connected to a nichrome wire that would heat up and burst into flames seconds after the timer activated. That heat source would then ignite the gasses in the room and go *boom*! The trick was to set the timer on a short fuse but give himself enough time to open the release valves on the cylinders and tanks then get as far away as possible without looking suspicious. Lalo accomplished all of this with three minutes to spare.

Before leaving the gas-filled storage room, he removed his rebreather to take one last look at his handiwork. Wiping the sweat from his brow, he smiled with satisfaction. Lalo then tossed his rebreather into the room, locked the door behind him, and set off to find Min-jun.

Staring at her watch, Marlana counted down the final seconds. "Three … two … one …"

As Lalo had promised, the blast was unmistakable, shaking the foundation of the entire facility. Rolls of toilet paper and cleaning supplies fell from the shelves as Marlana steadied herself against the door. The lights flickered inside the closet, and then the tiny room went dark as the fire alarm kicked on.

"¡Mierda!" she cursed.

Fumbling in the darkness to find the doorknob, Marlana entered the hallway to discover the emergency lights had activated. Bedroom doors began to open as sleepy-eyed workers appeared in their pajamas, wondering if there was genuine cause for alarm.

"¡Al toque!" Marlana prodded, hurrying up the hallway. "Get out!"

Just as she reached Rose's room, the door opened unexpectedly. Standing in the doorway, with a wicked case of bedhead, was Dr. Rose Landry.

Rose stepped back with a shriek, startled to find a dark figure blocking the doorway. Then she narrowed her eyes with confusion. "Nunez?"

Marlana nodded excitedly, putting her finger to her lips.

Rose was speechless. She stared at Nunez for a moment, not believing her eyes. Then she lunged forward and wrapped her arms around her friend.

"How did you find me?" she whispered breathlessly in Marlana's ear.

Marlana could feel Rose trembling and rubbed her back soothingly. "It was all Becky. Boxcar Willie was very clever."

Rose pulled back with a broad grin, wiping away tears of joy. She laughed. "I didn't think it would work." Then the chaos around them brought her back to the moment. "Wait, what are you doing here?" Noticing Marlana's housekeeping uniform, she added, "And what are you wearing?"

"No time to explain." Marlana grabbed Rose by the hand. "C'mon; we need to get moving."

"Where?"

"Outside," Marlana answered over her shoulder, pulling Rose down the hallway toward the stairwell. "Our ride is waiting."

"Holy smokes!" Salazar blurted as the eastern side of the compound exploded in a massive fireball. The rumble from the blast echoed for miles around and could be felt inside the SUV.

Wiggins saw it, too. Peering through his binoculars, a wide grin stretched across his face. He then raised his radio. "Condor, this is Zephyr. Over," he called.

"I read you, Zephyr. Go ahead," Warrant Officer Brewster replied.

"We are a go for extraction. Repeat, we are a go for extraction."

"Good copy, Zephyr. Condor is inbound, five-mike."

Lalo raced down the hallway, trying to mask the excitement and fear on his face. His timed detonation had gone off without a hitch. Now, as he dodged security personnel rushing to fight the fire, he made his way to the opposite end of the facility in search of the Asian man known as Mr. Choi.

When he arrived at the storage room where Min-jun was being held, Lalo found the door unguarded. He let out a breath of relief, grateful for not having to confront anyone from security. Jiggling the handle, he found the door was locked. A colorful expletive nearly escaped his lips, but Lalo caught himself in time to minimize his number of sins for the day. Undeterred, he eyed the deadbolt then fished around in his pants for his Swiss Army knife.

Lalo tried the tweezers first, bending one metal arm ninety degrees to create a tension wrench. He then pulled out the toothpick and tried fitting it into the lock. It was too big, so he retrieved the nail file and sanded down the tip. After a few attempts, the toothpick finally fit inside the lock. He then pushed the makeshift tension wrench into the keyway, applying pressure to the pins inside the lock. A few tries later, he heard an audible *click* and the lock released.

Lalo put his knife back in his pocket and opened the door. Rushing inside, he pulled up at the ghastly sight of Min-jun sitting in the middle of the room. The prisoner was bound to a chair and had clearly been worked over, his face a bloody mess. Horror dulled Lalo's reaction, and then he blinked back his shock.

Inching closer, he could not tell if Min-jun was alive or dead. His eyes were closed and swollen.

"Psst! Señor Choi?" he whispered.

Min-jun did not move. His ankles were bound, and his hands were zip-tied behind his back. Lalo could only imagine what Mr. Choi had been through.

Remembering their time crunch, Lalo stepped forward and tried shaking the Asian man.

Min-jun's eyes shot open, and he awoke with a jerk.

Startled, Lalo clutched his heart.

Now, fully alert, Min-jun stared fiercely at the stranger before him, expecting another round of torture. Then he realized something was amiss. Unlike the military fatigues the guards wore, Lalo was dressed like a mechanic and wore a name tag.

"Lay-low?" Min-jun muttered through his bloody lips.

Lalo crooked his head, scrunching his brow, then saw Min-jun eyeing his nametag. Feeling grateful that the man was alive and alert, Lalo replied, "Lah-low." He gestured to Min-jun. "Señor Choi?"

Min-jun nodded warily.

"Bueno."

Wasting no time, Lalo went to work cutting away the zip-ties with his knife.

As soon as Min-jun was free, he massaged his sore wrists. Lalo helped him to his feet.

"Ven conmigo, *por favor.*" *Come with me, please.*

Min-jun had no idea what Lalo said, but energized with a surge of adrenaline, he followed the mystery man, anyway.

Limping down the hall, Min-jun did not care who Lalo was or where they were heading. All that mattered was getting the hell out of this place before the guards returned. Then he remembered Rose.

"Wait," Min-jun called, halting in his tracks.

Lalo stopped and rounded on him with a look of confusion.

"What about Rose?"

Unable to speak English, Lalo shrugged. He then waved impatiently for Min-jun to continue.

"No," Min-jun insisted. "We find Rose."

"Min-jun?" came the sound of a female voice.

Min-jun turned around sharply to find Marlana Nunez and Rose Landry approaching. His face lit up, as did Marlana's, who rushed to him.

Ignoring his injuries, Marlana squeezed Min-jun tightly, pinning his arms to his sides. "We thought we lost you."

To Min-jun, her embrace felt like a million bucks. Knowing she had risked her life on his behalf left him speechless. Now he understood how all the people he helped defect from North Korea must have felt.

Min-jun's swollen eyes drifted to Rose. She smiled meekly in return, still unsure who this bloodied man was or what was happening.

"Rose?" Min-jun asked.

"Why, yes." Dr. Landry smiled, surprised the man knew her name.

"My name is Choi Min-jun." He bowed.

"C'mon, we'll get to know each other later," Marlana urged. "We need to get both of you out of here. There's a chopper waiting outside."

Rose raised her eyebrows. "You've got a helicopter?"

"Two, actually." Marlana replied with a scandalous grin. "Seems the U.S. government thinks you're both pretty valuable. Now, c'mon. Move it or lose it."

The foursome continued down the hall, with Lalo in the lead. He knew how to find the room where the exit was located, but he had never been inside before. They arrived at the door a few moments later. As expected, entry was controlled by a keypad, so Lalo fished out his trusty knife. He went to work unscrewing the keypad's cover plate so he could bypass the lock's tamper switch.

Meanwhile, Min-jun, Rose, and Marlana kept a nervous eye out. Marlana happened to glance at Min-jun. Taking in the extent of his injuries, she cringed at the sight of his face. Retrieving a rag from her housekeeper's uniform, she offered it to him.

"You okay?" she asked.

Min-jun accepted the rag, smiling faintly. "I will live." He wiped his face, using the rag to apply pressure to a nasty cut above his left eye.

Just then, Lalo bridged the contact point to the cover plate inside the keypad, essentially fooling the lock into thinking someone had pressed the exit button from inside the room. The door unlocked without having to cut any wires and no alarms were triggered. Grinning at Min-jun, Lalo pushed the door open and flipped the light switch on to reveal Mr. Renzo's dojo.

Nunez peeked inside at the sparring mat and wooden training dummy. "What's this?"

Min-jun recognized a martial arts room when he saw one. A sinking feeling came over him.

"Go," he said with urgency. "We must leave now."

No one argued.

Marlana took Rose by the hand and led her across the room. Min-jun followed with Lalo bringing up the rear. But, as Lalo went to close the door behind them, a three-inch dart came out of nowhere and struck him in the neck, just under the chin. Lalo recoiled and instinctively removed the projectile, but the poison had already entered his bloodstream.

Unaware of this, Marlana reached the exit door on the far side of the dojo and threw it open. Two MH-60M helicopters had arrived; one set down in the field while the second hovered high above the ground, providing overwatch. She turned to the others, elated to see that the crazy plan was going to work.

"They're here! Let's …" Marlana trailed off at the sight of Lalo staggering across the room.

With a bewildered look on his face, Lalo clutched his neck with one hand and held the dart in the other. His skin began to turn pale with a feverish sheen. He and Marlana made eye contact, and both knew something was terribly wrong.

Lalo stumbled forward, moving as if in a dream, almost mechanical, his eyes unblinking. His eyes then rolled back in his head, and he fell face-first onto the unforgiving concrete floor.

Marlana gasped, and then her eyes darted toward the entry. Standing in the doorway was Renzo, clutching his blowgun. He wore a cold, dangerous look on his face.

Hearing the *thud* behind them, Rose and Min-jun turned to find Lalo facedown with blood foaming from the corner of his mouth. Rose shrieked as Min-jun noticed Renzo in the doorway.

"Go," he told Rose and Marlana from over his shoulder, positioning himself between them and Renzo.

Marlana glanced outside. She could see the Navy SEALs disembarking the chopper on the ground. It was only one hundred yards away. "They're here. C'mon!"

Min-jun turned sharply, grabbed Rose by the arm, and steered her toward the exit. Without a word, he pushed both women outside then closed the door. Marlana pounded on the door, demanding he open it, but Min-jun ignored her muffled calls as he squared up against Renzo.

The element of surprise had come and gone for the two helicopters. Lalo's diversion had worked, but waiting for the hostages left them terribly exposed. Mathias's security forces soon discovered their arrival and responded in force. With guards redirected to the perimeter wall, a full-on firefight erupted, pinning the ground team down beside their chopper.

"We're sitting ducks!" Brewster, the Condor's pilot, screamed over the radio. "We need to move!"

Commander Diamond agreed. Despite carrying out a successful diversion, the two people inside the compound responsible for retrieving the hostages had missed their scheduled rendezvous. Now, as all hell broke loose around them, Diamond had to make the call to stay and fight or bug out.

"There!" Chief Ortiz pointed.

As Diamond emptied thirty rounds from his M4A1 assault rifle, he followed Ortiz's hand to the exit door in the perimeter wall. Two women—Nunez and Dr. Landry—were running toward them in a panic.

"Suppressing fire!" Diamond ordered, redirecting his team to provide cover for the women.

Just then, bullets flew near his head and ricocheted off the fuselage. He ducked, subconsciously counting his lucky stars the shots had not been three inches closer.

Dropping his empty magazine, Diamond fluidly popped another loaded one in its place and returned fire.

"Stringer, Croll, get to the hostages!" he ordered.

Without hesitation, both frogmen raced to help Rose and Marlana.

Diamond quickly surveyed the battlefield. Mathias's security forces held the high ground, using their perches along the perimeter wall to their advantage. Reinforcements had also arrived, leaving his team grossly outnumbered.

"Bishop, this is Condor," he called his overwatch. "Target the southeast corner! Fire for effect!"

Aboard the second helicopter, Corporal Siskel, the door gunner, sat behind his Dillon M134D Minigun and aimed at the southeast corner of the compound's perimeter wall. As soon as he pulled the trigger, three thousand rounds of 7.62x51mm ammunition spewed out of the six-barrel rotary machine gun in less than a minute, disintegrating the wall in a plume of gray dust and killing everyone in its path.

Meanwhile, the two Navy SEALS, Stringer and Croll, met up with Rose and Marlana at the halfway point. As Croll provided cover fire, Stringer yelled for Rose to keep moving to the awaiting helicopter. He stopped Marlana.

"Where are the others?"

"Lalo's dead!" she spoke over the sound of the rotors and weapons fire. "Min stayed behind to buy us time!"

Stringer gave her an incredulous look, but there was no time for more details.

"Get on the chopper!" he told her.

Stringer then tapped Croll on the helmet. "Fall back!"

As Rose arrived at the helicopter, Diamond paused his firing to help her aboard. She climbed inside bare-footed and took a seat. Turning back to his team, he noticed they were missing two civilians—Lalo and Mr. Choi.

Just then, a fast-moving object flew overhead. Diamond ducked. A split-second later, the rocket-propelled grenade struck the overwatch helicopter. Diamond spun around in time to see the Black Hawk in trouble. The RPG had disintegrated the helicopter's tail rudder, sending the aircraft into a deadly spin.

Both pilots fought gallantly to keep their aircraft aloft but, in the end, they were powerless to stop the inevitable. The damaged chopper lost altitude until the main rotor struck the ground then exploded on impact, instantly killing all three souls onboard.

Diamond looked at the blazing wreckage in horror. Knowing there could be no survivors, his first thought was to recover the bodies, but even that would be impossible. The fire prevented them from getting any closer.

As the barrage of enemy fire continued, Diamond made the call to save those within his control.

"Everybody aboard!" he told his team. "We're leaving!"

Marlana and the SEALs climbed into the helicopter with Diamond being last to step off the battlefield. As the door gunner continued spraying the enemy with his machine gun, Petty Officer Stringer helped Rose and Marlana buckle in. Seeing the terrified expression on Rose's face, he shook Marlana's leg to get her attention.

"She's in shock," he said over the chaos.

Marlana turned to Rose. Her friend had a blank stare on her face and shook uncontrollably.

"I've got her!" she replied, wrapping her arm tightly around Rose. It was the best she could do for now.

Stringer gave her a thumbs-up.

With everyone onboard, Commander Diamond barked to the pilots, "Go, go, go!"

Seconds later, the helicopter lifted off the ground. As they gained altitude, on the top of everyone's mind was another rocket attack. Fortunately for them, the RPG that brought down the first helicopter was a single-use model.

Watching the battle unfold from afar, Wiggins lowered his binoculars as Condor rolled away from the compound. Praying the helicopter had not sustained crippling damage, he breathed a sigh of relief once the SEAL team had cleared the tree line and was out of harm's way.

He then turned his attention back to the compound. Raising his binoculars, Wiggins focused on the field leading up to the exit door.

"Shouldn't we get going?" Hector asked, anxious to be reunited with his wife.

"Not yet," Wiggins replied, never taking his eyes off the target. "Lalo and Mr. Choi didn't come out."

Hector and Salazar raised their binoculars to join the search. In all of the chaos, neither had noticed the two men were missing.

"Condor, this is Zephyr," Wiggins called over the sat radio. "What's your status? Over."

Commander Diamond responded immediately. "Bishop is down. Three KIA," he replied soberly. "We extracted two targets, both females. Choi is MIA. He stayed behind to help the women escape, and I'm afraid your man, Lalo, is KIA as well. Copy?"

Wiggins sighed. "Roger, Condor," he replied with a heavy heart. "You did your best. Proceed as planned."

"Copy that," Diamond affirmed. "Condor, out."

As soon as the radio went quiet, Hector leaned forward from the back seat. "What now?"

Wiggins raised his binoculars. "We wait. I want to see how Mathias responds."

51

TAKANAKUY

Planet Earth
Satipo, Peru

The murderous glare burning in Renzo's eyes confirmed what Min-jun had already suspected—the man standing before him had an appetite for violence. He had seen it before while serving in the Korean People's Army. Some men hungered for power and would resort to violent means to attain it whenever necessary. Others were simply born with bloodlust, an insatiable desire to kill or maim whenever possible.

Renzo struck him as somewhere in-between the two. He was not a soldier, or at least he did not carry himself like one. Min-jun guessed Renzo had grown up on the streets, forced to fight to survive. Somewhere along the way, he had found favor with Edmund Mathias, a man who had given him everything. This made Renzo more dangerous than other opponents—he had everything to lose.

Min-jun was the opposite. He had nothing to lose. In fact, he welcomed death. His family awaited him in the next life. All he sought was an honorable death, preferably quick and painless, but it was clear that the Chachapoyan would offer him neither.

Renzo wanted retribution for what had transpired this night. Such a costly failure was inexcusable and jeopardized his standing with Mathias. The situation was still salvageable as long as Mr. Choi remained alive and in custody. Renzo knew he could not kill the man, but someone had to pay, and he knew how to exact his revenge in ways that would leave his adversary begging for death.

With the door behind Renzo remaining open, heavy footfalls could be heard racing up the hall. A guard soon appeared and came to a sliding halt in the doorway.

"Mr. Renzo, we're under attack!" he said, panting heavily.

Renzo cocked his head sideways, never taking his eyes off Min-jun. "Is the fire under control?"

Following his boss's eyes, the guard suddenly noticed Min-jun standing off to the side. Seeing the prisoner's restraints were missing, he reached for his sidearm.

"Sir, do you need my help?"

Renzo raised his hand to quell the guard. "What is happening with the fire?"

The guard darted his eyes between the two men. Gauging the tension in the room, he realized something personal and ugly was about to go down.

"The sprinklers were damaged in the explosion. It's spreading."

"Call in the local fire department, round up villagers, I don't care who you have to call," Renzo said coolly, "but get that fire under control. Understood?"

"Yes, sir." He felt compelled to offer his assistance once again. "Are you sure—"

"Leave us," Renzo cut him off. "And shut the door on your way out."

Once the door closed, Renzo unshouldered his carrying case. "Your friends are gone," he said as he began dismantling his blowgun. "There's nowhere to run. But if you surrender now, I promise you will live."

As he spoke, Min-jun surveyed the dojo. There was a sparring mat to his left, along with a Wing Chun wooden practice dummy in the corner, which offered some insight into his opponent. However, it was the mural of Roberto Puch Bezada, ex-convict turned martial arts expert, that caused Min-jun to reevaluate Renzo.

Since their first encounter, Min-jun had figured Renzo to be some kind of Bruce Lee copycat, judging by his attire. Yet, there was nothing in the dojo paying homage to the kung fu legend or his personal fighting style, known as Jeet Kune Do—The Way of the Intercepting Fist. This observation reminded Min-jun not to underestimate his opponent. He had to be prepared to adapt to whatever fighting style Renzo threw at him.

"I'll take your silence as a no." Renzo smirked, inwardly thrilled Min-jun chose not to surrender. He placed his case against the wall. "Here in Peru," Renzo continued, "we have an annual Christmas tradition called Takanakuy. You see, there are many remote villages in my country. Most are too poor to afford law enforcement, yet crime remains relatively low because neighbors respect one another and their property.

"But, of course, no one is perfect and differences do arise," Renzo explained conversationally as he came to face Min-jun. "That is how Takanakuy came to be. It is a fighting festival where villagers resolve their differences in public, mano y mano." He playfully threw a few air punches to mimic a fight.

"Takanakuy has passed for this year, I'm afraid"—Renzo frowned—"but lucky for you, Christmas has come early. If you can get past me, the door to freedom is right there."

Despite Renzo's heavy Spanish accent, Min-jun got the gist of his meaning. But only a fool would believe Renzo would simply let him walk away, especially after getting his ass kicked. Renzo's men would hunt him down like a wild animal. Then, once recaptured, Min-jun would be brought back to face more torture and interrogation.

Min-jun accepted Renzo's challenge by simply walking to the center of the sparring mat. Turning his body diagonally to face Renzo, he assumed a fighting stance with his knees slightly bent and hands balled into fists.

Renzo's mouth curled into a sneer, and he joined Min-jun on the mat. Out of mock respect, the Chachapoyan bowed to his opponent.

Min-jun ignored the gesture. This was a fight to the death, not a karate tournament. Instead, he remained laser-focused on Renzo. The person who landed the first blow typically had the advantage, so he had to be ready for anything.

Renzo shrugged off the slight and assumed a similar fighting stance.

The two fighters locked in on one another. Min-jun kept a serious, unreadable expression with his eyes narrowed and ever watchful. Across from him, Renzo carried himself with an air of confidence as he began circling Min-jun. His movement was fleet of foot, as if dancing around his opponent like Sugar Ray Leonard.

Min-jun reacted cautiously, shadowing Renzo's movements. With a swollen face inhibiting his peripheral vision, he knew he had to keep Renzo in front of him at all times.

As they circled, sizing up one another, Min-jun recalled his Kyeok Sul Do training, a North Korean martial art similar to Taekwondo. This technique focused on horizontal limb strikes and using melee weapons, such as a knife or blunt object. Min-jun had no weapons but strikes, he could do. He envisioned taking Renzo to the mat and beating him to a pulp, but all that was thrown out the window when Renzo launched a lightning-fast leg sweep.

The blow caught Min-jun unaware, striking him in the meaty part of the calf where the anaconda had sunk its fangs. A sharp pain ran up his leg, causing Min-jun to grimace between gritted teeth.

"Still tender, I see." Renzo smiled, relishing Min-jun's discomfort. He continued dancing about, toying with his opponent. The movement forced Min-jun to counter and keep pressure on his injured leg.

Noticeably limping, Min-jun ignored the pain and kept his feet moving.

Renzo followed by throwing a succession of discovery punches—a jab, then a cross, and followed quickly by a lead hook. He purposely held back on each, testing his opponent's defenses and gauging Min-jun's reflexes.

Min-jun blocked each punch with ease, which set up Renzo's second leg sweep. This time, Min-jun was ready. He blocked Renzo's low attack with his forearm, protecting his throbbing leg, but the Chachapoyan quickly reestablished his balance and responded by landing successive punches to Min-jun's face.

Already with a broken nose, Min-jun saw stars as the blows sent a stinging sensation right between his eyes. Staggering backward, he shook off the effects and recentered his balance. With a copper taste in his mouth, Min-jun wiped his lip. A smear of blood ran along the back of his hand. It was time to change tactics.

Pound for pound, the two fighters were nearly identical in height and weight, but age proved to be decisive. Renzo's youth gave him a definite advantage in speed and agility, so Min-jun turned to battlefield tactics. When being shelled by an enemy's artillery, one could either stay put and die, retreat out of range, or close the distance to make the artillery a nonfactor. The answer was obvious—get in Renzo's personal space.

That opportunity came when Renzo threw his next punch. Min-jun avoided a rear hook that narrowly missed his face, but it allowed him to step into Renzo's body. He grabbed Renzo's arm as it recoiled then flipped the Chachapoyan over his shoulder and threw him hard onto the mat. The move took Renzo completely by surprise.

As soon as he landed on his back, Min-jun was on top of him, throwing an unceasing barrage of punches to the face. Now the gloves were off, and the fight turned savage.

Min-jun continued wailing on Renzo, bloodying the Chachapoyan's unmarked face, but Renzo favored this type of no-holds-barred fighting. It was the Bakom way—vicious in nature, just like the streets of Lima.

Using one hand to try to shield his face, Renzo reached for Min-jun's groin. He grabbed hold of his opponent's testicles and gave them a mean twist. Min-jun howled in agony, clutching his privates.

This lapse enabled Renzo to shove Min-jun off and go on the offensive. The two men continued scrapping ferociously on the mat with Renzo proving he was stronger than he looked. In a flash, he had turned the tables. Min-jun now found himself on his knees, head down, with Renzo crouched behind him, swinging wildly at the sides of his head. The Chachapoyan landed several punches to Min-jun's ears and neck until Min-jun surprised him by throwing back his elbow. He heard the bone crack as the blow shattered Renzo's nose. Now they were even.

Renzo stumbled backward, allowing Min-jun time to get to his feet. Chest heaving, Renzo wiped the blood and perspiration from his face, red droplets spattering on the mat at his feet. Grinning sadistically, Renzo then reset his nose.

Laughing off what had to be excruciating pain, Renzo flexed his nostrils, and then his demeanor abruptly turned to rage. He charged Min-jun, tackling his opponent around the waist. Momentum carried both men to the edge of the sparring mat until Min-jun's back thudded against the concrete wall, nearly knocking the wind out of him. The jarring hit left his midsection exposed. Renzo capitalized on the opening and went to work on Min-jun's ribs, throwing body blow after body blow.

Cornered, Min-jun did his best to protect himself while looking for an out. He went straight for Renzo's eyes, clawing at his face. Renzo screamed as Min-jun's fingernails dug into his flesh, just below the eyelids. Renzo threw his arms up to break Min-jun loose and pulled back, his face a bloody mess.

Feeling his body weakening, Min-jun knew he had to end the fight now. Summoning what strength he had left, he spat bloodied saliva on the mat then attacked. He charged Renzo, who raised his fists to protect his head, but Min-jun caught him by surprise with a low, leaping roundhouse kick. Bringing his sweeping leg around with power and speed, Min-jun's foot found its mark right where the quadricep met the top of the knee. Renzo's leg buckled instantly with a bone-crunching pop.

With his opponent collapsed on the mat, writhing in pain, Min-jun went for the kill. He dropped to his knees and wrapped his arm around Renzo's throat in a rear-naked choke hold. The Chachapoyan had no defense in this position. His legs flailed about as he fought desperately to free himself from

Min-jun's vice-like grip. But like the anaconda, once Min-jun latched on to his prey, there was no letting go.

After a few moments, Min-jun could feel the life draining from Renzo. Finally, he whispered in his opponent's ear, "Shh, no noise."

Min-jun held this position until all the fight left Renzo. He then released him, rolling the dead Chachapoyan over, face-first on the mat. Chest heaving and muscles spent, Min-jun wasted no time picking himself up off the mat. He hobbled for the exit knowing it would not be long before the guards returned.

He threw open the dojo's emergency exit door to find himself on the outside of the compound. The area was lit up by exterior lights with the alarm still blaring. Shielding his eyes, Min-jun recognized the field before him. The smoldering wreckage of the downed Black Hawk was new. He hoped Marlana and Rose had not been onboard. If they were, there was nothing he could do for them now. Pushing that grim thought aside, Min-jun started across the field, limping his way to freedom.

Wiggins had seen enough. The sight of Mathias's compound burning out of control brought a satisfying smile to his face. As a firetruck from nearby Satipo raced toward the front entrance with its lights and siren blaring, he lowered his binoculars, ready to close down the op. Then a mysterious figure burst through the side entrance door near the smoldering helicopter wreckage.

Curious, Wiggins raised his binoculars. The man was covered in blood and clearly not one of Mathias's goons.

"Who the hell is that?" He pointed.

Salazar raised his binoculars and zoomed in. "Sweet Jesus," he muttered in Spanish. "That is not Lalo."

"Hector, is that your guy?"

Sitting in the back seat, Hector was distracted, thinking of his wife. He leaned forward between the seats and peered across the open field. "Holy shit, that's Min!"

"Go, go, go!" Wiggins barked.

Without hesitation, Salazar started the vehicle and floored the gas pedal, kicking up dirt in its wake.

Min-jun spotted the SUV bouncing down the slope toward him and assumed it was Mathias's men. He changed direction and limped toward the jungle, figuring he would take his chances in the wild. His heart sank as the vehicle gained on him; his broken body could not cover the distance fast enough.

As the vehicle neared, it cut off his path to the jungle and slowed. Desperately looking for options to escape, Min-jun glimpsed the silhouette of a man hanging halfway out the window. It was Hector Nunez.

A wave of relief washed over Min-jun at the sight of his friend.

Suddenly, the ground around him erupted in puffs of dirt as automatic weapons fire broke out. Bullets whizzed past Min-jun, and he instinctively shielded his face—for what little good that might do. He then willed his ragged legs forward toward the SUV.

Run, Min, run! his brain screamed.

Salazar turned the vehicle to block the incoming fire. As bullets peppered the SUV, blowing out the windows and spraying the interior with shards of glass, Hector pushed open the back door. He grabbed Min-jun and pulled him inside.

"Go, go, go!" Wiggins yelled.

Salazar pushed the accelerator to the floor, causing the SUV to donut in the wet grass. Overcorrecting the wheel, Salazar exposed the front of the vehicle to Mathias's sniper. A lone bullet cut through the air at supersonic speed and smashed through the windshield, striking him at the base of his throat and severing his spinal cord. Eduardo Salazar, aka Mongrel, died instantly.

Beside him, Wiggins had ducked the moment the windshield had exploded. When he turned back, he found Salazar slumped behind the wheel, his lifeless eyes staring back at him. Wiggins grimaced but kept his wits. Knowing there was nothing he could do to help the man, he instinctively jumped into action.

"Hector, steer!" Wiggins yelled as he dove under the steering column and slammed Salazar's foot on the gas pedal.

Hector muscled his way forward between the two front seats and grabbed the wheel. Beside him, Min-jun could do nothing but duck and cover.

With the engine over-revving and tires smoking, the SUV found traction and fishtailed across the open field. A deluge of enemy fire continued to rain down on them until they reached the hill on the far end and snaked their way back from whence they came. Cresting the hill, they lurched onto the single dirt road leading back to Satipo.

"We're clear," Hector called down to Wiggins.

Wiggins pushed the brake pedal, and the SUV came to a skidding halt, throwing himself and Hector forward. As soon as the vehicle stopped, Hector recovered and shifted the vehicle into park but left the engine idling.

"A little help," Wiggins said.

Hector grabbed the back of his shirt and pulled him up.

"Thanks," Wiggins said, wiping the sweat from his face. "We don't have much time."

Opening the passenger door, Wiggins hurried around the front of the vehicle to the driver's side.

Hector checked their six, knowing Mathias's men could not be far behind. He turned back as Wiggins opened the driver's door and unceremoniously dragged Salazar's lifeless body out of the vehicle and into the nearby grass. No words were said. There was no time.

Brushing glass off the seat, Wiggins climbed behind the wheel, and they were soon moving once again.

"If they come after us, we're screwed," Hector stated the obvious.

"Agreed. We need to get to the airport fast. I have a plane there," Wiggins explained as he fished around in his pocket and retrieved his phone.

With one eye on the road, Wiggins speed-dialed his Peruvian pilot. The phone rang repeatedly until voicemail picked up. Wiggins hung up and tried again, with the same result.

"Dammit! He's not picking up," Wiggins said in frustration, resisting the urge to smash his phone on the steering wheel.

"Who?" Hector asked.

"My pilot. He's probably hungover in some brothel."

"Hey, I can fly," Hector offered matter-of-factly.

Wiggins glanced warily at Hector in the rearview mirror. Judging by Mr. Nunez's colorful beach shirt, he had never pegged Hector as a pilot.

"Seriously, I'm retired Air Force," Hector reiterated. "I used to fly A-10s."

"Can you fly a twin-engine Beechcraft?"

Hector made a face, almost insulted by the question. "Of course, that's easy." He waved dismissively. "You got a flight plan?"

Wiggins shook his head, as if to say this flight was definitely off the books.

Hector shrugged indifference. "That's okay. We don't need no stinkin' flight plan."

Wiggins grinned thinly as Hector's Hispanic accent seemed more pronounced the more rebellious he became.

Turning serious, he added, "We're about two minutes out. As soon as we get to the airfield, you get the plane ready. I'll take care of your friend."

Turning to check on Min-jun, Hector cringed as he got his first good look at the man's battered and bloodied face. "Damn, Min, you okay?"

With heavy eyes, Min-jun mustered the strength to nod slightly.

Hector grinned and patted his friend's shoulder. "Hang in there, amigo.

We'll be out of this soon."

They arrived at the darkened airport moments later. Wiggins breathed a sigh of relief. Only a few exterior lights were on outside the terminal. The facility did not officially open for two more hours, so with any luck, they might be able to leave unnoticed.

He pulled up beside the Beechcraft still parked where they had left it the day before. Wiggins climbed out of the SUV and opened the plane's side door.

"Thank God," he muttered at finding the aircraft unlocked.

Peeking inside, he half-expected to find his pilot passed out onboard, but the man was nowhere in sight. That was probably a good thing. There was no time to explain that a small army was chasing them and they needed to depart immediately without logging a flight plan.

Hector finished removing the wheel chocks. He and Wiggins passed each other in haste.

"Spare keys are in the visor," Wiggins said as he went to grab Min-jun and their luggage.

"Copy that," Hector replied as he tossed the chocks inside the aircraft before climbing aboard.

Taking the left seat in the cockpit, Hector lowered the visor, and the spare keys dropped in his lap. He found the ignition key and placed it in the starter. Then he removed a set of headphones wrapped around the control wheel. Hector familiarized himself with the main instrument panel, then located a pre-flight checklist tucked in the seat's side pocket. He began running through the startup procedure.

Both engines were fired up by the time Wiggins had Min-jun loaded inside the aircraft and buckled in. As he went to close the side door, Wiggins noticed headlights speeding down the dirt road toward the airport.

"We got company!" he yelled over the propellers.

Hector responded with a thumbs-up then throttled forward.

Wiggins closed the door as the tiny aircraft rolled away from the terminal. The Beechcraft then taxied across the tarmac in the darkness. Hector kept the running lights off to avoid drawing attention. With sunrise still a few hours away, moonlight and clear skies provided enough illumination to light their path to the runway.

By the time they reached the far end of the airfield, Wiggins had joined Hector in the cockpit. He pulled on the co-pilot's headset and watched anxiously as Hector pointed the aircraft's nose down the runway and throttled up. The Beechcraft lurched forward and began picking up speed.

Wiggins looked to his right and peered out the side window. Three SUVs pulled up alongside their abandoned vehicle at the terminal. Mathias's men hopped out with automatic weapons and began firing on their plane. Bullets riddled the fuselage as the aircraft sped down the runway. Seconds later, Hector pulled back on the control wheel, and the Beechcraft took flight.

Once they were airborne, Hector watched the gauges for a few tense moments to ensure they had not sprung any leaks. Satisfied, he retracted the landing gear.

Speaking into his mic, Wiggins asked, "We good?" He dared to hope.

Hector gave Wiggins a sideways glance. "Depends." He grimaced. "We only have half a tank of fuel. Where are we headed?"

Wiggins thought for a moment. With Peru off-limits, he considered Bolivia. They were allowing the Americans to use their airspace but not land. If word got out that any of Peru's neighbors harbored the forces that attacked Mathias's facility, it could turn really ugly, really fast. That left only one option.

"How do you feel about landing on an aircraft carrier?"

52

TYRO

Planet Earth
The White House, Washington, D.C.

President Roger Fitzgerald groaned at the unwelcome knock on his bedroom door. He slowly opened his eyes and looked at the clock on the nightstand.

"Three forty," he grumbled. "You gotta be kidding me."

Beside him, the First Lady buried her head under the blankets to keep in the warmth as her husband rolled out of bed.

Sliding his feet into his slippers, the President crossed the master bedroom, yawning and stretching his arms overhead to help him wake for whatever waited outside.

Cracking open the bedroom door, Fitzgerald was greeted by the Watch Officer, Captain Wilkins.

"Mr. President," he said, holding out a Boeing Black smartphone, a highly modified and encrypted Android device built specifically for the United States government.

Squinting as his eyes adjusted to the bright lights in the West Sitting Hall, the President cleared his throat. "Tommy, please tell me we're not being invaded by aliens."

"No, sir. Sorry to wake you, but it's Director Ratliff on the line."

This can't be good, the President thought as he took the phone.

Knowing Operation Bold Fortress was underway, Fitzgerald hoped no news was good news, at least on the CIA front. He half-expected any midnight phone calls would come from a belligerent senator calling on behalf of Edmund Mathias, not Maxine.

The President stepped out of the bedroom and closed the door quietly behind him. "Thanks, Tommy. Standby one," Fitzgerald said as he crossed the hall to the adjacent dining room and closed the door behind him. He double-checked the caller ID, confirming it was Maxine.

"Hi Maxine. Let's hear it," he said, expecting the worst.

"Mr. President, I'm sorry to report we lost one helicopter, three crew members KIA. The second helicopter, carrying Dr. Landry, is safely away, along with all four SEAL team members. They should be landing on the *Washington* shortly."

"Just one hostage?"

"The second hostage, Mr. Choi, apparently stayed behind to buy time for Dr. Landry's escape. By the time he made it out, the second chopper had already departed."

"Where is he now?"

"Lima Station Chief, John Wiggins, picked him up. They managed to get away under heavy fire and drove to the local airport. They're airborne in a private plane."

Fitzgerald scratched his head. "So, what's the problem?"

"Fuel, sir. The plane they're in had not been refueled before departure, so our options are limited. Peru is definitely out of the question, and I'm reluctant to ask any of its neighbors. The damage to Mathias's compound was significant. When this goes public, sir, any known accomplices will face serious repercussions."

Fitzgerald had inherited a challenging situation in South America when he had taken office. Nearly every United States military base on the continent had been shut down for various reasons over the past two decades. Mending relations and regaining a foothold in the region had been a top priority with his predecessors but had been met with sharp opposition. For this reason, the President had to agree with Ratliff's assessment—they could not afford to ruffle any feathers at this time.

"What are you proposing?"

"I need you to authorize a civilian aircraft landing on the *George Washington*, sir. Admiral Danforth said hell no unless the order comes directly from you."

Fitzgerald ran his hand through his hair and sighed heavily. "And who exactly is flying the plane?"

"Hector Nunez, sir. He's a retired A-10 pilot but has never attempted a carrier landing."

"Most pilots haven't," the President remarked dryly. "All right. Let me talk to Danforth. I can't blame him for objecting. How much time do we have?"

"They'll be out of fuel in approximately twenty-seven minutes, sir."

"Understood. And when this is over, I want to meet the families of the downed helicopter crew. I don't want their sacrifice swept under the carpet."

"Yes, Mr. President. I'll make the arrangements myself."

Fitzgerald hung up then immediately called the White House switchboard. The operator assigned to the President's personal, encrypted line answered immediately.

"Yes, Mr. President. How may I help you?"

"Patch me through to Admiral Danforth aboard the USS *George Washington*."

USS *George Washington*

Admiral Rusty Danforth entered the darkened confines of the Combat Information Center in a mood that mirrored his surroundings. Ten minutes earlier, the Chief of Naval Operations—his boss—had floated a request from the CIA to allow a civilian aircraft to land on his ship. Danforth had dismissed the request as absurd. The safety of his crew and ship superseded the lives of three civilians, even if one was retired Air Force. His boss had understood, but something told Danforth that was not the end of it.

After stepping out for some fresh air to clear his head, Danforth was called back inside with an emergency message from the President.

Inside the CIC, he stood before a red secure phone mounted on the wall. Danforth checked his bearing before lifting the receiver off its cradle.

"Admiral Danforth here."

"Standby for the President of the United States," an operator replied. Seconds later, President Fitzgerald came on the line.

"Admiral Danforth?" said Fitzgerald.

"Yes, Mr. President."

"I'm not going to waste your time with pleasantries, Admiral. It's too early in the morning for that. I understand that what you're being asked to do violates every safety rule in the book. I respect your stance, but consider this, these are no ordinary civilians on that plane. One played a key role in averting the recent alien invasion. The other two have served our country and put their lives on the line, just like you and everyone aboard your ship. Now, be frank with me, Admiral, is there any chance in hell a carrier landing is possible?"

Admiral Danforth cursed inwardly. He knew there was precedence and assumed the President had been briefed, as well.

In 1975, at the end of the Vietnam War, South Vietnamese military and civilians had fled the country as the Viet Cong overtook Saigon. In a desperate attempt to save his family, Major Buang-Ly of the South Vietnamese Army had stolen a single-engine Cessna O-1 Bird Dog and had flown out to sea with little fuel and no radio or advanced flight systems.

Flying blind, he had come across the USS *Midway* that was holding station off the coast to aid evacuations. Major Buang had circled the carrier several times and dropped a handwritten note to the ship, asking for help. In response, all Army helicopters used to transport refugees were pushed overboard to make room for the Cessna. Major Buang landed successfully and was hailed a hero by many. Admiral Danforth knew this story well because Major Buang's plane was now on display at the Naval Aviation Museum in Pensacola, Florida, the same base where Danforth had earned his pilot's wings.

Danforth breathed out heavily. "There is precedent, sir. It's not without risks," he emphasized, "but it can be done."

"Then you have your orders, Admiral. Bring our boys home safely."

"Yes, Mr. President."

The call ended.

Danforth hung up the phone and immediately reached for a second line to his Air Boss, Commander Strand. He was in charge of all flight operations aboard the aircraft carrier.

"Strand, here."

"Strand, this is the captain. I've got an emergency situation. Prepare to receive a civilian, twin-engine Beechcraft. It's low on fuel and less than twenty minutes out."

Stammering a reply, the Air Boss acknowledged, "Aye, sir. Anything else?"

Looking out a large window from *G-Dub's* conning tower, Commander Strand peered across the flight deck at the MH-60M Black Hawk helicopter that had just landed. It was shot to hell but otherwise in good condition, and all aboard were safe and sound. The rest of the flight deck was clear of aircraft. Air operations were not set to begin for a few more hours, so the timing was fortunate. All he had to do was get the Black Hawk out of the way.

"Three civilians on board," Admiral Danforth continued. "The pilot is retired Air Force, flew A-10s back in the day. You can reach him at 243MHz," he added, referring to the emergency radio frequency used by the military. "Let's use the barricade on this one, too."

"Aye, Captain. Does it have a callsign?"

"Not that I know of," Danforth replied. The irritation in his voice made it obvious this order came from a pay grade higher than his. Thinking for a moment, the admiral added, "Designate them callsign, Tyro. Copy?"

The term "Tyro" dated back to World War II and referred to a new or inexperienced pilot. That told the Air Boss all he needed to know.

"Aye, aye, sir. We'll be ready."

With that, emergency landing protocols were set in motion. Fire and recovery crews were activated, including two rescue helicopters in case the inbound aircraft had to ditch in the drink. Meanwhile, since the Beechcraft had no tailhook to catch the ship's arresting system, a barricade webbing would be used instead of the standard cables to stop the aircraft once it landed on deck.

Stretching as high as twenty feet and extending the width of the flight deck, the barricade webbing was an emergency recovery system rarely used on aircraft carriers. The heavy nylon straps that made up the webbing tended to cause significant damage to airframes. It was only used as a last resort. In this case, with orders being orders, damage to the Beechcraft appeared to be a moot point. As long as the passengers arrived safely and the ship remained undamaged, the Beechcraft would probably be dumped overboard afterward.

The next twenty minutes were intense. Fresh off their hostage rescue mission, Warrant Officer Brewster and his SOAR co-pilot were hurried back to the flight deck to get their helicopter airborne before the Beechcraft arrived. Marlana, Rose, and the SEAL team gathered in front of an observation window in the ship's conning tower to watch Hector's landing.

"There he is," the Air Boss called out from behind a large pair of binoculars.

All eyes turned east and located the tiny aircraft set against the backdrop of a gorgeous sunrise.

Marlana squeezed Rose's hand nervously, prompting Rose to wrap an arm around her friend's shoulders. They watched together with bated breath, listening as the Landing Signal Officer on the flight deck communicated with Hector.

To help him get his bearings, Hector conducted a flyover for practice. The Beechcraft skimmed over the flight deck at what looked like slow motion compared to the F-18s and F-35s onboard. For Hector, it was fast enough. Despite his experience flying low-level strafing runs in A-10s, he had never attempted landing on a moving runway. This feat required twice as much focus.

The Beechcraft banked to starboard, and Hector performed a wide circle to line up for the real deal. There was not enough fuel for another practice run. Once he was on final approach, the LSO called out his distance and speed. Wind added to the challenge as thirty knot gusts bounced the tiny aircraft about.

Hector pointed the aircraft's nose to the centerline on the flight deck and dropped his landing gear as he started his descent. Seated beside him, Wiggins clutched the armrests, afraid to say anything for fear of jinxing them.

As the carrier's stern grew larger in the front windshield, Hector took one hand off the flight controls long enough to wipe the sweat from his brow. In his ears, the LSO calmly talked him down, with Hector only needing to make minimal adjustments.

Seconds later, the Beechcraft touched down and hit the unforgiving flight deck harder than Hector had intended. This caused the aircraft to bounce off the deck. Hector responded by pushing the nose down just as they became entangled in the barricade webbing. The aircraft came to an abrupt halt, throwing the passengers forward in their seat restraints. With the propellers caught in the barrier, both engines stalled and shut off automatically.

Inside the cockpit, a moment of silence followed as Hector and Wiggins sat back in their seats to catch their breath and gather themselves.

Hector's headset had been thrown off from the sudden stop. It was resting on the dash, and he could hear the LSO calling to him. He placed them back over his ears.

"Control, this is Tyro," Hector replied. "Go ahead."

"There you are," the LSO replied. "Good job, Tyro! You made it. Is everyone okay?"

Hector looked to Wiggins, who was rubbing his sore neck from a mild case of whiplash.

Wiggins gave him a thumbs-up.

"We're good," Hector replied. "Are we on fire?"

"Negative, Tyro. Welcome aboard."

Hector's shoulders dropped. "Thanks, Control. We owe you one. This is Tyro signing off." Hector removed his headset and tossed it back on the dash. He closed his eyes for a moment, then they shot open.

Min-jun!

Hector twisted around in his seat to find his Asian friend slumped over in his seat. He had been so caught up in flying that he had forgotten all about Min-jun, who had been quiet the whole trip. Hector quickly unbuckled and moved to the back of the plane.

Checking for a pulse, Hector let out a breath of relief to find that Min-jun was still with them. He then cradled his friend's head and gently helped Min-jun sit up. "Min? Hey, buddy, you with us? Open your eyes."

Min-jun stirred. He lifted an eyelid to glance at Hector, snorted, then fell back into a heavy sleep.

Hector grinned, then exchanged looks with Wiggins. Both men guffawed at the realization that Min-jun had slept through the entire ordeal.

"Man, I can't wait to tell my grandkids about this," Wiggins said, smiling with satisfaction.

Hector looked at him quizzically. "You got grandkids, Holmes?"

"No, but if I ever do, this'll be a killer story to share."

Hector laughed. "I know. I can't wait to tell the HOA."

Just then, a Navy deck officer opened the aircraft's side door and greeted them. They roused Min-jun and helped him out of the plane. An awaiting medical team loaded him onto a gurney and started an IV as Hector and Wiggins were escorted off the flight deck.

Marlana and Rose were at the tower's side door, waiting anxiously. As soon as Hector saw his wife, he rushed to her, and they embraced for a long moment.

When they separated, Marlana looked him up and down to make sure her husband was okay. Then she gave him a wry look. "You're never going to let me live this down, are you?"

Hector smiled from ear-to-ear. "Live what down? You're married to the top gun!"

53

ENDINGS

Planet Earth
The White House, Washington, D.C.

CIA Director, Maxine Ratliff, sat quietly inside the Oval Office, trying to gauge the President's reaction to her final report on Operation Bold Fortress. Across the desk from her, Fitzgerald read the report, twice, without giving Ratliff any verbal or visual cues to indicate how he would respond. In the end, the hostage rescue was a success, but with a heavy price—five KIA, including Lalo and Salazar, and one aircraft lost.

After his second pass, the President closed the folder and rubbed his eyes. "Have the funerals been scheduled?"

Ratliff cleared her throat. "Yes, Mr. President. The families requested burials at Arlington. Services are next week."

"Good. Do me a favor and give Sheri the details before you leave. Tell her to make room on my calendar for all three."

Ratliff nodded solemnly. "Yes, sir."

Fitzgerald sat back in his leather chair and eyed Maxine. She was having a hard time returning his gaze, which mirrored the tone of her report. The President empathized. These were not the first soldiers to have died on his watch and probably not the last.

"Are these your first losses?"

Maxine nodded.

"Bold Fortress didn't go off as well as we'd hoped, but it was still the right call. We have to look after our own."

Maxine shared the sentiment. "Yes, sir. Freedom does come at a cost. I just hope I live to see the day when Mathias pays his share."

"Here, here," the President seconded, pretending to raise a glass. Switching gears, he asked, "Tell me about Deputy Aguri?"

Ratliff sighed. She had hoped Jessica's involvement was in the past. "She's one of our best, sir. Pulling Mr. Choi to run recon was a mistake—she knows that now—but the two have a long history together of running similar ops. She'll learn from this."

"And Mr. Choi? Where is he now?"

Ratliff straightened. "On his way back to Montana, sir. He's being accompanied by Colonel Nunez and her husband. The doctors expect a full recovery."

"Good. What about Dr. Landry?"

"She should be home by now. Just to be safe, we've assigned her a security detail for the time being."

Thinking back to Ratliff's report, Dr. Landry had shared keen insight into Mathias's bold scheme. "So, Mathias has cut a deal with this Aiwan, Luna?"

"Correct, Mr. President. Satellite surveillance of Mathias's ship near Challenger Deep confirmed that Luna is onboard."

"He doesn't lack ambition, I'll give him that," Fitzgerald granted. "The report said the Aiwan helped build some kind of cloaking device to hide the crystals?"

"That's correct, sir. We're not sure how it works, but NSA is burning the midnight oil to turn up any electronic intel originating from Mathias's ship."

"I hate to admit it, but hiding the crystals is a brilliant idea," the President conceded, especially considering the potential threat of off-world harvesters returning to Earth. However, he cringed to imagine such technology falling into the hands of their enemies here on this planet. It gave a whole new meaning to the term stealth.

"Talk to Ernie and see what legal grounds we have under the laws of universal jurisdiction. *Reagan* is still in the area, and I'd like to see if we can get our people onboard to inspect Mathias's ship."

"Yes, sir." Ratliff scribbled a note.

A light on the President's phone flashed, discreetly notifying him his next appointment, Ambassador Nichols, had arrived.

Considering their talk about aliens, the ambassador's ears must have been burning out in the hall. With the U.N. Security Council voting to establish an Earth Defense Force, he and Nichols needed to formalize the administration's official position on the matter.

The President got to his feet and moved around his desk. Ratliff took her cue that the meeting was over and stood. Fitzgerald walked her to the door.

"One last thing, Maxine, has anyone heard from Captain Tan?"

Ratliff shook her head. "No, sir. I'm afraid not."

Fitzgerald frowned. "Well, let's hope no news is good news."

Somewhere in hyperspace ...

Ava lay unconscious on the metal-grated floor as the bounty hunter, Smythe, cleared out a storage closet he intended to be her temporary holding cell. Satisfied there was nothing left behind that could be used to aid her escape or be fashioned into a weapon, Smythe retrieved a handheld device from his belt.

The human's reaction to his toxin seemed to have affected Ava more than other species. Most would have awakened by now.

Pointing the device at Captain Tan, Smythe scanned her vitals. The best he could tell, she appeared stable. Human anatomy had never been recorded on his device, but based on similar species, she appeared out of danger.

Smythe grunted with satisfaction. He only needed her alive a little while longer. Once they were able to hack into the Reaper and were absolutely positive the failsafe was disabled, he would sell the human to a slaving outfit on Gomaiyus, or simply dump her in space.

In the meantime, he grabbed Ava by the back of her outfit and dragged her limp body into her new home. The door slid downward to close and lock. Double-checking he still had Ava's nano-ring in his pocket, Smythe departed.

He made his way to the freighter's main storage bay to check on the Reaper. Still locked in the arms of his ship's docking clamps, this was Smythe's first opportunity to take in the sleek-looking vessel. He had to admit he was impressed by its exterior, but that was not what made the ship so valuable. The devil was in the details. The real treasure lay within, and Smythe was determined to find it.

"Computer, lower the boarding ladder," he called to the Reaper.

No response.

"Reaper computer, acknowledge."

Still no reply.

Grumbling to himself, Smythe tried to reach the control panel underneath the Reaper's bow, but doing so invited a sharp pain to his midsection. He still needed to tend the wounds inflicted by Prince Kypa. That was next on his agenda, but first, he had to know the hand he had been dealt.

Smythe carefully scaled a wall-mounted ladder nearby. Rung by rung, he climbed until he could step onto the dorsal side of the Reaper's outer hull. There, he discovered the docking collar and manually opened the Reaper's interior hatch.

Descending inside the ship, Smythe stopped briefly inside the main cabin. With his blaster drawn, he visually checked the room's small confines then entered the empty cockpit. A deathly silence enveloped the Reaper as the bounty hunter cautiously surveyed his surroundings.

Satisfied, Smythe returned to the main cabin and descended the ladder to the engineering section. Before reaching the bottom, he noticed the orange glow emanating from the Magnetarite crystal.

Stepping off the ladder, Smythe approached the Reaper's engine core and eyed the crystal floating within the ship's containment field. He had seen Magnetarite before, but smuggling crystals had never been his forte. They were too rare a commodity for steady income. This one would fetch a small fortune on the open market, although it was small compared to others, which made him wonder.

Why would Krunig go to so much trouble for this crystal?

Just then, his commlink chirped.

"Go," Smythe replied.

"We should be safe now," Gort said. "I jumped three times just to be sure nobody tailed us."

"Good work. Contact Hiromi. Tell her we need to meet. I've got a new job that pays quadruple."

After a brief pause, Gort asked cautiously, "What about Krunig?"

"Let me worry about him," Smythe replied with ice in his veins. "Trust me; we do this right, and our bounty hunting days are over."

In all of their years together, Gort had never heard Smythe talk that way, nor had they ever reneged on a job. He trusted his partner explicitly, but acting against the syndicate invited a world of hurt.

"Something about this cargo isn't adding up," Smythe continued. "Find us a remote location to lay low for a while. Got it?"

"Sure thing, boss."

Smythe returned the commlink to his belt and eyed the orange crystal once more. If Hiromi could hack into the Reaper without blowing them all to atoms, they might be able to unlock the ship's secrets. At worst, they could extract the crystal and sell it. That alone paid more handsomely than the paltry sum Krunig was offering.

Smythe *hmphed* with disdain. His days of working for others were over. Time for one last score. But Gort was right; making enemies with Grawn Krunig and the rest of the Madreen Crime Syndicate was a dangerous proposition. They would be hunted to no end.

Perhaps it was Karma or a bad omen, but the thought of the hunter becoming the hunted triggered another sharp pain in Smythe's side. It was time to treat his wounds.

Locating the nearby exit hatch, he lowered the ladder. Smythe started down then stopped abruptly, thinking he had heard a noise.

Removing his cowl, his antennae probed the air, searching the ghost ship for anything out of the ordinary. He remained still on the ladder for a long moment. Then, realizing he was jumping at shadows, he dismissed his paranoia and retreated down the ladder.

The threat is out there, not in here, the ex-bounty hunter reminded himself as he schemed a way to cheat the largest crime organization in the galaxy.

Planet Earth
Arbor Ridge, Georgia

A black Cadillac Enclave, bearing government plates, pulled up in front of Rose's house just before noon. Sitting in the back, Rose peered out the window to find her driveway filled with cars. A big "*Welcome Home!*" banner hung from the garage.

Before departing the *George Washington*, Rose had been allowed to call her family so her arrival was not unexpected. Yet, seeing everyone gathered at the house reminded her of the old days when Joe had still been with them. A reunion was long overdue, something Rose decided to correct.

The SUV parked on the street. A serious-looking man in a dark suit, sunglasses, and an earpiece stepped out of the front passenger seat. Sweeping the area for threats, he then opened the back door for Rose. As soon as she appeared, the sweet voices of her grandchildren called to her.

"Memaw!"

Rose's face lit up as she rushed onto the front lawn to wrap her arms

516 | TODD HOSEA

around the youngsters. She marveled at how much they had changed in just a month. Meanwhile, the rest of the family joined her outside. They shared many hugs and kisses, and tears were shed, as well. The elephant in the room was the mysterious agent, standing off to the side and holding Rose's bag.

There were questions that needed answering, but Rose put them off for now. Top of her mind at the moment was getting inside to take care of one important task.

"Memaw's had a long trip," she told her grandsons. "I need to go to the bathroom."

Her excuse made the boys chuckle. Then they led their memaw by the hand into the house. Smiling uneasily at the mystery agent, Rose's daughter, Becky, collected her mom's baggage and followed the rest of the family inside.

Peeling herself away from the boys, Rose made her way to the back bedroom. She closed the door behind her and locked it for good measure, then went straight to the closet. Buried under her clothes, Rose was relieved to find her safe right where she had left it.

She dropped to her knees and unlocked it with her thumb print. A second wave of relief came at the sight of the wrist beacon Kypa had given her. Rose picked it up and eyed the device nervously. She had never imagined having to use it, but now was as good a time as any.

"For what it's worth," Rose said then cringed as she pressed the button, half-expecting an alarm to sound.

A red light, no bigger than a small pearl, began flashing quietly. Rose breathed a sigh of relief then placed the beacon back in the safe and closed the lid. She came to her feet and moved to the window, looking skyward.

"Kypa, I sure hope you're listening."

Planet Aiwa

The royal yacht exited Aiwa's atmosphere, escorted by six gunships. Passing the orbiting fleet, Kypa's personal transport continued onward to Pria-12, Aiwa's farthest moon.

Inside, Kypa sat on an examination table in the ship's infirmary, surrounded by Commodore Boa, Queen Qora, and Princess Seva.

"Are you sure you are all right?" Qora fretted as the medical officer finished his examination.

"I am fine," Kypa insisted, testing his jaw. His ribs were still sore from the bounty hunter's blaster shot to his chest, but he kept that to himself. There was no time for another quick dip in the healing chamber.

The medical officer completed his examination and concurred with Kypa's assessment. He released his patient then gathered his equipment and departed.

Neil appeared from an adjacent room, dressed once again in his nano-suit. On the floor at Kypa's feet, he noticed the scorched aquasuit. Their deception had almost worked. Wearing Neil's nano-suit underneath his own aquasuit had saved Kypa's life, but in the end, they were unable to rescue Ava or prevent the bounty hunter from escaping with the Reaper.

"So, where are we heading?" Neil asked.

"To my lab," Kypa replied, putting his feet on the floor. He was dressed in his golden robe for the time being. "I have a transport we can use to pursue Ava."

"Why not take gunships?" Seva reasoned.

"Indeed," Boa concurred, clearly not keen on Kypa's plan to pursue Captain Tan without armed escort.

"We cannot afford to spare any warships," Kypa countered. "Besides, we need to travel inconspicuously. I left a tracking beacon aboard the Reaper, so we should be able to find Ava. But, if they see us coming, we will never get her back."

Just then, the yacht's captain called over the commlink, "My Prince, we have arrived."

To his right, Kypa looked out the viewport to Aiwa's most remote satellite—the only uninhabited moon orbiting the homeworld.

"Thank you, Captain. Hold position and prepare a shuttle for immediate departure."

Kypa turned to his sister, taking her hands in his. "You know what must be done. Please look after Maya and the children while I am away."

Seva steeled herself and nodded. "They will be safe, I promise. You take care of yourself, brother. Both of you," she said to Neil. "And good luck finding your friend."

Queen Qora eyed Neil warily. Her son's choice of traveling companions was clearly not reassuring. She preferred a seasoned Aiwan warrior to accompany Kypa, not a man whose lack of fighting skills was dwarfed only by his inexperience traveling the cosmos.

Seeing his mother's reservation, Kypa gently turned her head toward him so their eyes could meet. "It will all work out. Trust me."

"How can you be so sure?" Qora pressed, trying to mask her fear of losing her son.

"Because it must," Kypa replied. "Ava would do the same for us."

Against her better judgment, Qora accepted her son's decision. Stepping back, hands clasped in front of her, she bowed her head without further objection.

Kypa signaled to Neil with a head bob that it was time to leave.

On the way out, he turned to Boa. "There is something I want to show you. Will you accompany us?"

His interest piqued, Boa accepted. "Of course, My Prince."

The trio made their way to the nearby lift. Kypa stepped inside and rounded to face his mother and sister. Seva smiled reassuringly, putting her hand to her chest in farewell just as the doors closed.

Kypa, Neil, and Boa rode the lift in silence, down to the yacht's landing bay. There, they stepped out onto the flight deck and made their way to a nearby shuttle. Waiting to meet them was Captain Areda, the yacht's captain. He held gun belts in both hands.

Areda bowed as Kypa approached. "As you requested," he said, handing Kypa and Neil each a gun belt with a handheld blaster tucked inside the holster.

Neil accepted the weapon with mixed emotions. It was his first blaster, something he had dreamed of since childhood, but this was no toy. Lives were at stake, and he hoped he would not need to pull the trigger.

"The shuttle is prepped and ready to leave," Areda added.

"Thank you, Captain. Commodore Boa will be accompanying us to the surface. Notify the gunships; we will need an escort."

"Yes, sir." Areda bowed dutifully then took his leave to carry out the order.

Kypa, Neil, and Boa boarded the shuttle through a side ramp. As Boa made his way to the cockpit, Kypa sealed the hatch and retracted the ramp. Moments later, the engines came to life and the shuttle lifted off the deck. Once they cleared the yacht, three gunships broke formation and followed the shuttle to the moon's surface.

Sitting in a crescent-shaped pilot's chair, Boa steered the shuttle on its descent to the coordinates Kypa had provided. Standing behind him, Kypa and Neil watched in silence as the desolate moon loomed large in the main viewport. They reached the surface moments later.

Dipping into an enormous crater, the shuttle entered a darkened cave too narrow for the gunships to follow.

"Hold position," Boa ordered their escorts.

Inside the cave, the shuttle's exterior running lights cast eerie shadows along the walls.

"This isn't creepy at all," Neil remarked dryly. "So, what's your plan?"

"You will see," Kypa replied mysteriously.

To Boa, he instructed, "Slow down. We are close."

They soon came to a dead-end. Facing a large rock wall, Kypa punched in a secret code on the commlink worn on his wrist. Outside, the holographic rock wall suddenly disappeared, revealing a metal structure embedded in the moon's rock walls. The exterior lights to Kypa's secret lab activated automatically, revealing two interior landing platforms situated behind an electronic containment field.

Neil was awestruck. "You built all of this yourself?"

Kypa shrugged modestly. "The structure is actually a converted cargo container. It took some time to hollow-out the rock wall, but once that was complete, I was able to assemble the container myself. Then it was just a matter of interior design."

Neil rolled his eyes. "You make it sound so easy."

"Actually, the lab took me nearly a full rotation to complete," Kypa explained. "Commodore, please land on the platform to the left."

"Aye," Boa acknowledged. The shuttle proceeded slowly and passed through the containment field that kept the internal atmosphere intact. They touched down seconds later.

"Thank you, Commodore," Kypa said. "Dr. Garrett and I will take it from here."

"You do not want me to stay?"

"That will not be necessary," Kypa assured him. "Now that you are aware of my lab's existence, I am entrusting its security to you."

Boa nodded. "As you wish, My Prince."

"I will contact you as soon as we locate Captain Tan."

Sharing the queen's misgivings, Boa was not keen on Aiwa's future king venturing off into wild space unprotected. But his protest was on record. This was Prince Kypa's decision, and if the tables were turned, Boa knew he would do the same for a friend in need.

"Call for reinforcements if you need us."

"I will. Thank you," Kypa replied appreciatively. With that, he led Neil outside.

Boa retracted the ramp as soon as they were clear then lifted off.

Kypa waved goodbye. When Boa was out of sight, he turned to Neil.

"Wait here," he instructed. "Do not move."

"Sure," Neil replied, checking his feet to see where he was standing. When he looked up, Neil saw Kypa crossing the platform to a set of controls in the back of the room. "I don't understand," he confessed, his voice echoing off the metal walls. "Why aren't we taking the shuttle?"

"I have something better in mind," Kypa replied from over his shoulder.

With a press of a button, the platform in front of Neil came to life. The floor slid open to reveal a hidden compartment underneath. Then he watched as a second Reaper prototype rose from below.

Neil could not believe his eyes. He approached the ship and ran his fingers along the bottom of the fuselage. "You built two?"

Kypa smiled, admiring his creation. "It seemed prudent at the time."

"Good thinking," Neil agreed. Lowering his hand, it came to a rest on the blaster holstered to his leg. "Hey, by the way, I don't have a clue how this thing works. Any chance I could get some practice shots in before we leave?"

"Of course." Kypa pointed toward the hangar's exit. "Just aim, point, and shoot. Captain Areda had the biometric reader on the trigger matched to your DNA. It will only fire when your finger is on the trigger."

"Nice safety feature," Neil remarked. He drew his weapon. It felt light and comfortable in his hand. "Just like this?" he asked, taking aim.

"You got it. Now fire."

Neil pulled the trigger, releasing a green bolt of energy that took him by surprise. The shot hit the hangar's containment field and dissipated harmlessly.

"Wow, that hardly had any kick at all. Just like my mom's old twenty-two."

Neil fired several more shots, trying to hit the same spot each time. He was no Doc Holliday, but pretty good for a beginner. At least now he stood a fighting chance against whatever dangers lay ahead.

"Well done," Kypa said.

Satisfied, Neil holstered the weapon. "Thanks, I guess we should get going. Are you going to change outfits."

"Later," Kypa replied. "I have been meaning to make my own nano-suit. I will take care of that once we get underway."

With that, Neil followed Kypa up the ladder leading into the engineering section. The ship was cold and dark inside. Only the soft glow of an orange Magnetarite crystal spinning behind its containment array offered any illumination.

Looking around, Neil noted how this prototype matched Reggie's design to a tee.

"Have you given this ship a name?" Neil asked as they ascended the steps to the main cabin.

"Not yet," Kypa replied. "But I will give it some thought."

They reached the cockpit, and Kypa pressed the power button by the door. The ship came to life. All of the internal lights and systems came online, including both chairs. Since this version of the Reaper had no previous settings for Neil on record, he had to make do sitting in the oversized excavator's chair.

"Give it a moment, and the chair will adjust to your body type," Kypa said.

As soon as Neil sat, the chair immediately began to conform to his body. "Pretty slick, Kypa. Is this an exact replica of Reggie?"

"Almost," Kypa replied. "This one has a few modifications that have yet to be field tested."

"Oh yeah? Like what?"

Just then, an alarm began beeping. Kypa took his seat in the pilot's chair and activated the HUD. Recognizing the signal, his brow furrowed.

"Rose," Kypa said with concern.

Neil rotated in his seat to face Kypa. "What about her?"

"She has activated the emergency beacon I gave her. I hope she is not in danger."

"Should we return to Earth?"

Kypa shook his head emphatically. "No, I am afraid Earth will have to wait. Ava comes first."

Neil agreed.

With that, Kypa powered up the Reaper's twin nacelles and lifted off. As the ship passed through the lab's containment field, he retracted the landing gear and piloted through the darkened cave. Moments later, they emerged from the moon's crater. The Reaper soared past the royal yacht and escort ships, heading toward deep space.

Kypa located Reggie's tracking beacon and plotted an intercept course. Now facing the unknown, the Reaper jumped into hyperspace with Kypa and Neil hoping it was not already too late to save Ava.

EPILOGUE

Planet Earth
Challenger Deep

Luna descended headfirst to the bottom of Challenger Deep, allowing the weight of the cloaking device to help carry her into the abyss. She reached the cave where Ava had first discovered the field of crystals and swam inside. With the device tucked under her arm, she used a special flashlight built to withstand the pressures at this depth to illuminate her path. Making her way into the cave's interior, Luna marveled at the large cache of magnetarite reflecting brilliant sparkles in the light.

The sight of the crystals briefly reminded her of home, but the euphoria was short-lived. She understood the significance of this find. Wars were started over deposits much smaller than this.

Knowing what she had to do, Luna set the cloaking device down in the middle of the cave. With a flip of the switch, the device came to life. The sides of the device opened to reveal a glass cylinder that glowed a bright white.

As Luna floated in the center of the cloaking field, she did not perceive any change in the environment. Around her, the crystals were still visible to the naked eye, as if nothing had happened. She double-checked the cloaking device, ensuring all was in order, then swam to the exit several yards away. Now outside the field's range, Luna turned back to face the crystals. Those nearest the device had vanished. She grinned with satisfaction.

Next, Luna retrieved a handheld control fashioned from the damaged Seeker. She aimed it at the invisible crystals and turned it on. The scanner read negative—no crystals detected.

Pleased with the results, Luna adjusted a setting on her handheld device, which expanded the range of the cloaking field. The rest of the crystals in the cave suddenly vanished before her eyes.

Luna exited the cave and scanned the area again from several ranges. Each time, she was met with the same results. The cloaking device worked as expected.

With her job finished, Luna was about to start back to the surface and report her success to Mathias when the thought crossed her mind to run. Tempted to make a break for it, the tracking bracelet irritating the skin around her ankle made her reconsider. Luna decided to stick to her original plan.

Reaching *Billy Bones* a short while later, she climbed the boarding ladder. Mathias and his security team were there to greet her.

"Well?" Edmund asked anxiously, handing Luna a towel.

"The cloaking device works," she replied. "The crystals are safely hidden, just as you wanted."

"Yes!" Edmund pumped his fist. "I knew you could do it."

"I should start working on a better scanner," Luna suggested. "There could be more deposits out there that we do not know about."

"Good idea, but first, let's drink to our success."

Edmund waved her to follow him. They exited the main deck and entered a side door that led into a luxurious cabin.

Inside, Edmund made himself at home behind the bar while Luna sat on one of the plush couches. Only the lead security guard remained in the room as Edmund poured himself a cognac on the rocks.

"Thirsty?"

Luna politely declined.

Edmund shrugged indifference then sat on the opposite couch. Lounging back with supreme self-satisfaction, Mathias sipped his drink. Luna sat quietly, watching him.

"You know," Mathias said, chomping on an ice cube, "I couldn't have done this without you. Great things are ahead for you and me. In fact, I have some ideas I want to run past you."

Just then, the security guard's phone rang. He recognized the caller ID as one of the direct lines from the facility in Satipo. He took the call, listening intently.

"My apologies," Edmund said to Luna, clearly distracted by the guard's hushed conversation.

"I understand," the guard said at last. "Hold one while I put him on." The guard gestured with the phone to Mathias. "Sir, there's been an incident in Peru. I think you should take this."

Edmund sighed heavily, not wanting anything to dampen his mood. He set his glass down on the table and crossed the room. The guard handed him the phone.

"Yes?" Edmund answered lazily. After a few seconds, his face morphed into rage. "What!"

Mathias shot an angry glance at Luna then stepped outside so she could not eavesdrop. As Edmund could be heard screaming into the phone, Luna eyed the half-empty glass of brandy only two feet away.

She leaned forward casually and began massaging her sore ankle. Making a furtive glance at the guard, she found him watching her closely. Luna smiled thinly and turned away. Then Edmund blurted several expletives outside that caught the guard's attention. As soon as he looked away, Luna seized her opportunity. She reached out in a flash, ran her long index finger around the rim of the glass over Edmund's residual saliva, and then settled back into her seat. The guard was none the wiser.

Mathias stormed back into the room moments later.

Instantly, Luna sensed the connection had been made. She smiled inwardly.

Edmund paced back and forth collecting his thoughts. Then, after a heavy breath, he threw himself onto the couch opposite Luna. He looked her over, contemplating his next move. Seeing his glass on the table, Edmund retrieved his drink and downed the last of it, wincing at the liquor's bite.

Luna tested her mental connection with Edmund and learned of the attack on Mathias's compound. But that was not all.

Rose escaped!

Luna fought to contain her excitement as Edmund closed his eyes and rested the glass of ice against his temple. The loss of Renzo hurt more than he cared to admit, but he could always find another fixer. At least all of his subterranean labs and precious research were still intact. Heads would roll in Washington, that he promised. For now, he took solace in knowing his long-term plans were still on track.

"Something wrong?" Luna asked.

"No, just a minor inconvenience," he lied. "Forgive me. Where were we?"

Luna narrowed her eyes ever so slightly. *You were talking about our partnership ... and you were going to remove my ankle bracelet.*

Edmund felt a slight tickle in the back of his mind. He opened his mouth to speak but stopped short, pausing as if questioning himself. Then he snapped out of it and replied, unfazed, "Ah, yes, we were going to discuss a partnership, if I recall. In fact, now that I think about it, if we're really going to trust one another, perhaps a leap of faith is in order."

Turning to the guard, he said, "Remove her ankle bracelet."

The guard looked perplexed. "Uh, sir, are you sure you want me to do that?"

Edmund waved him over, pointing to Luna. "I've never been more sure of anything in my life. Now get to it."

Reluctantly, the guard obeyed.

Luna leaned back and propped her foot up on the table. As soon as the bracelet was off, the guard backed a cautious step.

"Thank you, Edmund." Luna smiled. She then settled her eyes on him with a sparkle of the endgame. "I like the way you think."

AUTHOR'S NOTE

Greetings! I hope you enjoyed *Hunt the Reaper*. It was a lot of fun for me to write. If you would be so kind, please rate and review the book on the retailer's website where you purchased it. I'd love to hear your thoughts. Reviews help me promote the book to new readers and I use your feedback to grow as a storyteller. I really appreciate it!

Good news, there is more in store for Ava and the gang. Work is underway on the third and fourth installments of The Reaper Series. They promise to be just as fun and intense as the first two books. Be sure to check out my website (**www.toddhosea.com**) for updates and additional information about me and future projects. If you are on social media, please follow me on Amazon, Facebook, Goodreads, and YouTube.

Thank you so much for your support. Take care of yourself. Until next time, CAVU!

Best regards,
Todd

APPENDIX

CAST ON EARTH

Ava Tan – Pilot, Captain of the Reaper

Dr. Neil Garrett – Astrophysicist, National Aeronautical Space Administration

Dr. Rose Landry – Pathologist, Centers for Disease Control and Prevention

Lt. Colonel Marlana Nunez – United States Air Force (Husband: Hector)

Jessica Aguri – Station Chief, Sanhe, China, Central Intelligence Agency

Dr. M. Edmund Mathias – Founder and CEO, Mathias Industries

Roger Fitzgerald – President of the United States

Cathy Harrington – Vice President of the United States

Ernie Gutierrez – White House Chief of Staff

Ken Hreno – National Security Advisor

Russ Franks – Secretary of Defense

Bill Nguyen – Secretary of State

Admiral Susan Donnelly – Chairman of the Joint Chiefs of Staff

Guy Lannister – Director of National Intelligence

Maxine Ratliff – Director of the Central Intelligence Agency

Brett Brenham – Director, National Clandestine Service, CIA

General Anthony Garza – Former Chairman of the Joint Chiefs of Staff

Gary Sizemore – Former Director, Central Intelligence Agency

Haley Nichols – U.S. Ambassador to the United Nations

Henry Wiggins – CIA Station Chief, Lima, Peru

Eduardo Salazar – aka "Mongrel"

Luna – Aiwan engineer from Cirros

CAST ON AIWA (Ā-wuh)

Prince Kypa (Kī-puh) – Son of King Loka and Queen Qora

Maya (Mī-yuh) – Prince Kypa's mate (Children: Toma, Arya, Fraya)

King Loka (Lō-kuh) – King of the Five Realms and Warden of Eos

Queen Qora (Kor-uh) – Queen of the Five Realms

Princess Seva (Sē-vuh) – Daughter of King Loka and Queen Qora

Commodore Boa (Bō-uh) – Lord Commander of the Aiwan Military Forces

Smythe (Smīthe) – Bounty hunter

Gort – Pilot/mechanic (Smythe's business partner)

Commander Rega (Rē-guh) – Commander of the Royal Guards

Major Gora (Gor-uh) – Commander Rega's second in command

The High Court of the Five Realms

King Loka – Warden of Eos

Lord Zefra – Warden of Fonn

Lord Wahla – Warden of Dohrm

Lord Cara – Warden of Maeve (Māv)

Vacant – Warden of Cirros (Sīr-ōs)

Miscellaneous

Grawn Krunig – Underboss of the Madreen Crime Syndicate, Aiwan Sector

Grawn Supreme – Head of the Madreen Crime Syndicate

Ekator (Eck-a-tor) – Grawn Krunig's spaceport within the Mishi Nebula

Gomaiyus (Gō-mī-us) – Remote world known for its Pleasure District

Xipos (Zī-pōz) – Seahorse-like creatures native to Fonn

Zemindar (Ze-mīnd-ar) – Sea serpent on Aiwa

Krakadon (Krack-a-don) – Apex predator on Aiwa

Maxixe Magnetarite (Max-ice Mag-net-a-rīt) - Rarest of magnetar crystals

CPSIA information can be obtained
at www.ICGtesting.com
Printed in the USA
BVHW031940090223
658230BV00012B/50/J